BIRMINGHAM BLITZ

AND

BIRMINGHAM FRIENDS

Also by Annie Murray in Pan Books

Birmingham Rose

ANNIE MURRAY

Annie Murray graduated from Oxford in 1983. She has worked as a journalist and a nurse, has had short stories published in several magazines, and won the *SHE/ Granada Television Short Story Competition* in 1991. She now lives in Reading with her husband and four small children, Brummies all. *Birmingham Blitz* is the third novel in her bestselling Birmingham series.

Annie Murray

Birmingham Blitz
and
Birmingham Friends

PAN BOOKS

Birmingham Blitz first published in 1988 by Pan Books
Birmimgham Friends first published in 1996 by Pan Books,
under the title *Kate and Olivia*

This omnibus edition published 2003 by Pan Books
an imprint of Pan Macmillan Ltd
Pan Macmillan, 20 New Wharf Road, London N1 9RR
Basingstoke and Oxford
Associated companies throughout the world
www.panmacmillan.com

ISBN 0 330 43674 0

1 3 5 7 9 8 6 4 2

A CIP catalogue record for this book is available from
the British Library.

Printed and bound in Great Britain by
Mackays of Chatham PLC, Chatham, Kent

BIRMINGHAM BLITZ

For Mum and Dad,
with love and gratitude

ACKNOWLEDGEMENTS

Special thanks are due to the Birmingham people who generously gave their time to talk to me about 'their war': Elsie Ashmore and Nancy Holmes for their hospitality and frankness, Doris Burke who was a star and prepared to answer any number of daft questions, Rose and Jack Hall with whom I spent a great afternoon (Jack makes the best chips in Birmingham, if not the world), and Eric Langston for his welcome and his memories. A particular thank you also to Joe Mattiello who made himself available at unexpected moments and was a rich vein of information, and to my parents, George and Jackie Summers, who have frequently cast their minds back fifty or more years at a few seconds' notice.

Thanks also to Martin Parsons at Reading University, to Dr Rob Perks, Oral History Curator at the National Sound Archive, to Tony Doe and Concept Creative Productions.

There are a great many excellent books available about the Home Front during World War II and I drew on a variety of them, but none deserves mention more than Angus Calder's comprehensive and humane book *The People's War*. Thanks also go to Birmingham's Tindal Memory Writing Group which convened to produce *Writing it Down Before It's All Gone*, edited by Alan Mahar, which is a repeated source of inspiration.

NOTE TO THE READER

This story was originally conceived round the concept of the new and powerful influence of radio during the Second World War. Each chapter was prefaced by part of a contemporary song which in some way reflected its contents. Regrettably, because of the extremely high copyright costs of reproducing quotations from songs, these have had to be omitted from the finished book. However, readers who are familiar with the lyrics of the time might like to supply a suitable song for themselves as they go along.

A little happiness, a little sorrow,
May be awaiting you tomorrow –
That's what life is made of anyhow.

A little tearfulness a little laughter
And not a care for what comes after
There's nothing to be afraid of anyhow.

For the world rolls on the same old way
Just as night comes after day
And none of us can have a say about it,

So make the most of every minute
And get your sixty seconds in it,
'Cos that's what life is made of anyhow.

Ray Noble
(That's What Life is Made of)

August 1939

'Mom?'

Silence.

'MOM!'

'What?' That was her 'what the hell do you want *now*?' voice.

'Come up quick. It's Lola. She's dead.'

A pause from downstairs. We never usually called her Lola. Granny, Nan, filthy-old-cow, depending on who was talking, who listening. I couldn't call her Granny today somehow, not now she'd gone.

'Hang on a tick – let me put this on the gas. Genie? Sure she's not having you on?'

God Almighty. 'I'll ask her shall I? Lola? You dead, or what?'

'Don't be so cheeky.' I heard her footsteps across the back room. Then nothing. Above the mantel there was an oval mirror with a green frame, faded pink flowers stencilled round it. I realized she'd stopped, actually stopped to look at her reflection, her pale face which looked gaunt and scooped out under the high cheekbones, thin brown hair twisted in a knot at the back, wisps of it always working out of the pins.

She dragged herself up the stairs eventually, muttering, the martyr as usual. 'She would go on a Sat'dy morning when no one's around and your dad's off playing soldiers. As if I haven't got enough on my plate.

1

What're we going to do? Oh!' She clapped her hand over her nose at the door.

'She must've messed herself,' I said.

'As if I couldn't tell. In this heat too!'

She hadn't messed like that before as a rule. Not the full works. Just wet the bed, my bed where I'd had to sleep with her every night for three years, pressed up against the bugs on the wall waiting for it, the wet and stink and it seeping across, warm first, then cold.

Not taking her eyes off Lola, Mom backed over and flung open the window with one hand. We could hear kids playing out the back next door. Then she crept forward, face all screwed up, on tiptoe as if she thought Lola was going to explode or jump up and dance a polka. She bent over the bed, keeping her hand on her nose. Long, pointy nose like a pixie, my mom.

Lola's hands were lying outside the covers. They'd barely looked like hands for a long while. Had a hard life. They were red like mutton chops, the knuckles tight and swollen, and she used to nurse them in her lap when they throbbed. Mom picked one up like she would a dead rat (except she never would pick up a dead rat, she'd get me to do it), her face still looking as if someone'd forced a cup of castor oil down her.

'She's not breathing.' One hand was still pegged to her nose, the other groping about round Lola's wrist. 'She's gone.' Dropped the hand and let it fall back on the bed. Finally she loosed her nose, staring at Lola's grey old face. '*Shame*. Looks quite peaceful now, don't she? You'll have to clean her up, Genie, before we get her laid out. Can't let her be seen in that state, can we?' She was over at the door by now. 'I couldn't do it. It'd make me bad.'

*

So I washed my dead granny that baking hot afternoon. You have to do your duty to the dead, even though she was smelly and vicious and I hated her. She had disgusting habits. Taking snuff was one of them and she only had two hankies which I always got the job of washing out. They looked as if a dog had sicked on them and I could never get them any cleaner. She sniffed louder than water going down the plughole and gobbed into the fireplace, she soaked me in urine nearly every night and talked a load of gibberish. I'd kneel down in front of her to roll her stockings up her sickly white legs with the bacon-burn marks up them from sitting close to the fire all her life, the smell of wee rising off her. Sometimes she'd slap me, hard as she could round the face. Brought tears to my eyes. She'd squawk, 'Bitch! Common little bitch!' and I knew she meant Mom because she always reckoned Mom wasn't good enough for her darling babby Victor, her youngest and best. Mom wouldn't lift a finger for her so long as I was around to do it.

She was still wearing her corset, the colour of old cement, with bits of whalebone sticking out all over the place. I pushed her over on one side which was an effort because I wasn't much of a size, and skinny with it, and she was heavy for such a scrawny old bird. Shoving my shoulder against her, I managed to get her unlaced. She was trying to roll back on me all the time, with me gagging at the stink. I took off her lisle stockings, the interlock vest and bloomers and saw all the brown mess between her legs and up her back and in her scraggy little mound of hair down there.

While I was going over her with a rag and a pail of water (cold – Mom said, 'What's the use in wasting gas, she's dead, isn't she?') I thought, what would she have looked like when she was fifteen? And how with a name

3

like Lola Mavis she ought to have been in a circus act instead of working factories the length and breadth of Birmingham.

I bent down to squeeze out the rag in the water that looked like stewed tea but didn't smell at all like it, trying not to drip any on my frock.

'Oh my God!' I said, straightening up. My heart was pounding like a mad thing and sweat pricked under my arms because I'd have sworn on my own life she moved and I was out of that room and down the stairs as if my bloomers were on fire.

'Mom – she moved. She's not dead. I saw her titties going up and down!'

'*No.*' Her hand halted a wooden spoon in the air. 'You're seeing things!'

But we both tiptoed up the stairs and peeped into that room, not knowing what we were scared of except we'd both have screamed like billy-o if there'd been one tiny flicker of movement from her. All we could see were the grimy old soles of Lola's feet and the soiled sheet in a heap on the floor and the enamel bucket and there wasn't a sound as we moved closer. She lay quite, quite still.

We stood by the bed and suddenly Mom was tittering away like the Laughing Policeman and set me off. I thought this was a bit of all right, Mom being nice to me, us laughing as if we couldn't stop. But we did stop, very sudden, because we saw Lola's eyes had slid half open and she was watching the pair of us like an old parrot.

'For God's sake get her eyes closed,' Mom said, disgusted. 'I'll fetch you a couple of pennies.'

I pushed Lola's eyes closed and laid a penny and a ha'penny on top, which was all she could find. I covered her, pulling an old sheet up over her twisted feet, the wasted belly which had turned out twelve children, three dead, nine living, her papery old bosoms and her mean, crumpled face. I thought how a dead body isn't just the person who's left it a few minutes ago but a shrine to everyone they've ever been. And I also thought thank God I can have the bed to myself instead of perching on the edge waiting for the deluge.

There was a deluge then, because outside it started to rain like hell and the sky was so low it nearly scraped the rooftops. It felt like a promise of something, like God saying yes, I'll give you a chance, kid. Now you can make things right in your family. Now you can be happy.

Mom chose to name me Eugenie Victoria Josephine Mary Watkins (I don't suppose Dad had any say in the matter). At my christening at St Paul's Church in 1924, he leaned over my pram, a father for the first time, and I imagine his round face pink with pride.

'Look at her,' he said, chucking my cheek. 'She'll go far.'

Nanny Rawson, my other grandmother, stood just behind him, commented, 'With a gobful of names like that she'll need to.'

I don't know how far he thought I was going, but by 1939 none of us had got further than Brunswick Road, Balsall Heath, where we had a back door as well as a front and our very own flush toilet in the garden. I lived with my mom, my dad who was a bus driver, my little brother Eric, seven years younger (Mom's 'other mistake' as she kindly called him), and Mom's brother, Uncle Len. And Lola of course, up until now.

5

Nanny Rawson lived nearly half a mile away in Highgate, and Len stopped at home with her up until Mom's sister, my auntie Lil, had to move back in there with her kids and Len came to live with us. He wasn't quite the full shilling, Uncle Len. No one'd say why, so I took it for granted he must've been born that way. He was an enormous bloke. Didn't just come into a room, he took up half of it. He was all right. Sweet natured, and loved to hear people laugh. Not that living with Mom and Dad was ideal on that score.

He came to us a few months after Lola'd arrived, so our terraced house started to get crowded. Lola and I had had a room each. Mine was the little one at the end and Eric slept in with Mom and Dad at the front. But when Len arrived everything had to be juggled round.

'Eric'll stay in with us,' Mom decreed. She didn't object to Eric down at the foot of their bed on his mattress. I suppose someone else in the room helped keep Dad off her. 'And you'll have to bunk up with Lola at the end.'

'With Lola! But Mom – there's no room for another bed in there.'

'You won't need another bed. The one you've got now's three-quarter size. You'll have to share. It'll only be for a bit. She can't last much longer.'

This was appalling news. Lola was revolting enough round the house, but to have to share my bed with her! Being an innocent twelve-year-old, I protested, 'Well, why can't I share with Len?'

Mom glowered at me. 'Don't talk so silly. Len's a grown man and he needs a decent room to himself. And besides,' as she was turning away, 'he's not without a few funny habits.'

Typical of her, that was. Never explained things.

'Don't run backwards!' she'd shout at me when I was younger and capering along the pavement. 'I know someone who died doing that.'

I found out about Len's funny habits all too quickly. I barged into his room one day and there he was, kneeling on the floor in front of the chamber pot, unbuttoned, with his willy clenched in his hand, except it wasn't like a willy any more. More like a policeman's truncheon. He didn't even notice me, he had this grin on his moon face and whatever he was doing I could see he was enjoying it. I knew I'd best not say anything to Mom. I carried on sharing with Lola and kept out of Len's bedroom.

Len was no trouble though. I was puzzled to notice Mom'd do anything for him, because she certainly didn't display that attitude to anyone else, not even her pal Stella, and you can at least choose your friends. Len just sat about or went for little walks round the local streets. He played tip-cat and football with Eric and me. He looked through Eric's comics, *Desperate Dan* and *Hotspur*. He sat in the pub and laughed if someone else was laughing, and people were mostly kind to him. He never had a job in those days. Jobs were hard enough to come by for anyone. I grew ever so fond of him. He was more like a big, soft brother to me than a grown up man.

Dad couldn't make a fuss about him moving in because he had Lola there already, transforming Mom into one of the saints and martyrs even though I did most of the skivvying. He liked Len. Besides, he wasn't the sort to make a fuss. Quiet man, my dad. He didn't get up and bang on about anything much. Mom could've got away with murder, and often did. Emotional murder. Poison darts kept flying his way – 'Victor, you're useless, hopeless, no good to anyone ...'

7

She made it quite clear to Eric and me that pregnancy and birth had been the greatest trials of her life and that to compensate her for the ordeal of bringing us into existence we had to bother her as little as we could manage. We'd been through the ploys of trying to get her attention by loudness, naughtiness and breaking things, and nothing had worked for long, so we had to learn to put up with it and shift for ourselves.

Mom had days sometimes when she couldn't even seem to move herself, just sat in a chair staring at the walls. Life weighted her to the floor. She was literally bored stiff. Bored with my dad, my solid, reliable dad, who had not an ounce of lightness or fun in him but was all a husband and father should be – except whatever it was she wanted him to be. I know she never loved him – not even when they first got married. Lil always said Mom married him to keep up with her pal Stella.

When I used to hear them talking, Stella and Mom, about their lives, Mom'd say, 'And then of course I went and married Victor.' The way she said it it might as well have been, 'And then I died.'

A lot of women didn't expect more than they got, but she did. She was romantic and full of dreams. I reckon on those bad days, when her face was strung tight and her hair never came out of a scarf and she smoked and snapped and sighed all day, she was looking at her life those last twelve, thirteen, fourteen years and thinking, 'What a waste.'

For Eric and me there was Nanny Rawson. She was always there and always, after a fashion, pleased to see us. When Mom sat listless in her chair and said, 'Oh go out and do summat with yourselves,' we'd often as not shoot up the Moseley Road to our nan's, me holding Eric's little hand to keep him off the horse road. Nanny

Rawson'd give us a piece with jam if she had any and let us play out in the yard with the neighbour's kids. We'd stay until it was nearly time for bed. When we got home, sometimes Mom had cooked for us. Sometimes she was still sitting in her chair, the same cup of cold tea balanced on the arm.

Course, all the family were at Lola's funeral in their glory. Dad got back from his camp with the Territorials two days earlier. He joined the TA a year before, after the Munich crisis, which I suppose made him feel useful and got him out of the house one evening a week after a shift on the buses, and some weekends. Must have been restful for him. They were training him up as a signalman.

Life was barely worth living in our house the morning we buried Lola. Mom had given Dad hell ever since Lola passed on because he hadn't been there.

'I couldn't help it, Doreen,' he snapped at her finally. He must have been feeling guilty enough already. 'But I had to go. The way things are there's going to be a war – soon.'

'There's not going to be a war,' Mom sneered. 'They won't let it happen.' She looked suddenly frightened. 'They won't, will they?'

She'd been up since crack of dawn, a scarf round her curlers, cutting bread for sandwiches, eggs bobbling noisily in a pan of water. Good job it was only sandwiches because she wasn't the world's greatest cook. She got everything too dry or too wet and finished it off by burning it. Her rock cakes spread out into black coins of sponge, charred sultanas bulging out.

'Who's coming then?' I asked.

9

Mom sniffed. 'Don't know for sure. But some of *them*'ll most likely turn up.'

'Them' were some of Dad's long lost relatives, and she was going to show them what was what. Dad's brothers and sisters were all scattered about, some in Birmingham, some wider still. We weren't sure where and we never saw any of them. But Mom was determined that she was a cut above whoever might turn up so it was out with a tin of salmon and the house had to be spotless.

The coffin was in the front room taking up most of the space between the whatnot in the window with an aspidistra on the top in a brass pot, leaves snagging on the window nets, and the little china cabinet at the back end of the room. The chairs had been pushed to one side, and dead flies dusted out of the vases. Mom liked to keep the front room a bit special so we spent most of our time in the back round the table.

Thing about my mom was, she had dreams of everything all kippers and curtains out on one of the new estates. She'd say names like 'Glebe Farm, Weoley Castle, Fox Hollies' with a special look in her eye, sort of tasting them on her tongue. New houses with bathrooms and neat little gardens front and back. But she wouldn't go. It wasn't Dad stopping her. And we weren't half as hard up as some of the neighbours. Balsall Heath, just a couple of miles south of the middle of Birmingham, may not have been her first choice, but she could at least feel she'd gone up in the world because she had a back and a front room and a patch of garden, and she had a set of willow pattern china off the Bull Ring when many a household in the street were still drinking out of jam jars. And in the end she needed another kind of security – she'd never move too far from her mom, Nanny Rawson, in her back-house in Highgate.

It was Nan who'd arranged everything for Lola: the plot in Lodge Hill Cemetery, registering the death, the hearse. Mom had one of her times of deciding she couldn't cope. But she was the one in charge today, pinner over her nightdress, dispensing orders. The house filled up with shouting.

'Doreen – I need a shirt collar ...' Dad didn't tend to move when he needed anything, just sat tight and hoped it would appear.

'Here!' she hollered up the stairs from the back room. Could bawl like a fishwife she could, when she forgot she was trying to be respectable. She had a collar in one hand, loaf under the other arm, the top half buttered. 'It's starched.' Course it was. I'm surprised she didn't starch his underpants.

'Genie – I want you out scrubbing the front step before you think about getting dressed up. Eric—' thwack—'get your hands off. Look – the table's all smears now!'

'I daint mean to,' Eric snivelled, clutching his smarting ear.

'Genie – just get him out of here. Keep out of my way. And Lenny, sit down, will you? You're getting me all mithered. At least you're ready – even if it is hours before time.'

Len launched himself backwards into a chair so the cushion would've groaned if it were capable. His clothes were too tight and none of us had had any breakfast, but Len still had the grin stuck on his face that had been there since Monday when he got his first ever job, aged twenty-nine. He was going to pack shells at the Austin works, travel out on the bus, the lot, and he was so

11

pleased with himself he'd hardly been able to sit still since.

'You'd best go in the garden for a bit,' I advised Eric. 'I've got to scrub the step.'

'Can't I come and watch you, Genie?'

'All right. If you have to.'

I completed my chore in the morning sunlight, made hazier by all the smoke from the factory chimneys. The smell of manure rose from the horse road and there was a whiff in the air of something chemical. Eric stood leaning against the front wall, sniffing and idly scuffing his shoes against the brickwork.

'You'd better pack that in,' I said, 'or you won't half get it.'

Then I was allowed to get changed. I had one decent dress which Mom had knocked up on her old Vesta machine. First time she'd made me anything. It was a pale blue shirtwaister, and I wore it with a pair of white button-up shoes which were scuffed grey round the toe-tips and pinched at the sides, but I could at least still get them on. I felt awkward in that dress. That was partly because Mom had managed to get the waist too high. And I suppose I didn't think of myself as a girl – not a proper one, like my friend Teresa, and other girls who liked to dress up. I was so skinny, Dad used to say, 'We could use you as a pull-through for a rifle' – elbows and knees sticking out and my socks would never stay up. I was supposed to be a woman by now, getting 'bosoms' and acting grown up. After all, I was out at work. But it was all a flaming nuisance, to my mind. Your monthly coming on, rags chafing in your knickers. I didn't half wish I was a boy sometimes.

Downstairs in the back room I peeped in the oval

12

mirror. My face looked back at me from the yellow glass, big grey eyes almost too big as my face was so thin and delicate, pointy nose, though not sticking out as far as Mom's. My straight, straight brown hair was parted in the middle and hung thick over my shoulders. Auntie Lil used to say I was prettier than my mom. She may've said that just to rile Mom of course. I gave myself a smile which brought out my dimple, like a little pool by the right side of my mouth.

Dad emerged from the stairs and said, 'You look a picture, Genie. Be nice to see you doll yourself up more often.' I went pink. Dad seemed to be having trouble turning his head. Must've been the starch in that collar.

Mom'd been fussing on the way. 'Victor, your tie's not straight. Genie, you take Len into church and make sure he behaves himself. Eric, for pity's sake stop sniffing.' Poor Eric. Very snotty, my little brother. Whatever the time of year there was always a reservoir of green up his nose.

They were all waiting outside St Paul's Church in their Sunday best, a line of desperately polished shoes, and coats even though it was the middle of summer, giving off a smell of mothballs. Nanny Rawson had on a navy straw hat and her mud-coloured coat which she'd bought off a lady second-hand, saying you could get away with brown on any occasion. She was a wide lady, walked rocking from foot to foot the way you might shift a full barrel of beer. She had an ulcer on her right leg so it was thickly bandaged, and round, muscular calves as if someone had dropped a couple of cricket balls down inside her legs. To match her hair she had a

13

bit of a black moustache, which is more than my grandad had. Bald as a pig's bladder he was. But of course he'd been dead ten years by 1939.

There were a group of four people in shabby clothes and down-at-heel shoes who I thought looked ever so old, and when Dad went to them, red in the face, sweat on his forehead, I realized these were some of the uncles and an auntie we never saw. He shook each of their hands or slapped their shoulders, said, 'Awright are you?' and couldn't seem to think of anything else to say. Mom was looking down her nose at them, and they shifted about on their feet and looked embarrassed. I went and shook hands too, and one of the men looked nice and kissed me, and they said, 'Hello Eugenie,' the woman with a sarky note in her voice. I don't think she was my proper auntie. She just married someone.

Lil was there with her kids. She had a wide black hat on with a brim which we'd never seen before. Mom sidled up to her nodding her head like a chicken at the hat. 'Cashed in your pawn ticket in time, did you?'

Dad was saying, '*Doreen*,' pulling her arm. 'Remember who we're burying today, please.'

'I'm hardly likely to forget, Victor,' brushing his hand off. 'Since I was the one left to deal with it all while you were off playing soldiers.'

Dad's cherub face was all pink now, his voice trembling. 'How many times do I have to tell you, the Territorial Army does not play soldiers. Don't you realize just how serious ...'

Lil started putting her threepence ha'penny in too, her lovely face puckered with annoyance. In a stage whisper she started off, 'Don't forget, you stuck up cow, that some of us do a job of – Patsy!' She broke into a yell, catching sight of him leaping gravestones like a

14

goat. 'Get here – now!' That was our Lil for you. Scarcely ever got through a whole sentence without having to bawl out one of the kids.

'Pack it in, the lot of you,' Nan hissed at them. 'They're staring at us.' She tilted the straw hat towards the aunt and uncles whose eyes were fixed on us. 'Doreen – go in,' Nan commanded, still through her teeth. 'And see if you can keep your gob shut.'

'Come along, Eric.' Mom flounced off in her mauve and white frock, yanking Eric along in his huge short trousers which reached well below his knobbly knees.

Dad seemed flustered, not knowing who to sit with, and ended up following me in with Len. I took Len's hand. 'Come on – I'll look after you.'

He came with me like a little kid. No one wanted to sit in the actual front row so we filed into the second lot of pews. Len's knees were touching the back of the pew in front, his enormous thighs pressed against mine. It wasn't that he was a fat man, he was just built on a huge scale. He kept looking round at me, pulling faces and grinning.

'S'nice this, Genie, in't it?' I think he liked the candles and the coloured glass. He pointed to his fly buttons and said loudly, 'What if I need to go?'

'You just tell me,' I whispered. 'I'll take you out. Try and keep your voice down, Len.'

He heard Cathleen, Lil's three-year-old, laughing behind us, so he started laughing too – hor hor hor – hell of a noise, shoulders going up and down.

'Len.' I gripped his arm, nervously. 'You're not s'posed to be laughing. Lola's in that coffin up there.' I pointed at it, flowers on top, the lot.

'In there?' He pointed a massive finger.

I nodded. 'She's dead – remember?'

15

But that set him off even worse and I had to start getting cross and say, 'Now Len, stop it. You mustn't.'

Along our pew Mom was frowning across at Eric for pulling snot up his nose too loudly. Then there was a bawl from behind. Cathleen must've pulled Tom's hair and made him whimper and Lil had smacked him one low down on the leg hoping no one'd see. He blarted even louder and Cathleen was grinning away to herself under those angelic blond curls, the mardy little cow. Nanny Rawson, next to the aisle in our pew, swivelled round and gave them all the eye from under that hat.

A train rattled past at the back of the church. At last the Reverend started in on his prayers. 'We brought nothing into this world and it is certain we carry nothing out . . .'

I started to feel sorry for old Lola now I couldn't smell her. Dad was a bit upset and blew his nose a lot. He'd tried to do his best for her. After all, she was his mom, even if she was a miserable old bitch. He was forever telling us it was just her age. She wasn't always like that. Mom'd say, 'Oh yes she flaming well was.'

But I sat there and thought what a rotten life she must've had. Terrible poverty they lived in when her kids were small. A slum house, not even attic-high, two up, one down on the yard, with nine children in the house and never enough to go round. Didn't make her a kind person. Her husband did his best, from what Dad said, but he was a bit of a waster. My father was her little ray of sunshine. Bright at school and had always held down a job. The other kids drifted away and mostly stayed away.

I looked across at the coffin as we stood up and started in on 'Abide with me'. I thought about her old

16

wasted body in there. How she'd climb out of bed very quick and pull her clothes up to sit on the chamber pot. Sometimes I'd get a glimpse of something hanging down there, like an egg, white and glistening. She'd sit for an age, grunting and cursing, willing urine to flow the way you will a late train to come. Sometimes she'd put her hand up her, try and push it back and relieve herself, and she'd give a moan. Soon as she lay down again it'd all come in a rush and I'd be clinging to the edge of the mattress trying to keep as far from her as I could, almost crying at the smell.

Poor old Lola. Thank God she'd gone.

'I hope they don't notice I've eked the salmon out with milk,' Mom whispered, stirring the teapot in the kitchen at the back. 'Here, take these through, will you Genie?'

I carried the sandwiches to the front room, Mom's willing slave as ever. Willing because I'd have done anything for her if only she'd be glad I existed. She was being quite pally-pally with me today because she needed my help.

Everyone was crushed into the front room except Lil, who'd taken the kids out to let off steam in the garden. Eric and Little Patsy, a year his junior, were brawling on the grass like puppies.

It went all right, just about. Dad's brothers and sister were either silent or very very jolly and the uncles loosened their threadbare ties, asked each other for a light and stood about smoking and sweating. There wasn't the room to sit down. The auntie spent a lot of time peering in Mom's china cabinet. They ate all they could and went out saying, 'We'll have to do this again,' but all knowing the truth was that it'd be at the next funeral, and departed even more awkward than when they arrived.

So that left our family with the curling egg sandwiches and nubs of Madeira cake to get on in our usual affectionate way. I stuck with Len and brought him more helpings of food because he could eat for ever, his mouth churning away like a mincer.

Lil had brought the kids back in. She was a stunner, our Lil, and like a flypaper to men. Like Nanny Rawson she looked as though she had a touch of the tar-brush: she had tresses of black hair, almond-shaped brown eyes and olive skin, and today she'd got a dab of colour on her lips. Before she had the kids she sometimes used to put curl papers in her hair, and it hung in shiny black snakes down her back. Wild as the wind she was then, all high heels and make up. She worked as a french polisher in a toy factory, on gun handles and little carpet sweepers.

Mom'd always been jealous of her. Lil's looks of course, for a start, even though she was worn to the bone nowadays with the kids. Lil was chosen as the May Queen when they were kids at school and Mom's never forgiven her for that. But I think another part of her jealousy was Lil moving back in with our nan after her husband died. Well, I say died. Patrick Heaney was his name. Cheerful Big Patsy. Mom never liked him. Doesn't like the Irish full stop, and his other crime was to make Lil happy. Patsy got into a fight one night – more of a friendly by all accounts – but the other bloke knocked him over on the kerb and he had a nasty bang on the head. He was never the same after. Turned to the booze, had fits, couldn't get out of bed of a morning.

Next thing was they were dragging him out of the canal. It was a shame. Lil was in pieces. But at least while he was alive she really had something with Big Patsy that Mom'd never had. You could see it in their eyes. She'd sit in his lap, even after Little Patsy was born. Popped out a couple of kids in as many years.

But she couldn't cope on her own, what with holding down a job and the kids and their third child Cathleen being only a titty-babby. Poor Lil.

Cathleen sat on Lil's lap and started pulling at her waves of black hair.

'Leave off, will you?' Lil snapped. 'Never get a second to yourself with kids, do you? Can't even fart in peace.'

'Give 'er 'ere,' Nan said. She took the little girl on to her enormous lap and bounced her until she squealed.

Lil sat back, tired as usual. Her mouth turned down more nowadays. 'How about another cuppa tea, Dor, now that lot've gone?'

'You know where the kettle is,' Mom said with her usual charm.

'I'll get it.' I went to the kitchen and made tea, not that I expected any thanks for it, and when I got back they were arguing. Mom and Lil that is. Len was shuffling a pack of cards. He never played anything, just shuffled. He and Dad usually just sat waiting for the wenches to burn themselves out.

Our nan had a look in her eye I didn't quite like. She was sat forward. Cathleen had got down and was on the floor waving her legs in the air, showing off her bloomers.

'Because,' Nan was saying, 'it's the practice run Sat'dy, ain't it?'

'I'm not sending my kids nowhere,' Lil said, scraping at egg on Tom's face with her nails. 'Whatever Adolf bloody Hitler's planning.'

Hitler this, Hitler that, all we ever heard nowadays. I put the tray down, pushing plates aside. Everyone was keyed up about the thought of war war war.

'Your mom'll need you at 'ome,' Nanny Rawson said to me. 'You can look after your dad.'

'Why?' Lil looked at Mom. In a nasty tone she demanded, 'Where're you off to then?'

'With Eric.'

Eric looked from one to the other of them, mouth full of cake and a hopeless expression on his face. He knew he wasn't going to get a say.

'You mean you're sending him? To live with complete strangers?' Lil was on her high horse. She caught hold of Cathleen and cuddled her tight, doing her best impression of the Virgin Mary.

'That's what we're supposed to be doing, isn't it? Or d'you want your kids bombed and gassed like they say they will be?'

'But just sending him off … Poor little thing.' Eric looked about as depressed as anyone would be faced with the choice of bombing and gassing or being sent away to live heaven only knew where. 'Anyhow,' Lil said. 'You don't need to go to the practice. Not as if you're going with him, is it?'

Mom was silent for a split second. Everyone stared at her. She stuck her chin out. 'I thought I'd go.'

Dad sat up then. News to him, obviously. 'But Doreen …'

Nan was scandalized. 'You mean go off – leave Victor and Genie?'

'Not for good. I thought I could just deliver him. Have a look over where he's going.'

'But you're not allowed,' Lil argued. 'I'd be allowed to go, with Cathleen so young, but you're not – not unless you're a helper or you're ...' Lil looked ever so suspicious all of a sudden.

Mom stared back at her, brazen, nose in the air.

'You're never going to tell them ...' Lil started laughing a real nasty laugh. 'Oh I get it. Well it wouldn't be the first time, would it? After all, you were "expecting" when you got Victor to marry you, weren't you? Longest pregnancy on record that one. What was it? Fifteen months?'

Dad had gone nearly purple in the face, to the roots of his hair. Mom stabbed her knife into the last piece of Madeira cake as if she wanted to kill something. 'You bloody little bitch.' I thought she was going to slap Lil but Nanny Rawson was on her feet pushing them apart.

'That's enough from the pair of you.' She stood with her arms outstretched between them.

'She only said she was pregnant so she could beat Stella to the altar!'

'Well at least I've still got a husband – I'm not dragging my kids up in the slums.'

'But you don't give a monkey's about sending Eric off to live with Christ only knows who ...'

'That's why I'm saying I'm expecting you silly cow – so I can get on the train with him ...'

I went and sat by Eric, who no one seemed to have given a moment's thought to.

'Take no notice,' I said, putting my arm round him.

'Is she going to send me away?' He had tears in his eyes. 'Where am I going?'

'Somewhere nice I expect. In the country. See the cows and sheep. It'll be all right,' I told him, though I hadn't the foggiest whether it would or not. 'Here – want a game of snap?'

Eric nodded, picture of misery.

'Right, now sit yourselves down,' our Nan was saying. 'As a mark of respect to Lola, since we 'aven't seen much of that yet, we'll 'ave a song.'

'I'm not singing with her,' Mom said.

'That's what you think.' Nan got her squeeze box out from the corner and sat with it on her lap, legs apart, skirt pulling tight across her knees.

'She's wearing red bloomers,' Eric whispered to me, distracted for a moment.

'Doreen, Lil, stand up. You sing along too, Len,' Nan urged him.

I got the cards off Len and played with Eric, and Dad sighed with relief that they'd all stopped carrying on and the two loving sisters started on a song. Nan was fantastic on the accordion. She'd picked it up off her dad and she could play the piano too. Just about anything you asked in the way of songs. A gift that, that ran in the family until it got to me, apparently. Mom could have a go too, given the chance. She, Lil and Nanny Rawson all had good strong voices. People called them the Andrews Sisters, and they did a turn in the pub now and again. Times when they sang were mostly the only occasions when they weren't arguing.

So they stood in our front room with the sunlight fading outside and Dad lighting one fag after another to calm his nerves. They sang 'The Rose of Picardy' and 'Ta-ra-ra-boom-de-ay', blending their voices, and then that new song, 'The Lambeth Walk' everyone was mad about. Lil looked so pretty and not tired suddenly, Nan's

22

face was softer than usual and Len was swaying from side to side in his chair, face split by a smile, in heaven.

Mom looked almost happy while the music was going on. I saw Dad watching her and there were tears in his eyes. Shook me a bit, that. I wondered whether he was thinking about Lola, or about the fact that he might soon have to go away, or whether he was wondering the same as I was: why Mom couldn't find it in her to be happier with him – with all of us.

Come the end of that week we were in for a surprise. I was working in a pawn shop in Highgate, which disgusted Mom, but it was one of the best jobs I'd had so far. That week, as we stood in the little shop on the Moseley Road, we watched a crowd filling sandbags to shore up the factories opposite. Every day there were changes. That Friday I walked home after work and saw the last evening rays catching the bloated shape of a barrage balloon, a silky light coming from it. Some people, Mom among them, were still saying, 'Oh there's not going to be a war.' But if there was to be no war, what was all this for? Digging trenches in the parks, blackout curtains downstairs, and sending the kids away.

We'd had the gas masks months. One day when I got home Mom'd said in a grim voice, 'Look what's arrived.' There was a pile of boxes by the door. The masks were most off-putting. They looked a bit of a joke with their mouse faces until you put one on. When I pulled it over my face it was so tight, and the smell of rubber made you heave. The leaflets told us there'd be wardens round with rattles if we had a gas attack.

'I couldn't wear that,' Mom said, shuddering. 'Make me sick that would.'

Dad, standing in shirtsleeves at the door, remarked, 'I don't s'pose being gassed'd make you feel all that marvellous neither.'

I didn't really understand about war. Everyone was forever on about 'the Last One' but I wasn't born 'til nearly six years after it finished. All I knew was that everyone was living on their nerves. Mom was on at Dad because he might have to go away. 'What did you have to go and join the TA for? Other men of your age aren't being called up. How d'you think I'm going to manage without you here?' she'd wail. Tears turned on as well. There was a feeling about, excited and deadly serious at the same time, building up like the tension in a dog waiting to spring.

When I walked through the front door that evening I knew something was different. It was quiet, much more so than usual, but I could hear a voice in the back room. A man's voice. Posh. I didn't know who it was. I pushed the door open and before I'd had a chance even to open my mouth they all said, 'Ssssh!' without even looking at me. There they were, all sat round the table: Mom, Dad, Eric, Len. And in the middle of the table, shiny and new and absolutely gorgeous, there she was.

'Blimey! Whose—? What—? Whose is it?'

'Sssssh,' they said again. Len was making gleeful sounds, bouncing up and down in his seat.

The man's voice went on for a moment longer, then music started to trickle out into the room. I tiptoed closer and stared. It was a beautiful thing, almost a couple of feet long, encased in veneered wood with a dark grain across it as if it had been washed by the sea. On one half of the front was the speaker, the overlaid wood cut into a sunburst. On the other half, set into a metal surround, was the dial, with little ebony knobs underneath it. Out from it, louder now, were coming the sounds of violins and trumpets and other instruments all pitching in together, and it gave me a queer feeling. Made me want to cry suddenly though I didn't know why. Even Len went quiet.

I didn't get any sense out of anyone until Mom got up to put the kettle on.

'So – whose is it?'

'Len's. He bought it. First wage packet.' She moved her mouth close to my ear. 'We made up the extra for him – saw he had enough.' Her little brother. The one person in the world she'd kill to protect.

'Is that yours then, Len?' He looked as if he was going to burst, head nodding up and down like crazy.

'Pleased as punch he is,' Dad said. As if he needed to.

I squeezed Len's shoulder. 'Aren't you lucky? It's really smashing.'

Next day, Mom dragged Eric off to school for his evacuation rehearsal. The schools opened specially, even though it was the summer holidays. Mom had put away her ideas of being able to wangle a passage with him now it had dawned on her that Dad might have to go sooner than she'd realized. Eric had to go off with a small holdall for his clothes and a little bag for his 'iron rations' and his gas mask.

It was a peaceful morning in one way. Dad sat and read the *Sports Argus* and we didn't clear away breakfast for a good hour. Len settled himself down by his wireless and kept twiddling the dial, catching torn up bits of sound until he heard something he fancied.

I was supposed to be cooking lunch, but I sat down for a bit too, feeling that without Mom around I could leave my hair loose and straggly and no one would tick me off for the grubby stains on my frock. I stretched my legs out in front of me, seeing how skinny and pale they looked, and wished I didn't have a figure like a clothes-horse. But all the time worries about Eric kept flickering through my mind and I had a queasy ball of tension inside me. I thought about my family all being split up and suddenly they didn't seem so bad any more and I wanted things to stay as they were.

'Dad?'

'Mm?'

'If there's a war will you have to go straight away?'

He laid the paper down in his lap and looked ahead. Outside someone was having a fire and rags of smoke kept drifting past the window. 'Could be any time now, love.'

'Oh.' The music carried on quietly behind us.

Dad turned his head to look at me. 'I know I'm not all your mother would want . . .' He couldn't seem to finish that bit. 'You will look after her for me, won't you?'

I nodded and he looked away again. 'You're a good wench.'

That morning, while we were waiting and wondering, I heard a singer who was to become one of my favourites. Her voice came from the wireless strong and dark as gravy browning. We sat quite still while she was singing. The second she'd finished, Len pointed at the wireless and said, 'Gloria.'

'What you on about, Len? They said her name was Anne Shelton.'

He shook his head hard and pointed again. 'Gloria.'

I realized he meant the wireless itself, and I saw how

much it suited her. Glorious Gloria. From then on she was never known as anything but Gloria.

One Wednesday night we were all listening to *Band Waggon*, all in stitches at Arthur Askey, Len laughing at us laughing – hor hor hor – out of his belly. We had Gloria turned up high and I thought she was the best thing that had ever happened because before that I never ever remember us all sitting laughing together. Even Mom looked happy, and I saw Dad watching her, all hopeful.

And then she stopped. Right in the middle of it, no more Gloria. Len was out of his chair, wild at the knobs. 'Gloria ... Gloria ...' Not listening to Mom, who was trying to say, 'Lenny, it's OK, it's just the accumulator ...'

Len sank back on his chair and blubbed, fat slugs of tears rolling from his eyes and his shoulders shaking as if there was an earthquake. 'Gloria ... Gloria!'

'LEN!' Mom bawled down his ear. 'GLORIA WILL BE ALL RIGHT. WE NEED TO TOP UP HER ACCUMULATOR!' To the rest of us, she said, 'Listen to me. *Gloria*. Getting as bad as he is.'

She got through to him in the end and he stopped crying, but his face was dismal. He spent the rest of the evening with Gloria in his lap, lying across his thighs as if she was an injured cat.

I took the accumulator in on my way to work the next day. There was a cycle shop on Stoney Lane would top them up for you. I'd never given much thought to what was in them before, but I soon found out because the aroma of spilt acid in that shop made my eyes water. It was eating into the floor.

'You got a spare?' the bloke asked.

We hadn't, though I thought we'd better get one so's not to have this performance every time.

'I'll be back for it after work,' I told him.

So, come the evening I handed over threepence, and it would have been worth a shilling just to see Len's face when I walked in with it. Gloria was on again straight away in time for *The Six O'Clock News*.

Those last days of August we still waited and waited. It was like being held under water.

The groups of people gossiping in Nan's shop were saying, 'Let's get it over with if it's coming. Just let us know one way or the other.'

It was a time full of instructions. Leaflets through the door, the papers, and of course Gloria, who took our hands and led us into the war, giving out advice and information as we went. Hearing the voices which came from her was like someone sat right there in the back room with you. And she gave us relief from it, letting our minds slip away into plays and stories and songs.

The newspapers were different. On 31 August Dad brought home the *Birmingham Mail*. There was the banner across the front, stark in black and white:

EVACUATION TOMORROW ... BRITAIN AWAITS
HITLER'S REPLY.

September 1939

'Genie? can I come in with you?'

It was before dawn. I could just see Eric's outline in the doorway of my room.

'What's up?'

He came silently up to my bed. 'She's sending me away, ain't she?'

I pulled the bed open. 'Here – hop in.'

'Ain't she?' His toes were chilly against my leg.

'She thinks it's for the best. You don't want that nasty man Hitler dropping bombs on you, do you, Eric?'

His tousled head moved from side to side against my chest. I put my arms round him, scrawny little bit that he was, and pulled the sheet close round us.

'Little Patsy's not going.'

'But the Spinis are – Francesca and Giovanna and Tony – even Luke.' My friend Teresa's brothers and sisters.

'They'll all be together . . . I'll be all on my own.'

'You never know – you might be able to go with them.'

But he was already crying, snuffling like a kitten, a hand pressing on one of my titties, such as I had.

'Don't wanna go. I don't wanna.'

'Now Eric – it won't be for long,' I kept telling

him. 'It'll be for the best. Mom only wants the best for you.'

I lay holding him, hoping that was the truth.

Mom stood by the open back door with a packet of Players, blowing smoke across our thin strip of garden. I went out to use the privy. There were cobwebs under the roof, cut out squares of the *Gazette* on a string, and no seat. I sat on the cold white enamel feeling a breeze under the door. When I came out, a bird was singing. A thin mesh of cloud covered the sky but the air was growing warm. It was about six-thirty.

Mom stood with one arm wrapped round the waist of her cotton nightdress, her bit of stomach pushing out from under it, other hand holding the cigarette in front of her face. Her skin looked pasty, nose shiny with night sweat. She was often like that, miles away, but this time her expression was drawn and frightened. I didn't even think she'd seen me, until she said, 'What're we going to do?'

I stared at her. I was angry at her for sending Eric away, and angrier because I knew she was right: there was going to be a war and none of us knew what would happen, and we were all confused and frightened.

'How d'you mean?'

'I don't know if I'm doing the right thing.'

You're the mom, I thought, not me. What you asking me for?

'Mrs Spini's got four to send,' I said, stepping past her.

'Thought she wasn't going to.'

'Changed her mind.'

'Typical.' Tutting. 'Italians.'

I filled the teapot. Mom turned, slit-eyed, smoke unfurling from her nose. 'I'm only doing what I'm told, you know Genie.' She pointed in, towards Gloria. 'She – I mean they – say that's what we've got to do. This is an evacuation area. So we're s'posed to evacuate.'

'Well that's all right then, isn' it?'

'What are you looking at me like that for then?'

'I don't know.' I could feel the tears coming on. I turned away.

We heard my dad coming down. The stair door pushed open into the back room.

'It's right, in't it Victor?'

'What is?' He was stood there in his shirt and underpants.

'Sending Eric out of harm's way.'

Dad looked in some amazement into Mom's pinched, foxy face and saw that for the first time any of us could remember she was actually asking his advice. He pulled his shoulders back and stroked the reddish stubble on his chin. 'I should say so. If that's what they're saying.'

'Where is he, anyhow?'

'In my bed. Still asleep. He came in in the night, crying.'

'Shame.' Mom stubbed out her cigarette, grey ash dirtying a white saucer. 'Better get him up. It's an early start.' She went to the bread bin and fished out the stub end of a loaf. 'I'll make him a piece. He'll need summat on his stomach.'

Eric had to leave as soon as he'd had breakfast. His little bag and his gas mask stood forlornly in the hall. He clung to me, bawling his eyes out, and I was in tears myself. Hadn't thought how much I'd miss him, even

31

though he'd been stuck to me like my shadow all his life. There'd be no more Eric sneaking out after school with jam jars to sell for a ha'penny each, or driving us mad with that clattering go-cart of his with the back wheel falling off. No more walks to Cannon Hill Park to 'get him from under my feet' with a stale crust for the ducks. He suddenly seemed the most precious person I knew, my baby brother.

'Can't you come with me, sis?' he sobbed, already in his little gaberdine coat.

'I've got to get to work, Eric. Mom'll look after you. We'll see you soon.' Someone had their hands round my throat. 'Won't be for long.'

Mom didn't say much, couldn't. I did my best to hide most of my tears until they were away down the road. I stood waving him off, him turning, cap on his head, silver streaks of dried tears on his cheeks and new ones coming. He was twisting round, trying to wave, right the way to the corner. Then they were gone.

I had a proper cry then, upstairs. Dad had gone out the back. I suppose he was upset too. After, I blew my nose, pulled myself together and hurried to work. I thought of Eric all the way there, wondering where he'd end up, what it was like outside Birmingham, and what an unknown family somewhere would make of the arrival of my snotty-nosed brother, Eric Rudolph Valentino Watkins.

Palmer's was on the Moseley Road, its golden balls hanging outside. It was a dark little shop and stank a bit inside of course, of frowsty clothes and camphor, of the gas lamp that was kept burning most of the time so we could see to write out the tickets, and of Mr Palmer's fags.

He was already in when I got there. He was ever so old – seemed it to me – fifty-something at least, with half-moon glasses, a paunchy stomach and grey hair greased flat to his head. The whites of his eyes had gone yellow, maybe from smoking, like his fingers. He was a shrewd operator, Mr Palmer, but well capable of kindness.

'Ready for the Friday rush, Genie?' he said as I walked in, shivering in the dank shop in my cotton dress.

I liked Fridays. Payday – everyone coming to redeem the Sunday outfits they'd pawned on Monday for a bit of extra to see them through the week, and many would stop for a chat. We'd see them all back in the next Monday.

''Eere I am again,' one lady used to say. 'In out, in out, quick as me old man on a Sat'dy night.' Took me a minute or two to work out what she was on about.

'You get busy then,' Mr Palmer said. He was half way through a fag and didn't seem to be planning on shifting himself. I started tidying bits and bobs, dusting the crocks. He'd told me he'd never seen the place so organized before I came along.

That was my trouble with jobs. If I wasn't kept on the run I got bored. And not just a bit yawning bored, but screaming and running round the room sort of bored. I'd done all sorts: sticking Bo-Peep stickers on babies' cots, taking calls for a taxi firm where I got so fed up I gave the windows a going over in my spare time ... Soon as it got too slow my head filled with fog and my legs went heavy as brass weights. That was when it was time to look for something else.

As I was tidying I heard a click, and a voice said, '... we're on number twelve platform at Waterloo Station...'

My head jerked up. 'A wireless!'

Mr Palmer nodded, pleased with himself. It was at the end of the counter, a little box with a curved top and nothing like as grand as Gloria, but the reception was quite clear.

'Thought I'd bring it in,' he said, through a cloud of blue smoke. 'Didn't want to miss anything. Funny times these.'

'... the train's in,' the voice was saying, 'and the children are just arriving ... the tiny tots in front ... they're all merry and bright, we haven't had a single child crying and I think they're all looking forward to this little adventure ... The whistle goes, the children are looking out ... and in a moment this train moves out to an unknown destination ...' We heard the sound of the train chugging hard and loud, finally dying away. I thought of Eric sobbing his little heart out. Was he the only child in England not 'merry and bright'?

'You all right?' Mr Palmer asked. He twizzled the knob and the wireless went off.

I started to fill up a bit then. 'It's my brother Eric. He's eight. He's gone today.'

Mr Palmer tutted and shook his head. 'Terrible,' he said. 'They said they had it all sorted out the last time. Mind you, wench, it's for the best. They say this one'll start with bombing. If my kids were young I'd want 'em right out of it. Anyhow—' he winked at me— 'they reckon if anything happens it'll be finished by Christmas.'

The rush started, with all the Sunday best going out again, as if it was going to be just any old normal weekend. Then we heard Mrs Wiles coming. She lived round the corner on Balsall Heath Road and she'd bring in bundles for the neighbours. You could hear her coming from half way up the road, pushing the rottenest old wheelbarrow you've ever seen.

Mr Palmer turned to give me a wink. 'Oh – 'ere we go.'

The first we saw of her was her behind because she turned and shoved the door with it, too hard, so it flew open and the bell almost turned itself over ringing. She pulled the barrow down over the step with a loud 'thunk' so I wondered if that would be its last time, and stood blinking for a second or two, in her old man's cloth cap, a sacking apron and man's boots tied with string. She can't have been much different in age from my nan, but her face looked like an old potato.

'Mrs Johnson wants two shilling for this,' she said, picking up Mrs Johnson's bundle of washing.

Mr Palmer looked her in the eye over his glasses. 'One and nine.'

'Two shilling. She wants two shilling.'

'One and nine.'

Every week it was the same, and the look she gave him, I was laughing that much bent over the counter that I could barely write out the tickets.

'Oh you bloody fool,' she said, screwing up her leathery face. 'Oh, you old miser.'

They went through this with every bundle on the barrow. She counted and recounted the coins Mr Palmer gave her, and pushed them into a little pouch which she had tucked into her waistband.

This was all part of the normal performance. But what wasn't part of it was that this week she looked a lot more agitated than usual, couldn't seem to find her waist at all and was pulling at her long skirt as if she thought something might drop out of it. Then she started making funny noises like a guinea pig. Mr Palmer glanced anxiously at me.

'You all right, Mrs Wiles?' He pulled up the flap in the counter to get through and then just stood there while Mrs Wiles suddenly clutched at her chest, fingers clenched and head back pulling the chicken skin under her chin tight, and then dropped to the floor, pawn tickets fluttering from her.

'Oh Lor',' Mr Palmer said, looking down at her. 'Genie – what do we do?'

'Her pulse.' I ducked under too and knelt by Mrs Wiles's slumped body. 'I'll feel for her pulse. You go and get help.'

Mr Palmer charged out of the shop, probably faster than he'd moved in thirty years, and I found myself alone once again with a dead old lady. Because she was dead. I felt the faint pulse flicker, then disappear in her wrist. I folded her hands together over her chest, except one of them kept dropping off. Other customers started coming in.

'What's Mrs Wiles doing down there?' the first woman asked.

'She's dead.' My knees were shaking.

'Oh you poor kid! Did she just ...? Where's Reg Palmer?'

I shrugged. 'Gone to get help.'

By the time Mr Palmer came back with Mrs Palmer, who was fat and usually jolly but not at the moment as someone'd just died, there was quite a crowd in the shop, waiting with their tickets and standing round the walls because Mrs Wiles was taking up such a lot of the floor.

'Her son's coming,' Mrs Palmer said after tutting. 'He's arranging transport. In the meantime . . .'

Since we couldn't leave Mrs Wiles where she was, the Palmers and I stowed her behind the counter. Mrs P found an old sheet on a shelf.

'No one'll be wanting that back now,' someone remarked.

Course, there was barely room to move behind there, and I had to work with one foot on either side of her legs.

When things had settled down a bit Mr Palmer said, 'Oi – it's news time.' It was ten-thirty. He switched on the wireless.

The customers in the shop stood stock still as we heard it. Afterwards, everyone was coming in with their lips all in position as they got through the door to say, 'Have you heard? I suppose you'll have heard by now?' It was on everyone's face. 'They've gone into Poland. The Germans have invaded Poland. We're for it now.' One lady was crying. Her son was twenty and she hadn't forgotten the last war, lost two brothers.

What about my dad? I wondered. The air crackled with goings on, with nerves. I knew everything was changing and everyone thought it was very serious, that the kerbstones on the Moseley Road had been painted black and white for the blackout, that my brother had been taken from us.

It wasn't until the afternoon that Carl Wiles turned up to pick up his mom, and then not with very good grace. I saw Mrs Wiles carted out to his van like a sack of onions. I wondered if anyone had ever really loved her. And I thought, surely, surely there's got to be more to existence than slaving your fingers to the bone all your life and then dropping dead in a pawn shop and no one really caring whether you do or not?

The thought of Mom in a soggy heap was too much for me straight after work so I went to my nan's, which felt just as much like home. I knew I could tell her about Mrs Wiles passing on in front of me and she'd listen.

Belgrave Road was a wide, main street sloping down from the Moseley Road to the Bristol Road. Nan lived almost at the top, had done for years, in one of the yards down an entry behind the shops. As you went down the hill the houses gradually got bigger and bigger and at the bottom end there were some really posh ones. Nanny Rawson started her working life in one of those, in service to a family called the Spiegels, soon after the turn of the century. She didn't get paid in money, they gave her bits of clothes and food instead. She'd lived in three different houses in Belgrave Road, and, as Mom was forever reminding us, Nan brought up her three surviving children at about the same level of poverty as everyone else in the back-to-back courts of houses. Poor as grinding poor back then, after the Great War, not knowing from one day to the next if my grandad would be in work or out of it, drunk or sober. Their clothes shop was the heap tipped out in the yard by the rag and bone man.

'We couldn't shop three days ahead in them days,' Mom'd say (oh, here we go). 'It was hand to mouth. Your grandad was out of work and your nan in the factory, until she got that shop ... You got an ounce of jam at a time in a cup, if you was lucky. Your nan was up in the brew'us at five in the morning doing other people's washing to make ends meet.' Mom'd never forget it, scrubbing at the top of shoes with barely any soles on them, never knowing a full stomach, coats on the bed and the house lousy and falling down round their ears. Nan had struggled to give her kids better and Mom knew to hold on tight to what she'd got.

The road was full of the smell of hops from Dare's Brewery and the whiff of sawn wood from the timber merchant's down opposite Hick Street. On the corner stood the Belgrave Hotel, and Nan's huckster's shop was across the road with a cobbled entry running along the side of it which ran into the yard. The shop's windows had advertisements stuck to them for Brasso, Cadbury's, Vimto and such a collection of others that you could hardly see in or out. Her house, which backed on to the shop, was attic-high – three floors, one room on each, and in the downstairs you could walk through the scullery, lift up a little wooden counter and you were in the shop.

I was almost there when Nan's shop door flew open, bell jangling like mad, and two girls tumbled out shrieking and spitting like cats. One had a heap of blond hair and long, spindly legs pushed into a pair of ankle-wobbling high black patent heels. The other had crimpy red hair and a skin-tight skirt, scarlet with big white polka dots, and showing a mass of mottled leg.

'You mardy old bitch!' the blonde yelled into the shop at the top of her lungs. As she did so, she caught her heel in the brick pavement and fell over backwards, white legs waving. 'Now look what you've made me do, you fucking cow!'

The redhead was helping her up. 'You wanna watch it – we can have you seen to, grandma . . .'

Nanny Rawson loomed in the doorway, enormous in her flowery pinner crossed over at the back, face grimmer than a storm at sea. Bandaged leg or no, she was out of that door in a jiffy, giving the redhead a whopping clout round the face that nearly floored her. The girl set up a train-whistle shriek, as much from wounded pride as from pain, which brought people out of the shops to stare and grin.

'All right, Edith?' someone shouted. 'That's right – you give 'em one!' Nanny Rawson ignored them.

'Get this straight,' she barked at the girls. 'You may be Morgan's latest tarts but while you're in my shop you behave like proper 'uman beings and keep a civil tongue in your 'eads. Don't come in 'ere showing off to me. And if you want to come through and up my stairs—'

'They ain't your stairs, they're Morgan's,' the redhead retorted, hand pressed to her cheek. 'And there's bugger all you can do about it. 'Cept move of course, and do everyone a favour.'

Nan bunched her hand into a fist and the redhead quailed. 'Don't hit me again!' she pleaded, backing off.

The blonde had got to her feet by this time. Now I was closer I saw she had pale, pitted skin, thickly caked in powder, and can't have been that much older than me. If she'd been thinking of having another go at Nan she changed her mind, knowing she'd more than met her match, and turned on me instead. 'And what d'you think you're gawping at, you nosy little bitch?'

Nanny Rawson suddenly saw me too, and she didn't like her family getting involved with Morgan and his women. She rounded on the girls. 'Get inside there quick. For my own state of health I'm going to forget I ever saw you.' As they teetered back in through the door she shouted after them, 'Coming to him two at a time. It's disgusting!' There was a cheer from the bystanders which Nanny Rawson, on her dignity, completely ignored.

Her run-ins with the landlord Morgan and his endless parade of 'young trollops' had been going on since she started renting the place nigh on sixteen years ago, and she and Morgan, a scrawny, over-sexed weasel of a man, were growing old together. When Nan first got the shop she was desperate to keep the lease and was beholden to Morgan for keeping the rent low. Now she'd been here this long she wasn't going anywhere for anyone and Morgan knew he'd never get a better tenant. It had developed into a contest – who could hold out there the longest. But the fact that the only way to get to the upstairs was through the shop meant that Nan had had her nose rubbed in his preoccupations week in, week out, and even after all this time there was no chance of her accepting it.

As soon as the girls disappeared it was as if nothing had happened. Suddenly her face was full of doom. Hitler. Poland.

'What you doing 'ere?' she demanded.

'Come to see you, what else?'

'You don't look too good – seen your mother, 'ave you?'

'No. Why?'

She jerked her head towards the door. 'You'd best come in.'

Nan's shop had seemed like a magic palace to me when I was a kid. You couldn't see across the room much better than you could through the windows, there was that much stuff in there. She sold everything you could think of: sweets, kids' corduroy trousers, balls of string, gas mantles, mendits for pots and pans, paraffin, safety pins, scrubbing brushes. There were glass-fronted wooden cabinets where I used to bend down and breathe on the glass, see my ghostly eyes disappear into mist. Inside, rows of little wooden drawers held all sorts of bits and bobs, spools of cotton, hooks and eyes, ribbons. There were fly papers, brushes and paraffin lamps from the ceiling, and shelves round the sides and across the middle.

Nan folded her arms and stared at me. 'You'd best get home. Doreen'll need you. It's your dad. Soon as the news came out this morning they started calling up the territorials – 'e's already gone.'

'Gone?' I couldn't understand her for a minute. 'Where?'

'Into the army, Genie.' She softened, seeing the shock on my face. It was all too much in one day. Eric, Mrs Wiles, and now this. 'He's not far away. He'll be back to see you. Come on—' She led me by the shoulder, through the back into the house. 'Your mother'll cope while you have a cup of tea. It's just as much of a shock for you as for 'er, though no doubt she won't see it that way.'

I sat by the kitchen table which was scrubbed almost white. Nan's house was always immaculate, even with Lil's kids living there. She still prepared all her food on the old blackleaded range which gleamed with Zebo polish. She rocked round the table from foot to foot, rattling spoons, taking the teapot to empty the dregs in the drain outside. I looked at her handsome, tired face. Always here, Nan was. Always had been, with her hair, still good and dark now, pinned up at the back. She'd always been the one who looked after everyone: Doreen this, Len that, Lil the other. Slow old Len always here, round her, until he came to us. And now she was half bringing up the next generation.

I watched her pour the tea into two straight, white cups. There was shouting from the yard outside, getting louder, rising to shrieks. The sound of women bitching. Nan eyed the window and tutted. 'Mary and Clarys again.'

'You all right, Nan?'

'As I'll ever be.'

I went and looked out of the door into the yard. Two of Nan's neighbours, Mary and Clarys, were up the far end by the brewhouse, Mary with her red hair, hands on her hips, giving Clarys a couple of fishwifey earsful. Little Patsy, Tom and Cathleen had been playing round the gas lamp with another child. Usually there'd have been a whole gang of them out there. They'd stopped to watch, Tom, my favourite, swinging round the lamp by one straight arm.

'Wonder what's got into them two,' I said.

'Be summat to do with Mary's kids again,' Nan said. 'Right 'andful they are.'

The bell rang in the shop. Nan stood still, teapot in hand, listening as the door was pushed carefully shut. There were furtive footsteps on the front stairs. Morgan had arrived. His life was strung between his mom, who he lived with over his ironmonger's shop in Aston, and his bolt-hole here. Nan carried on with what she was doing, which nowadays was exactly what she would have done if Morgan was in the same room. It was the girls who could still get under her skin, but Morgan, so far as she was concerned, was invisible, like a tiny speck of dirt. He crept in and out with an ingratiating smile on his face, and what was left of his streaks of greasy hair brushed over so they lay across his head like something fished out of a river.

I sat back down and within minutes we heard Lil.

43

'Awright, awright,' she was saying to the kids. 'Let me at least get in through the sodding door.'

'I see them two are at it again,' she said, flinging herself down on the horsehair sofa, in the worn cotton dress she wore to work at Chad Valley Toys. She put a hand over her eyes. 'She wants to keep them kids in order she does. My head's fit to split.'

Nan handed her a cup of tea and stood in front of her, hands on hips. 'You having second thoughts?' There was silence. ''Bout sending the kids?'

'No I'm not!' Lil sat upright quick as a flash, then winced at the pain in her head. 'I'm not having anyone else lay a finger on them. Sending the poor little mites off to fend for themselves.'

At that moment the three 'poor little mites' roared in through the door at full volume. 'Mom! Mom! – what's to eat? We're starving!'

'Out!' Lil yelled over the top of them. 'Stop "Momming" me when I've only just got in. You can push off out of 'ere till your nan says tea's ready!'

The room emptied again. The voices had quietened down outside but Lil's boys started drumming a stick on the miskin-lids down the end of the yard. Lil groaned, then sat up and drank her tea, pulling pins out of her hair so that hanks of it hung round her face.

'That foreman won't leave me alone again. I'm sick to the back teeth of it.' Lil was forever moaning about men chasing her. It was such a nuisance, the way they wouldn't leave her alone . . . None of us believed a word. She loved every minute of it.

Nan ignored her. 'Victor's gone you know. Dor was up here earlier in a state. Called 'im up straight away.'

Lil stared back at her. 'Bejaysus.' She often said that. It was one of Patsy's sayings and she clung to it. 'I

44

didn't think it'd be so soon. They haven't said there's going to be a war yet. Not for sure.'

'Looks mighty like it though.'

'Poland,' Lil said with scorn. She lit a fag and sat back. 'Where the hell is Poland anyhow?'

Nan sat on the edge of her chair, sipping tea. 'I've cleared out the cellar.'

'What for?'

'What d'you think for? I'm not going out in those public shelters with just anyone. There's not much space down there but we can fit and it'll have to do. I've given it a scrub.'

'Charming. Reducing us to sitting in the cellar.'

'Want some bread and scrape, Genie?' Nan said.

'No, I'm all right, ta. Nan?'

'What, love?'

I told her about Mrs Wiles.

'Well, what a thing,' she said. 'I thought you was looking a bit shook up. Poor old dear.'

'Shame.' Lil took a drag on her cigarette. 'Be much nicer to die in Lewis's, wouldn't it?'

'Better not tell Doreen,' Nan said. 'She'll only say that's what you get for working in a pawn shop up 'ere.' Mom put on a show of thinking people in Highgate were common, which was rich considering she grew up there herself. When I got the job I didn't tell her for days.

'You'd better be moving on,' Nan said to me. 'Got to see to this blackout palaver tonight. Your mother never got it done for the practice, did she? She won't want all that on 'er own.'

'She's all right – it's light yet,' Lil said. She seemed to be coming round a bit now she'd got some tea inside her. 'Eric get off all right, did he?'

I nodded, miserable at the thought. Lil sat forward, her old sweet self for a moment. 'You'll miss him, won't you Genie love? But he'll be all right. He's a good boy.' She smiled at me prettily. 'You'll have to come round and see my lot when you want some company.'

I found Mom in tears of course, with Len taking not the blindest bit of notice. It wasn't that he lacked sensitivity. He'd most likely just given up by now. Soon as he got in from work he usually sat down by Gloria without even washing his hands unless we nagged him, and that was that.

'My boy!' Mom was carrying on behind her hanky. There was no sign of tea on the go. 'My poor little Eric. How will we ever know if they're looking after him properly?'

I felt impatient, although all day I'd had nothing but the same thought in my mind. 'Oh, I expect he'll have a grand time,' I said bitterly. 'Forget we exist.'

'But that's what I'm worried about!' Mom wailed. She flung herself up out of her chair, dabbing at her red eyes. 'First I've got no son, and now I haven't even got a husband!' She clicked the stair door open and disappeared upstairs, slamming it behind her.

'She's crying,' Len remarked.

'You don't say, Lenny.'

I was really fed up with her. Sometimes I'd have liked to be the one who could flounce about and cry and behave like a child. I got sick of being a mother to my own mom. I wanted someone to sit down and put their arm round me while I cried because my dad and my brother had gone away.

'I s'pose this means I'm cooking tea, does it?' I

snapped at Len, since he was the only person left to snap at, though I got no answer anyway.

There was liver in the kitchen. I started chopping onions. Len fiddled with Gloria until music came streaming from her. I felt a bit better. Len beamed. 'S'nice this, Genie, in't it?'

There was a voice kept coming on as I was cooking, saying we had to retune the wireless. Len was taking no notice, didn't understand.

I wiped my hands and went over. 'Len, the man says we've got to turn the knob to a different number.' Len stared blankly at me. I went and fiddled with Gloria's dial and Len got a bit agitated.

Just as I was dishing up, this voice said, 'This is the BBC Home Service.' I'd just called Mom down and we looked at each other expecting something else to happen.

'The what?' Mom shrugged and stepped over to look at herself in the mirror – 'What a sight' – then, as the light was waning outside, went round the windows, pulling all the black curtains she'd made. 'This should've been done earlier,' she said accusingly, pulling the ordinary curtains over them. 'I'll have to do upstairs tomorrow. Well this *is* going to be jolly I can see. Feels like the middle of winter.'

My liver and onions wasn't out of this world, though no worse than Mom would've managed, but she still turned her nose up at it.

'Gravy's lumpy. And how did you get the liver so hard?'

We waited, tensed up as the nine o'clock bulletin came on, but there was nothing new, nothing definite, except that Australia had said she'd support the Allies if war broke out.

'Who are the Allies?' I asked.

'Us of course.'

When we turned Gloria off, finally, to go up to bed, it was eerily quiet. There wasn't a sound from outside. Wasn't something supposed to be happening?

'I wonder what Victor's doing,' Mom said, turning all soggy again. 'How could he do it to me?'

Saturday 2 September. The day of waiting.

It had been a golden afternoon, the city's dark bowl lit by autumn sun. Two blokes whitewashing the entrance to an ARP post whistled at me on the way home. The balloons sailed in the sky, tugging gently on their lines.

What's up now? I wondered, stepping in from work that evening. The house was quiet again but I could hear music in the distance. They were out in the garden, Gloria too, on a paving slab with her accumulator. Someone was playing 'Somewhere Over the Rainbow' on the organ with twiddly bits.

At the end of the garden, next to the wizened lilac tree, its mauve flowers now brown, stood Mom, Len and Mr Tailor from two houses along. They were all looking at a big, grey loop of corrugated iron and two other flat bits which were leant up against the fence. The Anderson shelter had arrived.

''Ullo Genie!' Len boomed across at me. The others didn't seem to notice if I was there or not.

Mom was all worked up. 'Isn't this just the limit?' She lit one cigarette from the stub end of another and sucked on it like a sherbet dip. 'Isn't it just like Victor to go away the day before the shelter gets here. How am I ever going to cope with all this?'

'Look, love, you're awright – I've said I'll do it,' Mr Tailor said. He was always the philosopher, Mr Tailor. Maybe because he had a grown up son whose testicles had never come down. Nan said with something like that in the family there was no point in getting worked up about anything else. He'd most likely be there on his own deathbed in the same grey braces saying, 'Yer awright, bab – things'll look better in the morning.'

'I'll sort it out for you, soon as I've finished my own. I'm not going anywhere, am I? Too long in the tooth for that caper. Look – you just have to dig down and put this bit in the ground—' He pointed to the big curved bit which I saw was two sheets of metal bolted together at the top. 'Then you put the soil back over the top, these bits are the front and back, and Bob's your uncle.'

Len had already got the spade and was all for starting off.

'He could do it if I show him,' Mr Tailor went on. 'Big strong lad.'

Mom was hugging her waist. I could see the shape of the Players packet in the pocket of her pinner. 'Looks more like a dog kennel. I certainly don't fancy sitting out in that of a night.'

'It's tougher than it looks,' Mr Tailor said, slapping his thick, hairy hand on the side of it. 'I'll come and give Len a hand finishing it tomorrow – how's that?'

Mom nodded. 'Look, I've got to get in and finish these flaming blinds. Been queuing half the morning for the material . . .'

The organ music which had gone on and on stopped suddenly. 'Sssh,' I said. 'Listen!'

We walked back over the toasted daisies and stood round Gloria.

'This is the BBC Home Service ... Here is the six o'clock news ...'

Everyone stood still. Mr Tailor raised one hand in the air, flat as if he was pushing against an invisible wall.

The government had given a final ultimatum to Hitler. Withdraw from Poland or we declare war. They'd given him until the next morning.

When it was over, another voice said, 'This is Sandy MacPherson joining you again on the BBC organ ...'

'Not again,' Mom said. 'That bloke must be exhausted. He's been stuck on that flaming organ all day.' As she disappeared into the house she added, 'Why does that Hitler have to do everything on the weekend?'

The sun went down slowly, though not slowly enough for Mom, who was still toiling away on the Vesta, the reel of black cotton flying round on the top, cursing to herself.

Without being told, I picked up the idea pretty quick that I was cooking tea. I saw there was a rabbit hanging by its hind legs in the pantry. Mom said Mr Tailor had got it somewhere. Don't ask, sort of thing. 'That's for dinner tomorrow,' she said. 'Do summat with eggs tonight.'

When I'd got the spuds on, I went and stood out in the garden. Len was working like mad digging out turf and soil, dry though it was. He was droning some kind of tune and he didn't look back or see me.

I took my shoes off, felt the wiry grass under my feet and wondered what it'd be like to live in the country with nothing but grass and trees. I wondered about Eric. The street was so quiet. Usually it was full of kids playing, in the gardens and out the front.

And I thought this evening was like no other I'd ever known. Not even the night I left school when I knew I was going to a job next week and everything else would be the same, not like Christmas Eve, even though there was the same sort of quiet. Everything was shifting, you could feel it all around you, those balloons filling in the sky. No one had a clue what was going to happen tomorrow.

I didn't know whether to be excited or frightened.

Mom still didn't manage to black out the whole house by sundown. 'Cotton kept breaking,' she complained. She wasn't very good at sewing either.

We ate scrambled egg and potatoes. Len ate astonishing heaps of mash. It was a queer feeling sitting there with the windows all muffled. Made you feel cut off, as if you were in prison. And Mom decided for reasons of her own that we had to have the windows tight shut as well and nearly suffocated the lot of us.

None of us could settle to anything. Mom said she couldn't stand the sight of any more sewing. So we sat round Gloria and listened in. She was our contact with the outside world: Sandy MacPherson, records, news. Parliament had sat in emergency session. Len slouched, picking his nose.

'Don't, Len!' Mom scolded.

We sang along with 'We'll Gather Violets in the Spring' and 'Stay Young and Beautiful, If You Want to Be Loved.'

We wondered what tomorrow would bring. There was a storm in the night and I barely slept.

The Prime Minister was due to speak at eleven-fifteen. Mom was in the front at her machine again, tickety-tick,

51

and I, who seemed to be cook for the duration, was stuck at the sink. Len was out digging, the ground softened by the rain.

It dried out to a perfect, calm morning, though the air was humid. I could hear church bells early on, then they stopped.

Our dinner was going to be late.

'I can't touch that thing,' Mom said, pointing at the rabbit, its legs rigid against the door. 'Make me bad, that would. You'll have to skin it, Genie – we'll have stew this afternoon.'

What a treat. Didn't she always find me the best jobs?

I spread an old *Sports Argus* on the kitchen table. There were a couple of knives that needed sharpening and the kitchen scissors. It was a wild, brown rabbit with a white belly, and heavier than I expected. Its back legs were tied with string and it was sticky with a smear of blood where I touched it on one side. Its eyes looked like rotten grapes.

Before I got started I went and switched Gloria on and heard a band playing.

'What time is it?' Mom called through.

'Five to eleven.'

There was a ring of blood like lipstick round the rabbit's mouth. The ears felt very cold and there was a pong coming off it like fermented fruit.

It was a hell of a job to get the head off. Our knives sunk in deeper and deeper but wouldn't break the pelt. In the end I snipped at the neck with the scissors, but it took so long it made me feel panicky, as if I was fighting with it.

The news came on on the hour. There was a knock at the front door.

'Get that, will you Genie?'

'Can't – I'm all in a mess.'

I heard her sigh, like she always did if I asked her to do anything. Peeping into the hall I saw Molly and Gladys Bender from across the road. I knew Mom'd be thinking, oh my God. They both stood there with big grins on their faces, each of them the size of a gasometer, still in their pinners. Gladys was Molly's mom and by far the sharper of the two. They lived together and both did charring and you almost never saw them without a pinner or an overall. They both wore glasses and both had their hair marcelled and probably had done since it was fashionable sometime round the year I was born. Molly looked the image of Gladys except that Gladys, being twenty years older, had hair that wasn't exactly grey, but dusty looking, and Molly's cheeks weren't full of red wormy veins.

They were beaming away like a couple of mad March hares. 'We was wondering,' Gladys said in her blaring voice, 'Mr Tailor said there's to be an announcement – only, we haven't got a wireless . . .'

So all Mom could really say was, 'Why don't you come in then?' and called to me, 'Genie – get the kettle on, love.'

Love? That was a sign we had company.

'Don't mind Genie,' Mom said. 'She's doing our dinner.'

I caught a whiff of Molly and Gladys. There were grey smudges down their pinners and they always reeked of disinfectant and Brasso and sweat. Especially sweat, but it was always mixed in with all these cleaning fluids and polish. They sat down, filling the two chairs. Molly craned to see out to the garden.

'Oooh,' she said. 'Your Len's busy, in't he? We could do with borrowing him.'

They chattered away to Mom, who was as polite as she could manage. I got into the rabbit by snipping up from under its tail with the scissors – tricky with me being left-handed – along the soft white belly. With the first cut a round hole appeared like a little brown mouth and the smell whooshed up and hit me. Lola. I opened it up and there was a pool of muck inside, and round it, holding everything in, a glassy film of pink, grey and white, tinged with yellow. The kettle whispered on the stove. It was ten past.

'Shall I call Len in for you?' Molly asked eagerly.

'You stay put,' Gladys bossed her.

I called down the garden. Len dropped the spade and loped up to the house. I don't know if he knew why he was hurrying but he'd caught the atmosphere, something in my voice. He stamped his feet on the step outside.

'It's all right – nothing yet.'

I pushed my knife into the thin, tough film of the rabbit's insides. There was blood everywhere suddenly. Soft jelly shapes slumped into my hand, cold trails of gut like pink necklaces, rounded bits with webs of yellow fat on them, green of half-digested grass when I pulled on its stomach and it tore. I knew which bit the liver was, rich with blood, four rubbery petals like a black violet.

When I'd got everything out it had gone quiet next door. Nice of them to call me, I thought, washing my hands. Mom, Molly, Gladys, Len and I all stood or sat round, everyone's eyes fixed on Gloria.

'I am speaking to you from the Cabinet Room at Number Ten Downing Street,' the Prime Minister said. Words we'd never forget. The announcement of war.

'Now that we have resolved to finish it, I know you will play your part with calmness and with courage.'

When Mr Chamberlain had finished they played the National Anthem. Molly and Gladys struggled grunting to their feet. Then church bells pealed from Gloria, filling the room. We drank tea. None of us spoke for a time. No one knew what to say. Molly and Gladys weren't grinning any more.

'So it's finally happened,' Mom said at last. 'Len – you'd better go out and finish off. Mr Tailor's coming later.'

Len wasn't listening and nor was Molly, because they were staring hard at each other as if they'd never seen one another before, with great big soppy smiles on their faces. He walked backwards out of the room, tripping up the step into the kitchen.

'I'll have to watch him,' Mom said when Molly and Gladys had departed, thanking us endlessly. 'He may be soft in the head but he's all man, our Len.'

'I know,' I said.

Her head whipped round. 'What d'you mean, you know?'

I finally finished the rabbit, pulling back the skin from over the front legs like peeling a shirt off. The inside of the pelt was shiny and covered with hundreds of wiggly red veins like Gladys's cheeks. When I got the skin off it looked small and helpless like a new-born babby. Tasted all right though, come three o'clock, with a few onions.

We waited for the peril that was supposed to fall from the clouds. That's when people started staring up at the sky, heads back, eyes narrowed. The night war was declared I went out into the garden after it was dark. Mom was despondent because they'd announced in the afternoon that all the cinemas were going to close.

'Life's not going to be worth living!' she kept on. I wanted to get out of our muffled rooms.

I leapt out of the back door closing it as fast as I could so's not to spill any light. I walked down the garden. It was dark as a bear's behind out there. Everything was quiet, deathly quiet I thought, really eerie.

At the bottom of the garden I could just make out the hunched shape of the Anderson which Mr Tailor had put in for us that afternoon. Len had heaped the soil back on top. It was odd seeing it there. A web of searchlights danced in the city sky, but down in the garden you could barely see a hand in front of your face. No lights from the street, the houses, the cars. Nothing.

I stumbled on a hummock of grass. Then there was a sound. Must've been a twig scraping the fence but it set me thinking, and my heart was off thudding away.

No one knew when the Germans would come. We'd expected them down the street straight away. Maybe they were here already. Was that what I'd heard, someone moving about in the garden next door? Or maybe there was someone in the Anderson ... Someone just behind me with a gun ...

Panic seized me tight by the throat and I was across that scrap of lawn and struggling with the door handle so mithered I could hardly get it open. I landed panting in the kitchen.

'What's got into you?' Mom called through. There was a laugh in her voice.

*

56

One Sunday in the middle of September Mom was having one of her wet lettuce sessions. Lunch had been cooked by yours truly (I was getting a lot of practice). I'd done a piece of chine and Mom said, 'This isn't up to much, Genie. How d'you manage to make such a mess of it?'

So I said, 'Cook it yourself next time if you're so fussy.' She slapped me for that, hard, at the top of my arm. Sod you too, I thought.

I knew what was wrong though. Partly the feeling of anticlimax.

'You only have to strike a match out there at night and someone jumps on you,' Mom moaned. 'But there's nothing cowing well happening, is there?' You could tell she was under strain when her language started slipping.

Earlier in the week Dad had come home to tell us that his short period in Hall Green was finished and that they were being transferred for training outside Birmingham. He didn't know where. Before he went, suddenly younger-looking in his uniform, I saw Mom go to him, and they held one another. He stroked her hair and she clung to him.

'I can't stand it,' she sobbed into his chest. 'Can't stand being here on my own. I won't be able to cope.'

'You've got Genie,' Dad said. 'I'm sorry, love. I hadn't realized it would all be so soon.'

She seemed to have more respect for him now he had an army uniform on. And I hadn't seen Mom and Dad cuddling before, not ever. Made me cry too. And then Dad did something he'd not done since I was a tiny kid. He came and took me in his arms too and I saw there were tears in his big grey eyes.

'Goodbye, Genie love. Eh, there's a girl, don't cry

57

now. You're going to help your mom out, aren't you? I s'pect I'll be back before we know it.'

Len was starting to blub too, watching us all, and Dad gave his shoulder a squeeze and then he was gone. I dried my tears. Didn't like crying in front of Mom. It didn't feel right.

She'd been all right up until Sunday. Even though we had a letter from Eric:

Dear Mom,
    Ime well and I hope you are to. And Genie and Dad and Len. I was at one ladys and now Ime at annother. Shes qite nice. Shes got cats.
    Love Eric.

It was from Maidenhead. Mom sniffled a bit when she read it – 'Not much of a letter, is it?' – but then carried herself along being busy and was quite cheerful. She even had a mad cleaning session and the house was spotless. But finally she fell over the edge into gloom and sitting for hours in chairs without her shoes on.

So I left, and went to see my pal Teresa. She'd always been my best pal, ever since we were kiddies, although we were never at the same school. The Spini kids traipsed all the way over to the Catholic School in Bordesley Street. Teresa, who was always up to something the rest of the time, could dress up demure as a china doll on a Sunday with a white ribbon in her hair and go off to Mass at St Michael's with Vera's – Mrs Spini's – family, who all lived in the streets of 'Little Italy' behind Moor Street Station. It was like stepping right into Italy down there, with them all speaking Italian and cooking with garlic. I used to go with Teresa and see her granny sometimes. Nonna Amelia was a wispy old lady with bowed legs and no teeth who always wore black and spoke hardly any English. She used to suck and suck on sugared almonds from home and spit the nuts out because she couldn't chew them.

They had a back-house in a yard just along from my nan's, though not behind the shop as they'd tiled that part white like a hospital and turned it into their little ice-cream factory. The door of the house was almost always open, summer or winter, and usually there were kids spilling in and out. When I got there I could see the back of Micky, Teresa's dad, sat at the table in his shirtsleeves. He wore belts, not braces like my dad. I could hear their voices, loud, in Italian.

'Genie!' Teresa called, spotting me. Soon as I got there they switched to talking in English.

Their house was much like any other in area inside, with a couple of small differences. Near the door was a black and white engraving ('my photograph' as Vera called it) of Jesus, and over the mantel hung a tile, in a thin wooden frame. On its deep blue glaze was a handpainted figure of the Madonna and child, and beneath, the words AVE MARIA. I'd asked Teresa about it once, years ago.

'My nan in Italy gave it to Dad before he came here,' she said. 'She didn't want him to go, and she gave it to him as she kissed him goodbye. She said "If your own mother can't watch over you, remember that the mother of God is always near to catch you when you fall." Micky had never seen his mother again after walking out with that lovingly wrapped tile at the age of twenty.

'Anyway,' Teresa'd said. 'He met Mom his second day in Birmingham, so someone was looking out for him.'

Teresa pulled a chair out for me at the table between her and Micky.

''Bout time,' she said. 'We haven't seen you in ages.'

'Some of us work for a living you know.' Now I was at the pawn shop I worked most Saturdays. 'No time for gadding into town to try on hats in C&A. Come to think of it that might be a good reason for moving on!' I glanced nervously at Micky. You never quite knew what mood he was going to be in.

He frowned. 'I thought you were at that pie factory?'

'I was – for a week. There was this bloke opposite me with a great long dewdrop in 'is nose. I reckon there was more snot than meat in some of them pies. One week of that and I was off.'

The others groaned and laughed, even Stevie, Teresa's older brother who was usually either in a daydream about shiny new Lagondas or being a self-righteous pain in the neck. I saw Teresa looking nervously at her father for his reaction and I wondered if I'd walked into the middle of something. 'You wouldn't want your seat getting too warm anywhere, would you?'

'I have to be kept busy.'

'You've practically done the lot already!' Teresa said. She sounded envious, and her eyes strayed once more over to Micky. He was holding a hunk of bread in his strong hands, pulling off pellets and half throwing them into his mouth.

I looked round the table. 'It's quiet, isn't it?' And then wished I hadn't said the one thing they were all most likely trying not to think about. Vera's eyes turned to pools of misery.

But God, it was quiet. Normally when I went in there eight pairs of dark brown eyes turned to look at me, but now the four younger ones were missing and I felt the loss almost as if they were my own brothers and sisters. In terms of noise you barely noticed Eric being gone because he was such a mouse most of the time. Micky and Stevie weren't all that vocal, but those Spini women were LOUD. Even Giovanna at seven had a voice on her like a foghorn, and Teresa was about the noisiest of the lot. Great blast of a voice and sandpaper-rough as if she'd smoked forty a day since birth.

'I can hardly look at Teresa in that dress for wondering how they are and what they're doing.' Vera's homely face was crumpling.

The dress was crimson with a white lace collar and Vera had made three to match, so other Sundays Francesca and Giovanna had been turned out in theirs too, matching and all lovely with their dark hair, Teresa's long and loosely tied back, Francesca with plaits and Giovanna's in a pert, swinging ponytail.

'Will they be able to go to Mass where they've gone?' I asked.

Tears started running down Vera's cheeks. She shook her head and shrugged. 'Don't know, love. I told Francesca to ask, but with them down Wales ... Don't know that they're all that keen on Catholics down there. I can't stand thinking about it. At least they've been kept in twos – Francesca's got Luki, and Tony and Giovanna are together. I s'pose I should be thankful for that.'

'They'll be all right, Mom,' Teresa said, putting her hand on her mother's plump arm. She was such a happy woman usually. You'd see her in the shop even in the depths of winter, blowing on her hands to keep warm, songs billowing white out of her mouth. And she hugged and kissed those kids like no one had ever done to me in my life.

'I don't know why I sent them,' she went on. 'Nothing's happening. Only I kept on thinking about what they did bombing Spain and I thought it'd be the same here. Every day I have to stop myself going to fetch them back.'

'No good thinking like that,' Micky said more gently. 'The war's only just started and we don't know what's coming. Francesca'll see they're all right. She's nearly grown up now.'

I looked at Micky timidly. He was a moody so-and-so – tough as anything on his kids, though he'd barely ever said a harsh word to me. 'How's the Fire Service, Mr Spini?' I asked.

'Dad 'ad a bit of a shock this week, didn't you?' Teresa said cautiously.

We waited for a split second to see the reaction. And Micky's face broke into a grin, as did Stevie's. 'Oh God yes, the jump!' He blew smoke at the ceiling, smoothed a hand over his wiry black curls. He'd done his first two weeks in the Auxiliary Fire Service. 'They got us doing sheet jumps. That means you 'ave to go up the drill tower in the station. Everyone else is standing at the bottom holding out a sheet to catch you. If you're holding it you have to brace yourself to take the weight.' He clenched his fists, the hairy backs of his hands turned towards the floor. 'So you're up the top of the tower, sitting on this window-sill and the instructor's told you "Don't jump off, just step off." You're thinking Christ Almighty—'

'Micky!' Vera interrupted, eyes fierce.

'Sorry. But I was, I can tell you. I was thinking to myself, that's not a sheet down there, it's a pocket handkerchief.'

'So you jumped?'

'Didn't have no choice. My insides followed me down about five minutes later!'

'You should just thank your stars you don't have to jump out of aeroplanes!' Vera said.

'Well at least they have a parachute!' We all laughed at his head-shaking indignation.

Vera got up, clearing dishes already wiped clean with bread, scraping bones and wrinkles of fish skin on to the top one. She was not a tall woman, but rounded and comfortable, and Teresa looked very like her, although Vera Spini's long hair was blond – out of a bottle Mom said – but it suited her, even though her eyebrows were jet black.

Already it was half way through the afternoon. They could make meals last an age, the Spinis. Eating was a pastime as well as a necessity. Sometimes, Sundays, they were all still sitting round the table at four o'clock, spinning the meal on into cups of tea.

'Who wants ice cream?' Vera called from the scullery.

'Oooh!' I said. 'Yes please!'

'I didn't need to ask you, did I?' She smiled, bringing the basin of homemade ice cream to the table. 'You'd eat it until it came out of your ears.' She leaned forward and pulled my cheek affectionately between her finger and thumb.

'Only my ice cream,' Micky teased.

Vera faced him indignantly, hands on her shapely hips. '*My* ice cream? Listen to him. Who makes all the ice cream around here Micky, eh? Whose family has been making ice cream for three generations?'

'Yours, my darlin'.' Micky looked mock humble.

'I should think so.' Vera dug in the spoon. 'We had a few punnets of strawberries over so I put them in too.'

That set my mouth watering. Vera's mom and dad,

the Scattolis, were part of the community from Sora in the middle of Italy, one of the ice-cream families, and you came across Scattoli ice-cream cycles all over town. When Vera married Micky, a newcomer and a southerner, the family accepted him and helped set them up in their own shop. Old Poppa Scattoli gave his blessing not only on the marriage, but also on their using the family's ice-cream recipe for another string to the Spinis' business bow – provided they used the Scattoli name.

The ice cream was delicious. I was just sitting there relaxing, thinking how nice it was to be eating food that might've been made by angels, in a proper family with a mom and dad there and no rows, when Teresa had to go and say, 'I wish I could get a job.'

Micky's eyes swivelled round to her angrily and Vera and Stevie sighed. Teresa always had a way of offering the red rag straight to the bull. You didn't argue with Micky – except Teresa did – and the Spinis' ding-dongs had a way of blowing up on you sudden and harsh as a summer storm.

'We need you here,' Micky decreed, jabbing a stubby finger towards her. 'And first you got to learn 'ow to behave yourself before you go anywhere out of my sight on your own.'

'I am behaving myself.' Teresa was on the boil already, voice booming. 'He was a customer. I was only talking to him. What's wrong with that?'

'Talking to him!' Micky's voice was mocking. He sat back, waving one thick, hairy arm, his Brummie accent laid over his Italian one. 'You think you're just talking but I can see what he's doing with his eyes. And what you're doing with yours too. You make yourself cheap, girl, behaving like that. You give him ideas about yourself. If I see you doing that again . . .'

He stopped because for once he couldn't think of anything to say and Teresa stared back brazenly. She never went out anywhere he could stop her going, except to Mass, and she knew she was an asset in the shop. The customers loved her, listening to their moans, her big laugh ringing down the road behind them.

'Don't keep on, Micky,' Vera interrupted. 'You've said enough already.'

'But she don't take any bloody notice!' Micky roared. 'What do you want – eh? You got no respect!'

'You got my respect,' Teresa bawled. 'But how come it's always me?' She pointed at Stevie, who was watching her across the table with his heavy-lidded eyes. 'You don't say anything when he's going about with that lunatic Fausto. Or is it awright now to invite a mad man into the family and one who still thinks he's a Blackshirt as well – eh?'

'You've got Fausto wrong,' Stevie said with contempt.

Micky waved the air dismissively. 'The boy's a hot-head, a fool . . .'

'It's not fair!'

'Teresa!' It was Vera's turn to try and calm her down.

'But I'm sick of it! The men in this family do just what they like and expect us to stay at home and wait on them hand and foot.' She pushed her chair back and marched off outside, saying, 'It's like a prison here . . .'

Micky slammed his spoon down and left as well. I thought he was going after her but we saw him move past the window and head for the street.

Vera sighed. 'When will Teresa ever learn to keep her mouth shut?'

*

Teresa and I sat out on the back step, frocks over our knees.

'I s'pect Dad's gone over Park Street to the pub. I really hate him sometimes.' She squinted up at the sky. 'Wish they'd come if they're coming. We could do with a bit of action round here.'

'You're awful,' I said. 'Any rate, I didn't think that was the kind of action you were interested in nowadays.'

She stuck her tongue out at me as far as it would go.

'Come on then, tell us. Who is 'e?'

Teresa stuck a finger urgently against her lips and peeped round the door. Vera was washing up, had said Stevie should help so he was wiping, with his altar boy face on.

'Come over here.' Teresa pulled me to my feet and over towards the brewhouse and we stood with our faces to the wall. Her whisper tickled my ear.

'He keeps coming in the shop – from that sheet metal place opposite Frank Street. I'm sure he's taken a fancy to me.' Even at this distance she kept looking back nervously at the house. Micky and Vera thought Teresa was far too young to be thinking about boys.

Although we'd left school we were still treated as kids, weren't allowed out dancing, nothing like that. Teresa was barely allowed to set foot by herself. But the boys went for her. It wasn't that she was pretty exactly. She was shorter than me, small and round, whereas I was bony and boyish; she had Vera's looks, a snub nose, and her complexion wasn't all that marvellous. But what she had was a lot of life and a lot of laughs in her. And what's more she was ripe and ready to be swept off her feet, even though she was innocent as a day-old child, and looked it in that Sunday dress.

'He keeps coming in – I've never known anyone buy

so many apples – 'cept he comes and gets them one by one!' She burst into her infectious giggle. 'Ooh, sometimes I feel like taking off just anywhere, just for a bit of excitement!'

'So he's Prince Charming then, is he?' I couldn't help sounding sarky.

'He's all right. Nice enough. Bit skinny. I like 'em with a bit more brawn on them than that!'

'Brawn or brains – make your choice.'

'And he's got this great big Adam's apple – wobbles around when he's talking as if he's got a plum stuck down his throat …' The giggle turned into her loud, exuberant laugh. 'No, I'm being unkind. He's got a nice way with him. Oi – what's up with you?'

'Nothing.'

'Don't just say nothing—' She elbowed me but I pulled away, staring stubbornly across the yard. From the top-floor windows the Spinis' bedding was hanging out to air as usual, an Italian habit the neighbours still weren't sure about.

'B for Boys. B for Boring.'

'Well, you wanted to know!'

'Yeah, and you told me,' I snapped, crosser with myself than her because I was mucking up the afternoon. But God she didn't half go on. I wanted her to be happy – she was my best pal. But I wanted her all to myself as well. She was so restless and impatient. Even now she was tapping her feet against the grey bricks as if she wanted to be off and none of us were good enough for her.

'I don't know what you're always moaning about—'

'Who says I'm moaning?' she interrupted my outburst.

'If I had a family like yours I'd think I was in clover. You should try living with my lot.'

'Oh don't you start getting on your 'igh 'orse with me!' Teresa's temper had a shorter fuse than a banger on fireworks night. 'You're not the one stuck in the shop and minding little kiddies all the time . . .'

'Nor are you now, 'cause they're not here, are they?'

'And your dad doesn't come down on you like a ton of bricks every time you even open your mouth to talk to a boy . . .'

I was getting ready to say that's because he never noticed anything much I did but she was getting well warmed up now. 'Family this, family that. You can't get away from them ever – and if it's not them it's the sodding church.'

'Well how come Stevie doesn't mind?'

She made a big, irritated puffing sound through her lips. 'Because Stevie's pain in the backside little Stevie. He's like a policeman round the place and all he ever thinks about are cars and football.'

She relented and looked round at me. 'All I want's a bit of excitement. We'll be pals whatever. Boys don't make any difference.'

'I know,' I said, face all red.

Just then we heard footsteps charging along the entry. The Spinis' yard was a 'double knack' which meant there were two ways in, and there was an entry running along by the brewhouse. When I saw who it was my face blushed to my ears. Walt Eccles, Stevie's pal. I was scared stiff every time I saw Walt, by the way my knees turned wobbly and my heart went like the clappers and my insides churned with frightened, helpless adoration. An adoration I'd rather have jumped from the spire of St Martin's than let him know about. After all, Walt was two years older than us, which seemed like centuries, and why should he be interested in a gangly scarecrow like me?

The sun shone on his shock of gold hair and there was the usual cheeky grin on his freckled face as he came panting up to us, looking gorgeous.

'In a bit of a rush, are we?' I said, tart as I could manage, while Teresa smiled sweetly at him, as she would at anything in trousers.

Walt gave me his best ingratiating smile which filled me brimming over with panic. 'Nice to see you too,' he said. 'How're you then?'

'None the better for seeing you.'

He pulled a face at me. 'See you're full of charm as ever. Stevie in?'

'Somewhere,' Teresa said, waving into the house.

A moment later the two of them came out, off up to the park to kick a ball around. The blush rose in my face again, and I turned crossly to the wall. Teresa was giving me a really close, squinty look.

'You're sweet on 'im, aren't you?' Her face was full of devilment.

'I'm not!'

'Oh yes you are!' she bawled in her big husky voice, and jumped about triumphantly clapping her hands. Luckily the yard was quiet. 'Genie's sweet on Walt. Genie likes boys after all!'

I went all tight inside. Only half joking I pushed her up against the wall of the brewhouse, gripping her shoulders.

'One word to Stevie, or *anyone*,' I said between my teeth, 'and you won't live to see another day. And that's a promise.'

We were bored with the so-called war already. Every night we sat round the wireless, windows blacked, waiting. Mom hadn't been to the pictures for three weeks. It was Bore War. Sitzkrieg instead of Blitzkrieg. We wanted something to happen, and not just in the Atlantic. Something we could see.

Gloria kept handing out announcements. Keep off the streets. Carry your gas mask as at all times, etc. In fact recently she'd been a bit of a bore herself.

The proper programmes were back on now at least. *Band Waggon* now on a Saturday night, Len with his cup and saucer jigging about as they sang, 'Come and make a trip upon the Band Waggon – skiddeley-boom,' until Mom'd say, 'For goodness' sake give me your Bournvita, Lenny. It'll be in your lap, else.'

She was still low. Blackout, no pictures, supposedly in charge of the house, the uncertainty of it all getting on her nerves. Said she was scared to be out at night. Her so called pal Stella had moved across town with her husband and hadn't troubled herself to come back and visit so she wasn't around to have a moan to. Mom did crack her face at Tommy Handley sometimes.

One evening she got out of her chair and said, 'I've had enough of this. There aren't going to be any air raids. Let's have the last of the light before we all die of asphyxiation, never mind the flaming bombs.'

She threw open the blackout curtains and the waning light lapped across the room. We all took in a deep breath, thought something would happen. Nothing did.

The weeks passed. Poland surrendered. We clung to the music and wondered what was happening. We waited.

October 1939

'Well, that's that,' Mom announced. 'I'm not stopping in like this. I've had more than enough already.'

Mr Churchill had just announced that the war would last three years. How he knew that we didn't understand, but something about him made you believe it. And that did it for Mom.

'There's no knowing when your father'll be home for good.' That thought seemed to rouse her out of the depressed stupor into which she'd kept dipping.

Lil had just moved jobs, though she hadn't escaped the factory. She was learning welding at Parkinson Cowan, in overalls and with a snood over her hair, and kept on about how useful she was being to the war effort and humanity in general despite having three young children. She put on a good show of being irritated by a new set of admirers.

Mom decided that for the first time in fifteen years she'd get herself employed. She fixed herself up with a job on the telephone exchange, second shift of the day.

'But Mom – you'll have to come back from town on the bus late at night. You won't even go out as it is now.'

Apparently this didn't matter. 'I'll just have to manage.' She was excited all of a sudden, cheeks pink. 'You'll have to stop in and keep Len company.'

This was all quite a turn about for the woman who'd

refused even to go up to our nan's of an evening because she was too scared to come back in the blackout.

'I could be knocked down in the street and robbed,' she'd kept saying. 'There's a lot of it about you know.'

'So who's going to cook? And shop and clean?'

'Genie!' She laughed, looking back over her shoulder at her reflection in the mirror. 'You sound like an old woman. We'll get by. I'll be home mornings, and you know what to do by now, don't you? It's not as if we've got your father to feed.'

On the strength of the vast fortune she was about to earn she went out and kitted herself up with a couple of frocks and a pair of shoes with T-bars and a chunk of heel, and started on her new working life. The rest of us, who'd been at it for some time with no red carpet laid out, had to stand aside.

She went off at dinnertime, hair knotted low in her neck, in one of her new dresses and her small black bag over one arm, and came home at about half ten at night off the bus. She was full of it. The work, the people. It was fast, busy. And she was needed suddenly.

'They even have special gas masks for us with a little microphone at the side so we can carry on working.' She laughed. 'After all, in a gas attack the telephones would be essential.'

I could just imagine her putting on a posh telephone voice. She stood more upright now, strutted about as if she owned the place, and didn't sit in chairs and stare at nothing any more. Nor, from the first day, did it seem to cross her mind that there was such a thing as housework to be done.

I decided to have a go at something else myself. I was getting restless with all this change around me, and I needed a job which allowed me to start early and finish early, what with the shopping and cooking to do and often washing thrown in as well. Mom was at home all morning but she was barely ever up until gone eleven. She needed the time to recover, she said.

There was a job going at a firm in Cheapside called Commercial Loose Leaf. I walked through the sandbagged entrance up a gloomy staircase smelling of glue, to a cluttered little office above the shop floor. The gaffer was a middle-aged man with a tired, worried-looking face, thin hair and blue eyes like a little boy's.

'D'you know your numbers properly?' he asked.

'Oh yes,' I said airily. 'I was good at arithmetic at school.' Once again I showed my certificate and reference from the school.

He just glanced at them, not really interested. 'Just so long as you can count.' He gave me a quick look up and down. 'Table hand. You can start Monday.'

Well, that job nearly did me in. The company produced trade books and ledgers. To start with they put me to collating piles of paper covered with print about technical things I couldn't make head or tail of. The second week I was put on numbering. So this was the reason I needed to be able to count. The blue-tinged papers were all numbered by hand. You had to concentrate enough doing it so's you didn't lose your place and that meant you couldn't talk to anyone, but it didn't take up anything like the whole of your mind. The second night I dreamt of nothing but numbers.

We got used to a new routine at home. Suddenly we were a family where everyone had a job. I was working from eight in the morning until half past four. So after work I'd walk home and pick up any shopping on the way. Len came in soon after from Longbridge, so muggins here would cook the meal and wash up (Len wiping) and we'd sit in the rest of the evening until Mom came in. Occasionally Teresa would come down to keep us company.

'You're the one person who cheers me up,' I told her one night. 'It's an endless round of drudgery otherwise, and no one notices what I've done anyway.'

'Why don't you say something to your mom?' Teresa said, not being one to sit down under anything.

I shrugged. 'She'll only play the martyr. She's got her head so high in the clouds I don't think she even notices the rest of us exist any more.'

Teresa sat back with her legs stretched out, playing with a lock of her hair. 'You'll make someone a lovely wife,' she teased. 'With a flock of kids.'

I scowled. 'I'm not getting married. Not ever. I'm going to work as hard as I can and get rich and buy a cottage in a field next to a river, where there's no chimneys and no factories and no people, and I'm going to live there on my own for the rest of my life and grow flowers. Well – Len could come too if he wants.'

'Oh, I want to get married,' Teresa said. 'I think it's sad seeing a woman left on the shelf.'

'Sure you're talking about marriage and not just a white dress and a veil?'

'Oh Genie! You're such a flaming misery you are!' She laughed, exasperated.

'I just think you're better off on your own. I mean, look at my family. Who'd want to get hitched after seeing them lot?'

'Lil had a decent husband.'

'Yes, but what's the good of a decent husband if he's just going to throw himself in the canal?'

Teresa found this mighty hilarious for some reason. 'Genie, you're awful you are!' She sat up again. 'Guess what?' Then she was off again, giggling so much she set Len off and then I started laughing too, which came as a relief, although in the end none of us knew what the hell we were laughing about.

'My love life is about to begin,' she got out in the end.

'No,' I said. 'Not him? The Adam's apple?'

'That's the one,' Teresa managed to get out between guffaws of laughter. 'We're going out for a walk – Sunday. In Highgate Park.'

My eyes widened. 'Does your mom know?'

Teresa shook her head. 'I'll tell them I'm coming to yours.'

'But that's lies! How many Hail Marys is that, Teresa?' It wasn't like her to tell fibs, even if she was a bit wild.

'It is not as if we're going to do anything. Not real mortal sins or anything.'

'What's a mortal sin?'

'Having a babby when you're not married and killing someone and – you know, bad things. But I just want summat to happen. Some excitement. I get sick of being under Mom and Dad's noses all the time. Anyway, his name's Jack and he's seventeen.'

Determined not to look impressed I said, 'Well keep me posted. Don't go giving sweets to any strange men. And Teresa – don't make me lie for you.'

Why did I do it? I asked myself, cheeks aflame at the memory. Something made me. Something called living in hope. I'd been at Commercial Loose Leaf for a couple of weeks. Already I was half mad with boredom. We needed something for our tea and I had to shop on the way home. Sausages would be easiest for Len and me. Mom had a meal in the works canteen.

I went home via Belgrave Road, along to Harris's the butchers where Walt worked. It was a detour, but it made perfect sense to go there, didn't it? Because after, I could pop in and see my nan.

Walt was standing behind the counter in his striped, bloodstained apron, a pencil behind one ear, bright red against the shorn gold of his hair. I could see through the window that most of the stock had gone by this time of day. I walked into the tiled shop, my feet almost silent on the sawdust-covered floor, though the bell on the door gave me away with a loud tinkle. Walt was sharpening a knife and whistling as if he had not a care in the world.

'Can I help you, madam?' He half caught sight of me, then looked up properly, his freckly face spreading into a grin. The grin was laced with mischief that at first I was too blind to see. "Allo, Genie! What're you doing here?'

'Come for a pound of sausage, what d'you think?' I said, my cheeks pinking up, to my extreme annoyance. 'This is a butcher's if I'm not mistaken.'

I didn't know exactly why I was like that whenever I saw Walt, but I couldn't help myself. I lay in bed thinking about him, daydreamed about him for a proportion of my time that I would rather die than admit, but I simply couldn't let him know I liked him. I wasn't going to set myself up for being kicked in the teeth. What I was too stupid to realize was that he could see it as clear as day.

'I was only asking,' he said, pretending to be hurt.

'Sausage? There's a few left.' As he was weighing them out he said, 'Seen Teresa?'

'No I 'aven't. Not in a week. Don't get time for anything, do I, what with Mom working, Len working . . .'

Walt flung the sausages into the scale with a flourish, eyes fixed on the needle, which swayed back and forth. 'Just over,' he said. 'Seeing as I know you. How's the new job then?'

I gave him a sideways look. 'If you're looking for a new exciting life, don't go to Commercial Loose Leaf.'

Walt grinned again. 'Don't go on. You're making me jealous.'

As I handed over the money he closed his fingers over mine and held them. I managed to look into his eyes. 'You'd be nearer Jamaica Row there, wouldn't you?' he said.

It was true. We were a stone's throw from the meat market where I could easily have chosen to shop if I'd wanted. Feeling his warm hand on mine I blushed like mad and realized that was exactly what Walt had been aiming for.

I yanked my hand away. 'I'm allowed to shop where I want, aren't I? I've come up here to see my nan. If that's all right with you.'

I flounced out of the shop. Half way along the road I stopped, cursing. I'd taken off without the sausages. I stood there for almost a minute trying to decide what to do. I had to go back. I was going to look a right idiot whatever I did. Summoning what dignity I could, I pushed the shop door open. Walt stood there with my bag of sausages held out in one hand, with the kind of teasing smile on his face that made me want to curl up somewhere dark and never come out. I couldn't look him in the eyes. I grabbed the sausages, said 'Ta' in a sarky voice, and took off to the door as fast as I could.

'Genie.' His voice was soft suddenly, sweet, with a kind of longing in it.

I turned back, my pulse speeding up, and for one split second my silly little heart told me Walt'd been hiding his feelings. I was special to him ... As I looked round at him he must have seen it, my need and hope spraying out like sparks across the room.

And he was grinning, a mean, triumphant smile which made me shrink and buckle up inside. 'You still haven't got your change.'

I snatched the tuppence from him, dropped the sausages, had to fumble to pick them up and finally slammed out of the shop, cheeks ablaze.

'Bye bye beautiful,' he shouted, his mocking laughter following me along the pavement.

'You bastard, Walt Eccles,' I fumed, storming along the street. I was in too much of a state even to go and see my nan.

Life was peaceful in its way without Mom around. Len'd roll up his sleeves and get a fire going in the grate after work while I got the tea and we'd listen to Henry Hall or some other show. Then *The Nine O'Clock News*, after that old 'Jairmany calling, Jairmany calling' Lord Haw-Haw. He gave me the creeps at first, just the sound of his voice, but then we all just used to listen for the daft things he came out with. Then there'd be music and I'd do mending or tidying or handwashing – whatever else was needed – until Mom came in like the conquering hero and we'd have a cuppa with bread and butter. Then bed. That was our day, every day.

One night while Len and I sat waiting we heard the front door open and Mom's voice, high and animated in a way I'd almost never heard it before.

'Goodnight then – and thanks ever so much!'

The door slammed shut. She was in the hall taking her coat off and humming to herself. I went to look and she turned round and smiled at me. Which was all pretty unusual. She was unknotting a woollen scarf from round her neck.

'Brr, s'getting cold out nights now. Awright?' she said. 'Everything OK?'

'Who was that at the door?'

'Oh . . .' She kept her tone casual, hanging the scarf on the hook behind the door. 'He's a copper – seen me home a couple of times off the bus after I said I was scared in the blackout. He's very helpful.'

'That's nice.' I stood watching her, her lit up expression. I'd seen my own face in the mirror not long before, pale, with dark grooves under my eyes from exhaustion like an old woman. I felt wrung out and lonely, and I wanted her to look after me and be my mom.

'Got the kettle on? Hallo, Lenny love.' He nodded amiably at her. I went and lit the gas. Mom stood by the hearth, back to the fire. She rubbed her hands, started telling us about the 'girls' at work, jokes, things that'd happened. I sank into a chair. 'Aren't you making tea?' she asked eventually.

'I'm tired out. Can't you make it?'

Her eyes narrowed. She looked spiteful. 'You're tired? Huh. I get in from work in the middle of the night and you tell me you're the one who's tired.'

I was near to tears with weariness. After all, who was running this house with no help or thanks from anyone?

Sometimes I wish she'd just go, then there'd be just me and Len. Things were all right until she came home. But I wasn't going to show how miserable I felt in front of her.

She sank down by the fire in a martyred fashion and twiddled bits of her hair round her fingers as I got up to make the tea.

'Mrs Spini does the house and the shop,' I said. 'Always has.'

'I've got quite enough on my plate with your father and Eric away,' she snapped. 'Vera Spini.' She put all her energy into that sneer. 'Hair out of a bottle.' The way she said it dyeing your hair might have been crime of the century.

Then she turned plaintive again. 'It takes getting used to going back to work again and working shifts. I think I deserve all the help I can get.'

November 1939

Strikes me it's about time someone told Teresa the facts of life, I thought to myself. And who else is going to take the trouble but me?

Teresa was one of those girls who could give men the wrong idea. Too friendly, too vivacious, too downright appealing, but with barely the first idea of what it was all about, for all her talk of mortal sins. Of course most of us girls were innocent as morning dew until we strayed into marriage or trouble, but what with the trollops coming and going I'd long started asking questions, and Lil made it her business to get a few things straight with me when I left school.

'Your mother'll never be able to bring herself to do it,' she said. 'God knows, she spends enough time with her head stuck in a pile of sand as it is. But you ought to know, Genie. The factory's no place for an innocent kid like you. Specially with your pretty face.'

We were in Nan's house. Lil had chased the kids out to play.

'You're 'aving me on!' I said when she explained. 'Not with his willy!' My mouth hung open for minutes after.

Lil's cheeks went rose pink all of a sudden. 'I know it don't look much of a thing as a rule, but when they come on to you and get the least bit excited, it ...' She

81

gave me a vivid demonstration with her index finger. 'That's how they put the babbies inside.'

I sat there goggling at her. Her brown eyes smiled mischievously. I had so many questions I couldn't think what to ask first. 'But doesn't it feel – *funny* – them doing that?'

'Feels a bit funny at first of course. But you get used to it. Can be ever so nice . . .' Her face took on a dreamy look. I got the definite feeling this was something she liked talking about. 'Best feeling on earth at times, that's if you love 'im. But Genie . . .' She leaned forward solemnly and lowered her voice to a whisper. 'What I'm saying is, you don't want to do it with any old dog who comes along. Keep yourself nice for someone special. And make sure 'e's going to marry you before your knickers get below your knees.'

'Lil!'

'I'm giving you good advice, Genie, believe me. It's not nice to be a tart, and anyhow, you don't know quite where else they've been dipping it if they're that way inclined.'

Things were beginning to make a bit of sense, quite apart from the trollops. Len, for a start. That enigmatic smile that used to come over Big Patsy's face when Lil sat on his lap. And Lil was right. I couldn't for the life of me imagine Mom coming out with any of this information. For a second I thought of Walt and blushed to the roots of my hair.

Since, according to Lil, men were only after One Thing, I thought it was time Teresa knew. Which she didn't, I was sure. Her Mom and Dad treated her as a child and she was still safe in the bosom of home – or so they thought. Course they didn't know she was walking out late some Sunday afternoons now with Mr Sheet

Metal, supports-the-Villa Jack, using me as her alibi. Lil had given me such a vivid account of the male sex drive that I thought Teresa was in immediate danger of losing her virtue in Highgate Park.

I went to the Spinis' in the middle of Sunday afternoon when I guessed the marathon meal would be over. In any case, with only half of them there the heart had gone out of it. Only Vera and Teresa were in and Vera was sat at the table touching up the roots of her hair from the bottle of peroxide which Mom had been right about.

'Micky's pumping water out of air raid shelters,' Vera said, squinting at the little oblong mirror. Her dark eyebrows looked startling set against the bleached out hair. 'That's all they seem to have to do in the Fire Brigade. S'pose I shouldn't be complaining though, should I?'

Teresa had on her red dress from Mass and she'd dolled up her hair with a matching red bow. 'We were just going out, weren't we?' she said, looking meaningfully at me.

'S'pose so.' I didn't take too kindly to being treated as a decoy in place of some bloke.

'What're you doing here?' she hissed at me as soon as we were in the street. 'You know I'm meeting Jack.'

'All right, all right, I'm not going to forget, am I, the way you keep on?' Jack this, Jack that. The minute he'd come along he'd become far more important than I was. I didn't seem to be important to anyone nowadays.

We cut past the closely packed lines of houses and factories along Stanhope Street.

'Don't walk so fast.'

'I'll be late. I told him half past three.'

'But I've got summat to tell you.'

I suddenly felt like the guardian of Teresa's virginity, my imagination running riot about what she and Jack were getting up to.

'Hang on a tick.' She pulled me into an entry. 'Hold these for me a minute.' I found I was holding a handful of pins.

'What the hell are these for?'

Skilfully Teresa made a thick tuck in the red skirt, pinning it up round her bit by bit and shortening the drop of the church-length dress by a good six inches.

'You can't go around like that!' I laughed at her. 'You'll get them sticking in you!'

'Wanna bet?' She did her coat up round her with a grin, hiding the clumsy lump of material. 'There. That's better. Come on.' She pulled me along the road again. 'What you got to tell me?'

Once I'd blurted it out Teresa stood stock still on the pavement and just stared at me, brown eyes popping. I thought for a horrible moment she was going to come out with something like, 'Oh Genie, how could you think I didn't know? Jack's already had his evil way with me and I'm expecting twins . . .'

Instead of which she erupted into her huge laugh, bending backwards, then leaning forward doubled up. I ended up in stitches too just watching her. People were staring.

'Oh no!' she cried when she could speak. 'No, that can't be right, Genie. Where in hell did you get that from? That's the most horrible idea I've ever come across!' And she was off again, tittering away. 'You don't half come up with some barmy notions, you do.'

'But it's true!' I insisted. 'How else d'you think . . .?'

She moved closer, aware of ears flapping along the

street. 'A man kisses you a special way and then the Holy Spirit gives you a babby. That's what really happens. Come on,' she said, stepping out again. 'He'll be waiting. You keep out of sight, eh?'

'Charming.' I was stung by jealousy again. 'Don't believe me then. I just hope you don't live to regret it.'

'All he's ever tried to do is hold my hand,' she said smugly, disappearing round the corner. 'Which is more than anyone does for you.'

'I've got more bloody sense, that's why!' I felt like tearing her eyes out, the stupid cow.

Her voice floated round to me, mocking. '*Ciao*, Genie.'

I peeped round the corner. Standing by the gate to the park, waiting for her, was one of the tallest, gangliest blokes I'd ever seen. His hair was curly and a bright carroty red as if his head was on fire. I couldn't spot the Adam's apple, but it would've been hard to miss the great big daffy grin on his face as Teresa walked up to him. She'd forgotten all about me, that was for sure.

When I couldn't stand any more of Commercial Loose Leaf I got myself another new job in a little factory in Conybere Street, staining bunk beds which they made for the forces and the shelters. It was a small, dark place, all one room. On one wall there was a poster in big red letters which read: 'FREEDOM IS IN PERIL. DEFEND IT WITH ALL YOUR MIGHT. YOUR COURAGE, YOUR CHEERFULNESS, YOUR RESOLUTION WILL BRING US VICTORY.'

On one side a few fellers were knocking up the beds, then they came to us to be stained before the webbing was put on. It wasn't too bad. If it ever got a bit slack I went round and swept up or kept my hand in cleaning windows again.

'I've cleaned that many factory windows,' I told them, 'I'm starting to think I ought to set up in business as a window cleaner.'

'You're like greased bloody lightning you are,' one of the lads said to me. He had black curly hair, uneven grey eyes and his name was Jimmy. 'Don't you ever let up?'

'No,' I said. 'Not if I can help it. Gets boring. I like to be on the go.'

'I can see that.' He kept watching me dashing about, throwing me the odd wink.

The other girl working with me, a stodgy blonde called Shirley, said, ''E fancies you. See how 'e keeps on looking over here? You're in there, you know.'

'In there? What's that s'posed to mean?'

Shirley looked at me pityingly. 'Don't you want a bloke? I'd do anything to 'ave a bloke of my own.'

It was odd the way she said it. She might just as well have said she'd do anything to have a dog, a budgie, a house ... But I can't say I wasn't flattered by his attention. I pulled the belt tight round my overall and kept my hair brushed. I couldn't help thinking about what Lil had said about men and their willies. But then I'd go and look at a real live man – let alone these boys around me – and I couldn't quite put the two together. I thought maybe Lil was having me on after all. It really was beyond imagining.

Every week we had a letter from Dad, who was down south, somewhere with a funny name. He said he'd started off being billeted in a barn with rats running round his head of a night, the food was abominable and he seemed to spend most of his life digging – trenches, latrines, holes ...

He said he missed us and hoped he'd be back for Christmas, though the war showed no more sign of being over than it did of getting going.

Mom seemed a bit shaken by this news. 'It's funny, isn't it?' she said. 'Feels as if he's been away such a long time. I've got sort of used to it. As if he was never here.'

Eric wrote every so often and told us not a lot except that he was all right and Mrs Spenser was a very nice lady, and thanked us for the letters we sent him.

'Can he come home at Christmas, Mom?' I asked. 'We can't just leave him down there – not then.'

'Oh, I should think so,' she said vaguely. I had this feeling when I talked to Mom nowadays that most of her mind was out to graze somewhere else.

'Couldn't he stay home? Lots of other kids have - come back. There's nothing happening, is there?'

'What?' Her attention snapped back to me. 'Oh no – I don't think so, Genie. Not while there's any danger of bombs. I mean, they keep telling us to leave the children where they are. And in any case, there's no one at home to look after him, is there?'

I didn't dare ask why she couldn't just give up work. Was it that the country needed her or that she was enjoying herself far too much? After all, as she'd kept reminding us one way or another, we'd been getting in her way for the past fifteen years.

One night after work I got so fed up with doing bits of hand washing, and had a bit of extra energy for once, so I stoked a fire with slack under the copper and had a good go at it, pounding it with the dolly. When it came to mangling it I called Len to come in the kitchen and give me a hand. We just fitted into the room and he turned the handle for me.

'Things all right at work?' I asked him. 'You managing still?'

'Yes,' he said in his slow, thick voice. 'I like it. S'nice.'

'Good.' I pulled a snake of wet washing from the wooden rollers of the mangle. 'I'm glad you're happy, Len.'

He nodded enthusiastically, looking across at me, his eyes always appealing, somehow innocent. 'You OK, Genie?'

'Oh. . .' I sighed. 'Yes. I'm OK, Len. Ta.'

There were shirts and underclothes, the lot, draped all round the room by the time Mom got in. We heard the front door and felt its opening jar all the other doors in the house.

'Come on through,' I heard her say.

Len and I looked at each other. Her voice was so smooth, soapy bubbles of charm floating from it.

I saw the shock in her face as she came into the back, catching sight of her drawers hung out to dry by the fire. But she recovered herself quickly. Over her shoulder I could see his face – dark brown hair, swarthy, handsome and young – quite a bit younger than her actually. The shoulder of a copper's uniform. He was looking nervous.

'This is Bob,' Mom started babbling. 'He's just popping in for a bit. He's been very kind and escorted me home from the bus a few times and his shift's finished so I thought a cup of tea was the least we could do.' She gave a tinkly laugh. 'This is my brother, Len. Shake hands, Len.'

Len said, ''Ullo,' and did as he was told, dwarfing Bob's hand in his. Bob coughed and nodded at him.

Now he'd got himself into the room I could see he wasn't much taller than Mom, with a stocky, muscular body.

'Len's not quite – you know . . .' Mom was saying. She slid over that one. 'And this is my daughter, Eugenie. I had her when I was very young of course. Much too young,' she threw in quickly.

'Eighteen,' I added, pretending to be helpful. 'And I'm fifteen.' Mom glowered at me. PC Bob nodded again, even more nervously.

'Genie,' Mom said between her teeth. She gave a little jerk of her head. 'The washing – couldn't you just . . . Until we've finished . . .?'

'I've just hung it all out,' I said stubbornly. 'I've spent the whole evening doing it.' My hostility wasn't lost on her. 'You could go in the front.'

'It's icy cold in there.'

'Never mind,' PC Bob said quickly. He gave a stupid little laugh. 'I take people as I find them in my job. And I have got a family of my own, after all.'

'Bob's got two kiddies,' Mom said, seeing him to a chair. She turned up the gas light, peeling back the shadows. 'Kettle on, Genie?'

'No.'

She clenched her teeth again. 'D'you think you could put it on?'

We all drank tea while Len and I sat quiet and Mom chattered on about her job, my job and about Eric being away. She didn't talk about Dad. I watched her. She was like another person from the one we saw every day – alight, talkative, a bit breathless.

I had a good look at PC Bob. He knew I was staring at him but he couldn't do much about it. It's not that I dislike people on sight as a general rule, but I couldn't stand him. I could sense it with them. What was between them. And I didn't like it.

He didn't say much. Smiled in the right places when Mom laughed. He had a heavy-set face and dark, mournful eyes which hardly ever looked anywhere but at her. I knew she could feel it, that stare. I'm not sure he was more than half listening to what she was saying, and she was making less and less sense because of the charge his look had set up in the room. His eyes travelled over her as she talked. I think they were a sludgy grey but it was hard to tell in the gaslight. I wanted to get up and shout stop it. Stop staring at her like that. He was following her shape and she talked all the more as if to fight off the magnetic intensity of those eyes.

When he'd drunk up and left, at last, the force of his presence left a hole in the room, like the sudden silence when we switched Gloria off for the night.

Mom was in a dither, cheeks flushed. 'You didn't have to be so short, Genie,' she said. 'All he came for was a cup of tea.'

'Just make sure the house is tidy when I come in,' Mom instructed me at least once a day. 'Just in case.'

And he was soon back.

I made tea and sat watching them. No one was saying anything much and all you could hear were spoons in the cups and the fire shifting. Mom looked down at the peg rug by the hearth, at her feet, then up at Bob. He was sat forward on the edge of his chair in his dark uniform, sipping the tea, giving Mom soulful looks. When their eyes met she giggled.

God Almighty.

'What about some music?' Mom said in the end. 'No Gloria tonight, Len?'

'I told him to turn her off when we heard you come in,' I said.

'Oh, there was no need.'

PC Bob was giving a quizzical sort of frown. 'Gloria?'

'Our wireless.' Mom tittered again. I'd never seen anything like the way she was behaving. 'Len calls her Gloria. Go on Lenny – switch her on.'

Len lumbered to his feet and in a second there was music, something soft, violins. Bob sat there dutifully for a few minutes, pushing the fingertips of each hand against the other.

'Better be off home,' he said. At last. He put his cup on the floor.

'Oh yes.' Mom was sparkly still. 'Back to your little family. Never let you loose for long, do they?'

They both went into the hall, snickering like a couple of monkeys. It went quiet for a moment. I wondered what they were doing. I thought about walking through to the front just to annoy them, but then I heard her letting him out.

When she came back she saw me staring sullenly at her. Oblivious to this, she gave me a wide smile. 'He's such a nice man, isn't he?'

A week later when she was due home from work, I left Len shuffling a pack of cards in the back with Gloria on, and went to the front room. I left it dark, pulled back the corner of the blackout curtain and slid the window open just a crack. There were no lights in the road of course and I knew I shouldn't be able to see them coming from far. But the room was very dark as well, and my eyes were settling to it.

Not many minutes later I heard them. I couldn't make out the shape of them in the sooty darkness, but I could see the burning tips of two cigarettes, and I knew Mom's tone. Their voices were low and I couldn't make out any words at first.

They came and stood on the front step and I was scared stiff they'd see me or notice the open window. I felt it must be plain as daylight I was there. But even if they could have spotted anything much out in the cold damp of the evening, the only thing they were interested in seeing was each other. They came and leaned up against the window where I was sitting. Mom perched on the sill, so if I'd wanted I could have pushed my fingers through the slit and touched her coat.

'Least we don't have to worry what the neighbours are thinking in this,' she said, giggling.

Silence. Kissing. The blood pounded in my ears.

'Bob . . .' Her voice was wheedling now. 'You are going to be able to sort out your shifts, aren't you?'

'For this week,' he said, impatient. His mind was on other things. 'What about your kid? She giving any trouble?' His voice was a low growl. There was something hypnotic about it.

'Nah – she hasn't got a clue about anything. Anyroad – we said you'd got a family, didn't we?'

'Oh yeah.' He thought that was very amusing apparently. 'My family. My two kids! Come on Dor—'

Mom said 'Oooh' and gave a little squeal. Then it went quiet and I knew they were kissing again. After a bit Bob pulled away, giving an impatient sigh. 'I need more than this, Doreen. I can't wait for ever, you know.'

'Oh, I don't care what anyone thinks!' Mom

squeaked at him. 'I know I shouldn't, but I want it too – if only there was a way we could get on our own . . .'

Silence.

'You do love me, don't you Bob?'

Lord above, I didn't want to hear any more of this. I let the curtain drop, reminding myself I'd have to come back later to shut the window.

I was all tight and squirmy inside. As I sat with Len, waiting for her to come in, I thought of my poor old dad in a barn full of rats, of the way he looked at Mom, always wanting, always hopeful.

Cow! I thought to myself. You horrible selfish cow. I felt like killing her.

I didn't say anything. I started to think I was the only sensible person left around the place, what with Mom and PC Bob and Teresa going doolally over Aston Villa Jack and telling fibs to her mom and dad.

'Len,' I said to him one evening, 'at least I've got you. You've got more common sense than the rest of them put together.'

'Yeah.' Len swayed and grinned. 'You and me, Genie. You and me.'

The winter set in and our days of limbo crawled past. Work, work, work, was all life consisted of now. All day painting woodstain on the rough bunks with Jimmy the Joiner, as I called him, winking away at me across the small factory floor as he bashed the frames of the bunks together. I started smiling back. What the hell.

Then there were the evenings of enthralling drudgery and Mom fluttering in late, her brains gone AWOL for the duration. The war was still not showing any signs of getting off the ground so far as we were concerned, but we still had to live with all the disadvantages: creeping about in the dark, staying in, and food costing a bomb.

The only thing that cheered me up in the evenings now was Gloria, and when Nanny Rawson and Lil paid us an occasional visit, usually on Mom's day off. The kids'd erupt into our house, glad of a bit of extra space round them, and I'd always try and have something nice laid on for them – a bit of cake or some sweets, with the best one saved for my soft, brown-eyed Tom. Nan'd bring her squeeze box and we'd sit round the back room and drink endless cups of tea and talk about how much better things were 'before the war' – barely three months ago.

At the end of the month they came, full of news.

'Have you heard, Dor?' our nan said, plonking the accordion down on the table. 'There's bombs gone off in town.'

'Oh Lor,' Mom said with the kettle in her hand. 'Has it started? Are they over here?'

'They reckon it was the IRA again,' Nanny Rawson said. 'Blew a couple of phone boxes to bits. No one killed I don't think.'

'That's just what we need, isn't it?' Mom was climbing up on her high horse already. 'Them coming over here making trouble.'

Oh no, not the Irish again. That usually set Lil off and then they'd be at each other's throats ... But Lil wasn't even listening. Sometimes, especially when she was feeling low, she went off into another world. She was pulling the kids' boots off to dry by the fire. Cathleen was moaning on about something. Patsy'd brought a comic with him.

''Orrible night out,' Lil said absent-mindedly. Her face was pale with exhaustion, the dark hair scraped back. She struggled with the knots in Tom's laces, and I knelt down beside her and worked on the other foot.

'We're in for a hard winter I reckon,' our nan said.

'Got your torch?' Mom stood watching in her pinner, hands on hips.

'Course.' Lil sounded impatient. 'It's like looking up a bear's arse out there. And the flaming paper got wet though.'

Torches and the batteries to go with them were like gold dust. Nowadays you could use a torch so long as the light was dulled down with a sheet of tissue paper. Lil laid the crumpled sheet of paper on the tiles by the fire to dry out.

'We had about three people following us down the Moseley Road, all in a line.' Nan laughed. 'Just for one bleeding little torch.' She was wiping the accordion down. 'That won't've done it much good. Still – it's had worse in its time. Come on – let's have a cuppa before we get started.'

Mom beat me to the kitchen. She seemed mighty eager to please. Guilty conscience, I thought.

She came back in again with a few Rich Tea on a plate, and offered them round, hovering round her sister like Nurse Cavell. 'How're you bearing up, Lil?'

Lil looked round at Mom as if she'd just been spoken to by some barmy person. 'Awright, ta. What's got into you?'

Mom couldn't hide it, try as she might. The new look, the glow, the vivacity. She was lighter altogether. 'I wouldn't mind a bit of whatever it is you're on,' Lil said wearily. 'Patsy – leave Tom alone.'

'Here.' I pulled out a bag of aniseed balls. 'This'll

keep you lot quiet for a bit.' The kids' cheeks soon had satisfying bulges.

'Ta, Genie,' Lil said, then announced out of the blue, 'Any rate – I've put my name down for a council 'ouse. I'm sick to death of living in a rabbit warren. I want the kids to breathe in some clean air for a change.'

'But how'll you cope if you get one?' Mom asked, with a snidy edge to her voice. Glebe Farm, Turves Green, Weoley Castle ... Was Lil going to get the little dream house Mom had always fancied? 'You couldn't cope last time.'

Lil stuck her chin out. 'I was in a state, what with Patsy's – accident. And Cathleen was only a babby. Not long now and she'll be at school. I'll cope. I'll just have to, won't I?'

'Well, that'll remain to be seen.'

'Doreen,' Nan said, warning.

Mom, remembering she was the perfect hostess all of a sudden, poured tea, spooned in the condensed milk and offered round biscuits which the kids had to take the aniseed balls out of their mouths to eat, the red outsides already sucked white. Len chomped away, eating two biscuits at once.

'Ah – nectar!' Nan smiled, sipping the tea. 'That's better. Let's 'ave a bit of a sing-song now.'

Patsy lay by the fire with his comic and we fished out a few of my old crayons for Cathleen to scribble on some paper.

'You come and sit with me, Tom,' I said. Stuck between an elder brother and his temperamental baby sister I could see he was always hungry for affection. He came readily to sit on my knee.

'That's it – you go to Genie, she'll look after you,' Nanny Rawson said, sitting forward on her chair and settling the accordion on her knees. She smiled across at me as I hugged Tom tight, her dark brows lifting. 'Hey, Genie—' She frowned suddenly. 'You look all in. Is she sickening for summat, Dor? She's as thin as a stick, and ever so pale. Don't you think she looks peaky?'

Mom looked at me properly for the first time in weeks. Tears came into my eyes and my cheeks burned red. 'You're awright, aren't you Genie?'

I glowered back at her over Tom's head. If I was exhausted she ought to know the reason perfectly well, the way she was carrying on.

'You ought to take better care of her,' Lil said. 'After all, it's not as if you've got any others to worry about now, is it?' That was another of Lil's hobby-horses – she'd got more kids, more problems. I waited for the fight to begin but, to my amazement, Mom said cheerfully. 'Oh, she's all right. Just needs a bit of sun on her face like the rest of us, that's all. Come on, Lil – I feel like a real good sing tonight.'

They sang the rest of the evening away with their strong voices. It was a miracle because we got through that night without a fight, even though the fuse was lit more than once. Cathleen fell asleep on the floor among the crayons while they were singing 'When They Begin the Beguine', and Tom dozed on my lap. All the old favourites which Nan could pump out with an ease that never failed to impress me, never once looking down at her fingers.

I watched Mom as we went through 'An Apple for the Teacher', walking her feet on the spot in time with the music and snapping her slim fingers. Tonight she looked so vivacious, almost prettier than Lil. There was a spark in her eyes so that somehow you didn't notice the hard angles of her face. I thought of Dad watching

97

her with that 'Love me – please' look in his eyes. And I knew it was only through his going away that she'd been able to come to life again, come out from under it all, the years of wife and mother and nothing else and not really wanting it. Maybe she really couldn't help herself. But neither could I help my deep, burning anger at seeing her so carefree, so disloyal.

December 1939

It was evening and I was lying talking to Teresa up in the 'girls'' bedroom in their house which she now had to herself. There were two beds in there and nothing else – the big one which Francesca and Giovanna shared and Teresa's next to the wall. We had a bed each to lie across as we talked. Teresa's hair was loose, laid out in a dark swathe one side of her head.

'You shouldn't tell fibs to your mom and dad like you do,' I said to her. 'They've always been so good to you.' The Spinis would've been broken-hearted if they knew Teresa was deceiving them. Both of them looked so worn and tired at the moment.

'But they'd stop me seeing Jack. Dad's a bully. You just can't see it.'

'He's strict all right, but . . .'

Teresa half sat up. 'He's not just strict. He's not fair. Like last week – it was Nonna Spini's anniversary, my nan in Italy. We all had to go to Mass because that was the day she died and none of us have even met her. And he belted me one because I said I didn't want to go. And it's only because he feels guilty because he always said he'd go back to Italy and see her and he never did.' She lay down again with a thump. 'He just pushes things on us that are nothing to do with us.'

I sighed. We'd been having a bit of a laugh until she

got on to the inevitable Jack. She leaned over to me, tight-faced. 'You'd better not tell 'em.'

'Don't worry – I won't.'

Teresa was changing. I felt old and disappointed, as if such childhood as I'd had was dead and buried overnight. Even though the war had barely affected us in terms of fighting, we had all changed. It was as if we'd had a layer of something scraped off us and we acted more on our impulses than we used to. I watched my mom and my friend and felt like a disapproving old spinster.

Teresa couldn't talk enough about Jack. She was droning on about him again, leaning up on one elbow. 'He's ever so good looking when you get up close – lovely eyes. And so grown up. He's got a real cigarette lighter and he likes football. It's a great game, you know. He said he might take me to see the Villa play one day.'

'For God's sake, Teresa, you hate football!'

'I don't. It's just I've never had the chance to see it played properly – that's what Jack says. He says—'

'I couldn't care less what he says!' I exploded at her. 'It's all a bloody waste of time. Boyfriends. Getting married. All of it. It's stupid.' I found myself nearly in tears.

'You're just jealous.'

I hated her. I wanted to smack her smug face. 'Well, bugger you, Teresa. That's all I can say.' I climbed down from the bed. 'I'm off.'

I ran downstairs and shot through the room where Micky and Vera were sat by the table.

'Hey!' Micky said, as I was going to open the door. He was leaning forward on a chair pushed back from the table, cleaning his boots. Vera sat across from him with a darning mushroom pushed into a stocking, squinting in the gaslight. 'Going already?' he said. 'You just got here. Stay for a cuppa tea with us, eh? Kettle's on.'

I shook my head, choked up inside, looking down at the floor. I couldn't open the door and I couldn't speak.

Micky stood up. 'Genie? Hey darlin' – what you unhappy about?' At that, I burst into tears. Micky stood there at a loss and Vera came quickly over to me, making comforting noises, and pulled me into her arms, pressing my head against her soft body.

'Come on – you can tell your Auntie Vera. What's got into you? You and Teresa had a bit of an argument?'

I couldn't tell them. Not about Mom and Bob or Teresa and Jack, and how I was feeling inside. I was too ashamed. And I felt so silly blarting in front of Micky. When I looked across at him though, I saw such unexpected kindness in his eyes. But I just nodded, let them think it was just over me and Teresa squabbling.

'Teresa!' Micky shouted upstairs grimly. '*Vieni qui – subito!*' Teresa clattered down the stairs right quick. 'What you said to Genie to make her cry like this?' He turned to me. 'She's got a terrible temper on her, you know. You should take no notice.'

I was beginning to feel really stupid about this and I didn't want to get Teresa into trouble, but I just couldn't stop crying now I'd started, blubbering away like a little kid. Vera looked really concerned.

'You feeling all right?' She looked down into my face with her dark eyes, which made me want to cry again. 'Not sickening for summat, are you?'

Teresa was looking pretty scared. I suppose she thought I might've given the game away about Jack, but it soon became clear to her that I hadn't. 'Come on, Genie,' she said. 'What's got into you? I hardly said a word,' she told her father. 'Honest.'

The three of them all gathered round staring at me, so I felt obliged to cheer up and start smiling just to stop them looking so blooming worried. Vera fed me a cup of tea with a heap of sugar in it and Teresa kissed me. 'Pals?' she said.

I sniffed, nodded. 'Yep.' And felt a bit better.

As Christmas drew nearer I thought, at least Dad'll be home. Maybe he'll be able to knock some sense into Mom. Not literally of course. He was never violent. I just thought him being there might bring her to her senses. Can't really imagine what made me think that but I had to have something to cling to.

That day the week before Christmas had started off badly in the first place. I was already feeling run down, so much that even Mom noticed enough to say, 'What's up with you?'

At work a couple of days before, a whopping splinter speared into the thumb of my left hand. I thought I'd got it out, but found my hand swelling up enormously.

'That's a full-blown whitlow,' Mom told me. 'Looks bad that.' I'd made a linseed poultice to try and bring it on but my thumb was still throbbing like mad, felt about ten times bigger than it should have done and was making me turn feverish and light-headed.

Breakfast time wasn't improved by a letter arriving from Eric's foster mother, Mrs Spenser. I watched Mom read it. The letter had got her out of bed unusually early.

Behind her Gloria was pumping out *Up in the*

Morning Early, a new exercise to music programme. Mom's face was stony.

'. . . across . . .' the woman's voice chirped on. '. . . to the side . . . the left arm . . .'

'The cow!' Mom erupted, reaching the end. 'Who the hell does she think she is, telling me what to do about my own son? The nerve!' I took the letter off her.

'I have told Eric that you require him to be sent home for the Christmas holiday,' Mrs Spenser had written. 'I felt obliged to do so, naturally, but to be frank with you I am not sure that moving him again at this stage would be advisable. Eric seems most reluctant to go through the process of uprooting himself again, and I wonder whether it would not be better to surrender your own desires on this occasion and let him remain here until it is deemed safe for him to return to you permanently.

'I shall, of course, abide by your final decision.'

'"Require him to be sent . . ." I ask you.' Mom ranted on for a bit about Eileen Spenser: stuck up, condescending bitch, and a few other choice terms. Then the doubts sneaked in.

'Eric wouldn't not want to come home, would he?' Her face looked pinched and anxious. 'This is his home. Not with some woman in Maidenhead.' She was pacing around our little room. 'Of course he wants to come back. Doesn't he, Genie?'

'Course he does,' I said, feeling, in my sick state, as if the inside of my head was lunging around. I couldn't believe Eric wouldn't want to see us, even though it sounded as though he had a cushy number down there with this Mrs Spenser.

'I'll write and tell her what's what,' Mom said,

searching for a pen to do just that. All she could find was the wooden handle of one of my old dip pens from school with no nib and no ink.

Work didn't go too well. I couldn't use my left hand so tried to hold the brush with my right and I was slow and clumsy. I tried to keep busy, keep my mind off the pain, and crack jokes with the lads in the factory, but Even Shirley noticed I wasn't myself. 'You sure you're awright?' she kept saying, and I thought how it was strange that everything Shirley said sounded like a moan.

Come dinnertime I was feeling rotten. I went to stand up from my work place and the next thing I knew I was on a chair with my head between my knees and people fluffing round me. My right ear was hurting me now as well. Must've caught it when I went down.

'You'd best get 'ome,' Jimmy was saying, his face topped by black curly hair, swaying in front of me as I tried to focus again.

'You've gone green,' Shirley complained.

I groaned, sick and dizzy.

The gaffer said I should get off as well. It was a while before I cooled down and the inside of my head stopped throbbing and swimming about. After that I went cold and shivery.

I headed out into an overcast, freezing afternoon, hugging my hand up against my chest as if it was a kitten needing protection. It felt so swollen and sore I'd have screamed if anyone had tried to touch it. I cut through on to Belgrave Road and up to my nan's, thinking that if I came over faint again I could at least go in there for a rest. I thought about home, about curling up under the blanket on a chair with a hot cup of tea and the wireless on. The house to myself. Bliss.

And then I saw them, across the road. By the

doorway of Harris's, where of course I couldn't help my wretched eyes turning. They were standing just outside, Walt leaning one elbow up against the glass and her facing him sideways on. Some girl. She had copper-coloured hair, a sweet pretty face with an upturned nose, and was laughing away at something he'd said, the cow. He was smiling, talking, liked her a lot, I could tell.

He had to go and catch sight of me across the road, and in that split second I saw a vicious smile sneak across his face. He moved deliberately closer to the girl and shouted across at me, 'Awright, are you Genie? Nothing I can get for you today then?'

The girl frowned up at him, hearing the taunting in his voice. Yes, you just be warned, I thought.

'Found a better class of shop, ta,' I shouted back, then pulled my collar up round my face with my good arm and hurried past with my nose in the air and Walt's mocking laugh again to speed me along.

It gave me new strength to get home. All the way I was saying to myself, you're so stupid. You're such a stupid little cow, Genie. Why would Walt be interested in you? You've no looks like that other girl and you can't open your mouth to him without coming out with something tart or horrible. You deserve everything you've got. And after all, you don't care anyway, do you?'

But as soon as I was in the house I couldn't pretend any more and the tears came. I couldn't even find the crocheted rug I'd dreamed of sitting under. I sat in the cold back room hugging my throbbing hand and Janet, my old worn-faced rag doll I hadn't touched in years, feeling frozen and ill and as sorry for myself as it's possible to feel.

The next two days disappeared down a long dark

pipe full of confusion. Tossing from side to side in bed, conscious of nothing much except the agony in my hand and arm and unable to lie in certain positions because it hurt so much. Sometimes I knew there were people in the room. Len bringing me drinks of Beefex cubes which I sometimes drank and sometimes not. Mom's face, her voice – 'Genie? Can you hear me?' – trying to get me to take a spoonful of some stuff or other. Nanny Rawson knitting by the side of my bed on the hard chair, knowing her mainly by the rough black wool of her sleeve or her singing. A patchwork of dreams, cooking smells, bits of talk: Walt, the girl, 'bomb … IRA … doorway of Lewis's … mess … Eric … Victor …' Walt, *her*, that girl … Christmas carols and band music coming from Gloria downstairs. The lumps in the hot mattress swelled under me into molehills.

By the time I could sit up and eat oxtail soup and hold a cup of tea myself, Eric was there perched on my bed.

'You look bigger!' I told him.

'I get lots to eat. She's got chickens and a vegetable patch. And I got a nice comfy bed and she uses table napkins. And you don't have to go down the garden to spend a penny.'

He'd also grown a couple of new teeth since he left.

'Sounds a bit of all right then.' I noticed Eric was talking a bit different, putting his aitches on. 'You glad to be back?'

Eric looked down at the old blanket with a bleak expression and shrugged. Then he met my eyes and managed a bit of a smile. 'Yes. S'pose so.'

'Aren't you pleased to see me?'

He'd gone stiff and shy.

'Come on – come 'ere.' I pushed the soup bowl aside

and gave Eric a cuddle which he submitted to. He wasn't just skin and bone any more.

'Cor, Genie,' he said, pulling away. 'You don't half pong, you do.'

'Oh.' I was hurt. 'Well I've been stuck here for a bit.'

'You been bad?'

'I had a bad hand.' I pointed to the dressing on my thumb. 'It's getting better.'

'Mrs Spenser says, whatever happens, there's no excuse for not keeping clean.'

'Oh. Does she?'

Eric was looking round my room as if he'd never seen it before. I had a bedstead, an old rickety cupboard and a chest of drawers, a mirror that hung on the wall by a nail and a couple of old squares of carpet on the floor. Suddenly he got up and started kicking the chest of drawers with his boots, hard, until he splintered the front of the bottom drawer. 'Cheap!' he shouted. 'Everything's cheap and old and rotten.' His face was red and furious.

I started crying but he took no notice, just stood there with his fists clenched.

Eventually I said, 'Dad's coming home Sat'dy.'

Eric looked at me for a second, then turned and ran back downstairs.

Mom managed to wangle herself some time off work the night before Dad came home.

'I'm having an evening out,' she said, touching up her hair in front of the mirror in the back room. She had it hanging loose at the back and pinned up in a roll away from each side of her face at the front. 'Wish the dratted mirror was bigger.' She had to go right up to it to peer down and see if her dress looked all right. 'You'll be OK, won't you Genie? You got Eric for company now.' She was putting lipstick on, so it was mostly the vowels we heard.

I sat watching: Len was peeling spuds at the table and Eric was playing Shove Ha'penny, nudging at me to join in. Apart from his outburst to me, he'd just been quiet since he got home and Mom hadn't seemed to notice any difference in him.

'This is one of the things you don't want me to tell Dad about then, is it?'

She whipped round and gave me a really nasty look, eyes like slits. Then she tried to soften her expression. 'Now Genie, there's no need to be like that. It's just better if you don't say anything about Bob – your father'll only go and get the wrong idea.'

'Will he?'

She stared hard at me. 'Bob's just a pal of mine. Someone to have a chat to – bit of company. I'll just have to hope he doesn't . . .' She jerked her head in Len's direction but he was well taken up with his potatoes.

Come seven o'clock Bob arrived, in a suit this time, not his uniform, five o'clock shadow shaved off and a hanky dangling from his breast pocket. Smoothy bastard, I thought.

'D'you tell your wife you're on a late shift then?' I asked him. I wasn't going to act polite to him. He should've known better. They both should.

'Genie!' Mom snarled. 'Not in front of Eric. Say you're sorry.'

I didn't say anything, just walked off into the kitchen. 'Come on,' Bob said. 'Let's get out of here. Bringing your gas mask?'

'Nah,' Mom said. 'No point, is there?'

When they'd gone Eric said, 'Who's he then?'

'Just someone Mom knows. They go out sometimes. He's a copper.'

'Bob,' Len said.

'That's right, Len. Now let's just forget about them, shall we?'

'Mrs Spenser says—'

'Will you shut up about that cowing Mrs Spenser!' I yelled at Eric, finding my hand raised ready to hit him. He cowered in front of me which made me feel even worse.

We passed the evening, ate our meal, had Gloria on. I played games with Eric, trying to make up to him. Make him want to be my brother again. Come nine I put him to bed and waited for Len to go. I wanted to have a good wash and brush up for the next day with Dad coming home, especially after Eric's charming comment, but I wasn't going to do it with them about. I still couldn't find the yellow and green crocheted rug which I wanted to put on Eric's bed. Normally it was kept folded over the back of a chair.

I heated up two kettles full of water on the stove and filled a basin. The house was very quiet except for the clock ticking on the mantel. I switched Gloria back on low, so as not to disturb the others.

I wanted to wash my hair, which was limp and greasy and smelt sour as I hadn't washed it since before I was ill. I thought of Mom's rainwater bucket outside. Why shouldn't I have nice hair as well? God knows, I had little enough time to spend on my looks.

I opened the back door and let a wide slice of light fall on the garden, trying to see the bucket. Blackout – what blackout? Couldn't see it. I stepped outside. It was a freezing night. The air almost cut your face and I could see stars clear as anything. The bucket was down by the privy, but when I found it of course the water inside was frozen solid. Just my luck. I'd have to use the water I'd already got.

Then I heard the noise. It didn't scare me. Wasn't that sort of sound. It was a giggle and it was coming out of the Anderson. I crept down there and stood outside, breathing very light little breaths. There wasn't much to hear. Long bits of silence, whispering, then a burst of giggling. Mom's giggling. I'd heard enough. Shaking with anger, I went back to the house. I thought of bolting the side gate on the outside to spite them but I didn't want them traipsing through the house with me about to strip off.

Bugger the both of you, I cursed to myself, tipping water wildly over my hair. At that moment I hated the whole world.

'Long film was it?' I asked Mom next morning.

She'd stayed in bed late and came down yawning. She gave me a startled look, hearing the hate in my voice. 'We went dancing. At the . . .' She trailed off. Couldn't think of a porky-pie fast enough. 'It was really lovely.'

When I said nothing and just kept looking at her, she said between her teeth, 'If you dare breathe a word . . .'

When Dad got home she was all over him. Poor Dad was as pleased as punch. Thought she'd missed him so bad she'd decided she loved him after all.

He'd even brought a box of eggs from the farm where he was billeted.

110

'You brought those all the way back on the train?' Mom laughed. 'That's just like you, Victor – and look, only one broken.'

'Lovely and fresh too,' Dad said. 'Laid this morning I expect.'

When he saw our dad, Eric showed the first real signs of positive emotion we'd seen since he got back. Dad squatted down and Eric flung himself into his arms, face against the scratchy khaki uniform.

'That's a lad,' Dad said. After a moment he held Eric away from him and looked at him. 'You're bolting! Must have grown six inches since I last saw you!'

'It's the country. Mrs Spenser seems to be looking after him a treat,' Mom said smoothly.

'We'll play some football while I'm at home, shall we?' He gave Eric a playful punch. They'd never played football together before. Eric's face was a picture, lifted with delight. Dad looked younger and thinner in the face, with more life in him than I'd remembered. He looked over Eric's shoulder. 'Genie, you're growing up too.'

Shy suddenly, I went to be taken in his arms. Relief seeped through me and even my anger with Mom stopped bubbling and lay calm and still. Everyone was back. We could now at least pretend things were normal, that we were a proper family again.

'Here – I've got summat for you.' Dad pulled a little folded piece of paper from a pocket of his kitbag. 'Not much, but I thought they'd suit you.'

Inside were three ribbons, red, white and blue.

'Patriotic too,' Mom gushed. 'What d'you say, Genie?'

'Thanks Dad, they're smashing.' And they were. I

111

was so chuffed, not just with the gift but because he'd thought of me. A smile worked its way across my face and settled there.

'We're having Christmas here,' Mom said. 'Our mom and Lil and the kids can come over. We'll make a real celebration of it.'

Dad put his arm round her. 'That's my wench. It's good to be back where I belong.'

The Spini household was alight with celebration. The kids were home!

'And they're not going back, neither,' Vera vowed from behind one of the lines of washing strung across the tiny room due to the rain outside. 'Never again.' She poked her head out from behind a row of the damp children's clothes which she'd washed as soon as they arrived home. Her face looked shaken out and softer, the tension gone from it. 'Whatever happens, if anything ever does the rate we're going, at least we'll all be together.'

The tiny back-house seemed to have shrunk even further now it was full of children, all bigger than they had been when they left. The two younger ones, Giovanna and Luke, who was now nearly five, came home and settled in as if they'd never left it. Francesca, who was twelve, was glad to be back with Teresa and her mom and dad, although she seemed more moody and far more grown up than before. It was Tony who was finding it hardest to settle back.

'He keeps saying the house is too small,' Vera said dismally. 'The family he went to had a rabbit hutch not much smaller than our house.'

'He'll be OK – give him a chance,' Micky said. He

was happy now, sat at the table in the heart of the family, all his kids around him. 'Another three months and he won't remember he was ever there.' He gave Giovanna's cheek a playful pinch. 'Who's my beautiful girl, eh?' And she went pink and said, 'Gerroff, Dad!' the little ponytail swinging at the back.

It was Christmas Eve and I'd brought a few sweets for the Spini kids. They were all home after the rush in the shop, customers clearing the shelves of Brussels and chestnuts and potatoes. There wasn't room for a tree, but Francesca, who was now used to being in charge, was organizing the younger kids, making streamers, so they were up to their ears in strips of paper and flour and water paste at the table and squabbling over the scissors. Luke was sat on the floor smearing paste down his legs as if he was embalming himself. They fell on the sweets, jelly babies and fruit drops – 'Cor – thanks Genie!' through hardworking mouths.

Stevie was hooking bits of holly over the mantel, adorning a picture he'd got hold of of a shiny Lagonda. There wasn't room for Teresa and me to sit so we stood around watching. Vera was stirring pots on the stove and the room smelt of stew and was steamy with boiling spuds.

'What about a bit round here?' Stevie said to Micky, pointing to his Italian tile.

'Yes – go on. Put it there, put it everywhere!' Micky waved his hands, ready today to decorate his house, his life, everything.

Vera gave us all a cup of Tizer. Teresa was in a good mood too.

'Must be lovely having Eric and your dad home,' she said. 'Proper family again.'

'Ummm – 'tis,' I said. I hadn't told her about Mom

and Bob of course. I just couldn't. Even if I'd wanted to she hadn't had much time for listening lately.

Amid the chaos I whispered, 'How's Jack?'

Teresa's face clouded over for a second. 'OK – I think.'

'Haven't you seen him?'

'He's busy.'

'Take a hint then. He's had enough of you.'

'That's just like you, ain't it?' She managed to snarl in a whisper, which isn't easy. 'Making me think the worst. I knew you were jealous.'

'I'm not,' I lied. 'I just don't want to see you get your feelings hurt.'

'They won't be,' she said haughtily. 'I know what I'm doing.'

'You reckon?'

'Oi – you two aren't falling out, are you?' Vera scolded. 'You staying to have a bite with us, Genie? There'll be enough.'

'Can't, Mrs Spini, thanks very much. Got too much to do at home.' In fact that brought me up sharp. 'Blimey. I've got to go.'

All the family kissed me and wished me a happy Christmas. Vera pushed a small packet into my hand.

'That's for you, love. You deserve a little summat. And these are for the family.'

She sent me off with a bag of fruit and a warm happiness fizzing inside me.

That night I tucked Eric up in bed. Now I was better he was sharing my bed, which I didn't mind at all. I quite liked it. After all, he wasn't Lola. I sat on the bed beside him.

114

'Look – I've put you this old stocking here for Daddy Christmas.' I laid it at the foot of the bed. I was puzzled he hadn't asked for one. Last year he'd been on about it for days. 'You need to get to sleep quick – he won't come if he knows you're awake.'

'There's no such thing as Father Christmas,' Eric retorted. 'Mrs Spenser says. She says it's just a story made up by grown ups and I'm too old for it now.'

'Mrs Spenser's got a lot to say for 'erself, hasn't she?' I snapped. Then I was sorry and patted him. 'You just get to sleep and see what happens.' There wasn't much to put in it but I'd gathered up a few bits and pieces.

As Eric dozed off to sleep I sat there feeling very low in myself. Damn you, Mrs Spenser, I thought, for nothing like the first time. Even if my childhood seemed to have long vanished, I'd still wanted to share what was left of his. To have something pretty and magical and more than real life to believe in. Reindeer on the roof and bells and a white world when it wasn't really snowing. I still half believed in it all myself. But now even that was gone.

Mom did us proud over Christmas. She put on such a good show that even I was lulled into forgetting what a deceiver she was. She adorned the house with a tree in the front room, mistletoe (of all things) in the doorway of the back room so Dad kept bashing his head on it, and tinsel all along the mantel, which Len loved. He kept going and stroking it.

We had turkey and trimmings. Len and I sat and peeled spuds, scraped carrots and put criss-crosses on the stalks of sprouts. Mom took over the main cooking for once and did her best to get it all the right consistency and a colour other than black. She filled the turkey's behind with sage and onion and the craw with a cooking apple. She was like another person, bright and chirpy and singing carols along with Gloria and the rest of us, stirring the gravy, pink-cheeked and happy looking. Dad was allowed to go in the kitchen and put his arm round her waist. I watched from the back room.

'Love you, Dor. You know that, don't you?' This, by Dad's standards, was an outburst fit to be put on stage.

She said, 'Oh Victor,' in a half-reproachful voice but she turned and kissed him and he touched her hair.

Before lunch Nanny Rawson and Lil brought the kids over and they all came in singing, 'Ding dong merrily on high' out of time with each other and laughing, and Patsy was shouting with excitement. Tom came straight over to me. Nan had brought her accordion. She had a bad chest but was cheerful. Eric seemed happy enough to see his cousins.

'You're looking very pleased with yourself,' Lil said to Mom, and she didn't sound spiteful about it for once.

Mom was feeling so well disposed to the world in general that she even invited Gladys and Molly over after dinner to listen to the concert on the wireless put on for the boys in France. They had taken their pinners off and wore flower-print dresses in the same material and had dabs of rouge on their cheeks.

'This is ever so kind of you,' they kept saying. They'd brought over cake with a scattering of dried fruit and a little packet of butterscotch.

Molly made a beeline for Len who was sat at the table and plonked herself down right next to him, smiling away like mad. Most of the butterscotch went by Molly's hand straight into his mouth, which was definitely the way to Len's heart.

It was grey and cold outside but cosy in the house. We listened to the concert, opened our few presents and drank ruby port, the scraped turkey bones still jutting up on the table. Vera's present to me was a pretty hairslide, Mom had talc from Dad and there were chocolates. Gracie Fields was singing 'The Biggest Aspidistra in the World' as Gladys fell asleep in the armchair with her legs apart. Molly barely took her eyes off her until she was letting out little snores. Then she shifted her chair even closer to Len's, giggling and peeping round into his eyes. Their two hands crept together and lay there like ham joints on the pale blue tablecloth. Mom pretended not to notice. Molly slipped the last square of butterscotch into Len's mouth.

Dad was due to leave in the New Year. It'd been a happy week, the happiest I could remember in a long time, since way before the war ever started. Lots of singing and talking and people being nice to each other. I kept trying to forget it was a lie. That the glow on Mom's face was put there by a stocky copper called Bob several years younger than both her and my dad.

On New Year's Eve we joined in auld lang syne along with the people singing on Gloria. We listened to the King's stumbling voice: 'I said to the man who stood at the gate of the year, "Give me a light that I may tread safely into the unknown." And he replied, "Go out into the darkness and put your hand into the hand of God. That shall be to you better than light and safer than a known way."'

We looked over the year's dark rim into the unknown of 1940.

January 1940

Once Christmas was over we came down to earth with a crash. Dad had to go and so, apparently, did Eric.

'D'you want to go back to Mrs Spenser?' I asked him.

Mom was watching us like a hawk. 'He's got to go, there's no two ways about it. "Leave the children where they are." That's what they're saying.' For a moment she squatted down next to Eric and looked into his face. 'You do understand, don't you love? It's for your own safety. It's not 'cause we don't want you. I wish you could stay.'

Fortunately I had the wisdom to keep my mouth shut about the Spinis. 'But d'you *want* to go?' I asked again.

Eric shrugged. 'Dunno.'

'Oh Eric, spit it out!' I nudged his arm impatiently. 'You must know whether you want to or not.'

'Don't mind going,' Eric said. 'Mrs Spenser's all right.'

'I've told you,' Mom snapped, straightening up again. 'He's going.'

Ten whole days of Bob deprivation had left her nerves properly frayed. The sugary act she'd managed for Dad was beginning to wear off too and she was being short and snidy with him again. Now Christmas was over there was nothing to look forward to but being back where we were with more work, more blackout, more drudgery. Mom at least had a grand reunion with Bob to look forward to, so she was better off than the rest of us.

Dad knew he was bound for France and he was a bit emotional. I didn't see Mom shed any tears for him, although she was smoking her fags end to end the morning he went. He set off very early so he could take Eric on the way and meet the dreaded Mrs Spenser. So the two of them got togged up, Dad in his uniform, which suddenly made him stand up straighter, his kitbag over one shoulder, and Eric as before with the gaberdine, little case and gas mask. Mom and I weren't yet dressed.

Dad came and gave me a big tender hug and I felt like bawling and saying, don't go because everything's going to be terrible once you've gone. But I didn't, I just hugged him back and swallowed on the lump in my throat as I felt his newly shaven cheek against mine. He stroked my head like I'd seen him do Mom's. 'Tara, Genie,' he said, looking into my eyes, and I saw his were watery. Then he hugged me again. 'Be a good girl now.'

All I managed to get out was, 'Bye Dad.'

Eric clung to me and I tried to talk in a normal voice, still sounding as if I had a bad cold. 'Be a good boy for Mrs Spenser, won't you? I s'pect you'll be 'ome again in no time.'

Len gave Eric a bear-hug and Mom, Len and I stood out the front as the two of them walked off down the street into the pale dawn, hand in hand, Eric swinging the gas mask from its string. At the corner they turned and waved a last time.

Mom let out a big breath, said, 'So . . .' and went indoors.

That very evening Bob was round again. Must've

been psychic. Later on in the night I had a dream about the pie factory and the bloke with the leaking nose. In my dream, Bob had fallen into a gigantic mincing machine and scraps of blue uniform kept turning up, pressed tightly into the pies. I woke feeling quite happy the next morning.

Teresa managed to tear herself away from Jack long enough to come with me into town one Saturday. Big of her.

'It's blooming freezing, isn't it?' she said as we cut down Bradford Street to the Bull Ring. She pulled the collar of her old blue coat close round her. Our cheeks were pink and raw.

'S'going to snow. Gloria said.'

The sky looked grey and full.

'Jack said too.'

'Oh well – must be true then.'

'Cheeky cow.' She decided not to take offence, which made a welcome change. 'Here, what you going to get? I'm going to Woollies to buy a lipstick.'

'Lipstick?' I'd had in mind some new knickers from off a stall in the Bull Ring. 'You can't wear that!'

'Who says?'

'You'll look like a tart. What'll your mom say?'

'She won't see. I'll put it on when I'm out. Jack can kiss it off again.'

'Yeeurgh! Thought you said you got babbies if you kissed.'

'Hasn't happened so far,' Teresa said smugly. 'Anyhow – I've decided you were probably right about what really happens. Now I've got a bit more – experience.' She went ever so red in the face all of a sudden.

120

'What experience?'

'Never you mind.' Her cheeks aflame.

'You *haven't*, have you?'

She was shaking her head like anything. 'Course not. It's just—' She put her mouth by my ear. 'Once when we were having a kiss and cuddle he pulled me close and I could feel it there against me. As if it was waiting.'

'So what did you do?'

'Nothing! What d'you take me for?' We both got the giggles a bit then. We turned up past St Martin's Church.

'When are you going to let me meet wonder boy then?' I practically had to shout over the din in the Bull Ring.

'Oh – sometime,' she said, casual like. 'Don't want him running off with you, do I? You and your big soulful eyes.'

I was still recovering from this remark as we made our way through the bustling and pushing and shoving in Spiceal Street. There was a tight bunch of people round a bloke stood on a box who was throwing socks into the crowd.

'Here y'go – three pair a shilling. I'm practically giving 'em away. Don't for God's sake wear 'em and then bring 'em back, will yer?' Lots of laughter and repartee from the crowd. There was the usual collection of people hanging round the statue of Nelson and someone playing a trumpet, a melancholy sound, and all the stalls of fruit and veg and cheap clothes and crocks and some people getting a bit scratchy with the crowds round them. There were some uniforms mingling in with the rest, on their way up and down to the station, and kids crying and stallholders yelling and smoke from cigarettes curling into your face on the freezing air. The sky was so dark and heavy that some of the stalls already had naphtha flares burning on them.

We went to Woolworth's, catching whiffs of fish from the market next door. Teresa bought herself a sixpenny lipstick called 'Lady Scarlet' and put some on straight away.

'It does make you look like a tart.'

'Ta very much.' She preened in front of a little round mirror in the shop. 'I just want to grow up. I'm fed up of being treated like a kid.'

I sighed and she looked round. 'What's up with you?'

'I wish I was a kid still. A little tiny babby who doesn't know about anything.'

Teresa saw my downcast face. 'D'you want to do your bit of shopping?'

'Nah. Shan't bother.' Couldn't face the idea of buying camiknickers now somehow.

'Let's go to the Mikado then – have ourselves a cake?'

On the way round there we passed one of the emergency water tanks ready for all the fires this war was supposed to set off. Some clever dick had stuck signs on saying 'NO BATHING   NO FISHING'.

The Mikado was a lovely café and was packed as usual. It was a big place with an upstairs, did lunches and teas, and the windows full of cakes invited you in. You walked into a warm, fuggy atmosphere of steam and the sweet smell of all sorts of cakes, people with bulging cheeks wiping cream from their lips with rough little paper napkins, and cups and saucers chinking.

Teresa and I took our trays upstairs after we'd passed through the agony of choosing a cake. This was just before things were rationed and we'd come to appreciate it even more later. What to have? Chelsea buns you could unroll into a long, currant-spotted strip, flaky

Eccles cakes dark inside, chocolate éclairs squirting cream at every bite? I settled for a cream doughnut and Teresa had a custard slice which erupted with yellow gooiness every time she stuck the dainty little fork into it.

We hung our coats on a proper coatstand and took a table by the window, looking out over the Saturday bustle of Birmingham's Martineau Street. Everywhere people were milling about with bags of shopping.

Teresa and I grew drunk on the sweetness of the cakes and got the giggles. I tried to forget everything at home and we sat and laughed and reminisced. Teresa was her old jolly pre-Jack self, and I looked at her dancing eyes and lipsticky mouth which had faded in the onslaught of custard and thought, she really is my best pal and that'll never change. And I was in a quite good mood until suddenly Teresa said, 'Seen Walt?'

'No.' I couldn't help sounding sulky. 'Why would I have done? You're the one whose brother's pally with him, not me.' I slammed my fork down too hard on the tea-plate and a lady stared at me.

'Come on, Genie. You know you like Walt. You're your own worst enemy, you are. You're not going to like this but I'm going to say it—'

'He's walking out with another girl. I know, ta.'

'How?'

'Seen 'em.' I kept my eyes fixed on my plate.

'Oh Genie.' Teresa was all sympathetic in a superior 'I'm so lucky to have gorgeous Jack but poor old you' sort of way which got right under my skin. She leaned forward. 'She's not reliable that one. I've heard things about her.'

'So what, anyhow,' I said savagely.

'He does like you, you know he does.' Teresa was

grinding on at me. 'If you didn't do everything you could to put him off. Why can't you be nice to him instead of eating him alive every time he speaks to you?'

'I don't like him now anyway. He's a pig.'

'How come then?'

I wasn't going to tell her about him making a fool of me. Twice.

'What's her name?'

'Lisa.'

'Bully for her.'

'Well you asked.'

I didn't want to know any more. Didn't want to think about it any more either. The afternoon was spoilt.

'Fancy going to C&A?' Teresa said when she'd drained her teacup.

I shook my head, staring at the endless movement of people outside. As my eyes focused on the faces, I noticed one shambling along who was nearly a head taller than everyone else, gangly, head aflame with red curly hair.

'Isn't that . . .' I said, before I had time to think.

'Who?' Teresa craned her neck, following the direction where I'd been looking. I saw her eyes widen. 'It is,' she said. I could hear the hurt in her voice. 'It's Jack.' Her cheeks went red, clashing with the fading lipstick. 'He told me he had to work this afternoon. Was doing an extra shift. That's why I came . . .'

'With me?' I finished for her, pushing back my chair. 'Well thanks a lot, Teresa. It's always nice to feel second best to some carrot-top who doesn't give a monkey's about you in any case.'

She was peering round the window-frame, following him as he disappeared. 'Was he with anyone? Did you see?'

'No, I didn't as a matter of fact. But it proves one thing. You can trust your beloved Jack about as far as you can spit.'

'It's just a misunderstanding,' Teresa said, lower lip trembling. 'Course it is. He wouldn't lie to me. Not Jack.'

But I couldn't help a guilty feeling of triumph at the sight of Teresa's crumpling face.

Next time I saw her of course, Jack had wormed his way out of it. Fibs? Him? Downright porky-pies? No – it had slipped his mind, he wasn't working after all, and being a model son he had to run some urgent errands for his mom.

His devoted, starry-eyed girl told me this in all seriousness, face ashine. 'I knew it'd all be all right! He's explained everything.'

'Teresa,' I said, 'if you'll believe that, you'll believe anything.'

The thing I hadn't told Teresa was that I did have an admirer in Jimmy the Joiner.

I paid him a bit more attention. Smiled sometimes. After all, I wanted someone to want me. In fact I pretty desperately wanted someone to want me. Number one on the list would have been my own mother. But I wasn't going to show it or go begging for it from anyone. I managed, me. I could cope. Didn't need anyone. That's what I wanted to say to everyone. Scared the life out of me, all that wobbliness every time I saw Walt. And the terrible stabbing jealousy when I saw him with Lisa or whatever the hell her name was. I didn't dare think what would happen if I gave in to feelings like that. But Jimmy was different. Apart from the fact he wasn't unpleasant as such, I had nothing in the way of actual attraction towards him at all. Except for being a bit flattered. It gave me a warm, stroked sensation that anyone was taking an interest.

Since I didn't feel anything except a helping of curiosity, I wasn't worried enough to be nasty to him. In fact I started to get a thrill saying 'Hello Jimmy' when I came into work and seeing I had the power to make a red flush spread over his pale, underfed-looking face.

'Rationing starts today,' Mom said, though I could hardly have missed the fact since Gloria had been on and on about it. The week's ration was to be: bacon, 4 oz.; butter, 4 oz.; sugar, 12 oz. We were already registered with all the right people. Thank heavens we were with another butcher and not Harris's, I thought with a shudder. Didn't need my nose rubbed in it.

'We'll have to make sure we don't have that Molly over every five minutes, living off our ration,' Mom said. She was ironing at the table. Now there was an unusual sight. I should've had a photographer in. 'She seems to be coming over here a lot.'

She didn't know the half of it. Molly was over just about every evening when Mom was out at the telephone exchange. She seemed to have got out of Gladys's clutches, and instead of being dragged into premature old age had decided to *live*. The dabs of rouge got thicker. She brought boiled sweets. She had a cousin worked over at Cadbury's and got her cheap chocolate so she brought that along as well and saved all the best bits for Len, even some with nuts in. Once Len was home from work he and Molly parked themselves in front of Gloria for the evening, enormous in their chairs, sucking and champing away on barley sugars and Dairy Milk with serene smiles on their faces. They never said much to each other. Barely a word in fact. Whatever was on, they listened. *The Nine O'Clock News*, they tuned into Haw-Haw, concerts, records, *ITMA*. They cheered the house up no end, chuckling away when anyone laughed on the wireless, Molly's titties heaving up and down. I thought how their dimensions suited each other.

And Gloria had just given us a new treat: the Forces Programme which was put on for the lads in France, but we could tune into it at home as well. I wondered if Dad'd hear it and felt cheered by the thought that he might. It was like a link with him. Gloria's music was the one thing that could lift my spirits on these chill, dreary days. All those bandleaders, their music like shiny sparkling trails through the house, making you want to sing, to move your body – Geraldo, Joe Loss, Ray Noble, Glen Miller. I was in love with them all, though I had no idea whether any of them looked like the Hunchback of Notre Dame. And my Anne Shelton, and the Mills Brothers with those sweet, melancholy voices. I wanted to be tucked into bed by 'Goodnight Sweetheart' and dance till I was drunk on happiness to 'In the Mood'. They did what they did for me for Len, for Molly, and for countless other people. They made life worth living.

It started snowing. I say snowing. It was snow such as I'd never seen in my life before. Heaps and swathes and layers and banks of it clogging up the town and blown across the parks. The old'uns were all saying, 'Can't remember snow like this since ...' – though each of them seemed to recall a different date. Gloria said it was turning into the worst winter for forty-five years. Everything was muffled and the sky seemed to sink lower as if it was creaking under the weight of it all. Buses, already crawling along in the handicap of the blackout, were now going so slowly they were almost going backwards. Everyone was even friendlier than usual and Mom had to buy herself a new pair of boots to get to and from work.

'Feels safer somehow, doesn't it?' Mom said, when the snow had been falling for some time. 'As if they couldn't get at us with all this wrapped round.' She stood staring out of the back window.

'It's so cold though.' I was crouched by the fire, turning this way and that to try and feel the warmth on every bit of me. 'I was frozen in bed last night. Where's that crocheted blanket of Nan's gone?'

Mom picked up her bag and started fiddling inside it. 'What blanket?'

'You know. The yellow one.'

Mom shrugged and made a show of checking through her coins. 'It's so flaming dark on the bus you can't see what change they're giving you ... Maybe Len's got it.'

Since Len had already gone I couldn't ask him, but there was no sign of it on his bed.

'That strip of baize we had in the front room's gone too,' I told her.

Mom frowned. 'D'you think that Molly's light-fingered?'

'No, I don't.' The thought hadn't crossed my mind.

128

It was hard to imagine Molly being light-anythinged. 'I s'pose it'll turn up.'

One night Len and Molly started kissing. After some sign between the two of them which I must have missed, Len knelt down on the floor in front of her. Molly spread her legs apart to let him come near and they locked their lips together. And that was that. For ages. I was ever so embarrassed. Seeing people kissing like that's enough to make you jump out of a window even from the top floor, and they didn't care whether I was there or not. They didn't even notice.

But what could I do? Len had his eyes shut and Molly's brawny hands were clamped behind his back, so I went into the kitchen and did the washing up. Mom would've had a fit if she'd known about them. But then who was she to complain? Everyone else seemed to be at it, so why shouldn't Molly and Len have a go, even if they were both as thick as butter? So I just left them to it.

When I crept back in later Molly was sitting on Len's lap. She beamed at me, her red face pressed against Len's, and he was in some sort of dreamy trance as well.

'Awright, Genie?' Molly said. 'Don't mind us, will you?'

'D'you want a cuppa tea?'

'Ooh yes,' Molly gasped, as if she'd just run ten times round the block. She lurched off of Len's knee. 'I made a few biscuits – 'ere.'

She handed me a paper bag containing four crumbly biscuits. 'Two for Lenny,' she said, planting herself opposite him.

Soon after there was a loud hammering at the front. The three of us looked at each other.

'Stay in your own chairs,' I said, running to answer it.

Lil was in a right state. Her coat collar was pulled up round her throat and her hair and shoulders sparkled with snow.

'It's taken me a bleeding age to get here,' she panted, steaming in past me. When we got into the back her eyes looked darting and scared. 'It's your nan. She had a fall earlier and they've taken her up the hospital. She's done summat to her leg. Where's Doreen?'

'Work.'

'Course. I'd forgotten you're on your own every evening.' She nodded at Molly. 'Len – our mom's hurt her leg. Fell on the ice.' She spoke slowly so he'd take it all in. Molly made some sympathetic noises and then, surprisingly, seeing she'd be in the way, took herself off home.

'I'll wait and tell Doreen,' Lil said.

It was ten o'clock. 'She should be half an hour or so.'

Lil went and stood by the fire. 'Jaysus, my legs are shaking.' After a moment she burst into tears and sank into a chair. 'I've never seen Mom like that,' she sobbed. 'She was on the corner of Moseley Road. She'd been to see Mrs Briggs – the one who's got pleurisy – and she fell on the way back. When they came to get me she was lying there making this horrible noise. I can't get it out of my mind. It was the pain – she sounded like a dog whimpering. Someone from the hotel got her an ambulance and it took ages and ages to come. Mom went quiet and I thought she was dead.'

I went and knelt down by Lil and watched her,

wondering if I should take her hand. I was scared. Len sat, looking stunned.

'It's all right.' Lil looked quickly across at him. 'She's not dead. She'll be OK. She's done summat to her knee. But when they put her on the stretcher to go in the ambulance, someone shone a torch in her face and she looked so old and her eyes were full of fear. I've never seen her like that before.'

She was sobbing even harder now. I felt so sorry for her and for our nan I nearly started crying myself. I went and poured her a cup of tea. She hadn't even taken her coat off and was still hunched up in its grey, prickly warmth.

'You said Nan's going to be all right, didn't you?' I asked cautiously. I felt very young suddenly. I wasn't exactly sure what was up with Lil but I put it down to shock. Len leaned forward and took her hand and Lil suddenly threw herself into his arms, laying her head on his big strong chest.

'I hate being on my own,' she cried in a desolate voice. 'I want my Patsy back. I want him so bad. Why did he have to do it?' She tried to say a few more things that got lost in sobs and gulps. Len rocked her back and forth. 'I can't stand it,' Lil said. 'I can't go on. I need someone to be with. I hate sleeping in a lonely bed every night and doing all the worrying for all of us on my own. It's too much, day after day. How'm I going to manage now?'

When she'd calmed down a bit I said, 'Who's with the kids?'

'Mary, from next door.' That was a sign of how bad things were if she'd entrusted her kids to Mary Flanagan.

Lil suddenly seemed to lose all the energy that had

driven her here in such a state. She sniffed, sat quiet back in her chair and drank her tea. But it was still all going round in her mind because after a while she said, 'Mom won't be able to manage. I'll have to give up work and run the shop.' She sighed. 'I hate that bloody factory, but I'm making better money now than I've ever done in my life.'

'Or I could,' I said. It sounded like a nice idea to me. There was no point in suggesting my own dear mother. I knew that just wasn't going to happen.

'I can't move out now,' Lil said gloomily, only half hearing me. 'Not even if they offer me a council house. I'll be stuck in Belgrave Road for ever.'

'No you won't. Nan'll get better.'

Lil looked at me, dark eyes filling again. 'When she was laid there in the road I saw what it'd be like without her at home. And I thought how she's had it hard, what with me coming back to live and Len ... And Doreen and me not getting on. I wanted to make it up to her. She's been a good mom to us ...' And she was off again.

The mantel clock said ten twenty-five. 'Mom'll be in soon,' I said, desperately.

But she wasn't. We all sat and waited. Lil was tapping her foot on the tiles round the hearth. By a quarter to eleven I had this nasty suspicion turning round in my mind.

'Probably the weather,' I said.

Ten more minutes passed and I was getting in a panic. How could she, tonight of all nights? She had to be somewhere with PC Bob, but I couldn't tell Lil that because the most God Almighty amount of shit would hit the fan if she was to find out about that, specially the state she was in tonight. I sat tensed with terror at the thought of hearing the front door and Mom, in her flirty voice, asking Bob in for a drink.

Once it reached ten past eleven Lil stood up. 'I'll have to go and let Mary get home. What the hell's happened to her? Is she often this late?'

'Oh, sometimes she is,' I said quickly, praying Len wasn't going to say anything.

'Will you be all right?'

'We'll be OK, just as normal,' I said. I was nearly laughing with relief that Lil was going. 'I'll tell her, soon as she gets in.'

When I opened the door to let Lil out Mom was standing on the other side of it with a kind of smirk on her face which she wiped off right quick when she saw us.

'What's the matter? What're you doing here?'

When Lil told her, Mom was about as upset and flustered as she deserved to be. We all stood crushed into the hall.

'I'll go straight up the hospital and see her tomorrow,' Mom said. She hadn't taken her coat off either.

'Visiting's afternoons,' Lil told her in a chilly voice.

'Oh – well, Genie can go after work, can't you love?'

I was going anyhow. Didn't need her sending me.

Lil disappeared along the road, her muffled torch playing on the icy ground. I shut the door carefully and turned round and stared at Mom. She had guilt not just written, but carved in massive gullies all over her face.

Eventually, with a shrug, she said, 'We just went out for a drink.'

I kept staring really hard at her eyes. How could she? How could she?'

'What, Genie?' Her face went all sharp and spiteful.

'I didn't know, did I? How could I know what was going to happen? Don't barge past me like that ...'

I'd heard enough of her already.

'I have too much of your cheek sometimes ...' she shouted up after me.

I didn't say another word. Just went up and shivered myself to sleep in bed wishing to God I could have a new life, new family, new everything.

The next morning brought a blue sky without blemish, grey clouds wiped away and the sun brilliant on the snow. Before Mom was up I opened the back door and went out. From the kitchen to the privy the snow had been well stamped down by us tramping back and forth. No one, so far as I knew, should have walked on the thick pie crust of snow towards the bottom of the garden where the Anderson sat smooth and rounded as an igloo. But of course I found footprints, not filled in by any night snow, leading from the side gate to and from the shelter. Two sets. I followed them, pressing my feet into the bigger ones with their rugged prints. Round the door of the shelter it'd all been stamped down. There was a cleft in the snow at the edge of the roof as if someone had rested their hand there.

I pulled the door away and looked inside. In the confined space a piece of thick canvas had been laid out to cover the frozen floor. On top of it were a Tilley lamp, a variety of covers and materials: a thick grey blanket I'd never seen before, the strip of green baize, a couple of pillows and the yellow, orange and green crocheted blanket of Nan's which had long been missing from the back room.

February 1940

Life got a bit better after that because Lil took up my offer and I said goodbye to Jimmy the Joiner and Shirl, and went to look after my nan and help run her shop.

She was properly laid up and Lil was earning better money than me. I was happy. Nan let me come and go as I needed to. She understood about Mom. Not Mom and Bob of course – I hadn't said a word to anyone about that. Just about the way Mom used me.

'She don't deserve you,' she said to me, laid back on the horsehair sofa with her leg, rigid in its plaster cast, stuck out in front of her. She'd done some horrible thing to her knee.

'Summat to do with cart-lidge they said up the 'ospital. They say it'll take weeks to heal. Flaming nuisance.'

It'd knocked the stuffing out of her. Her face looked thinner and more lined. Sometimes I found her asleep, head lolling back on the sofa, which was unheard of for her as a rule. But she was always on her dignity. She'd never come down in her nightclothes. When I arrived in the morning she was always dressed. I suppose she must have hoisted herself up off the bed to put her dress on, rolling a stocking up her good leg – good except for the ulcer dressings. She always sat and pinned up her hair.

'I've taken to coming downstairs on my backside,' she said. 'I'm not up to hopping at my age.'

I looked after her as if she was a queen, which she was in my eyes, as she'd never been anything but good to me. I wasn't the only one who thought so – the neighbours drifted in and out of the back door like flies, wanting to know if she needed anything. Hot-tempered, red-headed Mary Flanagan came almost every hour trailing an assortment of her seven kids behind her. She'd tried evacuating them once but they'd all come home.

'You awright there, Edith?' she'd say. 'You shout me if you need anything.'

And in the shop it was always, 'How's Mrs Rawson?' and then they'd say, 'I bet she's glad of your 'elp, bab. I couldn't borrow you for a bit, could I?'

'You're golden,' Nan said to me sometimes, watching me work. I scrubbed her quarry tiles on my hands and knees. I blackleaded the grate, did her washing in the brewhouse when it was our turn, and hung it steaming across the freezing yard. I cooked for her, I ran errands, I scuttled back and forth to the shop whenever we heard the click of the door opening and the bell ringing out.

I felt grown up. I'd just turned sixteen after all, even if that hadn't been much of an event. I served in the shop. I sorted stock, arranging jars of sherbet lemons and throat drops – there were still sweets to be had then – and bars of Lifebuoy and blue Reckitt's powder in packets and piles of enamel buckets. It was peaceful in there most of the time, except once or twice a week when Morgan made his forays through to the upstairs with a selection of trollops in tow. Once the girls arrived there were bangs and squeaks of the floor and giggles and thumps from the bug-ridden rooms upstairs. It was no good suggesting to Nan that she move. There was a time when I just didn't understand this attitude. But it was so much part of the fabric of life at her house I barely gave it a thought now. There was Nan, and there was Morgan. That's how it was. Nan would roll her eyes to the ceiling and tut a bit at the louder noises, but we mostly just had to ignore them. Besides, people being the nosy so-and-sos they are, the trollops were surprisingly good for business.

I adopted Nan's policy towards Morgan, that he was like a mote of dirt passing through, unseen under my nose. That is until he started coming in a bit early – before his girls – and fixing his pale eyes on my chest.

''Allo my dear,' he'd say, wiping his sweaty forehead with a hanky. The strips of hair hung down like pondweed. 'You are growing up fast, aren't you?'

'Nan, he keeps talking to me,' I reported.

'Right,' she said.

Next time he turned up, sneaking in and pussyfooting about instead of going upstairs, grinning at me with yellow smoker's teeth, Nan's voice roared through from the back.

'You filthy bastard, Morgan!' He actually jumped. It had more impact her being invisible, like God's voice out of a cave. 'You as much as speak to my granddaughter again and I'll 'ave your bollocks twisted round the back of your neck!'

'No offence intended, my dear,' Morgan said to me, retreating hurriedly to the stairs.

I kept the place immaculate, took people's money or filled in the strap book so they could pay later. I checked with Nan. She knew them all and trusted most of them. She'd been known to land a punch on the jaw for bad debts. I tore round the place like a whirlwind and I loved it. I was doing it for my nan and I could decide what I wanted to do and when and do it as fast as I liked. I had a fierce mixture of anger and love inside me and I was like a fury.

Sometimes Cathleen trailed round after me, or Nan tried to keep her amused. There were the other kids to deal with when they got home from school. They came and sat by the hearth, hands blue from the cold walk home, and I gave them each a cup of tea and cut them a piece to eat so they were in a good mood by the time Lil got home. I got high marks from Lil because I saved her a lot of chores.

Nan was none too happy though. She wasn't fed up with me, who she couldn't find enough praise for, but because sitting about on her backside wasn't exactly her style. She tried to teach Cathleen to knit but the kid was too young and flew into a tantrum and was happier with a bag of clothes pegs. But Nanny Rawson was bored, so I asked Len if he'd be very very kind and let her borrow Gloria for a bit while she was poorly? It took a bit of persuasion of course, because Gloria was meat and drink to him. But he did love his mom, and in the end he nodded his heavy head when I said we could all have our tea over at Nan's of an evening so he could hear Gloria too.

One morning I trudged over to Nan's through the slush, water seeping into my old boots, carrying Gloria, with the accumulator hanging from one arm in a hessian bag. Nearly flaming killed me. I had to stop every few yards to rest because my muscles were aching so bad, balancing Gloria on people's front walls and switching the accumulator from arm to arm.

I was standing by St Paul's churchyard with Gloria resting on the wall when a voice said, 'Need a hand?'

I nearly dropped the thing.

'Er – oh, hello,' I said. 'Yeah. Ta.'

Walt took Gloria off me with ease and the accumulator suddenly felt light as a sparrow on its own. I rubbed my arms as we set off.

'Where you off to with this?'

'My nan's.'

'I 'eard about her accident. She bad?'

'She'll be all right. Bust up her knee. She's fed up not being able to get about.'

'I'll bet. You brought this to cheer 'er up?'

Why the hell was he being so chummy all of a sudden?

'It's Len's – my uncle. I nearly 'ad to put a gun to 'is head to get 'im to borrow it 'er.'

I gave a laugh, to show I could be light and joke. He was nothing to me now. I didn't care. I'd seen Walt in his true colours, putting me down the way he did, and now he was walking out with that Lisa girl I found it perfectly easy to be civil to him and show I didn't care. I wasn't out to waste my affection on someone who'd taunt me and put me down. That'd be a sign of things to come all right. So talking was easy all of a sudden. Walt was even laughing at my jokes as we walked to Nan's house.

When we got to the shop I said, 'All right, Walt, ta. This'll do.'

'Might as well take it in for you,' he said. 'Not much further is it, and I can't put it down in the wet.'

But he stopped me before we went in.

'Genie—' He was the one blushing now. 'We got off on the wrong foot, didn't we? I was wondering. D'you fancy going to the pictures – with me?'

I could feel my face taking on a wide-eyed innocent look. 'But Walt, you've got a girl to walk out with. Lisa, ain't it?'

Walt looked at the ground, embarrassed. 'Not any more. I'd rather go with you.'

Oh, would you now.

'Sorry. I can't go out. Mom's working evenings and I'm busy.'

'What about a Sat'dy matinée?'

'No ta,' I said, ever so politely. 'To be truthful I wouldn't go out with you if you were the last man on earth.'

He decided to stop helping me after that.

Nan of course was up and dressed. She was amazed. 'Is that Len's wireless?'

I nodded, a smile spreading ear to ear. She looked ever so pleased and I knew I'd done something good. 'He said you could have it while you was laid up. I'll set it up, shall I?'

Between us we wired it to the accumulator and Gloria was off, jollying the place along no end. Nan cheered up straight away. 'Isn't it marvellous?'

By the end of the day, during which Gloria was barely switched off, Nan said, 'I think me and Lil ought to see about getting one of these.' She nodded at the kids who were sat next to *Children's Hour* sucking bulls' eyes. 'And it doesn't 'alf keep them quiet.'

I was tingling from more than one sense of triumph.

Soon after, I popped into the Spinis' one dinnertime and walked slap bang into a family row. The Spini family's disputes had two things which outdid even the most ferocious yard fights in the area: one was fluency, the other was volume.

I could hear it coming when I stepped out the front of Nan's, voices all the way down the street, and there was a gaggle of people gawping in the Spinis' doorway to watch the fun. Their rows seemed to work better in Italian, so none of us could understand a word, and even if we could the four of them were all yelling at once.

I went and pushed through the nosy parkers until I was just inside. Vera was holding her ground on one side, arms waving in the direction of Micky, who was wagging an infuriated finger mainly in the direction of a box heaped with turnips, and I couldn't tell who he was actually shouting at. Stevie, in a white apron, his sleeves rolled up, was framed by the back door leading into the ice-cream-making room where he had presumably been interrupted churning the 'Scattoli's Outstanding Ices'. He, like the others, was shouting and wore a heavy scowl, although that wasn't unusual.

Close by was the tall young man with a drooping black moustache, a nose curved and slender as a knife blade, who Teresa had such scorn for. Fausto Pirelli. He was watching, wearing a superior kind of expression, saying nothing.

And in the middle of them all stood Teresa, between two sacks of carrots as if they were protecting her, like sandbags, from the blast coming from all around. But she was doing her fair share of shouting too.

They must have found out about Jack, I thought, and I wasn't quite as sorry as I should've been.

But no. Teresa was off again, hair hanging down, hand out in front, slapping at the air with the back of her hand. In the midst of all the Eyetie I heard the words 'war effort'.

Suddenly catching sight of me standing there, she yelled in English, 'Ask Genie, since you think she's such a model daughter. Go on, tell 'em, Genie. She goes out to work in factories and there's no trouble. Nothing. All the time you treat me like a child and I'm sick to death of it. Sick of it!'

The row suddenly switched into English. 'We just want to protect you,' Vera said. She didn't seem on the boil as much as Micky and Stevie, who were doing their injured male pride bit. 'We want to keep the family together.'

'Well that didn't stop you sending the kids half way across the country, did it? You soon did that when you decided it was the right thing. So what's wrong with me just going out to get a job up the road somewhere?'

'No one's going anywhere unless I say so,' Micky decreed. His face was thunderous. 'I'm not having you going off behind my back. You stay here, you work here and that's an end of it – finish.' He swiped his hand across as if cutting his own throat and made as if to walk off, but found the door blocked by all the gawping passers-by, so he turned and had another go. 'That's the trouble with you young people. You got no respect for your families now. You got to keep respect – do as you're told.'

'You're stupid, Teresa,' Stevie started up. 'You're being selfish. You should act more responsible instead of being so childish.'

'I'm not childish!' Teresa shrieked at him, arms waving. 'I'm just sick of you all running my life for me. "Teresa you can't go here …" "Teresa you've got to do this …" And anyway, Stevie, what's all this got to do with you? Why don't you shut your trap and take your bloody ice-cream cart out? It'll give us all a rest.' She waved an arm at Fausto Pirelli. 'And take Mussolini here with you!'

That did it, they were all off then, Fausto too, who

142

was totally enraged all of a sudden, and no one could get a word in edgewise for minutes at a time.

Then, in a tiny chink of quiet, Teresa said, 'But they've given me the job!'

'Tell them you can't do it—'

'Go on – let 'er get a job,' some woman shouted from the doorway. 'It's all for the war effort.' No one took the blindest bit of notice of her.

I could see they were going to start off all over again. This one could go on for hours. So I pushed my way out and slipped back to Nan's, their voices following me down the street.

'What happened?' I asked Teresa, tiptoeing back in later.

'My daughter, she wants to just go,' Vera said, one hand scooping through the air like a plane taking off.

'She got her own way – as usual,' Stevie said, grumpy sod that he was.

Teresa put her thumb up and grinned. 'I'm going to have a go. It's Green's, over in Sparkbrook, making army uniforms.'

'You'll be kept busy then.'

She waited till Stevie had moved out of earshot, then hissed at me, 'The factory's right by Jack's house.'

'Oh,' I said. 'Bully for it.'

Jimmy the Joiner walked back into my life one freezing Saturday with a ring of the shop bell. I ran through, ducking under the dividing counter, and there were Jimmy and Shirl.

'Genie!' Shirl greeted me as if I was her long lost, best ever pal, and I found I was really pleased to see her. I'd quite missed her voice droning on down my ear.

Jimmy was giving me a shy smile and his squiffy eyes were warm and friendly. I wasn't sorry to see him either. 'We thought we'd come and see how you was getting on,' he said. 'T'ain't the same at work without you, Genie.'

This was gratifying to hear. 'Come through and meet my nan,' I said.

Nan was friendly, as she was to people she expected to approve of. 'Sorry I can't get up and do anything for you,' she said. 'It's not me at all, sitting about like this.'

'Oh no, you must rest,' Shirl said.

Shirl's pale hair was soft and curly and she had thick pink lips and enormous blue eyes. Everything about her was round, her behind, the shape of her legs, her cheeks, her big heavy titties. She was another of those that made me feel scraggy and boyish. But there was something very comforting about Shirl. Cathleen was hovering by her and Nan seemed to feel it at once.

'Come and sit by me,' she said to her. 'Genie'll make us a nice cuppa tea.'

'Lovely place you've got 'ere, Mrs Rawson,' Shirl said in the sort of voice most people put on to tell you someone's died. Nan knew perfectly well her house was just like thousands of other back-houses, if perhaps more spick and span, but she seemed chuffed all the same.

Jimmy sat quiet. He'd hardly taken his eyes off me since they arrived. I kept looking at him out of the corner of my eye, not sure whether I liked him or not. There was something awkward about him, his very pale skin, dark hair curling at his white neck, and when he looked at you he almost squinted in a way which made my flesh creep a bit. But on the other hand I'd seen worse. And he'd come specially to see me, and not many people ever did that.

'She's a good girl, our Genie,' Nan said, nodding across at me as I lit the gas. 'She's been a right little gem to me.'

'We miss her,' Shirl said, taking Cathleen up on to her lap and stroking her plump hands. 'It's not the same at the factory without her buzzing about.'

They sat and drank tea while Nan gave Shirl a blow-by-blow account of the fall, the doctors, the hospital where she'd spent four days.

''E said 'e didn't like the look of my knee at all,' she was going on. ''E said, "I shall 'ave to consult with my colleague." Those are the exact words he used.' Shirl gave every sign of loving it all, and cuddled Cathleen. I could picture Shirl with loads of kids.

Jimmy kept sneaking looks at me. Once he winked and I smiled back. Yes, he was all right Jimmy was, I thought. I'd missed his attention.

Outside in the yard when they were going, Cathleen still clung to Shirl's hand.

'Jimmy's got something to ask you, Genie,' Shirl said.

Jimmy shuffled his feet. 'D'you fancy coming out with me, Genie?' Then, thinking he'd been a bit short, he added a quick, 'To the pictures or a walk or summat?'

I thought about Walt. Stuff Walt.

'I would, Jimmy,' I said. 'Only it's hard for me to get away, what with my nan and my uncle and my mom.'

His face dropped.

'You two go,' Shirl said. 'I'll come and sit with your nan Sat'dy afternoon, that's if she's no objection. And I can play with little Cathleen here.' She pinched Cathleen's cheek. 'I'd like that. We got on ever so well.'

145

We consulted Nan and she looked pleased. 'It's time Genie 'ad a bit of life of her own for a change.' She turned a sterner eye on Jimmy. 'As long as you both know 'ow to behave yourselves.'

Next week Jimmy and I walked down the Cannon Hill Park. I wore my best green winter frock and huddled in my coat. Truth to tell I wasn't feeling at my best. I had a cold and a blocked nose and it had been an effort to come out. But I decided to think positive, to like Jimmy's loping walk and his voice, which came out sounding deeper than you'd expect from the size of him.

Almost as soon as we were on our own he grabbed my hand, which took me aback. Bit pushy, I thought, when he'd always seemed a timid sort before. But he turned and smiled at me and said, 'Don't mind, do you? I've been wanting to hold your hand ever since I first saw you.'

Course, if someone says something like that you don't resist, do you? And it was a nice feeling, special, having someone close. His hands were warm even in the cold. The snow was thawing slowly and there was wet everywhere.

'You're ever so pretty, Genie.'

'Me?' I laughed, pleased as punch. Sometimes I just wanted to be a proper girl. 'Go on. I'm not.'

'You are. Your eyes are like – like – well, they're – nice. And the way you get that dimple when you smile.'

We walked round watching the ducks on the small lake. The park stretched wide around us, sloping down to the swimming baths at the bottom, full of leaves now, and chunks of ice. It was a shock to see green again after all the days of white. There were still hard mounds of snow with grey crusts on top melting slowly down the slope.

Jimmy told me he had four sisters and a brother and his mom was deaf, had to lip read.

'What about your dad?'

'Oh . . .' he said, almost as if he'd forgotten about him. 'He's reserved occupation – Heath's, the foundry.'

'Mine's away,' I said, suddenly proud. 'In France.'

'Wish mine was,' Jimmy said with feeling. 'He's a bugger – pardon me.'

I wasn't sure what to say to that. There are such a variety of ways of being a bugger and I wasn't sure I wanted to know the particulars.

And Jimmy said, 'I don't want to talk about 'im. What d'you like doing best?'

I had to think hard about that one. 'I don't seem to get the chance to do anything much these days. I like going to see my friend Teresa. When she's got the time,' I added gloomily.

'I like football.'

Oh Gawd, not another one. 'You don't support the Villa, do you, by any chance?'

'Nah – never. Blues.'

That was something, although whether he was going to carry on about Aston Villa or Birmingham City wouldn't make much odds to my passing out with boredom in the long run.

When he got me up by the trees at the quiet, top end of the park, he caught hold of me and kissed me like I'd seen Len and Molly doing. I had a bit of trouble with that because I didn't think to breathe in before he started and my nose was all stuffed up. His big slimy tongue popped into my mouth and he was sucking away at my lips and I found myself thinking Jaysus – like Lil would have said – is this right, us getting on to kissing so quick? I couldn't do anything back except cling on to his shoulders struggling for breath as he pushed his body against me. In the end I had to pull away and take in a big gasp, which Jimmy took to mean I was so overcome with emotion I couldn't stand any more. Which was pretty near the truth, only not quite how he thought.

When I turned round again after fixing some sort of smile on my face, he was giving me a grin brimming over with triumph. 'You're my girl now, Genie.'

Len was coming to Nan's straight from work now, early evening, so I could cook for all of us with Lil, and get it all over in one go. It also meant he could have a good old listen to Gloria before we had to go home. It was much nicer this way, sharing some of the chores with Lil. She was being as nice as pie to me as I gave her so much help with the kids, dunking them in the tin bath by the fire for her once a week, clearing up the mess after and keeping them entertained. She taught me a few tricks to help the cooking go better, like taking the custard off the heat to start stirring it so it didn't heave up into lumps like it usually did. Mom never told me anything useful like that even though she'd once worked in the Bird's factory in Digbeth, and you'd think she'd at least have picked up how to make the stuff.

That night we had stew with loads of dumplings. Lil showed me how to make them really nice with suet. We all squeezed round the table, except for Nan who couldn't get her leg under it. It was cosy with the fire and Gloria and the dim gaslight and we all ate hungrily.

'Feels a bit like Christmas, doesn't it?' Nan said. 'Shame Doreen's not here as well.'

148

My eyes met Lil's. We couldn't bring ourselves to agree with Nan on that one. My feelings of fury at the way Mom was carrying on had grown worse and worse.

Len and I walked home together after, holding hands for safety: the street was so dark and it was beginning to freeze again. We had our torch but didn't bother carrying the gas masks any more.

'I'm glad you're here, Len,' I said. 'I'd be scared stiff else.' He was so big and slow and solid.

One hint of sound from outside our house brought Molly to her door. 'You're back then?' she called across the street.

Couldn't really disagree with her there. Sometimes it got on my nerves a bit, her pouncing on us like that. But you couldn't dislike Molly. She was inoffensive and as generous as she could afford to be. And she made Len happy.

'Doesn't Gladys mind?' I asked as she came over. I was struggling to find my key in the dark.

I just saw Molly put a finger to her lips, rather coyly. 'She's asleep. Didn't see me go.'

As I went to the front door I heard a faint knocking noise from the side of the house. There was a breeze and the entry gate was unfastened. Anger twisted in me, and dread.

'You go in,' I said to Len and Molly, unlocking the door. 'I'm just going to shut the side gate.'

They weren't listening to me anyway, so wrapped up were they in each other.

I tiptoed down the little alley between our house and the next into the back garden and slid across the wet grass. I knew it. Noises from the Anderson. Even more blatant noises than before. It was horrible. Molly and Len, Jimmy, now this. Something exploded inside me.

I pelted back round and in through the front door, steaming in past Len and Molly who were in each other's arms but still alert enough to look round in amazement at me.

'Len!' I commanded him from the kitchen. 'Get in 'ere a minute.'

I had an enamel pail in the sink, the tap full on so water was rushing into it at the full strength of the old plumbing. Len stood watching. When it was three-quarters full I dumped it on the floor in front of him.

'I want you to do a piddle in there. The biggest one you can manage.'

Nice thing about Len was, he never asked questions. Just unbuttoned his flies and obliged, with Molly watching, eyes on stalks, over his shoulder.

I flung open the back door and stomped down the garden, leaning well over to one side to balance the pail. On the way I stopped and scraped what dirt I could from the top of the flower bed, hurting my hands on the icy ground, and chucked that in too.

From inside the Anderson I could still hear loud, indecent sounds. They wouldn't have noticed if the whole bloody Luftwaffe had come over that night.

I could barely see a thing but it was so small I couldn't possibly have missed. I yanked the front aside and sloshed the bucket of wee-wee stew in on top of them.

'Bob's your sodding uncle!' I yelled. And left them in a wet, shrieking, effing and blinding heap inside.

Mom's rage knew no bounds. To begin with. She called me every name under the sun, once PC Bob had dripped off down the road refusing to stay another moment to be treated like this, etc. etc.

'You *stu-u-upid*—' she screeched, dragging the word out long, '—selfish, evil little cow!' She was shivering in the back room, lank strips of hair hanging on her shoulders and her red dress daubed with soil, clinging to her. 'I wish I'd never – never even *seen* you in my whole life. I'm cowing frozen – and Bob could catch his death . . .'

'There was wee in there as well.' Thought it best to tell her. Otherwise she'd never know, would she?

'WHAT?'

She'd stormed into the house without even noticing Molly sprawled on top of Len in one of the chairs, the top buttons of her dress undone. They hadn't wasted any time. Molly strugged to her feet like an upturned beetle and skedaddled, right quick.

'Who in the hell d'you think you are?' Mom ranted on. Quite a bit of pacing up and down the room went on, except being such a small room any pacing turned more into pigeon stepping. 'Interfering. Passing judgement. What's Bob going to think, me having a daughter like you?' She was working herself up. 'He might never come back and it'll be all your fault.'

'GOOD!' I shouted. 'I hope he dies. I hope he catches pneumonia or falls under a bloody bus. He shouldn't be here at all. He's not my dad, and you shouldn't be carrying on behind Dad's back. You're a disgusting tart, that's what you are.'

That was when she started hitting me, the bitch, stinging slaps round my face again and again until Len had the wit to grab her arms and stop her. I bit my lip until it bled. I wasn't going to cry for her. I hated her.

It was she who burst into tears then, sobbing and snivelling and carrying on while Len and I just stood there staring at her. I put my hands to my smarting cheeks and my heart was completely hardened towards her.

Until suddenly she said, 'You don't understand, Genie.' She looked up, sharp face all raspberry blotches, appealing to me. For the first time trying to tell me something she truly felt. 'You don't know what it's like to find someone you can really love. To be lifted out of years of feeling dead and buried, and scared stiff you might lose it again. You've seen how he looks at me. I've never in my life been wanted like that before – ever.' She was sobbing again at the thought of it.

'Dad wants you.'

She looked down and I knew she was ashamed. 'But I don't want him. God knows, I've tried. I just don't. He makes me feel buried up to the neck. Always has.'

I started crying then. Didn't know where it came from, all of it. Frightened Mom a bit I think, the way I howled. Scared me too. It was like a pain pushed down so far I didn't know it was there, all gushing out. I didn't want to hate her. She was my mom. Your mom's the one person you can't hate or it eats you inside. She's like the North Star and you always need that right direction.

And for once she forgot herself and put her arms round me, and I sobbed and bawled and couldn't stop. Len came and hugged the both of us together like a gorilla.

'I'm sorry, Genie,' Mom said in the middle of it. I could feel her tears dropping on the top of my head. 'I can't help it. I just can't help myself.'

March 1940

My Dear Doreen and family,

Well at least the weather's warming up slowly
and we wake with the birds now – they've started
singing at last! We can still see clouds of our breath
on the air first thing too. Roll on spring proper. So
now my only complaints are that I still haven't
found a pair of boots that fit properly and that I
wish I could be at home with you. We're still here
waiting to find out what proper soldiering, as the
lads call it, is all about.

One new thing – they've issued us with special
day passes to go into———. I went, Saturday, with
Dickie, the pal I told you about who comes from
Stechford. It was an experience. Very smart and
pretty with flowers at the windows and people sit
out and drink on the pavements. We tried some of
the wine they sell. It's some rough stuff – I'd rather
have a pint of Ansells!

I've read so many books since we've been here.
The lads pass them round. Otherwise it's card
sharping and letters. Thank Genie for the chocolate
– a proper taste of home. How is Gloria doing? The
wireless in our billet stops us feeling too blue. Today
I heard Vera Lynn singing 'Somewhere in France
with You' and it made me pick up my pen to tell
you, my Dor, how much I miss you.

Glad to hear Edith's knee is on the mend. I'll write again soon. In the meantime, try and keep in good spirits, won't you?

Your loving husband, Victor.

I liked letters from Dad, knowing he was safe and hearing about new places he'd been. Mom always read the letters of course, but she'd put them down on the table without a word. After, she'd be scratchy and short for a bit.

Bob stayed away for a week after our little set-to. Don't know whether she told him to or whether he was in a huff or scared I might go for him with the carving knife. Whatever the reason, he kept his distance and all was rosy. We had Gloria back – Nanny Rawson and Lil had bought a little set of their own – and Mom was being extra specially nice to me. She ran me up a new dress on her machine and it actually fitted me. It was navy with white polka dots and a little matching scarf to go in the neck. She visited our nan twice a week. She even did some cleaning. I found her up early one morning sweeping out the back room.

'I know I've been a bit neglectful, Genie,' she said a couple of days after our fight. 'And your nan says you've been a proper treasure to her.' She even brought me up tea in bed, which was an unheard of luxury. Suddenly I felt like someone's daughter.

One morning she sat on the edge of my bed, her hair loose, and said with a coy little smile, 'So who's the lad courting you, Genie?'

Can't say I'd thought of it as courting exactly. But Mom was trying to be my friend and I wasn't getting much change out of Teresa nowadays.

'His name's Jimmy Davis. He was at the factory in Conybere Street.'

'Nice then, is he?'

"'E's all right.'

'Bring him home to meet me, Genie.'

As I nodded she put her head on one side so her hair fell in a fine, straight sheet. 'You're not getting up to anything you oughtn't, are you?'

What a question. 'No,' I said, thinking, no more that anyone else round here anyhow. Jimmy was keen on kissing. Ever so keen.

'What about Len and Molly?' she asked suddenly.

'What about them?'

'Are they behaving themselves? I don't want any trouble on my hands from them two.'

'They're all right.' She may have been my pal all of a sudden but I wasn't going to go and spoil things for Len. 'They keep each other company in the evenings.'

'So long as that's all they're doing.'

'Mom?'

She raised her eyebrows.

'Is Bob ever coming back?'

'Genie – I've told you.' She gave a big sigh. 'I love Bob. He loves me.'

'But what about my dad?' My voice turned squeaky and tearful. 'What're you going to do?' It felt as if the world was falling apart.

She got up and went over to the window, stood with her back to me in her white nightdress. 'I don't know. Can't seem to think about it. I keep hoping it'll just sort itself out, one way or another.'

I was crying quietly behind her. 'But what about when Dad comes home?'

'I've told you—' She turned to me again, half angry but near tears herself. 'I don't know, do I? This has never happened to me before. Don't think I don't feel badly about your father. He's a good man and he don't deserve it, I know. But I can't throw away what I've found. Bob's come along and I feel as if he's saved me – saved my life.'

''E hasn't really got a wife and kiddies, has 'e?'

'No.' She at least looked ashamed of this lie. 'He hasn't.'

I pushed my face down into the prickly blanket, hugging my knees, rocking back and forth. 'I want my dad. I want him home. I want things to be all right again.'

She sat by me, even stroked my back. 'I'm sorry, Genie,' she said eventually. 'But Bob's the man I love.'

After his short bout of quarantine, Bob was back and I was faced with an offensive of charm.

'Hello Genie,' he said when he first came back one Saturday morning, his tone sounding as if I, not Mom, was his long lost love. He produced a bunch of daffs from behind his back like a conjuror with a rabbit. 'These are for you. To make friends.' He stuck a really sick-making smile on his brawny face.

'You'd better give them to Mom. Flowers make me sneeze.' I flung the bright yellow blooms on the table as if they were dog muck.

Bob clenched his teeth but he didn't say anything. He stood in the back room with his hands in his trouser pockets. I didn't remember inviting him in but he seemed to be there anyhow.

'All right are you, Len?' he said in the stupid, jolly

voice people seemed to think they'd got to put on with Lenny just because he was a bit simple, as if he needed humouring. Len grinned obligingly. But then Len'd have grinned at Adolf Hitler if he'd happened to pop in. He was like that. Bob turned round and about, jingled coins in the pockets of his loud checked suit. I stood watching him, po-faced.

He tried again: 'That's a right pretty frock you're got on there, Genie.' Then he coughed. 'Very nice.' I glowered at him. 'Your mom knows I'm here then, does she?'

'No.'

'How about telling her then? There's a good girl.'

'Mom!' I yelled up the stairs without shifting myself. '*He*'s here.'

She looked ever so nervous when she came down. She had her hair up and was wearing a pretty, tight dress which hugged her waist and her small bosoms. Bob's eyes swept up and down, devouring her, dirty sod.

'I've got to go,' I said. Nan was expecting me.

'We'll all have to go out together one day, won't we Bob?' Mom said brightly. 'To the pictures or something. Get to know each other better. You'd like that, wouldn't you Genie?'

I didn't even bother answering that one.

Teresa was rather full of herself. Working outside the family business had turned her head.

'Don't know what you see in it,' I told her, since for the moment I was finding more freedom working in my family's business than out of it. 'Clocking on, and at someone's beck and call every minute of the day.'

'Yes, but it feels like a real job. And I feel as if I've grown up.'

'And you get to see Jack? When am I going to meet lover boy then?'

Teresa hesitated. Even with her olive skin she blushed easily. 'Yes – I see Jack,' she said, very offhand.

What was going on here then? 'I thought that's just what you wanted?'

'I did – do. Only . . .' In her eyes I could suddenly see a funny little gleam. 'Oh Genie – there's the most gorgeous feller at the factory. It's mostly girls there of course – but he brings all the supplies in and he's forever stopping for a chat. Specially with me.' I could well imagine. I could hear Teresa's wonderful, life-giving laugh echoing out across the factory floor.

'But Teresa, I thought Jack was the be all and end all, your one and only—'

'Oh, I'm still walking out with Jack,' she said hastily. 'Only I can't help liking Clem. He's got the most beautiful green eyes.'

Oh yes, green eyes? I didn't believe in green eyes. I mean I couldn't put my hand on my heart and say I'd ever in my life seen anyone whose eyes were truly green.

I was hanging on to what I had with Jimmy. Which wasn't much. But I needed someone. Truth was, after his opening outburst of affection and that first breathless kiss Jimmy hadn't poured out much in the way of feelings. In fact he never said very much at all.

A typical date with Jimmy went like this. We usually went out on a Saturday. Shirl came to be with our nan, even though Nan was better and hobbling about with a stick.

Jimmy and I would meet, him grinning away in anticipation. He'd take my hand and sometimes we'd go to a matinée at the Carlton, or if it was fine we'd walk in the park. And I'd try to get him to talk. I told him my nan was better.

'Oh well – that's good.' End of that conversation.

'I might look for another job soon.'

'Oh ah.'

Another attempt. 'D'you still like me, Jimmy?'

'Course. Wouldn't be 'ere else, would I?'

I was even forced to ask about football. Problem was, we just hadn't got anything to say to each other. Was this something I was supposed to mind, I wondered? I thought about married people I knew. Mom and Dad had never had a lot in the way of conversation, other than what was needed to get by. Lil and Patsy had at least had a laugh together. But what I wanted to know was, was this the very best you could expect? I'd hoped for something a bit more like being friends with Teresa. Getting on, feeling the warmth and excitement of seeing her, laughing together. Was it normal to find your mind wandering when a man kissed you and to be thinking up a shopping list in your head, or wondering why it was Jimmy's mouth often tasted just a bit of rhubarb when it wasn't even in season?

After he thought we'd indulged in enough pleasantries, Jimmy set to with the real business of the date so far as he was concerned. It'd be back of the cinema as the picture flickered on high above us (I'd try to twist into a position so I could at least watch it as well, over his shoulder). Or in the park, or a doorway on the Stratford Road monkey run while near us, girls snatched handkerchieves out of the boys' breast pockets – you name it, Jimmy took his chances. Blimey, the hours I spent locked, more than half bored, in Jimmy's grasp. Sometimes he got bold and tried to worm his fingers into my coat, inside my dress, but I wasn't having that.

'Oi – you can get out of there.'

He'd give me a sheepish grin and those lips would come close again. So far none of it was like Lil said. Certainly not the best, dreamiest feeling in the world. Frankly I'd rather've had a more tasty sort of gobstopper like a bag of Brazil nut toffees. Except that he was there and he wanted me and kept coming back for more.

Maybe I'm not normal, I thought. Teresa seemed to get a lot more of a thrill out of a man than I did. Perhaps all my housewifery and careworn life and all that was going on at home had made me old too soon?

Bob, like the proverbial rash, was back with a vengeance. Our house was nothing short of a knocking shop and it was getting me right down. First of the evening shift was Len and Molly. They didn't seem to be pushing the boat right to its full limits with sex, but having those two snogging in front of me half the evening was a disturbing enough sight. Didn't know where to put myself. If we'd had a proper coal shed I'd have gone and sat in it.

I did as many things to distract them as I could. I got them playing rummy, gave them things to eat, made endless cups of tea, switched Gloria on. I was cooking our meals back at our house by now, but sometimes I went out to my nan's, prepared to brave the walk back later through the black streets rather than face the canoodlings of Len and his Moll. After all, he was thirty now. I was just in the way.

Second shift, on nights they could manage it, were

the other two love birds. Now they'd moved into the house, the Anderson shelter not being the ideal place to carry on a romance, particularly because as the ground was no longer frozen it was sometimes ankle deep in water. I saw the first signs of trouble when the crocheted blanket appeared again, folded over the back of a chair like it had always been before.

Thing was, Mom was still being uncannily nice to me. She did the ironing and brought me the odd treat when she could: sweets or bits of clothes, some new black shoes with a bow on the strap. I knew perfectly well it was hush money, bribes to keep me sweet, but at the same time I couldn't bear to lose it. The price was knowing she took Bob up to my father's bed while I sat and cried downstairs and Len, alone by this time of night, comforted me.

'S'all right Genie, s'all right.'

'It's not sodding well all right,' I'd sob, cringing in myself at the slightest sound from upstairs. But they were quite quiet, I'll grant them. Len and I put Gloria on loud as we dared and tried to drown out even the slightest sign that they were there. I did a lot of that in those days – blocking things out, closing my eyes, my ears and my very heart.

Some nights when I thought Bob was coming, sickly sweet as he was to me these days, I just stayed over at Nan's and slept on the prickly horsehair sofa by the dying heat from the range and the ticking of her clock.

It didn't take Nan long to catch on. 'I'm not a fool, you know, Genie. What's going on with Doreen?'

I couldn't meet her eyes. 'Nothing, Nan.'

She sat quiet for a minute, the stick resting by her leg, her breathing loud, wheezy on her chest. 'Is she carrying on behind your dad's back?'

161

I couldn't tell her a real lie. Not Nan. I just sat there, wanting to die of shame.

'Genie?'

'She's got a – friend.'

'Thought so. She'd been like a bitch on heat since Christmas. I noticed it then but I gave her the benefit of the doubt.' Nan pursed her lips, face grim. 'Selfish little cow. Always been the same when it came to riding roughshod over everyone else.' The extent of her anger took me by surprise.

I was relieved Nan knew, but frightened to death at the same time. Mom'd never forgive me for letting it slip and if she found out I'd lose her again, just when we were getting on so well.

'She says . . .' I began timidly. 'She's never been happy with my dad.'

'Happy? *Happy*.' She turned the word round and about like someone looking for the chip at the edge of a saucer. 'You show me someone who thinks they are happy. A marriage is a marriage and that's that. Wasting time dwelling on whether you're happy or not is a sure way into trouble.'

I looked at her tough, lined face. Mom had told me that Grandpa Rawson used to bash her about till sometimes her face was almost unrecognizable. I wasn't sure whether her missing teeth had dropped out with each child born or whether they'd been knocked from her gums by his fist. He didn't restrain himself any better when she was carrying a child. She'd miscarried two on account of his violence. But even when she managed to lease the shop, when she had more money and could've got shot of him, she carried on, steadfast, in a marriage she'd chosen. 'Where would leaving 'im have got me?' And then he died. If there was anyone,

Mom always said, who deserved heart failure, old man Rawson was the one.

'Don't say anything to 'er, will you?' I begged. 'Not at the moment. Things are all right really.'

'Are they?' Nan's voice was sarky as it ever got. 'So what're you doing sleeping here on my couch?'

I saw Teresa now and then. I wasn't sure about the latest of what she was up to and at the moment I didn't really care. I presumed she was thinking up all the backhand ways she could manage to meet Jack or Clem or whoever the hell it was. Good sodding luck to her.

One night though, she came round to Nan's.

'I was hoping you was still here.' She looked a bit down. 'Fancy coming to ours for a bit?'

I suppose I wasn't very gracious greeting her. My mind was back in Balsall Heath, wondering anxiously what might be going on in our house.

'You go on,' Nanny Rawson said. She was standing ironing at the table which was swathed in an old, singed blanket. 'Do you good to have some young company.'

At the Spinis' I found Teresa's Dad in a bad state. He was downstairs, in a chair by the hearth, but his face was very pale, his skin clammy, and he seemed only able to talk in a whisper. Opposite him sat Fausto Pirelli, the young man who'd been in the shop that day they were all yelling at each other. His shadow fell on the wall beside him, nose like a hawk's beak. He was talking, on and on in Italian in a soft, earnest voice, with a frown on his face. Micky seemed agitated, kept trying to interrupt, but when he tried to speak it ended in a bout of agonized coughing.

Vera, standing by Micky's chair, looked worried to

death as well, and exhausted. 'Micky was called to a factory fire yesterday,' she whispered to me. 'It was over Bordesley way, some chemical place, and he said the fumes and smoke were evil – choked him. He only just managed to get out. It's done something terrible to his chest.' Her eyes filled with tears. 'I hate seeing him like this. Micky.' She leaned down and touched his hand, 'please go to bed.'

'Later,' he managed to say, trying to smile at her, and indicating with an angry nod of his head that the other man was still talking. The anger was directed at him.

'Fausto,' Vera implored the man, and the rest was in Italian, but I could see she was begging him to go, to let Micky rest. He flapped his hand impatiently at her, saying, '*Subito, subito* ... straight away,' and not moving.

The smaller children were in bed but Stevie and Francesca were at the table, not doing anything but listening and watching. Stevie's eyes were absolutely intent on Fausto's face.

'Brew up, Teresa,' Vera ordered quietly. I could see how tense she was.

'What's going on?' I asked, following her into the scullery.

'That stupid idiot.' She jerked her head. 'His family comes from the same place as Dad's in Italy. They're talking about what's happening there – Mussolini ... Fausto still reckons he's a Blackshirt, even though he can't find many to agree with him. They don't like all that round here. He doesn't even really know what it means – he's all hot air. But Stevie looks up to him – thinks it's big talk. Fausto hasn't got a father of his own, he's dead, so Dad feels responsible for him. He's worried he's going to get into trouble.'

'Trouble?'

Teresa shrugged. She seemed distracted, stood with the empty kettle in her hand as if she couldn't think what to do with it, so I took it off her and went out across the yard to fill it and set it on the gas.

'You worried about him?'

'Who?'

'Your dad.'

'Yes – but the doctor said he should be all right. Needs time to let his lungs clear again. It's not that, it's – Jack found out about me and Clem.'

'What was there to find out about you and Clem?'

Teresa looked down at the floor in shame, face hidden by her dark hair. 'We started to get a bit keen on each other and I went out with him a couple of times. And with Jack living so close to the factory and that, I knew I was going to have to tell him and he was so angry and said he never wanted to see me again.'

'Well what d'you expect? Anyway, that's all right, isn't it, if it's Clem you want to see.'

'But I don't know if I like Clem very much any more. He's ever so cocky.' She sounded very sorry for herself. 'And I'm going to end up with nobody.'

A wave of great weariness came over me. What a load of stupid rubbish it was. All of it. Men, women, girls, boys, love, romance. It was all a silly story put out at the pictures and in sixpenny romances to make us think such things were possible and then cast us in the deepest blue depression when we were brought nose up against real life.

'Oh Teresa,' I said. 'For God's sake just pull yourself together.'

I went out and sat with Vera Spini, watching Fausto

165

as he talked on urgently. He seemed very strange, as if something was burning him up inside. And I listened to Vera's worries, which at least had some proper substance to them, leaving Teresa to sulk in the scullery.

April 1940

The spring was here with all its usual fevers enhanced, worse luck for me. And then the Flanagans' roof fell in, two houses away from Nanny Rawson's. I was out with Mary Flanagan, hanging out my nan's washing and basking in a little thread of sun which had managed to reach in and light up the far side of the yard. One minute there was the Flanagans' house, large as life, in tightly squeezed back-to-back line. The next, there was a massive great crash and glass shattering and, for what seemed an age afterwards, things groaned and shuddered, tinkled, smashed and finally settled, and sworls of thick dust rose up choking us. Minutes later, when the dust finally sifted down out of the air, we could see through to the street outside and there were people standing looking. My washing, needless to say, was black again.

'Jesus, Mary and fecking Joseph!' Mary was gasping over and over. 'My house – will you look what's happened to my house!'

Then panic set in. 'Where's Geraldine?' Mary laid her hands on each of the other two of her small children who were still at home, reassuring herself. 'Eamonn, where was Geraldine? Was she in the house now, was she?' She was screaming at the boy, shaking him. There was plaster and dust all over her red hair.

All the neighbours were out of their houses. They

stood round, numbed. No one seemed able to move. The thought that six-year-old Geraldine might be trapped under the weight of the house was too terrible to take in. Then people started saying 'What about Mr and Mrs Griffin?' and everyone wondered whether the elderly couple who lived in the front-house had been crushed under it, until Mr and Mrs Griffin were spotted out in the street with a crowd round them.

A small bang was heard from the end of the yard and Geraldine, a child with hair as bright a red as Mary's, emerged unconcerned from the privy saying, 'Mom, what was that noise?'

Mary dashed to her and whacked her one soundly round the ear. 'You eejit of a girl! What did you think you were doing in there? Sure I thought you were dead.' She clutched the bewildered girl against her great big chest, clinging to her while Geraldine bawled from the walloping she'd had. 'Where's our house gone, Mom?' she sobbed over Mary's shoulder.

Mary stood up again slowly and turned to face the fact that she had seven children, a husband away in the RAF and no house. The slum houses in that area were built back in Queen Victoria's day to give the worker bees who manned the factories a place to live, or at least exist. They were jerry built – the state of some of them was so bad it defied description – and Mary's, after the harsh winter, the weight of the snow and then the thaw, not to mention the landlord swiping slates off the roof every time the rent was overdue, had finally given up the ghost.

Mary was silent now and deathly white in the face. As everyone in the yard normally did in a crisis, she turned to my nan.

'Edith – what in the name of heaven am I going to do?'

Nan hobbled over and took command. 'For a start what you'll have to do is go to the Corporation and get on the list for another house. With seven kids they'll have to get summat sorted out for you. In the meantime ...' She looked round the yard with the kind of expression on her face no one would dare disagree with, even Mary's next-door neighbour and sparring partner, Clarys. 'We'll all make sure you're all right, won't we?' There were nods, some more doubtful than others. 'We can fit some of you in,' Nanny Rawson went on.

Where on earth? I was thinking, listening to my nan setting example by what I thought of as rash promises.

By the evening it was sorted out. Lil's kids stayed on in Nan's attic bedroom. Nan persuaded Lil to move in with her and freed up the second bedroom for Mary Flanagan and her two youngest kids. Geraldine and one of the lads were taken in by another neighbour, the other kids by a third. And so, the teeming yard at the back of Belgrave Road, already overcrowded, ramshackle and insanitary, managed to redistribute itself with one less house to go round. The only person driven completely barmy by it was my auntie Lil, who already thought her own kids quite enough to cope with, ta very much, without having extras foisted on us.

'How about a trip to the Lickeys?' Jimmy said, and at the time I couldn't think of anything better. It was a gorgeous spring, the skies powder blue, sun warm, any last nip on the air long gone now, and the trees uncurling their leaves to the spring air looked like a miracle after the winter we'd had. Even the yard behind our nan's seemed a less drab place with sunlight streaming off the newly washed windows.

Course, just as the world seemed the most precious and lovely the spring can make it, Hitler's troops started to move across Denmark into Norway and we sat round Gloria waiting to hear the latest. In the newsreaders' solemn voices we heard names which were strange on our lips, ones we'd never heard before – Narvik, Trondheim – bringing the world in on us. You could feel suspense in the air.

Jimmy and I rode the 62 bus out to the Lickeys. The Lickey Hills are a beautiful, wooded ridge on the south edge of Birmingham where the trams and buses terminated after the long, tree-lined swoop along the Bristol Road. This was the place where hordes of factory-pale, work-weary Brummies would congregate on holidays and weekends to escape the claustrophobic closeness of the city's walls and alleys, to feel they were in the country and picnic with the sun on their faces if they were lucky.

Jimmy started trying to kiss me on the bus.

'Oh, gerroff, will you,' I said irritably. 'Not in front of all these people.'

Jimmy leered at me. Love, or at least a shortlived infatuation, is blind, I thought. His wonky eyes had given him charm and appeal at first. Now they looked as if they were squinting at me all the time, full of unwelcome lust.

'No one's looking.' There were loads of kids on the bus which kept stopping to pick up more passengers until it was crammed full. People were clinging to each other in the aisle and there were shrieks of laughter when we swung round a corner.

'I don't care. You should behave yourself when there's people about.'

'What – so I don't 'ave to when we're on our own?'

'Don't you ever think about anything else?'

It was well warm enough for my summer frock and Jimmy only had on trousers and a grey shirt that had once been white. We had a bag with bread and butter and cake, apples and a few lumps of cheese and bottles filled with cooling tea. I was excited. A trip to the Lickeys was a really special day out.

We passed through Northfield, Longbridge, to the terminus at Rednal where the bus disgorged us all. Mothers in hats yelling at gaggles of kids, all with too much to carry, headed off in excitement for the paths to Lickey Hill or Cofton Wood.

I'd have liked to go to the park with its ornamental pool, swans riding their reflections in the glassy water, and peaceful, dreamy paths and flowers. But no. Jimmy had other plans. Grabbing my hand, he said, 'Come on – let's get shot of all this lot, shall we?' and dragged me off to the tracks that led off through the woods. It wasn't that difficult to get away from the other day trippers. The Lickeys had paths winding all across them and through the trees. Many of the families out for the day walked as short a distance as possible and settled on the grassy hillside with a sweeping view of the surrounding counties, picnicking and lazing while their kids played round them, and hardly shifted all day.

Truth to tell, I was already wishing I could have come on my own. I could feel coming over me the bored restlessness I felt more and more with Jimmy, making me want to tear about shrieking or thump someone, preferably him.

'Come on.' I pointed to a place on the grass with

rings of families in view. 'This is a nice spot. Let's have our picnic here, eh?'

'Nah.' Jimmy pulled me on further and further, into the woods. 'Don't want to be surrounded by people, do we? This way . . .'

He dragged me right out to the edge of the place somewhere, finding a spot in the woods which no one else apparently thought was the great beauty spot of the Lickey Hills because no one else was there. It was pleasant enough, light darting in through the leaves, never still, and leafmould and twigs on the ground. But it wasn't exactly the scenic view I had in mind. And I knew what he wanted. God, I was fed up at the thought of wasting a day in the Lickeys stuck to the end of Jimmy's lips.

'Now I've got you all to myself, 'aven't I?' He chuckled. 'Come 'ere . . .'

I saw those lips coming towards me again, a light stubble on the white skin above them.

'Will you just lay off and let me eat my dinner in peace,' I snapped.

'Well, you're not much company, are you?'

'Can't think about summat else for a change? Or don't you have anything else in your head at all?'

'What I've got's all 'ere,' he said, patting his crotch.

'So I've sodding well gathered.' I shifted away from him and opened the packet of sandwiches. Boredom perched on me like a gigantic bird. I wished Teresa was here. Not that she was better at the moment, but with a bit of work you could get her mind off men.

At least he let me eat for a bit.

'Find you were hungry after all, did you?'

Jimmy grinned. 'Nice cake of your nan's.'

'She's a good cook.'

'My mom's cooking's terrible.'

'So's mine.'

We laughed together. He was talking to me, which made a change.

'I bet yours has never cooked a hen with the feathers on like mine did once.'

'She never! What the hell'd she do that for?'

'She was the worse for it – the drink, you know.'

'She drink a bit then, does she?'

'Yep. Don't blame her. If I was married to a bastard like my dad I'd get kalied all the time as well.'

'What's he like then?'

Jimmy dug a dirty thumbnail into his apple. 'Our mom relies on him, see, not being able to 'ear. And he treats her like the lowest form of life. Brought the clap 'ome to her once – never been the same since, she 'asn't. She was expecting a kid at the time too. She lost that one.' Jimmy took a big bite of the apple. 'If he died I'd cheer.'

I watched him, glad at least to feel something for him again, even if it was only sorry. Some fellow feeling. And I was hoping at last here was someone who would understand what was on my mind.

'My mom . . .' It was costing me to speak and I wasn't even sure he was listening. 'She's going with another bloke. Brings him to our house. I hate him.'

Jimmy said nothing, just munched on the apple.

'It's horrible, isn't it?' I persevered, watching his pale face.

Jimmy hurled the apple core away over into the trees. 'Come on. Let's do it.'

'What?'

'The whole thing. Fucking. Properly.'

'Jimmy!' The very word gave me the heebie-jeebies. It sounded so *rude*. 'You don't use words like that.'

He was shuffling closer to me. 'Sorry.'

'Should think you are. It's not nice.' I was sitting clenched up tight, knees against my chest.

Jimmy slunk his arm round my back. 'What d'you want me to say instead?'

'Something nice and romantic. Say how you feel about me.'

'Well, you're all right, you are. I've told you. I like you, Genie.'

'But d'you feel anything more than that? D'you love me, Jimmy?' It felt important that he did, that it wasn't just One Thing he was after.

His face loomed closer. 'Yeah, OK Genie. I love you. Now give us a kiss.'

I gave a big sigh. What price affection. He kissed me for some time, then undid a couple of the buttons on the front of my dress and wriggled his fingers inside.

'Don't,' I tried to say, but he wasn't having it. He squeezed until I squeaked with pain. I was mortified. Didn't want his hand down my dress. His eyes had started rolling about and he looked so queer with his white face close to me and his body rocking up and down beside me as if he had a horse under him.

There's got to be more to it than this. Lil hadn't had those dreamy eyes on her just for this. And how long'd we got to sit here doing it for? What a complete waste of the afternoon when we could've been out in the sun. And then I started thinking about home, Mom and Bob doing this. I felt sick.

Jimmy started fumbling about in his clothes. ''Ere,' he said, ''ave a feel of this. This is 'ow much I want you.'

174

He yanked at my hand, rubbed it against him.

'No!' I said, pulling away. It felt hot and sticky. 'Don't be dirty.'

He scowled. 'All right then. If you're going to be like that, we'll do it another way.'

Hands on my shoulders, he shoved me back so my head was in a pile of leaves and twigs. He pulled my dress up and got his hand down my knickers, poking around hard and clumsily. Lying along me, half on, half off, he ground his body up and down, faster and faster. It didn't take long. He tensed up, eyes squeezed shut, hurting me with his hand and I called out in pain.

When he got off, my blue dress was all wet and sticky.

'You pig,' I said. 'You horrible, disgusting pig.'

'Go on.' He half turned away, buttoning himself up again. 'That's what you wanted. Next time I'll give it to you proper.'

I felt very cold suddenly, and shivery, sat huddled up, clutching my knees tight. The world was a nasty mean place.

'Let's go. You wanted a walk, didn't you? Bit of sun on your face?'

I spread out the skirt of my dress, all gluey and wrinkled. 'What's my mom going to say?'

Casually, Jimmy picked up one of the stera bottles we'd brought our tea in. It was a third full still, and he poured the rest of it in my lap. The blood-warm tea seeped through and trickled between my thighs.

'There y'are. Now she'll never know the difference, will she?'

*

'There's no need for you to keep my nan company no more,' I told Shirl. 'I'm not going to be seeing Jimmy again.'

'Oh.' The smile dropped off Shirl's face but I was too wrapped up in my own mortification to take in how downcast she looked.

'Got fed up of 'im, 'ave you? Thought you would. Not got a lot going on upstairs, 'as 'e?'

I shook my head.

'So – you don't need me round then? I mean I don't mind ...'

'No,' I said, very short with her. 'There's no need to put yourself out any more.'

She took me at my word and walked out of our lives again. I didn't give it a lot of thought then because it was absolute mayhem up at Nan's, with Lil's lot and the Flanagans roaring in and out. Nan was getting better. She was taking over from me again day by day and I knew I'd soon be booted back out into the working world. She bore the Flanagans with her usual stoicism – 'The Corporation'll sort them out a place soon enough.'

But it was Lil who was doing her nut. The price of fags had gone up by a ha'penny a packet, the government was behind the factories to up production (especially aircraft – Len was on extra long shifts) and to cap it all the house was nearly full to bursting.

'Your life's never your own,' she moaned regularly. 'At work you don't have time to turn round hardly and when I get home I can't see across the room for mad bloody kids.'

And the Flanagans were wild. After all, we only had two of them, but the mess they made was indescribable. The boys were bedwetters, so there were smelly sheets to be dealt with every day, dirty clothes left in heaps, Patsy, Tom and Cathleen's things all turned upside down and scattered round the place, and the constant noise of them charging in and out. Mary seemed helpless to control them, try as she might. How the hell did she cope normally? we wondered. They started to make Lil's kids look like angels with haloes.

It was getting Lil down and I felt sorry for her. She was growing sourer by the day and I thought she deserved better.

I went to see Vera Spini one day. The shop was quiet and she was out the back making ice-cream, her face sagging with exhaustion. She wore a white cap on her head to keep her hair out of the way.

'Let me help, Mrs Spini,' I said, going to the churning handle.

They boiled the ice-cream mixture in the copper until it was like custard, which stood overnight covered with muslin cloths to keep any flies out. The next day it'd go in the churning machine, a long cylinder which was kept cool by electricity. There were blades inside to turn it round and it got paler and paler yellow, smelling sweet and turning into food from heaven when you were used to lumpy tapioca.

'How's Mr Spini?'

'Not too good.' She stopped turning and pulled the cap off. Her pale hair was dark at the roots as if it was planted in soil. 'He hasn't managed to do anything much for the past two weeks. I'm ever so worried about him, Genie.'

She wiped her dry, workworn hands on a cloth and

tried to force a smile. I'd never seen her do that before. Not force it. But there were no songs on her lips today, no hymns or Santa Lucia.

'Here, come and see him. He'll be glad to have a bit of company.'

'Me?'

Vera looked at me in surprise. 'Course. He'd love to see you. He's got a real soft spot for you, Genie. Always has had.'

This was news to me all right and it didn't stop me feeling scared. I'd hardly ever seen Micky without Teresa around.

'Stevie!' Vera shouted into the yard. 'Come up front for a bit, will you? I'll not be long.'

In the house, Micky was sitting by the fire huddled in his coat, watching Luke push an old wooden horse with rough little wheels along the floor. His body looked thinner, his face was drawn and sick looking and he had several days' worth of greying stubble on his cheeks. There was a newspaper on the table and a cup with tea dregs in it.

'Genie!' He really did look pleased to see me and I felt warmed by it. In fact he looked nothing like as stern as usual. 'Come and have a sit down with me. I'm stuck here, useless to everyone at the moment.'

'You're telling me,' Vera mocked him.

'Feeling any better, Mr Spini?' I asked, perching on the edge of a chair by the table.

'A bit.' He ran a hand over his wavy, pepper and salt hair and nodded insistently at his wife. 'I do. She don't believe me. Makes you think though. I don't know what was in that smoke but it nearly did for me, I tell you.' And he was off, coughing again. He didn't sound well, whatever he said.

178

Vera stayed long enough to brew up a pot of tea, sugaring a cup for Micky and placing it tenderly on the table beside him before going back to the shop.

'You got time to sit for a bit?' Micky asked.

I nodded.

'It's very nice. Long time since you sat and had a chat. Now you're a working girl.' He laughed, then coughed. I couldn't say I ever remembered sitting having a chat before, but I wasn't going to argue. But what in heaven were we going to talk about?

'You OK, Genie? Everything all right at home?'

'Yes,' I lied.

He looked into my eyes with his dark ones for a moment then stared at the back of the door which Vera had closed for once.

'I've been sat here all this time – so I've been thinking. Never get the time on a normal day.' He stopped. I waited for him to keep talking, not sure if I was meant to ask, and then I saw he was struggling to keep from coughing.

'I remembered something from when I was a little boy in Italy – about seven or eight. I had a special place for myself. No one else knew about it.' He stirred the tea and took a sip, slurping it. 'Of course everyone knew about it – but no one except me knew it was special. Our village was outside Castellamare, and the church where we said Mass was high on the cliff and the land round it looked out over the water – that's the Mediterranean Sea. Beautiful blue it is. There were a few trees on that piece of land and one was an olive tree with a very old, twisted trunk where I used to go and sit. It was at the far end, away from the church, so the old ladies who came in and out to clean the church or say their rosary couldn't see I was there. I used to feel the

179

trunk of the tree behind my back and the land in front of it sort of dipped down towards the sea. There'd be salamanders – little lizards – running up the tree and there were crickets in the grass. You ever heard the noise crickets make, Genie?'

I shook my head.

'The grass was a dry, wiry kind that scratched at the back of your legs. Sometimes I sat there as long as an hour, hoping no bigger boys would come and find me. The sky was always blue – that's how I remember it, and you could smell salt on the wind. And because I was alone and all I could see was sea and grass and sky it gave me room for all these dreams to pass through my head. I felt very big sitting up there, as if I owned all the world and I could do anything I wanted.'

He laughed again suddenly as if he'd said something daft, because he never talked like this normally. Certainly wouldn't have done to his own kids. The laugh ended in a long bout of coughing and his lungs sounded as if they were half full of liquid. Each breath was a strain for air and his face went red. Luke stared up at him. When it'd passed he said, 'D'you have a place like that, Genie?'

I shook my head. 'There's no room for that here, is there?'

Micky tapped his head with one thick finger. 'There is in here.'

I thought of my house all for me, by the river with fields and trees and flowers. 'I s'pose I do then, yes. Only it's not real.'

'It don't matter. When I want to dream of something outside all these houses so close together I can go back to my tree. So you're looking at a crazy bloke who spends his morning sitting under a tree thousands of miles away!' He seemed embarrassed now, after saying all that. Luke jumped up and pulled at his father's leg and Micky lifted him up on to his lap, Luke watching him with a finger in his mouth.

Seeing the newspaper on the table, Micky picked it up and handed it to me. 'Here – another good reason for sitting under a tree.'

It was the *Mirror*. With a black-rimmed nail, Micky pointed to one column:

> There are more than twenty thousand Italians in Great Britain. The ... Italian is an indigestible unit of population ...
>
> Even the peaceful, law-abiding proprietor of the back street coffee shop bounces into a patriotic frenzy at the sound of Mussolini's name ...

'In Italy we have the *Fascio*,' Micky explained. 'The Fascist Party, pretty much like the German Nazis. So they think that because we are Italian we must support Mussolini ... I can't think of anyone now who is a supporter – well, except young Pirelli, or he likes to think so anyhow ...' Micky shook his head.

I read the last part of the newspaper column: 'We are nicely honeycombed with little cells of potential betrayal.'

'But what does it mean?'

He must have seen the worry on my face because he reached over and patted my arm. 'I hope it don't mean nothing. I've been here far too long to worry about.

'Come and see me again if you get time, eh?' he said, as I got up to leave. 'I'll be on my feet soon. Oh – and by the way, Genie. Teresa. She getting up to anything she shouldn't be?'

I shook my head, panic stricken. Why did people have to keep asking me such blooming awkward questions?

'Not that I know of.'

He looked into my eyes for a moment, then smiled. 'All right, love. Thanks for coming to see me.'

I wanted to say something nice but couldn't think of anything. In fact what I really wanted to do was go and put my arms round him for being kind, for making me feel special. I didn't do it, but I knew I'd never see Micky Spini in the same way again.

'Tara,' was all I said. 'Hope you get better soon.'

Mary Flanagan's kids were not the easiest to get to bed. I'd thought of Mary as someone intimidating, forever yelling and carrying on, until she moved in with my nan and I saw her trying to control her kids. It was pitiful.

One night when I was round there the tension of having two families living under one roof was reaching breaking point and although the Corporation had promised to rehouse Mary 'at the earliest possible opportunity' so far there was no date.

'Get up there and stay where I put you or you'll be feeling my hand across you again,' Mary was bawling up the stairs in her deep, throaty voice for about the tenth time. Downstairs I was trying to deal with the devastation the kids had caused while they were still up.

Lil sat on the couch chewing her nails as if she'd like to gnash someone's head off. I could tell she was bubbling inside like a boiler about to explode. She was a stickler for getting her own kids to bed in good time, and once they were there, that was where they stayed, and no messing.

Not long after, despite Mary's threats and pleas and bribes, we could still hear feet padding back and forth upstairs, then the clattering and squeaking of the bed-frame as the two boys bounced on and off it like little rubber acrobats.

Nan and I exchanged glances in the scullery.

Lil suddenly snapped. 'Christ Almighty, would you listen to them! They'll be waking Cathleen again if they carry on like that. What's the matter with them? Why the hell can't you get them to do as they're told? They're like bloody animals.'

'I'm doing my best,' Mary snapped from the bottom of the stairs. 'Don't you talk about my kids like that. Eamonn, Colm – I'm coming up to give you a hiding so I am!'

'They're unsettled,' Nanny Rawson said. She was washing up, I was wiping. 'Poor kids've been split up. They're not used to it.'

'I don't bloody well care.' Lil was on her feet, brown eyes darkened further with fury. 'I've had enough of it. If they come to live in our house they should do as they're told. We want some peace, no sodding kids running round the place all evening. Some of us have a job of work to do as well you know!'

Suddenly there were wails from upstairs. 'That's it!' Lil exploded. 'That's Cathleen. Move, will you.' She pushed past Mary who was at the foot of the stairs. 'They've really done it now.'

'Don't you touch my kids!' Mary spat at Lil's back, following her up the stairs.

'I wouldn't touch your poxy kids if they were the last ones on earth. I'm going to see to mine now they've cowing well gone and woken her up.' But as she passed through the boys' room we heard her bawl at them,

183

'GET INTO BED AND STAY THERE YOU LITTLE BAS-
TARDS' at the top of her voice as she went up to
Cathleen.

We could hear Cathleen's weary, half-awake screams
downstairs, and it took Lil some time to get her settled
again. Eventually she came back down, but the Flanagan
boys were still up there tripping the light fantastic with
Mary yelling helplessly at them.

'At least Cathleen's gone off again,' Lil said through
clenched teeth. 'I just can't stand any more of this, I
really can't. Come on, Genie, I'll take you home.'

'It's hardly even dark,' I protested. 'I'll be all right.'
My mind was doing gambols over and over, trying to
think what time it was and what exactly might be going
on at home.

'It's only nine.' Lil glanced at the clock. 'I can take
you along and sit with you for a while. Have a bit of
peace out of this madhouse.' Lil was already walking
out into the spring evening.

'Just drop me at the door,' I said. 'I'll be all right –
really. I've walked back much later than this.'

'Do I smell or summat? I've told you – I'll come and
keep you company. See Len. Wait till her in there's got
her act together.'

My mind was racing madly ahead. What the hell were
we going to find if Molly was over at our house? And
then I remembered. How could I have forgotten? They
wouldn't even be there. Len and Molly had gone to the
pictures – big excitement – and wouldn't be back until
after ten. Thank you sweet Jesus.

Lil was carrying on down my ear, sorry for herself,
her voice hardly changing tone. Moan tone. 'I'm that
tired I can hardly get about these days. If it's not work
it's the kids. Sometimes I ask myself why I go on with

184

it all. Why I don't just go and do the same as Patsy did and jump into the canal?'

'Don't say that. You don't mean it, do you Lil?'

'I do. Some days I really do. I mean what's there ever going to be for me now? My life's over. Only you can't do a thing like that to your kids, can you?'

I didn't blame her really. Only I was so relieved, after those moments of outright panic, to think the house would be empty when we got back, I was almost ready to dance down the road.

'Things'll get better, Auntie Lil. You'll get a nice new house and move out – have a garden for the kids.'

'At the rate Mary's getting hers it'll be the turn of the century before they find me one,' she said despondently. 'And I'll be dead by then anyway.'

The house was dark. Blacked out of course, but there were no lights on inside when I opened the front door, finding myself grinning like an idiot with relief.

'Come on in,' I said. 'I'll put the kettle on.'

'Doreen got anything stronger? Drop of port?'

'Dunno. I'll look.'

I lit the gas light in the back room with a spill and found a tipple for Lil. I'd put the kettle on as well and was trying to poke some life into the fire when we heard it from upstairs. Clear and loud and horribly unmistakable.

'Jesus,' Lil said. 'What the . . .?'

I couldn't answer her. I went straight to a chair, pushed my burning face into it and pulled the cushion over my head as my mother's cries upstairs reached fever pitch. Knees tucked up on the worn seat of the chair, I curled tight into the smallest speck I could manage.

But Lil was at me, poking my back.

'Genie . . . Lift your head up. Genie!' She yanked me out of the chair by one arm. I wouldn't look at her, just covered my face with my hands, squinting out between my fingers. Lil hissed at me. 'Who is that up there?'

'It's Mom.' What an admission, my mom behaving like that.

'I know. I can hear that much. But who the hell is that with her?'

'Bob.'

'Who's Bob when he's at home?'

'A copper.'

Lil mouthed air like a fish. 'Well how long's this been going on?'

I shrugged. Couldn't think. I couldn't think of anything. The noise had calmed down upstairs.

'The little bitch.' Lil advanced on the door to the stairs.

'Lil no, don't! You can't!' But it was like shouting into an avalanche.

My legs were trembling so much as she stomped upstairs that I had to sit down, waiting for all hell to break loose above me. I kept thinking over and over, what are they doing here? They're not supposed to be here. How could they do this? How could they?

The fight Mom and Lil had that night outdid anything I could ever remember before. Lil was fit to burst with outrage, righteous indignation, fury at being related to such an obvious trollopy bitch of a sister and, though she'd never have admitted it, pure, grass-green jealousy. And Mom – also outrage at being burst in upon while she lay stark naked in candlelight, her head lifting in panic off Bob's King Kong hairy chest when she heard feet on the stairs. And anger and mortification at being caught in the act of complete, undeniable adultery.

The shouting, sobbing, cursing, slapping and recriminations went on and on. Some time, at about the eye of the storm, Bob slunk downstairs, half dressed in socks, drawers and shirt, looking like an ape in clothes. He pulled on the other bits, the trousers, jacket, even tie, as I sat crying. His shoes came flying down the stairs on the force of Lil shouting, 'Take these with you, you filthy bastard, and don't ever come back!'

Bob never said a word to me. Didn't even look at me. He let himself out and left them to it.

May 1940

It was soon after that Mom started being sick. Course, not having had a babby myself, the sight of someone heaving over a bucket every morning didn't automatically make me suspicious.

'My cooking's not that bad, is it?' I said to her.

All I got in reply was a lot of groaning. Some mornings she'd say finally, 'Oooh, I can't go to work in this state. I feel terrible.' And she'd crawl back up to bed and stay there until the middle of the afternoon. She did a lot of crying as well. A real lot.

I started to get worried. 'Shall I get our nan?'

'No!' She found the strength to push herself up on one elbow. 'Don't you dare say a word to anyone. D'you hear?'

'But you look terrible.'

She did too – face greeny white and clammy, hair in greasy strips. The room smelled stale and sweaty.

'I'll be better in a while. Just get me some water, and don't breathe a word to anyone.'

By the evening she'd dress and come downstairs, unsteady on her feet, eat a little bit and sit, silent most of the time. This went on for days. The time that for the rest of us was really the beginning of the war almost passed her by. Suddenly Gloria's news bulletins were once more the most important notches on which we hung our day. We listened in to *The Nine O'Clock*

News in the evening like religious fanatics, shutting up anyone who dared open their mouth to interrupt.

Hitler invaded the Netherlands. More names of places we'd never heard of. More realization that there was a world out there where things were happening. Bombs fell somewhere outside Canterbury. And Mr Churchill became Prime Minister. I liked him. Nearly everyone did, I think, with his way with words. Made you feel carried along and full of strength, not like the others, all muttering away.

'We have before us,' he said, 'an ordeal of the most grievous kind.'

But he made you feel noble, chosen in some way to do it, as if the fate of the world rested on us, each of us. Even Lil, the great sceptic, was impressed. ''E makes you feel it might all be worth it, doesn't 'e?'

Life was beginning to gleam a bit brighter for Lil. Or at least it was going to revert back to what it was before. Mary Flanagan and her kids were to be rehoused in Stanley Street.

'A front-house too, if you please!' Lil said. But she didn't really care whether the Flanagans were being moved into Buckingham Palace so long as they were well out of her hair.

Mom finally admitted one morning, between bouts of sickness, that she was going to have a babby. She was crying when she told me.

'I can't keep it to myself any more, Genie. You're my daughter' (she'd noticed!) 'and I've got to tell someone.' She lay back weakly sobbing into the pillow.

I was right out of my depth here. 'Is it – er. . .is it Bob's babby?'

''Course it's Bob's!' she wailed. 'How many men d'you think I've been with the past few months?'

I felt sorry for her. I did, really. Because I knew she didn't find having babbies any joy, and to cap it all this one was a little bastard and it wouldn't take the neighbours long to work that out for themselves.

'Are you going to tell 'im?'

Mom sobbed even louder. I sat down on the bed and touched her shoulder. 'D'you want a cuppa tea?'

'No, I don't want a cuppa tea! How's that going to help anything?' Then she softened. 'Sorry, Genie. No ta.' She looked bleakly across at the window. I saw dots of white light in her eyes. 'I want to tell him. I want everything to be all right – for him to want it. But after what happened . . .'

Since the Big Fight with Lil, neither she nor Bob had been near the place. 'I'm scared he won't ever want to see me now . . .' And off she went all over again.

'D'you want me to find 'im for you? Where does he live?'

'You can't go to his house,' she said, wiping her eyes. 'He still lives with his mom and her sister, and he says they're both proper tartars. Look, he works at Moseley Police Station – if you could take a note?'

The note said, 'I've got to see you. D.' I made a detour on the way to my nan's, going to Moseley first.

That night we heard the Germans had bombed Rotterdam. Everyone thought thousands and thousands of people had died, the doom-laden faces were back in my nan's shop – 'We'll be next' – and everyone started dusting off their gas masks again. Len had to take a cactus in a pot out of his and we sent him off with it again every morning. It was a shock. It was near, and getting nearer. The Dutch capitulated and the next thing was they were moving into France, into Belgium, Antwerp, Liège, Brussels, names falling like ninepins.

'They're saying at work,' Lil told us, 'that all the Germans've got to do is fly over. Some of 'em might even be here already. You got to be careful who you talk to.'

Straight away I had a mad, beautiful daydream that 'Uncle Bob' was really a Fifth Columnist spying for the Nazis who would soon be unveiled as the traitor he was, humiliated and tortured in public, then strung up in the Bull Ring to meet as slow and agonizing a death as possible.

Shame life isn't that simple. When he finally turned up I let him in, still in his uniform.

'Awright, Genie?' He was very short with me, pushed past into the hall. We'd had no warning of him coming. Len was still at work at one of his endless shifts at Austin Aero. Luckily Mom was up and dressed and had managed to get some soup down her. She was wearing an old dress, and had dragged a comb through her hair. I didn't get a chance to warn her, what with old Charmschool barging in like that. I heard her say 'Bob!' startled. She struggled weakly to stand up and held on to the back of the chair, smiling so sweetly at him, really trying hard.

'What d'you want?' I couldn't quite make out his tone. It wasn't angry or abrupt, more cautious and slippery.

'I er, didn't get a chance to say sorry. About what happened. My sister ...' She gave a little laugh. 'Can't ever get away from your family, can you? One way or another?'

Bob didn't look particularly amused. 'Is that it? I haven't got a lot of time tonight.'

'Bob, please.' Mom's eyes filled with tears. 'Don't be like that. It was our fault. We shouldn't have been there

– not then. Genie wasn't to know ... Look, Bob, stop—' He was starting to turn away. 'I've summat to tell you. Genie – leave us alone, will you? There's a good girl.'

I went upstairs, feeling sick at everything that was happening. I didn't want PC Bob anywhere within shouting distance of our house.

It didn't take her long to tell him. Didn't take him long to get to the front door either. Within minutes I heard it slam, and Mom's howls of despair from downstairs. I found her lying along the hall on her front, arms stretched out as if she was heaving on an invisible rope, trying to pull Bob back.

'Oh please, *please* ...' she moaned, until the words gave out to sobs with no sound coming at all.

Then there was a great banging on the door. I stepped over Mom. There was Molly, a big grin on her pork pink face. 'Is Lenny in yet?'

'No, he sodding well isn't!' I yelled at her, guilty for it before I'd even finished. 'Sorry, Molly. No, he'll be back later tonight.'

Molly peered in between my legs at Mom's head on the floor behind me. 'Everything all right, is it Genie?'

'No, Molly, it's not,' I said savagely, and slammed the door in her simple face.

'Nan, there's summat you're going to have to know.'

Mom told me to tell her and Auntie Lil, because she couldn't face doing it herself. I told our nan first. Didn't want Lil there ranting and raving.

We had a few quiet moments in the shop. Nan was

sorting through sugar coupons. She looked round at me. I could see she was sort of steeling herself for something she half dreaded already.

'It's Mom. She's expecting.' My cheeks were aching hot. I couldn't look Nan in the eye. 'The babby's Bob's.'

Nan bent her head and pushed the coupons into her battered tin cashbox, her fingers working fast and nervously. I watched her strong profile, dark hair swept round, half covering her ears. 'Nan?'

'What?'

'Did you hear me?'

She bent to push the cashbox under the worm-riddled counter. 'I may be a lot of things, Genie, but I'm not deaf.'

'I just thought you'd say something.'

Nan stood up. She looked tired. 'What d'you want me to say? That she's a fool? That she's throwing away a perfectly good marriage? Your father may not be a Rudolph Valentino if that's what she was after, but 'e's been a good husband to her. 'E's a worker. 'E's never laid a finger on 'er and 'e's looked after you and seen you all right. What more does she want?' She passed a hand back over her forehead. 'I don't know.'

She let herself through into the house at the back. I heard her moving the kettle on the range and wondered where it was Nanny Rawson kept her feelings about all the horrible things that happened. She must have had a hump hidden somewhere where she could store and absorb them like a camel.

I followed her through. 'Mom's bound to ask what you said.'

Nan didn't even turn to look at me. 'No point in me

193

killing the messenger is there? Tell 'er she knows where 'er family are. We ain't going nowhere.'

'Is there any news, love?'

Vera had run up to Nan's shop in a pair of battered old slippers for a packet of fags.

'I didn't know you smoked.'

'I do today.' She bought matches too and lit up straight away.

'The last letter we had was all wiggly,' I told her. 'He said he was writing in the wireless truck while they were moving along. Said he'd seen German planes dropping bombs and a great big crater where they'd blown up a farmhouse.'

Vera grimaced. I wasn't sure if it was at what I'd said or the cigarette. 'I bet your mom's worried ain't she, poor thing? If there's anything I can do to help . . .?'

'Ta.' I couldn't think of anything at all I could say about Mom's state of mind at that moment. When Dad's letter came she cried and cried.

'Poor Victor. My poor Victor.' Tears of remorse. She'd almost forgotten he existed over the past months and now she could see he wasn't so bad after all.

I changed the subject quickly. 'Mr Spini any better?'

'He's awright – it's taking time.' Vera shrugged. 'Teresa's the one who's trouble – always wanting to be somewhere else away from us. She doesn't do as she's told and she makes Micky furious.' Vera was starting to wave her arms. 'We don't know what she's getting up to. She won't listen to us. She and Micky had a set-to the other night because he tried to make her stay in and she disobeyed him. If he was in better health she'd've more than felt his hand across her.' She sighed heavily.

'As if there ain't enough to worry about. What she needs is to find a Catholic boy like her – one of the lads from St Michael's. Mixed marriages only cause trouble.'

'Oh, I'm sure she's not thinking of getting married!' I laughed. Vera's mind always ran on to the worst possible. Teresa marrying a Protestant!

She smiled suddenly, sheepish. 'You think I'm stupid. But she don't tell us what she's doing or where she is. It's not right. I wish she could be more grown up and sensible like you, Genie. D'you think you could have a word with her?'

Mom was managing to pull herself together by dinnertime these days, have a bit to eat and get to work.

'The babby won't show for a bit yet, so I'm not going to get asked any awkward questions. If I don't get out I'll only sit here feeling sorry for myself.' This came as a bit of a surprise to me because I'd thought that was exactly what she would do. What with Bob taking off and his bun in the oven I thought she'd be about ready for the canal herself. But after a few days of pure misery while she mourned her rejection by PC Bob and leaned on me as if I was an iron doorstop, she became almost cheerful. I was baffled. She started going on about my dad.

'I've never given Victor enough credit for what he's given all of us,' she said one evening. 'He's been a good husband and father – not like some. And he's given me you and Eric. It's time I acted like a proper wife to him.'

I was so relieved she wasn't in the depths of despair at this point that I didn't think to ask her what she imagined Dad was going to say when he came home to find this little cuckoo in the nest. Surely she wasn't going to con him again with one of her record pregnancies?

Lil, who'd already had her say in no uncertain terms, came to the conclusion that that was exactly what she was going to do. 'He was here December,' she said in her sarky voice. 'And the babby's due about next December. So it'll be a good three months shorter than the first time, any rate. Poor old Victor, he must love her, God help 'im.'

'Well don't you go interfering,' Nanny Rawson told her. 'We've enough trouble already without you letting fresh air in your gob out of place.'

In the meantime, I got myself a new job. Nanny was recovered, barring a stiff knee. 'You want to get out and earn yourself some more wages,' she said. 'I'm all right 'ere now.'

Lewis Broadbent's foundry was an old family firm with a good reputation in the back streets of Highgate. In peacetime they made brass plumbers' ware – taps and sink bases, washers and screws, but for the war effort the firm had gone over to making caps for shells and petrol cans, and other small parts.

A middle-aged woman called Doris with jet-black hair and watery brown eyes showed me round the factory, which was hot from the furnaces where they heated the brass, and noisy with the clank of metal and the chunking of the pressing machines.

I was taken on in the warehouse at the back as a checker. It was a wide, not very well lit area with rows of women working at long tables. Doris slotted me into a work place at the end of a table and showed me how to look over the parts, searching them for mistakes or rough bits.

'See this one—' She showed me the inside of a petrol cap. 'The thread's not taken properly. You'd never be able to screw that up.'

After checking, we had to wrap the parts in tissue paper and a layer of brown paper and string and pack them in tea chests to go to other factories needing the parts.

It kept me busy enough, that did. We were all working flat out and quite honestly it was nice to get away from my family for a bit. I began to see Teresa's point. Out in the warehouse I was almost the babby of the place. There was just one other girl anywhere near my age, a year older, very pert, called Nancy. She had little freckles on her nose and auburn eyebrows plucked to a thin line. The other women were mom's age and older. They treated me very well and looked after me in a motherly way. In between chat about the job I learned about their families, those with good husbands and bad, those with none at all, who was in a reserved occupation, who'd signed up, and about their children, mother-in-laws, landlords. And about the Broadbent family who owned the factory. Everyone seemed agreed that Lewis Broadbent was second only to God, that his wife Betty was a scheming hypochondriac, his two daughters no better than they ought to be and his son, who was in the RAF, had the sun shining out of various bits of his anatomy. Nancy went silly at the very mention of Joe Broadbent's name.

''E's all set to take over the factory when this lot's over,' one of the women said, waving her hand over the petrol caps as if they were the war itself.

''E's got no airs and graces though, Joe, has 'e? Comes in and knuckles down to any job 'e's given. Knows how the place works backwards.'

'You'd hardly believe 'e was related to the two sisters, would you?' Nancy said bitchily.

'Ooh, she's got her eye on 'im all right,' someone teased and Nancy looked round coyly.

'Just hope they look after 'im in the airforce . . .'

The talk turned, and then one of them said to me, 'You got yourself a nice fella, 'ave you, Genie?'

I shook my head, not looking up.

'Go on – why not?'

'Don't tease her – she's only young yet,' a voice said.

I thought with a pang of Jimmy, and of Walt. I'd messed up my chances good and proper with both of them. Oh well, I thought, giving a shrug inside myself. So what. Who cared anyway?

When it came to Dunkirk it was everyone's news, everyone's war suddenly, and for those last days of May no one could talk or think of anything else. Gloria was on for every news bulletin whenever anyone was in. Mom, still sick, was in a shocking state.

One evening when it was all going on, Auntie Lil turned up. She came to bury the hatchet and not, for once, in the back of Mom's head.

'You still bad, Dor?' she asked, sweet as jam.

Mom was sitting writing to Eric, and Lil's sympathy sent her all weepy. 'I've not been into work I feel that terrible.' Her appearance had gone all to pieces. She was gaunt, her skin the colour of porridge.

'Come on now,' Lil said. 'Genie and I'll help you, won't we love?' She pushed Mom back down into a chair. 'You need some company – get Stella over for a chat.'

'She don't care. Never seen her for dust – some friend that one,' Mom said despondently.

'Never mind. You just stay there and we'll see to everything.'

'I thought you hated me!' Mom sobbed.

'What's done can't be undone,' Lil said. 'Here – I brought you a bottle of stout for later. Buck you up.'

Lil was a busy sort. Spun round the place doing housework as if it was a race. She'd always been like that. Patsy and Tom, who'd come down with her, were out in the garden playing in the evening sun. Before I could blink hardly, Lil had brewed up tea, dusted and tidied downstairs, rinsed and hung out a bucket full of washing and was all for setting in on the cooking.

I watched her as I worked on carrots and parsnips for our tea, her sleek body bending and straightening in the garden as she pegged out, shouting to the boys now and then. Her life had been the same for so long, I thought, and wondered if it'd ever be any different for her, for any of us.

'How is Eric?' she called to Mom as she came in with the empty washpail.

'He's all right.' We could hear the emotion in Mom's voice. She was never more than a breath away from tears these days. They seeped up into her eyes at the mention of all sorts of things: Dad, Eric, the babby, the war, going to work, sometimes even the thought of getting up in the morning. 'He doesn't write much. That Mrs Spenser's got her claws into him – Victor said when he took Eric down there she had ever such a nice house and she nearly jumped on Eric as if he was her own.' She gave a little wail. 'It's not right. I feel as if I've lost him.'

Lil pulled a grim face at me and went in to her. 'Never mind,' she soothed. 'You know he's safe, and at least he's happy where he is. You've no worries on that score.'

'But he shouldn't be happy – he doesn't belong there. You wouldn't send yours off, would you?'

I took them another cup of tea, then retreated into the kitchen. Patsy and Tom were playing down round the Anderson which was now sprouted over with dandelions. Some had already gone to seed and the boys were blowing dandelion clocks. I had a peculiar feeling for a minute which was so strange it took me a while to work out what it was. I was happy. Just for a little flash of time. Seeing the boys there looking carefree like kids should be in the last of the sunshine on these calm, clear-cut days of spring, and Auntie Lil here and people being nice to one another.

But then I heard Lil say, 'What are you going to do, sis?' and the little spark of harmony which lit those few seconds was snuffed out because Mom was crying again and trying to speak and Lil was saying, 'Ssh ... ssh ... there.'

'I've been so bad,' Mom was pouring out to her. 'Such a fool. But I loved him. Really loved him, and I've never had it before like that, you know ... But he never loved me. Not really, properly. It was all a lie ...'

'Yes.' Lil's voice was desolate. She knew only too well what it was to be left alone. 'He was using you, sis.'

'I want to get back to what we had – me and Victor. I mean it wasn't all I've ever wanted but it was good enough. If I lose that I'll have nothing.'

'But Doreen, the babby. It's not just going to go away.'

I held still in the kitchen listening.

'No, but ...' I heard her hesitate. 'He might be away ages and the babby'll be born in seven months. I could hand it over. There's people would take it off me – adopt it. And he'd never know. Nothing would have changed then, would it?'

'Doreen!' Lil was dreadfully shocked. 'You can't go on like that, deceiving him. He's your husband!'

'But what else can I do?'

'The truth'll find you out, Dor. The neighbours aren't blind and deaf, are they? Some bloody busybody's bound to say summat even if it ain't out of spite – although the chances are it will be. What about Gladys and Molly for a start? They've not enough sense between them to keep their mouths shut. You're just going to have to tell him the truth.'

'No. Oh no, I couldn't do that!'

I pictured Dad's face if he knew, the twisted hurt in it, and she must've seen it the same way.

We heard Len at the door then and they had to stop talking.

'Awright Len?' Lil said. 'Been at it since the crack of dawn, have you?'

I heard Len making pleased-sounding noises. Then a click and Gloria was on. There was news due. 'Ssssh,' everyone said.

The Germans had reached the Channel coast. The British Expeditionary Force as well as Belgian and French troops were surrounded in a small pocket of ground inland from Dunkirk.

The days as we waited were so beautiful. So lovely it hurt. It looked all wrong for disaster and dread and knowing great calamities were happening somewhere far away. By 24 May the BEF was completely cut off. Those of us who had people there could think of nothing else. What was happening to my father? Were they safe? What was going to happen next? Even for those who could look at the thing less personally, the fact was, the Germans were only twenty or so miles away from the south coast, looking at us across a tiny vein of water.

Over that weekend, when they began the evacuation of Dunkirk, the skies were clear and lovely and people watered their vegetable patches and sunned themselves in the park, wore cotton frocks and held cricket matches. That was the oddest part of the whole thing, trying to hold together in your mind that these things were happening in the same world.

The nights were horrible, broken, patched with bad dreams, and waking it hit you, thoughts coming in a rush – 'Oh God, oh no!' – like black water filling a drain.

On the Monday the Belgians capitulated. They were bringing troops out of France by the thousand every day. Mom was in such a state of agitation she scarcely knew where to put herself. She managed to carry on working most days, which helped keep her mind occupied. But at home she paced the floor, couldn't keep still.

'I feel as if I'm going mad,' she cried. 'I wish they'd get it all over with. This waiting's worse than anything.'

She'd got all the options worked out by now with the clear-cut selfishness of a true survivor.

'If he gets killed I'm going to be a widow on my own. And if he comes back he's going to find out about the babby and everything'll be ruined anyway. He can't come home now. He just can't!'

June 1940

There was no other conversation in those days. Nothing else on anyone's lips. Walking home from work I'd hear the muffled sounds of wireless sets through open windows. The women at the factory were marvellous to me. 'Any news, Genie?' every day. Ever so kind. ''Ow's your mother?' People who saw Mom thought she was jumpy with sleeplessness on Dad's behalf, desperate for him back. I couldn't tell them it wasn't quite like that.

I loved being at work, away from her. She wasn't feeling well still, wasn't sleeping. 'What if Victor comes back? What if he doesn't?' I found it a strain being with her when I was in a state of nervous exhaustion myself. I felt sick almost all the time.

We all sweated it out. The weather was boiling. Every day Mom shrunk a bit thinner. She carried on confiding in Lil and I'd never seen them so close. As for Len, we barely saw him. When he wasn't at the Austin he was off somewhere with Molly. Nanny Rawson was a pillar of strength as ever.

'Come over to ours and have a sing-song,' she insisted to Mom. 'Take your mind off it.'

'Oh no, I couldn't,' Mom said. 'Not singing. Not now.'

'You should,' Nan said. 'Works wonders for you.' She and Lil still played in some of the pubs round and about.

I went anyway, and sat singing with Nan and Lil on an evening that felt like the middle of summer with the door open so some of the neighbours stood round in the yard and chimed in with us. And Nanny was right, a bit of 'Knees up Mother Brown' and other old favourites did take your mind elsewhere for a bit.

But we were still being swept along with the fleets of Dunkirk. All the little vessels, fishing smacks, tramps, paddle steamers, shrimpers and tugs that had gone to support the naval ships and channel steamers to get the boys home. It made you nearly boil with pride inside. Made defeat seem like victory, although really now we were right up against it and we knew it clear as anything. But all I wanted to know then was, are they bringing my dad? I was praying all the time, 'Please God, please . . .'

They started trickling home. Gloria told us how in the Kent gardens along the railway, people stood waving them back. By 4 June the evacuation was over. They'd done all they could and the Germans were getting too close. No more ships were going.

When the men started coming in from the coast, there were heroic stories about their welcome, the programmes of washing and feeding and entertaining them all. We heard of arrivals in Birmingham. We waited and waited, Mom like someone preparing to be fired from a cannon.

'Mom asked if there's anything you need?' Teresa said when she appeared on our doorstep.

It was my mom's day off from work and she was slouched in an old dress with a pinner over the top and her hair all over the place. Teresa looked really taken aback at the sight of her, and seeing Teresa, Mom straightened up and tried to pull herself together. 'Nothing you can do,' she said. 'Waiting's the only thing – ta.'

Teresa, in contrast to Mom, was looking lovely. The sun had only to come out for her skin to light up brown and the days had been tropical. She had on a bright yellow dress with big orange flowers dotted across it and her black hair was hanging loose.

'You look nice,' Mom told her. 'Haven't seen you in ages.' She had to pretend with Teresa. It seemed to do her good, having to act like the pining, faithful wife. 'Sorry I'm such a mess. Got other things on my mind.'

'You must be ever so worried, Mrs Watkins,' Teresa said, sitting down opposite her, dark eyes full of concern.

'Oh I am,' Mom was saying demurely. 'But we're still hoping. There's more coming back all the time.'

She was being a model Person Taking It Well. 'How's your job?' she asked Teresa.

'Boring. Wouldn't mind a change to tell you the truth. Stevie says it serves me right.'

Stevie would, I thought.

Teresa told us about some of the antics they got up to to liven the place up. Her voice rang round our house. Must've shocked the walls. They weren't used to happy sounds.

'Hope you don't mind me having a laugh, Mrs Watkins,' Teresa said.

'No, you go on,' Mom urged. 'Good for us to hear you.'

When Len came back he joined in at the sound of her. Said that after tea he was going out with Molly.

Teresa being there kept Mom together all evening.

We ate boiled beef and spring cabbage – 'Hope you don't mind our sort of cooking,' Mom said – listened to Gloria's music and news bulletins and talked and joked. Teresa even made Mom laugh with her infectious energy. After dark, Len came in looking pleased with himself. Mom gave me a look full of meaning and I tried to ignore her.

'Where've you been, Lenny?' she asked him.

'Out,' was all she got in reply, while he twiddled Gloria's knobs as he had no doubt just been twiddling Molly's.

Teresa ended up staying over. 'Mom'll know where I am.' It was like the old days, before Lola, when she used to come and sleep the night, weekends sometimes, when there was no school the next morning. The more we'd been together that night the more I felt we could be close again. She hadn't even mentioned blokes all evening. But there was this great lie and pretence going on in front of her and it made me really uncomfortable.

She bunked up with me on the bed in my room. It took her ages to get ready. I lay down in my thin white nightdress, watching her. She peeled off the sunny yellow dress and laid it over the chair. Underneath she had on a cotton petticoat, old but still surprisingly white, or it seemed so in the candlelight, and her skin looked dark against it. She stood facing me, using my hairbursh to brush her hair forward, first over one shoulder, then the other, then holding it up luxuriously with two hands and letting it fall down her back, bosoms lifting as she raised her arms. Her body tapered down to narrow hips. She smiled at me, eyes dotted with little candles, and laughed her chesty laugh. She's beautiful, I thought. Not pretty, but beautiful.

'Haven't done this for a long time, have we?'

I shook my head, shy of her suddenly. She looked so grown up.

'Hope I'll fit in.'

'You will. You're nothing like the size of Lola. Here—' I pulled the covers back.

She half lay in bed, leaning over on one elbow to blow out the candle on the chair beside her, hair falling forward. It was very dark then, with the windows blacked out. I couldn't even see her outline, only feel the warmth of her next to me. I smiled in the dark.

'I feel like a little kid again,' she said.

'Just what I was thinking.'

'I wouldn't want to be though, would you? A kid I mean. Not for anything.'

I was still wondering about this when she said, 'Sorry I behaved like such an idiot over Jack.'

'And Clem.'

'All right. And Clem then.'

'S'all right.'

'Genie? What about Walt – d'you still like him?'

'Haven't seen him.'

'But if you did?'

'No.'

'Never mind, there'll be someone.'

I thought about Jimmy, his body pushing down on mine. The tea hadn't all come out of my dress and Mom had been livid.

'I don't think I care all that much.'

'We just haven't met anyone good enough for us.'

'That must be it. Anyway, there's always us. Pals?'

'Pals.' After a moment she said, 'Your mom's being ever so brave. If it was my dad away I can't imagine how Mom'd cope. Or me.'

'It's a case of having to.'

'Course. All the same, I think you lot are tougher than us. All too emotional, Italians.'

I couldn't lie to her any more, not being there so close to her. And I wanted to stop feeling so alone. But my heart was pounding so hard at the thought of bringing it all out that I couldn't speak and I was shaking.

'What's up with you?' Teresa said.

'I want to tell you summat . . .' Then I was crying so much I couldn't get it out.

Teresa turned on her side and wrapped her arms round me and I hugged her back, feeling her full chest against my skinny body. She felt lovely. She kissed my cheek and I kissed her too.

'Go on – you can tell Teresa. What's got you worked up into this state all of a sudden?'

'It's Mom. None of it's how it looks. She doesn't really want my dad back because she's having a babby and it's not his.' I told her all about it then, spilt it out, about Bob coming to our house in the winter and how he took to his heels as soon as he knew she was expecting. 'Mom's scared about my dad coming home and him finding out. She's been in a state for ages . . .'

'I'm not surprised,' Teresa said. 'Oh my God, Genie, that's terrible. Your poor, poor dad.'

'Promise you won't say anything to anyone,' I begged her. 'I shouldn't be telling you really, only I couldn't help it. You won't, will you?'

'Of course not. On my life.'

She let me cry myself out and eventually we settled down to sleep, with her curled round behind my back. She felt warm and comforting and she wasn't bossing me, wasn't after anything like Jimmy. Lying there with her was the best, warmest feeling I'd had in a long time.

I was at work the morning Mom saw a man in army uniform move into view in front of our window, then stop, looking up at the house. Her legs turned to jelly. She was sure at once it was Dad. 'Even though I could see it wasn't,' she said later. 'I couldn't move. I was convinced it was him. I mean who else would it be? But he was the wrong height and everything.'

Another person stepped into the picture, a neighbour, who spoke to the man, who then came to our front door. Mom opened it, shaking. She saw a face with thick black eyebrows and a grubby khaki uniform.

'Are you Doreen Watkins?' To her nodding he announced, 'My name's Dickie Carter. Army pal of your 'usband's.'

Mom asked him in, gibbering questions. She made tea and sandwiches.

'Didn't know if I'd find him 'ere,' Dickie said. 'We promised each other, whoever got home first, we'd go and see each other's missis and let 'em know.' He ate the bread ravenously. 'I ain't got back over to my missis yet but I sent a message, and she knows I'm on my way.'

'So – Victor's coming home?' Mom asked. Dickie must have seen a white, stricken face in front of him.

He nodded, chewing away. 'Last time I saw 'im 'e was about a mile from the beach. Not far at all. But see, it was chaos at the time – pandemonium. All sorts of stuff blocking the road, lorries and that, things going off all round us ...' Dickie carefully didn't give us all the details he might have done about the bodies of men and horses in the road. We heard about that later. 'Any rate, I never saw 'im after that. Thing was though, we was so close. We 'ad to walk a couple of miles along the beach. Bloody 'ard going across that soft sand and we was all in after the miles we'd come already. There were lines of blokes everywhere so it'd have been easy to miss 'im. Somehow we never caught up with each other again. I reckon 'e'd've got to a boat though. Not much doubt about it. There was all sorts of stuff coming in to get us out.'

'You haven't see him though – over here?'

'No, I ain't, but that don't mean 'e's not 'ere. There's blokes being sent about all over the place. I came through Reading but 'e could've gone anywhere else. But I reckon 'e'll be back.'

When he'd eaten and drunk as much as was on offer, Dickie set off to go back to his missis. 'Don't you worry, Mrs Watkins,' he told Mom. ''E'll turn up sooner or later.'

'I don't understand it, Genie,' Mom said to me. 'If he was back over here, he'd've got a message to us, wouldn't he? Or written a letter. He was always writing letters.'

She was like a Jumping Jack. The slightest sound and she was at the front door to see if it was him coming. There was nothing could be done to set her mind at rest. She didn't turn up for work again and they were already getting browned off with her being so irregular. She was a bag of nerves. Seeing Dickie, a real live returner from Dunkirk, she was now convinced Dad must be on his way.

When I got home from Broadbent's and heard the news I was excited. I wanted my dad home, whatever mess Mom had got herself in. I wanted him fair and square. By the time I got in she'd obviously been at the port bottle and wasn't quite steady on her feet.

'I can't stand this waiting,' she said. Her cheeks were an unnatural, shiny pink.

'Let's go to Nan's.' I couldn't cope with her here on my own all evening.

'What if he comes back when we're out?'

'He'll guess where we are. It's got to be better than just sitting here.'

On the way she insisted on calling in at the Outdoor for ale. 'Mom and Lil'd like a drink I s'pect,' she said.

Nanny Rawson and Lil were all agog hearing about the appearance of Dickie Carter. Another Dunkirk survivor had come home to Belgrave Road, everyone crowding round to hear the tale he had to tell, and we were still waiting for our family hero. Mom had to repeat the details at least three times.

'Is Uncle Victor coming home then?' Tom asked.

'We hope so,' I said.

Mom was already the worse for drink by the time we got there and she kept on tipping it back as the evening wore on. Nanny Rawson was full of an indignant tale about an unusual customer she'd had in the shop that day. She sat with her stocky legs stretched out, leaning down to rub her injured knee as she spoke.

'She stopped outside in a great big car. Come in 'ere with five pound wanting to buy up all the sugar. Told me she came from Henley-in-Arden if you please.' Nan laughed. 'Voice like a glass chandelier.'

'D'you give it to her?' Lil asked.

'Hadn't a lot to give her. But she was prepared to pay well over the odds.' Nan shook her head, laughing suddenly. 'She was wearing a fox fur stole. Beautiful it

211

was. Must have wondered where the 'ell she'd found herself when she came in 'ere.'

'The nerve though,' Lil said. 'They think they can just buy anything, some of 'em.'

Mom was knocking back the beer and Len was eyeing up Nanny's little wireless set. 'Can we 'ave it on?' he said hopefully. It may not've been Gloria, but in his eyes it was better than nothing.

'No,' Nan said. 'We'll make our own music tonight. Lil and I did a spot down at the Eagle last night and it cheered us up no end. Run up and get my squeeze box, Patsy. Otherwise we'll forget how to do it.'

Patsy clomped up the bare wood of the stairs in his heavy Mail charity boots and hairy socks to Nan's bedroom where she kept the squeeze box. We all sat round, the house seeming almost spacious now there were no Flanagans hurtling about. Tom sat close to me on the couch, Lil next to us with Cathleen asleep across her lap, looking angelic enough now her eyes were closed. Len joined in the singing with unpredictable shouts. All Nan's old favourites.

'I wish you could come and live with us, Auntie Genie,' Tom said to me. 'Here – d'you want to see my marbles? I swapped 'em with Wilf at school.'

'Go on then.'

Tom showed me five scratched marbles. He was pleased as anything. 'He collects cards so I give him the ones I had off Auntie Doreen.'

Mom gave her cigarette cards to Tom now Eric wasn't here. Mrs Spenser was paying for Eric to have piano lessons. He lived in another world.

I cuddled Tom to me as Nan's fingers leapt across the keys of her squeeze box, oom-pa-pa, oom-pa-pa.

Mom got up, said she was going to the lav. Her face

was sickly white and she couldn't walk in a straight line. Lil was saying, 'Steady on, Dor. How much've you had tonight?'

She got as far as the door and leaned up against it, faint, saying, 'You'd better get me a bucket,' but it was too late and she was bent over pouring her guts up into the yard, making little moaning sounds in between.

Lil and Nan got her inside and sat her on the couch with a bowl.

'Len!' Nanny ordered. 'Get a bucket of water and wash down the yard.'

'What's the matter with Auntie Doreen?' Tom asked me, and at the same time Lil was on at me saying, 'How much did she have before you came out?'

'I dunno exactly,' I said. 'She had a bit of port I think.'

'More than a bit by the looks of it.' Mom was lying back on the couch now, head lolling.

'I'll make her a cuppa tea,' Nan said. 'The state she's in I don't know as you'll get her home tonight.' She went over and put the kettle on the heat. We could hear Len sloshing water about outside.

Clarys' face appeared round the door. 'Everything awright, is it Edith? Only I saw Doreen looking ever so poorly.'

Lil marched over to the door. 'Everything's tickety-boo, ta, and if it wasn't, you poking your nose in wouldn't make it any better, would it, so why don't you just go in and get on with your knitting?'

Clarys retreated in a huff.

'No call to be so rude,' Nan said, spooning tea. 'We've still got to live with her tomorrow.'

'Nosy bitch,' Lil was muttering.

Len came back in and switched the wireless on as if

to say he deserved it after that charming job. Music streamed out. Glenn Miller, 'In the Mood'. Mom was asleep, snoring. I was ashamed of her.

'She been bad again this week?' Nanny asked me.

I nodded.

'She's bound to be, what with the babby and the worry,' Lil said. 'And if Victor's coming home any minute . . .'

'She's not going to be able to keep it in the family much longer,' Nan said, advancing on Mom with a cup of black tea. 'She always shows early.'

'Let her sleep it off,' Lil suggested. 'She can stay here.'

'She needs summat on her stomach.'

I felt frightened watching my nan sit Mom up, saw her flop as if she was dead, head rolling forwards, unable to open her eyes.

'Give us a hand.'

Lil went over as well. Patsy, Tom and I stood watching, the other side of the table. Lil held Mom's head as Nanny tried to force some of the tea down her. She spluttered and dribbled and murmured, 'Hot.' Eventually, after tipping tea into the saucer and back a few times, they got her to drink some before she subsided back on to the couch. She looked terrible. I felt tears come into my eyes. My life felt like a mirror that had been shattered. I just wanted my dad to come back and make everything all right.

No sign of him. It was a terrible week. The women at Broadbent's tutted round me, and about me.

No one spoke the worst but I knew they were

thinking it. If he's not home by now he must be dead. Surely. It couldn't have taken this long?

At home the strain of living with Mom took its toll. She was falling to pieces and I wasn't far from it myself.

'It's not knowing,' she sobbed one evening. 'I just can't stand not knowing whether he's alive or dead. I just want to get it over with one way or the other. But they'd tell me if he was dead, wouldn't they? There'd be a letter or a telegraph.'

I still clung to my hope that he was alive, maybe in hospital.

She couldn't get through the days without drinking. She still managed to get to work – slept it off in the morning. But as soon as she was home she'd go straight to it. She started on what she had in the house – that bottle of port. But it wasn't long before that was gone and she had to buy more, gin this time, downing it quick, with tears, not pleasure. But at least she was still drinking it nicely then, out of a glass. She'd say, 'Oh – that's better,' and plonk herself down, half gone with drink and tiredness, and just sit there until it was time for bed.

It was a lonely life, even with the kindness of the women at work, of the Spinis. Len was barely ever in in the evenings now, either because of work or Molly. He'd slope in and have his meal, and on these warm, sultry evenings he and Molly took off until after dark. Never said where. They must have gone and walked in the parks, gas masks and all. I found myself missing Len's presence even though it was a relief not having him and Molly in the house together.

I was left with Gloria for company. *Hi Gang! Garrison Theatre*, *Band Waggon*. Without them I might have gone off my head in those days when part of my mind was always listening for a bang at the front door, for Dad's voice in the hall.

But it didn't come. Still didn't come.

A few little notices started to appear in the *Birmingham Mail*. They tore at your heart. Did anyone have information about ...? Know the whereabouts of ...? People's sons, brothers, husbands, who had not, as hoped, walked in off a train from the coast and Dunkirk. Mom put one in. It was peculiar seeing his name, Victor James Watkins, in the paper like that. As if he was just another name, nothing to do with us.

While we were waiting, a whole new lot of trouble broke out. On 10 June, Italy declared war on Hitler's side and suddenly no one was supposed to like Italians any more. The papers had already stirred that one up, as Micky had shown me. Now the headlines were screaming, 'INTERN THE LOT!'

I went straight to see them that evening. The house was full of people, the older ones sitting on the available chairs, the others all standing round. Vera's family, except for her mom, two other elderly men, a woman with thick black hair swept back in a bun, her arm round Vera's shoulder, and some younger men including Fausto Pirelli. All the talk was in Italian. Bottles of Micky's wine and tumblers stood on the table.

'You all right, Genie?' Teresa asked.

I nodded.

Vera took my hand for a moment and squeezed it. Her face looked strained. 'Any news?'

The other woman was watching me, her dark face serious. 'Her father's missing in France,' Vera told her.

The woman tutted, shaking her head. 'A terrible thing – I 'ope you have better news soon, darlin'. Don't lose 'ope. You must always have 'ope.'

It was hot and airless in the room. Normally they'd have kept the door open but that night it was closed, maybe because they felt safer that way. The air was full of cigarette smoke and loud talk. Stevie was over by Micky looking solemn and grown up. Teresa and I stood by the door.

'Should I go?' I whispered to her.

'No, course not. You're all right.' She put her mouth closer to my ear. 'They're worried. They think people will be arrested.'

'But there's no one here who'd do any harm, surely?'

She shrugged. 'Even today at work someone made a nasty remark about my name. I suppose I'm Italian now whether I like it or not.' She sounded bewildered more than upset.

Suddenly Fausto leaned over the table, raising one of the thick glasses half full of red wine. His sharp-featured face looked quite bonkers, I thought, eyes blazing with fanaticism and the effects of the drink. The men round him, Micky included, all started shouting at him at once, telling him, so far as I could make out, to shut up.

But Fausto wasn't going to shut up. He lifted the glass even higher, slopping some of the wine on the head of a bloke sitting next to him. '*Viva l'Italia!*' he shouted. '*Viva il Duce!*'

Two of the younger men, one an uncle of Teresa's, moved in and took Fausto by the shoulders, forcing him towards the door.

'What did he say?' I hissed at Teresa.

'Long live Mussolini,' she said without turning her head, too busy watching what was going on. 'Dad's not going to have that. Fausto's such a bloody idiot. Doesn't spare a thought for anyone else.'

Micky pushed his chair back and stood up. He talked so well with his hands that I didn't need to understand the rest. Get him out of my house. Out. Now. D'you want to get us all arrested?

Fausto was led out of the house by two of the men. As they stumbled past the window we could see his mouth was still going.

That night, Teresa told me, there was a loud hammering on the Spinis' door. Micky went down, pulling on his trousers. The rest of them listened, frightened, at the top of the stairs.

'Micky?' It was a neighbour. ''Fraid you got some trouble out the front, mate. Someone's broke your windows.'

They all went out, except Giovanna and Luke who stayed asleep, and stood in the street in their nightclothes staring at the shattered front window of the shop, the big hole in the glass with jagged splinters round it. Stevie was cursing, Francesca crying. Vera stood with her hands on Tony's shoulders in silence.

'We should have stayed in the Quarter,' she said, shaking. 'Then at least we'd all have been together.'

Micky didn't say much, just kept running his hand through his hair.

'It might have been someone trying to break in?' Teresa suggested. 'Or kids?'

'No. We know why it is.' Micky's voice was quiet, but angry. 'I don't know what to think. I suppose we get it glazed again tomorrow. But maybe now this is going to happen every night? We're in the wrong camp, even if we have spent most of our lives here. We're the enemy all of a sudden.'

There were to be no more church bells. No more of the usual pattern of chimes across the Sunday city. Only if we were invaded. That was to be the warning.

The Germans were closing in round Paris. It was over a week now since the evacuation of Dunkirk ended and we hadn't heard anything. Our newspaper clipping about Dad was starting to go yellow at the edges.

Mom was having to wear her loosest clothes already, though she could still easily get by as not being pregnant. But being a skinny woman she did show early. She put her hand to her stomach a lot. Her face was permanently sullen and sulky as if life had cheated her. Of everything.

The day after Italy declared war, she went out into the garden in the evening. She'd only had one glass of port so far. That performance at Nanny Rawson's had brought her up a bit sharp. 'I'll have to watch myself.' I went out and found Mom staring at the sky, the last bronze light on 'our' barrage balloon. From inside we could hear Gloria playing 'When You Wish upon a Star'. Mom was standing sideways on to me and I thought I could see the little bulge of the baby growing inside her.

'Victor's dead.'

I didn't say anything. I didn't want to hear those words.

'He's dead. I know he is.' She whipped round. 'Genie – whatever am I going to do?'

We stood there, both in agony, but not touching each

219

other. I wanted my dad so badly, wanted the solid, sensible bit of our family. Mom blew about like a feather and I couldn't trust or rely on her. Everything was breaking up. No Dad, no Eric, and now she was going to bring a babby into the house whose father I could murder with a smile.

'At least he'll never know,' she said, all wrapped up in herself as usual. 'He'll've died thinking I was a good wife to him. I can keep Bob's babby.' Then, voice going high, she went on, 'But how on earth am I going to manage? We'll have no money, and another babby and no man to look after us . . .' That old bogyman poverty, the cold, aching, eking-out struggle she remembered from her childhood, leered up over her shoulder.

'You've got me, Mom. I can earn money now, don't forget. And Lenny.'

She squatted down on the grass suddenly, hands over her eyes, head bent. 'I've messed up everything, Genie. Every single thing I've ever done I've made a mess of it.'

'Mom . . .'

She didn't look up.

'He might not be dead . . .' I still hoped that, prayed it. Until we had some sign or letter we'd never properly believe it.

She got up suddenly without another word and went into the house as if someone had called. They had. The gin bottle.

On the Wednesday that week, in the evening, the police moved into Park Street, Bartholomew Street and the others which made up Birmingham's Little Italy, arresting a man from every house and carting them off to the police station. Among them was Vera's elder brother, Teresa's uncle Matt Scattoli.

'They thought it was a bit of a joke at first,' Teresa told me. 'Some of the lads anyway. A group of 'em went down there all full of themselves and the police said if they didn't get off home they'd arrest them as well.'

'Have they let them go now?' I asked.

'Oh no. No one knows what's happening. They haven't got themselves sorted out.'

'Well what about your dad?'

'God knows. They haven't come down our way. He's in the Fire Service, Mom keeps saying. What would they want to arrest him for?'

The Germans moved into Paris and the French surrendered. The newsreader's voice was very sombre, seeming to come out of a big echoing silence behind him. After the news they played trumpets.

The heat and breathless calm made the atmosphere electric. Waiting. Rumours all the time. They've landed on the coast at Margate! No – they hadn't. Planes overhead! They were ours. Leaflets came fluttering through our doors again, 'don't give the invader anything'. Strangers were remarked on, even invented. Previously normal behaviour seemed suspect and all sorts of tales spread based on hearsay. They might parachute in dressed as nuns. Look out for hairy-knuckled nuns!

Even the newsreaders started telling you who they were. 'This is the — o'clock news, and this is Frank Phillips [or Stuart Hibbard or Alvar Liddell] reading it.'

The rumour-mongering reached such a pitch that the government released a whole collection of posters to try and keep us quiet: 'Careless Talk Costs Lives'. This was our turn now. Us. We were next in line now the French had gone. Would we have Germans marching down our street, kicking down our door with their jackboots?

Lil said, once France had fallen, 'Well at least we know what we're up against now.'

But we didn't. Not really. That was the trouble, and our imaginations were on fire.

'Have some dinner with us, Genie – there's enough,' Vera said.

It was Sunday and the Spinis were all squeezed round the table as usual, except for Stevie who was out with the ice-cream cart. Mom was at work, trying to redeem herself by turning up regularly, and so was Len, so I'd come looking for company.

The door to the yard was open and it was quiet, everyone in having dinner. I could see the tap across the way, shining drops falling fast into the blocked drain. The Spinis' yard always stank of drains.

Micky Spini seemed relaxed enough, his health improving by inches. He sat at the table in his shirt-sleeves, in one of his quiet moods, just staring ahead at the table as if he had things on his mind. He smiled at me though, when I came in. Vera had cooked beef, pink in the middle, liver-coloured at the edges, and there were potatoes and peas. It was nice to be in a proper family again with a dad, and a mom who could see further than the bottom of a glass.

'Sorry to hear about your windows,' I said to Micky. 'You had any more trouble?'

He shook his head. 'Not so far.' They kept talking about Uncle Matt and the others still held by the police. Everyone was edgy.

'No news, Genie?' Vera said to me as usual.

'Mom doesn't think he's coming back. He'd've come by now if he was coming, wouldn't he?'

Vera stared at me wide-eyed and tried to make comforting noises but I could see she'd been thinking the same. What else was there to think?

'What about Eric?'

'He still writes. Sometimes. Seems to like it down there. His handwriting's come on a treat.' I sniffed and Teresa reached across and squeezed my hand. 'Can't see him wanting to come home after all she'd done for him down there.'

'Course he will!' Vera said indignantly. 'Home's home. You're his family. Not Mrs Whateverhernameis down there.'

I didn't contradict her but I wasn't sure any more. About anything.

'And how's your mother bearing up?' This was always Vera's conversation. Family concerns. She knew Mom hadn't got any time for her but close family ties were what she'd been brought up on.

Teresa's eyes met mine. I couldn't tell Vera about Mom's other predicament. She was kind all right, but sins were sins and she wouldn't have had any cotter with what Mom had been up to.

She brought in ice cream flavoured with vanilla pods.

'It's made with unsalted margarine. There's nowhere near enough butter about.'

'It's not the same,' Teresa said. 'Doesn't have the creaminess.'

223

'No, it's OK. You're imagining it,' Micky said, sliding it over his tongue.

'I'm not. D'you think I can't tell!'

Already the argument was growing heated. Micky splayed his stubby hands, palms up. 'You put two plates side by side. You'd never be able to tell the difference.'

'I can't tell the difference,' Francesca said.

'You see?'

'She doesn't know!' Teresa was shouting by now. 'She can't tell if she's eating lemon drops or bulls' eyes. She's got no sense of taste at all!'

All the kids were tasting now, making their own comments at full volume. Personally I thought Teresa was right but decided to keep my trap shut about it.

'My tongue must be more sensitive,' Teresa said. 'It tastes of margarine. It tastes cheap.'

'Cheap!' This caused uproar. One of the Spinis' full-blast ding-dongs was just getting warmed up, Luke banging his bowl on the table since he couldn't manage anything loud enough with his mouth to enter the competition.

'What d'you think, Genie?'

'I can't remember what it used to taste like,' I was saying, when we all realized there was a shadow across the doorway. Two shadows. Men in dark suits with bowler hats. One red-faced and fat, everything about him round, even his nose, the other tall and gangly. Laurel and Hardy to a tee. But their faces weren't anything to laugh at at all. Their coming slashed into the afternoon. The shouting switched off.

Micky stood up, nervously rubbing his hands on his trousers. 'Can I help you?'

Without being invited they stepped in, and looked

round the tiny room at the ice-cream-smeared faces of the children and at the Spinis' tidy few belongings: the shelf with their remaining bits of chipped crockery that weren't on the table, the worn pieces of brocade draped over the mantel, Vera's 'photograph' of Jesus. They wore sneers on their faces. Considering how hot it was they had ever such a lot on, and the fat one's face was perspiring. It seemed a long time before anyone spoke again and it all felt bad before they'd even opened their mouths.

Eventually the fat one said, 'Are you Michele Spini?'

Micky nodded.

'I am instructed to arrest you under Regulation 18B as an enemy alien to this country.'

Vera let out a gasp and put her hand over her mouth.

'But for God's sake, I've been here eighteen years!' Micky protested. 'My wife was born here, and my children. I'm in the Fire Service.' The agitation started him coughing again.

'That's as may be. But you haven't been here *twenty* years or more, have you?' The thin man stood up very straight and recited pompously, 'We are given leave to take into custody anyone believed likely to endanger the safety of the realm.'

The two of them went to Micky and took him by the arms. 'So let's not waste any time about it, eh?'

'No!' Vera cried, standing in front of them, barring the way. 'You can't do this. It's all wrong! You've already arrested all the wrong people. My husband loves this country. He'd fight if he was the right age. You're making a mistake.'

'Vera,' Micky said quietly. 'It'll be all right. We'll get it sorted out.'

'You've been consorting with known members of the Italian *Fascio*,' the thin one said. He pronounced it 'Fasho'. 'We have Mr Fausto Pirelli in custody already.'

I heard Teresa make an explosive noise of outrage.

'But it's Sunday today,' Vera carried on. 'You can't arrest him on a Sunday!'

'I'm afraid we can, Mrs Spini,' the fat one said. He nodded at his colleague as if they were about to set off and then said, 'Norman, we haven't searched the house.'

'Ah yes,' said the one called Norman. 'The house.'

Vera sank to a chair as they released Micky and started going through their few possessions. The fat one went and peered up the stairs.

'You ain't going up there!' Vera said. 'There's nothing there.'

'Is that so?' Next thing was his fat arse climbing up to Micky and Vera's room, feet clomping on the floor above. Vera covered her face with her hands.

The thin one was pulling drawers open and shut, and yanked one so hard that it came out and fell on the floor. The side fell off the drawer and Micky and Vera's small collection of papers slid out in a heap. Giovanna started to cry and set Luke off. Teresa picked him up and cuddled him on her lap and Giovanna ran to her mother. Tony sat staring.

'Hoi,' Micky called out. 'Watch what you're doing. What you looking for anyhow?'

'We'll know when we've found it,' the thin one called Norman said. He had squatted down and was rifling through the papers, a look of disgust on his face.

Teresa suddenly erupted from behind the table, still holding Luke in her arms.

'What the hell d'you think you're *doing*?' she bawled at him. Luke was so startled he stopped crying for a moment. 'Coming here, scaring our family, breaking things and insulting us. Who the bleeding 'ell d'you think you are?'

Micky hurriedly laid a hand on her arm. 'Teresa, be quiet. Now!' he ordered, the exertion making him cough again.

'D'you know why he's coughing like that?' The man just stared at her with a flat expression. 'He was in a fire, trying to save a factory, and his chest'll never be the same again. How many times've you done summat like that, eh? You smug bastards. He'd die for this country my dad would. And yes, we do know Fausto Pirelli – he's an ignorant jumped up little shite with a bleeding great chip on his shoulder and anything he thinks or does is nothing to do with us. So why don't you just get out of our house and leave us alone? We haven't done anything.'

The fat man appeared from the stairs. What with Teresa yelling and the kids bawling the racket was getting pretty overwhelming.

'What on earth's going on?'

Teresa turned on him. 'Satisfied now you've had a good nose round, are you?'

'Can't someone shut this wop tart up?' the fat one said and I saw the blood of fury pump into Teresa's cheeks. He jerked his head at the other policeman. 'Come on. Let's get out of here. Mr Spini—' They went and caught him by the arms again. 'You'll be coming with us.'

'No!' Teresa roared. 'No – you can't do this!' Vera watched helplessly. Teresa shoved Luke at her and went to her father, gripping his arm.

Micky's face was grey. He spoke calmly. 'Teresa, *cara*, it's a mistake. I'll go with them and get it cleared up.'

'What – like all their other mistakes?' Teresa retorted. I heard the strain of tears in her voice but she wasn't going to let herself go in front of them.

They ignored her and started to take Micky from the house. He turned his head at the door. 'Don't worry, Vera. It'll be OK.'

We saw them as they took him past the window, his ashen face turned down towards the ground.

Churchill said this was going to be our finest hour, but it didn't feel like my finest hour at all. It felt like the worst time of my entire life.

My mom was only just holding together and I was strung between her and the Spinis. Stevie had returned home to find his father gone and went straight down to the cop-shop only to be banged up as well. They'd be able to see them in a day or two, Vera was told.

A week passed. Vera and Teresa were down at the police station in Steelhouse Lane every day. Eventually they were allowed one visit and they saw Micky, Stevie and Uncle Matteo for a few minutes. None of them had a clue what was happening. Vera said they were all trying to be cheerful, but no one would tell them anything. She was getting more distraught by the day.

Then she found out they'd been moved and they wouldn't say where. The house swarmed with Italians, many in the same position, others offering sympathy or just coming for a nose. Vera was up and down to her mom's. Her eyes were sunken with lack of sleep and she looked as if she'd lost pounds in days.

Teresa gave up her job and came home. 'Mom needs me – and the little'uns.' So she was back among the fruit and veg, keeping up an amazingly cheery front with the regulars who didn't desert them because they were Italians and suddenly on the wrong side of the war. And I saw a new Teresa, one who was even stronger than I'd thought. Her face looked as sleepless as Vera's, but she pinned her hair back, dressed as nicely as she could and accepted everyone's sympathy.

'They've got to find out sooner or later that Dad shouldn't be there,' she said. 'We've got to keep going for 'is sake.'

She gave me strength. I had to do the same for my own dad. And I noticed a new gentleness about the place. Not just the Spinis. It's not just nostalgia talking to say this. It was nearly everyone. People cared more about each other now we were all in trouble. They'd go out of their way, do anything for you. Even Mom managed to think about Vera and what she must be feeling.

'What the hell are they playing at? That Micky Spini may be an Eyetie but what harm's he ever done to anyone?'

On 22 June the French signed the German Armistice. Mr Churchill expressed grief and amazement. The impossible was happening. The hot spring days passed agonizingly slowly.

Sometimes of an evening when I'd done all the chores I couldn't stand to be near Mom, her sitting there lifeless, half in a stupor, as if the world had already ended. I'd go up and lie on my bed, on the rough blanket, and look out at the light evening, the barrage balloon's silver tail. I often thought back to a year ago when everyone was home, squabbling, it's true, and looking daggers. But remembering it from where we were now, even with Lola there it had been normal. Blessedly normal.

I had to hold onto my dreams like Mom used to cling to the stories of the picture shows she saw. Mr Churchill said that if we could stand up to Hitler and beat him our lives would move forwards into 'broad sunlit uplands'. I liked the sound of them, those broad, sunlit uplands. They stretched out in my mind covered in golden corn and poppies and yellow and white flowers, with a warm breeze blowing and bare legs and the sweet, sweet smell of the fields.

July 1940

I heard the news over the factory wireless.

'Oh my God!' I was stuck to the floor like a statue.

'What's eating you?' Nancy snapped. Her voice was always tart as vinegar when she spoke to me and I could never make out why. What'd I done? 'Bunch of Nazis and wops,' she went on. 'Good riddance to them, I say.'

I was too upset to pay too much attention to Nancy. The appalling news was sinking in. The Germans had torpedoed a ship called the *Arandora Star* and sunk it off the coast of Ireland. The vessel had been carrying 1,500 German and Italian internees bound for Canada, and it looked as if an awful lot of them had drowned. Vera and her family still had no news, not of Micky, nor Stevie, nor Uncle Matt. For all we knew they could have been on that ship.

'What's up, Genie?' Doris leaned round me. 'There's surely no one of yours on there?'

'I don't know.' I was numb just then. 'That's the trouble. Could be.' I struggled to keep my eyes on the screw pitches of the brass caps in front of me.

Doris and the others were making sympathetic noises.

'Poor kid,' I heard someone say. 'Another thing to cope with.'

'While you don't know there's still hope,' Doris's deep voice came to me.

'Didn't know you was one for mixing with Nazis

and wops,' Nancy said. Now she'd picked on that phrase she was obviously keen to work it to death. 'Did you, girls?'

'Shut your trap, Nance,' someone said.

Nancy gave them her coyest smile, which was designed to melt hearts, and I felt like slapping her one. I turned on her. 'What do you know about it, you ignorant little bitch? Just you watch what you're saying.' I marched round to her side of the table. 'You're talking about my best pal. One more word out of you and my nails'll be making a pretty pattern on your face. Got it?'

'Did you 'ear that?' Nancy turned in exaggerated outrage to the others.

'You asked for every word of it, Nance,' Doris said. 'So just shut it, eh?' The others agreed with her. None of them liked Nancy, despite her pretty looks and winning ways. Didn't take anyone long to work out she was as two-sided as a half-crown.

'You'd better pack it in the lot of you,' another voice said from down the far end. 'Mr Broadbent's about today and you don't want him 'earing this carry on, do you?'

We certainly didn't. I went back to work, picking up each bit of moulded brass, trying to check it as thoroughly as I could. Mr Broadbent was a kind, straight man and I'd do the very best for him I could. When I glanced up I could see Nancy looking hate at me along the table, her auburn curls pushing out from under the snood we had to wear. Even in the dull light from the grimy factory windows I could see she had rouge on her white cheeks, and her thin, heavily plucked eyebrows made her face look wrong somehow – cheap, like one of Morgan's trollops. I saved that insult up for the next time I might need it and gave her my best 'and bugger you too' look down the long table.

If I could have kept my attention on all the most horrible insults I could think of to hurl at Nancy it would have been much the better for me. But I spent the day in the most agonizing state of mind, imagining terrible things. I kept seeing Micky and Stevie and Theresa's jolly Uncle Matt struggling in the waves, sinking down and down until they were lying on the bottom of the seabed but somehow never dead, always alive, peering helplessly up into the murky water.

After work it was still warm and sunny. I found Teresa packing up the shop for the day. She was wearing the orange dress with the splashes of yellow on it. Without saying anything I picked up one of the boxes from outside and carried it inside for her and together we gathered up the empty crates on which they arranged the pyramids of fruit.

When we'd finished both of us straightened up and I looked into her stricken face. She was holding on tight, I could tell. She couldn't seem to speak. After a moment she shrugged despairingly.

'Oh Teresa – come 'ere.'

We stood in each other's arms and Teresa held me very tight as I did her, our cheeks pressed together.

'We don't know they were on that boat,' she said fiercely. She squeezed me to make the point more strongly. 'We've got to believe they're not – 'til we know for sure. But we haven't heard from them . . .'

I saw her pull her mind away from that thought.

'You're brave, Teresa. Much braver than me.'

She shook her head. 'Not brave. It's just, if we think of the other, of what might've happened, we can't go on. Mom says the same.'

Teresa bent to bolt the doors of the shop, the orange dress tight over her hips. I thought how grown up she was, now she was allowed to be.

'Genie—' She stood up, hesitating. 'It's just – we're all going to Mass now. Would you come?'

In all the time I'd known Teresa I'd never once been to Mass with her. In fact I'd not often been to church at all. Mom and Dad certainly weren't regular attenders, just went sometimes at Christmas. I had been on occasion with Nanny Rawson who barely ever missed a Sunday. Mom said she used to go to get an hour's peace from my grandad and his keeping on, but I reckon it was more than that. I don't know how you'd carry on the way Nanny Rawson did, keep steady, without faith in something or other flickering inside, and the religion she'd been given was Church of England. Sound and solid and no lurching from one extreme to the other. No fripperies, preferably no smells and bells, and what little I'd seen of church was along those sober lines.

The Catholic religion was seen by people like us as something very different from ours. Foreign, baffling, full of dread. The Pope and lots of what Nan called 'paraphernalia' like statues and incense and rosary beads. She'd been up in arms when Lil announced she was marrying Patsy, until she saw that even though he was a Catholic he was no more religious than she was and probably less so.

So it felt peculiar to be walking across towards Digbeth to Mass with the Spinis.

'Are you sure they won't mind?' I whispered to Teresa. Vera was beside us carrying Luke, and Teresa was leading Giovanna by the hand.

'Course not. People'll be pleased.'

Vera's face was drawn and stony and none of us had said much on the way across town except Luke who kept chattering, and we took it in turns to answer. All Teresa said to me on the way was, 'Now I know what it must be like for you.'

St Michael's was in Bartholomew Street, near the railway. Inside it seemed very dark after the bright afternoon and I liked the strange smell in there, the whiffs of wax and incense and floor polish. It was stuffy and cosy and the candles made me think of Christmas.

A row in front of us sat the little stooping figure of Nonna Amelia, Vera's mom, and beside her Vera's other two brothers, Marco, with his pretty wife and two children, and Paolo who wasn't married. Their hair was black as crows' feathers and clipped very neatly round their ears. Nonna Amelia had a black lace mantilla over her white hair and when I looked round I saw Vera, Teresa and Francesca were wearing them too and they looked pretty. Nonna Amelia turned and nodded at me, a warm expression in her eyes. A moment later she swung round, passing me a dark green handkerchief embroidered with white at the edges. As I took it from her gnarled hand, Teresa whispered, 'Put it on your head.' Nonna Amelia nodded as I laid it softly over my hair.

Most of the women I could see were kneeling down holding rosary beads and the Hail Marys were rattling out at top speed. I was surprised how quiet and well-behaved the kids were. Luke sat wide-eyed next to Vera, sucking his thumb.

235

A bell rang and the priest suddenly started speaking from absolutely miles away down the front somewhere and I wondered why they didn't get him to shift forwards a bit so we could all see him. '*In nomine Patris* . . .' Everyone was crossing themselves and I was completely lost after that. Couldn't understand one word of it. And it looked to me as if he'd lost quite a few of them there because they just carried on all the way through with those rosary beads as if nothing was happening at all, not seeming to take the blindest bit of notice. I mean in my nan's church people tried at least to look as if they were listening.

But I started to feel really grateful for being there. Normally at this time of night I'd be pelting about at home cooking tea with people on at me. My heart was so heavy and at least here I had some time to think. All these people came to my mind, Micky and Stevie and Uncle Matteo, and my own dad, and my mom too, until I thought I'd burst with sadness there in that church. Vera's face looked so grieved, and I thought about Mom struggling on at work and all that had happened to us. I'd wanted to believe that if I tried really hard I could somehow make things right. Make my family all right. Now though, I saw there wasn't much I could do about anything except to hope and pray.

After lighting candles at the end of Mass the family gathered outside the square-fronted church. Nonna Amelia shuffled out on her little bowed legs, supported by the arms of her two sons, the mantilla pulled softly back to lie on her shoulders. She wore little black mules on her feet and a black shawl, and rosary beads the colour of gunmetal hung from her waist. She had not put on mourning clothes for her son or her son-in-law. Mourning colours were her permanent state, her everyday clothes since the death of her husband, Papà Scattoli, eight years earlier. With her hunched shoulders it was hard for her to raise her head completely straight and she looked more at home in a chair than standing.

I'd always liked Nonna Amelia, even though I could barely understand a word she said. This was partly with it being in Italian, but also because she had no teeth. Her lips had shrunk into a web of deep wrinkles all pointing inwards round the little dot which was all you could see of her mouth, like water being sucked down a plughole. She was all there, Nonna Amelia, even though she didn't sound it, because the words came out all soggy, as if she had a mouthful of sawdust. Her eyes were sunken and brown like a little monkey's but glowing with life. There was a slight tremor to her neck which made it look as if she was nodding wisely at whatever was being said.

All of us went ceremonially to kiss her velvety cheeks and she nodded at me kindly and mumbled a greeting as I handed back her hanky, just as if I was one of the family. Her son Marco stayed with her while his wife and Paolo distracted the kids, Paolo throwing Luke high in the air so he gurgled, and tickling Giovanna and teasing her by untying the bow in her hair.

The rest of them gathered round Vera. Marco put his spare arm tightly round her and for a moment she said something to him in a low voice and leaned gratefully against him, closing her eyes. Her two sisters embraced her as well, their eyes full of concern, of fear.

There were similar groups along the pavement. The attendance at Mass was far higher than usual that evening. The priest came out and mingled among the crowd. He was Irish, not Italian. A priest would visit once a year or so from Italy and preach a sermon in Italian and this was always an occasion. But this priest was able to give them his sympathy none the less. A lot of the people there were still in their work clothes, the men in boots and caps, women in old everyday frocks, not like their Sunday best. I stood by Teresa as people milled back and forth, all talking in Italian. I didn't need to ask Teresa what they were talking about.

You could see the shock and worry that the sinking of the *Arandora Star* was causing in the Quarter. Some of the internees, especially the younger ones, had been released and sent home not long after they were arrested. Some families had heard from their relatives that they were safe in transit camps, but there were a few others in the same position as the Spinis, who had seen and heard nothing of their men since their last hurried visits in Steelhouse Lane police station, and they all knew that the very worst outcome, the news they most dreaded, was far from out of the question.

People kept coming to talk to Vera and Teresa, nodding to Nonna Amelia who had earned a lot of respect and liking in the district. She barely spoke, her eyes moving from face to face from the support of her son's arm, but her silence seemed to speak of their pain more than the words of those around her.

A young man came up to Teresa and put his arms round her shoulders for a minute. He looked older than us, had a head of black, curling hair. Immediately the two of them were off, gassing away, and I watched, puzzled. Teresa seemed to know him well, was at ease with him. There was none of the dizziness I'd seen in her over Jack and Clem. She talked to him as she would have done Stevie or Tony. He did a lot of the talking, seemed worried.

Teresa interrupted him. 'Carlo – this is my friend Genie. I s'pect she's had enough of hearing all this Italian.'

'Sorry.' He smiled, held out his hand. Two blazing blue eyes looked into mine. He was so handsome, even dressed in his old work clothes. 'Nice to meet you, Genie.' He frowned at Teresa. 'I've heard of Genie, haven't I? How come we never met before?'

Teresa shrugged. 'She doesn't come to Mass. We've been pals for years. Her nan lives up the road from us. Hey, look—' She nudged Carlo and pointed.

Three men were standing together, one of them, the oldest of the three, talking loudly at the others, arms moving back and forth, touching the fingers of one hand against his forehead then beating the air.

'Fausto Pirelli's uncle,' Teresa explained. 'Sparks flying there all right. They think Fausto's being moved to Brixton. They send the real naughties there.'

'All this fuss about Fausto,' Carlo said scornfully, 'He knows nothing about politics. He's all hot air. Come to think of it.' He nodded his head towards the uncle. 'How did he slip through the net himself? If they took your dad?'

Teresa shrugged, eyes still on Fausto's aerated uncle. 'What's the matter with the stupid bugger?' she snapped suddenly. 'I'd rather know Dad and Stevie were in Brixton than—' She stopped, struggling to control herself. I squeezed her hand.

Carlo looked round at her and said softly, 'You all right, Teresa?'

She nodded hard. 'Have to be.'

239

Carlo suddenly pulled her close to him, his arm round her shoulder.

The air was cooling, the street full of shadow now. People were starting to drift hungrily home. There were cooking smells in the air from houses near by.

'*Ciao*, Carlo,' Teresa said, pulling away rather carelessly from him.

'*Ciao*.' He raised his hand, watching her. Suddenly it was as clear as day to me. Any idiot could have seen from the smile he gave her what he felt for her except, quite obviously, Teresa herself.

I don't remember you talking about him before,' I said as we began the walk back with the family.

'Carlo? I've known him years. I must've mentioned him, haven't I? The family are always there at Mass. He works in the terrazzo trade with his dad – laying floors and that. We used to do Italian classes at the church as well. I s'pose he was just part of the furniture.'

'He looks absolutely gorgeous,' I said, trying to raise a laugh in her.

'I s'pose he is.' Teresa sounded offhand, her mind elsewhere. 'Says he wants to join up but he's not sure how they'll treat him in the British army.'

Giovanna was chatting away on the other side of her, getting no reply. 'Uncle Marco says I can go to the park on Sunday with Adelina and Maria.' She gave a little skip. 'Just girls. Just me. Not Tony or Luke!'

I tried to answer Giovanna's babble since Teresa so obviously wasn't paying any attention. When we got to Gooch Street the shops had long closed, the blinds wound in, and the air was full of the smell from the brewery.

'I've been so stupid,' Teresa suddenly burst out, making me jump. Her face was fierce. 'All that matters is my family. I'm going to do everything, *everything* I can for them.'

'D'you know I've always envied you your family?'

'Have you?'

She'd never seen it up till now. They'd always just been there too, like air.

The days passed still bringing no news for any of us, not of my father, nor Micky Spini. Since there was no choice in the matter we kept on doing what we had to do, day in, day out.

Very early one morning when I was barely out of bed and Mom certainly wasn't, there was a great banging on the front door. Still in my nightdress I snatched up the crocheted blanket from a chair and flung it round me as I sped into the hall. Dad! was my first illogical thought.

Gladys was talking before I'd got the door properly open.

'You'd better get yourselves ready for a shock!' she informed the street at the top of her voice.

I was confronted by her and Molly, both already dressed in enormous frocks, baggy as potato sacks and covered with splodges of coloured flowers. Gladys was holding Molly tightly by the arm as if she might be of a mind to take off.

'Come in,' I said as they steamed past me though the hall, Gladys flicking the blackout curtain by the door out of the way as if it'd personally insulted her. She was off again before I'd got the door shut.

'Right goings on.' She dragged poor Molly along with her. 'And then what do I find?'

'Sit down,' I said. 'I'll get Mom.'

'You'd better do that,' Gladys called after me sanctimoniously.

Mom was no longer sick nowadays, but she still found it devilishly hard to shift herself out of bed of a morning and I had trouble rousing her. She rolled over and looked blearily at me. 'Gladys Bender? What the heck does she want this time of day?'

'She says we're in for a shock.'

Her face tightened immediately. Victor. News about Victor, and already she was half out of bed, twisted round too quickly and winced. Then she tutted, relaxed. What did Gladys Bender know about anything?

When we got down Gladys didn't even give her a chance to open her mouth. She propelled herself out of her chair and pointed at Molly, who was sitting hanging her head.

'It's not you should be coming down, it's that brother of yours!'

'Sssh,' Mom said tiredly, flapping a hand as if to shoo away the noise.

'This one 'ere's in the family way and your Len's the Jack Rabbit that got 'er that way. So what've you got to say about that then?' She just managed to fold her arms over her mountainous bosoms. In the light from the window I could see her specs were all smears.

We hadn't got anything at all to say. Not a thing for quite a few seconds.

'No,' Mom got out eventually, any wind she'd had in her own sails expelled completely. 'That can't be right. Molly, that's not true, is it?'

'Days it's been going on now. She's off her food, sick every morning. She's 'ad a go already today, isn't that right, Moll?' Gladys leaned over her, shouting.

Molly lifted her head and you could see from her face

242

she wasn't feeling any too well. Her normally pink cheeks were white and her hair was hanging lank and straight.

'But it can't be Lenny,' Mom stuttered, blushing heavily. 'Surely he hasn't been ...?' She was looking at me and the blood rose in my cheeks. 'Genie?'

I didn't say anything.

'Genie – you knew all about this, didn't you?'

'I never! I never knew Molly was expecting!'

'What's been going on?' Mom was shrieking at me.

'What d'you think's been going on?' Gladys retorted. 'My Molly's got a bun in the oven that's what—' She tapped Molly heavily on the shoulder. 'And it didn't get there by itself.'

'Well it's not my fault, I wasn't even here,' Mom said. 'How was I supposed to know what they've been up to? You should keep your daughter under control. I can't be watching Len every moment of the day. There's a war on – I've got a job to do!'

'Oh, and you don't think I 'ave?' Gladys was hands on hips, cheeks plum red.

It was turning into quite a shouting match and no one was taking any notice of poor old Molly, as if she was a sack of turnips they were haggling over, so I went and sat down by her. 'You all right, Molly? Feeling bad, are you?'

'I want Lenny,' she said tearfully. Poor old Molly, I'd never seen her miserable like that before, with everyone shouting about her head and not really knowing what was happening to her.

Just then, woken by the racket, Len appeared, shirt hanging out, hair standing on end, only half awake.

'Ah,' Gladys said accusingly. ''Ere 'e is.'

It all went quiet suddenly. Len stared round at us,

rubbed his eyes like a little kid, then looked at me as if I should explain everything. Then Mom was looking at me too. So it was up to me again was it, to take responsibility? I was damned if it was.

''E's got to know,' Gladys said, back in the arms-folded-over bosoms position. 'So you'd better get on with it.'

I stared hard at Mom. This isn't my job. Not this.

'Len ...' Horribly embarrassed, she took Len's arm and he turned his great head and frowned at her, struggling to get every word. 'You know you and Molly—'

'Molly!' Len pointed suddenly as if he'd only just seen she was there. 'Ullo Molly!'

'Len, listen. You and Molly like each other a lot, don't you?'

Len nodded very hard.

'Well, Molly's having your babby, Lenny. It is his, isn't it?' she hissed at Molly who stared back, then nodded.

Len still looked as if he'd got caught fast in a monkey puzzle tree and couldn't get out.

'Molly's got a babby in her tummy,' Mom spelt out slowly. 'And it was you that put it there, see?'

'And don't try saying it weren't,' Gladys threatened.

Len moved a few steps closer to Molly. 'You got a babby, Molly?'

Molly nodded again looking scared, poor child that she was. The two of them seemed stuck, Len standing there, Molly in the chair, not knowing what to do.

'Well, there's nothing for it,' Mom said. 'We're going to have to get this sorted out one way or another. I s'pose the next thing is to fix a wedding day.'

244

Molly gazed across at us as if she just couldn't believe what she'd heard.

'Wedding day, Molly? How would you and Len like to get married?'

The light dawned. Slowly, bit by tiny bit, Molly's mouth turned up into a whopping great banana of a smile.

The factory was abuzz with excitement. Doris was full of organizing a lunchtime show and trying to bludgeon as many as possible into a performance of a sort. It was amazing how much work they could get done while their minds were on other things.

'Come on, Agatha,' Doris wheedled. 'You've got a few rhymes up your sleeve. And Joan – you can do your trick with the bottle and string.'

'Oh not again!' Joan groaned. 'Everyone'll be sick to the back teeth of that.'

'No – you can't see that one too many times.' Doris was writing her down in a little notebook regardless.

'Don't know why you're bothering,' one woman said. 'More trouble than it's worth.'

'You old misery.' Doris's cackling laugh rang round the warehouse. 'Got to 'ave some fun from somewhere. What with tea going on the ration as well, there won't be any pleasures left at all soon!'

Her laughter moved closer to my ear. 'Right, Genie – put you down for a song, shall I?'

'I've got no voice!'

'Oh you 'ave, bab, I've 'eard you singing round the place – when you 'ad more to be cheerful about any rate. Sweet little voice you've got. From your nan I expect. It is 'er I've heard up the Eagle, isn't it? And your auntie – oi–' She held on to my arm and called out to the others for agreement. "Ow about Genie gets 'er nan and 'er auntie and your mom is it? – over 'ere? The Andrews Sisters of Balsall 'Eath!' She laughed again. 'That'd liven us all up.'

'They couldn't – they're all at work,' I said, not sure they'd agree even if they hadn't been.

'I could sing with 'er,' Nancy butted in, jealous of the attention I was getting.

'Sorry, Nance,' Joan said. 'Not meaning to be rude or nothing but you've got a voice on you like a pair of clapped out bellows. I should stick to the day job if I was you.'

Nancy scowled viciously.

'Eh – I tell you what, girls,' Doris said, clasping my arm even harder. 'Let's make a real go of it and 'ave it of an evening. Get Genie's nan along with 'er squeeze box, 'ave a bit of a drink and that – what d'you reckon?'

There were cheers and a few scattered handclaps.

'Go on – we could do with a bit of a laugh.'

'It'd get me away from the old man for a night any rate!'

'You could bring 'im along.'

'Not on your life I won't!'

'But there's no room for a proper concert here,' someone pointed out.

Someone suggested the yard at the back and they were chewing over how it could be cleaned up when Doris cut in with, 'I know – the roof!'

Broadbent's had a flat roof with a parapet running round it.

'But we'll never get a piano up there – it's four floors!'

'Oh yes we will,' Doris said comfortably. 'Course we will.'

There was a hubbub as everyone started making plans and picking the day, which was quickly chosen as the Friday, giving us two days. Doris with her little notebook, was jotting down names before they could even volunteer.

While this was all going on, out of the corner of my eye I saw someone come in through the door from the factory at the front and stand quietly waiting, watching what was going on with a smile on his lips. I half guessed immediately who he was, and it was only seconds before his presence was noticed by the others, and Nancy in particular, who let out a shrill, excited screech, 'Look,' She pointed. ''E's back!'

Instant excitement to top up what was already there. Joe Broadbent was surrounded by a bunch of chattering women, the older, more motherly ones kissing him, and more forward ones making smart-alec comments and others just standing round chatting and giggling, demanding why he wasn't in his uniform. A few of us carried on with our work, listening to the others.

Nancy, of all of them, was by far the most forward. God Almighty, I'd never seen anyone behave like quite such a tit. Blushing, leering, simpering, she hung round him as he tried to make his way into the factory. It was sick-making. She was throwing questions at him like confetti and tagging his name on to each of them in such a syrupy way that I saw some of the other women grimacing.

'How've you been, Joe? How's it feel to be a pilot, Joe? Have you flown lots of planes? Have you got your wings yet, Joe?'

On and on until someone else said, 'Oh leave off, Nancy – you're enough to give anyone a headache.'

I'd heard more than a bit about the famous Joe while I was at Broadbent's and I was curious too, thinking he probably wasn't all he was cracked up to be, because they hardly ever are, are they? Tucked away in the background I had a chance of a good look at him.

He was tall, a head at least above most of the women, and the first thing I noticed was the way he had of tilting his head forward when he spoke to them, fixing everyone's face with his eyes, their questions holding his attention. Even Nancy's, for a while anyway. He didn't talk down to them as if they weren't worth the trouble, just like his dad didn't, and his manner was easy, standing with his hands in the pockets of his brown, worn-looking jacket. He had fair hair, half way between blond and brown, cut very short of course, forces standard, which looked a bit strange on anyone in civvies. His long, thin face was pale, tired I thought. But smiling out of it were dark brown eyes, the liveliest and kindest I'd ever seen.

I was affected by Joe immediately. He was a clever person, I knew. He'd been to grammar school and before the war had been due to go on to technical college, even university. This was an awesome thought for all of us because opportunities like that were way off the edge of our horizon. He seemed so grown up at nineteen, so admirable, yet for all that, so far as I could see, so very approachable. I'd never come across anyone like him before.

Nancy was proving difficult for him to shake off as he did his round of the warehouse, stopping to have a word with everyone on the way. He seemed to remember everyone's name, their family, their circumstances.

It really was a family firm and some of those women had been there years. Broadbent's was known as a good employer – fair, kind and reasonable.

'Nancy – get back and get on with your work,' Doris ordered her eventually. They were all browned off with her by now. Nancy pulled herself away with enormous effort as if she was strung to Joe by a piece of elastic and went pouting back to her place. With great ostentation she took the snood from her hair, which she proceeded to shake out, a long auburn mass of it, wavy down her back. She pulled her fingers through it, looking to see if Joe was watching her, and once she'd seen his glance turn her way she began coiling it briskly round her hand and put the covering back on it, patting it to make sure little wisps of her fringe were peeping out at the front.

'Quite finished, 'ave you?' Agatha said, sarky.

'Now here's someone I don't know,' I heard Joe say. 'Who's this then, Doris?'

My heart was beating so fast when he came up to me.

'This is Genie, the new checker,' Doris told him. 'Been here a few weeks. She's a good'un she is – Genie, Joe Broadbent. He's home on a week's leave, from the RAF,' she explained carefully, as if I was deaf and hadn't heard anything that had gone before.

'Nice to meet you, Genie.' I realized suddenly that he was holding out his hand to me. I wiped my left hand on my overall and held it out and then of course remembered it was the wrong one and had to start all over again. I felt such a scruffy little mouse in my overall and snood with draggly bits of hair falling out of it and my dirty hands, but I managed to look up at him. The smile that met me in his eyes gave me a feeling I'd never forget. Something that dug so deep in me I didn't understand what had happened except I felt dizzy suddenly and new. Those dark eyes, striking against the light hair, held an expression that was so open, so sympathetic. After a few seconds I was able to smile back with all the warmth I felt.

'How d'you do, Joe,' I said, taking his hand. My heart was going so, I thought it must be showing, rattling my body.

'You getting on all right here, are you?'

'Very nice, thanks. It's by far the best place I've ever worked.'

My hand was still in his and slowly he released me. I noticed the rubbed look of his jacket. It was old, a favourite probably.

'Course, a lot of things have changed here since the war. They'll have told you that?' He glanced round at the others. Nancy was watching us, hard.

'Oh yes,' I said eagerly. 'You used to take maps.' Flustered, I lowered my eyes. 'I mean make taps.'

When I looked up he let out a loud laugh which after a moment I joined in.

'You're not scared of me, are you? Good heavens, there's no need to be.' With the laugh still in his eyes he leaned forward, resting his hands on the table. 'If it's so good here, tell me where else you've worked then.'

'You got half the afternoon to spare, have you? The worst place I ever worked was a meat factory ...' I found myself babbling on, telling him about the pork pies and the bloke's nose and the woman whose finger got grated in with it too. And I told him about the taxi firm and the pawn shop and a couple of the others, although I kept some of the list back so's he didn't think I was a complete waster.

He laughed a lot at what I was saying which gave me

courage and I relaxed and was able to talk more like my normal self.

'Why so many?' he asked.

'I get bored easily. Not here though,' I added quickly. 'I like it here.'

Still chuckling, he said, 'Seems I've led a very sheltered existence! You've managed to put me off pork pies for the rest of my life any rate.'

'I never said what they did to the sausage—'

'No, please!' He held up one hand to stop me. 'I'm surprised you lasted as long as a week there. Half an hour and I'd've been hanging up my overall I should think.'

After a bit more chatter Joe said, 'Well I'd better let you get on, or Doris'll never let me hear the end of it.'

He hesitated. 'See you around, Genie.'

When I looked across at the clock I saw with disbelief that we'd been talking for twenty minutes. It felt more like two.

He stayed a bit longer, exchanging pleasantries with a few people. I could tell he was pleased to be back. Two or three times I felt his gaze on me, and I couldn't stop myself watching him, following him with my eyes. I knew exactly where he was all the time he was in there. I watched the way he walked, his long straight back, his gestures, the way he moved his head.

As he left, going out again through the factory, letting in the clunking noises of the machines, his eyes found me again. Feeling the blush rise in my cheeks, I thought, it had to be a coincidence: he couldn't really have been seeking me out.

But as soon as the door shut, Agatha said, 'Ooh Genie!' Whatever else she might've said was interrupted

251

by Nancy who was round to my position in seconds and grabbing me by the throat.

'Just you keep off 'im!' Her face was all screwed up. ''E's mine,' she hissed, silly little cow that she was. 'Mine, OK?'

I seized her hand and jerked it away from my throat which was sore where she'd clawed at me. 'What'd you do then, eh? Buy 'im at the Co-op?'

'Get back to your place, Nance,' Agatha ordered her. 'And keep your catty mitts off Genie. What the 'ell d'you think you're playing at?'

For the rest of the afternoon Nancy gave me looks of such poisonous hatred along the table that I began to wonder if she was a bit barmy. But it didn't touch me. Nancy Hogan could go take a running jump.

'Will he be coming to the show on Friday?' I asked Doris.

She grinned at me. 'Who would that be, Genie?' She relented quickly. 'As he's home I'd be very surprised if he doesn't.'

'I'm working Friday,' Mom said when she got home that night, unsteady with exhaustion.

'Can't you swap?' I called through from the kitchen. 'Everyone else's going.'

Nanny Rawson never took much persuasion to play and sing. It was her one escape from the house, the endless work. And Lil said she'd come and bring the kids.

Mom sat in an armchair, leaning down, rubbing her ankles. 'No, don't think so,' she said listlessly.

I heard her get up and pour herself a drink. Suddenly I was full of angry determination. I wanted this so badly, wanted us all singing there together on Friday, and I wanted Joe Broadbent to see us. Without Mom's high-reaching voice which complemented Lil's deeper one, it wouldn't be the same.

Standing by the kitchen door I watched her sit down with a glass half full of gin.

'You managed to sort your shifts out all right when it suited you to see Bob.'

She hesitated, looking round at me, the glass to her lips.

I held her gaze, stared back. 'Do this for me, Mom. Just for once, do something for me.'

She took two gulps, shuddering slightly at the strength of it. At last she said, 'Oh well – all right then.'

I'd never been on the roof at Broadbent's before, but anyone could see it'd been transformed. A group of volunteers had stayed on after work the night before to make the place ready, and considering the drabness of a smoke-stained factory roof, they'd performed a miracle. It was surrounded on three sides by a brick parapet, and the fourth abutted a tall, thin building, higher than Broadbent's, occupied by Cobham's, a firm of tool-makers. So there was a blank wall facing us, only broken by a couple of filthy air vents. Across that they'd fixed old sheets made into a banner, painted in red and blue letters on the white, which read 'Showtime at Broadbent's – 1940'.

There were already a good number gathering up there. I looked round with our nan, Lil and Mom (no Len – the pull of Molly was even stronger than that of a sing-song) and the kids, who thought being right up there was the best thing ever. I lifted Cathleen up and we looked across at the roofs of factories and houses, some below so we could see all their loose tiles, others on the same sort of level. You could see the spire at St Martin's in the Bull Ring, and Cathleen pointed at the shining barrage balloons which seemed so much nearer from up here.

'Don't think I've ever been this high up before,' Nan said, still breathless from all the stairs.

Mom looked over the edge, dreamily. She was wearing a loose dress, sensitive about being seen to be pregnant, and she'd evidently decided to join in tonight, to play along.

They'd swept the tarred roof, which still felt spongy underfoot from the warm day, carried up trestle tables and what chairs and stools could be begged or borrowed, and arranged them in rows facing the wall and banner. Wonder of wonders, to one side, stood a piano.

'We borrowed some muscles,' Doris said, coming up to us. She said how excited she was to meet the family, Nan especially. 'This is my 'usband, Ray.' She indicated a massive bloke next to her, built like an all-in wrestler with the broken nose to match. In fact he was a boxer in his spare time. I had a strong feeling I'd seen him somewhere before. 'Knew 'e'd come in 'andy some time,' Doris laughed, and I could see our nan warming to her.

Doris admired Lil's kids, picked up Cathleen and cuddled her as everyone did, with her pretty looks.

'She'll be another like Genie,' she said. 'Bet she gets away with murder with them big eyes.' Cathleen stole the show at this point by putting her arms round Doris's neck and squeezing her face against hers.

'When're we on then?' Nan asked. She'd put her squeeze box down at the side of the piano.

'You'll be called,' Doris said. 'Ray 'ere's our master of ceremonies for the evening. 'Ere Ray – get Mrs Rawson and 'er family a drink, will you?'

There were a couple of barrels of beer, courtesy of Mr Broadbent, and a whole assortment of cups and glasses on the table. We'd brought a few ourselves, as well as sandwiches to add to the collection.

'Tizer for you kids?' Ray said. As he was opening the bottle with a 'swoosh' noise, I couldn't help myself keep looking round at the stairs, every time there was the movement of someone arriving. I knew that until the Broadbents were here the place wouldn't feel complete.

Nancy came up with another girl who I thought looked like her sister. She was wearing a black dress with huge pink roses on and dashes of white in it, with a nipped waist. I saw Nan stare at her. 'Is that that Nancy you were on about? Looks a bit of a hussy to me. And that's a lower neckline than's good for 'er – she could catch a cold down there.'

Some people had already sat down on the chairs and boxes and a few other kids had arrived, so Tom and Patsy were chasing round with them and Lil just let them get on with it. She'd gone over to the piano where Tony, one of the lads from the main factory, was tuning up on it, improvising, feeling his way into songs. He was good, had the touch, and Lil leaned with one arm against the top of the upright humming bits she recognized, winking down at him. He was such a young feller I could see he was dazzled by her, this gorgeous woman with red lips, raven hair and sequins on her dress. He stopped for a minute and they talked, then tried out the openings of some songs together. Not to be outdone, Mom went over with her tumbler of ale and joined in. I was proud of them both.

Please Mom, I thought, don't drink too much tonight. Just don't let me down.

I stood beside Nan, who'd taken a seat to rest her knee. A cheer went up as a trail of coloured bulbs which'd been strung across the top of the banner lit up, bright as boiled sweets although it was still golden daylight.

'This is one show'll have to be over by blackout time!' Ray announced.

'Let's get on with it then!' another voice shouted. 'What's all the hanging about for?'

More claps and cheers. The place was filling up and they were getting impatient. We all wanted to break the hard lines of ordinary days. We wanted to laugh, to sing and forget.

Mom and Lil came over, gathering up the kids, and stood by me and Nan, leaving the seats for other people. As the piano struck up again Nan turned to me. 'You look very nice tonight, Genie.'

I had to bend my head to hear her and smile. 'Ta Nan.' I had on the polka dot dress Mom'd put together, with its little scarf and I'd curled the ends of my hair and pinned it so it hung nicely round my ears.

Ray, Doris's husband, looked more the type to be handy with his fists than his wit but he stepped forward to do his bit as Master of Ceremonies and erupted into a patter that took us all by surprise and soon had everyone laughing and cheering.

Nan leaned over to me. 'I knew I knew that feller's face. Used to work the Bull Ring, selling crocks or summat. Haven't seen him in a while.'

When she said, I remembered him too. 'He's on munitions now.'

'And our first number tonight,' he was shouting in

his gravelly voice, trying to beat the catcalls and whistles. 'I tell yer, if yer don't settle down you lot, there won't be time for any bleeding show!'

More cheers and raucous laughter but the message seemed to have sunk in. Gradually they got settled down. But when I looked round I saw Mr Broadbent arrive at the top of the stairs, a woman behind him I'd never seen before, blonde, with sharp, rather haughty features.

'That them?' Mom whispered to me.

I nodded. 'She must be one of the daughters.'

Behind me I heard a voice say, 'I s'pect Mrs B's got the other sister at her beck and call at home.'

In the front row people were standing and shuffling along as Ray commanded, 'Make room now, ladies and gents, make room there.'

As they moved to the front I saw the one thing that I needed to see before whipping my head round to the front so it wouldn't be obvious I was staring. Joe was following behind them. He was here. My heart answered, speeding up.

Mr Broadbent senior and the daughter accepted seats in the front row, she looking like a chilly-eyed cat and Mr B with smiles to each side.

'Another space here!' someone called in a voice that sounded decidedly like Nancy's.

'That's all right,' Joe's voice came from close behind me. 'I'm happy to stand, thanks.'

My skin was up in goosepimples, knowing how close he was to me. As Tony struck up on the piano again I found courage and turned round.

'Hello again, Genie. OK if I stand here?'

'Course. Can you see over my head?'

He gave a laugh. 'With plenty to spare.'

257

The first person on stage was one of the main factory workers called Dick. 'This is Dick Busby,' he kicked off, 'talking to you from a munitions factory somewhere in the Midlands,' which earned him a clap before he'd even got started on his string of corny jokes, trying to sound like Arthur Askey. He told them pretty well in fact and bowed himself off.

Then it was Joan's turn. She was plump, middle aged, apple cheeked, and waddled forward with a length of white string, an empty milk bottle and a deadpan face, and proceeded to perform a series of antics. After a few minutes of this there wasn't a person in the audience who wasn't laughing until they ached and not one of us could have explained why. I could hear Joe behind me and after a few more manoeuvres from Joan we were all helpless with it. Eventually she gave a sniff as if we were all completely beyond her in our stupidity, wound up the string, picked up the bottle and marched off to the loudest possible applause.

'By special request from our pianist here, we're now going to 'ave a song. I'd like to call upon Mrs Lilian Heaney!'

Lil went up to the front wearing a blush that only made her look more ravishing than ever. The silky green dress she wore hugged her lithe figure, its sequins winking in the sunlight. She'd pinned a dark crimson rose behind her left ear and stood swaying to the rhythm of the piano. She sang a couple of Cole Porter numbers. After the first one, into which she poured all the longing of her own sad heart, because that was the gift she had, I felt Joe's breath on my ear.

'She's a real find, isn't she? Who is it?'

As I was turning to answer he moved forwards into Lil's place.

'That's my auntie Lil.'

'Your aunt?' He looked at me, then back at her. 'She's got real talent.'

I smiled, pleased for Lil as her rich voice poured out over the Birmingham rooftops and her fairytale face to go with it cast spells in people's mind. The clapping was at least as loud as for Joan with her bottle and string. Joe moved respectfully out of the way when she came back to us. I saw Mom whisper something to Lil.

There were more jokes, some told to laughs, others to groans, while helpings of ale were passed round and we polished off the last of the sandwiches. Poems, some politer than others. The pianist played dance music on his own. Nancy got up, eyes fixed on Joe, to do a gypsy dance which went off a bit half cock but could've been worse. Just about. She gave me a filthy scowl as she flounced back to her seat to not exactly rapturous applause.

'We 'ave some guest performers here tonight. We can't give you the Andrews Sisters from Hollywood but we do 'ave our very own Andrews Sisters of Balsall Heath! Let's hear it for Doreen, Lil and Genie and their accompanist, the much esteemed Edith Rawson!' He put his hands together and led the applause and we went to the front, Nan carrying her stool. She settled herself on it with the accordion, arms through the straps.

Lil, Mom and I arranged ourselves round behind her and Lil did the introductions.

'We've got a number of songs for you tonight—' This was interrupted by clapping. They were all getting pretty merry out there, and this was a special night. They were going to milk every second of enjoyment out of it before the dreary return to the factory.

We started off with sing-along numbers like 'Knees

up Mother Brown' and 'The Lambeth Walk' and everyone joined in at the top of their voices, stamping and
clapping. We spun 'The Lambeth Walk' on faster and
faster until we were all falling over ourselves with the
words and laughing and Nanny Rawson's fingers were
a blur on the keys of the squeeze box, her right foot
madly tapping the rhythm. It was going fine. The whole
evening had gone well and I knew I had wings, lifting
me specially, because Joe Broadbent had stood behind
me all the way through. He'd sought me out. I saw him
watching the four of us, all so colourful – Mom in red,
Lil sea green, me blue and Nan also in a royal blue dress,
all so different but with our voices blending. I saw Joe
was smiling, singing along with everyone else. Please
God, I thought, don't let anything go wrong tonight . . .
just this once.

After the rapturous end of the song Lil held up her
hand to quieten them. 'Right, you've had your fun. Now
it's time to settle down for summat more serious.' There
was a good-natured groan from out front. 'We're going
to turn the tempo down now and turn our thoughts to
– ' she drew the word out to raise a laugh, 'lu-u-urve.'

'Oooh!' everyone responded.

Nan struck up and Lil sang the verse of 'The Very
Thought of You', her voice rising to bring the rest of us
in for the chorus, and then our voices chimed in,
harmonizing, Mom quite in control tonight, her voice
high and lovely.

I'd barely ever sung with them in public before,
although at home we sang together in the normal course
of things. We hadn't practised, there was no time for
any of that, but I found I could move easily in time to
the music and the songs were so familiar it came as
naturally as singing in a bath tub.

When that was finished Lil stepped forward again. 'And now, since she's our excuse for being here at all, we're going to hear from the little'un.'

With a huge jolt I realized it was me she was on about.

'She don't usually sing with us, this one. Says she hasn't got a voice.' There was a pleased laugh from in front of us, although the only face I fixed on at that point was Nancy's and hers was full of spite.

'We think it's about time she joined the troupe. So, judge for yourselves, ladies and gentlemen. We'll help her along from the back of course, but now I give you my lovely niece – we're all very proud of her – Eugenie Watkins. Step forward, Genie!'

Heck, I hadn't been expecting this! But I couldn't exactly let them down now, could I? Even Mom was smiling. I moved nearer the front of the stage, my suddenly damp hands smoothing the front of my dress, but I hoped, looking more composed than I felt.

'Let's hear yer, Genie!' someone shouted.

I gave a little bow and turned to Lil with a grin. 'I'll get you for this afterwards.' Everyone laughed. More quietly I gave her a choice of song.

It went almost silent then, and into the quiet Nan struck up on the accordion. The sun was setting, had sunk behind the factory walls and the air was smoky. The faces in front of me had fallen into shadow.

I sang an old song, a beautiful song, 'I'll Be with You in Apple Blossom Time', and when I'd gone through a few of the lines I heard Nan, Mom and Lil join in with me and felt them hold me up, give strength to my voice, which was tuneful enough, but weaker and smaller than theirs. I've no idea how I sang, how it sounded, but I know I tried to do it the way Lil did, pouring everything

261

I could into it. That song promised things would turn out happily in a time of flowers and it was something all of us ached for. Things had to get better. And while I stood out there I thought my family should spend all their time singing because the songs went through and out the far side of everything else and let everyone be happy together.

I sang the final notes of the song and bent over in a bow. When I stood up I caught Joe's gaze fixed on me. His eyes were full of a quiet seriousness, but when he saw me looking he smiled back at me and raised his hands to show how hard he was clapping.

'Wasn't she lovely?' Lil quizzed the audience, and they roared back. 'Shouldn't she sing with us all the time, eh?' Another outburst of agreement. My cheeks were on fire. So was my heart, to tell the truth. 'For anyone who doesn't already know it, Genie's a great kid. And I'm going to give her the choice of our last song tonight.'

'Make it something jolly!' someone shouted. They wanted something to jump around to. OK, we'd let them have it. 'What about "Run Rabbit"?'

And so it was, and we went back to our places still singing. I felt proud to bursting. Joe's obviously admiring expression had given me a rare pride in who I was and my family. We may have been a complete mess in every other way but this was something we could do. It was us at our finest and I'd been included too. As I moved to my place I saw Joe's sister, Marjorie, lean towards her father and make some comment. Joe was still clapping.

'That was so good,' he said as I reached my place. This time it was he who seemed more shy of me.

Mom touched my shoulder as she passed me and found me a smile. 'That was lovely, Genie.'

'Have you really never sung like that before?' Joe asked, lips close to my ear.

'Only at home. I leave the performing to the others usually.'

'It was tremendous – listen, you can hear everyone loved it!' Only now were they winding down the clapping.

Joe made sure he stayed next to me this time and Mom and Lil squeezed in closer to the wall. The sun was going down fast now and very soon the coloured bulbs glowing there against the brickwork would have to be switched off.

After a couple more numbers, both saying we were a hard act to follow, Tony played 'God Save The King' and everyone stood and blasted it out, loud as they could.

'Come on you lot,' Ray shouted. 'Once more – and make it so that bleeder Adolf can 'ear it this time!'

When it was over everyone was suddenly milling about picking up chairs and clearing the trestle tables or trying to get to the stairs. A few were detailed to stay on and finish off after the rest had gone. The light was dying and there was a rush to get it finished, make the place dark.

Mr Broadbent and his daughter came up to us as we were shuffling towards the stairs.

'That was a real treat,' Mr B said kindly. He was a smaller man than his son, with his hair now steely grey but the same very dark brown eyes. His face always looked lined and tired. 'I'm glad you could all come. I didn't know we had such a budding little talent in the warehouse.'

'It were a pleasure,' Nanny Rawson said.

Even the sister smiled. She didn't seem all that bad up close. Probably just shy. 'It was really nice,' she managed to say.

And then they were gone, carried along in the tide moving into the stairwell, and Joe turned to say a quick goodbye which felt snatched and unfinished. Fittingly, as they vanished, the necklace of coloured lights went off, leaving us with only a shred of moon to see by.

At the top of the stairs I felt someone push up next to me and grab my arm, pinching it. 'Proper little bitch of a show off, aren't you, Genie Watkins?' Nancy dug her nails into my wrist. 'You've spoilt everything, you 'ave. I 'ate you.'

'Get off!' I yanked my arm away. 'You're hurting me, you barmy cow you. Why don't you just get home and hang up that chest of yours, Nance, before it falls out the front of your dress?'

'What was all that about?' Lil asked when I'd shaken Nancy off.

'Nothing,' I said. 'Nothing that matters anyhow.'

People didn't hang about outside. We all had homes to get to and work to do and the street was dark and deserted now except for us.

'We'll come down your way,' Mom was saying to Nan. 'It's not the quickest, but we might as well all stick together.'

'Coming for a cuppa?'

'Nah – best get back to Len,' Mom said. I guessed it wasn't tea she was interested in either.

We'd only got to the end of the road when we heard footsteps running up behind us.

'Someone's in a rush,' Nan said. We all pressed into the side.

The running slowed.

'Hello? Is that the Watkins family?' His voice. 'I wanted a quick word with Genie.'

We wouldn't be a minute, I told the others. I persuaded them I'd catch them up, and we were left alone. I could barely see his face in the moon's tiny threads of light.

'I couldn't go just like that. I told them I'd left something—' I could hear his quick breathing. He was nervous. 'Would you think of coming out with me, Genie? Say tomorrow night?'

Mom was sitting there staring at nothing, miles away.

'How do I look? Mom?'

'Very nice.' Sounded as if it was all too much effort for her to speak.

'The dress is smashing. Thanks again for making it.' It was the blue and white one again. I had nothing newer.

No answer.

'Look, Mom—' I went and squatted by her chair. 'I'm sorry to go out and leave you tonight, but Lenny'll be home soon. And you have said you could do with a quiet rest.' Umpteen times in fact.

She nodded but I could tell there were tears not far away. We'd already been through how it wasn't all bad, what good form she'd been in at the show.

'But I'm cut off from everyone – everything,' she moaned. 'I feel as if I'm locked in a cage . . .'

Now she was getting worked up. 'It's all right for you,' she said, jerking her head from side to side against the back of the chair in frustration. 'It's all bloody right for you, isn't it? Even that fathead Len has someone . . .'

I stood up, backing away from her. 'I've got to go. I'll be late. I promised . . .'

'He won't want you!' she shrieked after me. 'What would he want you for? He'll think he's too good for you, you wait and see!'

I started off along the Moseley Road before realizing I'd forgotten the little scarf that went with my dress, and by the time I'd torn back to get it I was in a proper lather. Joe and I had arranged to meet in Moseley Village, about midway between where we each lived, and I ended up running half the distance as I was so afraid of being late.

That mile and a half or so was torture for me. I was already in a state of nerves and Mom's kind sentiments ringing after me pulled me right down. At the concert everything had felt right and full of promise. Joe's smile, his eyes so obviously finding me, those short hours of forgetting all the grief happening to us. A dream world. Now all I could think of were bad things. Mistakes and hurts like Walt and Jimmy. The way they'd taken my hope and need and crushed them without a thought. Maybe I was all wrong again, clutching the end of a rainbow which would melt in my hand? There were all these differences between us: Joe was a grammar-school boy, older, his mom and dad had a nice house in Hall Green, and I was just a very junior pair of hands in his dad's factory.

But I had enough hope left to keep my feet, in their white buttoned shoes, trotting up the hill into Moseley, panting.

I'll know this time, I thought. When I see him again I'll be able to tell whether I've got this all wrong.

After all my running and fussing I got there early. It wasn't yet six. But when I turned up towards the gates of the church I saw Joe was already waiting for me. He'd come. That at least. He had his hands in his jacket pocket and was leaning against the wall, but when he saw me coming he straightened up and freed his hands quickly in a way that made me see he was just as nervous as I was and it gave me courage.

He smiled. 'Began to think you weren't coming.'

'But I'm early,' I protested, pointing up at the hands of the clock. 'Look, it's only five to!'

'I suppose I just hoped you wouldn't stand me up.'

'Not if I said I'd come.'

'You sound out of breath.'

I joked. 'Didn't dare be late, did I?'

We were at a loss then and stood looking at each other, and it seemed Joe's eyes penetrated deeper than the surface of my face. It was like someone stroking me, trying to know me. The feel of someone looking at me like that suddenly made me want to cry.

So's not to, I grinned at him and said, 'So – we going to stand 'ere all night then or what?'

Joe looked at me steadily. 'We could go to the pictures if you like. Or as it's a nice night, how about a walk?'

'Oh yes, a walk.' After all, what was the point in sitting staring at a silver screen? That was for escape from life, and now we had life spread in front of us to move about in.

'There's a private park.' Joe pointed across the Moseley Road. 'My mom knows someone down there'd lend us a key.'

'Is there? I never knew.'

We borrowed a key from a thin, weary-looking

woman called Mrs Munro who lived at one of the grand houses in Chantry Road, promising to drop it in on the way back, and she let us walk through a well-organized looking garden. At the bottom was a little wooden gate, and then the sloping edge of the park.

'Isn't it lovely?' I said as we walked down together under the trees. 'Fancy this being here all the time and me not knowing.'

'It's certainly tucked away,' Joe agreed. 'Seems a shame it's private really, but then that's why it's so quiet. It's not all that big though. We could go on somewhere else if you like.'

In the dip at the bottom was a little lake. There were trails of white, cottony seeds on the grass and birds chattered loudly in the trees around us.

'Loud, aren't they?' I laughed. 'Sound like my nan's neighbours gossiping.'

'Jackdaws I expect.'

'They the ones that pinch things?'

Joe laughed. 'They're the ones.'

At the bottom a path ran round the water and in the middle of it was a tree, its roots forming a tiny island. Water birds bobbed and skimmed around it.

'Those are ducks,' I pointed. That was about the limit of my knowledge. 'What about them then?'

'Moorhens.' Joe squatted down near the edge, watching another group of nervous brown birds. 'Nice little things them. Always look a bit worried. Specially when they're out of the water walking about.' He watched them for a few moments, smiling, then straightened up. 'Shall we go round?'

The path followed the curves of the lake, shady with trees on one side, more open the other. At the top of the hill you could see the enormous, elegant houses, with their balconies and fancy woodwork and ornate trees growing around them. I wondered what they did with all the space they had in there.

Joe started asking me about myself, my family.

'I still can't believe that was the first time you'd sung with them. You looked such a natural. And what a family!'

Yes, what a family, I thought.

'First time properly in front of an audience, but I've sung with them all my life. Lil dropped me in it as a matter of fact. But we sing at home all the time, or at least we did before . . .'

'Before what? The war?'

'Mainly.' I didn't want to tell him too much. The less the better for now.

Joe was silent for a moment. 'Doris told me – I hope you don't mind, Genie – that your father's missing.'

'Yep. Missing. Maybe. Or dead.'

'Sorry. I shouldn't have asked.'

'No, it's OK. Not a secret, is it? We don't know, that's all, one way or another. Be easier if we did 'cause then at least we could adjust to it. We're not the only ones though.' I told him about the *Arandora Star* and the Spinis.

'God, how appalling! Yes, I remember hearing about that. But they still don't know where they are?'

'No. It's killing Mrs Spini, Teresa's mom. Very family minded they are. She can't sleep. Teresa's the one holding them all together.'

'What about you?'

I wasn't sure what he meant by this, what he'd seen in Mom. He was sharp, Joe was, even though Mom'd put on a pretty good act that night.

'Someone's got to be in the house,' I said stiffly.

'Mom's got her problems.' I told him about Lenny, risked telling about Molly, and his reaction wasn't shocked like I feared. 'And I've got a brother, Eric – he went with the evacuation. But he's eight years younger anyway so he's a bit young to take on much even if he was here.'

'That's not so young. That'd make him what? Ten?'

'No, he's only eight.'

'But that means – you can't be only sixteen! I thought you were nearly my age, specially with all those jobs you reeled off to me.'

'That was only some of 'em too!' But I was anxious now. 'Does it matter?'

'No, of course not. I'm just – crikey, that means you're younger than that dreadful Nancy!'

We both laughed then, easier together. 'In years anyway,' Joe added.

We talked a lot about our families that night, and never did move on anywhere else. We walked carefully, side by side, round and round that lake I don't know how many times and for all we noticed we could've been in the Bull Ring.

It seemed the factory's version of Joe's family was exaggerated to say the least. Joe sounded surprised when I asked about his mother's illness.

'She's not an invalid or anything. What gave you that idea? She just suffers from terrible headaches rather often. So the house has to be quiet and she just lies in the dark until it's over.'

He told me the younger of his two sisters, Louise, was still at school, and the older one, Marjorie, worked for a machine tools firm over in Witton, secretarial, and they thought, was on the verge of getting engaged.

'She's such a dark horse it's impossible to know what's going on with her.' Didn't sound as if they were close, but there was nothing in his voice to say she or her sister were the whinging vixens that Nancy and the others had made out.

'And you're set to take over the family firm?'

'Eventually. Dad's got a lot of go in him yet. But yes, I like it. Good enough way of earning a living. That's if things turn out.'

We both knew what things turning out meant. Joe went quiet and the silence stood out after we'd been talk, talk, talk all this time. I'd told him far more than I'd expected, stopping short only at Mom's pregnancy because it seemed too much to load on him, for him to have to accept. I was afraid of what he'd think. And, while it would seem disloyal to Mom as well, I also couldn't help thinking how like her it would be to come between us and spoil things. We talked so long it was almost dark, and the birds on the water were faint shadows, making plopping or quacking sounds somewhere to the side of us.

Joe put his hand on my arm for a second to stop me after these moments of quiet. 'Genie – look, I've only got a week at home. Less now in fact. I'll have to go on Wednesday night to be there for reveille Thursday morning.'

'What's revalley?'

'Oh – when they get us all up, reporting for duty. It's just I'd like so much – would you feel able to spend some more time with me? I don't want to seem pushy, but after this week I don't know when I'll be home again, or where I'm going next now I'm a flyer—'

I almost needed to laugh again, cover how much I

was feeling for him, because I wanted to say, 'I'd go anywhere with you, do anything,' and I was afraid. But I managed not to fall into joking.

'Course I'd like to.'

Joe nodded and I saw he was relieved. 'Would tomorrow be too soon?'

'It's my day off.'

'So have you got time, or . . .?'

'I can't think of a single other thing I'd rather do instead.' I still wasn't joking.

In what was left of the light I saw a smile spread across Joe's face. He had such a giving smile, with no falseness in it, and I knew I wanted to see it directed at me for the rest of my life.

'Good,' Joe said. 'Excellent. Neither can I.'

For once I put aside all that was happening at home. I was going out and that was that. This was more or less what I told Mom. They wouldn't starve, that was for sure, one way or another.

Joe suggested we hire bicycles. He'd given his away earlier in the war and I'd never had one, so we went to the Ladypool Road, and set off on two enormous pushbikes with saddles it would've been difficult to match for hardness and lack of comfort.

'I thought we could go along the canals,' Joe suggested as we set off. The canal system criss-crosses Birmingham and you could get on the paths and go for miles. Personally I didn't care whether we cycled round the Midland Red bus depot all day so long as it was with Joe.

The pushbikes turned out to be a disaster.

'Blimey,' Joe said after only about twenty yards, 'this

one's a boneshaker all right. Shan't have any teeth left by the time we get back.'

The chain soon came loose on mine and did it so regularly after that that I was soon spending more time off the bike than on it, and both our hands were black with grease.

'It would've been better just to walk, wouldn't it?' Joe said, exasperated as we had to stop and fix the chain on my tricky mount for the umpteenth time. He seemed flustered. 'I'm sorry, Genie – this isn't turning out to be much fun, is it?' He ran his hand through his hair in annoyance and left grease on its pale strands. 'It was a daft idea.'

I looked up at him from where I was bent over the bike, as I seemed to be able to fix the thing more easily than he could. 'What you on about? It doesn't matter, we'll get there. Bikes are always like this, aren't they?'

'Well, mine wasn't. Look, let's not let them ruin the day. Shall we take them back and walk instead? I wanted to see you, not deal with these blasted things all day long.'

So we walked the bikes back the scant mile we'd gone out of town to the bike shop, got cleaned up and went to join the canal in town. Joe gave a sigh of relief as we went and I realized he'd got himself more het up than I realized about the bikes, it not working. I suppose he wanted me to think well of him, and couldn't get it into his head that these sort of hitches were just normal life to me. The few days out I'd ever had with Mom, Dad and Eric had always been full of disasters great and small. These ranged from falling in rivers or cowpats to losing Eric or forgetting the food, and everyone moaning and being evilly bad-tempered because we all wanted to do different things and couldn't agree or afford to do any of them. This was nothing in comparison. And the company was the best.

Despite all the factories along the canal, stretches of it were very pretty, with grass and buttercups along the path, and bindweed, keck, mauve fireweed edging the railway tracks. Joe was much better on the names than me, liked to name flowers, birds, animals and seemed to know them all.

'I haven't done this for years and years,' I said, dimly remembering it from a time when the grass came almost up to my waist. 'There's never enough time for anything like this, that's our trouble.'

We walked along all morning, talking easily, pointing out the barges in all their bright colours, painted with roses and castles, jugs of flowers and birdcages, and the canal women in their bonnets.

'I wonder what it'd be like living on here,' Joe said. 'Seems very romantic but I'm not sure I'd like it for long.'

'Oh, I would. Nice little space, no one bothering you. I've always fancied living by a river, seeing trees every day and fields.'

'None too many fields round here!' Joe laughed.

We settled to eat our lunch in a pretty spot, smelling the canal water and hearing trains thundering past somewhere behind us, though not exactly sure any longer where we were.

We ate our sandwiches and some cake Joe's mom had sent along, swishing away the odd wasp, playing with strands of grass, shedding seeds.

'I'm ever so sorry about the bikes,' Joe said.

'You're not still on about those flaming bikes!' I gave him a playful nudge.

'You really didn't mind, did you?'

'No, I didn't. I couldn't care less as long as ... Look, it's been smashing so far, OK?'

Joe reached out suddenly and stroked my cheek with the palm of his hand. 'I wish we had more time ...' He looked away from me, at the rippling colours of the water. 'Then maybe I could be more sure of not making a fool of myself.'

'You won't do that.'

He heard the solemn tone of my voice and looked back at me. 'Won't I?'

As I shook my head he reached out and touched my face again. 'Don't look so sad.'

'I'm not sad, Joe. I'm anything but sad.'

His arms came round me and gently pulled me against him. 'After I met you, that first day, remember? I couldn't stop thinking about you. That was why I asked Doris about you. Genie—' He moved his arm up, rested his hand on my head so I could feel the warmth of it through my hair. 'You're lovely, d'you know that?'

I turned my head and looked at him deep into his eyes, making sure, quite sure, although really I already was, that he was speaking the truth, not giving me flannel, not teasing. And then I pulled him to me, this man, the one person in my life who really wanted me. I felt the beat of his heart against me and I knew I was safe with him.

When he said my name again, making me look up, we kissed, and my arms slid up round his neck. And for the first time I answered that kiss and loved it, and not once did I find myself thinking about groceries. At last I began to get an inkling of what it was Lil had been going on about all this time.

*

I stopped being the one who was responsible that week and spent every possible moment with Joe. He managed to get round his father, who had a soft spot for me already, and talked him into giving me a day off the day before Joe had to go back, though I didn't tell Mom about that. We took a tram out to the Lickeys. It was a beautiful day and we had the place more or less to ourselves. And blimey, wasn't it different from the last time!

This time I had a day of wonder, seeing all the lovely parts I'd missed when dragged along by Jimmy. We walked arm in arm round the green water of the lake.

'That's my dream,' Joe said. 'To have my own lake so I could keep birds. Imagine having something like this in your back garden!'

We wandered through the woods, smelling the pines, and found a warm patch of grass between sun and shade where we had our picnic and stayed on and on afterwards in each other's arms.

Joe lay back against a tree trunk and I lay on my front, half across him, looking and looking at him. He closed his eyes for a few minutes, face turned up into a little pool of sun. I watched him, holding on tight to every moment, trying to remember every line of his face, his slim, pointed nose, the dark eyebrows, his lips . . .

I moved up and kissed him. 'You comfy?'

'Not very.' He straightened his head, opening his eyes.

'Well, move then!'

'I might if it wasn't for this sack of potatoes slumped across me!'

'Charming!' I shifted myself over to lie on the grass

and Joe lay down and settled next to me, pulling my head onto his chest.

'I was trying to memorize everything about you,' he said. 'For when I go back. Big blue eyes—'

'They're grey!'

'Are they?' He leaned round and looked. 'No – blue! Well, somewhere in between. Long brown hair, high cheekbones, sweet face . . . But none of that's you, is it? I could describe you, but it wouldn't be you.'

'I was doing the same. I don't want you to go.'

'Why don't you want me to come to your house?' Joe asked suddenly. He'd offered to pick me up from home that morning and Mom would've been in.

'No,' I'd said, quick as a flash. 'I'll meet you in Navigation Street and then we can just get straight on the tram.'

I didn't want her anywhere near him this week, spoiling things. I wanted to keep this just for me. Ever since she'd known I was going out with Joe, that I'd found something of my own, she'd been poisonous with self-pity.

'Don't know how you can go gadding about like you do with your dad missing. You ought to be ashamed of yourself.' She was worried and frightened about everything I knew, but she wasn't taking this away from me.

'My mom's not always the easiest. Specially not that time of a morning. I just thought it'd be better if I came out on my own.'

Joe leaned up on one elbow. 'But I must meet her properly some time. It doesn't seem right.'

'There's plenty of time for that. Can't we just enjoy today without bringing her into it?'

'It's just, the way I feel about you I want everything to be right – with everyone. My mom and dad are happy we're walking out together and I'd like yours – your mom that is – to be as well. See?'

'I don't think my mom's got much idea how to be happy about anything.'

I must've said this in a bleaker voice than I intended because Joe rolled over and took me in his arms. He kissed my face then drew back, eyes searching me. 'I wish I didn't keep seeing you look so sad.'

'But I've told you, I'm not sad. I'm happier than I've ever been in my whole life before and that's thanks to you, Joe.'

He carried on looking at me for a time and then spoke the words his eyes were already telling me. 'I really love you, Genie.'

'And I love you more than anyone ever.'

We held each other so close. All the love I had ready to pour out on someone had found a place to settle.

'I never knew it could be anything like as nice as this,' I said. Joe's face looked happy. We kissed again, feeling the sun through closed eyelids.

That day drifted past in a haze. I had no idea at any point what time it was and I couldn't have cared less anyway.

But we couldn't shut everything out. Late in the afternoon we sat high on the hills looking back towards Birmingham. We had heard planes on and off that afternoon and there were ragged vapour trails across the blue. We had no idea then, but that very day as we sat there, Hitler was giving orders for the invasion of Britain. The first knocks of the Battle of Britain had already begun but it felt far away and unreal then. Gloria had given us news of dogfights over the Channel, the reporter making it all sound like an afternoon's football match.

'So don't you know where you're going next?' I asked Joe. I sat with my hand on the hard muscle of his thigh. I wanted never not to be touching him.

'I'm not certain. Down south I'd imagine – things are looking bad.' He never talked very much about the RAF or what it was like. 'I'd rather forget it all when I'm home with you,' he said. 'It's all too uncertain. Your mind can't quite take it in.'

'This is the best day of my life.'

Joe turned to me. 'So far. Think of it that way.'

'No. The very best ever.'

'Teresa was here,' Mom said when I got back late. She was drunk as a lord, only less gracious, her voice slurred.

'When – this morning? What'd she want?'

'I don't know. Didn't let her in.'

'You *what*? Why not?'

'Couldn't face it.'

I stared at her in disgust, hands on my hips. I could see she was barely awake now.

'Didn't feel like entertaining your friends at ten o'clock in the morning, if that's all right with you.'

Ten o'clock? It must've been something urgent for Teresa to have left the shop. I had to go to her, late as it was.

'Where's Len?'

Mom gave a nasty laugh, slumped back in the chair, her hair hanging loose. 'Where d'you think? Over at Molly's getting his leg over with never a thought.'

'You make me sick,' I said, heading for the door. 'Don't you ever think about anyone except yourself?'

'You're a fine one to talk,' she shrieked after me childishly. 'Takes one to know one!'

Despite the dark I ran most of the way to the Spinis. I felt I'd been woken up roughly from a dream, real life battering its way in at the door again. It was nearly eleven, but I had to see them and there'd be no time the next morning. I ran down the entry and saw there was still light showing downstairs in their house.

Teresa opened the door cautiously. When she saw it was me she stepped straight out and flung her arms round me.

'They're safe!' She was all aquiver with joy even now. Loosing me, she pulled me into the house and it was then I saw she wasn't alone. Carlo was sitting there with her.

'Mom's asleep,' Teresa explained. 'It was all too much for 'er – she's hardly had a wink since the ship went down. It all caught up with 'er tonight. Carlo's stayed on to give me a bit of company.'

Teresa laid a letter in front of me. 'Look – from Dad. They've been in Sutton Coldfield all this time if you please!' She laughed and I could hear a touch of hysteria in her voice, the days of pent up tension only still releasing themselves now.

Micky's letter was short. It said he and Stevie were in a transit camp which was 'not very comfortable' and that he'd been 'a bit unwell', whatever that meant. Uncle Matt had been moved on somewhere else a couple of days ago but Micky and Stevie were still waiting. Micky made a joke about holiday camps and sent his love. I felt my eyes prickle with tears when at the end of this short letter, after messages of love to his family, he'd written, 'and to little Genie'.

I looked up at Teresa. 'Oh, thank God.'

*

280

I went to the station with Joe on the Wednesday night, holding tight to every last second with him. Walking tall in his uniform, kitbags on his shoulders, he looked older, and I suddenly felt shy. In such a public spot for farewells as New Street Station it was still possible to find privacy because the place was so crowded, so full of traffic and clamour that it made you feel alone. Service people and their loved ones, people just travelling in civvy street, all of them were wrapped up in their own rush for a train or struggle with an awkward piece of luggage, with their goodbyes.

Holding Joe's arm, I passed through the crowds with him, banging against bags and haversacks, arms and shoulders clad in blues and khaki, through the cigarette smoke and shouting, the Tannoyed announcements and the hissing and chunking of other trains moving out, until we found Joe's. We'd cut it rather fine and Joe looked relieved he hadn't missed it.

Saying goodbye was awful. I couldn't stand it, felt I had to pull back, close in everything I was feeling, not let it wash over me so that it didn't hurt so much. I found suddenly I had nothing to say, and stood there next to Joe as minutes tore past, desperate for him to stay but incapable of even speaking to him.

Joe put his bags down and took me by the shoulders. At first I couldn't look at him.

'Genie – tell me you'll wait for me? You'll be here?'

I shrugged. 'Course I will. Don't be so daft.' I was awkward, angry almost, fighting back tears. All I really cared about would get on that train any minute and disappear to God knows where.

Poor Joe tried again. 'I love you, Genie. You do know that, don't you?'

I glanced into his eyes, then down at his boots, nodding. The whistle shrieked along the platform.

'This is it then.' He couldn't seem to let go of me. 'I'll have to get on . . .'

He bent to pick up his bags and move off. Turning, he said, 'See you then.'

The hurt in his eyes sliced through me but I couldn't seem to move. People were pushing past, scrambling for the carriages, shouting, snatching hurried kisses.

Joe was throwing his bags through the door, leaving them to the risk of being trampled on by all the boots clattering up and down.

Straightening up, he turned and his eyes found me again, me standing there all knotted up inside with my arms crossed tightly over my chest.

'Genie!'

He was going, really going. Another whistle cut the air like a scream.

'Joe. *Joe!*'

I tore to him, shoving and fighting past people, not caring, and pulled him into my arms, covering his face with kisses, frantic to tell him, to show him. 'I love you, I love you – I don't want you to go . . .'

Joe gave a shuddering laugh of relief, holding me so tight, kissing me back. 'Thank goodness. My love,' he called me. His love.

As the train moved off, I, like lots of other people, ran a few yards with it, kissing his hand through the window, hearing his laughter. My last sights of him were his dark eyes meeting mine, lips blowing a kiss, then his arm with all the other arms like bristles waving out along the train, until I wasn't sure any more which one was his.

August 1940

Joe, my Joe as I thought of him now, was posted up north, while every day the news from Gloria was full of the Battle of Britain. But at the moment, Joe was safe. And as the days went by I discovered he was a letter writer, and he wrote to me as often as he could, every two or three days.

'My dear sweet Genie ...' He'd tell me a bit about the routine of the squadron – what he was allowed to tell without too much of the censor's blue pencil butting in. All day-to-day things. But by the end he always found something else to say – something specially for me. Things he might have been too shy to say to my face. And those bits I'd read again and again until I could remember every word. I'd recite them to myself in my head in the factory or in bed at night, trying to remember his face properly, the feel of him close.

'I never knew what it was to be truly happy until I met you ... Every day I think of that night I heard you sing ... I'll be home to you on the first train when they'll let me ... You have taken a piece of my heart from me ...'

And I wrote back and found it easier to say on paper what you really think because you don't feel such a tit doing it. It was just hard to find words for it all, when I wanted to fill the letters with 'I love you. I love you. Thank you for loving me ...'

'When I used to work at the pawn shop,' I wrote to him once, 'this lady came in one day and passed away in the shop, right in front of me. And there've been all the other bad things that've happened, like Big Patsy taking his own life, my Dad going missing and my Mom never being happy. And now I've got you. I can't explain this properly – it'll come out all wrong. But things feel different. It's not that everything's all right suddenly of course. But it's as if before, there were all these bits hanging off. Like a tatty old mop. But now I've found the bit that holds them all together, the handle, sort of thing. Are you laughing reading this? I'm just trying to tell you that knowing you're there makes everything feel hundreds, thousands of times better than all my favourite dreams.'

Most of the news I told him would be about the factory because they were the people he knew. 'Nancy knows about us,' I wrote soon after he'd gone. 'She's really got it in for me, but I don't care.'

That's how it was then. Nothing seemed to get through to me, yet at the same time I could afford to be kinder somehow. Which was a good job, because if I hadn't had the protection of Joe's love my poor mom would've driven me completely round the bend.

Her emotions were like a big dipper ride, only the dips were a hell of a lot longer and wider than the heights. She was drinking of course. The first drink mellowed her and she could be almost pleasant. Then the slide began. Mainly she was sorry for herself. And angry – with anyone and everyone. Everyone's life looked rosier than hers.

One day the post brought a letter from Joe for me that set me singing inside (I didn't dare sing out loud in front of Mom) and one of the much rarer ones we had from Eric.

> Dear Mom,
> I hope this letter finds you well? I am in good health thank you. I am doing well at school and making progress on the piano. Mrs Spenser says I may be able to start on the violin. Her cat Lucy has had kittens and one is going to be mine.
> Are you and Dad and Genie and Len all keeping well?
> With regards from Eric.

This made her cry like anything. 'He didn't write that himself. She's just told him what to say – to his own mom! "Regards" – to us! He's not my little Eric any more. He doesn't even know about his own dad, but what use is it me telling him anyway?'

Eric did seem such a long way off, and not just in miles. Mrs Spenser had no kids of her own and was lavishing what she had in the way of middle-class comfort and opportunity on this kid she'd had foisted on her. I suppose we should've felt grateful really. But it was nearly a year now, a long time in a lad's life, and he seemed like a stranger to us.

But it was Joe's letters, the smiles they brought to my face, that Mom could stand least of all. She was used to me courting her, needing her to love me and hungering after it, and now I'd turned to someone else.

That night her despair was terrible. Len sat watching her, his big eyes frightened as Mom got more and more drunk and her tears drew lines of black mascara down her face, which she smudged with her fists. She sat on the edge of her chair, hands clenching and unclenching, crying, sometimes flinging herself back in the chair, jerking about like a child in a tantrum, only much more pitiful for the age of her. I just didn't know what to do.

'It's all right for you!' she yelled at me. She kept saying that, accusing me.

'Why is it all right for me?' I didn't dare touch her and I didn't get any answer. She just mewled and sobbed.

'Wasser matter with 'er, Genie?' Len said.

'Lenny—' I spoke as calmly as I could manage. 'Go and get our Lil, will you?'

It was late, and I knew as Len plodded off that Lil was going to be anything but pleased, but I was scared of Mom. I couldn't cope with all this on my own.

'Mom—' I sat down by her when he'd gone. 'Look, why don't you ask to give up work? You're getting too tired all the time.'

'Oh yes,' she snapped at me, voice thick with drink. 'Then what'll I do? Sit here all day?'

'There's loads to do here. If there was someone at home it'd make things a lot easier. There's the house, and I've no time to shop. The off-ration stuff is all queues and Saturdays're terrible for that now. It'd be a help to all of us – we mightn't all be so tired all the time.'

'Huh,' was all she said, but I did at least feel she was listening. There was a lull, before she started getting all in a state again.

'Where's your dad? I want him. When're we ever going to know if he's coming home or not? You tell me that. I can't go on like this ...'

Wearily I went and set a kettle to boil in the kitchen,

partly to get out of her way. When Lil arrived she wasn't nearly as mardy about it as I'd expected, and she was all dolled up.

'S'all right,' she said cheerfully. 'I'd only just got in anyhow.'

'Where've you been then?'

Lil took me by surprise by giving me a wink and putting a finger to her lips. 'That'd be telling. Anyhow, sssh for now.' She went to Mom. 'Oh Dor – you can't go on getting yourself all in a state like this. It's no good for you or for the babby.'

Mom cried exhaustedly. 'I can't go on,' she murmured into Lil's shoulder. 'I just can't.'

Lil looked at me over her head, her eyes troubled. Len stood by the door.

'Ta, Lenny,' I said. 'Tell you what, you could take Gloria into the front for a bit, how about that?'

Relieved, and hugging his beloved wireless to his chest, he escaped, and we heard music drifting through from the other room.

Lil prised Mom off her and tried to look into her face, though her head was lolling.

'Look, Dor.' Her voice was sharp now. 'You've got to pull yourself together. You can't go on like this. You're making yourself ill.'

'I can't,' Mom groaned. 'Just can't.'

'You've got to. You don't have a choice. What about the babby? And Genie here?'

'But what about me?' Mom was wailing.

'You're supposed to be their mom. And there's Len's wedding. You can't just cave in now!'

The kettle was gushing steam. By the time I'd made tea things'd gone quiet and I went back in to find my mom falling asleep across Lil's lap, her breath jerky as a sobbing child's.

Molly and Len's wedding arrangements were causing quite a kerfuffle. This was partly because Gladys Bender was making sure they did, quite apart from everything having to be done at such short notice because of it being a wedding with a shotgun pointing at its head.

Gladys pestered us from morning till night, whenever anyone was in. She'd never in her dreams expected her enormous, not quite all there daughter to find a mate, and now she'd got the chance, Molly was going to be MARRIED, and married with bells on.

'Oh-oh, here she comes again,' we'd say, seeing Gladys steaming across in her slippers. A door slamming somewhere across the street was enough to send us scuttling to the window to see if we were about to have another lethal dose of her.

Then she'd be hammering at the door as if we were all deaf, and when we let her in, would often be as red in the face and beady with perspiration as if she'd run a couple of miles to get there. In she'd come, us grimacing at the smells of sweat and disinfectant. We put up with her self-righteous tyranny day after day because we had to: we were Len's family and he'd got Molly into trouble.

'I thought it'd be right for you to see to all the food afterwards,' she announced. This was half past seven one morning. 'Since I've got my hands full and there are more of you with a wage coming in like. And I've got all the trouble of the dress and Molly to look after in her condition . . .'

'Well, she is your daughter,' Mom snapped. 'And it takes two, doesn't it?'

There's the pot calling the kettle black, I thought. Felt like saying to Gladys, I've got one to look after an' all.

Gladys folded her arms, pulling herself upright so that a good inch of greyish petticoat showed from under her stained red dress and pinner.

'It's snowing in France,' Mom murmured, but this was completely lost on Gladys.

'You saying you're not happy with all I'm doing?' she bawled at us. 'D'you want to give Molly and your Len a good send off, eh? Or don't you think they're worth it?'

'We can do some food, can't we, Mom?' I looked nervously at her. Even as I said it I already had a feeling 'we' was going to mean 'me'.

Mom nodded, yawning at the same time. This was a bit early for her to start a slanging match. 'Lil'll give us a hand. Not as if there'll be crowds, is it?'

'There might be quite a number actually,' Gladys announced, now we'd safely volunteered. 'After all, I'm one of fifteen and there's no one'll want to miss seeing our Molly tie the knot.'

On the Saturday I went to Nan's for a conflab. The kids were at the table filling their faces with liver and onions and spuds and Lil was cooking more for her and Nan. The kids were staring at her and I stared too. What'd come over her? She was by the range, stirring gravy with a metal spoon and humming, actually humming.

'You swallowed a budgie or summat?' I asked her.

Lil turned, laughing, and gave me another wink.

'No, that'd be the sensible thing to do,' Nan remarked, limping in with a bucket of slack. The coal hole was in action again since there'd been so many months of not having to shelter in it after all.

I looked from one to the other of them. Only one thing would put that glowing pink in Lil's cheeks which had been pale and tired for so long.

'Who is he then?'

Lil laughed like I hadn't heard her laugh in years. 'Can tell you're in love all right. Takes one to know one, doesn't it? How is Joe, Genie?'

'All right.' I blushed as Lil came closer to look in my eyes, teasing. 'He's doing fine.'

Suddenly she stooped towards me and kissed my cheek, her dark hair brushing my face. 'I'm glad for you. Really glad. He's very nice. I'd soon tell you if I didn't think so.'

'You've hardly met him!'

'I met him at the show that night. His eyes hardly left your face.'

'Who's this feller of yours then?'

Lil went back to the gravy. 'His name's Frank. Met him when we were playing at the pub down Bissell Street.'

'Proper charmer 'e is,' Nan said drily, stoking the range. She didn't like men to be charming. Charm to her meant snakes in the grass, blarney and insincerity.

'He's not!' Lil said. 'Well I mean, yes, he is – but not how she means.'

I was sitting by Cathleen who was idly letting me feed her little squares of liver. 'What's he do?'

'He's a mechanic. Got a garage out in Kings Heath.

290

And he's part-time ARP. But there're a couple of little things he does on the side.'

'Yes, I bet there are.' Nanny Rawson straightened up, holding her back. 'No one's shoes should be as shiny as them 'e turns up in.'

Lil laughed in exasperation. 'Oh Mom! Frank's all right. He's not selling anything – not as such. He's interested in fortune telling, tarot, that sort of thing.'

I frowned. 'I thought it's only women do things like that?'

'Oh, he doesn't actually do it himself. He's got a room – lets it to this woman. He knows all about it himself though, how it's done—'

'I wonder what else she's selling while she's at it,' Nan retorted.

Lil started to get a bit shirty. 'I've had enough of this. You've condemned the man when you don't even know him. And he's very good to me.'

'Well, that's all very nice,' Nanny said. 'But you find out what 'e's after before you get in any deeper, because you can be sure there'll be summat. Now that's quite enough of this in front of the kiddies. Want some jam on that, Genie?' she said, seeing me eating bread and scrape.

'No ta. Let Tom have it.'

Tom gave me his handsome smile, gappy with missing teeth. There came a banging on the door of the shop. Nan's face turned thunderous. 'It'd better not be,' she growled.

'I'll go.'

Morgan. As I slipped into the shop I could see him through the glass, and the outline of the girl with him. When I opened up the door I saw she was a lot older than she appeared from inside, in her little girly clothes, and she looked browned off with the whole set up before she'd even started.

'Forgot my key,' Morgan said in his castor-oil voice. 'Sorry to disturb you.'

'Not half as much as you'll disturb us in a few minutes no doubt,' I said, standing well back as they went in as if they were a passing stink bomb. They disappeared quickly up the stairs.

'Was that that bastard Morgan?' Cathleen lisped in an interested sort of way when I went back to them.

'Cathleen!' Lil exploded, although neither of us could help a smile.

Nan leaned over to her. 'It'll be mustard on your tongue next time if I 'ear any more language like that. Now off to bed with you all if you're finished.'

Nan had made sure, since Lil came back, that the kids slept in the back bedroom away from the dividing wall with Morgan's part of the house at the front. They were such tiny houses and the noises travelled with barely an obstacle through the walls and floors.

Cathleen was still up in the attic in a cot with Lil.

I changed her – the kids had nightclothes now Lil was earning better – and took her down for a drop of milk which she sat on my lap to drink, next to the range, quiet now with heavy eyes and suddenly sweeter. I kissed her soft cheek and stroked the fine blond curls. 'You sleep now, Cathleen. You're a tired little girl, aren't you?'

Once I'd carried her up to bed I went to see the boys, and read from an old book of ghost stories, Tom's hand resting on my arm.

'Now I've scared you witless you can get some sleep,'

I said when I'd finished. The springs creaked loudly as they climbed into bed. 'Night night.'

Downstairs, before the kids had even settled, we were soon aware of another set of bedsprings under strain on the floor above.

'How many's up there?' Lil hissed to me while Nan was upstairs. She didn't like any mention of them up there, any admission they existed.

'Only one.'

'Makes a change. Usually takes two to get him going nowadays.'

We heard Nan's slow tread at the top of the stairs and Lil made a face. 'You coming singing with us now you've got the courage? You enjoyed it, didn't you?'

'I can't leave Mom.'

'You've left her tonight. Anyroad, you don't need to leave her, she can come.'

'She won't though. And I haven't left her at home. She's at work.'

'Genie – look, Dor's in trouble, there's no doubt, and we're all sorry for her, the babby and that. But if your dad's not coming back she's just going to have to knuckle down and get on with it. It's terrible – I know 'cause I've done it. But she can't expect you to take over the running of her life for her. Because if you'll do it, she'll let you. That's what she's like, always has been. One for sitting back and letting everyone else do it all. But you've got your life to lead as well, so don't let her take it away from you. She's already wrecked Len's—' She stopped abruptly as Nanny Rawson walked in.

'But I still don't think I should leave her. Not when she keeps getting in such a state.'

'She may be in a state,' Lil said drily, 'but she's just going to have to get out of it.'

Nan was dishing up liver and spuds for us. 'Let's get going on Len's wedding,' she said. 'After all it's not just Molly's wedding, it's his too, and he deserves the very best we can give him.' I saw her eyes meet Lil's, and there was a hard look in them I didn't understand. 'He's owed that much.'

So, with years of practice, we ignored the thumps and squeaks from upstairs. The wedding was booked for a Monday, ten days away, and everyone was arranging the day off. Gladys had said, 'Molly can't possibly be showing if we do it that soon.'

Lil had snorted at this. 'She's such a size she could get to nine months without anyone being the wiser.'

Although Lil had pledged to do anything she could to help, she was full of doubts about this marriage. First of all was the fact that Len and Molly were, for the time being, going to carry on living where they were, in their separate homes.

'Don't seem right,' she said.

'Lenny seemed well put out at the idea of moving in with Molly somewhere,' I told her. 'Don't think it'd crossed his mind that anything might actually change. He wants to stop at home with us.'

'There's no houses to be had,' Nan said.

'What's Dor got to say about it?' Lil asked, grimacing at the colour of the tea. 'Proper maid's water this is.'

'Not much.'

Lil was still looking disbelieving. 'What about – where're they going to sleep and that?'

Nan gave her one of her looks.

'Search me,' I said. 'All they talk about at the moment is clothes – Molly's dress.'

'Who's this woman who's making it then?'

'A Mrs Van der Meyer.'

Lil frowned. 'That a Kraut name?'

'No, Dutch, and anyhow he's dead. She's a widow. Anyroad, Molly's not going to let any of us within a mile of that dress before the day.'

'Course not. Bad luck else, isn't it?'

'If you ask me,' Lil said, 'the whole thing's bad luck.'

For the time being Vera Spini was like a person reborn. When I came to the shop that Saturday after the good news I heard her singing. She looked younger suddenly. There was colour in her cheeks, she'd touched up her hair again and it was twisted into a straw-coloured knot behind her head.

'That's a happy sound,' I said. 'Nice to hear you. More like before the war.'

She was bustling around the shop with a broom and turned to smile at me.

'I can't say I'm not worried. It's all wrong what they've done – he shouldn't be there. There's no trial or nothing, so what are we supposed to do? I get so angry thinking about it. But for now—' She stopped and leaned on the broom. 'They're all alive. That's all I can think about.' Her expression turned bleak for a second. 'I don't know what I'd have done ... This is daft thinking about something that hasn't even happened.' She carried on sweeping. 'D'you want Teresa? She's round the back.'

'Is Carlo there?'

Vera looked round at me with a mischievous smile. 'You've noticed then?'

'He seems to be round a lot.'

'Well, he's not here now. Lovely boy he is. I just wish Teresa would open her eyes and see the lad's crazy about her. But that's Teresa for you, always facing the wrong way when it matters. He'll be gone and she still won't get the message.'

'Gone?'

'He's joining up.'

Teresa was washing the floor in the house so I climbed on a chair to talk to her, watching her egg-timer shape from behind as she knelt, circling the scrubbing brush on the tiles.

She looked up and grinned through black curtains of hair. 'Thought you were up to your eyes in wedding dresses.'

'Oh no – Gladys is in charge of all that. We know every stitch and tuck of it, except for the fact we've never seen it!'

'She wearing white?'

'Oh, I don't know about that!' Both of us laughed. 'Can't really, can she, in her position. You are coming, aren't you?'

'I wouldn't miss it for anything.'

'We're decorating the church tomorrow night – me and Lil. I've been down the Bull Ring buying up the flowers.'

Teresa asked cautiously, 'How's your mom?'

It was such a relief to have someone I could tell the whole truth to. 'She's bad. In a right state most of the time, Teresa. I can't get through to her at all since Joe and me . . .'

Teresa stopped scrubbing and sat back on her heels, pushing her hair out of the way with her arm. 'You really serious about him?'

I nodded.

'I can see you are. You're different. How does it feel, Genie?'

'What?'

'Loving someone – really.'

How to tell her? The very best best. 'What about Carlo?'

'I've always liked Carlo – a real lot actually. It's just I've known him so long. He's always just been there, like Stevie—'

'Up till now,' I interrupted.

She looked into my face. 'I'm very fond of him. He loves me, has for a long time, so he says. I suppose I thought it'd be more dramatic. Like in the pictures. He's always so polite. He hardly touches me—'

'A gent?'

'I s'pose. Shy of changing things, I think. I know I don't want him to go. I do know that much. By the way—' She stood up and lifted the bucket. 'Have you heard about Walt?'

'No,' I said stiffly. 'What?'

'He's got a girl into trouble. Run off to join up and left her instead of facing the music.'

'But he's too young to join up! He's only seventeen.'

Teresa put her head on one side. 'D'you know, since they took Stevie, and all the trouble we've been through with it, he never once came in to see us. No "How are you, Mrs Spini, any news about Stevie?" Nothing. Some friend he turned out to be. That girl's better off without him. So I don't s'pose lying about his age'll come too hard to him, do you?'

Lil and I did our best with the church. The flowers I bought were a whole mix of colours, and as well as those, Mr Tailor from down the road let us have some out of his garden which was decked out like a flower show every summer. It was from him we had a bundle of wheat which he grew because he liked the look of it and tight yellow rosebuds which made Lil say wistfully, 'Aren't they lovely? They're my favourites, they are.'

Mom half-heartedly offered to help, but she still had sewing jobs to do on Len's suit for the next day so we left her to it. Lil and I carried our buckets and ribbon and scissors down the road and let ourselves into the church in the evening light. Peach-coloured rays were shafting in through the west window. The atmosphere was stuffy and filled with the smell of floor polish.

Lil eyed up the wrought-iron flower stand. 'I'm not sure I'm very good at this. We'll have to hope for the best.' She turned to me. 'I want Len to have the best. Have we got hymns and that?'

'Mom's sorted it with the vicar. She wanted "Lead us, heavenly Father, lead us". She said that's a good one for a wedding.'

We managed, after a few false starts, to cut and arrange the flowers in a magnificent spray on the stand, and put vases of flowers round to decorate the altar and sidetables. We tied sprays of wheat ears with yellow ribbon and attached them to the ends of the pews.

'Looks like a harvest festival,' I said, tying bows and flattening them the best I could.

'No it doesn't.' Lil backed down the church, surveying what we'd done. 'It looks beautiful. Molly'll love it, bless her. Time something nice happened to her.' Lil was coming round much more to the idea of the wedding now she'd got caught up in the spirit of it.

'You've changed your tune.'

298

'It's just – seeing it all, like this ... D'you remember my wedding – Patsy's and mine?'

'Course I do.' I was seven when they married. 'Wouldn't forget being a bridesmaid, would I?'

Lil shook her head. 'I was so happy that day. It really was the best day of my life – well, maybe except the ones the babbies were born. Not even a wedding beats that. My poor Patsy. I hope he don't mind me going about with Frank.'

'D'you really like Frank, Lil?' I asked shyly. Now I was with Joe it seemed we could talk woman to woman.

Lil picked up a long curl of leftover ribbon and started winding it round her fingers. 'I do, yes. At first – well, still really, because it's only been a few weeks – I couldn't stop thinking about Patsy. Comparing them, and feeling bad at being with someone else. As if Patsy was watching, talking to me in my head. I've felt that on and off since he died. At first he was always saying, "Why didn't you stop me? Why did you let me do it?" My own guilt talking, I s'pose. But I know really it wasn't my fault, wasn't anyone's. It was all an accident. Anyhow, after a bit I'd hear him saying more ordinary things, just like chat. That was nice, for a bit.' She gave a little laugh. 'Now though, it's more as if – how can I say it? – he's still there and I love him, but he's not part of now. I can see Frank without being ashamed. I can love both of them.'

'Our nan doesn't take to him, does she? I'd've thought she was a pretty good judge.'

Lil gave a snort. 'Mom? Are you kidding? She may be a good judge of some things, like how much stew a bag of scrag end'll run to. But when it comes to men ... I mean look who she married! And she was wrong

299

about Patsy, wasn't she? Had him down as a navvy and a waster. No, if you want advice about men, Genie, come to me, not my mom – and not your mom neither, come to that!'

We both laughed, but Lil with an edge of tears. 'Sometimes I just want to feel someone's arms around me so bad I ache with it.' She caught hold of the broom. 'Best get on. Be dark soon.' I followed her round with a dustpan and brush, and we went to search for a dustbin out the back of the church.

'Your Joe now,' Lil said, shooting flower stalks into the bin. I felt myself blush. My Joe! 'He's a good'un I reckon. You could do a lot worse than him, and you deserve to be happy, Genie. God knows, you do.'

The wedding morning dawned bright and we were all up and running like headless chickens before we were half awake. Our nan was down by half six carrying plates of stuff already cut with muttoncloth over them, I was brewing up tea for everyone and there were eggs on the go in a pan. Mom and Nan started laying up the table at the front, talking about beef and chicken sand-wiches. We'd saved everything we could for that wed-ding, and lots of people had chipped in. We'd already done a trifle of sorts and there was tinned fruit, and Gladys was being very mysterious about the wedding cake, which was another aspect of things she'd taken on herself.

She soon made an appearance of course.

Mom rolled her eyes to the ceiling. 'Go and answer the door before she knocks it down, Genie.'

Gladys sailed in with a tray of little cakes. 'Straight out of the oven,' she boomed. 'I've been up since four.'

The smell of them drifted in after her, sweet and delicious, and they looked soft and golden. Good job our mom didn't volunteer for that bit.

'How's Molly?' Nan asked.

'Got her 'ead over a pail at the moment,' Gladys reported to anyone in the whole neighbourhood who might happen to be listening. 'She'll be awright with summat on her stomach though.' She wiped her hands on her pinner and lowered her voice, which was a relief. Looking round at us in grand triumph she said, 'We've got the dress. You're in for a surprise.'

We all stared at her. Were we supposed to ask questions?

'Can't wait,' I said since no one else opened their mouth.

'Anyroad, this won't get the babby a new coat,' Gladys said as if we were all in a plot to waylay her. 'We'll see you later.'

'Gladys,' Mom called across after her. 'Any idea how many you've got coming?'

Disappearing into her house, she called, 'Oh, quite a few . . .'

We had to get Lenny out of bed and get some breakfast down him. Nan had starched him a collar and she fixed it all for him, pushing in the studs. 'Chin up, Len. It's a bit tight,' she said, struggling. Len's huge face loomed over the tight collar which was biting into the side of his neck. 'How d's it feel?'

'Awright.' He was grinning, which was more or less what he'd been doing non-stop ever since we first got him up. She helped him into his trousers and jacket, fastened his tie for him, soaped his hair flat and combed it. 'Now – let's have a look at you.'

My nan stood there in front of her enormous,

damaged son, looking him over from his plastered down hair to his newly blacked shoes. I saw a nerve in her face twitch. I bet she never thought she'd see this day. Her Len getting married. She licked her lips to bring the tremble in them under control and, pulling out a hanky from the front of her dress, she looked down so her eyes were hidden.

Finally she said, 'You'll do.'

The wedding was at eleven. At the last minute I was still putting whitener on my shoes and searching for gloves. But we walked down to St Paul's in good time, Mom with her arm through Len's, explaining to him for the umpteenth time that when the service started he was to wait at the front for Molly to walk up to him, and then the vicar would do all the other things they'd practised.

'Remember what you have to say when he asks you the questions, Len?'

'I—'

'Do. I *do*, Len. That's all you have to remember.' She made him repeat it over. 'Anyway, Mom and I'll be sitting right at the front so if you need any help you just look at us, right?'

'Church looks very nice,' Nan said approvingly as we walked in, and it was true. The blaze of colour from the spray at the front, edged with the half-open yellow roses, looked beautiful, though Mom didn't bother to say so to us. Everything had to be perfect for her precious Lenny's wedding day but she wasn't going to hand out any credit for it. The only thing she said to me on the way in, in a melancholy voice, was, 'I wish Victor was here.'

Our side of the church was empty until we arrived. Nanny Rawson's sister over in Aldridge said she might get there but we never saw any sign of her and no one else knew it was happening. But over on Molly's side there were quite a few there already, all dolled up.

After a few minutes the lady organist started up and we saw more and more trickle in on the Benders' side. Nan, next to me, was watching them from under the same hat she'd worn to Lola's funeral, only this time she had on a flowery frock instead of the mourning-coloured coat. I knew she was sizing up the numbers, wondering if they were all coming back to the house and if we'd got enough food.

There was a tap on my shoulder. 'Genie!' It was Tom, all scrubbed and in his school shorts and jumper. 'Can I sit with you?' He didn't need to ask. As he squeezed into the pew he opened one hand and showed me a shiny shilling.

'Look what Frank gave us. Patsy's got one too, and he gave a tanner to our Cathleen.'

'Blimey, lucky you!'

I turned round full of curiosity. Lil was coming down the aisle towards us with Patsy and Cathleen. She looked marvellous, in a sunny yellow dress which matched the roses, her lips glossy red and her hair swept up with a few curling tendrils hanging down, and I was struck again by just how beautiful she was. It was so hard to believe Nanny Rawson had looked similar in her youth. Cathleen was holding Lil's hand, wearing a little pale blue pinafore dress with white rabbits appliqued on, which I knew Lil had stitched herself. But my glance soon shifted from her to the man whose face I could see over Lil's left shoulder. I saw immaculate, shiny black hair, a thin black moustache, and as they came nearer, a sharply pressed suit. He was following Lil closely, looking coolly down at the rest of us.

'Crikey!' I whipped round to my nan. 'Is that Frank? 'E looks just like Clark Gable!'

'That,' Nan said, thumbing determinedly through Hymns Ancient and Modern, 'is what I'm worried about.'

Lil, Frank and the other two children settled in the pew behind us and after a moment I turned timidly to have a peep. Lil gave me a gorgeous smile and a surreptitious wink. Frank was looking at me and Lil leaned over and touched his hand. 'This is my little sister, Eugenie.'

He held out his hand to shake mine. 'Very pleased to meet you.' And he smiled.

I felt rather wobbly. The resemblance was so striking I thought any moment he'd say, 'Frankly my dear, I don't give a damn.' But instead he said, 'I'm Frank.' I stared back at him hard and couldn't see anything in his eyes to make me suspicious so I smiled back and said hello.

Just then, behind them, Teresa came in and, to my surprise, I saw Carlo was with her. She gave me a little wave and they sat in the third row. I couldn't help wondering how things were going with Carlo.

The organ struck up louder and everyone stood. Mom pushed Len out to the front where he waited, lost looking for a moment and then, as he caught sight of Molly, beaming like a sunflower opening out. Everyone on both sides swivelled to see the bride.

There was a gasp from all round. We couldn't help it. All of us watched, riveted, as she swayed along the aisle on the arm of one of her uncles, since her dad had been dead years.

As they came closer I heard Nan mutter, 'God Almighty.' Afterwards Lil said Molly was the nearest thing to a jam roly-poly on legs she'd ever set eyes on. The dress was simply enormous. It had every possible combination of frills and leg-of-mutton sleeves and bows and flounces that you could ever imagine all crammed into the same space together. The sleeves made Molly look as if she'd been blown up with a bicycle pump, the layered skirts flounced hugely over her backside and the neck, cleavage, sleeves and skirt were all trimmed with huge floppy bows. Not only that, although the dress was white – a bit cheeky of Gladys, considering – the edges were piped with a bright raspberry-coloured material and half the bows were made of the same colour. On her head she wore a little white cloche hat with a long gauze veil trailing from it which was, at the moment, down over her face. Actually she looked more like an enormous summer pudding with only some of the juice soaked through the bread.

But she was Len's Molly, and his face was brimful of delight. The fact she looked good enough to eat would be a bonus in Len's list of priorities.

The uncle was quite a size as well, and the two of them had rather a squeeze to fit along. It was only once they'd passed we saw the bridesmaid behind, a girl of about nine, in a dress of a terrible bright acid blue. Nan looked at me and I could hear her thoughts: What could have possessed them? But the child, unlike every other member of Molly's family, was extraordinarily pretty, with long, wavy chestnut hair, striking light blue eyes and the longest eyelashes I'd ever seen. A real beauty. It was like seeing Snow White with all the dwarfs around her.

The service sped past. I could tell Mom was on edge, sober as a judge today, afraid of Len putting a foot wrong. But he said his 'I do's' with such feeling that there was a ripple of laughter from behind him. He fed the ring on to Molly's pudgy finger and was allowed to lift the veil and kiss her. Molly turned, smiling coyly. They were married. I wanted to clap.

Outside we deluged them with rice and confetti and they looked like the happiest pair of people I'd ever seen.

'Heaven help us if all that lot come back,' Mom panted as she and I sped down the road ahead of everyone else. The few photographs had already been done. 'We'd better keep some of the sandwiches back so they don't all go at once.'

The minute we were back in the house she was swigging at the gin bottle.

'Mom!'

'What? God, I needed that. What're you staring at?'

'Don't get drunk, Mom. Not today – please.'

'Don't be silly – course I shan't.' She let out a titter, putting the top back on the bottle. 'I just wanted a little pick-me-up. I don't get drunk, do I?'

'Not half,' I muttered, checking the things laid out on the lacy cloth.

'Think of our Len, married!' Mom's voice was high with nerves and excitement. Suddenly she burst into hysterical-sounding giggles, hand over her mouth. 'Oh, that dress – have you ever seen anything like it?'

I had to laugh with her then. 'It was a bit loud, wasn't it?'

Tears of laughter trickled down our faces. 'How're we going to cope with her here?' Mom spluttered. 'It'll be like having a minesweeper in the house—'

'And that bridesmaid – talk about Reckitt's blue!'

Mom wiped her eyes, trying to calm down. 'Pretty little thing though, wasn't she? Oh dear, it's good to have a laugh. Come on though, Genie.' She started flapping again. 'They'll all be here in a minute. How on earth're we going to manage for glasses?'

'Someone'll have to go round the pubs, see if they can spare us any.'

Soon we heard the first knock on the door, but it was only Nanny Rawson and Lil with the kids. Lil went off round to the neighbours and pubs begging use of more glasses, plates and cups. Mom was spreading more bread and Nanny Rawson took over the sandwich factory so by the time Molly got there we were as ready as we'd ever be.

Molly filled up most of the hall and with Gladys and Len trying to squeeze in too there wasn't a hope, so Mom shifted them all through into the garden. Then there followed a thick stream of Gladys and Molly's relatives and it looked as if every last one of her fourteen brothers and sisters had turned up, along with bits and bobs of family and children, so the place was soon heaving with them all. When Frank arrived I was impressed to find he'd stayed back to show people the way. He looked even more like a film star when set against Gladys's clan.

Looking at Frank carefully, I could see he was quite a bit older than Lil – forty-something probably. The suit was smart and you could have looked in the black toe-caps of his two-tone shoes to put your lipstick on. How Nanny Rawson was going to loathe those shiny shoes!

'How's it going, Genie?' He pushed in through the throng of the front room where they were already lighting fags and drinking beer. I had a good look at his face again. I felt protective of Lil. She'd had enough on her plate. He was gorgeous, but was he a chancer? The smile in those steely grey eyes was warm enough, so I gave him the benefit of the doubt.

'All right.' I smiled. 'Lil's still rounding up glasses somewhere..'

'Anything I can do?'

'Beers?' We'd got a couple of barrels in.

'Right you are, Genie. And anything else you want – just give me the word.' And he really did knuckle down and help, seemed like a worker all right.

Nanny Rawson came in holding two plates of sand-wiches high so they didn't get knocked. 'Right!' she boomed, and everyone went quiet. 'There's more of you than we bargained for today which is awright. It's very nice. But you'll have to go easy on the grub and make sure everyone gets a share, awright?'

After that the party got into full swing and I went round offering food to a large number of people who looked very like Gladys and others of her relatives who looked totally different. Molly and Len stayed in the garden with a crowd, including the blue bridesmaid who was dashing about playing tig with Patsy, Tom and some other kids. Molly looked very hot in all her finery. Seeing me, she swooped down and clasped me in her arms so I was buried in bows, frills, bosoms and cheap scent. Up close I felt the dress was made of cotton.

'So you're my little niece now, Genie!'

I smiled. 'S'pose I am. You look lovely, Molly.'

Lenny and I had a big hug too. 'You did well, Len. We could all hear you.'

'I'm married now,' he announced.

'You are. And soon to be a dad,' I added more quietly.

'Never thought I'd be the one getting married.'

I squeezed his hand. 'I'll get you some grub.'

Inside, the house was full of chatter and smoke. Teresa and Carlo were there and I realized I hadn't had time to see them, but I caught Teresa's eye and grinned and waved as I went through the back room. In the front, Frank was still in charge of the beer and I heard him say to Nan, 'I hope you're going to give us a tune later, Mrs Rawson.'

'We'll 'ave to see.' Nan gave him a look as if to say when she did it wouldn't be as any kind of favour to him.

And then a noise broke through all the celebrating, a high, rising and falling whine.

'God Almighty!' Lil cried, 'It's an air raid!'

No one knew what to do. We weren't in practice for this. A bomb had come down last week across town but we had no routine.

'Well we won't all fit in the Anderson,' I said. Found I was giggling and didn't know why.

'Get Len and Molly in there, and the kids,' Nan said. 'The rest of us'll just 'ave to make do.'

For the next few minutes there was a low-level panic. Some of the guests went off saying they'd find a public shelter and Gladys pointed out that she had a cellar, so a few of her kin went across with her. Mom made sure she got into the shelter outside saying she was going to keep an eye on Molly and Len.

'Now isn't that just typical,' Lil hissed down my ear. 'I mean it's not as if she's got to worry about Molly getting pregnant now, is it?'

But in the end they found room for Nan as well. The rest of us sheltered in the little cupboard under the stairs – where I found myself with Lil and Frank – and under the tables front and back.

The raid went on for three and a half hours, and if it hadn't been for the absurdity of the situation and us all being together it would've been absolutely terrifying. The planes sounded so loud and close and when they were really overhead we all stopped talking and held our breath. We heard the crash of explosions in the distance.

'So it's really happening, isn't it?' Lil said as we crouched, ears straining, in the tiny space where there was barely room for the three of us.

'If I'd stayed out you could've had a lot more fun, couldn't you?' I said to them and Lil gave me a pretend slap on the cheek. 'Hey girl – what d'you take us for?'

When there was more of a lull we'd poke our heads out and call to the others under the tables. At the front were some of Gladys's family, who kept climbing in and out, polishing off the remains of the food, and Lil said it was a good job we'd still got the cake, 'if we ever get out of here.'

In the back room, under the smaller table, were Teresa and Carlo, and after the first time I popped in and found them wrapped tight in each other's arms, I thought I'd better just leave them to it. We heard their voices now and then, talking Italian mostly, and Lil winked at me. 'Lovely language, isn't it? Makes everything they say sound romantic.'

'Don't think they need the Italian for that by the look of things,' I said.

'Really?' Lil stretched out, put her head round the door, then drew back grinning. 'Ooh, I see what you mean!'

Frank told us jokes and stories to take our minds off it all, making us laugh. I was still trying to work him out, wasn't sure. He looked such a spiv, but at the same time in his face there was something worn and vulnerable that you didn't expect. And he did seem genuinely to care for Lil. By the end of the raids, what with all the laughs he gave us, I was more or less convinced.

The sun was low in the sky by the time the All Clear went, and we all crawled out to find the table empty.

'Greedy sods,' Lil said. 'Honestly.'

Gladys came back with her little band, although the lot who'd gone to find another shelter never reappeared and must've gone to the pub. Everyone was in a mad mood after the hours cooped up and we had a lot of laughs, ate trifle and evap and little cakes, then Gladys trotted back over to get The Cake.

When she stood it on the table everyone clapped and laughed. There were two tiers and on the top, moulded out of icing, was a little figure obviously meant to be Molly, with pink colouring piped round it something like her dress, and silver horseshoes at her feet.

'Where's the one of Len?' someone asked.

'You didn't want to crush the cake, did you?' another voice shouted. And amid the laughter and the cheers that everyone truly meant for them, Len and Molly cut the cake, each of them holding the knife with one of their enormous hands, both smiling madly and Molly's glasses misting up.

We hadn't got to the stage in the war when people were reduced to icing cardboard cakes. This was a real one with fruit and candied peel and it tasted delicious.

As the evening wore on, those who were left sang, led by Nan and Lil who dragged me in with them as well. Mom managed to get through the evening with barely a sniff at a bottle. Len and Molly were the picture of young love on chairs in front of me, Molly still in her amazing frock. And I don't know exactly what changes took place under the table in our back room that afternoon, but as we were singing, Teresa and Carlo sat smiling and holding hands, their shoulders touching like a couple of budgies. Life would have been perfect, really perfect, if my dad and Joe could have been there too.

Later that week my mental peace was blasted right apart by a letter from Joe telling me he was being re-posted down south, which could mean only one thing. He was going to join the fighters over the south coast and I could not rest easy again. The day I got his letter Gloria reported the RAF as having lost thirty-four planes that day. There was more bombing to the east of Birmingham. The war was real now, and drawing closer. We were on the alert for raids. When the sirens went the tradesmen harnessed their horses to the back of the carts to stop them bolting. Nanny Rawson had cleared the coal hole and started to get back into the shelter mentality. But I wasn't really worried about the raids. My own safety didn't feel all that important. It was Joe I worried about, day and night. Gloria was on overtime and one night when the accumulator went in the middle of the news I found myself screaming at her.

And there was Nancy carrying on. She was as nasty to me as she knew how, and had been ever since she found out for sure I'd 'stolen' Joe from her. She tried to turn the other women in the place against me by telling malicious tales.

The others knew where Joe was and gave me a lot of sympathy, which drove Nancy into even sorer vexation.

'What're you asking 'er for?' she snapped one day when someone enquired about him.

'Because she's the one Joe's writing letters to,' Doris said, 'whether you like it or not, Nance.'

''E's not!'

'Course he is,' Agnes said. 'Ain't 'e, Genie?'

I nodded. 'A couple of times a week.'

Nancy suddenly came at me round the table, hands like claws. 'It was all right before you came along. 'E liked me best!'

She was held back by two other women, both telling her to pack it in.

'I'm going to give 'er one, the sly bitch!' she shouted, struggling.

I was wound up tight with worry as it was, and sick to death of her stupidity and all the spite I'd had off her.

'Joe doesn't even like you, Nance,' I shouted at her. 'And I'll tell you another thing. You don't care about Joe. You don't care about anyone except your pathetic little self, and while you're here having a go at me he could be out there getting killed. That's what I'm carrying with me day after day, because I love Joe and he loves me and there's nothing you can do about it.'

I'd hoped my voice would come out strong, but instead it sounded as desperate as I felt.

'Shame,' someone said. 'Poor kid.'

Doris took a firm hold on Nancy. 'One more spat like that my girl, and you'll be looking for a new place to work, make no mistake. I'll not 'ave it in 'ere.'

Nancy walked out of that factory at the end of the day and Doris never had to send her packing. We never saw her again.

The Blitz began for us at the end of August. The Luftwaffe shifted from the daylight raids to night bombing. They bombed the Market Hall in town, leaving desolate, smoking rafters and a terrible mess in the place where we loved to go shopping. I felt as if this must be a film or a dream and I would soon step out of it. But there wasn't a way out.

The next night we spent mostly in the Anderson: Mom, Len and me. As they came over they felt very close, and I can't say the shelter made you feel all that much safer. Less, if anything. What if there was a direct hit? For hours we listened to the drone of the planes, the whistles and bangs of the bombs and our ack-ack guns firing now and then.

I'd thought Lenny might go to pieces. We all jumped at every explosion at first. But Len just perched there with us as if this was normal. He'd always loved fireworks. It was Mom's nerves that took it badly. As we sat there in the light of the hissing Tilley lamp she kept digging her nails into my arm and sometimes, when something landed close, she let out a squeak or a cry. 'Oh, I can't stand it in here,' she cried. 'Can't stand it another minute. I'll go mad.'

I didn't choose to remind her of a time when she'd stood it in the shelter very well of her own accord.

In the middle of it all she said suddenly, 'I can feel it – the babby! I just felt it move.' She put her hand to her stomach and stared at the little dancing flame. 'What on earth sort of life am I bringing this child into?'

September 1940

'It's a year today since war broke out,' Mom said gloomily into her morning cuppa.

I was at the table with Len, both getting breakfast down us quick so's to get off to work, though I hardly felt like eating. Mom didn't seem too bad this morning though. I thought maybe she was trying to take Lil's advice and pull herself together.

There was a rattle at the front door which set my heart pounding. Post. Joe. Would there be a letter for me today? My first and last thoughts of the day were of him, and so many in between. Every day Gloria gave us a reckoning of the number of planes lost and pilots missing. I was constantly worried.

Mom was already out of her chair. 'I'll go. You get on with it.'

She padded off into the hall in her slippers and I heard her give a little grunt as she bent down. She moaned as if in pain. When I got there she was sliding down the wall on to the green lino in a faint, the letters slipping from her hand. In those seconds relief spread through me like warmth: Joe's writing on one of the envelopes.

'Mom?' I sat her up with Len's help and we propped her with her knees apart, head between them. She groaned again, her face white.

I picked up the other letter. A card in fact. *Recovering*

from wounds. Prisoner of War. France. Alive! My father was alive!

'Len, it's from Dad!' I shrieked.

'Victor?' A slow grin spread across Len's face.

'Yes, of course Victor. Mom – he's alive!'

She was going into shock. 'Oh God,' she kept saying in a distraught voice. 'Oh my God.'

We got her into a chair and I squeezed more tea out of the pot but her hands were trembling too much to take the cup. I told Len to get off to work and cooled a helping of the tea for her on a saucer and she finally got some down her.

'Go back to bed for a bit,' I told her. 'Give it a chance to sink in.'

Her mind was jittering, racing. She grabbed my hand. 'I'd just got used to the idea of having my babby. Of keeping it ... I'll have to have it adopted now.' She stared hard into my face, wanting an answer from me. 'Won't I?'

'My sweet Genie,' Joe's letter said. It was written, I could see, in a very great hurry. 'The pace of life is very different here at ——. This'll have to be quick I'm afraid. Scarcely time to eat or sleep. Can't go into detail. Enough to say I'm on a crash course – but not literally so far!

'Just to let you know all's well. Longing to see you – you've no idea how much. Keep safe and well my sweetheart, until I see you.

'All my love, as ever, Joe.'

This short letter, tucked in the pocket of my dress, seemed to glow against my thigh all day and sometimes I took it out to read if I had a spare moment. I was loved, really loved by someone, and it was the best feeling in the world.

I was so excited that day I could barely keep still. 'My dad's alive!' I told everyone. At the factory they shared it all with me as if they were part of my own family. In fact with a lot more enthusiasm come to think of it.

Nanny Rawson scarcely said a word to start with, just carried on serving out the kids' tea.

'Uncle Victor?' Patsy said. 'He's been taken prisoner? By the Germans? Blimey!'

'Sit down,' Nan said sternly. 'Just get to the table.' She lifted Cathleen on to a chair, handed her bread and a bowl of soup and started absent-mindedly spooning it into the child's mouth.

'It's hot, Nan.' Cathleen spat it out. 'And I can feed myself.'

I could tell Nanny Rawson was turning things over in her mind but there was no use hurrying her. She poured me a cup of tea, then sat on the sofa in her pinner, thoughtfully rubbing her bandaged leg.

'I had a letter from Joe today too.'

'Oh ah.' She got up and beckoned me into the scullery. 'Eat up, you three.'

'Your mother all right?' We were squeezed in between the stone sink and the wall.

'She passed out. The shock. Said she'd have to get the babby adopted. She won't, will she Nan?'

Nan rolled her eyes to the ceiling. 'Daft mare she is.'

'D'you think it'd be for the best?'

'No. I don't. That's my grandchild she's casting off. Parting with your own flesh and blood – most un-natural. I'll 'ave to talk to 'er. Victor's a reasonable man, not like some.'

Lil burst in through the back door, face alight with smiles.

'All right, Genie!' she half sang. The kids looked round, mouths hanging open in amazement. ''Allo kids, what's up?'

'Victor's alive,' Nan said.

Lil flung her bag down, the smile wiped off. 'Oh dear.' Then she saw my face. 'Sorry, Genie. Good news really, in't it?'

'Yes, it is,' I said crossly. Teresa had flung her arms round me with joy as soon as I'd told her. There was a chance for us all now, that's how I saw it.

'How's Doreen taken it?'

We went through it all again in the scullery, the ifs and buts. Lil thought like Nan. Adoption was right out.

'How can she even think of it? Giving away a babby you've carried in you? Two wrongs like that aren't going to make a right whichever way you look at it.'

When this had been chewed over Lil whispered to me, 'Can you stay and give your nan a hand with the kids? I'm off out.'

I grinned. 'Course. Len'll slope over to Molly's if he gets hungry.'

After a quick bite Lil prettified herself, not that she needed to, being gorgeous already. She changed into the shimmery green dress, put her hair up and her lipstick on and she looked like a Persian queen. Although her life was as exhausting as ever, the colour had come back to her cheeks and her hair was glossy.

'You look really pretty, Mom,' Tom said, watching her with admiring eyes. 'You going out with Frank?'

'How did you guess?' Lil smiled into the glass by the door. 'That OK with you?'

'Yeah – 'e's awright Frank is.' He'd long bought the kids' affection with pieces of silver.

''E gave me a spinning top,' Cathleen piped up, enthroned on her potty in the corner by the stairs.

''E said 'e'd play football with me!' Patsy cried.

Lil laughed happily, kissing each of them, which was an unusual occurrence at the best of times. Indignantly Patsy wiped lipstick off his cheek. 'I'm glad you all like him 'cause I think we'll all be seeing a lot more of him.'

'What I want to know,' Nanny Rawson said, 'is where 'e gets 'is money from. I mean mending cars and the ARP – not places where you find a crock of gold, are they?'

Lil turned. 'What money?'

'Well it's obvious 'e's got money – the way 'e's dressed and that—'

'Mom,' Lil said patiently. 'Frank hasn't got that much money. What've you got that into your head for?'

'It's 'cause he looks like Clark Gable,' I teased. 'Nan thinks he's a film star.'

'Oh Mom.' Lil gathered up her coat. 'I thought you was the one who didn't hold with judging a book by its cover?'

I was alone in the house when Mom came in that night. Len had decided to stop over at Molly's. Her eyes were circled like a panda's from exhaustion.

Instead of heading straight for something alcoholic as she did every other night, she sat down on the edge of a chair in the back room, stone cold sober.

'What's up, Mom?'

'I've got to think,' she said in a far-away voice. 'Think things out.'

I wished I could tell her it'd be all right. That Dad wouldn't mind. But he would. Course he would.

'I went to the Welfare this morning. The woman said I couldn't give up a babby for adoption without my husband's consent. I didn't know what to do. I couldn't say, "He's in France", because I knew how she'd look at me and I couldn't tell her about its real father.'

There was a long silence before she said, 'It felt such a little thing I did, going with Bob. And it's turned into all this.' Bitterly, she added, 'Hasn't given him much trouble though, has it?'

On 7 September London had its first big air raid. Four hundred and thirty people died in London that night, so many we could barely take it in.

But the Battle of Britain wasn't over yet and Joe was still flying while those Germans were making up their mind exactly what it was they were playing at. Were they going to invade or not?

I had a letter from Joe sounding tired out, but full of affection. This affection that felt like a miracle, still unbelievable. Then nothing. Every day I rushed to the front door, waited, heart going like mad. Got to the point of crying with fear and worry when there was nothing. He'd been writing every other day when he could. Something had to be wrong. Of course it had to be. Things didn't go right for me.

'Joe – oh Joe, where are you? Write to me and make it all right again!'

I was choked with emotion but like everyone else, tried to keep it down. Always waiting, things out of our control.

''Eard from Joe?' the women asked.

'No,' I snapped, not meaning to turn on them. But they understood, kept quiet then, with knowing looks at each other.

On the Tuesday Mr Broadbent came in, so everyone suddenly put on that extra-busy look like they did whenever he put in an appearance. He took no notice, headed straight for me.

'Could I have a word a minute, out there?' He jerked his head at the back door, face terribly solemn.

The other women's eyes followed me out and they all had disaster written in them. He'd heard something, I knew it. The kind of telegram only moms and dads or wives are sent. I didn't want to follow him, didn't want to hear it.

We went out into the yard at the back and closed the door on the warehouse. I couldn't control myself any longer.

'Joe's dead, isn't he? You've had a telegram?' I couldn't help it. My heart felt swollen fit to burst.

'No, Genie love!' Mr B was overcome. 'It's all right – we haven't.' He put an arm round my shoulders as if he was my own dad. He wasn't that much bigger than me, smaller than Joe by nearly a head.

'I was only going to ask you if you'd heard from 'im, that's all. He's a good lad for letter writing but I'm sure 'e'd write to his young lass more than to us.' He was trying to sound light-hearted, make a bit of a joke of it, but I could hear the worry in his voice and this didn't help me, though I was grateful for his kindness.

I shook my head, tears pouring down my face. 'I haven't had a letter since Friday.'

'Oh,' Mr Broadbent said soberly. 'I see.'

Words were swirling round in my head. Where are you Joe? I can't bear it, I just can't bear it.

322

'Look.' Mr B rallied himself. 'They're very busy, under a lot of pressure. He'll get in touch when he can, love. I'm sure there's an explanation.'

The explanation, the only one possible it seemed, hung in the air between us like a cloud of flies and Mr Broadbent looked sorry he'd spoken.

'Just hold on, Genie. The moment I hear anything I'll let you know, all right? And you do the same, eh?' He patted my back. 'You take your time now, as much as you need, before you go back in there.'

The endless, gnawing worry took away most of my happiness in knowing Dad was alive. Nothing compared with the way I felt about Joe, how we'd had this bit of time together that was almost too good to be true. I couldn't talk to Mom about it, she was too wrapped up in herself. Only Teresa knew how sick with worry I was. Carlo had left for his army training and she came round to see me of an evening sometimes, knowing I'd just sit and fret.

'I know now,' Teresa said to me as we sat together that evening. 'Seeing the way you're feeling. If I thought something'd happened to Carlo I'd be exactly the same. Funny how I never saw him before, right there under my nose. Always trying to get away from the Italians and be different. This lot has made me see us all properly, the good that's there. I was such a stupid little cow, wasn't I?'

I managed a grin. 'I wouldn't put it quite that strong.'

'Hear that?' Teresa said. 'Wasn't that your door?'

There was another, louder knock.

Mr Broadbent was outside in the dusk, face all smiles, handing me a folded piece of paper.

'You'd never believe it – blooming postman delivered this wrong. It came two days ago and they put it through at 87.'

I must've just gawped at him.

'We're number 37,' Mr Broadbent explained. 'Joe didn't write it any too clear. He must've been in a rush. We've not been living there long, so they didn't know to pass it on to us. It's OK, Genie. Joe's all right.'

When he'd gone I opened it.

I'll write properly when I can. I love you. I love
you. I love you.
    Joe.

I sat down opposite Teresa and burst into tears.

The daylight air battles petered out in the middle of the month. The Germans had worked their way through attacking the coastal convoys, the airfields, the control centres, and now they turned their attention on the cities. London was getting it every night. Churchill made his famous speech about 'Never in the field of human conflict was so much owed by so many to so few.' They were heroes of the age, those flyers.

I was so proud of Joe, but I never had a minute's peace. His letter was like having him back from the dead, but I was sure that would never happen again. I knew he was alive and safe each time he wrote, but by the time it reached me? And the next day, and the next? I felt so unworthy of him I just could not believe he'd survive and come back to me.

This was different from anything I'd felt before. Frightening, because I couldn't just brush it off like I could with Walt or Jimmy. Joe had marked my heart and I couldn't get away from it.

That week Mom handed in her notice at work and a day or two later she was summoned to the Labour Exchange. She came back fuming with humiliation.

'D'you know what that hoity-toity little bit said to me? Cut-glass accent she had, can't have been much older than you. "Well, Mrs Watkins."' Mom was pretty good at taking off other people's voices. '"Are you quait sure you heven't got yourself in the femily way in order to get orf war work? Surely at your age you wouldn't normally be plenning to enlorge your femily?" Stuck up little bitch. What's she doing in a soft job like that anyhow? She could be in the army or summat.

'Anyhow, I told her she could keep her airs and graces and not talk to her elders and betters like that. She didn't like that, I can tell you.' Mom was roving round the room tidying, slamming things down on the table.

'Did they say you could give up war work though?'

'Yes, in the end,' she admitted grudgingly. 'Bugger this cowing war. Your life's not your own any more, is it?'

Music while you Work was blaring out as usual. 'We'll meet again . . .' and 'Bless 'em all' – thank goodness for the jolly ones because they didn't touch me. Horrible, being wrung out by music all day long. I wished they'd switch the flaming thing off half the time. My eyes and hands worked automatically, head down, not joining in with the jokes. They kept trying to cheer me up, bless them, but even though I tried to put on a brave face, nothing worked. I'd had one more very short note from Joe, but I'd got myself in such a state I was always consumed by worry.

'Genie!' A call passed along the warehouse. I hadn't seen the yard door open wide enough for his head to poke round. 'Mr B wants you out the back.'

All those eyes watching and my legs watery, nearly letting me down. If it was good news about Joe he'd have come right in. Run and told everyone, because after all everyone loved him, not just me.

By the time I reached that door I was trembling so much I could barely get it open. Someone helped, twisted the handle, shut it behind me.

My first breath on the other side of that door I gasped in so hard you could hear it. He was standing waiting for me across the yard, half smiling, uncertain. The time he'd been away felt so long.

'Oh—' I gasped again, grinding my fist into the middle of my chest. For a moment I couldn't speak. Breath came in jerks and pants.

'Genie . . .?'

I didn't remember crossing the yard. I might've flown for all I know. I was holding him, squeezing his arms, pressing his cheeks between my hands, pulling him to me tight, kissing and kissing his lovely face.

He didn't speak at first, calmed me with his hands, taking me by the shoulders to hold me at arm's length, and we looked at each other. His face was thinner, cheeks covered with a day's growth of stubble, dark eyes full of emotion. He pulled me to him and held me so tight.

'Joe, Joe—' My tears flowed, like fear dissolving down my face. 'Oh my God, are you all right?'

326

He nodded. 'I'm fine. On top.'

'You're here.' I couldn't let go of him, couldn't stop saying it again and again. 'You're here – really here . . .'

'Yes—' He sounded as if he couldn't believe it himself. 'Finally made it.'

'Don't ever, ever go away again,' I demanded.

Joe was holding me, laughing as Mr Broadbent came back out smiling, the worry lifted from him. He even looked taller. I mopped my eyes.

'Thought I'd leave you both for a bit,' he said. 'Betty, my wife, telephoned to say Joe'd got home and I said she'd better send him up here quick because there was someone losing a lot of sleep over 'im.'

Joe smiled properly for the first time. 'Thanks, Dad. But I was coming anyway.'

He only had four days and we spent every possible moment we could together. At the end of the week, while I was at work he stayed at home with his mom and sisters, catching up on sleep after the punishing weeks he'd been through. But he was young and very fit and he bounced back.

His first evening home Mr Broadbent asked me to come over and spend some time with them.

'Are you sure you don't just want him to yourselves?' I asked, uncertain about being included in the family like this. I knew Mr B was OK with me but I wasn't sure about the rest of them.

'Course not. And anyhow, if we don't get you along we shan't be able to tie Joe into his seat long enough to get anything out of 'im!'

I was nervous about meeting Joe's mom and his sisters. What on earth were they going to think of me?

Marjorie, the sister who'd been at Broadbents' show, opened the door of their recently built house in Hall Green with its fresh-looking white window-frames.

'We were just finishing off tea,' she said. I saw she had Joe's dark eyes and the same pale hair and skin. She did have an aloof manner but I think it was shyness, and she was trying to be nice to me.

'Sorry. Am I too early? I could go and walk round for a bit . . .'

'No!' She thawed further and laughed. 'We're expecting you. I'll never hear the end of it from Joe if I send you off again. Come and join us.'

Joe was coming out to meet me and introduced me to everyone – his mom and Marjorie and Louise. And he made it very clear I was someone special, brought me in as if I were royalty.

Marjorie was soon to be twenty-one, according to Joe, though as we sat round that evening I kept looking at her, trying to take this in. I couldn't help feeling I was older than her. There was something cardboard about her. Amiable enough, but with a bit missing somehow. She seemed like someone who was afraid of life, even her own shadow.

Joe sat beside me on their sofa and I basked in being close to him. Mr and Mrs Broadbent were in chairs on either side of the little tiled fireplace. Mrs Broadbent was, over all, a very pale woman. Looked as if she'd had a bad shock, the colour of her. Her hair was white-blond and her skin ashen and thin-looking so that you could see the veins in her neck. I was trying to puzzle out how she'd managed to build up the vile reputation she had round the factory. I came to the conclusion that because she was beautiful and fragile-looking she was like a red rag to a bull for some of those women. They were expected to be tough, coping, hard-working, whatever time of the month, stage of pregnancy or chronic illness they were suffering. Mrs B looked like one of those Victorian women who might get the 'vapours'. Actually her health seemed quite all right. Her manipulative illnesses must have been a factory legend that started small and swelled into something much bigger.

The fact was she was quiet and shy and pleasant and I was grateful to her that she didn't seem to mind me. After all, if she'd been half the snob she was painted as being she'd've objected to her son courting a factory lass. Maybe she thought it'd all blow over and he'd grow out of me, but either way, she was kind to me.

'I hear your father's been in contact,' she said, passing me an oatmeal biscuit. 'What a relief that must be.'

'Oh it is. Couldn't believe it when we heard. It's been so long, and no one telling us either way.'

'Like someone else we could mention.' Louise, Joe's younger sister, nudged him with her foot. She wasn't much older than me, with jet-black hair, Joe's cocoa-brown eyes and a lot of spark to her. She was in her last year at the grammar school. Her hair was cut in a pageboy with her fringe long and dead straight, level with her eyebrows. 'Next time just send us a piece of paper every day with a cross on or something, and then at least we'll know the Jerries haven't had you for breakfast.'

'Sorry,' Joe said, for what was obviously far from the first time. 'I did my best. It's not my fault if the postman can't read . . .'

'You've always had illegible handwriting,' Louise retorted, slouching back in her chair. 'Why *do* boys always write so much worse than girls?'

I wanted to tell her to shut up and leave Joe alone but

fortunately his dad did it for me. 'Leave 'im, Louise,' he said. 'Anyway, I thought you were off out?'

'I am.' She pushed the last piece of biscuit into her mouth and got up. 'The pictures with Laurie. Won't be late.' She nodded at me. 'Cheerio, Genie, nice to meet you.'

Marjorie drifted off as well, leaving the four of us sat round on their coffee-coloured furniture. They didn't make me feel awkward and I liked the way Joe and his dad talked to each other, man to man. Joe often turned to smile at me as we talked. I was still reeling from him coming home, didn't care where I was or what we did as long as I could be with him. Mrs Broadbent asked me about my family and later she made drinks of Bournvita.

As it grew late Mr B said, 'Are you going to run Genie home?'

'Can you drive?' I was impressed with that. No one else we knew had a car except the doctor.

'I'll give you a demonstration, shall I?' Joe took my hand to pull me up.

When we'd climbed into his father's Austin, me looking round the inside in amazement, he said, 'It's good to be home, but I've been dying to have you to myself.'

We waited while his dad gave us a wave and closed the front door, then Joe took me in his arms and I rested against him, smelling his familiar smell mixed with the leather of the seats. Our lips found each other's.

'I thought so much about what it would have been like if you hadn't come back,' I said, looking up at him. 'It felt as if anything good in my life had ended.'

Joe stroked my head against his chest. 'I thought about it too – about losing you. You've had raids here already, haven't you? And there'll be more if London's anything to go by.'

'Didn't you think about yourself – what danger you were in?'

'Only when I let myself. You can't too much. Hardly ever at Tangmere – otherwise I wouldn't be able to do the job. You don't think about dying. You get through every day, somehow. You have to be nearly as much of a machine as the planes.'

I didn't want to press Joe too much on the subject. Wasn't even sure how much I wanted to know anyhow. He'd said he was in an air crew at Tangmere and that towards the end of it all, Tangmere and Kenley had been the only sector airfields left to handle the defence.

'It's over anyway, that part,' Joe said. 'Let's think about the future.'

He started the car and drove across to the Stratford Road.

'How d'you fancy a day out tomorrow?'

'With you? Nah, don't think so.' I grinned at him as we pulled up outside our house.

'Cheeky hoyden!' He leaned over and tickled me until I was begging him to stop. 'Dad might lend us the car.'

'The car!' I sat up straight. A car to drive anywhere we wanted! 'Pick me up as early as you can,' I ordered him. 'I don't want to miss a single moment.'

Apart from the Lickey Hills, which just about counted, I'd never been out of Birmingham before. Joe drove us out to Kenilworth, me in a state of high excitement.

'There's a castle,' Joe told me as I was bouncing up

and down on the seat next to him. 'And lots of country round to walk in. That's if the car's still in one piece to get us there by the time you've finished.'

'I can't believe this, Joe,' I kept saying as we drove out along the Coventry Road, and Joe laughed again at my fidgety happiness as the edges of Brum faded behind us.

'It's not a very marvellous day,' he said, leaning forward to look up through the windscreen. 'Doesn't look as if it'll rain though.'

'I don't care if it does.' We laughed. Laughed a lot that day.

Now we were out of town I was full of exclamations about the fields, the fresh smell of the air, old cottages in the villages, cows and sheep, and the fresh hay bales spilling out of barns. All of it was exciting to me, like travelling into a story book.

'Oh Joe, I want to live in the country,' I said, overcome by all I could see and how lovely it all looked, even under a cloudy sky. 'I know it seems strange, no pavements and chimneys and shops and that, but I wouldn't miss them. Not if I could have all this.'

Warwickshire seemed at least as good as heaven that day.

Joe parked up the car in a narrow side street in Kenilworth and we walked through the little town with its pretty houses and generous green space in the middle. In the gardens there were still roses, beds of marigolds, golden rod.

'It all looks so small, doesn't it?' Joe said.

'It's beautiful,' I sighed, and Joe laughed.

'You're nice and easy to please.' He put his hand in the pocket of his jacket, and with his spare one, drew my hand through the crook of his arm. He leaned round and kissed me. I didn't care that it was in the street where people could see. I was proud to be there on his arm and I didn't give a monkey's who was watching.

We walked around, close together and very leisurely all morning, talking and laughing. We had a fish dinner in the Queen and Castle (a big treat), before going to see the real castle, not far away, at the edge of the town.

As we walked round inside the shell of the castle walls, where it felt very quiet suddenly, or set out along a path into the fields, I held my hand in Joe's, or sometimes slipped it into the pocket of his coat where his change rattled against the silky lining.

'I don't even know why you're wearing a coat this time of year – must be a born pessimist!'

We walked across the fields, climbing stiles, as the sky turned to lead, and watched the cows grazing, wondering when the rain was going to come. It wasn't long before enormous drops started to fall. Right away everything smelt lovely in the wet.

'Oh no!' Joe groaned, getting all bothered like he had over the bikes. 'Here, Genie. You have my coat.'

'No, I'm all right. I don't mind!' The rain made me feel wildly happy and reckless. It was heavy but warm, and the sound of it was all around us like a loud rustling. I turned my face up and held my arms to the sky, half dancing along the path.

'It's raining, it's pouring, the old man is snoring—'

I didn't care if I got drenched to the skin. I tore along, feeling it dash on my face and sink into my scalp through my hair.

Seeing me, Joe must have decided there was no point being worried, and he ran behind me and took my hand.

'Look!' he called out. 'Over the other side – we can shelter.'

The field we were running across was pasture for cows. It had clumps of enormous thistles with purple tops and there were cowpats all over the place. I was glad to see the black and white cows were all huddling right at the other end. Joe and I ran together, careful where we put our feet, laughing and whooping as the rain streamed down our faces.

'Crikey, what a downpour!' Joe shouted.

He felt very strong and fast but I kept up easily, even though it was all uphill, feeling as if I had an iron body and could have just gone on and on running.

The barn at the border of the fields was almost full. Joe picked me up and lifted me on to the ledge of straw bales which was about up to my chest, then climbed up himself and at last we were under cover. The rain was still coming down like mad, sweeping sideways across the slope of the field. We looked round, then at each other, and laughed again.

It was perfect. The stack was packed like a staircase, the bales at the back and sides piled right to the roof of the barn, but with a wide-stepped gap up the middle presumably designed so you could climb up to reach the ones at the back. It might have been made for us. The light was dim as we climbed further towards the top of the stack and the rain thundered on the roof. We settled down together surrounded by the fresh, prickly bales of straw, water seeping from the ends of our hair.

Still getting my breath back, I lay and looked up at the darkness. 'This is the most wonderful, exciting thing I've ever done.'

Joe turned and smiled at me, shouldering his coat off.

'I suppose you think that doesn't say much for the rest of my life? And that'd be about right. But it's doing this with you. That's the thing.'

He leaned over and wiped my face with his hand-kerchief, his own still shiny with water, eyes on mine. 'Some people would have let it spoil the whole day. Not you though.' Teasing, he pressed his little finger into my cheek as I smiled. 'Dimples.'

He mopped his own face, then absent-mindedly opened up the white square and laid it out flat on the other side of him, although there wasn't much hope of it drying. I think he was looking for something to do. Neither of us spoke for a time.

Things changed in those moments. I went from wild, crazy happiness to feeling solemn suddenly, affected by Joe's closeness to me. I watched him, wondering what he was thinking.

Joe had never said or done anything to offend me in any way. We'd kissed of course, touched outside our clothes, but he was always considerate and tactful. He'd never pushed me to do anything more than I wanted. I suppose he thought I was more innocent than I actually was, coming from households like ours and Nan's. I knew promiscuity led to punishment, like it had for my mom. That it was cheap and wrong to think of going with a man before you were married and that he'd probably think so badly of me if he knew what I was thinking . . .

Yet as I lay looking at him my whole body was full of longing. I found I was trembling with love for him and with need. I knew that at my age I shouldn't be wanting what I did then, from Joe. And as he turned and lay beside me all this desire and confusion must have shown in my eyes because I couldn't hide it. He leaned over me and in his eyes I saw the same struggle between thought and emotion, the same overwhelming longing.

I reached up and put my arms round his neck, shaking.

'Are you cold?'

I shook my head. 'No. Not cold.'

He understood me and half sat up again. 'Genie, the way I feel about you, I'd give anything, anything – But you're so young. I keep forgetting that. I don't want us – you especially – to do anything we'll regret.'

I sat up and put my arms round him again. Here he was. Now, in my arms. 'We could be dead soon. Either of us.'

Joe looked down at me, eyes full of emotion. 'I didn't know this feeling could be so strong. Wanting you all the time. I know I couldn't write, but you were in my mind so much. I kept thinking of you – your body.'

'And I did. I remember thinking I don't know you – all of you – what your shoulders are like. Your legs. And you might never come back and I'd never know. It's like a dream all this, Joe, to me. You've got to believe me – nothing anything like as good as this has ever happened to me before.'

Joe held me close. 'I love you, Genie. More than I can – anything I say never feels enough.'

'Joe—' My cheeks were burning suddenly. 'I'm only afraid of having a babby.'

He blushed then, fiddled with a wisp of straw. 'I can prevent it. Forces issue.'

'I want to tell you something.' Heart beating hard, I spoke all in a rush. 'Now, so I'm never hiding anything from you. It's my mom. She's having a babby and it's not my dad's. I need you to know, that's all. That's one of the reasons things are difficult at home. I never told you before because I was ashamed and scared of what you'd think.'

He let this sink in. 'Well, whose ...? No, it doesn't matter whose, I suppose.' He kissed my hair. 'But it's not your fault. It's nothing for you to be ashamed of.'

'But when it's your own mom—'

'Look, you've nothing to worry about with me. It's not for me to judge her.'

'People will though. They do.'

We lay kissing and touching, both of us trembling, pressed tight together as if we could each slide under the other's skin. The hard, pummelling downpour had eased but it was still raining steadily and the light came to us as if through cobwebs. I could sense Joe's excitement and I sat up in our little half-lit funnel between the bales and undid the buttons of his shirt. His shoulders were slim, pale and strong as I'd known they would be. He sat up to pull off the shirt and I put my face to his chest, soft with hairs, and breathed in the smell of him, felt the pulse of his blood.

He undressed me with shaking fingers and his shaking made me love him more. I thought how I would never in a million years let Jimmy do this, see any of me, let alone down there, the private place between my legs, and I felt very shy even with Joe. But I trusted him as he peeled off my blouse, then my damp little camisole, hesitating before touching my tiny bosoms as if he hardly dared.

When we were both fully undressed we touched each other's bodies. I felt his warm breath on my skin. Our eyes kept finding each other's, talking with no words. When Joe's hands moved between my thighs I heard his breath catch and this desire, his need to keep control, made me lift myself to him, legs widening.

We lay there afterwards on the scratchy straw, warming each other. 'Joe, my Joe,' I said again and again, my arm tight over him. 'You're all I've ever wanted.' The small amount of light cast deep shadows on the dips and hollows of our bodies. Joe pulled the dry side of his coat over us.

'Has its uses, you see.' Then he said. 'My love. My love.'

There was silence, except for the rain.

'When I was a kid,' I said, 'and it was raining outside – at night like – I used to lie there and think of all the people out in it. Not just people. Cats and dogs, anything that had nowhere to go. And I used to wish I could bring them all in, know that everything was safe inside under shelter. I had this doll, Janet. I've still got her – she looks pretty rough now – and I'd cuddle Janet and talk to her and pretend we could rescue everyone. We had soup made, the lot, in our game!'

Joe squeezed me. 'Be nice if everything could always be safe.'

'I feel safe with you.'

Talking and staying silent in snatches we held each other until we heard the rain stop, then dressed, shivering, back in our wet clothes. When we climbed down from the barn on the sodden grass mingled with loose straw, a movement caught Joe's eye.

'Look, Genie!'

From across the field a long, ungainly bird pulled itself into flight, huge wings beating with what looked like an enormous effort, and long, thin legs trailing. It looked like an old man in a panic.

'Heron,' Joe said, eyes following the slow path of its flight until it disappeared over the bushes into another field. 'Wasn't it lovely? Marvellous they are, I think. What bit of luck spotting one today.'

I put my hand in his, sighing. 'I don't know about so many things. You'll have to teach me.'

Joe turned and took me in his arms again. 'With pleasure. Genie?' His face was serious. 'What we just did. I wouldn't want you to think it didn't mean anything more to me. One day I want to be able to wake up with you in a bed in our own home. Our marriage bed.'

On his last day, I asked Joe to come to my nan's. It was Sunday afternoon and everyone was there: Nan, Lil and the kids, Frank, Mom, Len and Molly. Mom was deadpan but in control, although I kept eyeing her to make sure. I wanted Joe to meet my family properly now because I trusted he'd accept us for what we were, even though going there meant taking him to a slum house, however clean.

'Hope you'll take us as you find us,' were Nan's first words to him when we arrived. She was smiling, had met him before of course, and was impressed. And he did just what she asked.

One thing was worrying me though. I didn't want Joe having too many shocks at once. In a moment's opportunity I took Lil aside. 'Any sign of him up there?' I rolled my eyes at Morgan's ceiling.

'No, and there shouldn't be with any luck. I hear he's got back trouble.'

'Ah, now I wonder why.'

'Cheeky girl,' Lil dimpled at me. 'But it's all right. I think you're safe.'

With everyone there it was a tight squeeze of course, but we all fitted in. Joe talked to Mom and managed to get some joy in reply and he seemed to cheer her up a bit.

It was a wonderful afternoon. Cups of tea and cake, sing-songs led by Nan which had Molly and Len rocking from side to side putting the chairs in danger, Len yelling out bits of song. Lil made me sing solo, and Joe, who was obviously thoroughly enjoying himself, egged me on too.

'You know you can do it – and I want to hear you.'

I liked the old songs – 'Apple Blossom Time' again and 'Maid of the Mountains', and Joe led everyone clapping me.

'Come on, let's hear you now!' I challenged him, and after protesting he couldn't sing, in the end he and Frank clowned about together singing 'Some Day I'll Find You' and 'The Little Dutch Mill'.

Seeing the two of them together, Frank with his dark Hollywood looks and Joe's fair, handsome face, Lil linked her arm through mine and squeezed it, giving me a wink as if to say, 'We've done all right there, kid.'

The two of them finished, bowing from side to side as if they were in the Albert Hall, then Frank snuck up behind Lil. 'Here, I want to show you summat.'

He stood at the back of her and laid his hands on her head, feeling around.

Lil squealed. 'What the hell are you playing at? That feels really funny. Eh, pack it in!'

'You can tell a lot from feeling the shape of someone's head,' Frank said, kneading Lil's skull. 'I've learned a bit about it from a pal. It's a branch of science, you know.'

'Oh ah,' Nan said, rubbing her bandage. 'So's flying to the moon on a magic carpet.'

'Gerroff will you!' Lil stood up, poking him in the tummy.

'Awright.' Frank gave in. 'C'mere Joe, boys. Who knows some tricks?'

Patsy and Tom crowded round, keen, and Joe sat watching Frank dealing cards with a flourish, a fag hanging jauntily from the side of his mouth. Even Mom laughed at his antics and Lil stood at his shoulder. Only Nanny Rawson was giving him sceptical looks and sniffing over her teacup as if to say 'Huh!'

Some time in the afternoon we heard planes, and we all stiffened and went quiet except for Joe and Frank, who rushed out to see, looking for the formation, but they'd already passed.

'No siren anyhow,' Lil said. 'Must've been ours.'

But it seemed to remind Frank of something. He looked at his watch. 'Got to go.'

Lil frowned. 'Where're you off to?'

'Couple of things to see to, that's all.' He gathered up his cards, then leaned forward and kissed her. Our nan scowled so you could almost hear it. 'See you tomorrow.'

Lil looked disappointed, but there wasn't a lot she could do about it. I suppose she wanted things settled, wanted married life again.

Later in the afternoon we had a visitor. A little black and white terrier with tan eyebrows and bright liquid eyes was peeping in at us. Joe, sat by the open door, was the first to notice.

'Who's this then?' he said. 'Hello Mister!'

'Never seen him before.' Lil snapped her fingers at him. 'C'm'ere!'

The small, wiry body came in, wagging a stump of black tail so hard its whole body snaked from side to side, face turning fast from one to the other of us. Then it launched itself into Len's lap.

341

'Oi!' Len laughed as the terrier pushed its wet nose against his ear and Molly leaned over and rubbed at him roughly with her big meaty hands.

'Well where did he come from?' Lil said, bending over to stroke the rough, fidgeting back. 'Not from round here, is he, Mom?'

'Not as I know of,' Nan said. ''Ere – get 'im off the table!'

There were shrieks of laughter as the dog leapt skidding off the table and went round the room sniffing at everyone's legs.

'Ooh, he's tickling me!' Mom giggled. 'He's a proper livewire, ain't he?'

Then he was in my lap, scratchy tongue on my face, and I cuddled him. He felt warm and comforting. Joe reached round and stroked him and looked into the dog's face and I saw a kind of communication there that he seemed to have with all creatures. Patsy, Tom and Cathleen gathered round, squabbling about who could stroke him next.

'Wish we could keep him,' I said.

'I s'pect he belongs to someone,' Lil said. 'But he's nice, isn't he?'

'Could be a stray.' Joe was still making a fuss of him. 'If you haven't seen him before.'

Our nan got up to put another kettle on. 'Looks well enough fed, doesn't 'e? We'll just 'ave to see. Really and truly we need 'im round here like an 'ole in the 'ead.'

I didn't want that afternoon to finish. I kept shutting my mind to the terrible thought that not only would it have to end but that Joe was leaving today. We'd come

342

so close and now we'd have to be torn apart again. All afternoon we were close to each other, nearly always touching, legs, shoulders, hands, or Joe's arm round me.

As we all left Nan's, the dog followed.

'He likes you, Genie!' Lil called from the door.

'He's got good taste,' Joe whispered.

'You're not going to get rid of him in a hurry.'

'Go on – go home!' Mom turned and swished at him with her hand. He stopped for a moment, puzzled, then followed again as soon as we started walking. 'Shoo!' she tried again, but it was pretty half-hearted. I could see she'd taken a shine to him. And there was no stopping Molly turning round, chuckling and calling to him, giving him every encouragement.

When we got to Brunswick Road he was still there like our shadow.

'Oh, can we keep him, Mom? Please? He'd be company.'

'Well ... I s'pose if he belongs to someone he'll take off home later.'

But he ran into our garden at the back, sniffed around and cocked his leg as if he owned the place.

'He staying then?' Len asked.

'Dunno.' Mom's eyes followed him as he did a tour of the Anderson's roof. 'But he looks as if he might have it in mind.'

I couldn't face the railway station with Joe this time, so we said our goodbyes more privately, on the way to his house, where he had to go and change and get his kit. But it was even more terrible than before. Hard as I tried not to I cried this time, just wanted to hold on to him and drink him in, make up for all the time I

343

wouldn't be able to touch him or have him close. The nearer the moment came for us to part the less we spoke, but this time it was not fraught and unsure, just full of longing for things to be different. And I still had my feeling of not deserving him, a sense of doom, that this was too good to last.

When we said goodbye Joe held me close, chin resting on my head, and my arms were tight round his waist. He kissed the top of my head, and I could tell from his silence he was as emotional as I was.

'Ssh,' he said after a while. 'Don't cry, Genie. I'll be back soon, you'll see. We'll be together. And one day we'll be able just to stay together without all this.'

I reached up and put my arms round his neck so our cheeks were pressed together. Then we kissed as if it was the last kiss in the world.

'You're everything to me, Joe.'

He smiled down at me and I loved that smile so much my tears started falling again. 'You're part of me, Genie, you always will be. I love you.'

When at last I had to watch him walk off it was with a terrible tearing feeling, as if a piece of me was being snatched away and taken into the hands of an evil force that might not let me have him back.

October 1940

The leaves started to crisp and fall and Mister was still with us. From the day he followed us home he was a fixture. Now and then he used to wander off and we thought we'd lost him, but sooner or later we'd hear him bark out the front and Mom'd say, 'Oh-oh, here comes trouble,' and she was nearly as glad as I was to see him back.

I called him Mister because that was the way Joe greeted him that day and when I thought of Joe holding and stroking him it was like some contact with him apart from his letters, which were what I lived for these days.

Whenever I got home from work, Mister was there, jumping to greet me like a mad thing, panting and licking, on the teeter for food. I'd try and find him some scraps, telling him about my day almost as if he was Joe.

The bombing started gradually at first. They were taking more of an interest in us up in the Midlands, but it was like the lull, that early part of October. Mom was calm for a bit then. It was as if she'd put herself through so much agonizing and worry that her mind had blanked out. She was quiet, moved round the house doing odd jobs, went shopping in a loose dress she'd knocked up, slept and wrote letters to Eric. She smoked and drank, but for the moment, not as much as she'd done before.

She knew there was talk about her, bitching on the street, and they didn't trouble themselves to keep their voices down either. Mrs Marshall, Mrs Terry, Mrs Smith. You'd've thought they had enough to do with themselves without poking their noses into other people's lives. They got a thrill out of calculating the length of a pregnancy and talking about it loudly as we went past. We just looked hard faced and ignored them. But it was horrible, and you got to dread going out.

Teresa's Carlo came home on leave and one Saturday night they came over to see us. I liked Carlo, warmed to him. He was a year younger than Joe. His wiry black hair was cut shorter now, he had those striking blue eyes and a loud infectious laugh. He told us about some of the ragging he'd had as an Eyetie in the British army, though he seemed to be able to throw it off. Teresa, who was looking as beautiful as I'd ever seen her, sat close to him, and it was obvious she was just plain crazy about him. She kept turning, smiling into his eyes, and there were moments when the rest of us might as well not have been there. I was so happy for her, for them both.

Len and Molly were with us, Molly looking even more enormous already, although she still had four months or so to go with the pregnancy. Len sat between her chair and Gloria on the table, alternating between fondling each of them.

'Ssh!' Mom said, holding a hand up. 'Listen!'

A tiny, nervous voice was coming out of Gloria.

'It's Princess Elizabeth!' Teresa said. 'Ah – listen to that.'

We listened in wonder. We'd never heard her voice before. She was broadcasting a message to the evacuees.

'My sister Margaret Rose and I feel so much for you,' the high, cut-glass little voice was saying.

Mom scowled heavily as the Princess talked about the 'kind people who have welcomed you to their homes in the country'. By the end, as the little girls said their goodnights, she was dabbing her eyes with a hanky. 'Oh my poor Eric!'

'Oh, don't upset yourself, Mrs Watkins.' Teresa leaned forward and took her hand. 'Eric's safe as houses, ain't he? And it looks as if they were right about the bombing now, don't it? So he's probably well out of it.'

Mom tried to smile back. It was hard to resist Teresa. She could deal with my mom far better than I ever could.

'I know,' she sniffed. 'It's just hard to feel someone else's bringing up your son.' She rallied herself. 'Any more news of your dad, Teresa? And Stevie?'

Teresa's face fell. 'They've been moved, we think. There was a lad came home not long back – lived up by my nan. He's only fifteen, should never've been taken in the first place. Says they're moving them but he doesn't know where. Mom's ever so worried about him again now, because of his chest. I mean we don't know what conditions they'll be in – sleeping out and that.'

Carlo stroked his hand down Teresa's back, trying to reassure her.

'If only we knew more. We've had no letters for ages and we don't know what's going on or where they are. Sorry.' She tried to smile. 'I don't want to put a dampers on the evening. We've all got our worries, haven't we?'

I put my hand down and stroked Mister's black and white back, remembering Joe's hand doing the same. We certainly did all have our worries. But for those brief hours, things were as OK as they could be.

Our days had already been broken into by the chilling rise and fall moan of the air raid siren. But none of those interruptions – the scramble we made to the cellar at Broadbent's, smoke canisters going off outside to screen the factories, the singing to pass the time – compared with the night raids.

Birmingham's Blitz began at full strength in mid-October. There was a raid every night after that for the next two weeks.

We weren't ready for the first raid. At the sound of the siren, Mister put his head back and set up a shrill howling. Maybe it hurt his ears – it certainly jarred ours – but his high yowl made it all even more nerve-racking.

'Can't you shut 'im up?' Mom snapped. She couldn't seem to think what to do, just kept picking things up and putting them down again. 'Give him summat to eat – anything so's he'll pack that racket in.'

Not having a routine for this yet, we grabbed hold of things we thought might be useful – a lamp, Thermos, rugs, coats – and struggled down the garden into the shelter, seeing the searchlights criss-crossing in the sky. We had no idea how long it might go on for.

Len sat perched for a while on one of the shelves that made thin bunks on each side as the planes droned closer and closer overhead, then lay down and went to sleep, his bent knees hanging over the edge because the bunk wasn't long enough for him.

Mom and I sat side by side on the other bunk facing him across the narrow gap. The planes came over in waves, the noise growing louder, our hearts beating faster. It was like standing on a railway track, knowing there's a train coming. With every explosion outside, our heads ducked. If it was close enough you felt the impact under your feet. And all you could do was sit there, waiting.

It took me a little while to notice what a state Mom was in. That first night as they came over she was feverishly smoking and biting her nails but she was quiet. She'd lit the lamp and her eyes, stretched with fright, reflected back the flame. When it'd gone on for a time she said, 'Jesus – I wish I had something to drink.'

I reached down for the flask. 'There's some tea—'

'A proper drink!' she half yelled at me. 'It's bloody horrible in here. They're going to hit us, I know they are.'

'It'll be all right,' I said, though my legs were rubbery with fright. I cuddled Mister, who was more scared than I was, to steady myself. 'We're supposed to be safe in here.'

Mom gave a harsh laugh. ''Bout as safe as an empty peach tin.'

'Why don't you try and get some sleep?'

'Sleep? You barmy? How the hell's anyone s'posed to sleep through this lot? Well, 'cept him of course.' She jabbed a finger resentfully at Len.

It was terribly frightening. More than I could've imagined. My hands were sweaty, stomach all churned up. It was like being alone in all the world with the bombs. The rest of the city might as well not have existed.

I was exhausted too. To the extent that it was beginning to fight with the fear and to win. Mom could sleep this off tomorrow but I had to be at work. Tiredness could make you fatalistic. Whatever would happen would happen. You had to sleep, just had to. That was my first taste of the half-awake, half-asleep state you found yourself in during the raids. Asleep and yet not. Still half aware of the planes, the screams and thuds of the bombs in the soapy haze that your over-stretched mind had become. And whenever Mom thought I was nodding off she poked me awake. 'Don't leave me alone in this, Genie. I can't stand it.'

When it stopped and the sky went quiet, the All Clear finally sounded its two minute relief and we crawled up out of that damp hell-hole feeling as if we'd come out again into a different, miraculous world where there were stars in the sky, the shapes of houses round us, still standing, and fresh air. We were not just alive, but reborn.

'Oh, I can't go back in there again,' Mom said, stretching her arms to the sky. 'Never again.'

But we were back in there that night and for many nights after. This was the striped existence of the bombing raids. The days full of brightness, sunshine and fading leaves on the trees casting yellow light. After sitting there in the dark of the night, terrified and weary, the possibility of death coming at you all the time, the light of day was like an enormous cheer breaking out. We're alive. ALIVE. Everything felt bigger and more vivid than usual, the sky close and blue, our house bolder and more solid, the colours of flowers a cause of wonder and every building in the city, however functional, a great work of art. Every day we came out into the rank smell of smoke across Birmingham, looking round to see what had been destroyed in a city that until then we hadn't realized we loved with a passion.

From the second night Mom made sure she had a bottle of the kind she preferred with her. Len tried bringing Gloria in but she crackled and beeped and didn't seem at all happy in the shelter, and what with all the racket outside we couldn't have heard her anyway. So he stowed her under the stairs in the house after that.

The strain began to tell on us. Even in the daytime there were enough hazards. Dread of daytime raids, though they'd mostly stopped them now, unexploded bombs left over from the nights and glass blown out by the blast, the checking and rechecking that everyone was all right, had survived the night.

But it was the nights, those hellish nights. Mister, made distraught by all the noise, would burrow as deep as he could into my lap. Len sucked barley sugars, or hummed to himself, which drove Mom round the bend. She spent the time swigging gin, trying to drink herself into oblivion. And I sat in there with them all, so glad of Mister to cuddle, thinking of how it must have been for Joe up in those planes, holding on to the thought of him and trying to swallow the panic which rose in me like bile.

'Can I have some?' I asked Mom one night as she held tight to the neck of the bottle. No messing with glasses for her now.

'Go on then, have a sip. It'll make you feel better.'

I took a mouthful, felt it burn down inside me and gagged. 'Ugh – it's horrible.' My stomach was already to pot from fear and lack of sleep.

More than once Mom drank until she passed out and I was left alone, as Len could sleep through anything. I sat holding my dog, counting the seconds between each whistle of a bomb and the crunch of the impact, trying to keep a hold on my mind out there in the dark garden, with only this tiny metal hub between me and death.

When it was time to crawl out, blinking and squinting

as the door opened, I had to shake and shake Mom, and more than once just had to leave her there to sleep it off.

Another time she woke wild and hysterical, as if her dreams were a worse hell than the raids themselves.

'No,' she screamed at me, 'I can't go on – can't stand it—' clawing at me in a crazy way, and I was frightened. Her hair was loose and her face crumpled with drink and tiredness. I wasn't sure she was even really awake.

'Look,' I said desperately. 'Why don't you just go back to sleep for a bit?'

To my surprise she did lie down again and close her eyes. I think she spent most of the day asleep now, because there wasn't much sign of anything getting done except her managing to get to the Outdoor for more drink. We were lucky if we got a meal down us before the sirens went off again. Sometimes we ran down with steaming plates and ate in there off our laps.

One night, when we got to the shelter, she found that the gin supplies were disastrously low. There were only a couple of fingers left in the bottle.

'Christ – I can't get through it with only that.' The skin of her face looked thicker nowadays. She was puffing out with the pregnancy, but the boozing can't have helped. 'I'm going to have to get some more.'

'You can't,' I begged her. 'You'll just have to make it last.'

She looked at me as if I was a prison guard. 'You're getting a bit of a bossy miss round here nowadays, ain't you? Don't leave much room for me, does it?'

'I'm not!' I said, hurt. 'And anyhow, there'll be plenty to do when that one arrives.' I nodded towards her bump.

'Oh yes, that one.' She drank from the bottle, then gave a crooked smile. 'D'you think it'll be a boy or a girl? I bet it's a boy, don't you? And what do I call him then? Bob? Or Victor? Bictor, or Vob?' She laughed her stupid drinking laugh.

I thought, Lil wouldn't have been like this. Lil would've coped. But then Lil wouldn't have got herself in this mess in the first place.

'Do us a favour, Genie?' She had to speak loudly now, over the noise outside.

'What?'

'Go down the Outdoor for me and get some more?'

There were planes overhead. I stared at her in disbelief.

'I'll go for you,' Len said.

'No you won't, Len,' I snapped at him. 'They'll be in the cellar anyhow. They don't just stand there selling gin day and night in this lot. None of us is going anywhere.'

Mom pouted like a child. There was a long silence then, except for Mister's frightened whimpering and a tired moth battering against the lamp. Mom was sulking and I was too furious with her to speak.

With every wave of planes passing over I felt my heart bang harder until it was almost a pain. You couldn't move, you couldn't do anything about it – you just had to wait it out. Sometimes I wished I was old enough to be a warden, so's to get out there and do something.

It was a heavy raid that night. The first wave brought incendiary bombs, 'breadbaskets' of them rattling down to set the city alight, turn it into a beacon for the heavy high explosive bombs following close behind. The smell of smoke found its way to us. What was burning tonight? What would be left when – *if* – we got out of here in the morning?

Mom didn't have enough drink to knock herself out. She sat slumped on the bunk, leaning against the crimpy wall near the front of the shelter, staring at Len who was now sleeping like a princess in a fairy story.

I was so stung, so angry at what she'd asked me to do, I couldn't let it go. In the end I burst out, 'So you think more of a bottle of booze than you do me?'

She frowned, focusing on me slowly. 'What?'

'You'd send me out in this – just to get booze for you?'

She nodded in a befuddled sort of way and for a moment I thought she was too far gone to answer me. But eventually she said, 'Well that's me for you all over, ain't it?'

There was a sudden escalation of noise outside and both of us ducked, cringing, protecting our heads with our arms. The impact was loud and horribly near, shaking the ground, and the crashing and whooshing outside seemed to go on for ever.

'God, that was close,' I said as it started to die away. It was hard to straighten up. You got stiff and crumpled with fear.

In the lull that followed Mom nodded across at Len. 'I suppose you know why he's like he is?'

'Like what?'

'Like he is.' Her voice was harsh. 'Soft in the bleeding head, what d'you think? Thought your nan might've let on to you.'

'No. I always thought he was just born that way—'

'Nah, he wasn't born like it.' She shook her head as

hard as a Punch and Judy puppet. 'It was me did that. Ain't it always?'

She talked with her eyes fixed on Lenny's face.

'When he was born I was two – two and a half more like. He was a big babby, always was huge right from the start. And he was like six Christmases rolled into one for me. He was my dolly, my babby, he was going to be my best friend. And he was. I was all over him, all the time. Mom didn't mind. I took him off her hands and that suited her. She needed a hand, she was that pushed, what with the house and all the extra work she took in and our dad being the way he was. So Len was as much mine as he was hers really.

'Anyroad, he grew. I'd cart him about – course, he was heavy and I was a skinny little thing. Then one day when I was turned four Mom said she was going out to take some things up for a Mrs Brigham who lived in another yard up the road. The lady'd just had a babby and she wasn't any too good, so Mom was helping her out, the way she always has. She said to me – I can still hear her – "I'll only be a few minutes. Don't come up. You stay with Len."

' "But Mom—' I started arguing with her. "I want to see the new babby. Can't I come with you?"

' "No," she said. "You stay put. You'll only be in the way. Mrs B's not herself and she won't want me carting you two up there as well."

'And off she went. I was furious. I remember punching the couch downstairs with my fists, shouting, I was that cross. Don't know why I wanted to go so much really – there were always babbies about. But I s'pose I saw myself as a kid who was good with them and I wanted to be counted in.

'So in the end I wrapped my arms round Lenny, sort of in a hug, and picked him up. And I ran up the road after Mom. With his big head in the way I couldn't see where I was going and he was such a weight. I tripped and fell down right on top of him. His head went down with a bang on the pavement. Knocked him out. He wasn't quite two then, and he'd been starting to chatter on, but he never said another word after that – not for about five years, and he was never the same again. The doctors said he had brain damage . . .'

I could see it all, the little girl hoiking her baby brother along the road. Nan's face, the anger that even now she couldn't help spilling out on occasion when she spoke of her eldest daughter.

'You didn't mean it though, did you Mom?'

She shook her head, crying now, like the frightened child who'd done the deed. 'Course not. I wouldn't have hurt him for the world.'

I crept closer and sat by her, not quite daring to take her hand.

'Look at him.' Her cheeks were wet. I wondered if her tears tasted of gin. 'He's going to be a father and he's still only a kid himself. Thanks to me.' She looked at me. 'I deserve them hitting me after all the things I've done. One of these nights they'll get me.'

'Mom, no,' I said, frightened. 'Of course not. You didn't do anything on purpose. You're just . . .' I trailed off. Just what? Unlucky? Careless? Foolish? 'You've just had some accidents, that's all. You've had enough punishment.'

Later in the night, when she'd quietened, we felt sleep coming over us even though the raid wasn't finished. It was more distant and I found I'd blanked out for a time, I didn't know how long. It could have been seconds or hours. But then they were hard over us again and I was suddenly awake. The battering of noise was back, the planes, ack-ack guns with their tennis-like rhythm, the whining and crashing. I sat up, wide awake. The lamp had gone out.

Mister was still lying beside me, but I stretched out on the bunk. Mom wasn't there.

'Lenny?' I shouted across to him. 'Where's Mom? Where's Doreen?'

'She's your side.' He must have been awake already because he sounded alert.

'She's not.' I wondered if she'd tumbled on the floor. 'Mom? Where are you?' I felt around in the dark. Nothing.

'Len, take Mister. I'm going to see out there.'

I wrenched the door open and stepped up into the crazed, coloured world outside. The sky was copper streaked with yellow and red, and puffs of white from the ack-ack fire. Fires across the city – beacons to guide the bombers – were filling the air with acrid smoke and the searchlights scratched at the sky with their cold beams. The explosions of light now were from the foul-smelling high explosive bombs.

But my eyes were fixed on Mom. She was standing with her back to me half way down the garden in her nightclothes, staring up at the glowing sky, her arms stretched out in front of her, open, as if she was in the act of embracing someone. Just standing there, quite still.

'Mom – for God's sake!' I ran to her, wondering if she was asleep or awake. Her pale nightdress stuck out at the front over her belly and I realized she'd taken off her coat. She must have been frozen. Her eyes were open.

'What're you doing?' I bawled at her. 'Come back in for Christ's sake.'

'I thought I'd just get it over with,' she murmured, so I could only just hear.

There came the most massive bang from very close by that snatched the ground from under us and we curled on the ground like babbies, our hands over our heads. I squeezed my eyes tight shut. The noise seemed to go on for ages and ages, the crashing and splintering and explosions of glass. When we stood up, instinct guiding our hands to our bodies to check everything was there, tongues of fire were shooting up from the street behind our house. There was already the sound of fire-engine bells somewhere near.

Mom and I dashed into our dark house. There was glass everywhere, front and back, strewn like a hard, crunchy icing on every surface we touched as we groped our way through to the front. I heard Mom gasp, cutting herself. The blackout blinds at the front were in tatters and through them we could see that a great swathe of the opposite side of the road was gone. Just matchwood and rubble, burning, and more to see than usual of the sky.

Mom's hands went to her cheeks, breath sucking in. 'Oh, look!' She was gulping breath in and out and couldn't speak for a moment. 'They got it – not me ... Someone else got it!'

When the light came we could see it all. The three of us walked out dumbly into the dawn, only half dressed, to see our familiar street changed utterly. We stepped over fat hoses squiggling along the road, leaking feeble arcs of water and lying in a mouse-brown mess of wet plaster and brick dust, and more glass crunched under our feet.

'Lord above, look at it.' Mom stood with her arms folded, a rough dressing on her cut finger. 'God in Heaven.'

Gladys and Molly's house was still standing, as were those on each side of it, but not much further along a great block had been blasted out of the terrace, the inside walls of some still left standing pointing jaggedly up, with their pathetic strips of wallpaper, their picture hooks and damp stains, and the rest of the houses smashed to charred rubble, bits poking out at all angles like spillikins.

There were people out all along the street. Len rushed across and banged on Molly's door and after a time Gladys opened it and the two of them came out, already dressed as they'd most likely been all night. The pair of them looked as tired and dishevelled as we must have done. In the quietest ever voice Gladys said, 'Wasn't it awful? Just a few more yards this way . . .' and she looked along at the shattered houses, her eyes filling.

Len put his arm round Molly, who huddled close to him. Along the street a vicar, shabby old mac flung over his cassock, stood comforting a man who was watching the rescue squad, his face full of fear and desolation. They'd already been working out there for several hours, and the flames had all been put out. We could hear sawing and drilling and the men calling to each other. A team was waiting with stretchers. Other neighbours were gathering round. Mr Tailor from our side of the road stood out in his braces, and everyone was squinting in the shocking sunlight, no one saying, but all of us thinking, as we stared glumly at the houses opposite, 'Who's in there still? Who's dead?' A horrible, dank smell hung over everything, of wet, charred wood and plaster, wisps of grey smoke still floating in the air like the ghosts of those already dead. And mixed with this, the sickening smell of gas seeping from broken pipes in the houses.

One of the gossips I recognized from down the road was standing in front of what had been her house, two toddlers clinging dumbly to her coat and a baby yawling in her arms.

'Look,' Mom said. 'Mrs Terry.'

We went to her, seeing her shivering, the shock on her face.

'We was in the Anderson,' she said. 'In the Anderson. The Anderson at the back.' Their faces were brown with grime like panto gypsies but they all seemed unhurt. There was a mobile canteen at the end of the road handing out tea and we led her down, handing her carefully over the rubble because she didn't seem able to look out for herself. As we waited for our turn they carried a stretcher past to a grey ambulance, the face covered by a sheet. We all watched, no one speaking, but somehow we couldn't take our eyes off it.

Those who could go had already been taken to first aid posts, but the workers were still having to follow the trail of the buried or dead, listening for moans, tiny gasps, any flicker of life entombed under the houses. I heard a voice somewhere saying loudly over and over that we had to boil all our water. The bombing cracked and destroyed water pipes and the water wasn't safe.

As Mrs Terry sipped her tea, handed out by the cheerful woman in the mobile canteen, we stood trying to offer her comfort by our presence, not knowing what else to say. Mom held the babby for her, trying to quiet it.

'You can come back to ours and rest for a bit,' she said. 'They'll find you a place to go after, won't they?' None of us were sure. We couldn't think straight and it was all too new. Later we'd be able to gather our wits and ask one of the wardens where she could go.

Mrs Terry shook her head. She didn't know anything. She was in a state of paralysis. But she did hold out her arms to have her babby back. The two kids were chewing on the canteen's stale buns, both of them unnaturally silent.

A shout went up from amongst the wreckage. 'Here! There's someone under this lot!' There was urgent activity, equipment carried over at a jerking run, men sawing, lifting chunks of masonry, throwing out objects here and there when they got further down, a clock, a clothes-horse, a skein of baby-pink wool. It seemed to take so long. After a time they called a nurse through to give an injection.

'Morphine I s'pect.' Mom shuddered violently, arms folded tight. 'Christ, imagine being under there.'

As we watched, a man appeared in the street in trousers but bare at the top, blood dark on his head and stains of it on the shoulder underneath. His feet were bare as well and he was turning his head frantically from side to side as if looking for someone. One of the ambulance crew led him gently away.

'I've got to get over to your nan,' Mom said. 'See if they're OK.' She was agitated suddenly, pulled her fags out and was about to light up, hands shaking.

'No!' The warden almost flung himself at her, knocking it from her hand. 'Can't you smell the gas? You'll have the whole bloody street going up!'

'Sorry,' Mom said. 'Oh I'm sorry, I never . . .'

But he was too busy to listen to apologies and had already gone.

We were leading Mrs Terry and her children down towards our house when a murmur rippled through the straggling group of neighbours, a low moaning sound of everyone breathing out together. The rescuers were now pulling a body from the house where they'd heard the tiny sounds. It was a woman, and at the sight of her I saw Molly turn and bury her face in Len's chest with a whimper of distress. So slowly and tenderly they lifted her out, as if they were handling some treasure precious to their own lives. She was unconscious now, drugged out of her agony by the morphine, but how and what she had suffered these hours was more than any of us could bear to imagine. Her face was almost untouched except for a few small cuts, and the upper part of her body appeared unscathed, though it was hard to tell as she'd been trapped down there and could be crushed. But when the bomb came down she'd fallen, and been trapped by the weight of her house, next to where the fire burned in her little grate. For these past hours the heat of it had smouldered along the lower portion of her body so that all that remained of her feet were gnarled things like charred twigs which crumbled, dropping in small bits as they moved her, despite all their carefulness. The clothes on the lower part of her seemed melted round her like black tissue paper. Her head lolled to one side.

She can't live. Everyone must've thought the same. Not after that. I knew her face. Mrs Deakin, a widow in her late sixties who'd always been kind. I saw the nurse who'd given her the injection turn from the sight of that grilled body on the stretcher and take deep controlling breaths. She was young, with light freckles on her nose.

Silently we led Mrs Terry to our house, where yellowed leaves piled gently against the door as they would on any October morning, except that today they were mixed with ash and glass.

After work that day I hurried across to Belgrave Road. There was a lot of damage in the area, gaps and mess where before it'd been whole. Life itself was wobbling. I had to rush because sometimes they came over as early as six and the sirens'd be off, barely giving you time even to get home.

Teresa and Vera had volunteered their house to the WVS as a respite point where people could be taken temporarily for rest and help.

'Otherwise we're no use to anyone, are we?' Vera said. 'It's the least we can do.' It gave them a sense of purpose, and they both seemed lifted by it.

At Nan's they were already preparing for the raid. Lil had made a makeshift bed for herself and Cathleen under the table. The others would go down the coal cellar and they had coats and shoes rowed up and blankets ready.

Lil, cooking chops, was in a state about Frank. 'He was on yesterday and he's on tonight. Thinks he's got a charmed life. God, I do hope he's careful with himself after that lot last night.'

Mom'd told them about our street, but the other news on everyone's lips that day was the Carlton Cinema. A bomb had come down in front of the screen when the place was packed. Killed nineteen.

'They say they were just sat there as if they were still watching the film,' Lil said.

'That'll be the blast.' Nan was filling a flask with cocoa. 'Does odd things. D'you know, Genie – when we came up this morning every window in the house was open?'

I looked round. 'All the glass is in.'

'No breakages. But they were all open. Wouldn't credit it, would you?'

I only stopped there a few minutes, but in that time it would've taken an idiot not to notice there was something wrong with Tom. He wasn't himself at all. I tried talking to him, making jokes, but he was pale and very jumpy, poor kid, very sunk into himself.

'This is all making him bad,' Lil whispered to me. 'I don't know what I can do for him.'

I could do no more either, except give him a cuddle and say goodnight to go and face the next round. The days which had seemed such hard work before now seemed like a rest cure compared with the nights.

And then it stopped. After two weeks of raids every night, suddenly there were days of no siren, no Mister howling, no shelter. It felt really peculiar. The bombing had so quickly become a way of life. But all the same you couldn't relax because there was no guarantee it was over. They might go and bomb somewhere else but they'd be back, and we never knew when. The siren could go off any time. So throughout those days there was still the same fluttering heart and acid stomach. A couple of times during the raids I'd been woken suddenly from a quick snatch of sleep and been sick, such was the shock to my system. Even on those nights of quiet I kept waking, blood rushing, ears straining, not being used to a full sleep.

One morning Mom came down, grey faced with tiredness and nerves. 'I've decided. I'm never going out in that shelter again.'

I gave a sarky laugh, readying myself for work. 'Not till the next time.'

'No. Never.'

'Mom?' I walked round and peered into her face but she was looking out somewhere way beyond me, one hand absent-mindedly stroking her big belly as if it was too tight and she needed to ease it. 'You all right?'

There was a long silence and I nearly asked again. But then, more firmly than I'd expected, she said, 'I'll be all right.'

Something about her bothered me, though I couldn't say what. It wasn't as if I wasn't used to her being lost to me, depressed or drunk, but she was stone cold sober this morning and she frightened me, nearly as much as she did when I'd found her standing out in the garden holding out her arms to embrace the bombs.

I put tea in her hands. 'Why don't you go over to Nan's today? Have a bit of company.'

'Don't fuss, Genie.' She spoke dreamily. 'Just get off to work.'

To start with she was on my mind that day. I couldn't get Mrs Deakin out of my head either, the horrible thing that had happened to her. I tried to think, Mom'll be better once the babby's over with and born. Give her something else to fix her mind on. I was beginning to look forward to that, a babby in the house, whoever its father was.

It was a busy day at the factory with all the work and talk and the women asking me if I'd heard from Joe.

Yesterday's letter from him, safe for the moment with his squadron, was folded close to me in my pocket. I thought of us making love and blushed, blushed even more when they noticed and teased me. It had brought us even closer. I had no shame, no sense of wrong. Not with Joe. And not now during this war when you couldn't take anything for granted. You took what you could and were grateful.

I wanted to go round to Nan's at the end of the day and look in on Tom, talk more to Lil about him. But by the time work finished I felt I ought to get home to Mom. Some instinct I had, that made me run half the way there in a cold sweat, not stopping to queue for any food. I don't know what I was afraid of. I suppose I expected her to get drunk and have an accident one day. Fall when there was no one in.

When I clattered in through the front door, Mister came at me like a cannon ball, yapping and jumping round my legs in ecstasy, licking whatever bits of me he could reach.

'Mom, where are you?' I needed to hear her voice.

There was no answer, but then she hardly ever did bother to answer when I called.

To my surprise she was in the kitchen standing by the stove. Cooking of all things. And the place looked as if she'd had a tidy up too.

'Thought it was high time I did a meal,' she said.

I was all smiles of relief. 'You feeling better?'

'I'll be OK.'

I picked up Mister who was still frantic for attention beside me. 'D'you go to Nan's today?'

'I popped over. Picked up a few things on the way

back.' She was stirring the pot, looking so frail standing there in the gaslight, pregnant, her hair loose, seeming younger than her years.

'We'll wait for Len,' she said. 'He can eat with us tonight, not at Molly's.'

She'd done stew and spuds, even a kind of egg custard for pudding, and the three of us sat together round the table, Gloria playing to us. Mom didn't drink. Not a drop all evening.

'Quiet without Jerry, isn't it?' I said. We were still waiting, could hardly believe it was another night free.

'When all this is over,' Mom said to Len all of a sudden, 'you and Molly'll have to get yourselves a little house somewhere.'

'If there's any left standing,' I joked.

She looked solemnly at me. 'And you and Joe. He's a very nice boy, Genie. The sort who'll really look after you.'

'And we'll look after you too, Mom. Don't you worry. And little'un in there.'

She just gave a bit of a smile at that, as if to say it wasn't her that mattered. She was so calm. Perhaps I should have seen that as odd but I was just glad. Things felt normal, whatever that was nowadays.

We sat listening to Gloria and then Mom took herself off to bed. As she passed by my chair she rested her hand on top of my head. 'Goodnight, Genie.'

I was the last up. I switched the lights off and left Mister snoozing by the remains of the fire.

The high wailing sound woke me and I was out of bed, completely awake, pulling on the coat I'd left at the foot of my bed. It stopped. Started again. It was only then I realized it wasn't the siren but the other noise we normally heard along with it. Mister was howling, somewhere outside. I went and opened my window over the garden.

It was very dark and I could only hear, not see him, howling and whimpering under my window.

'Mister? How d'you get out there, boy?'

There were more yowls as he heard my voice and the rasp of his claws scratching against the back door.

'OK. I'm coming.'

Going to the door, I wondered whether I'd dreamt him being by the fire when I came up, or whether Mom'd been down, put him out and forgotten him. But as soon as I was on the landing I smelt it, that stink of the mornings after the raids, the mean, seeping smell of gas. I tore down the dark stairs.

When I opened the kitchen door the rush of it set me coughing and gasping. I could hear it hissing in the dark and the thoughts going round in my head were, who the hell, who'd been so stupid as to come down and leave the gas on in the middle of the night? I groped towards the back door and heard my feet knock into glass, bottles crashing together. Then I tripped over her legs and fell across the floor, banging my head and side. I got up and struggled with the back door key knowing now, knowing what was happening, taking gasps of air as I got the door open, sick with the gas. Mister tore inside and disappeared somewhere into the front of the house yelping and howling.

Everything was automatic now, with a kind of perfection born of instinct. My steps across the kitchen, one hand over my nose and mouth, the other going to exactly the right dial on the cooker to shut it off.

The hissing stopped. With more strength than I

knew I had, I bent and pulled out the dead weight of my mother's body from where she was lying, head resting on her crossed arms in the greasy base of the oven.

November 1940

Mr Tailor was the one I went to for help, after I'd knelt in the black kitchen, feeling along her wrist. My finger-tips found the veins slanting across her bones and a tiny pulse like a bird's.

I was retching from the gas and sobbing out all sorts of stuff to her. 'Don't die. Don't do this ... Don't you bloody well go and die on me ...'

The smell was still awful in there – there wasn't much of a breeze coming in – so I lifted her under her flopping arms, her feet bumping down the step into the garden and the cold air. I found the crocheted blanket and laid it over her. Mister was running in circles in the garden, barking.

I went and picked him up, so glad he was there. 'We've got to get help, boy.' I ran down the road with his soft head pressed to my face.

Mr Tailor was marvellous. Didn't make a fuss. He found a working phone box and dealt with the ambu-lance, while Mrs Tailor was kindness itself in the face of my shaking. She made me sweet tea. I clung to my little dog and couldn't stop my teeth chattering. They asked no questions. Most likely guessed most of it in any case. They took me to my nan's, said they'd go round to Len first thing. It was three in the morning and I had to tell Nan what had happened. Nan sat down and stared ahead of her. It was Lil who did the crying for all of us.

She was a long time in hospital. At first I was just scared she'd die, and she came very close. Death's door, that's what they say, and she was on the step, hand raised, knocking. She lost the babby. The labour came on with the shock and was born dead, much too small for this world. They said it was another little girl, although she'd thought it was a boy. She haemorrhaged badly and had to have a blood transfusion. For days she lay barely conscious and we'd sit with her in that ward at the Queen Elizabeth. Dots of light flashed round my eyes from exhaustion and I couldn't keep my food down. They were bombing every night again now and we crouched in Nan's house thinking 'What if they hit the hospital?'

But Mom didn't know about these worries. I'd sit watching her white, sunken face, wondering what I was going to say to her when we could talk again. Nan kept bringing in things for her to eat, bits of fruit, little custards or junket she'd made. But she never even had a response from Mom, let alone got her to eat anything. I'd grip her hand but got no squeeze from her in return. Only later we found out why. As she regained consciousness the doctors said she'd lost the use of the right side of her body – the right arm completely, the leg showing little flickers of life.

The first time she came round while I was there, her eyelids seemed so heavy she could barely prise them open as she bubbled slowly back up to us. Her right eye wouldn't open.

'Mom.' She croaked the word, coughed, tried again. Only half her mouth was working. 'Oh, God, Mom – Genie—' She couldn't say any more. Tears seeped down her face.

'Mom, oh Mom ...' I could only bow my head,

resting it on her, and cry too, overcome by her misery and my own shame.

There was Mom and there were the raids. That was what made up our lives. Nan and I went to the hospital every day, Lil when she could. I told Mr Broadbent my mother was ill. He told me to have days off, take my time. 'The others'll rally round,' he said.

I was staying at Nan's and Len was at Molly's. All other aspects of life faded into the background. Something happened to me during those days. Everything had changed from my life before, like a coin flipping over. The thought of seeing Joe appalled me, revolted me even. No, never again. Such things were not meant for me. This was family, and only family. And not even my family knew the depth of pain I was carrying in me over what had happened.

I couldn't look my nan in the eye. I'd let her down. Let us all down. I hadn't looked after Mom properly. That had always been my job. I was the one who saw her out there, arms out, calling to the bombs, and I should have known how near the edge she was. I should have been able to save her.

Nan did what had to be done, though she'd aged in a week. I thought she was angry with me. I couldn't stomach food, kept being sick at odd times. I wished I could be like Lil and let it all out. Lil could say all the things she needed to say, 'Poor, poor Doreen – fancy us not knowing she was that bad. Was she bad, Genie? And the poor little babby ...'

But it was my nan I couldn't stand to be near. I couldn't bear the grief pushed down in her as she ran the shop still, day after day, in her pinner, her jawline held proud, listening to the grievances of her customers. She didn't let on about her own.

By the early evening the sirens were screaming and it was a terrible rush to get some food, get organized. The minute it started Mister was howling and Tom would be curled up under the table quivering and refusing to move.

'I ain't going in that coal 'ole – I'm never going down there again!'

The poor kid. When he was awake he was terrified and when he was asleep he was thrashing about screaming with nightmares and wetting the bed. He nearly jumped out of his skin at the slightest sound.

So we arranged it that I'd stay up with Mister and Tom under the table. I was happier up there in any case, what with my sudden bouts of sickness, and because I was happier away from Nan, couldn't face her. I also wanted to do the best I could for Tom. I told him stories and we both looked after Mister, who was just as scared as he was, or we lay curled up together, the darkness in the house made even thicker by the heavy table above our heads, while the sky was set on fire outside.

This particular night as we lay there I said to him, 'D'you know what day it is today, Tom? It's fireworks night!'

We both managed a bit of a laugh at that. 'Don't exactly need to bother with it this year, do we?'

Tom clung to me, shaking, as the noise escalated outside.

'I wish it'd stop,' he said. 'Stop and never come back.'

'So do I.' All the time I was thinking about the hospital, what a big target it was. At least Nan's house was small.

When the All Clear went, some time late in the night,

my muddled brain didn't know how much time had passed. Tom had finally fallen asleep, his arm across me, and I lay there listening to his breathing, his restless muttering. Poor kid.

There was light moving in the room and I heard Lil taking Patsy and Cathleen up to bed. It went dark again. After a time Nan's slow tread came up the steps and through from the scullery. She went to the range and struck a match to light a candle. Her shadow moved nearer the table and I shut my eyes, sensing her bending to look under at us, taking it that we were both asleep. After a moment I heard a spoon chink against a cup and knew she was taking Turley's Saline to settle her stomach. I waited for her to move the candle and find her own way to bed, but instead of that she went and opened the door. Picking up a chair she carried it outside, came back in to put her coat on and blow out the candle, then disappeared again, quietly latching the door.

When she didn't come back in I moved Tom's arm off me and crawled out from under the table. My insides churned and I stopped, wondering if I was going to retch, but it passed. I felt my way to the window and moved the blackout curtain. There was a tiny piece of moon in the sky and I could see stars. And right the other side of the glass criss-crossed with tape I could see the back of Nan's head. She was sitting out there, quite still.

It took me quite some minutes to pluck up the courage to go out to her. But I couldn't go on living with her the way I was. Not with the shame I felt. She didn't turn her head when she heard the door open, was looking up at the moon, her hands folded in her lap, and I stood there by her shoulder.

'Can't you sleep, Genie?' She spoke very quietly.

'No. Tom's gone off, though.'

She nodded slowly.

'Nan—' My heart was like a throbbing pain. I needed her forgiveness, for her to say it was all right, although it wasn't, none of it.

She waited.

'Nan, I'm sorry. I'm so sorry – I know it was my fault.'

She seemed really startled and looked right round at me. 'Genie love? What've you got to be sorry for?'

I wished so much that I could cry. I tried to make the tears come, to ease it, but they wouldn't. 'I let you down. I was supposed to be looking after her. It was my job. I should've been able to save her.'

'But bab, you were the one that *did* save 'er.'

'But before – I should've known ... I should've woken up. But the day before she seemed better than she'd been—'

Nan gave a sigh then, the great breath of someone pressed by a heavy burden.

'There's no blame on you, Genie love. She's been a poor mother to you in many ways and you've been better to 'er than she ever deserved. It's a hard thing to 'ave to say about your own daughter but it's the truth. When I think back, 'ow things might've been different, what I could've done ...' She shook her head and brought up one hand, clenched in a fist, to her lips, the elbow resting on her other arm.

I thought of Lil's saying, 'Kids – when they're young they break your arms, and when they're grown up they break your heart.'

I saw that all this time she'd been blaming herself as well. I don't know if Nan's heart was broken. She'd had enough in life to chip it all right, from her dead babies and my rotten grandad right the way through to this, and it all sank somewhere deep in her like a stone so the world never saw what she was feeling. I'd have done anything, anything to make her feel better.

After a week at Nan's I went back to work. There was nothing much I could do at home and I felt I owed Mr Broadbent, but I was nervous about facing them all, or disgracing myself if I was sick without expecting it. It didn't happen all that often, maybe once every day or two, but it was always very sudden. Just happened, not much warning. Put me right off eating.

'How's your mom?' they all asked, and I made up something about how she was poorly and getting better.

'You awright, Genie?' Agnes asked me. 'You're looking terrible. You're all skin and bone.'

The others agreed. 'You want to get some flesh on them bones, girl. Joe'll think we're overworking you when 'e comes back!'

Course, everyone was tired and jumpy, not just me. The sound of a car engine in the road'd make you start violently. Every noise felt like a bomb coming to get you, even in the daytime. I just tried to smile at them through it all, praying my innards would behave themselves, at least while I was here.

I went back to our road, dreading the house. I called in on Len, told him Mom was OK. At home there was a letter from Joe. I picked it up and stared at it. His writing seemed like something so foreign to who I was now. I couldn't open it, couldn't stand to read his words of love when I felt so hateful. I knew how terrible it was not hearing, that I owed it to him to write back straight away, but I couldn't. There was nothing in my head except the bombing and what had happened to Mom. I had nothing to give Joe in a letter. Nothing to give him full stop. And I'd been a silly little fool, living in a dream world to think I could be with someone like him. I may have had Nan's forgiveness, even if she thought none was needed, but I couldn't forgive myself.

I put the letter in a drawer up in my room, still unopened.

It came on when I got to the front door, a sudden rush so I only just made it back into the kitchen, retching over the bucket, nose and eyes running, until I was empty and wrung out. I sat on my heels on the floor after, too weak for a while to get up. If only I could cry instead of this. Stop feeling so numb. This was my punishment. I didn't deserve Joe and now I'd lose him. If he wanted to know how I was he'd have to ask his dad. He wouldn't get an answer from me. Not from someone who'd died inside.

On 13 November there was a daylight raid on the Austin Aero factory, but thank God, Lenny was safe. On the night of the 14th the Luftwaffe flattened Coventry, bombed and burned it to the ground. Nowhere else disappeared as thoroughly as Coventry. As Teresa said to me after one of the endless, terrifying nights when they'd been over us, 'What the hell will there be left when they've finished?'

The night they bombed Coventry was a rest for us, but they were soon back. I was at Nan's all the time. That day it was her and me went up the hospital. Mom just lay there, face white as the sheets, her one open eye blank and empty. She had no energy to give it any expression. But the blankness looked like an everlasting sadness that no one would be able to take away.

We always tried not to look at the women in the other beds round us, with their rasping lungs or odd swellings. Sometimes you just couldn't stop yourself looking round, your eyes pulled by a noise or a smell, but we'd try to fix everything on Mom. We never knew what to say to her though. Nan put her coat on to go up there like a suit of armour, always as smart as she could manage, hat on too.

That day, nestling in the bag she always carried, was a carefully wrapped little cup of egg custard, carried delicately as if it were the actual shell of the egg. She fed it to Mom with a teaspoon, Mom half sitting up, bending her head forward, bits of custard slipping back out of the right side of her mouth.

'This'll 'elp get your strength back, Dor,' Nan kept saying. 'We'll soon 'ave you out of 'ere and back 'ome where you belong.'

Mom's good eye looked at her. 'I want to go home,' she whispered, mouth twisting against her will.

'Soon, Mom.' I took her hand, my heart thumping. I was almost afraid of her. 'They say a bit longer – maybe next week.'

'When you're a bit more yourself,' Nan said, stowing the little cup from the custard back in her bag.

What was 'a bit more herself' going to mean now?

'I've brought you a drop of beef tea. Will you have some?'

Mom closed her eyes as if in revulsion. Nan's face twitched. She put the bottle back in her bag and sat turning her wedding ring round and round on her finger, cuddling the bag on her knees as if she thought some-one'd nick it if she put it down for a second.

I picked up Mom's brush and stroked it over the hair round her face. She hated to be a mess. Her eye flickered open and closed. She was falling asleep.

On the bus home, full of smoke and the smell of stale old coats, Nan and I sat without talking. Nan's hands were clasped tight round the handles of the bag. The lights were very dim in the bus, and when tears started rolling down my face I didn't think anyone would see. Just a few tears I was going to allow myself, but something caved in in me on that bus ride when I thought of my mom so far away from us and so sunk in despair she might as well have been dead. I even wondered whether stopping her when I did had been the right thing. I'd kept her alive into something worse. I started sobbing and couldn't stop. I was too far gone to control myself, just pushed my face into my hands, trying not to make too much noise. All the fear and guilt and worry of the past fortnight came over me and I couldn't help myself. I was only sorry for embarrassing Nan.

''Ere, bab.' She didn't tick me off like she might have had things been different, just leaned over and gave me her hanky and that made me cry even more. She took one of my hands and hers kept clenching and unclench-ing on mine. When we were nearly back into town she led me off the bus and crossed over to the bottom of our road where she stopped me, took the hanky and mopped my face.

With no warning I was heaving, sick in the street. I rushed to the gutter, so glad it was dark, and stood there gulping in misery when it was over.

Nan led me by the arm. 'There now. You shouldn't

be in a state like this, that you shouldn't. Let's get you 'ome—'

Next thing, the air raid warning was cutting her sentence in half and everything was forgotten in the fear that noise brought up in you. I took Nan's bag off her to carry – it was hard for her to hurry with her bad legs – and as fast as we could we raced up the hill, terrified of being caught out in the road. The last tears dried on my face.

'Thank God,' Lil said as we came in. The room smelt of stew. Tom was curled up under the table and Lil, in a tizzy, was trying to persuade Patsy to take Cathleen down the coal hole, and dishing up plates of food.

Coat off, Nan started sorting out saucers and stubs of candles for the cellar.

'Fetch me a couple from out the front, will you Genie? We shan't get far with these bits.'

The sirens had stopped by now and although we were all doing things we were straining our ears to hear the planes coming, those minutes between the two usually one mad rush of getting ready.

I ducked under the counter into the shop, holding up one lighted candle stub, fumbling for new ones on the crowded shelves. It didn't take me long to realize there was an argument going on outside. Morgan's voice and no mistake, right outside the shop door, and a girl, pleading with him, it sounded like.

Pulling back the bolts I opened up to the moonlit night.

'Ah,' Morgan said, seeing me. 'Course, you've closed early tonight. I couldn't get in.' We weren't supposed to bolt him out but Lil had shut the shop right up without giving it a thought.

'Course we're closed – there's a flaming raid on in case you hadn't noticed.'

As I appeared, the girl made to take to her heels but Morgan grabbed her by the arm, and although she couldn't get away she wrenched round away from us, hiding her face. Seemed a bit timid this one, not like some of the brazen hussies he brought along.

'Don't be silly now,' Morgan said to her. 'You can't go rushing 'ome – as Miss, er ... Miss Genie 'ere says, they'll be over any moment.'

The planes moved into the range of our hearing as he spoke.

'Get in then.' I stood back to let them past, making sure he didn't so much as brush against me. He kept hold of the girl, who from what I could see was plump and quite young, and she kept her face pushed down in her coat collar.

'What the hell're you doing here tonight?'

'Thought there wouldn't be a raid.' Morgan let go of the girl now I'd shut the door and rubbed his hands together.

'Course there wouldn't be a raid. Why should there be a raid? I mean they only smashed the living daylights out of Coventry yesterday.' Must admit, I was rather enjoying myself. 'I don't know how we're going to fit you in. You can't go up there, can you? Mrs Rawson's really going to love you turning up.'

As I turned to lock the door, the girl gave out a noise like a whimper and moved over to me, speaking with her head still right down. I thought she seemed a bit odd. 'Let me go,' she whispered. I could hardly hear her. 'I'll just go 'ome.'

'You mad? Hark at them out there! It's the daft

381

bugger you came with wants his head looking at. See –
he don't care about you. He's in there saving his own
skin already. You come on in. I dunno what you've
heard about my nan but I s'pect even she'll call a truce
in this.'

'I can't.' This time it was almost a sob. I picked up
the stub of candle on the saucer and held it by her face.

She cringed away from me. 'Don't.'

'Shirl?'

Turning away, she put her hands over her face. 'I'd
no idea in the world 'e was going to bring me 'ere,
Genie, honest I didn't. He just said it was somewhere in
Highgate. I couldn't believe my eyes when it was your
nan's . . .'

The first bombs were falling and I rushed her through
the back and under the table with Tom. Shirl sat crying
and I put my arm round her. Nan must've told Morgan
he could shelter under the stairs if he was prepared to
clear himself a space, because we could hear him banging
about, moving out Nan's enamel wash pot, the bucket
of sand and stirrup pump, some old crocks and something that fell over with a crash which might've been a
clothes-horse.

From feeling so down before, my emotions swung
right the other way and I suddenly got the giggles,
hearing Morgan's muffled cursing from under our stairs.

'Hark at him,' I spluttered to Shirl, who actually
managed to look me in the face for the first time and
mopped her eyes, seeing I wasn't about to have a go at
her. Some other hard object came flying out with a
clatter, we heard Morgan say, 'Bugger it,' and I was in
stitches as the planes came over, Tom clinging to my
legs, still holding on to Shirl, the old wood smell coming
from the worm-eaten table.

There was a bang from upstairs, no explosion, just a real big thump from the roof and the planes passed over, followed by more.

'Mrs Rawson—'

I half crawled out from under the table and saw Morgan's scrawny figure standing over the entrance to the coal hole, his shadow enormous on the wall behind him.

'I think you've 'ad one of them incendiaries come through your attic . . .'

'What do you mean *my* attic?' Nan's voice came back loud and clear. 'This is your 'ouse, Morgan, not mine – you'd better get up there with that bucket of sand mighty bloody quick.'

So there was Morgan forced into being the big man, creeping off up with the bucket. We didn't know where it'd come down but he went to look up on his side. I imagined his gloomy attic with the white light of an incendiary up there sputtering like a firework.

'Just hope he knows what he's doing,' I said to Shirl. I kept trying to be light and cheerful because I was embarrassed for her, but I didn't want her to think I was going to hold anything against her, even though it wasn't exactly normal behaviour to turn up at my nan's as one of Morgan's trollops. But now wasn't the moment for explanations. We were all too busy listening to the movement of the planes. Keep going, you found yourself thinking. Just keep on going. Go somewhere else . . .

Next thing was, Morgan came crashing down the attic stairs, first the bucket, him following, effing and blinding his way down making a hell of a racket until he landed with a groan in the shop.

Shirl looked at me. 'D'you think we'd better look?'

'Not cowing likely. Not with this lot.' Bombs were falling, proper explosives. 'He'll be all right.'

He came through a minute later, groaning and cradling his right arm with his left. I peered out from under the oilcloth.

'I think I've bust my arm,' he moaned.

'For God's sake get under the stairs!' I yelled to him and retreated back in to save my own head. Shirl had her arm round Tom.

'D'you put it out?' Nan's voice boomed up from the coal hole. 'Or couldn't you even manage that?'

'Heartless bitch,' Morgan mumbled, backing into the stair cupboard. 'Oh Christ, my arm!'

The house shook, the windows rattled and a lump of something fell from the ceiling.

I saw the gaslight flicker. 'Blimey, this is a bad one.'

Even with all the noise, we could hear Morgan groaning and carrying on. 'Serves him right,' I said. 'Oversexed little bugger.'

Shirl turned away, embarrassed again. I thought how different she looked tonight – hair all fluffed up, heavy eye make-up and lipstick.

It didn't suit her. She had a sweet face normally.

'What the hell're you playing at, going with him of all people?' I suddenly found myself shouting at her.

Shirl shrugged sulkily, still holding on to Tom who trusted her instinctively, despite the tart disguise she was wearing. 'He was nice to me.'

'*Nice* to you!'

When there was a lull, she said, 'There's only me and Dad at home, see, and he's never had any time for me, even before Mom died. My life with him's like a servant's – nothing else. He isn't even there at nights

384

most of the time because he works a night shift now. But even when 'e is ... 'E hardly treats me as if I'm human, Genie. Never a word except "Get this – fetch me that. Sit down and fucking shut up." He kicks me out of the way as if I'm a dog. On my life, Genie. I wouldn't lie to you. I've been so lonely, specially since you went. It was so nice with you at the factory, and I used to love coming 'ere.'

I swallowed. All along I'd thought she was doing me a favour.

'I met Eric down the pub—'

That knocked me back a bit. All this time I'd never known Morgan had the same name as my brother.

'I know he's not God's gift, 'ow 'e looks and that. But 'e'll spend time with you. Say nice things—'

'To get what he wants.'

'He comments on how I'm looking and that. No one's ever done that before. Dad never even looks at me. I'm sort of invisible so far as 'e's concerned. Anyhow, after a bit Morgan started asking me to dress up for him a certain way – like this – because you know I don't as a rule. Next thing was coming out 'ere. I knew what 'e was after and I'd have given it 'im. I was that lonely and that grateful.' She looked at me with her huge eyes. I remembered they were china blue in proper light.

'I've never done it before, I swear to you. I s'pose you haven't the faintest what I'm on about, 'ave you Genie? What with all your family round you.'

'I had no idea things were so bad for you. I do know what you're on about, sort of. But Shirl, *Morgan*. I mean, he's vile.'

'Beggars can't be choosers.'

'But why should you be a beggar? You're so pretty and kind – I bet loads of blokes'd give their right arm to go out with you—'

Another moan came from the stairs cupboard. Shirl rolled her eyes. 'Sounds as if someone already 'as.'

That really set us off then, even Tom too, watching us, and Shirl and I were helpless with laughter and for a time the stupidest little thing set us off.

'Oh, I'm glad you're here,' I said to her, wiping my eyes.

It was a long, long raid that night, nearly ten hours of it until we heard the All Clear. There were some lulls when we crawled out and had a drink. Nan managed to fix up a makeshift sling for Morgan using an old strip of sheet, with a look on her face when she had to touch him like someone clearing a dead frog out of a drain. Morgan had to put up with whatever treatment he got and sat quietly sipping Bournvita. Seeing her with him then it dawned on me why she'd put up with him all these years. Amid all the hurts and setbacks of her hard life, which had, I think, cast her lower than any of us had guessed, Morgan was the one person she could always guarantee feeling superior to.

'Much damage up there?' Nan asked him.

Nose pointing into his cup, he nodded, swallowing.

'Your side?'

'Yep. Great 'ole in the roof. Room's in a hell of a state.'

'Shame,' Nan said. 'Well, that'll cramp your style for a bit, won't it?' And sparks of triumph glinted in her eyes.

*

386

We were all exhausted next morning as much from tension as lack of sleep. Morgan drifted off saying he was going to get himself seen to, which Nan shouted after him was not before time. We sat round trying to rouse ourselves with weak cups of tea, because sleep or no sleep, there was work waiting.

Of course Nan would normally have blown a gasket at the first sight of Shirl in Morgan's thrall, but what with all the goings on in the night she'd had time to calm down. We'd spent most of the hours talking, Shirl and me, and it'd been a huge relief for me so that once again I felt it was her doing me a favour. I told her about Mom, about how I felt. Swapped my shame for hers. I didn't talk about Joe though, couldn't even speak his name.

Between us we'd come up with a kind of plan.

'Nan – Shirl's not happy at home with her dad hardly being there nights and that and I've said she can come and live with us, back home, when Mom comes out of hospital. I could do with the extra help.'

Nan considered this, looking sternly at Shirl. 'You know what I think of the company you're keeping. You'd better mend your ways. For your own sake as much as anything.'

Shirl blushed a heavy pink and looked down at the floor. 'It was the first time, Mrs Rawson. And the last. You can be sure of that.'

Nan kept the kids home from school and they were already back in their beds sleeping the morning away. We heard Tom crying out in his sleep.

Lil tutted, leaning towards the mirror to put her

lipstick on. 'I ought to get him away from here. It's making him really ill.'

The three of us, Lil, Shirl and I, set out for our different factories in the morning's custard-coloured light. It was raining, but even in a downpour you'd have that new-born feel of it being a miracle after the long, threatening night. Even in all my sadness and worry I felt my spirits lift. This was now, today, and I was alive.

But there was so much devastation outside. Houses down along the road and all the morning shock and horror of it, the way everything looked squalid, and stank even worse. The wardens were on the street with the rescue squads, helping and reassuring. Someone said they'd hit the BSA over at Small Heath and a lot had been killed.

'I hope Frank's all right,' Lil said.

Vera and Teresa were out too, Vera helping a woman along the road with cuts on her face, taking her to their house. Teresa came over to me, hair scraped up in a hurried ponytail.

'How's your mom?'

'Same really. They're talking about her coming out next week.'

'How're you going to manage? You handing in your notice?'

'I might,' I said.

I hadn't decided until then, but even as she asked I knew that's what I was going to do. Mom needed me and I found seeing Mr Broadbent very awkward now. Sooner or later he was going to ask why I wasn't writing to Joe and I couldn't answer. If I was going to be unhappy it was no more than I deserved, but I didn't want to have to explain to him. Or to the other women who kept asking about Mom.

'You all right, Genie?' She touched my shoulder.

I turned away. 'Yeah. Better get on.'

'Genie?'

I looked round at her again, noticing properly the strain in her face. 'Nonna Amelia's very bad. They don't think she's got long. I thought you'd want to know.'

'Oh Teresa,' I said helplessly. Because that was the only way we seemed to be able to feel now about anything. Helpless.

The next heavy raid on Birmingham wrecked a lot of the water mains. Instead of us boiling water after the raids there was now none at all for a period and they were having to send water wagons round. Without a hot cuppa first thing in the morning after a raid you felt hopeless. Couldn't cope with the exhaustion, the jangled nerves and all the awful and weird goings on in the Blitz. The way everything was turned inside out, terraces ripped open like dolls' houses, showing everyone's private rooms. You heard stories about people caught on the toilet by a bomb, tales of relatives who'd died years ago appearing out of the dark, rumours of Fifth Columnists. All this was a bit much without Brooke Bond in the morning.

In the middle of all this chaos, Lil dropped her own bombshell. She was leaving her well-paid job at Park-inson Cowan, and Frank, who so far had survived the raids like a cat with nine lives, was going to 'set her up.'

'He's got me a little place in Hurst Street,' she told

us, aglow with excitement. 'The rent's a pound a week and he's going to pay it for me to start with. Till I get going.'

'Setting you up as what, in 'igh 'eaven?' Nan hadn't really got started on her yet but you could see it was coming. The world had truly gone mad.

'A phrenologist and clairvoyant.'

Nan opened and shut her mouth quite a few times before she could get going, like an old pair of bellows. 'You *what*?'

'He's been teaching me.'

'But he's a mechanic!'

Patiently, and with what seemed an astonishing steady sureness given the barminess of it, Lil explained. All this feeling of our heads that had gone on lately was practise for the real thing. Add to that knowledge of tarot cards and palm lines, throw in a crystal ball, and Lil was in business.

But this was only part one of the grand explosion. Parts two and three were to follow swiftly on. Two: there was another wave of evacuation from Birmingham and she'd decided to send Patsy and Tom.

'Look at the state of Tom,' she said. 'He can't sleep without screaming, can hardly talk to you without twitching. He's as thin as a rake and it can't be doing him any good at school. Patsy can go and keep him company. And I'm not just sending him anywhere. Frank's got an auntie lives over in Stoke and she says she'll have 'em while things are bad.'

Before Nan had had a chance to field that one, we were on to part three. 'And I'm moving in with Frank over the garage. Me and Cathleen. It's not far, and Kings Heath's not getting bombed anything like as much as over 'ere. Don't worry, Mom. I'm not going to be leaving you on your own all the time. Frank'll be out so much with the ARP anyway we'll probably be here as much as we ever are now!'

I went back to our house to pick up letters. I never opened the ones from Joe. I gave Mr Broadbent my notice, speaking to him formally, not meeting his eyes. He was my employer, nothing more.

'But why, Genie?' He ran his hand through the white-streaked hair, absent-mindedly smoothing it down.

'It's Mom. I've got to look after her. There's no one else.'

'I'm sorry, love – serious as that, is it?'

I nodded, looking down at the floorboards.

'That'd explain it. Joe said in his last letter he hadn't heard from you. If you'd said, we could've arranged more leave for you.'

'It's all right, thanks. I'll need to be at home for good now.'

Mr Broadbent came round from behind his desk towards me and I felt myself cringing. I set my face, chin out. Don't be nice to me, I shrieked inside. Don't give me sympathy or try to soften my feelings, because if I let myself go under any of this I shan't be able to bear it.

'Genie? You don't look at all well yourself, love. You've got so thin.'

It was true. There were pits under my eyes you could crawl into. 'Everyone's tired, aren't they?' I still couldn't look at him. 'You can't be anything else with the nights the way they are.'

I think he was probably a bit hurt, certainly puzzled, by the way I was behaving. But he was too nice a man,

Mr B, to try and force his way past my wooden determination.

'You're sure this is the right decision? Everyone'll miss you.'

'I'm quite sure.'

They had to carry Mom into the house that Friday when they brought her back. Two plump women were in charge of the ambulance and they laced their frozen hands together, gripping each other's wrists, and made a kind of chair to lift her between them. I had a fire going inside and offered them tea but they said no, they had to go. Seemed to be relieved to be out of there. I didn't blame them.

Lil, who'd already given up work too, was with me, though Shirl hadn't moved in yet. I couldn't have stood it my own. Lil was in enough of a state about the boys going off the next Monday, and seeing Mom there with her arm hanging all floppy by her side, and that dead half of her face, she started crying all over again.

'Oh Dor – Dor.' She knelt down and put her arms round Mom's waist, resting her face in her lap, shoulders shaking.

Mom looked down at Lil's sleek head, and after a moment she brought up her good hand and started stroking Lil's hair.

She looked across at me as I stood watching, torn up inside, wishing I could cry as easily as Lil.

Mom's lips were moving. 'I'm sorry,' she whispered, then managed it louder, her own tears falling now. 'I'm so useless to everyone. I'm sorry ... sorry ...'

*

Shirl moved in over the weekend. Just packed her bags and never told the old man where she was going.

'Teach 'im a lesson,' she said. ''E'll be round to fetch me back else. 'E can learn to fend for 'isself for a bit.'

I was so glad she'd come I hugged her. Even though I'd given up my job and could manage the house I was scared to be alone with Mom. Even Nan visiting when she could and Len popping in to escape from Gladys carrying on at him were not enough. Mom was like someone who'd been trapped in a dark well full of icy water and the coldness of it still billowed out from her. I was scared of catching her chill.

Shirl was one of those people who's happiest looking after others. Even with her doom-laden voice she could give off cheer like catkins shedding pollen. She was still working of course, but come the evening she'd be rattling the front door to be let in and I'd feel relief rush through me.

''Ere y'are.' Most days she'd thrust something into my hands, flowers or cheap meat. 'Been over the Bull Ring. Thought these'd 'elp.' It was her way of showing gratitude even though there was no need. My thankfulness was a giant compared with hers. I'd just about stopped being sick now Mom was home.

Shirl and I'd cook together, chat. She'd tell me about her day. She brought news to us, what buildings were down across town. And she stopped me brooding as much as I'd have done left to myself. I never mentioned Joe to her. I thought I could cope, just about, with these other things. With Mom. But I couldn't talk about Joe. Couldn't allow myself to think about him. I thought of Mister as my dog now, shut the memory of Joe's hands stroking him out of my mind. His letters were in a drawer, unopened. Soon he must stop writing and then that would be that. I could forget those kind of hopes, thinking I could have love like that. I didn't know the state I was in, couldn't see it for myself.

I had a job to do here, that's what I thought. And it was going to take everything I'd got. The doctor said that in time, Mom could recover. Perhaps not completely, maybe not the arm which was too dead. But she could learn to walk and probably to talk properly again. Only time would tell. She could get about on one leg holding the furniture with her good arm, steadying herself with the other foot. It wouldn't take the full weight, but she had some feeling in it. She had to arrange the position of her right arm with the left one, bending it to rest in her lap when she sat down. And she sat for hours, not even trying to talk, listening to Gloria.

If it was the last thing I did, I was going to make sure she got better. Looking after her was my job, and up to now what a miserable mess I'd made of it. But this time I was going to give it everything. I had to save her.

Saying goodbye to the boys, Tom especially, was terrible. I couldn't bear the thought of losing him as we seemed to have lost Eric.

'Soon as it stops we'll come and get you,' I told him, hugging him tight. Tom nuzzled his face against me, seeming younger than eight.

'Promise, Genie?' He looked up at me, those melting brown eyes full of tears. He was trying so hard not to let them fall.

'I promise.' I was struggling too, holding back my own tears. I may have longed for the release of it on lots of occasions but this was no time to start blarting. 'It'll be an adventure. You know, when I went out of Birmingham—' I came out with that without thinking and stopped short. My day out with Joe in Kenilworth. How long ago that seemed! It had happened to someone else. I couldn't think about that now. 'It was beautiful. You'll see. And you'll be able to write and tell me all about it and I'll write back.'

Lil and I went to put them on the train and waved them off, their little faces at the window, Tom's glum, Patsy full of bravado.

'So like his dad, our Patsy,' Lil said.

I comforted Lil. Nanny Rawson was livid with her and had been since she'd announced her intention, as Nan put it, 'to pack your kids off so you can play about with That Chancer of yours.'

'But Mom,' Lil had said to her, 'things are so different now. If you find a bit of happiness why not hold on to it and bugger the rules?'

'That's all very well,' Nan retorted. 'But whose rules are you living by now, eh?'

'It's not like that, Genie,' Lil sniffed as we walked through town on the way back. 'I'd have sent Tom anyhow, the way he was. And Frank says he wouldn't have minded them living with us. He likes kids. Wants some of his own.' Lil blushed, looking away.

'Nan knows really that they're better off out of it,' I told her. 'It's you living in sin she can't stand. You'll never see eye to eye on that in a million years. She's waiting for lightning to strike you.'

Lil looked sober. 'Like Doreen.'

When I got home I found Mom had got up and moved. In the still, silent way she had about her now, she was standing with her back to me, leaning on the doorframe which led out of the back room, staring across the kitchen.

'Mom?' I hurried to her.

Her eyes were fixed on the cooker and I felt terror rise in me. She was thinking about it. She's going to do it again! Jesus Christ, no.

'I can't remember.' She brought out the words, turning to look at me. Her face was so thin now, her open eye looked enormous. It was terrible seeing her face in that state. The worst part. 'Don't remember doing it.'

'Mom, come and sit down.' I helped her to the chair, her leaning on my shoulder, hopping and shuffling. 'I'll make a cup of tea.' She seemed glad to sit down and as I filled the kettle I told her the boys had gone.

'Poor Lil,' she said.

When I brought her the tea she whispered, 'This is no life, Genie.' I thought she meant her own reduced, miscarried, crawling-about existence, and I opened my mouth to tell her again how much better she was going to get, when she added, 'Not for you.'

I knelt down and took her hand. 'I don't mind, Mom. I just want to help you get better. You're my mom, and that's all that matters, honest it is.'

She shook her head, wouldn't believe it. 'How's your Joe?'

I managed to bring a smile to my face. 'He's all right, Mom. Things are fine. Really they are.'

December 1940

Shirl and I stood outside Lil's shop in Hurst Street. It was a narrow, scruffy frontage, squeezed between other shops, with filthy maroon paint flaking off the woodwork and its old sign, saying 'Stubb's Pawnbrokers', roughly whitewashed over. The golden balls had gone from outside though. Lil had evidently given the windows a going over but it still looked seedy and depressing.

'Bit of a dump, innit?' Shirl pulled the ends of her mouth down comically. 'I thought this was supposed to be 'er big break?'

'Well, give her a chance. She's only been here a week.' I was trying to be brave on Lil's behalf. She deserved some sort of new start, even if it did feel she was leaving the rest of us in the lurch.

On the pavement in front of the shop an old piece of blackboard had been leant up under the window. Chalked on it in swirly writing were the words: 'Liliana – Professional Phrenologist – 2/6d, 5/-, 7/6d.'

'Flipping 'eck, not cheap, is it?' Shirl exclaimed.

Underneath in smaller letters it read, 'Tarot, Fortunes, Palm Readings.'

''Allo girls, come on in!' Frank stood in the doorway in his shirtsleeves, although it was freezing, looking miraculously handsome. 'Lil!' he shouted into the shop. 'Your Genie's 'ere!'

'Cor, look at 'im!' Shirl hissed at me. ''E's a bit good to be true, ain't 'e? Can see why she'd risk 'er everything for that.'

I nudged Shirl hard with my elbow to shut her up and Frank stood back to let us in. It was dark inside and made even more gloomy by the winter day outside.

Lil, though, was looking anything but gloomy.

'Blimey, Lil. What do you look like?' I stood back staring at her, laughing. My auntie had been transformed into a gypsy. She had on a very full skirt in blues, reds, orange and green and a blouse which was just as bright with pink, orange and black flowers. She had her hair pinned up and a red silk rose, which matched her red lips, fastened over her left ear, and there were big gold earrings clipped to her earlobes. She pulled the skirt out at each side, curtsied, then twirled round on the wooden floor so it billowed out like a parachute.

'What d'you think of 'er?' Frank said, sounding like someone who'd just bought a new motorcycle. 'Looks right for the part, don't she?'

She did look gorgeous of course, but so strange and different I wasn't sure what to make of it. Was this Frank's influence, changing her, making her into someone else? And was what they were doing all a con anyway?

'This is it,' Lil said, turning round to look at the room. 'What d'you think?'

Course the place was very like Mr Palmer's shop in a way, only a bit bigger. The room was painted the colour of milky tea and there were long, filthy marks along the walls where shelves must've been taken down, and damp stains on the ceiling, which was flaking. There was still a counter at the back with oddments of clothes and crocks left by the previous owner, and Lil and Frank had put a table and two chairs in the middle of the room. On the table was a tiny vase with another silk flower stuck in it, and a crystal ball.

'Ooh,' Shirl said. 'Can I 'ave a look in?'

'You can look, but you won't see much,' Lil said.

Shirl bent over the table squinting into it. 'Well what d'you see then?'

'Oh, you'd be surprised.' Lil laughed mischievously. 'I had this woman in yesterday, said she could see mountains in the crystal ball. Convinced, she was. Said she'd always had this dream of going to Switzerland. "I'm going to go!" she said. "After the war's over." So there's one very happy lady thinking she's going to see the Alps. D'you know what it was?' She pointed over the counter. 'See them egg-holders?' Upside down on the counter was a white china holder for a half dozen eggs. 'It was them she could see reflected in the glass!'

We all laughed, Frank loudest of all. I mean it was funny after all, but I couldn't help wondering about it. 'Well, is any of it true then, what you tell 'em?'

'Course,' Frank said, through a fag he was lighting. The cigarette hissed and crackled between his lips and he pulled it out and glared at it. 'Christ! What are these things they're passing off for fags nowadays? It's a proper profession. And it'll be a good little earner. She's got quite a talent for it your auntie 'as.' He winked at Lil. Shirl was poking around in the leftovers from the pawn shop.

'Has Nan been to see you?' I talked to Lil. Wasn't any too sure about Frank these days. He was taking over a bit much for my liking.

'Nah, not on your life.'

'Well she wants to see you.'

Frank tutted. 'Never lets up, does she?'

I turned on him. 'She's Lil's mom. And she was looking after her long before you came on the scene.'

'Oi, Genie, no need for that,' Lil said. I saw Shirl look round at me. 'Frank didn't mean anything, did you?'

Frank gave me his most charming grin. 'Course not, no offence, Genie. She's a great old stager your nan.'

I stared hard at him. Cracks were showing here. No one, as Nan kept pointing out, should have a smile so bewitching or shoes you could see to powder your nose in.

Some woman came in then with an anxious face wanting her palm read, and Shirl and I took off to do our shopping.

'Go and see Nan,' I said to Lil before I went.

She touched my arm. 'Don't fret. It's all right, Genie – things are OK. I'll go tonight.'

'I just hope she knows what she's doing,' I said to Shirl. 'Our Lil thinks she's the world expert on men, but I can't say I'm any too sure about that one she's got there!'

The other person in our family who was happy as Larry was Len. Molly was coming up to seven months pregnant and was like the side of a house. Her big belly fascinated Len. Actually it fascinated Shirl too and she was forever leaning over Molly, asking questions about how it felt, was it kicking and all that. Len was a funny mixture of behaviour with Molly. He could ignore her for ages at a time while he fiddled about with Gloria, chuckled away at wireless programmes and forgot even to answer her as if she plain didn't exist. Other times he was all over her, feeling the babby moving whoever else was about, and stroking and kissing her as if she was a dolly or a pet dog until sometimes she got a bit sharp with him.

'Aw leave off, Lenny, will yer?'

Mister loved Molly and had been in the habit of curling up on her enormous cushions of thighs when she was around.

'Ooh!' Molly cried, shaking with laughter one evening when Mister leapt up in a great hurry and shot off her lap. 'The babby's kicked 'im off of me! 'E's going to be a footballer 'e is!'

The two of them often came over and sat with us, eating anything in sight, Gloria on, completely comfortable with everything in a way I never saw in anyone else. No restlessness, no question about Mom or worry about the way she was. No discontent. Nothing. That was Len and Molly – happy in chairs, for ever.

They were there when the siren went early on that month and Mister leapt up – this time off me – and howled, head back, the black and white fur across his throat stretched tight.

'Oh Lor,' Molly grunted, struggling to get out of her chair and not managing. 'Pull me up, Lenny. I'll 'ave to get over to Mom's.'

As she went, Lenny taking her along, Shirl and I started organizing. Tea in a flask. No booze. Light, coats, rugs.

'Len,' I called, hearing him come back in. 'Come and help with Mom.' But he lumbered in, picked up Gloria before anything else and stowed her under the stairs.

'My God,' I said to Shirl. 'What happened to women and children first?'

'No—' Mom was struggling to speak. 'I'm not going. Not out there.'

401

'Please, Mom, come on. We've got to.'

'NO.' She pulled her bad arm in close with the other one and leaned forward, curling in on herself.

What with the siren going and Mister howling and my nerves already in shreds before all that, I felt as if I was going to explode.

'What the hell am I s'posed to do?' I raged at Shirl. 'I can't force her, can I? What does it matter if we go out there anyway? We could all get killed whatever we do.'

Shirl took over, squeezed my arm. 'You're awright, Genie,' she said, sounding like Mr Tailor. She bent over Mom. 'Mrs Watkins, we're going to take you to the shelter. You can't stay 'ere.'

Mom hadn't the strength to resist us for long but I could feel the distress coming from her and I felt terrible. But I couldn't help thinking about Mrs Deakin and we struggled down the garden and got her inside. I put the Tilley lamp down on the floor and we laid Mom on one of the bunks, covering her up well. She turned her face away towards the corrugated wall.

Len brought Mister and closed us in. As the door shut I thought about tombs. Mister whimpered and came over to me.

'I'm so glad you're here,' I said to Shirl for the umpteenth time.

Her big eyes shone in the lamplight. 'Not 'alf as glad as I am, I can tell you.'

'What does your dad do – in the raids I mean?'

'Oh, 'e'll be all right. The factory's over Duddesdon – they've got a shelter there.'

'What, so you was on your own of a night?'

'Went round the neighbours – they've got a cellar. But I'd much rather be 'ere with you, Genie.' She turned her head. 'We're OK, aren't we Len?' she said, squeezing his arm. She nodded across at Mom and mouthed at me. 'She awright?'

I reached round, took Mom's good hand and held it. 'You asleep, Mom?'

She made a little noise so I knew she wasn't.

'You warm enough?'

'I'm OK.' It was a hoarse whisper.

When I turned back to Shirl I could see the pity in her eyes and I didn't know if it was for Mom or me. But seeing someone else looking in on my life made me feel so terrible about everything, the way it'd been broken and changed. First Big Patsy, Dad and Eric – even Lola, I felt sad about her – Mom and Bob and the dead babby, and Joe. But no, not Joe. I wasn't even going to let myself think about him . . .

Shirl made jokes to try and keep us going and I tried to laugh, thankful to her because it wasn't as if she had a lot to laugh about either. We talked in short bursts, going quiet when the planes came over, shrinking our heads down into our necks and cringing until they passed. A couple of times as it was going quiet Len put his arm round Shirl, and she said, 'Oh, you're a devil, you are.'

And I held Mom's hand and felt her silence like a leaden weight behind me.

I found Nan alone in her house the next day, down on her hands and her one good knee, the other bent up in front, blackleading the range.

'Here, let me do that.' I took the cloth and polish off her and tried to rub off some of my outrage at Lil on to its black surface.

'She said she was going to come back. Sod her! I

mean it's not as if Frank would even have been in with a raid on!'

'It would've been too late for 'er to come with the raid already started.' Nan had managed to pull herself stiffly to her feet. 'And anyroad, I'm awright. Take more than a load of Jerries to frighten me, I can tell you.'

She looked tired though. 'It's just not right you being on your own. Lil should know better.' I found I was shaking with anger, wanting to scream with it. There was never anything you could do about anything. I wanted to come and keep my nan company of a night, but how could I with Mom the way she was? And going into her house felt awful – no Lil, no kids running round.

Nan waved a hand at me to shut me up. 'How's your mother?'

'Same.' I was scrubbing like mad at the range.

'You're all skin and bone. You still being sick?'

'No.'

She absorbed this, then said. 'Morgan was bombed out last night – 'is place over in Aston.'

I stopped and looked round. 'D'he get out?'

'Oh, that sort always do. Rat out of a sewer. 'E was in the cellar, not a scratch on 'im. 'E was over earlier to see what state the room up 'ere's in again.'

'He's never thinking of moving in here?'

'Not unless he wants rain on his face every night. D'you know what 'e 'ad the nerve to ask me?' She didn't sound all that outraged, just exhausted. ' "You being on your own now, Mrs Rawson, I was wondering if you could spare me one of your rooms for a bit?" Rubbing 'is hands together how 'e does.'

'Nan, you never . . .?'

404

A wicked twinkle came into her eyes. 'I told him I only ever live with men if I'm married to 'em, ta very much. That drained the colour out of 'im I can tell you.' She let out a big laugh and it was good to hear her. ''E says 'e's lost his business and 'e can't do any repairs till 'e gets the insurance and there's no telling 'ow long that'll take. So that'll keep 'im out of action for a bit!'

'Nan!' I laughed with her.

Wiping her eyes, she said, ''E's 'aving to find somewhere else to move in with his Mom!'

'God, you can't imagine him being anyone's son, can you?' Remembering, I pulled a letter from my pocket. 'This came today. I haven't shown it her.'

Eric's letter contained the usual wooden scraps of news that we'd had to get used to, but in the middle he wrote, 'Mummy says I can stay here for good if I want to.' Mrs Spenser had let him leave it in. She'd obviously wanted us to see it.

'Mummy?' Nan flared. She stared in disbelief. It wasn't just Eric thinking of Mrs S as his mom, it was him sounding like a toffy-nosed twit into the bargain.

'She can't do that, can she? She can't just keep him?' I was tearful all of a sudden. 'Soon there'll be nothing left.'

Nan gave my shoulder a pat. 'She can't just keep 'im, not unless—' She broke off and I knew she was thinking of Mom, of what sort of life Eric was going to come back to here. He wouldn't be getting piano lessons, that was for certain. I could see the grief in Nan's face, just for a quick flash. 'No. She can't just do as she likes.'

Teresa and her Mom were spending as much time as they could over in the Quarter because it was obvious

405

Nonna Amelia was dying. But Teresa found time to call in and visit us and ask if I wanted to go and see the old lady for what would surely be the last time.

Teresa hadn't seen Mom since she'd come home. Mom hated anyone in the house, couldn't stand to be seen in her state. And Teresa couldn't keep the shock out of her face.

'It's terrible, Genie,' she said as we set off towards town. 'Is she going to get any better?'

I told her the little bit of hope we had. Even talking to Teresa I felt at a distance from her, and fiercely protective of Mom. I was almost sorry I'd let Teresa see her. Mom wouldn't go out at all, didn't want the neighbours' tongues wagging any more than they had already. Teresa was an outsider in this. It was Shirl who'd come in and got involved and I felt closer to her nowadays, and somehow that was another sad thing. I could tell Teresa didn't know what to say to me and I couldn't speak to her. If I asked about Carlo she'd be bound to bring up the subject of Joe, so I said nothing and walked along with my old friend feeling distant and tense.

Vera was already at Nonna Amelia's house with her sister and the youngest of the children. They greeted me warmly, but whether in Italian or English, everyone was speaking in hushed voices, as if Death was already in a conversation with the old lady that they were afraid to interrupt.

'You want to see her?' Vera led me upstairs, treading very quietly on the staircase. Teresa stayed down. Vera showed me into the room and then, to my surprise, left me and went down again. Soon I knew why. Communing with the dying's best done on your own.

There was no light in the room. It was a grey, overcast

day, and the curtains had been half drawn, leaving a gap of only about eighteen inches between them. Nonna Amelia was lying in her enormous bed with its high wooden bedstead in such deep brown wood it looked black. The only part of her to be seen was her face because the rest of her was well covered up with sheets and blankets, an eiderdown and a brocade coverlet. They seemed to have piled everything possible on top of her to try and keep the warmth in her tiny, shrunken body.

I could barely even see her face in the dim light and I moved closer to the bed. Her white hair was swept back behind her head which was resting on a white pillow slip embroidered with green leaves at one edge. I licked my dry lips and went to stand right by her. I didn't feel frightened or sad, just awed. Like a tiny, new-born babby, she was already half somewhere else that the rest of us have forgotten, with this life we know still just clinging to her. Now those wise, dancing eyes were closed there was only a shrunken, bony face, the skin yellow, the Nonna Amelia we knew blown out like a match. But she was still there. I could hear her breathing.

'Nonna Amelia?' I whispered, putting my face close to hers. 'It's Genie – Watkins. Teresa's friend. I don't know if you can hear me. I just wanted to say—' What the hell did I want to say? What do you say to someone when you know it's the last thing you'll ever say to them? And if she could hear me she most likely wouldn't understand a word.

I pulled up a chair and sat leaning forward towards her. For quite a time I didn't say anything and that was OK. But then in a funny sort of way I felt as if she was listening to me, not like her, the old her, but just a sort of presence there to listen, like a priest or a statue.

'I wanted to say—' I hesitated, then looked away from her face and kept talking. 'I've always looked up to you, Nonna Amelia, because you're the sort of person who everyone loves. D'you know that? You might not have noticed, like Teresa hadn't until the war came – I expect you have though, because so many things have happened to you, haven't they, to make you wise?' I talked in fits and starts, not sure half the time whether I'd said something or just thought it. 'All I can say is I envy you your life because you've made a lovely family who all respect and love you. That's all I've ever wanted really, to have a family who are happy and who love me. But I can't seem to make it happen however hard I try. I thought, just for a little time – the best time of my life—' As I said this my throat started aching and I had to stop and swallow hard. 'I thought I might be able to have it with Joe. I tasted what it might be like . . . But now I know that was only a dream . . . I've wrecked everything and I know things don't happen for me like that, and it's all falling apart round me and I can't keep it together . . .'

Words kept coming out of my mouth, about Mom and Joe and how bad I was feeling. Words I couldn't have said to anyone else. I felt she was listening, but maybe that was because I wanted someone to. After, I leaned down and kissed those cheeks, soft as flower petals, staring into the shadowy face of this old lady whose life was laid out in front of me.

A light sigh came from the bed, a lift in the breathing, little shudders in the rhythm as she breathed out. I stood up and managed to smile at her. 'Thanks, Nonna Amelia.'

It was a moment before I saw that had been her final breath. No, it couldn't be! I lifted the covers and felt around in a panic for a pulse in her frail wrist. Nothing. I hardly remembered getting downstairs.

'She's gone, Mrs Spini,' I said. 'I was just standing there, and—'

It was expected, but still a shock. Vera's face tightened and she gave out a long breath almost as her mother had done. I was upset and embarrassed. I wasn't family. I was the wrong person to have been there. Why did old women have to keep choosing to die suddenly when I was around?

But Vera stepped forward and embraced me, kissing my face on each cheek before she went upstairs. 'I think it was a compliment to you.'

Thick clouds and foul weather saved us from bombing that week but also meant that the day of Nonna Amelia's funeral was cold and wet. Whatever the weather the Italians were going to send Nonna Amelia off with all the pomp and splendour they could gather together.

I paid my respects to her again once the women had laid out and clothed her in a stiff black dress. Now she was dead her face looked like someone else.

They carried her to the Requiem Mass at St Michael's in a horse-drawn hearse. The six black horses, blinkered and adorned with noble black plumes, gleamed in the rain, their breath snorting out jets of steam around them, and walked with high steps as if they sensed the honour of the occasion.

Vera's brothers and other friends of the family carried wreaths to the church, the biggest taller than they were themselves, and there was an enormous crowd inside. She had been very much loved, that old lady, for her kindness, and very much respected.

Teresa walked in with Vera and the other girls, all in their black lace, and Nanny Rawson limped beside me. Nan could swallow her misgivings about Catholics generally for the sake of this family in particular.

The strain was showing on Vera's face. As we settled in our pews, Nan steadfastly refusing to bob up and down to the High Altar or any of that, I whispered, 'If only Mr Spini was here. It's so hard on her, in't it?'

After the solemn Mass Nonna Amelia was taken off to Witton Cemetery with the closest of the family. But we called round later to join in the wake, the men and bottles ensconced in the front room, the women in the back, some of them crying as if they were there with the job of letting out grief on everyone's behalf.

We sat with the women for a time, everyone in black, accepting food and drink. Teresa came and sat by us in her black crêpe dress, looking worn out.

'You all right, love?' Nan said to her.

'I'm OK, ta. Thanks for coming both of you.' She seemed a bit distracted I thought, in a bit of an odd mood, because through all the tiredness and formalities she looked somehow excited. While the other women were talking loudly she moved closer to me. 'I've got summat to tell you.'

I looked round at her.

'Carlo's asked me to marry him.' I hadn't imagined it then, that light in her eyes. He'd written to her, couldn't even wait to come home and ask.

'He's such a hothead,' Teresa said affectionately. 'Not quite the same as going down on one knee, is it!'

I didn't have to ask what the reply was going to be.

'But at your age – what does your mom say?'

'I'll be seventeen soon and she adores Carlo. Always has. I s'pose if it wasn't for the war she'd tell us to wait,

410

but she was so scared I'd go off and marry a Prot and leave her, she's quite happy. A good Italian Catholic boy with his family in the Quarter, she's not going to let that one slip past!'

I flung my arms round her. 'I'm really happy for you, Teresa. Nice to have some good news for once.'

'Well, good luck to you both,' Nan said when we told her, though we had to keep our congratulations low as no one else was to know yet. Even despite the sadness of that day Teresa did look happy and settled in herself.

As we left she kissed me extravagantly and hung on to my arm, hugging it. 'Maybe you and I should make a double wedding?'

Gently I pulled away. No one was going to see the ache in my heart, not now. I covered it with a laugh. 'Bit tricky that one, ain't it, since neither of us are Catholics!'

That Sunday afternoon I answered a knock on our door to find Mr Broadbent standing there. His car was parked across the road. My knees went weak.

'Genie?' He looked ever so uncomfortable having turned up like that. I couldn't ask him in. There was Mom asleep in a chair and out of pride I didn't want him seeing her. And I guessed why he was here. I just couldn't let him near me because if he said too much I knew I'd cave in completely. I stood stiffly in the doorway, my expression closed tight as an iron door.

'Sorry to bother you, love,' he said. 'I know it's a bit funny me calling. But Joe's very anxious about you. Said he hasn't heard a thing from you for ages and he asked me to check and see if you were all right.'

I swallowed, looked past him seeing the ground was

wet outside and it was filthy still, mess from the street's wreckage continually trodden back and forth. 'I'm awright.'

Mr Broadbent seemed so embarrassed I felt guilty, but I couldn't help him.

'He keeps hearing about the raids of course. It's not as bad where they are, nothing like.' He paused. 'Are you sure everything's all right, Genie? Only Joe's wondering why he hasn't heard. He's upset and worried. You mean a lot to 'im.'

I shifted my weight from one foot to the other, arms folded tight, stared over Mr Broadbent's head across our smashed up street.

'I can't write,' I said, holding on tight to myself inside and out. 'Just can't. You'd better tell Joe he's made a mistake. Tell him to forget me.'

'Oh.' He stroked his hand back over his hair. 'I didn't know it was like that.'

I was moving back into the house.

'But Genie – wait, love . . .'

'Love' undid me. 'Got to go. Mom's calling.' And I shut the door. Leaned on it, gulping, and closed my eyes.

Tuesday. And there was Lil at Nan's, sobbing her heart out, and Nan's face clenched like a rat trap with 'What did I tell you?' written all over it. It took me quite a time to get the whole sorry story. Nanny Rawson, it seemed, had been right about Frank with a vengeance.

'That didn't take long, did it?' Nan said. 'Talk about living in Cloud Cuckoo Land – people like that believe their own lies.'

Lil sobbed even harder.

'So you mean he's got another woman?' I said, trying to put together the bits of information dribbling out between Lil's snuffles and sobs.

'I – I was so sure about him,' she wailed. 'How could I have got it all so wrong? How could he tell me so many lies?' She had no make up on and her lids looked naked, pink and puffy. She put her head in her hands, so betrayed and dejected. I looked at Nan, framed in the window's dying light. She folded her arms, glanced at Cathleen who was on the floor with a rag doll.

'Not only is lover boy already married with a kid, 'e's got this other trollop set up across town – where is it? Hockley or somewhere – doing all this fortune telling and that . . . Only she's a bit more to 'im than 'e was letting on before!'

'And there's a flat over the top of that one,' Lil wailed. 'I reckon she sees more of him than I do!'

'Christ,' I said, 'how does he manage it?'

Nan frowned at my blaspheming.

I didn't know whether I was surprised or not. I mean I was, by the facts, by Frank's cunning, his sheer energy. But somehow not by the actual truth of it. He was much too good to be real, too charming, too slippery.

'So how did you find out, Lil?'

'Oh—' She waved a hand tiredly, as if that hardly mattered any more. 'He didn't come home.' She gave a harsh laugh. 'Not that that should surprise me, by all accounts. Anyway, he'd been on duty, or so he said. So I went up to the ARP post. I mean it's not as if we've had any raids, is it? They were ever so funny with me at first, wouldn't say a thing. Didn't know where he was. So I was going, then one of them came after me and said Frank'd been in an accident. They'd gone into a bombed out warehouse and Frank'd had a load of stuff come down on him and done his neck in bad. So I go carting up the General to find 'im ...' She sat twisting her hanky round and round. 'I'm sat there by the bed when this bird walks in, looks at me as if I stink and says, "Who the hell are you?" So I say, "Well, who are you?" And she says—' Lil's voice broke again. '"I'm his wife." They've got a little lad an' all, six years old, called Bertie.'

'Well, what about the other woman?' I could feel rage rise in me for my poor auntie Lil. What I wouldn't do to that smarmy ...

'She, his wife, knew about her. Suspected anyway. Didn't know about me.'

Did now though.

'The raids gave him the perfect excuse,' Lil sobbed. 'He was always telling us he had to be somewhere else. And the flat over the garage was a bit bare, but I thought it was just his bachelor way of life.'

Nan's fury twitched in her cheeks. She sliced bread for Cathleen, loaf under one arm, with a look of it being Frank's neck.

'Oh Lil,' I said. We put our arms round each other and I stroked her back. Sweet, loving Lil. It knifed me through to see her so hurt and destroyed, so alone all over again.

'How could he do it?' she sobbed, shaking. 'How could he? What have I done to deserve this? How could he lie to me and me not know – and to her? Poor cow's got a kid and she's saddled with him. The worst of it is ...' She pulled away from me and sat up wiping her eyes with the wet hanky. 'I really loved him. I still do. I mean if he walked in here and spun me some tale about it was all a mistake and none of it was true I'd have him back, I would.'

Nan yanked the blackout viciously across the window. 'Then you're a bigger fool than you look.'

'Can't all be like you, can we, Mom?' Lil said, without aggression. 'Some of us have to believe you can have something better.'

Nan didn't rise to that, just slopped tinned pears in Cathleen's bowl.

'What're you going to do, Lil?' I said softly.

She sat very still, staring into the fire. 'I dunno. Oh God. I suppose I'll have to come back here – if Mom'll have me.' She didn't look at Nan. 'Go back to Parkinson Cowan or somewhere. The factory. Right back to square one.'

When I left them, feeling guilty that I'd be so late home, I was bursting inside. I had a tight feeling in me from pent up emotion about everything that had happened, and seeing Lil in that state of betrayal and lost hope had brought it all to the surface. We were all so stuck, waiting, and not knowing whether what we were waiting for was going to bring more pain and more disaster into our lives. We could lose the war, my mom was stuck in a mockery of what was once her body, I'd rejected a good man who loved me because of my anger with myself – and now this. Now I'd seen Lil fall victim to Frank's self-obsessed greed and lust.

It was already dark as I stormed along the Moseley Road, trying to release some of the feelings. If it was light I'd have run. This time of the evening there was too much danger of colliding with someone or knocking myself out on a lamp-post. But the sky was clear and there was a moon. Bomber's moon, I thought. *God.*

It was as if my thoughts set it off. The sirens wailed

round me so loud and horrible I wanted to scream myself. People out on the street started rushing and I could see threads of light from torches moving fast, combing the pavement.

I needed to get home quick. At least Shirl was there. Wonderful Shirl. She'd get Mom and Len organized. But the thought of the shelter, of sitting still in there when I was so frantic with anger and frustration was hateful.

Turning the corner of St Paul's Road I could just make out that someone was standing there, and as I passed, in the quick yellow flare as a match was struck, lighting the end of a fag into a glowing orange bead, I knew those features. Dark brows, heavy-set face. Bob. My rage boiled over.

'You bastard! You shit-faced bastard!'

With all the fury of my compressed emotion I flung myself at him, taking him completely by surprise, yelling and screaming against the noise of the siren. I tore my nails down his face with every bit of my strength, kicked at him, grabbed something, his hand, took the fleshy bit above the thumb knuckle in my mouth and bit right into it until I felt it crunch.

'Aaagh – what the *fuck* . . .?'

He caught hold of me, easily stronger now he'd got his act together and was furious and in pain, pinned my two hands together, pulled out a torch and shone it in my face.

'You! You little bitch!'

With pleasure I saw blood on his cheeks. I drew up a big gob of spit and let him have it in one eye.

'Christ.' He had to wipe it with his shoulder, moving his grip to the tops of my arms, pinning them to me hard.

416

'Get off me.' I struggled, fighting him. 'Don't you touch me.'

'You evil little bitch, you—'

'My mom nearly died because of you. She was having your babby, the one you ran off and left her with, you lump of dog muck. She put her head in the gas oven and now she's a cripple thanks to you. I hate you! I hate you ... Get your fucking hands off of me. I've got to get her into the shelter – she can't walk properly. Let me go ...' I was sobbing and cursing, beside myself, and Bob relaxed his grip on me. I twisted free and started running.

'I hope they get you—' Through my tears I screamed at the sky. 'Come on you stupid Jerry bastards – come and get this one!'

They were overhead, the planes, but I just kept running. This area was a favourite of theirs of course. They thought a lot of the factories were here instead of on 'shadow' sites like Castle Bromwich. They were after the BSA – Birmingham Small Arms – the big munitions factory which made motorbikes in peacetime. They'd already hit it but they were back for more. Looking up through my tears, I saw planes pass black in front of the moon. That wave of bombs fell over to my left, further north. It sounded as if there were a lot of them out tonight.

I tore along Brunswick Road. Thank God for Shirl, I thought again. If she'd not been there I'd have been too late. I dragged my hands impatiently across my wet eyes. There was no more time for emotion.

The house was dark of course, like all the others. There was no point in banging on the door so I ran to the side gate, struggling with the latch, caught my sleeve on the fence and then stumbled down the garden. There were more planes and the whistle and crunching boom of the explosions. Even before I got to the shelter one came down very near and I threw myself down, curled up. The ground snatched under me and the sky lit up. I heard glass breaking.

'Shirl. Shirl!' I yelled. 'Get the door open for me!'

She couldn't hear me over the racket. They'd be worried about me. Head down I covered the last few yards, pulled the front off the Anderson and flung myself in. To find it empty and dark.

There should have been matches but nothing was there. I felt around every inch of the floor but couldn't find them. It was pitch black.

'Damn! Damn you, Shirl. Where are you? Why aren't you all out here?'

I felt my way up on to one of the seats and perched on the edge, once more boiling over with anger and frustration. Did I have to do everything? And I wanted Mister, the distraction of comforting him in my lap and being able to think about him and Mom instead of my own skin.

The shelter seemed to close in round me. I had a picture of it in my mind as a flimsy bubble, thin enough to give off rainbows in the sun, out here under all the bombs. I didn't like being alone in the dark. I pulled my legs up, resting my heels on the edge of the berth and curled tight, hugging my knees.

When it lets up a bit I'm going in, I thought. Couldn't do it now, it'd take too long to move Mom. She couldn't just run down the garden like the rest of us. I wondered where Len was. Maybe he was at Molly's and Shirl hadn't been able to manage on her own?

I lost track of time. I wasn't sure exactly when I'd left Nan's – I guessed it had been about half six – or how long I'd been in the shelter. Seemed like hours. I couldn't keep my mind on anything but how scared I was, because it was all too much, much worse on your own. My mind did something it'd done before during the worst raids, it sort of closed down until I was repeating just one word: Please, please, please . . .

One came down very near. The ground shook and I pulled my head tight on to my knees, hearing myself moan with fright. Clifton Road at the back, it sounded like, though the noise could mislead you. I was thinking who did we know, did we know anyone in Clifton . . .?

I didn't hear it coming, not that one. Just knew one minute I was sat there, the next I was choking, buried, my mouth and nose full of soil, earth over me, terrible the close fit of it, buried alive. Every muscle of my body was clenched in a mad, fighting panic, wrenching and twisting, spitting, coughing, savage with desperation for a clear unclogged breath. In a second I found I could move, so it wasn't a deep cover. Clawing with my hands, I felt air above and I fought my way out, hawking and spitting, feeling the soil crunch between my teeth, the horrible thick plugs of it in my nose and its tightness on my face, weighing down my lashes.

The door of the shelter had been blown right inside and was jammed in at a tilt, so I had to crawl past it to get out, forcing my shoulders out into the garden.

The next thing I remember was running up and down the street under an orange sky, not knowing what I was doing. A warden loomed from the shadows yelling at me, 'Get under cover! For God's sake get in!'

'Our house—' I stood pointing, lost. It only took one look from him. He steered me to a doorway. 'You can't hang about. Got anywhere to go?'

And then I was tearing along the Moseley Road

again, a road that had seen so many ordinary days, ducking in and out of doorways as the sky seemed to tear apart above me.

We were down there as soon as the All Clear sounded, even though it was still dark, holding on to each other, Nan, Lil and me, braced for the sight.

They were working on our house. The air was full of dust which coated the inside of your mouth and once more there was the queasy-making smell of gas, but today we noticed these things only in the very far back of our minds. Morning dawned slowly, the colour of an old net curtain, and with the light more and more people came out into the road, watching and murmuring to each other. An ambulance waited near by.

We stood in silence. There was nothing to say. We had long ago done the things we could do: called at the Benders' house; no, no Len. He'd stayed home. Lil, the only one of us who could function at all, ran, jumping the hoses, to one of the wardens and grabbed at his sleeve. He listened, shaking his head. Couldn't tell her anything. Not yet.

As we stood there with Gladys and Molly a nurse with red hair came to us from the ambulance, seeing who we must be, and spoke to us in a reverent sort of voice. 'Maybe it's better if you don't watch. It can be distressing. Would you like to come and wait over here?'

But we couldn't move, shook our heads dumbly. Cups of tea were given us by people whose faces we didn't even see. I didn't remember drinking except suddenly I was holding an empty cup, until someone took it away. I heard Molly sobbing.

It took a long, long time, eyes straining, listening to the grunts and shouts of the rescuers, feet crunching on glass and rubble, sometimes the noise of a saw or drill on the cold morning air. And we could do nothing except stand and wait.

'Quiet!' The man who seemed to be in charge of the team eventually waved his hands. 'I need quiet. I can hear something.' Silence came down like a chopper. We all strained our ears and heard tiny mewling noises from somewhere in the wreckage. The men looked at each other. I knew as soon as they did that that wasn't a human sound. It was a dog – Mister, alive somewhere in all that. My spirits lifted for a second. But what about the others? What about Mom, Len, Shirl? What we all wanted to hear, what we yearned for from the depths of our being, was to hear their voices crying for help so we knew they were alive. But apart from Mister's frantic scratching and whining, there was nothing to hear from inside, just quiet. Deathly quiet.

They brought Shirl out first, covering her bloodied face with a sheet. We couldn't see the rest of her. I gripped Lil's hand. There was no need to ask if she was dead. With each body they brought out, so carefully, so painstakingly, a ripple, that low murmuring sound passed through the scattering of people, a sound of horror and sympathy, a long, wordless, human breath.

Mom was next. It took them some time to bring her out. They did their best for us, closing ranks, their backs to us as they arranged on the stretcher the parts of her they had salvaged, shielding her, and us, before they could decently cover her. They didn't look at us as they carried her away. Nan's hand came up and clasped over her mouth and stayed there, her eyes fixed on the house as they carried her children out. She didn't move. She was waiting for Len.

They had to move more rubble from the brown, crumbling heap that was our house. Mister didn't let up whining. Some of our things were scattered in the road, looking small, dirty and humiliating. Scattered bits of furniture, shreds of a chair cover, the mantel clock with its glass shattered rolled out into the road, pink-backed playing cards turning over in the breeze. Shirl's black bag. *Oh Shirl.*

Len's fleshy, schoolboy body was soaked in blood. When she saw them bring him, Molly threw herself forward, taking the rescue team by surprise, falling on him, a great howl coming from her that seemed to crack the air apart. 'Len – Lenny – my Len – no-o-o-o-o.' She kissed him again and again and came up with blood on her face as they prised her away, belly shaking with sobs. Gladys drew her into her arms, her child with child.

When they brought Len to the ambulance Nan walked forwards, pulling her coat round her. Lil and I followed.

'It's better if you don't—' the nurse started to say.

Nan held up a hand to stop her. 'It's awright, love, I'm not going to make any fuss. Just give me a minute – there's no harm.'

She pulled the sheet back and looked at him. Len's eyes were half open, his face cut by glass but not disfigured.

'Good lad.' She ran her rough hand over his matted hair. 'You've been a good 'un, Len. A good son.' She gave him a last, long look, then covered his face again and started walking away.

'Mom.' Lil took her arm. Nan's eyes were glassy. She was in shock, we all were. 'Where're you going?'

'Home. There's nowt to stay 'ere for, is there?'

'I've got to stay,' I said. 'For the dog.'

Mister was freed shortly after from the cupboard under the stairs and he tore out still yapping hysterically. When I called to him he rushed into my arms in convulsions of quivering, and licked my face. It was only then my own legs started trembling, and it was all I could do to stay standing.

Later that day there was a knock at Nan's door. It was Mr Tailor. His house was still up.

'I'm sorry, love,' he said to Lil. 'Sorry what's happened, and for barging in on you like this. Only they found this – under the stairs, so it's kept safe. I thought you'd like to 'ave it before some bugger nicks it.'

In his arms was Gloria, plus accumulator, without a scratch on her.

'The King's 'ere,' Mr Tailor said as he went. 'Walking round town. Come to see the damage, I s'pose.'

We laid Gloria on the table. Nan sat by her, stroked her hand over the dusty veneer. Slowly, lovingly, she touched the knobs. Then she laid her head on her arms and wept.

I was ill after that and the days disappeared. My throat was so painful I could hardly even stand to swallow water. It must have been all the soil and muck I'd had in my mouth, and I had a very high temperature and delirium. A lot of the time I couldn't remember what had happened in a direct way, but all the sensations and dreams wrapped in that hot, twisting fever were threatening, sometimes shapeless, sometimes clear, always awful.

In one of my dreams Mom was back in our house as it had been. She was speaking to me and I knew what she was saying was the last thing I'd ever hear her say, but however much she strained and forced her slack mouth to shout, she couldn't make me hear her. I sweated with concentration trying to remember the last living thing my mother would say but I always failed.

There was another dream. Again I was in our house. Pieces of my mother were lying in a chaotic jigsaw puzzle round the rooms and I had to put them together before – before what I didn't know. Before it was too late – for something. I ran from room to room picking up an arm here, a hand or foot there. I had to save her. The horror of the dream was knowing all the time I wasn't going to make it. Once when I dreamt that dream it was Joe, not my mother, whose limbs were lying scattered.

Again and again I woke trying to scream, my throat a ring of fire, and Lil would come to me, trying to quiet me, her hand cool on my forehead. Day and night I couldn't stop my hands from shaking.

I don't know how my nan got through those days. I was so sick, and it was Lil who held on, who was strong for us all. She knew bereavement, perhaps knew how to survive.

'It's all right, Genie love.' She held me all the times as I mumbled out, feverish, all the things I blamed myself for. Kept going on about Shirl, Shirl's dad.

'None of this is your fault, love. None of it. The only person to blame for all this is Adolf bloody Hitler. That's who's the cause of all of it. You stop blaming yourself. You've been a really good kid and no one could've done more than you. You've just got to get yourself better now.'

The fever left me and I lay in bed weak and thin as tissue paper, looking round at the bare walls where Tom and Patsy slept when they were here. I barely had the strength to move and my throat still felt as if I'd been gargling with gravel.

'Look.' Lil came in one day carrying a card. 'From Victor – from your Dad.'

She held it in front of my eyes. A card from a POW camp addressed to Mom. His health was good, it said. At the bottom he sent 'Best regards to yourself, Genie, Eric, Len, Edith, Lil and the rest. Happy Christmas. Yours ever, Victor.'

I looked up at Lil. 'Of course he doesn't know. We'll have to tell him.'

She looked away out of the window, her eyes very sad. 'Yes we will. Poor old Victor.'

Teresa came and her face in the doorway looked scooped out and deathly white.

'You better, Genie?'

'Think so, ta.' I hid my trembling hands under the covers. 'Bit wobbly still.'

'Your nan says d'you want a drink?'

'In a bit. What's up?' I pulled myself up on one elbow, disturbed by the way Teresa looked.

She sat on my bed. 'Stevie's home.' Her voice broke up and she spread her hands over her face, distraught. Only after a few moments she managed to say, 'Dad's dead.'

'Your dad – dead?'

She lowered her hands despairingly. 'They didn't even bother to let us know. Probably didn't think a wop traitor was worth it.' I'd never heard such hate in her voice before. 'They just sent Stevie out to do it for them.'

'When, Teresa? What happened?'

'Stevie says a fortnight ago. He caught pneumonia. No one'd do anything, although Stevie went on and on at them – said Dad's lungs were already bad and he needed attention. They didn't get him to hospital until it was already too late.' She thumped her fist on the bed, her face twisted with anger. 'No one was there when he died. None of us. Not even Stevie.'

'Oh God, Teresa. I'm so sorry.' I thought of Nonna Amelia's death, all the family waiting to hand her gently into it. And Micky so much younger, shouldn't have died at all. Micky who was told the Mother of God would catch him when he fell.

Teresa wiped her red eyes. 'I've been to see you before but you was too poorly. You looked really bad.'

'Felt it.'

'I'm sorry – your mom, Lenny ... It's terrible, Genie.'

I nodded. 'Your dad, Teresa – he was good to me.'

'I know. I knew when he'd gone – what I'd missed. And then when I got to know Carlo properly I started wanting to know all about his life over there, Dad's childhood, his mom and that. I used to get fed up with him trying to tell me – I was so arrogant. I thought, when he gets back I'll be able to ask him . . .' She trailed off, wiping her eyes. 'Oh, what's the use?'

She shifted closer and we put our arms round each other.

'God, Genie, you're skinny!'

'I can feel your bones too.'

We rested our cheeks together.

'When Carlo and I get married, will you be my bridesmaid?'

I squeezed her. 'Course I will.'

I stayed in just about all the time, mostly up in my room, often lying on the lumpy bed but not asleep, not exactly awake, but in a weak, dreamlike state brought on by my illness. When I thought about moving I had to concentrate hard to make an arm move or a leg. Mister often came and lay on my bed to keep me company and I liked his warm weight by my feet.

Now and then I found the strength to go down, even outside. But people stared, and once I had Clarys bitching at me in the yard. 'I hope you 'aven't brought your bombs with you.' People believed that, that the bombs followed you. Not that we were having much in the way of bombing at the moment anyhow. But I stayed in. It was freezing out. Now and then I sat down by the fire, Mister at my feet. I switched Gloria on, stroked her sometimes. She was all that was left of home as it had been.

Lil and Nan were just getting on with it. Keeping going. The shop opened, the jobs got done, Nan's hair was suddenly almost white, the skin looser on her face. Lil too looked very haggard, but everyone was gentle. We knew we were all we had.

Now I'd surfaced I started to remember other things. That it was nearly Christmas for one. And that Lil had lost Frank. She never mentioned him, just came and went, looking after me and Cathleen like an angel. She even tried to decorate the house up a bit for the season.

'What're you going to do, Lil?' I asked her, watching her hang snippets of holly on the mantel. I was huddled in my nightdress and a coat by the fire. 'You going back to the factory?'

She stood back to eye up her decoration. 'No.' I saw her chin come out, determined. 'I've been doing a lot of thinking. I may not be able to have Frank, but one thing I've got out of all this is that shop. I was doing well at it – got a bit of a flair for it.'

'But Lil, is it real? It looked like a big con, that lady thinking the egg-holders were the Alps and that?'

'Depends on your attitude,' Lil said seriously. 'Course you can trick people. Tell 'em any old rot. But there's a skill to the cards and the palm reading and the rest. You can use your instinct. Really try and feel your way into a person, who they are. I can do it – I know I can. People trust me. Sort of open up to me. I'm going to keep the lease and make a go of it. Make it nice inside with a little grotto for the crystal ball and the palm readings. I've coped on my own before and I can do it again.' She grinned at me suddenly. 'Not as if Frank's the only bloke in the world, is it?'

She frowned then. 'Why aren't you opening your letters, Genie?'

Our post came redirected now, from the old house.

'Letter. There's only been one.'

'Well – one then?'

I shrugged, looking down, pulling the old brown coat close over my knees. 'Don't, Lil.'

428

'Don't what?'

'I don't want to talk about it.' I'd thought he'd stopped writing. I was glad. It was over. But then this other one had come.

Lil knelt down in front of me, staring up into my face. 'You loved him, Genie. Don't shake your head at me. It was clear as anything.'

I stood up, pushing her away, my throat aching with tears.

'I told you, I don't want to talk about it. You don't know what you're on about. Just leave it.'

I went up to bed again, swallowing hard, Mister following me, his claws loud on the wood stairs.

We got ready for Christmas out of habit, even though there was nothing to celebrate except the lack of bombing. The night air had been a lot quieter lately. You could sleep right through if habit allowed you. Preparing for Christmas was a way of remaining steady, keeping some of the normal things going when the rest had been smashed apart.

Nan ran the shop, accepted people's condolences and put up with blokes coming and going to mend Morgan's roof. Morgan was desperate to get back his access to a private place away from his elderly mom as soon as possible and he kept coming and eyeing up the work, demanding to know how many days it would take. It was a sign of how things were that Nan made not a murmur. Even the thought of Morgan creeping back and forth had suddenly become a sign of longed for normality.

We didn't speak about Mom or Len much. We all knew what had happened to Mom and no one wanted to bring it out in the open. It was too terrible. Nan hadn't even been able to see her at the end. In secret shame I wondered how Mom's life would've gone on if she'd lived. Would I have kept finding her eyeing up the gas oven until one day she finished it that way for good?

Instead of talking about Len, we talked of Molly. She was heartbroken, poor thing.

'We'll have to give her any help we can,' Nan said. 'After all, I'm the babby's grandmother, aren't I?' It was clear to see that if there was ever a little babby going to be swamped with doting nans, this would be the one.

On Christmas Eve we sat round the fire, Nan and Lil drinking hot toddies. Cathleen, full of excitement, was allowed up late and the rest of us were doing our best for her, although I could tell Lil was low. She and Cathleen were missing the boys and it'd really hit home tonight. She'd sent parcels for them out to Leek and was toying with the idea of bringing them home.

'It's not over yet,' Nan said, swirling her drink round to cool it. 'Now you've sent them you might as well wait till it's safe for 'em – even if it is *his* aunt. She's good to them by all accounts, and you don't want Tom all worked up again.'

'So you don't think I was all wrong sending them?'

'No. Even if your reasons were dodgy at the time.'

'I do hope they're all right,' Lil fretted.

'They sound it. Sure you don't want a drop of this, Genie?' Nan offered.

'No ta.' I stuck to tea. Mom'd given me a horror of drink. I'd have signed the pledge the way I felt about it. And I still wasn't well. I felt feverish again tonight,

430

turning hot and cold, my hands shaking so I could only just control the cup.

'Look at the state of her,' Lil said. 'You poor kid.'

I tried to give her a smile.

We had carol singers round, kids mostly, and stood outside the front door listening, door closed because of the blackout. Their feet crunched on the frost and I was shivering.

'Once in Royal David's City,' they sang, not quite in tune but well enough to make you fill up. Made me think of those stories of the last war – the Christmas truces, carols floating across the trenches. How blooming peculiar the world was.

The singing brought our emotions to the surface and we couldn't stand much of it. We gave them a couple of coppers to get rid of them. We hadn't sung together at all. Not without Mom and Len. Back inside we were all quiet, full of that swell of emotion that Christmas brings, but for each of us this time, an unbearable amount worse. It brought us up against all we'd lost. I knew everyone was thinking of it.

In the end Lil said, 'You're going to have to take her place now, Genie. Should we sing, Mom?'

We both looked at Nan. Her jaw tensed. 'No,' she said quietly. 'I don't think so. Not yet.'

We got Cathleen ready for bed, eyes still bright with excitement, like a Christmas angel herself in her little nightdress. I thought of how she used to sleep in her raggedy vest and bloomers before the war when times had been so hard for Lil.

'You get off to sleep now,' Lil and I told her. 'Or Father Christmas won't come.' Lil had bought her a puzzle and a cheap little ornament, a mermaid with a shiny blue tail. She was going to love it.

On the way down from saying goodnight to her I came over dizzy and had to sit down quick to stop myself falling downstairs. Lil looked at me anxiously.

'You're not right yet, are you? Nowhere near.'

'No. I feel pretty bad. I'm going to turn in too.'

I lay in the dark feeling the fever come over me in hot waves, shivering one minute, pushing the covers off the next, sea-tides of hot and cold pushing me back and to. Thoughts seemed to clang into my mind harder than usual, chopped up, distorted by fever. Thoughts of how this house felt like a home to me, always had, downstairs, Nan's shop, how I'd once dropped a drawer full of reels of coloured cotton and they'd bounced and spun off all over the shop going 'plok-plok' on the floor and it seemed to take for ever to pick them up. The sound echoed loud now in my mind. Eric had been there, a babby then, crawling round the floor, and he stopped, mouth wide open, head turning this way and that and not knowing which one to watch. Everyone paraded through my mind – Dad, Len, Mom, Bob. That fantastic feel of Bob's thumb crunching between my teeth.

I was asleep yet not asleep. I knew Mister had jumped off my bed and pattered off downstairs. He was barking for a time. Gloria must've been on. Music, then voices talking on and on. I wasn't sure how much time had passed, and whether I'd slept in the middle of it.

There was a light in the room, the unsteady glow of a candle, very vivid. Not a dream. Lil come to look in on me. Very drowsy, my eyes kept opening and closing.

'Can I have some water?' I managed to say in a hoarse whisper.

I thought I heard her talking, low voices, and I said, 'What?' Then the cold cup came to my lips as I half sat up, cold suddenly, teeth knocking against it. I opened my eyes, sipped. 'Ta.'

Not Lil. Was this a dream? Joe sitting on my bed, face full of anxiety. I heard myself gasp.

'Genie?'

'Joe. Joe?' In my weakness I lay back in the bed and found I was already crying. The wave broke over me, a great wash of tears that I couldn't hurry or stop. I heard the forgiveness in his voice even when he'd said so little, I saw it in his face, and it began to release everything. The terrible loss, the pain and fear and guilt of these past weeks that had been locked down in me, keeping him out, punishing myself as unworthy of him.

He knelt by the bed and took me in his arms as I sobbed hoarsely. 'It's all right.' He held his cool cheek against my burning one. 'It's all right now, my love. Sssh, my sweet one.'

'I'm s-s-sorry, Joe. I'm sorry. I'm sorry.'

I felt him take in a deep, shuddering breath and I clung to him, this miracle of love and forgiveness who'd appeared out of my dreams.

'Mom's dead. And Len.'

'I know. Your auntie Lil told me.'

I frowned, all muddled up. 'When?'

'Just now. I've just got in. From the station. I wrote and said I was coming . . . I know, you've had a terrible time.'

'Did she tell you Mom tried to gas herself?'

His head jerked back, horrified. No, she wouldn't have done.

'I felt so bad. So ashamed. I let everyone down. I thought you were too good for me. That's why I didn't . . . couldn't . . .'

'Sssh, Genie. It's OK.' He soothed me like a little kid

433

and that was just how I felt. I wanted someone to be my mom, my dad, my love, all in one. He sat me up and held me on his lap, stroking my hair.

'I didn't write because I thought—' I was still sniffing and gulping. 'I don't know what I thought. I just hated myself and it made me think you couldn't want to see me again.'

'I was worried.' There was a flash of hurt, of anger. 'Your letters were what kept me going, see. But Dad said he'd been to see you and said something about your mom being bad so I thought maybe you were too busy to write.'

I looked up into Joe's face. Mr Broadbent hadn't passed on my message. Not what I'd really said. Maybe he hadn't wanted to hurt Joe. Or did he just plain not believe me?

'Soon as I got here I had to come and prove to myself things hadn't changed. And of course when I got to your house, I saw—' I could hear tears in his voice. 'Jesus, I thought you were dead, Genie. You were dead and that's why I hadn't heard anything. When I saw your house – smashed up, gone – I felt as if everything had been destroyed, everything I'd hoped for, all we talked about doing together. Torn apart. It was the worst moment I can remember, ever.'

Wretched, I stroked his face and he took my hand and kissed it hard, a lot of times.

'I'm sorry, Joe. I'm terribly sorry.'

'No – I just wish I'd known. All that's happened . . .'

'D'you really love me – still, after all this?'

'I could never not love you.'

I held on to him so tight. 'I thought I'd lost everything. Almost everything. And then suddenly, oh Joe, you're here.'

We kissed, his lips pouring new life into me. We sat there quietly in each other's arms. I didn't know it was possible to feel so happy while I was so sad.

'You're very hot,' Joe said, feeling my head and neck. 'Your nan said you've been really bad. She's been worried about you.'

'She must be,' I said, cuddling against him in a haze of joy. 'Otherwise she'd never've told a bloke to come up into my bedroom!'

After a time Joe tucked me back in bed and kissed me. I put my arms round his neck. 'Don't go,' I said sleepily. 'I might wake and find I dreamt you.'

'You didn't dream me. I'll be back, love, every minute I can be.' He watched my face. 'I can't believe my luck. Now we've just got to get you better.'

'Oh, I'll be better now. I'll be better tomorrow!'

My eyes followed him to the door, candle in his hand. He turned, his lovely smile across the room more powerful than any medicine. 'See you tomorrow. Good-night, sweetheart.'

On 1 January 1941 the BBC launched a new programme called *Any Questions* which became very popular and was later renamed *The Brains Trust*. That day, I spent in my nan's house, my home for now, with Nan, Lil and Cathleen, and Joe on the sofa by my side, my bony hand held in his. Gloria sat, newly polished and shiny on the table, the voices pouring out through her sunburst. Mister was on my lap, a fire in the grate, tea in our cups.

Joe's eyes met mine as we first heard the posh, chattering voices and we laughed. I leaned into his arms and felt his kiss on the top of my head.

'Hor hor hor' laughed the chappies on the wireless. Lil's eyes filled, although she was smiling. She looked round at us all. 'Wouldn't Len have loved this?'

BIRMINGHAM FRIENDS

For Peta, with thanks

ACKNOWLEDGEMENTS

I should like to express my warmest gratitude to the following:

For particular help with the research for this novel by generously giving their time and conversation: Mrs Iris Deathridge, Mr Terry Leek and Dr Marcellino Smythe.

My agent Darley Anderson for his galvanizing encouragement, faith and friendship.

My editor Peta Nightingale for her sharpness and dedication and for keeping going with it in testing circumstances.

All those at Macmillan involved in the various stages of production and promotion – in particular my copy editor Penny Rendall and illustrator Gordon Crabb.

Belatedly and long overdue to my former editor Jane Wood.

Birmingham's Tindal Street Fiction Group: Gaynor Arnold, Alan Beard, Julia Bell, Mike Coverson, Stuart Crees, Godfrey Featherstone, Barbara Holland, Alan Mahar, and Penny Rendall for their ongoing support and expertise.

Finally, and above all, my family: to John – and to Sam, Rachel, Katie and Rose. Thank you.

In fact in almost every family, one sees a keeper,
or two or three keepers, and a lunatic.

Florence Nightingale

Prologue

ANNA

Birmingham, 3 August 1981

My mother is dead.

Anna repeated these words to herself, still trying to make it real as they walked along the cemetery path under the dripping trees: rain had fallen briskly after a hot day, clouds piling suddenly across the blue. Smoke was still wafting from the squat chimney of the crematorium. These places removed death so far from you.

But she had seen Kate dead. The day of the Royal Wedding, when the hospital was festooned with red, white and blue, flags waving on the ward TV and everyone carrying on about Diana's dress. The nurses put a yellow rose between the papery flesh of Kate's hands. And they prepared Anna for days before by avoiding her eyes, by which she knew for certain Kate was dying. It was obvious anyway. The cancer sucked her down to a tight-skinned puppet, eyes closing against the world. Astonishing that a woman as big as her mother could ever shrink so thin.

She sat quietly touching Kate's arm for an hour or more after she died, though the moment it happened she knew her mother was gone, absolutely. Mom. Strange and silent. She didn't know then that the changed form on the bed was more of a stranger than she imagined. Kate was the one person of whose past she thought she could be certain. She had known it the way a child knows the rhythm of a fairy story, secure and unchanging for thirty-four years. Until yesterday. Why couldn't she have said something before it was too late?

'Sure you wouldn't like me to drive you, my dear?'

Anna smiled, squeezing the fleshy arm that was linked with hers. 'No, I'm fine thank you, Roland. And I'm sure it's me who should be offering you. You're the one who's been of most support to her.'

The chubby cheeks next to her creased into a melancholy expression. Now his hair was so thin on top, Roland's face seemed even more naked and expressive. 'Not a lot I wouldn't have done for the old girl – you know that.'

'I know. You've been so good. Thank you.'

'Want to be on your own for a bit?'

She nodded. 'Yes. I think I do. I'll go and face the house. But it'd be lovely to see you again – soon. I haven't been coming back often enough, I know that.'

Roland gave her hand a final pat as if to absolve her from any sense of guilt, put his little tweed hat back on his head, and with his usual supreme tact walked on ahead of her. She watched, eyes full of affection. He was squeezed into an ancient black suit, a fraction too small, and the hat looked quite incongruous with it, but that was all Roland – one of the things for which they had loved him.

Not wanting to run into anyone else, she followed swiftly past immaculate borders of marigolds to the wrought-iron gates. As she reached her car, the clouds started to let rain fall.

*

2

The cutting from the *Post* about Kate's retirement was pinned to the noticeboard in her kitchen with a yellow-tipped tack.

'"Aunt" Kate to retire after forty years', it read, and beside the caption a photograph of Kate's round face beaming at a baby in her arms. She was restraining the plump hand that was reaching up towards her face.

'He was a little demon,' Kate had told Anna, laughing. 'He was determined to pull my glasses off!'

> Kate Craven, known as 'Aunt' by generations of the city's children, retires this week after nearly forty years' Health Visiting.
>
> A motherly, if often outspoken character, Kate will not be forgotten by the many women whom she has advised and supported over the years.
>
> Her career began in 1938 as a nurse at the General Hospital and in her time she worked in most areas of South Birmingham, as well as being an ardent promoter of Health Education in schools.
>
> From her final post at Poplar Road Clinic in Kings Heath she was given a send off today by staff and parents.
>
> 'She's a lovely lady,' said one mother of three. 'Flexible, honest, and always kind. Everyone will miss her.'

Anna stared at the picture again, the smile on that round, generous face. *What is all this? What have you kept from me?*

The phone started ringing. She knew it was Richard. She should have unplugged the thing.

'How was it then?' he said. She could picture him standing in the hall of their house in Coventry, still in his casual social-worker clothes, moss-green cords, brown jacket, shirt open at the neck. No tie of course.

3

'It was a ball, what d'you think?' He should have taken the day off and been there with her.

'Sorry.'

Anna didn't say anything.

'So you're not coming back tonight then?'

'No,' she agreed flatly. 'I'm not coming back tonight. Nor tomorrow. I've got all the house to sort. There's no point in driving up and down now it's the holidays, is there?'

'If you say so. Only I could do with the car. It's a bit awkward.' There was a sigh in his voice, but then he always sounded rather long-suffering on the phone.

She tried being conciliatory. 'All right, I'll come over tomorrow night. I'll be able to use Mom's car – OK?'

'I could cook,' Richard offered.

'That'd be nice,' she said, thinking she'd believe it when she saw it. 'How was today?'

'A pain. Delays in court all morning. Gerry Kinsella this afternoon.'

Gerry was one of Richard's most intractable probationers. Normally she'd have felt obliged to ask about it. Today she didn't think she'd bother.

Richard sighed wearily. 'I suppose I'd better go and find something to eat then.'

'Yes, you had, hadn't you?'

Anna put the phone down hard and said to it, 'You've just lost your mother, Anna, so how are you feeling? Well funnily enough I'm pretty cut up about it, Richard. Really nice of you to think of asking.'

The box, with its card pinned to the top, 'FOR ANNA', was in one of the bedroom drawers.

She had not been long in the house when she started prowling restlessly round the rooms, as if to make absolutely sure it was empty. The bedroom door opened with a squeak and she felt her palms sweating, somehow nervous of invading Kate's privacy. It was a pretty room: floral curtains and bedspread to match in soft pinks and greens, and a cream carpet with sprigs of pink roses. Kate had moved into this house only a year ago, preparing for retirement and a bigger garden. Anna remembered the austerity of her mother's room when she was a child, the brown lino and old iron bedframe, the lodgers.

She opened the wardrobe and looked inside, but found at once that she couldn't bear it. Kate's clothes, her shape, the skirts limp and slightly pushed out at the back from being sat in, the broad, still creased waistbands. And shoes, her second, very personal skin. Kate's shoes, squatting there in the bottom of the wardrobe, defeated her. She lay on the bed, her hair draping her face like a shroud, and cried. She hugged the flowery quilt with its familiar scent, trying to feel her mother's once plump arms round her, soothing her out of the pain of her own death.

It was after this she found the box, a carton covered with Christmas wrapping paper. Inside were a photograph, two letters and a thick bundle of paper pushed into a pink file. These were all tied together with the thin white elastic Kate used to thread through Anna's school socks to keep them up.

She had never seen the photograph before. It was from an old newspaper, the paper yellow and the print grainy. She knew at once that the two children in the picture were Kate and Olivia. There had evidently been bright sunlight in their eyes, adding crinkled noses to their smiles. It was quite obvious which was which. Kate's wide, friendly face, the glasses, well-defined eyebrows above them, her dress looking a bit too small. And Olivia, beautiful right from the first. Anna squinted at the image. She had never seen any picture of Olivia before. She was thin, shorter than Kate, with a mass of wavy hair and dark eyes which dominated her face. Her dress was of a pale, frothy looking material. Anna thought she could just make out the tips of Olivia's fingers round Kate's waist. Beside the two of them stood a very tall dark-haired man, and behind, a ring of people watching a roundabout, its movement slightly blurred in the picture.

Handwritten in the margin were the words, *Onion Fair. Birmingham 1929.* The girls had been eight then, though the writing in blue biro looked recent.

Anna picked up the shortest of the letters. It was on a good quality sheet of blue paper. Beneath the Birmingham address appeared a mere lineful of words written with beautiful evenness: 'I'm here to stay now. *Please*. Olivia.'

Anna's heart started to beat faster. So often at story-time in her childhood: 'Mummy, tell me a story about you and Olivia when you were little girls.' And Kate had seemed to relish this talk while Anna sank into sleep. Idyllic summers spent in the languid gardens of Moseley, their endless talk, piano playing, their laughter and games. Talented, lovely Olivia, who was killed in the war in 1944.

Anna looked up slowly, frowning. The date at the top of Olivia's letter was December 1980.

She reached for the pink file.

6

Part One

Chapter 1

KATE

Birmingham, 1929

'Kate Munro!'

Miss Pardoe's voice rang down the school corridor. I jumped guiltily, wondering what I'd done wrong. When Mummy spoke to me in that tone it meant Trouble. I had forgotten for a second that that was the way Miss Pardoe always talked.

'Come here,' she commanded. I walked up to her, trying to interpret the expression on her handsome face. At least she didn't look cross. 'It's all right. You're not going to be punished. I've a little job for you. Olivia Kemp has been taken ill, and I'd like you to go and sit with her until she goes home. You'll find her in the lost property room.'

I scowled at Miss Pardoe's back as she strode off towards the staff room. Just my luck.

The lost property room was a narrow hole next to the changing rooms with a cold stone floor and a stained enamel sink on one wall. There were a couple of hard, ink-stained chairs inside and a small cabinet screwed to the wall, always locked and containing a rudimentary first aid kit. Apart from that there were two disintegrating baskets into which were thrown any items of lost

9

clothing or kit found round the school. The room stank of sweaty Aertex and rubber pumps, and there was only one high little window, so it was gloomy as well as smelly.

And on top of that it had to be snotty, top-of-the-class Olivia Kemp. Although we were in the same class, I'd mostly kept out of her way until now. For one thing Olivia was glorious to look at, skinny, with those huge brown eyes like a puppy's and thick, curling brown hair. I was plump with hair that was neither blond nor mousy but somewhere in between, and I had to wear specs that crouched across my nose like black crows. Olivia sat in the corner desk at the front of the class, head bent, working and working, or listening with wide eyes and what seemed exaggerated intentness to whatever the teacher was saying. She got marvellous marks and we all thought her frightfully stuck up. And she was Councillor Kemp's daughter. Everyone in Birmingham had heard of Alec Kemp. He was the youngest yet one of the most prominent councillors in the city, and a very handsome one at that. You could see where she got her looks from.

I had enough friends to pair off with in class or at games if I needed to – Marjorie Mantel and Celia Oakley were always available. Now I actually came to think about it I wasn't sure who Olivia's friends were. She seemed to keep people at a distance. But I was sure she had much bigger fish to fry than me. Shame one of them hadn't been landed with the job of looking after her. I hoped her mother would be quick. No doubt she would be utterly ravishing and think to herself what an ugly lump I was while being sweetly polite to me.

I flung open the door of the little cell-like room so

violently that the brass handle banged hard into the wall behind it. Olivia was sitting on one of the two upright chairs, feet in white ankle socks and black shoes, not touching the floor. On her lap was a white enamel bowl. Her eyes widened as I crashed into the room. She looked very small alone there in the murky light. I could see her eyes were full and her cheeks wet.

'Oh, it's you.' Quickly she rubbed the backs of her hands across her eyes as I shut the door behind me. 'I do feel rotten.'

I stood opposite her, hands on hips. 'Miss Pardoe says I've got to look after you.'

Olivia looked up at me doubtfully. 'You look very cross,' she said. 'Actually, you very often look cross.'

Did I? I wondered, intrigued by this observation. Against my will I felt sorry for her. 'I'm not cross. I say, you do look awfully seedy. D'you still feel sick?' It would be rather interesting to see Councillor Kemp's daughter being sick in a bowl.

'Not at the moment.'

We eyed each other warily. I sat down on the other chair, opposite her.

'I suppose they've sent for my mother?' Olivia looked across at me. She had tears in her eyes again.

'I expect so,' I replied gruffly. 'Doesn't she like you being ill? My mother says we make enough mess when we're well.'

In fact I said this mostly to cheer her up, our times of illness being those when Mummy seemed to find us most tolerable.

Olivia giggled suddenly, a rippling, infectious sound, and surprisingly loud. 'D'you like your parents?' she asked.

I thought about it. My parents felt like shadows who hovered round the edges of my life. My father was forever working. 'No, not all that much,' I said.

Olivia looked perturbed for a second at my response, then she gave a strange smile, her teeth almost bared. 'My parents are absolutely marvellous.' Her expression changed to one of curiosity. 'D'you always say what you think?'

'Mostly.' No one else at home did, so I felt I might as well.

Olivia considered this. 'You can probably get away with it because you're rather plain. If you're pretty, everyone seems to expect such a lot of you.'

'Thanks very much.'

She clapped one hand to her mouth, eyes wider, laughing with embarrassment. 'Golly, I shouldn't have said that. I didn't mean it really. I think you're nice.'

'That's all right.' For the first time I smiled at her. She wasn't really a bit stuck up, not the way I'd imagined. 'Anyway, it's not true – that I get away with it, I mean. I always seem to be in trouble with Mummy, and she thinks my brother William's the bee's blinking knees.'

Olivia was quiet and I realized she was only half listening to me.

'Are you going to be sick again?' I felt slightly less hopeful about it now.

Olivia nodded miserably. Her face had gone very pale and her forehead had broken out in a sweat. Her head lolled forward, her thin hands clutching the bowl tightly. Surprised at myself, I went over to her, put one hand on her shoulder and with the other held back some loose wisps of her hair. I could see ginger lights in it. Green liquid gushed suddenly from her mouth into the white of the bowl. She retched and I felt the force of it go through her. She gulped and panted. I fetched her a cup of water.

'Here.' My feelings of protectiveness took me totally by surprise.

'Ugh.' She wiped her mouth and sipped the water as I emptied the bowl into the old sink and rinsed it out. 'That was horrid. Thanks though. I feel better.'

From that morning on, we were inseparable.

My life changed when I got to know her. We were besotted with each other in the way young girls can be. Both of us had been lonely and needed someone to talk to. We loved each other's company. At home there was only William, and sometimes Angus from next door. Marjorie Mantel and Celia Oakley were pale substitutes for such a friend. I felt butterflies of excitement in my stomach at the thought of seeing Olivia. She was above all things lovable, and for that you could forgive her a great deal.

As well as being in the same class she lived less than half a mile away from us. We'd sit in her huge bedroom on Park Hill, its bay windows letting in sheets of sunlight, happy for hours, talking and laughing together. Often I don't think we even knew why we were laughing. It was just pleasure in being together.

I loved that room. It was such a pretty, girlish place, stuffed full of things: a flowery chair on which dolls and teddies and other animals snuggled together, their glass eyes or button replacements peering out between each other's furry limbs, a grand doll's house on a table, her shelf stuffed with books and her cupboard and drawers full of pretty, feminine clothes. We weren't allowed pets at home, but they even let Olivia keep her two budgerigars in her room, and they flapped around and rang their little bell in a cage near the window.

'Don't they keep you awake?' I asked her.

'No, silly. I cover them up and they go to sleep on their perches.' Even this made us laugh.

Best of all, though, was Olivia's little dressing table with its dainty drawers, its embroidered mats on the top and its bright, slanting looking-glass. The ones in our house looked as if someone had gone over them with sandpaper and they made your face look squiffy. The top of the dressing table was covered with all her pretty things, her silver-plated brush and comb, her jewellery box from which tumbled a muddle of hairslides and combs, necklaces, rings, and a little woven basket with a few of Elizabeth Kemp's discarded lipsticks and powder compacts. She had perfume and ribbons, she had cushions on the bed and pretty prints on the walls of flower fairies and some chubby children playing with a spaniel pup.

My own room was comfortable enough, but very plain. Candlewick bedspread, my old doll and my favourite teddy, Bosey. A small table, books ... And usually the only other rooms I saw were William's, which was very dull, and Angus's, with his model aeroplanes everywhere and the smell of adhesive. Olivia's room seemed a place of enchantment.

And she made me feel like a girl.

'Come on, Katie,' she'd say. 'Let's make ourselves up.' She'd daub my face with rouge and powder, pencil in wobbly lines along my eyebrows and smooth on lipstick with a flourish. Then I'd do her, once she'd taught me how. My mother never wore make-up, except the odd dab of powder which she applied as a kind of nervous habit like some people smoked cigarettes.

14

Then we'd sit squeezed side by side on the silky-seated stool in front of Olivia's toilet mirror, our faces close together, admiring the effects we'd created. At other times we did clown faces. Or Livy would just paint her lips thickly with scarlet, and pout and roll her eyes at the glass until we were both laughing so much we couldn't paint anything straight.

We played the piano together. We helped each other with our prep from school. Although she was usually top of the class I was sometimes able to help her, especially with arithmetic, which boosted my confidence no end because William was always held up as the one with the brains.

And most importantly, I could tell Livy anything.

'You're so lucky having a brother,' she said to me wistfully one day.

'No I'm not. I hate him.'

'You don't.'

'All right. Not hate. But he's such a smug boots. He's always got to have done something marvellous all the time. He has to be best. And he's smug to Angus too, and Angus is really good at some things and much kinder than William.'

'Well I think it's nice. Much better than being the only one all the time, like me.'

But I felt that being on your own would be quite all right if you had parents like Olivia's: a beautiful, sweet mother like Elizabeth Kemp with her soft, blond looks, and Alec Kemp. The amazing, glorious Alec Kemp. He was the most exciting man I had ever met. For the first time in my life he and Olivia made me feel pretty. Since I met the Kemps I felt I had become a different person: more appreciated and contented than I had been since I was a very small child.

Chapter 2

I remember the shiny perfection of that day.

The Onion Fair – and with Olivia and Alec Kemp! We sat in the back of his Bentley, every line of it sleek and gleaming, singing, 'We're going to the fair, the fair, the fair,' to the tune of 'The cat's got the measles . . .'

'I want to go on everything!' Olivia cried, bouncing excitedly in her seat as we swept towards the centre of Birmingham.

'Oh, I expect we can arrange that,' Alec said easily from the driver's seat. The two of us shivered and giggled with delight.

Olivia was wearing a very pretty dress in cream broderie anglaise, a matching strip of the material holding back her wild hair. My dress was of course much plainer and more 'serviceable' as Mummy would say, in blue and white gingham. But I did have a beautiful tortoiseshell slide to fasten my hair, which Livy had given me. She was forever giving me things.

She peered out of the window. 'Are we going past the factory, Daddy?'

'No,' Alec Kemp replied, steering the huge, smooth-running car along the cobbled streets. He had a deep voice and was proud of his Birmingham accent. 'No need today. We're going out for some fun, aren't we, girls?'

I stared at the back of his neck, the dark brown hair

cut in a precise line above his white collar and beautifully tailored suit. It was a surprisingly sober suit for his tastes, in grey worsted. He seemed so much bigger than my father, who always had a stooped look as if other people's problems were actually fixed heavy on his shoulders. Alec Kemp stood very tall and he was jaunty, engaging, with large brown eyes and a vivacious face.

People turned to stare at us as the Bentley eased to a standstill at the edge of the Serpentine ground in Perry Barr. The two of us must have looked very small sitting on the plush back seats, peering out eagerly, our feet not touching the floor. Most people came to the fairground by bus or tram, but we were arriving with Councillor Kemp.

'Will people recognize him?' I whispered.

'Of course.'

Of course. Pictures in the *Mail* and *Gazette*, always immaculately dressed in expensive suits with suave, black hats, or clad in vivid Prince of Wales checks. He would smile genially from the photographs, his image of himself carefully presented.

'Will you have your picture in the papers today?' I couldn't resist asking him.

'We'll have to see,' he said. 'I could have my photograph taken with my daughter and her lovely friend perhaps?'

I squirmed with pleasure. Alec Kemp had a way of making you feel like a princess in gold slippers, even if you knew you really looked more like one of the pumpkins.

The fairground was already packed and milling with people. As we walked from the car we could hear shouting and screams of laughter from some of the rides, the throb of hot engines driving the roundabouts and a

17

band playing. Everywhere we looked was a blur of curved, coloured movement: merry-go-rounds turning and the twirl of dancing skirts and lights flashing on the machines and sideshows. And smells: a delicious mixture of potatoes baking, fried onions, cigarettes and sweat and the sharp whiff of blue smoke from the engines overlaid by sweetness of candyfloss.

'Don't get lost now, girls,' Alec said. 'I'd have one heck of a job finding you again in this throng.' With his pipe jutting from the side of his mouth he took our hands and I felt the smallness of my hand in his huge palm. I was almost bursting with pride. As we walked along he smiled and raised his hat to people, took his pipe out of his mouth, loosing us each time and then reaching for our hands again. The smell of his tobacco smoke wafted down to us. I looked up at the tall, athletic figure beside me. I saw women of all ages blushing as he smiled and spoke to them.

One young woman approached him, smiled coyly and said, 'Aft'noon, Mr Kemp.' And Alec replied, 'Good day, Violet.' She walked away giggling with her friend, casting backward glances over her shoulder.

'How does she know you?' Olivia asked.

'She's from the works,' he told her.

Alec Kemp was one of Birmingham's darlings. Born and educated in the city, he had won his way to grammar school and become a self-made man without ever leaving the place. He had taken over his father's mediocre firm and used it to prove himself. Kemp's was squeezed into a plot of land behind Birch Street, near the heart of Birmingham, round which were crushed streets of grimy dwellings, and tiny workshops and chimneys pouring out black smoke into the already speckled air. But Alec's reward for economic prowess had been to move from

18

the terrace in Sparkhill where he grew up, to one of the huge, ornate houses gracing the streets of middle-class Moseley. And this was considered quite fitting for a young, successful man so obviously destined to become one of the city's aldermen, and particularly one who had taken the condition of the city's housing so much to heart. He had already completed a successful campaign to demolish one of the decaying blocks of Victorian slums in the Birch Street area and build innovatory flats to house the occupants. His campaign slogan was 'Prosperity and Responsibility'.

And it's Livy and me who are with him, I thought. No one else. I felt more presentable than usual, wearing that frock instead of the cut-down pair of William's shorts that Mummy so often dressed me in. If only I didn't have to wear my ugly specs . . .

Alec treated us to everything that afternoon. 'Here, you'd love a go on this,' and 'Come on girls, I remember this one from when I was a kid.' He lengthened his stride towards the biggest merry-go-round with the horses gliding up and down so high above us, its banner reading 'Rides for Young and Old'.

'I wish Daddy was like your father,' I said excitedly to Olivia. 'He'd never spend money on things like this.'

Olivia grinned mischievously. 'He's all work, work, work. That's no fun, is it?'

My father was forever working, busy with his patients or in the study. Reading, writing: Christian ethics, papers on improving the health of the nation. His work as a doctor and his Christian Socialist principles didn't leave him much time for leisure. Quite unlike this glamorous, thrilling, all-providing Father Christmas who was Olivia's father. No wonder Elizabeth Kemp adored him so. How could you not envy her, being married to such a man? Largesse flowed from his fingers, pouring out over the whole city.

The horses slowed suddenly, people climbing down before they had stopped, and it was our turn. We rode together on one of the painted horses, knees gripping the cool smooth flanks. I sat behind, my arms tight round Olivia's waist, and her hands gripped the twisted metal pole. We laughed and screamed to the loud music. 'I'm flying!' I shrieked, and Olivia just giggled and giggled.

He took us on the helter-skelter and the Big Bens, the steam yachts which swung up until they were at right angles to the ground, leaving your stomach behind as they came down again with everyone screaming. We laughed our way helplessly along the shuddering cake walk. He bought us hot potatoes, balloons, furry stickfuls of candyfloss.

'It's like eating knitting,' I said cheekily, and Alec lunged for it, teasing me. 'All right. If you're going to be fussy, I'll have it!'

But Olivia stopped suddenly, taking in the sight of one of the traction engines which pulled the trailers, right in front of us. It was a brilliant emerald green, the sunlight catching its polished brass funnel.

'I've got to go on one of those!' she cried and, candyfloss still in hand, she dashed across the dry ground, wisps of her hair and her cream skirt flying behind her. I followed, letting go of Alec Kemp's hand, scared for a moment by her impulsiveness. Only days ago I'd watched her climb the parapet of a little bridge over the River Cole, scrambling up, shouting triumphant, then falling. She was unhurt but wet and scared. But she could make you frightened for her. Sometimes I wished I could tie her down. I felt staid and solid beside her.

'That's not a ride, Olivia!' Alec shouted. He strode after us. 'Come back. You'll get lost.'

But she was already standing next to the majestic machine. She had to have what she wanted. By the time he reached her she was already climbing up into it. We could hear its throb, the power of it. She was chatting to the men working the engine, who smiled back, captivated but bemused, caps on heads and their hands black with grease.

'We've told her we can't move it, sir.' One of them climbed down to speak to Alec Kemp, who raised his hat to him. 'Not now, in this crowd.'

'That's quite all right. She shouldn't be up there,' Alec replied. I saw him slip coins into the man's hand. 'Thank you.'

That was the one cross moment. I had seen the panic in his face as Olivia dived into the crowd. Now he gripped her so hard that she yelped. When he let go there was a pink, suffusing mark on her arm.

'You must never go off like that again, you silly girl. D'you hear?' I could hear the anger like needles in his voice. 'Now stay close to me all the time or you'll get into trouble.'

Olivia stared at the ground, lower lip thrust out. I could tell she was near tears.

'I'm sorry,' she said in a little high voice. 'But it was so exciting.'

'Never mind, princess.' Alec recovered quickly and swung her up into his arms for a moment. 'Daddy doesn't want to be cross. Come on. Let's go and find something else you can have a go on.'

21

The photograph was taken after one of our merry-go-round rides. A young fellow with sticking-out teeth and a badly fitting suit approached us with his camera. 'Councillor Kemp, I'm from the *Gazette*. Could I trouble you for a picture?'

'Of course. It's no trouble, is it girls?' He smiled amiably. Courtesy to everyone, he maintained, was the trick. He was a great one for presenting the right image. 'Would you like the girls in as well?'

'That'll be a treat,' the young man said, squinting into his lens. 'Stand nice and close together now.'

We were both still alight with the thrill of it, standing warm together, arms wrapped round each other's back, utterly friends and absolutely happy.

The picture made the evening edition.

* * *

OLIVIA

They moved the piano forward in the drawing room, left music open on it and a vase of huge chrysanths on the top, which spread a heavy scent through the room.

'Don't make me,' I begged Mummy. 'Please. I don't want to I can't.'

'Oh, Olivia.' Mummy knelt down beside me immediately. Her face was white. She implored me with her eyes. She had to make me, had to, for him. 'Daddy's so proud of you. Do it for him, please, my darling. You must do things for Daddy to make him happy.'

She put her arms round me. She was so thin and pale. I could smell her cologne. 'Please Olivia, my pretty darling. You're so clever.'

She cupped my face in her hands, stared into my eyes and she was frightened, I knew. She stroked my hair as if I were a pony. I had no choice. I was only ten and they expected me to play in front of all those people: councillors, aldermen, even MPs like Neville Chamberlain.

'We'll ask Kate to come along and keep you company,' Mummy said.

It was 1931, the summer leading up to the formation of the National Government. They were all smug and expectant, of course, much talk of the eclipse of Socialism, Ramsay MacDonald having fluffed it. Waiting like vampires to do their duty for King and Country.

Daddy held a party, which meant giving orders for a marquee, terracotta pots with cascades of geraniums and busy Lizzies spilling from them like blood, lanterns strung between posts in the garden for when dusk came, and days of frenzied preparation of food. Mummy was pretty and charming but she was a draper's daughter. She had a little green book called *How to Entertain*, and kept it by her bed like a Gideon Bible. The responsibility made her eyes bulge. It took away her sleep.

I went to talk to Lady and King, my budgerigars. They were in my bedroom. I was allowed them there as long as I kept them clean. Lady was an unpromising-looking creature, pale sulphur colour with a smudge of green down one wing. King, though, looked perfectly splendid. A green-patterned bird, he lived up to his name, mottled with black and majestic. But they were such mute birds. They made sounds but they didn't speak. I wanted them to talk to me.

Sometimes I got angry with them. 'Say something. Speak, will you? Say, "Pretty Livy." Don't just sit there looking stupid like that!'

They'd chatter together sometimes, harsh, shocking outbursts of noise like dried beans falling on lino, but usually when I wasn't in the room. I'd listen from outside, hearing them gossiping, confiding things between them or fighting over the seed. They fluttered around in a frenzy, pattering their droppings down on the floor of the cage for me to clear up. When I went in they'd go silent suddenly, as if I was interrupting something.

It was like that that morning. As I climbed the soft, red stair carpet, I could hear them chirruping from the other end of the corridor. I tiptoed, my feet making no sound. I stepped over the raised, creaky board on the dark landing, knowing exactly where it was. I even held my breath when I reached the long strip of light by my bedroom door. They were hopping round the circular cage, chatting like an old couple reminiscing. Cosy, it was. I stood at the door listening, feeling angry. One of them rang the little bell I'd hung in there for them. They hopped and fanned with their wings.

Slowly and silently I slid into the room. They didn't see me at first. When my shape and movement came to their attention they stopped. They sat quite still, watching me warily, like they always did.

'Go on,' I said sweetly, squatting down beside the cage. 'You don't have to stop because of me. Keep talking – I like to hear you.' I pressed my nose against the bars. They fled to the opposite side of the cage and stood on the bottom, shifting nervously from one horrible naked pink foot to the other. I hated to see their scalded-looking skin and the way they were so scared and shifty.

'All right,' I wheedled. 'If you've got nothing to say, I'll talk to you. Daddy's having one of his parties tonight and there's a big tent on the lawn in case it rains, though it doesn't look as if it will. And all the important people Daddy knows are coming. And he's going to make me play the piano in front of them and I don't *want* to! I HATE THEM ALL STARING AT ME!'

My shouting made the birds panic. They crashed around the cage, nowhere to escape to, their wings clumsily hitting each other, beaks open and vicious. Sometimes I thought they might peck each other to death to escape me.

'It's all right, I'm sorry,' I soothed them. 'I'll tell you something nice now. Something that makes it better. Katie's coming. My best friend Katie. You like her, don't you? She doesn't scare you. She's coming to keep me company and stop them all pressing in on me with their eyes. Katie doesn't mind it. She doesn't see it. She loves me.'

And I loved her. How I loved her

'Much more than you ugly little pigs,' I said to Lady and King. I stuck my tongue out at them.

Dear Kate. She was so overwhelmed by it all. So impressed. Her family were restrained and colourless. She was always wide-eyed and in love with us, her round face pink at a word from Daddy. He charmed her as if with a magic pipe and she lay squirming at his feet. She was so sweet. Of course she was plump and she had to wear those dreadful glasses, but she was a darling behind all that gruff self-protectiveness. Win Munro never gave her an ounce of self-esteem. She had no idea how to say anything warm or caressing. It was my parents who did that for her. And Daddy was so fond of Kate back then, giving attention in a way that he never normally did to women who weren't beautiful.

But you couldn't not like Kate. She was full of innocence and fortitude. She'd go to the ends of the earth for you in her tight cotton frocks and buckled sandals.

'Gosh, Livy, it's beautiful!' she cried, looking round the garden with her mouth open. The wisteria was hanging in flower and there were garlands of lilies round the entrance to the marquee. The servants were on the run, Dawson and O'Callaghan heaving a huge side of cooked meat on a platter.

'My feet are killing me already,' O'Callaghan moaned. I hadn't got the measure of O'Callaghan yet, she was a new one. The maids were always coming and going. Except Dawson. Dawson was a very sensible woman. She'd learned: she lived out and had a small child and no husband. She hung on to her job with us.

It was already nearly dusk when the guests arrived. Lanterns glowed between the leaves in the garden. Mummy had dressed me in a white bridal frock like Betty McNamee wore for her First Communion. Kate's dress was pale green and as frumpy as ever, poor thing, but I could never lend her one of mine because she couldn't fit into them.

'It's gorgeous, Livy,' she said wistfully to me. She wasn't jealous. That wasn't Kate. She just admired. Her heart was so whole. She didn't see bad things and I didn't want to make her. I needed her to believe in us, in our fairy tale, so we could have her wonder, her adoration.

We stayed at the edge of the crowd, darting to the table to fill our plates. Kate ate, I picked at the food, the meats and sweet tomatoes and eggs and prawns trapped in aspic. I gave my most angelic smiles to those who stopped me and spoke.

'You're not eating much,' Katie said, as we sat in our spot near the shrubbery and watched.

I was sick with nerves. 'Oh, I've seen the food going past under my nose all day,' I said. 'Dawson and O'Callaghan gave me some bits to eat. I've no space left.'

We gazed up at the shadowy figures around us, the men in their dark suits and the shimmering, coloured silks of the ladies' long dresses which swished across the grass as they walked. I pointed to a tall, lean man talking earnestly near us. 'Neville Chamberlain,' I told Kate. 'Look, there's his wife over there.'

'She's gorgeous,' Kate breathed, peering over at Annie Chamberlain, swathed in pale violet silk. 'Look at that dress.'

We took in fragments of conversation. There was much talk of the election and the downfall of Socialism, and of riots breaking up meetings of the New Party. Labour's darling MP for Smethwick, carried on shoulders through the street after the 1929 election, dark and dashing with a red rosette, had soon fallen foul of the Prime Minister, Ramsay MacDonald. Oswald Mosley's meetings in the Bull Ring were now broken up by hecklers, bottles and chairs flung into the crowd by irate members of the Labour Party.

'Quite extraordinary, Mosley's lot seem to be,' a voice said. 'Bunch of thugs. Fearful tribe.'

Oswald Mosley had become the *bête noire*, but of course the Tories weren't complaining. I was fascinated by Mosley. He was so attractive. There was something diamond hard about him, and everything dark: his hair, clothes, heart, black and dangerous as a cobra.

'Olivia?' Daddy's voice cut across the chatter of the guests. 'Have you seen my girl? Where are you, Livy?'

I loved him so much I wanted to run into his arms, do anything I could to please him. My daddy, my handsome, adoring father. I was all to him, his kitten, his princess. He wanted to show me off in front of his friends. The piano. I felt my stomach lunge and buckle.

'Olivia?' Kate cried in alarm. I stood retching in the darkness behind the blossoms of buddleia, its drugging scent all around me. The guests couldn't have noticed.

Wiping a spot of my mess from my shiny black shoe on to the grass, I walked from behind the leaves, standing up very straight.

Kate was big-eyed. 'Here, drink this.' She handed me her glass of ginger beer.

'Been over-eating, Olivia?' Daddy teased softly. He loomed over us both, immaculate in his evening dress. Kate beamed up at him. 'Come on now, they want to hear you play.'

The piano was my passion. I knew I was good, brilliant perhaps. It was something I was sure of, deep in me. But my music was precious, intimate. I liked playing for myself, and for Kate, not for strangers. But I had to do it to make him happy.

A semi-circle of them were sitting, polite and expectant, in the drawing room, skirts carefully arranged, on chairs and on the sofa, some of the men standing and smoking, wafting the smell of it round the room. As I walked in and the talk lowered I could hear the ladies exclaiming to each other how pretty I looked, what a darling child.

I tried to pretend they weren't there. I walked to the piano and sat down, closing my eyes for a second. But when I opened them I saw Kate had slipped into the room and was standing blushing by the door. I remember feeling aggravated by that. They weren't looking at her, so why was she all tomato red?

'Tell us what you're going to play, Olivia,' Daddy prompted me.

I looked up. They were all smiling. Lipstick lips, moustaches, rows of teeth. I knew I looked sweet and pretty and small. I was too short to reach the pedals.

'M-Mozart,' I said. The stammer was deliberate of course.

I chose something easy and rattled it off, badly. Three sonatas played perfunctorily. I kept my face down, my heart pounding. The music did nothing for me. I wasn't lost in it. I was outside it and hating those people. Hating them all.

Of course they all clapped. They had to. I boiled inside. Clapping something bad. Hypocrites.

'Bravo!' a voice boomed.

'What a lovely child.'

'Credit to you, Alec!'

My feet took me across the cream Persian rug and out of there, running up the stairs to my room and my sleeping birds. Kate followed me. Moments later I was sobbing, held in her round, comforting arms.

Chapter 3

'Livy? I love you.'

'You shouldn't say that.' Olivia sat up abruptly in her bed across the room. 'Girls aren't supposed to love girls. Not like that.'

'Not like anything,' I protested. 'Why d'you have to twist things? I just love you. You're my best friend.'

Olivia relented and rolled sleepily across the bed again, grinning through strands of hair. 'Funny old thing. I love you too.'

I lay back on the firm pillow. I was so happy. On holiday with the Kemps – in a hotel! I stretched and wiggled my toes, the dry grains of sand scratchy between them. The cotton sheet felt delicious against my bare legs. I couldn't see anything clearly because my specs lay on the chair next to the bed. The light in the room was a blurry green, filtered through curtains which wafted by the open window, through which we could hear the waves.

Our first full day there and everything about it felt right. The sun was shining and only tiny puffs of cloud shifted slowly across the sky. We had swum and climbed on the rocks all morning while Elizabeth Kemp lay back in a chair on the sand and Alec had taken a boat out. We were now resting to let our lunch go down before swimming again. And the best thing of all was that we'd talked and laughed together all the morning, just her and me as close as close.

Before lunch we walked up the steep path from the beach to the cliff top, our legs scratched by gorse as we climbed the path of compacted mud, small stones rattling away from our pumps. We found a place to sit on the wiry grass which topped the headland, and looked out over the hazy blue of the estuary, tiny white sails in the distance.

Olivia sat leaning back on her hands, her legs stretched out in front, the warm wind blowing her hair back from her face.

'I found a piano in that back sitting room in the hotel,' she said. 'So we shan't have to do without playing after all.'

'No music.'

'But we'll remember it, won't we?'

When she said we I knew she really just meant herself. She sat for hours at a time in front of the piano at home, whereas I was forever looking for excuses to get out of practising, and Mummy didn't pay too much attention to whether I did or not.

'It'll be something to do after dinner,' Olivia said. 'If we're not already done in from all this fresh air.'

She leaned her head back and closed her eyes. I could see the shape of her eyes moving restlessly under the lids. I sat watching her. Both of us had changed in appearance since we first became friends, but we had spent so much of our time together that I barely noticed Olivia's looks alter any more than I did my own. Since she had been away at school in Staffordshire and I didn't see her for weeks on end, though, I'd begun to notice things. Livy's voice, which was deep and strong, had

31

become even more forthright with a confidence that the school had given her, its Birmingham intonation fading. Her hair was thicker and glossier. She was thinner, had a waist suddenly, and breasts. Curiously I looked down at my own body. I'd certainly not been short-changed on that front. Just like my Granny Munro. My legs looked much pinker and rounder than Olivia's slim ones.

'I wish they hadn't sent you away to that school.' It was far from the first time I'd made this complaint. 'It's not the same without you around.'

I was waiting for Olivia to agree and say how much she missed me during the term time and how there was no one else at school who was half such a good friend. This familiar conversation was like a ritual seal on our friendship.

But this time Olivia said, without even opening her eyes, 'Well, it could be worse. Gets me away from them at least.'

'Who?'

'Mummy and Daddy, of course.'

'But they're marvellous, your parents!'

Olivia started laughing, sitting up hugging her knees, her body shaking.

'What? What did I say?'

'Oh, Katie. You're so innocent, aren't you?'

I felt cross suddenly. Olivia was putting on that superior tone she sometimes used, as if the fact that she was a mere six months older let her into all sorts of adult secrets.

'I'm not,' I said sulkily. 'Granny Munro tells me all sorts of things.'

Olivia laughed again. 'How is your mad granny?'

'She's not mad,' I protested, with a reluctant grin. 'She does it all on purpose.'

Granny Munro, Daddy's mother, had come from Scotland to live with us only three months ago, after my grandfather died. She had made up a little bit for Livy not being around. Already she had appeared at the breakfast table with no clothes on, told the local grocer's that she needed biscuits and cheese on tick because we wouldn't give her any money and set up a trestle table at the front of the house in Chantry Road in order to hold her own jumble sale because she had brought too many possessions to Birmingham with her. She was driving Mummy nearly demented.

'It's been really fun having her living with us,' I said. 'She tells me all sorts of things Mummy would never dream of saying.'

Olivia had lain back suddenly, head among the blades of grass, her eyes closed. 'Lucky old you,' she said in a bored voice. I felt rather hurt and didn't bother telling her any more.

She'd never explained what she meant about her parents, I thought, lying on the warm bed. Perhaps it wasn't anything. Maybe it was just one of those Olivia things to say, making a drama out of nothing much.

'Livy?' I lifted my head, resting it sideways on my tanned arm.

'Mmm?'

'Let's take the boat out later?'

Olivia nodded, eyes closed.

I took a deep, contented breath, enjoying the smells of the little hotel: floor polish and cabbage and Rinso on the sheets. I'd have liked Angus to see the place. In fact I was feeling so well disposed towards everyone that I'd almost have liked William to be there.

I knew Olivia's parents were having a rest in the next room. They had the very end room along the corridor

33

facing the sea, and ours was next to it. A touch ashamed of myself I tried to imagine Alec and Elizabeth Kemp lying together on the bed which I'd glimpsed that morning through their door. Elizabeth would have unpinned her soft, fair hair. Perhaps she would have changed into a loose gown for taking a rest. My imagination skated quickly over Elizabeth's slight body. Beside her I pictured Alec's darker, more robust one. His handsome face with those brown dancing eyes would be close to Elizabeth's. Was he leaning over her? I wondered. I thought I could hear their voices through the wall. Was he about to kiss her? Would he then do *that* to her? What Granny Munro had told me about that I knew my parents could not bring themselves to mention?

For a moment I allowed myself to imagine Alec Kemp leaning over me, his lips moving closer to mine ... Of course Alec was my best friend's father and I was a rather lumpish fourteen-year-old with thick spectacles. But he was also the prince in every story. Kiss any frog, I thought, and it would transform instantly into Alec Kemp.

I heard a door open, close again. Growing sleepy I followed the faded pattern of dog roses and convolvulus on the wallpaper, hearing the rustle of the sea. As my eyes closed and I began to drift into sleep I heard noises from next door and was suddenly awake again. The sounds were soon unmistakable. I held my body absolutely still, listening, me heart starting to beat very fast. The sound of weeping was so desolate, so intense, and it could only be coming from Elizabeth Kemp. At first her crying was quiet and muffled. I waited, expecting to hear Alec's voice comforting her, but there was nothing except these terrible broken cries. For a few moments

34

Elizabeth sobbed loudly and uncontrollably before the sounds died down. Then there was silence.

When I woke, Olivia had already gone.

I stood by the window, enjoying the salty air and looking for her. From below came the sounds of children shouting, a dog barking, a boat's engine in the distance somewhere. The hotel was sited in the angle of a narrow bay with only a few cottages for company and a narrow road passing through. Round the headland was a small holiday town, which could be reached by the road or a short ferry ride.

The tide was out and shadows from the cliffs were already beginning to edge across the sand. Everything had turned the richer colours of late afternoon and children were busy digging on the wide shiny platter which was now the lower half of the beach.

The memory of Elizabeth Kemp's crying shifted uneasily round my mind. I had always liked Elizabeth. She was very gentle, a timid person who I had scarcely heard utter an angry word since I'd known her. She wasn't a vibrant woman. She was unsure of herself and she provided a counterbalance to Alec, his restlessness and drive. But there was a sweetness about her and she always gave me a warm welcome. Above all she obviously loved and admired her successful husband with wholehearted devotion. So what could have brought on such broken-sounding grief? I tried to persuade myself that I'd been mistaken and the noise had been coming from somewhere else.

The boat was drawing closer. It was the ferry. The red paint on the hull became visible, the engine droned louder as it advanced on the low stone jetty, pulling in with a churn of reversing engines.

As the passengers climbed out, a movement caught my eye, something known, familiar. Alec Kemp walking the tapering jetty among them, jumping down athletically. He was dressed in navy trousers and a white shirt, unbuttoned at the neck, and already his arms and face had lost their city pallor. He looked tanned and healthy. He held a cigarette in one hand; on his face was a look of satisfaction, amusement even. When he reached the hotel he stood, facing the beach, to finish smoking. I knew instinctively that there was something wrong in his being there. I drew my head in quickly, closed the window and waited a few more minutes before going down to find Olivia. By then he'd gone.

Olivia was down near the sea, scraping wet sand out of the blue rowing boat, *Serenade*, which Alec had hired for the week. The breeze puffed out the yellow blouse she was wearing over her swimming costume. She was not alone. Three boys were standing round her, and as I drew closer I saw that they were much our age, perhaps older, locals by the look of them, who were watching Olivia, giving unwanted advice, bantering with her. Olivia had let her hair loose in a wavy curtain down her back. Uncertain, I went and stood by them, wishing they'd go away.

'Need a bit of help pushing her off?' one of the boys said in his curvy Devonshire accent.

'We'll give you a push off all right!' another said, and they all sniggered. 'Want us to come along with you?'

To my surprise, Olivia, instead of telling them to get lost, was smiling impishly at them. 'I don't think you'd better come in the boat,' she said, 'but we could do with a bit of help getting going.'

'Getting going!' the third lad echoed, and they all

laughed raucously as if she'd said something funny or dirty.

'This your friend is she?' one of them asked, eyeing me up and down. 'Shouldn't think you'd need much of a hand with her to help you.'

I scowled at them. I didn't like being compared unfavourably with Olivia. I stood there awkwardly, dressed in an ungainly old pair of William's shorts.

'Ooh – she don't like us!'

To my fury, Olivia carried on smiling and humouring the boys long enough to let them help us drag the boat the final few yards to the sea. The bow slid into the water, rising and dropping suddenly as the force of each wave broke over it, and we clambered in.

'Right, here you go,' the boys shouted, standing thigh deep in the water, the edges of their shorts wafting with the water's movement. The boat was already well afloat, but they pushed us off, cheering and waving exaggeratedly as Olivia started to row. She stopped and waved back. I kept my hands by my sides, frowning.

'We didn't need those idiots!' I exploded furiously as soon as we were a distance from them. 'Why did you let them?'

'Oh I know we didn't, but you have to keep them happy, don't you?' she said in a pettish voice. 'Anyway, what's eating you?'

I didn't answer. I watched the water curl away from the oars. Peering down I could still see pebbles and sand on the bottom and trails of green weed. I screwed up my eyes against the white light on the water. I hated it when Olivia was like this. She had suddenly gone into what I called her witch mood, when she was sharp and mean and stirring up trouble and I couldn't get near her.

After a while I said, 'I saw your dad. He'd been to the town.'

For a second Olivia hesitated, frowning, the oars stilled at right-angles to the boat. Then, abruptly, she carried on rowing.

'Can I have a go now?'

We swapped places and I started off, enjoying the pull against the water, the feel of using all my strength. I dug in hard, trying to force the boat fast across the bay.

'Don't pull down so deep,' Olivia snapped. 'You'll catch a crab.'

'Look. What's the matter? What've I done?'

'Nothing.' Olivia stared down miserably into the bottom of the boat. 'You haven't done anything.'

The breeze helped propel us back towards the beach. Soon the prow jerked the boat to a halt against the sandy bottom and it tipped sideways so we were forced to jump out.

'One, two, three, pull!' we cried, hauling the little boat along the beach with exaggerated effort. Several times we fell over backwards and lay side by side, helpless with laughter, the sharp words forgotten, our hair getting thick and gritty with sand.

'Come on, you daft thing,' Olivia giggled weakly. 'Or we'll never get it up there.'

The beach was in shade now except for a slice down one side. Picnickers were packing up their windshields and Thermoses.

'Girls!'

Shading our eyes, we saw Alec Kemp moving towards us with his long stride, the dark trousers flapping round his legs in the breeze. I was squatting down next to the boat. Olivia stiffened.

'Don't move.' He grinned at us. 'That'll make a lovely picture.' He raised his Brownie camera, legs bent slightly and elbows out to get the angle right, and clicked down the shutter. 'One more.' Another click. 'There. That'll do nicely.'

He helped us position the boat up by the sea wall and we went to the hotel. As we crossed the road, quiet as it was, he took our hands as if we were small children before walking across. I was thrilled.

We ate each evening in the dining room of the hotel at tables with stiff white tablecloths and vases of miniature silk roses. It was a family hotel, not a posh establishment, but it had a wine list and tried to keep up certain standards. I was allowed to drink wine – wine! Alcohol was something my parents didn't hold with.

It was several evenings into the holiday and it had been raining most of the day. We'd woken to a fine mist of it over the sea and had barely been out all day. And it was mackerel, shiny metallic blue across our plates, the eyes still in. Fish made Alec Kemp irritable, if he hadn't been already. He liked to do everything properly and with style, but boning fish defeated him.

'Blasted things,' he said, pushing small bones out between his teeth with what seemed to me disproportionate fury.

Elizabeth had come down to the meal with her face clearly blotchy and pink from recent tears which even the carefully applied powder could not hide. I hadn't heard her crying again since that first day and had tried to forget what had happened, but seeing her that evening, the sound of it resurfaced disturbingly in my mind. She had composed her face now in its habitual lines: gently upturned lips, her glances towards Alec conveying, so far as I could make out, only attentiveness and appreciation. But her left hand fiddled restlessly with the string of seed pearls at her neck.

Elizabeth usually spoke very little as we ate. Alec liked to perform. Elizabeth would watch him, the smile fixed on her lips, letting him entertain us all.

Alec would tell stories about his Birmingham childhood – he and his two brothers – or the way he had taken over the firm, Kemp's Foundry Supplies Ltd, from his father and built it into something that really counted. There was no doubt he was doing well. The 1930s were such a desperate time for many people, but while laid-off miners were demonstrating on Birmingham's streets and queues reached round the corner from the Labour Exchanges, Kemp's Foundry Supplies was prospering. We'd all heard much of what Alec said before, but we let him talk. The couples and families at the other tables were talking quietly, except for one where the children were squabbling over bread rolls and cutlery.

'The old man didn't have the know-how to make the business really thrive,' Alec might say. 'He didn't lift a finger to improve the products. Of course in the end all the customers started to move to the firms that did. That's business. So I had to win them back – and more. And that's what I've done. You have to remember that, young Katie. If you want to get on you have to keep on your toes.'

Sometimes he leaned across the table and very softly sang 'K-K-K-Katie, beautiful Katie...' to me in a wooing voice which made my cheeks go red as I squirmed with pleasure and embarrassment.

But this evening there seemed to be barbs at every point in the conversation.

'Flaming fish.' Alec slammed his knife and fork

down. 'Flaming, bloody mackerel.' He pushed his chair back and lit a cigar.

'You should persuade your father to take a bit of a holiday,' he said, the cigar nipped between finger and thumb. 'Works far too hard.'

'He never seems to have the time,' I told him. 'I wish he would. He's always working. I don't think he'd know what to do if he wasn't.'

'Not good for his health though, is it?' Alec took a long pull on the cigar. 'He's a quack. He ought to be the first to know that. Sand, sun, fresh air – all the pleasures life can give you. Keeps a man, well, on top, so to speak.' He smiled engagingly at Olivia and me, but there was a glint in his eye, something I couldn't read but which made me feel uncomfortable.

'Alec.' Elizabeth's voice held a warning, though she was still smiling. Her hand gripped the pearls, knuckles whitening.

Alec's dark brows sank into a frown. 'I bet that idiot Parker's making a right balls-up of everything.'

'Kemp's will be quite all right without you,' Elizabeth reassured him. As she moved her hand to lay it on his sleeve I noticed the startling blue of the veins in her thin wrist. 'Even if Reg Parker doesn't get everything quite right, he can't possibly undo all your success in one week, can he? Don't worry, darling.'

I looked at Olivia, who was pushing peas on to her fork. For a second she glanced up and caught my eye, then looked away with determined nonchalance over towards the lights on the far wall with their little tasselled shades. I saw the blood rising in her cheeks.

'I wonder what all these people do for a living,' Alec said aggressively, looking round the room. 'What they do to deserve a holiday by the sea.'

Olivia clenched her teeth tightly together and stared at her plate. I could sense panic around me and I was filled with sudden dread, though I had no real idea why. I knew I wouldn't be able to finish my food.

'Daddy.' Olivia's cheeks were flaming. 'Don't start here. Please.'

Alec angled his body close to Olivia, who flinched visibly away from him.

'Well, you provide some of the conversation then, since you don't like mine.' He leaned back pretending to be genial and conversational. 'We could talk about – pets, let's say. The care of birds, for instance. Budgerigars in particular.'

I was bewildered. Olivia's beloved birds had become ill and died months ago. She'd cried over them for ages afterwards. Why was he being so cruel now, baiting her as if suggesting she hadn't looked after them properly?

'Livy loved those birds,' I said indignantly. 'She did everything she could for them.'

'Oh yes,' Alec agreed smoothly. 'Absolutely everything.'

Olivia swallowed, spots of red burning in her cheeks. 'I was thinking,' she said in a high, fluttery voice. 'It's funny being here with different servants. No Dawson or Radcliffe.'

'Your mother's missing them I think,' Alec said. He was unsmiling, spoke very deliberately, watching his wife's face. 'Bit of female company round the house. Even if they are common little tarts.' He spat the words out.

'Alec.' There was an appalled, begging note in Elizabeth's voice and her eyes were full of tears.

'They know how to please, though.' His tone was casual now, almost chatty. 'Never had cause for complaint, have we, darling? Worth bearing that in mind, Katie. Always be eager to please. Gets you places.'

Elizabeth stood up and left the room, walking through the stares of the other diners. Olivia was sitting rigid in her seat. I felt sick.

'Look.' Alec was suddenly sheepish. 'Sorry about that, Katie. Olivia? You're not cross, are you? You know your mother never is much good at taking a joke!' He tried to laugh it off. 'Never mind us, Kate, don't take any notice. Have a nice pudding, eh? I'll go and get her.'

Olivia stared stonily at her plate as Elizabeth followed her husband back to the table. Her expression was completely collected as if nothing had happened. We sat through the rest of the meal, Alec back to his ebullient, entertaining self. I felt very edgy still and could not help glancing at Elizabeth Kemp. But if it had not been for Livy's mutinous silence I might have begun to think I'd dreamt it all. Alec was affable, able to bring out jokes. And Elizabeth's face wore its mask of gentle, affectionate amusement.

'Livy?'

We were preparing for bed after the meal.

'I don't want to talk about it.'

'But what did . . .?'

'I said I don't want to talk about it.'

'Is it – are they often like that?'

Olivia stood with her back to me, pulling her dress on to a coat-hanger. After a moment she turned, suddenly giving me a dazzling smile which also managed to convey bafflement. 'Whatever do you mean?'

* * *

43

Did they really never know I heard them? Of course they assumed my deafness, my innocence. And when Daddy was aroused he bellowed, locked in his own needs and urges. I listened to their ritual through the smooth wood of the door, through keyholes, cracks between hinges. My room was safely far away, they thought, at the opposite end of the house. But I was there: nights when the maids had left or were up in bed and occasional afternoons when they assumed I was well occupied elsewhere.

Why did he pursue it? I used to wonder. Why humiliate them both? Sexual intercourse petrified my mother. I suppose my mind couldn't take in the contradiction that he really did love her and want her. That the others were all substitutes, not additional pleasures.

That afternoon they thought I was asleep in the gazebo. Carelessly they left ajar the door to their delicate nest of a bedroom, its windows edged with draped chintz the colour of clotted cream, stained with bright crimson flowers.

'It's been so long,' he begged. I had a wider viewing strip than usual. I had learned to move absolutely silently. He was kneeling at her feet naked, offering himself to her, his erection a dark branch in front. I called his penis his pleaser. I didn't know the proper name for it then. 'Please, my darling. I need you so much.'

'No. Don't, Alec. No.' Mummy's voice came out as a moan. I could just see the edge of her silky, peach-coloured gown and imagined her with her arms clasped across her breasts, shutting him out, her face distraught.

'Let me just touch you. You know sometimes if you relax you can ...'

'No – I can't.'

'You won't have a baby – you know you won't. It's all right.'

'Please, Alec, why must you do this? It's so horrible, I can't bear it. Go to anyone you like if you have to but please leave me.' Her voice was high and tearful.

'But you're my wife, Elizabeth.'

She moved over to the bed and backed up against the pillows, pulling her knees up. She looked so little with her wispy hair all hanging down, sitting there, cornered.

'Come on,' he wheedled. 'Just unfasten it, that's a good girl. Just lie back. There. Isn't that nice? You like this, don't you?'

He latched his mouth on to one of her breasts. She gave a whimper of distress. I suppose he fooled himself it was pleasure.

'Now – there's a good girl – ' His voice was low and hypnotic. 'Just open up now – let me in and it will all be all right.'

I couldn't see their faces. He had climbed over her, his body, strong and agile, already moving above her.

'No!' she cried.

I pulled my arm across my mouth and bit into it, hurting myself, listening to their sounds.

'I've got to,' he grunted. 'You've got to let me. You cold bitch!' His voice rose to a great roar. 'Let me in – *now*.'

Her sobs filled the room. I bit myself harder, harder. 'I can't. I can't bear it.'

'Touch me then, quickly for God's sake – hold me. Tighter. That's it – yes – harder ...'

45

Something I hadn't seen before. He came with his pleaser spurting between her tiny hands, his noises ecstatic, angry, all at once. There were a few seconds of silence. My arm was smarting, indented with deep pink curves.

Mummy cried and cried. She always did.

'I'm sorry, Elizabeth.' He lay contrite beside her. 'I'm sorry, my lovely. Stop that now. Stop.' Then loudly, 'Stop that fucking noise can't you, you stupid cow?'

He moved from the bed and I knew he would leave the room. I whisked along to my end of the house taking in tiny shallow breaths.

When I closed my bedroom door behind me the birds grew silent. Lady fluttered up from the bottom of the cage to one of the wooden perches, shifting her claws back and forth along it, her eyes black and cold like pellets in her yellow face. King was clinging to the bars, his bill hooked round one of them, gnawing at it.

I leaned against the door, watching them. King suddenly made a flurried movement as if something had startled him and launched himself, feathers fanning violently, until he landed on the bottom. They had no practice in using their wings properly. There wasn't the space. I saw then how they'd never move from there. Never do or be anything else.

'You're stuck in there, aren't you?' I said softly, sliding across the carpet to them. 'Nothing you can do about it in there all day every day, is there?'

Their dark eyes fixed me with metallic stares. They didn't care what I was saying.

'It's not right, is it?' I unfastened the door of the little cage and reached inside. King panicked again, wings beating madly, their cool draught against my hand. He

46

flapped round and round, evading me. Lady sat quite still as if frozen.

Carefully I lifted her from her perch and drew her out, one hand cupped round her body, the other underneath, supporting her gnarled feet. Her little life pulsated against my palm. I squeezed her, my fingers pressing tighter and tighter until I was shaking and the effort made me dizzy. Lady struggled for a few seconds but I had her too hard and I kept holding her with all my strength until she was still. Her little head flopped to one side. I laid her in the bottom of the cage. Then I chased King. He didn't want to come but I was faster than him and I killed him too and left him lying beside Lady. Their beaks were touching. They looked as if they loved one another.

Dawson found them like that. I came in later and found her standing bent over the cage.

She turned her brown eyes on me. 'Oh, Miss Olivia, what on earth've you done?'

Mummy and Daddy said the birds had both caught a chill. They kept telling me so.

I was so happy when they sent me away to school.

* * *

Chapter 4

Granny Munro was standing quite naked in the drawing room.

'Kate!' My mother's voice from the wooden balcony was shrill with barely concealed rage. Strands of greying hair hung limp on each side of her thin cheeks as she looked down at the upturned faces in the garden, our eyes screwed up against the bright summer sun. 'Get in here quickly. She's doing it again!'

The vicar was due round any minute, I remembered. One of Mummy's parish meetings. I threw down my cricket bat and ran towards the house. Even Olivia perked up. She had been pouting on the bench in front of the hollyhocks because William had caught her out. She and the others weren't supposed to know about Granny, but of course they did.

'She must've taken all her clothes off again!' Olivia cried, almost clapping with delight.

The four of them left in the garden watched as I scurried into the house. They stood in silence, unable to resist trying to hear what was afoot: Olivia, William looking embarrassed and Angus and John from next door.

The house felt very dark and cool as I ran inside. Mummy emerged from the kitchen and seized my arm.

'Do something with her quickly,' she hissed, unrestrained now we were alone. I was startled, feeling her hand on my arm. We hardly ever touched each other. 'The wretched, selfish old woman. This is too much. Mr Hughes could be on the doorstep for all I know.'

Clenching her hands into fists to try and quell her frustration, she retreated back into the kitchen. She must have thanked heaven for the nets in the front windows, or anyone passing along Chantry Road might be treated to a glimpse of her mother-in-law. It wasn't just embarrassing that she was standing there starkers like that: it made it look as if Granny wasn't being cared for properly, and Mummy was supposed to know about taking care of people.

I tiptoed nervously along the tiled hall. The drawing-room door was not quite shut and I tried to peer through the crack between the hinges but my specs got in the way, so I pushed the door a little further open.

Granny was standing with her back to me. She had not a stitch on. Her hands were clamped to her waist, and she was taking in deep breaths through her nose and letting them out through her mouth like a steam train mustering force. Though I'd never in my life seen Mummy naked, the sight of Granny was something I was growing used to. Sometimes I helped her dress, and very often I sat perched on a cork-seated stool as steam curled round the bathroom, and kept her company while she bathed. In fact that was when we had our best talks.

I could talk to Granny Munro about anything. What was such a relief about her was the way she was so straight and open, just came out with it when she was thinking something. And I could tell her so much, like how I got fed up with Mummy lumping me in with the boys all the time and never buying me anything pretty like Olivia had and how I wished Angus was my brother instead of Wonderful William.

She'd tell me stories about her childhood and her life in North Berwick with Grandpa Robert and how she swam in the grey foamy sea every day up until she left. We said things to each other we knew mustn't be repeated.

'When you get to my age,' she'd say, soaping her vanilla blancmange of a belly, 'and you've had as many children as I have, you get past modesty and all that sort of nonsense.' Then, with a conspiratorial little smile, she'd add, 'I don't suppose your mother will though, do you?'

Despite this, it was odd seeing her there in the drawing room. I smiled, half in amusement, half pity. Sarah Munro had always been a big woman – I was left in no doubt from where I'd inherited my solid figure – and had not shrunk much in old age. The years had just made everything droop a bit. Her bottom was large and squashy and her back covered by sagging folds of flesh. But she stood good and straight, her soft, steely-grey hair still neatly pinned up. She was a strong woman for seventy-five.

I suppose I'll be like that one day, I thought, looking down at Granny's plump, mottled legs.

I clicked the brass door-handle to give her a chance, let her know she wasn't alone. Granny whipped round, glowering, her long, pink breasts swinging as she moved. I saw she still had her half-moon glasses on the chain round her neck. When she saw me her expression lost some of its defiance.

'Ah, it's you.' Her Edinburgh accent was broader than my father's, who had long moved south, the tone of her voice surprisingly soft. 'I suppose you've been sent to tame me?'

I, at fourteen, was the only one who could 'deal with' Granny Munro. Even her son, doctor or no doctor, could make little headway with her.

'Mummy's afraid Mr Hughes'll see you.'

Granny's broad, pink face broke into a grin. 'I'll bet she is. The sight of me would be enough to give that namby-pamby little preacher a turn.'

Anxiously, I peered back into the hall to see if Mummy was coming, but there was no sign of her.

'Granny, look, I'll help you get dressed, shall I? You'll only get into more trouble if you don't. Shall we go upstairs, and I'll bring you some tea up afterwards?'

'I suppose if I stay here I'll be shot at dawn. Or it'll be rat poison in the tea. That'll be the next thing.'

I gathered up the clothes that she had apparently not just discarded but hurled all round the room: garters and bloomers, the heavy dress and shift and her stiff whale-boned corset. Her stockings had landed on the standard lamp.

'I'll check the coast is clear and then we can get back upstairs.'

The doorbell rang as we were crossing the hall. My mother dashed out from the kitchen and made frantic flapping motions at us, her body taut and furious.

'Oooh,' Granny said, stopping in full view of the front door and clasping her hand to her chest, 'I think I can feel a funny turn coming on.'

'Just get up there,' Mummy snarled at her, gesturing at Simmons our maid, whose eyes were goggling, to wait before opening the door.

Granny suddenly dropped the pretence and shot with impressive speed up to the first floor.

'Why d'you *do* it?' I panted when we were up in her

room overlooking the garden and I was rolling her stockings up her legs.

'Got to get someone to take notice of me somehow, haven't I?' she said petulantly, perched on the pale blue candlewick bedspread. 'Locked away up here.'

I clicked my tongue. 'You know you can come down any time you like.'

'Yes, but with her around ... Heavens, no wonder your father's wrapped himself up so tight in his work.'

I'd heard these complaints so many times now that I didn't rise to them. 'I'll go and fetch you some tea now, shall I?'

I settled her in the easy chair in what was in fact a light, comfortable room with many of her possessions round her. I carried up tea and slabs of shortbread and stayed while Granny enjoyed them, sitting with the window open over the garden. It had gone quiet outside. I sat on an upright wooden chair, my tanned legs spreading over the seat.

'I gather you managed to behave yourself while I was away?'

'You deserted me.' She looked at me out of the corner of her eye with mock reproach.

'It was only ten days.'

'And it was lovely,' Granny stated.

'It was ...' I hesitated. Since the holiday I had tried to push the disturbing elements of it to the back of my mind. 'Yes, it was lovely.'

Granny ruminated on her oblong of shortbread.

'I'd like to marry someone like Alec Kemp,' I said, dreamily.

Granny snorted. 'Nonsense. He's a Tory.'

I giggled. 'And he's married already.'

'And he's old enough ...'

52

'. . . to be my father!' I finished for her, laughing.

Granny sat re-stirring her tea. She dropped the spoon noisily into the saucer and said, 'No. The one you ought to marry is Angus.'

'Angus?'

'Yes, Angus. If ever I saw a nice boy it's Angus.'

'But he's only fifteen.' Set beside the glamour of Alec Kemp, Angus seemed a mere child.

'And you're only fourteen.'

'But Angus is just a friend. I mean he's just, well – Angus. And he's so quiet and serious all the time.'

Granny shrugged. 'You don't want to get married. Get a job instead. Far better paid. If I hadn't got myself married and tied down out in the sticks I'd have had a much better time. Out there, marching with them all.' She held her arm out as if to indicate a column of militant women parading through the garden. It was a cause of continuing regret to her that she hadn't been able to take an active part in the Women's Suffrage movement. She switched into her rhetorical tone. 'Marriage is pure slavery anyway. Look at your mother. Frustration, that's her problem. Don't think I don't sympathize, because I do. Much too full of ideas to be married, that one.'

Suddenly she flagged, and sank back in the chair. 'Where's my book? You get out with your friends. I'll be good, I promise.'

The others had moved down to kneel round the pond at the far end of the garden. They had a net and a bucket and were looking for tiddlers. Butterflies were slowly folding and unfolding their wings on the buddleia.

As I walked across the lawn, I saw Angus coming back in from next door carrying another net. There was a gate between our garden and the Harveys' which enabled us to pass freely between them.

Angus was a tall, slim boy with a pale complexion and dark brown hair cut very short at the back but longer at the front so that it tumbled over his forehead. He had serious eyes and a more uncertain manner than William's, whose body had a kind of physical arrogance about it. Like me, William had inherited a solid figure, but in him it was expressed in muscle: a brawny torso, thick, rugby-playing legs and a broad, freckled face topped by wavy fair hair. Angus was much lighter and more delicate looking, and dressed as ever in the careless Harvey way, in long baggy shorts and a buff-coloured shirt that looked a size or two too big.

William and I tolerated each other just about, but I always liked Angus better. William was self-confident, an achiever both in class and sports. Angus appeared less certain of himself and William often put him down.

'Oh, come on,' William would shout, exasperated, during a cricket game. 'If you're going to bowl at least put a bit of elbow into it. Even Katie could do better than that!'

And Angus would try harder, very seldom rising to William's needling. It took me a long time to realize how much he minded it.

'Is she all right?' Angus asked. He sounded concerned, and I was grateful to him for being so and for not poking fun.

'She's had a cup of tea. I waited with her for a while.'

Angus nodded. 'Poor thing. She's missing Scotland I expect. My mother says she's welcome to call round at our place any time, you know.' He gave me his sudden smile which made his grey eyes crinkle at the corners.

'We thought we'd go into the park. We were waiting for you.'

The gardens on our side of the road all shared their boundaries with a private park which had a lake in the middle.

As we neared the pond, Olivia looked up from where she was kneeling beside William on the rough slabs round the water.

'About time!' she called, jumping up. 'Let's go! There's nothing to catch in here. Come on, William.'

To the equal astonishment of me and William, who was nearly sixteen and felt himself to be above our company nowadays, Olivia thrust her arms through each of ours and pulled us with her to the gate at the bottom of the garden. William strode along, apparently unable to resist but looking most uncomfortable.

We walked down the leafy path and round the still water of the lake to a shady spot from where you could look back up to the line of Chantry Road's huge, ornate houses, their windows catching the light of the afternoon sun. Leaves rippled white, green, yellow. Moorhens and mallards slid over the surface of the lake. The boys started off with the nets. Olivia and I lay on our stomachs on the cool ground waiting for a turn and looking down into the dark water.

'I look like the full moon,' I sighed. My round face shuddered in the water's surface. 'Except the moon doesn't wear specs.' With her big dark eyes and long wavy hair Olivia looked like a wispy Ophelia in the water. 'I wish I was pretty like you, Livy.'

Olivia smiled. She could be a minx when attacked but when I made a comment like that it brought out her better nature. 'You've got a lovely face. All sort of big and generous.' She called out to the boys, 'Come on – let us have a turn now, won't you?'

I took one of the long-handled nets and dipped it into the water. It came up containing nothing more than a coating of green slime.

'Try again.' I found Angus at my shoulder. He watched seriously as I dipped in the net and on the fourth attempt brought it up with something tiny flapping in the bottom amid the leaves and weed. Carefully we turned the net out into the enamel bucket. I saw the deft, precise movements of Angus's slim fingers. Heads together, we watched the tiny, almost transparent creature struggle into the water.

'We shall let it go, shan't we?' I asked.

'Oh yes – it'd be cruel not to.'

For a second I became aware of Olivia watching us, her brown eyes puzzled. Suddenly she twirled round, floral skirt dancing about her legs, and skipped over to William.

'William, will you help me? I can't seem to catch anything either.'

William picked up his bucket looking surprised, walked over to Olivia and squatted down, his thick legs bent up on each side of the pail. Olivia inclined towards him as if she had a secret to tell him, and William, startled, jumped back and overbalanced, sitting down suddenly.

Olivia let out peals of giggles. 'What are you doing?' she cried. 'Here – let me pull you up.'

'I can get up myself,' William said crossly, with a flushed face.

She kept on at him all that afternoon: 'William, will you help me? William, walk with me. Will you carry my bucket?' I couldn't understand this sudden attention paid to him, nor his passive response to her clamouring. If I'd carried on like that I was quite sure he'd have told me to leave off. Finally he did say gently to her, 'Can you leave me alone for a bit now, Livy, eh?'

Pouting slightly, Olivia stepped over to me.

'William's being rather mean.' She turned her head to look at him over one shoulder, coquettishly, strands of her chestnut hair half covering her face.

'Just leave him alone for a while,' I replied, carefully moving my net through the water. 'Anyone'd think you've got ants in your pants this afternoon.'

I was so absorbed in helping Angus to release some more tiny fish into the bucket that it was some time before I noticed Olivia was crying.

'Hey, what on earth's the matter?' I flung an arm round her slim shoulders, but she wriggled uneasily.

'Come over here,' Olivia said. She seemed all twitchy and strange. We left the boys and walked back up slowly under the trees towards the garden.

'I feel so peculiar,' Olivia sniffed. 'It's – Katie, I got my – you know – today.'

I turned to her, baffled.

'My – when you become a woman.' Olivia seemed to have to wring the words out of herself.

'Oh,' I said. 'Gosh. I see. Your periods.' Thanks to Granny Munro I knew all about those. 'Bad luck. Is it making you feel rotten then?'

'No. My tummy hurts a bit. It's sort of gripy, down here.' She laid a hand on the lower part of her stomach. 'But it's not that. I feel awfully queer. I've never felt like this before. As if I want something very badly but I don't know what it is.'

'Oh,' I said again. I hadn't the remotest idea what Livy was talking about.

'And when I told Mummy about it, she got all cross and then started crying. It's made me feel awful.'

I was astonished. Hoping to cheer Livy up, I said, 'Never mind. Let's go in and have some tea before you have to go. Mrs Drysdale's made shortbread and there's chocolate cake.'

Olivia burst into tears all over again.

'What's up now?' I cried.

'I don't know.' She was wiping her face with her hanky. 'It's just how I feel.'

When we got inside, Mummy seemed to have calmed down. Her meeting was over.

'Well, you look like a wet weekend,' she said briskly to Olivia in her best nursing sister tone. 'Where are the boys?'

'Coming,' I said.

We sat in the kitchen and Mrs Drysdale poured tea for us all from the big brown pot with its green and orange knitted cosy. I loved the kitchen. It was warm and steamy in winter with the range going full blast and cool in summer with its dull red quarry tiles and shady atmosphere.

We all sat round the table, Mummy with her thin body quite upright, as if she had a steel bar up the back of her blouse. She had fastened her hair up again at the back and it waved neatly round her face. She was wearing a moss-green cardigan which had a tie of braid at the neck.

'You've got so much on, Mummy,' I exclaimed, looking at her. 'It's such a boiling day!'

'It may be outside,' she replied as she sliced up the moist cake, a smooth ridge of butter icing between the two layers, 'but I've been in sorting out this parish work.'

'Oh yes,' I said. 'Sorry. I forgot.' I always seemed to say the wrong thing.

'Your father's going to be late.' I wondered why she was even commenting on the fact since Daddy was late almost every day. 'Sometimes I don't know why he doesn't take a truckle-bed and go and sleep in the surgery.' She checked herself, remembering that Mrs Drysdale was still working over by the sink. Mummy pointed at the ceiling. 'I take it she's quietened down?'

'She's all right,' I assured her, glad I'd managed to do something right. 'And she's promised faithfully to be as good as gold from now on.'

'Well,' Mummy said drily. 'I'll believe that when I see it.'

Chapter 5

'Can I come with you, Daddy? Please?'

He hesitated over his boiled egg, not meeting my eye. William was scraping his toast with irritating loudness so that charred black crumbs dusted his plate.

'I don't think so,' Mummy intervened abruptly. 'You haven't been down there for years. You're too old.'

'What your mother means,' Daddy said, his manner less harsh than Mummy's, 'is that you might find some aspects of it rather unappealing at your age. You were just a little girl when you used to come before.'

Occasionally as a small child I'd gone down to the surgery with Daddy and sat in the corner of the drab waiting-room with my colouring pad and crayons, amid all the coughing and sighing and complaining about things I couldn't understand. I was curious, hungry to see my father's other life. It was the very fact I might now be able to make more sense of it all that attracted me. And Granny had supported me. I think she hoped it might bring Daddy and me closer.

'And the patients wouldn't like it either,' Mummy said, sniffing. She had a heavy summer cold and would have been feeling very sorry for herself had she ever permitted indulgence in such emotions.

'I think you should go,' William said, taking an enormous mouthful of toast and speaking through it.

'The sight of you would shock them all into feeling better. Either that or finish them off altogether.'

'William!' Mummy said.

I scowled, and Daddy pretended the conversation wasn't happening, a tendency of his which I found hugely aggravating.

'This is not just a game,' I said. 'I really do want to come.' In my enthusiasm I knocked over my egg cup and Mummy tutted.

My father wiped his mouth with his napkin. 'No one'll object,' he reassured Mummy. 'Katie seems interested in looking after people. You do wonders with your granny after all, don't you?'

My mother buttered her toast in silence.

'You don't mind, do you Mummy?'

She looked up, tight-lipped. 'Why should I mind? I'm just thinking of your health – all those germs. But your father's the doctor. I was only a nurse, after all, so what do I know?'

Having to abandon her job as a children's nurse on marrying Daddy was a sacrifice about which she had never ceased to feel bitter.

Daddy pushed back his chair, ignoring this remark as he tended to blank out all such expressions of emotion. 'I'll be leaving in ten minutes.'

I sat in the passenger seat next to Daddy, nervous at being alone with him. We turned into the Alcester Road, the Austin shuddering on cobbles and tramlines, swooping downhill from the fresher air of Moseley towards the lower-lying, smoky atmosphere of Balsall Heath, two miles from the middle of Birmingham. Daddy's surgery was on the inner edge of this area, in St Joseph's parish, with its hotch-potch of dilapidated back-to-back houses, and workshops and factories all squeezed in together, its life altogether louder and more public than in our suburban street. What would it be like to live here? I wondered. I was seeing everything with new eyes today, alert suddenly to these differences. Both my father and Alec Kemp moved daily between these two contrasting areas, both able to afford houses in prosperous, tree-lined Moseley. The surgery was in the Birch Street area, only streets away from Kemp's Foundry Supplies.

I eyed Daddy's profile, his neatly trimmed dark hair, the little moustache and tired blue eyes, every line of him dutiful and serious.

He cleared his throat. 'I gather you managed to settle your grandmother down yesterday,' he said in the objective voice he always used when speaking of her, sounding as if he was discussing one of his patients.

'She took all her clothes off in the drawing room again.' I saw him flush slightly and wondered if I'd said the wrong thing. I couldn't always work out what I was supposed to say to my parents. One minute they were talking about patients and illnesses and bits of bodies, some of which I knew you didn't refer to, even in Latin, in polite company. Then at other times if you mentioned something, especially if it was to do with the family, they'd go all stiff and embarrassed. It was very confusing.

'Why did Granny come and live with us? She could have managed on her own, couldn't she?'

'It seemed the most practical thing, after your grandpa Robert died. North Berwick's a long way off and it made sense for her to be near her family.'

'But we're not her only family.'

'We were the ones who were able to have her. The

others have commitments which made it impractical for them.'

'But I don't think she's very happy. And she and Mummy can't stand one another.'

Daddy was silent for a moment. I looked out as we passed the ornate red-brick bathhouse on the Moseley Road.

'It always takes families time to adjust to new arrangements – particularly people who are above a certain age. Three months is not a very long time in that situation.'

What situation? I wondered. We were talking about Granny, not some situation. I sat in silence. Whatever the reasons she was here I thanked God she had arrived, like a bracing gust of wind from north of the border.

We turned into a side street and parked outside the surgery. I squinted myopically at the brass plaques. *Dr. W. Munro*, and underneath, *Dr. J. Williamson.* I hoped I shouldn't see sour, bad-tempered Dr Williamson.

'It needs a polish,' I said.

'Well, there's a little job for you then.'

A line of people were already waiting outside by the step. Daddy raised his hat and greeted them. One of the women, tight-faced, held a silent baby. An elderly man was coughing, bent over by it, his lungs sounding drenched.

The waiting-room was dark, the walls painted brown. There were wooden benches against three of the walls and in one corner stood a small table and two chairs. In the fourth wall a door, through which Daddy disappeared, led out to the two consulting rooms at the back, and there was a little trapdoor for the dispenser.

I was just settling myself down at the table when my father reappeared, hurrying across the waiting-room.

'Dr Williamson is going to handle the start of surgery. I have some urgent calls to make. Won't be too long.'

'Oh, let me come. *Please* let me!' It seemed very important that day that I see everything.

He had no time to spare for discussion. 'Come on then, quickly.' He was already going out of the door. 'None of them is too far. It'll be easier to walk.'

It was a humid day, warm and cloudy, threatening storms. We hurried along the crowded pavement of Birch Street past rows of shops, their blinds slanting out over the pavement. Everything seemed colourful, absorbing. Each shop gave off its own special smell: the warm, fleshy smell of sides of meat padded with yellowed fat, fresh bread and burnt currants, the tangy sweetness of strawberries and the bitter smells of metal and rubber from the hardware shop. Mixed with this was the ripe whiff of horse manure from the road.

I followed Daddy into another side street, hurrying to keep up with him, he striding and I trotting.

'Here we are.' He knocked on the door of a house. 'You'd best stay outside, I think. Old Mr Fenton has his bed downstairs now.'

The house was run-down and filthy, the windows so thick with grime that they must have let in very little light. There were signs that the paint on the bleached window frames must once have been blue.

A woman with a large, sagging face and a wart sprouting whiskers on her left cheekbone appeared at the door. The rest of her hair was wrapped in a washed-out brown scarf. As the door swung open a waft of stale air hit us, stinking of sweat and urine. I shrank back.

'Oh, it's you, doctor,' the woman said lifelessly. 'He's bad today.' She talked of a turn in the night, said she was sorry for having to bring the doctor out. My father gently dismissed the apology.

The woman left the door ajar and I peered in. I could see a bed with a heavy wood headboard, covered by old grey blankets. Propped against the pillows was a yellow face, so shrunken that it seemed not to be living at all but a mask, something out of an old tomb. The head was bent back slightly so that the nose pointed at the ceiling. The old man was struggling for breath, his lungs making a terrible rattling sound.

I had expected to feel afraid or repulsed, but I found I was looking at him with a detached kind of pity. He was dying, clearly. He appeared to be at a distance from us already, as if death had moved in and taken possession before life was extinguished.

I watched my father bend over the bed and take the old man's hand tenderly from under the bedclothes to feel his pulse. He spoke a few soft words. 'Easy now,' I heard him say. His daughter stood at the end of the bed with her arms folded across her large breasts.

Daddy turned to her. 'There's nothing more I can do, I'm afraid. You're doing the best that can be done.' The woman sighed and nodded stolidly and kept thanking Daddy before we left.

As we approached the next house, two children who had been waiting on the front step came running at the sight of the doctor, cheeping like young birds: 'It's the babby – he's took real bad!'

They were both girls, both dressed in very worn gingham frocks, too big for the elder girl and too skimpy for the younger.

'Our mom's worried it's the diphtheria or she'd have brought him to you.'

I stepped into the house with Daddy. The room was spotlessly clean, though with very little in the way of furniture. There was the black iron range, a table and two wooden chairs.

The young mother was pacing the cold bricks with bare feet, the baby in her arms. His eyes were half open and he was breathing in quick, panting breaths.

Daddy gently opened the child's mouth. In a voice that was low but urgent he said, 'Kate – outside. Now.'

I watched from the doorway with the other girls, whose eyes moved enviously over my dress.

'You were right Mrs Smith,' Daddy told her. 'It is diphtheria. Little Tom is very ill. We'll need to get him to the fever hospital.'

He spoke further of the child needing a hole in his windpipe to help him breathe, and of arranging transport, a blue-windowed diphtheria van. When we left I had even more trouble keeping up with him. He strode down the street, lips pressed tightly together. I wondered once more whether I'd done something wrong.

In the end I asked timidly, 'That baby was very ill, wasn't it?'

'We ought to be able to do something.' The words burst out of him. 'We ought to be able to prevent children from getting terrible diseases like that. It's a scourge – it's dreadful. I can't bear to see it.'

I'd never seen this grief in him before. I felt like crying myself, and could only trot along silently beside him.

He looked down at my miserable face and suddenly smiled. 'Hey now. Don't you go worrying, Katie. It's not your fault.' He laid his hand on my shoulder for a moment. 'Come on. We've one more call to make.'

I waited downstairs in a filthy room in one of the back-houses, facing out over a yard strung across with washing. The room was very dark and stuffy and on the table were the remains of what looked like several days' worth of meals. The old oilcloth was soaked with spilled tea and the remains of some kind of stew. There were plates covered with congealed gravy, several jam jars with a crust of dried tea-leaves at the bottom and an old heel of bread. The floor was strewn with food remains and dirty clothes from which rose a rank, sweaty smell. And there was another terrible odour about the house which I couldn't identify but which turned my stomach.

Across the table from me a scrawny girl who I thought was about thirteen sat picking her nose and sniffing, her brown hair in two rat's-taily plaits. Round her feet a baby crawled on the floor, its nappy hanging heavily round its bottom and stinking of faeces. The child's face and limbs were streaked with filth. I found myself bearing in mind one of Mummy's nursing sayings: 'Always breathe through your mouth.'

'What's the matter with your mother?' I asked her.

'She's took bad after the babby,' the girl said matter-of-factly. 'Can't get out of bed no more.'

'This baby?' I pointed at the infant who was now sitting down, having found an old scrap of bread to chew off the floor. Shiny worms of snot trailed from his nose.

'No, the littl'un – she 'ad 'im last week.'

As we spoke I became aware that the sound I could hear of a small baby crying was coming from upstairs.

'Have you got any other brothers and sisters?' I asked. I supposed the girl must think me awfully nosy, but she didn't seem put out by my asking.

'Ar – there'm six of us. Three older 'uns, me, and then me dad buggered off, an' then Bob moved in an' she 'ad the two babbies.'

'Oh,' I said, barely able to imagine such a household. 'So is Bob out at work?'

'Nah. 'E's buggered off an' all.'

We heard Daddy's tread on the bare boards of the stairs.

'Now Lisa,' he said carefully to the girl. She had a certain spark to her and was evidently taking everything in. 'You know your mother is very poorly?'

Lisa nodded.

'She's got childbed fever and I'm afraid she's so sick that we're going to have to take her into the infirmary. She says you've been helping her a great deal, but she's fretting about you missing work and about little Sid here.' He glanced at the youngster by his feet who was staring up at him with enormous blue eyes. 'She said your neighbour Babs Keenan would look after you both but she's not well at present. So what I'd like you to do now is to clean Sid here up a bit. A new napkin at least, eh? This afternoon I'll come back and take him on a little journey in my car. You'll have him ready, won't you, Lisa?' Looking at me he said, 'He's coming home with us for a few days. Just until Mrs Keenan's herself again.'

At the surgery I heard him explaining to Dr Williamson. 'Puerperal fever, poor woman. In a shocking state – she should have been in days ago by the stench of her. The child didn't look too hopeful either.'

When we drove home in the car with baby Sid Blakeley, he wasn't looking in a much better condition than he had been that morning. Lisa had evidently tried to give his face a wipe over because the dirt was smudged and differently distributed. She had changed his nappy but this one was now nearly as full as the last, and the ammonia smell of it filled the car. I held the child beside me on the back seat.

'Hello, little fellow.' I smiled at him. The boy turned his pasty, snub-nosed face towards me with interest. He had not seemed disturbed by being taken away from home. I pushed my little finger into his palm and he gripped it tight. I giggled at him, leaned my face close, and he reached up and tried to snatch at my specs.

'Oh no you don't!' I laughed, pulling my head back. 'I like him, Daddy!' There were no young relatives in our family so babies were a new experience. I liked Sid's little fat wrists and soft, dirty feet. 'How old is he?'

'About a year.'

'His sister – she's younger than me, isn't she?'

'Oh no – couple of years older. She's been out at work for a time now.'

As we drove back up into Moseley I asked, 'Daddy, why did you become a doctor?'

'I suppose for the reason anyone does. Because I wanted to help people who were sick to get better.'

'Do you like people?'

I couldn't see his face but heard the rare smile in his voice. 'I suppose I do.'

'Does Mummy like people?'

'I would think she does, yes.'

'She doesn't always seem to.'

'Now, now.' He stopped the car outside our house.

The questions I hadn't asked him were, how long is the baby staying for and, above all, won't Mummy be *furious* with you?

I carried the smelly child into the house and went

nervously upstairs to find her. This was the greatest moment of surprise of the whole day.

She took one look at the little boy and launched herself straight back into her element. 'Right. The first thing that child needs is a jolly good bath. Go and get it running, Kate. I don't have the baby bath any more, but at least he can sit up by himself. Not too hot – dip your elbow in. And a new bar of Sunlight. Here, give him to me.'

She took Sid to her with no sign of hesitation, filthy as he was. 'Hello, young man.' She looked intently into his eyes as I watched in astonishment, seeing a new softness in her thin face I had barely remembered her capable of. 'What you need,' she went on, 'is a wash and a good big bowl of something to eat. Do you like porridge, eh?' Seeing me in front of her still, she said impatiently, 'Go on. Stop dithering. This child needs looking after. And when you've run the bath, go down and ask Mrs Drysdale to put some porridge on for him.'

Sid appeared later with a face of a quite different and more wholesome shade, and bolted down a dishful of sweet porridge. My mother settled him down to sleep in William's and my old cot. To my surprise she had pulled out from various recesses in the house almost all the paraphernalia needed for looking after a baby: cot, sheets, blankets, bottles, terry nappies and toys.

'Why on earth did you keep it all?' I asked.

'Well, as you can see,' Mummy said stiffly, 'you never know when it might come in handy.' Of course she couldn't express the fact that she simply couldn't bear to part with these things.

I went to Granny's room to tell her the news. 'I've had a simply marvellous day!' I was glowing with it all. I plonked myself on a chair beside her. Her cheek was pushed out by a sweet she was eating.

I told her about the surgery and the visits to the houses.

'It was all so interesting, seeing all those people. And Daddy was so different from how he is at home.' Granny was listening attentively. 'D'you think I could do something like that when I grow up?'

'With a family like yours,' she said serenely, holding out a little white paper bag, 'I should think it would be almost a foregone conclusion. Bullseye?'

Sid Blakeley stayed in our house for only four days before Babs Keenan called at the surgery to say she was ready to take him home. But for a short time he turned our house upside down. Though he couldn't speak, he was able to express himself, his needs and his joy with a directness of which no one else in the house was any longer capable. His small body and nose-wrinkling grin softened the lines of my mother's face and pulled unusual smiles from my father. I even found William now and then chasing him about the room, both of them on their hands and knees. As for me, I was besotted. And I took secret pleasure in reciting to myself the new words I'd learned out on the rounds that day: diphtheria, puerperal, buggered.

Chapter 6

A humid night in August. There was no breeze to stir the curtains at my open window, and I was lying restless, under a sheet. The sound of the front doorbell startled me out of my half sleep. It sounded twice, long and hard. For a few seconds I lay listening, trying to guess the time. It was already dark and felt like the middle of the night. A door opened downstairs. Daddy and Mummy must still be up.

Out on the landing I saw my mother moving quickly down the stairs, still dressed but with her hair pinned up for bed. The old wooden cased clock on the shelves by the stairs said ten past eleven. I peeped round the banisters into the hall.

They opened the door to Elizabeth Kemp, her face very white, eyes like huge dark wounds against her skin. She had on a cotton dress with a white shawl half covering it. Her pale hair was loose at her shoulders like a young girl's and in her agitation she had evidently not thought to put on a hat. I watched, absolutely still.

'I'm sorry. You've got to help me.' Her voice was low and hoarse. 'I shouldn't have come here. I know you're not my doctor, but I don't know where else to turn.'

She started to cry, weak, tired-sounding sobs. My

mother steered her into the study and Daddy went in behind, shutting the door.

'What's going on?' William was standing sleepily at my shoulder with only his pyjama trousers on. 'Did I hear some sort of rumpus down there?'

'It's Elizabeth Kemp – crying her eyes out,' I whispered.

'Why?'

'Don't know. Can't hear now anyway. Ssh – let's go down and listen.'

'Kate, we shouldn't . . .' That was William for you. Rather stodgy.

But he followed me part of the way down the stairs. I stood at the bottom, listening so intently that even my own breathing felt like an interruption.

For a time the three adults in the study talked in low voices. There were questions, answers, short exchanges, but I could only hear the tone of their voices and not the words. But suddenly there came an anguished outburst from Elizabeth that sent William and me haring back to the top of the staircase.

'I can't. I can't do it. I just couldn't bear it!' And the sobbing began again.

'Whatever's the matter with the woman?' William asked. 'I've never heard anything like it.'

For a second I felt annoyed at his superior tone, his implying that Elizabeth was making an unnecessary fuss about something. Of course our own mother behaving in this way was quite unimaginable, but I felt churned up inside by the sounds of such terrible unhappiness downstairs, even though I had no idea what the matter was.

After more quiet talking the door opened. We squatted down, one at each side of the top step, hidden by the carved wood of the banister. I was astonished to see that Mummy had her arm round Elizabeth's shoulders.

In an exhausted but formal voice Elizabeth Kemp said, 'Thank you for your advice. I'm sorry to have put you in such a difficult position.' She glanced distractedly at a half sheet of paper she was holding. 'I'll do something as soon as I can. Next week.'

With a strange gentleness my parents closed the door behind her and Mummy turned and leaned wearily against it. She looked unusually vulnerable, standing there like that in those hairpins, her emotion all clenched up inside.

In a high voice she said, 'Heavens above.'

My father shook his head sadly. 'Sometimes I wonder if the middle classes don't have it worse. All this business of keeping up appearances.'

'Thank goodness we've not had that to contend with.' Mummy sounded close to tears. Daddy went over to her and took her in his arms and she leaned against him, both of them standing in silence.

Unused to witnessing such intimacy, William and I avoided looking at each other. As our parents moved apart, the two of us shot into our bedrooms.

* * *

OLIVIA

Before she had me, Mummy gave birth to her first baby at home. I know because she told me, early on sometime. Though she very seldom spoke to me of her feelings, there was no one else she could confide in, only her little girl. Who was too young. She couldn't seem to let

74

things out gently. Her words were like shards of glass coughed up from her throat. She was in labour for five days, and the baby, who would have been my elder brother, was born blue and without breath. They had to stitch her up inside, tight like a hessian sack.

So when she was expecting me she chose to go to hospital. She waited for me, settled on stiff white sheets. Although I was small I wouldn't come out. She lay on her labour bed for four days with her feet up in leather stirrups while the doctors tried to decide what to do. The pains were mild at first. Then her body pressed down tighter and tighter and she was in agony back and front but they wouldn't let her move. She cried out, 'My baby's dead.' One of the nurses slapped her and said, 'Pull yourself together.' They wouldn't let her eat.

On the third day when they unstrapped her legs she tried to jump out of a window. The next day they cut me out by Caesarean section and by a miracle I was still alive. They told her one of my hands was tightly gripping the umbilical cord. They instructed her not to have 'relations' with Daddy for four months after. She swore never to let him touch her again. She didn't quite manage that.

Usually she is sitting in the drawing room. She hasn't been well these last weeks. She seems exhausted and her face is white.

'What bad luck to be off colour while the weather's so good,' Daddy jokes. 'Poor old girl. At least you've got Olivia home to keep you company.'

Dawson eyes her knowingly. Later I realize you can never fool Dawson.

I come skipping down Chantry Road from my piano lesson at Mrs Weiss's cosy house, wearing my little leather sandals and a silk frock. I've had a lovely afternoon and I want to tell Mummy about it. I run inside, leaving Dawson to pull the door closed by its cold iron knob.

'Mummy? Mummy?'

My feet thud up the stairs and Dawson looks up at me from the hall with her dark, handsome eyes. 'You should leave her to sleep, Olivia,' she calls, but there's a smile in her voice. Along the dark corridor, shadowy after the brilliant day outside and the more so because their bedroom door is closed. My feet slip on the red carpet.

'Mummy?' I knock. There is silence. Softly I turn the handle and push the door open. I stand in the doorway unable to move.

The bed has turned red. Even her hair is soaked almost to the roots as she lies askew across the covers, her eyes closed. Her face is chalk white, the cheeks drawn in tight. She still has a satin slipper on one foot.

I cross the room. By her feet is the deep blue and white chamber pot, full to overflowing with blood. Next to it on the floor something long and sharp, streaked red.

I find my voice. 'Dawson!' I scream. 'Dawson!'

It was only when my mother went secretly to a doctor that she realized how much an abortion would cost. She had no money – none of her own. Without asking my father for the price she could not even contemplate it. Rich as we were, her choice was as limited as so many others in her position and she resorted to the same thing: a sixpenny knitting needle.

If I had not been at home she would have died.

*   *   *

Within a fortnight of her visit to our house, Elizabeth Kemp suddenly became gravely ill. I could get almost nothing out of Olivia.

'She's in a private nursing home,' was all she'd tell me. She sat, pale and tight-lipped in one of the cream chairs in the Kemps' beautiful drawing room.

'Can I come and see her?'

'No, I told you. She's very ill. She can't have visitors.'

'Well, when will she be better?'

'I don't know.' Olivia put her hands over her face and burst into tears. 'I wish I knew. I just want her back home.'

'Your father must be able to see her, surely?'

Olivia looked guarded suddenly, as if afraid. 'Yes. Sometimes.'

When Alec Kemp came home later that afternoon his face was grey and exhausted.

If Granny Munro had any idea of what was happening in the Kemp household she chose to keep silent. She was blunt, but not brutal. And she was in the same position in the house as a child: an eavesdropper, not a person responsible enough to be automatically party to information, though she was shrewd enough to guess most of it.

By the autumn of 1936 she had settled in much better. She was keeping her clothes on and she and my mother had reached an uneasy truce.

One Saturday William and I were talking to her while she tidied her room – or at least I was in there and William had to come barging in as well.

'Goodness, Granny,' William said. 'What a mess.'

'I think it looks rather nice,' I said loyally, staring round at the tottering staircases of drawers she had removed from the chest, the rush-seated chairs tilted over on the bed amid the letters and diaries, the full skirts of dresses in sea blue and grey and her tweeds, the tangles of pearls and heavy amber and jade beads, all of which she was evidently trying to sort into piles. William blushed at the sight of some of her more personal items of underwear: huge brassières and corsets and bloomers strewn across the bed.

'Ah, spotted my dreadnoughts have you?' she laughed. 'Poor William. I tell you what, you go down and fetch us up a nice cup of tea and Katie and I will have them stowed away by the time you get back.'

With relief, William squeezed out of the door.

'The poor lad, I shouldn't tease him so,' Granny said, winking at me over her glasses. 'But he is a bit of a stiff fellow, isn't he? Very like his father, I'm afraid, and his before him.' She sighed, folding an enormous pair of pink bloomers. 'You don't really remember your grandpa Robert, do you? He was a good man. Truly good. You can't argue with that sort of goodness – it wouldn't be fair.' Her face wore a wistful expression. 'But oh, I did long to let up occasionally and do something really wild and *bad*. I'd have to go for a good stump along the beach or a bracing swim to get it out of my system and then I'd feel better. Until the next time, anyway.' She smoothed down the bloomers and picked up another pair. 'You know, Katie, you can spend all your life keeping your feelings packed tightly away. I'm not sure it's always the best thing. Trouble is, after years of doing it you don't have much practice at showing how you do feel.' She peered at me with her watery eyes, looking suddenly sad and vulnerable. 'I know I rather overdid it when I first came here.'

I went and flung my arms round her. She smelt of camphor and rose water. 'Granny – it's been absolutely lovely since you came. You're the best thing that's ever happened!'

And she laughed tearfully and hugged me back.

In the evening when Daddy went to look in on her there was clearly something wrong. She was lying at an angle across the bed in silent distress. She had spent most of the day seeing to her room and it was immaculate.

'Win,' Daddy shouted. 'It's Mother.'

I came running immediately. 'What? Granny, what's wrong?'

I knelt down and took her hand. It felt cool and clammy, like the feet of those birds Olivia used to have. She was trying to speak, but nothing came out that made sense. 'Granny, Granny!' I sobbed, leaning my head against her fulsome body, feeling the stiff corset under my ear through the silky stuff of her dress. 'Don't be poorly, Granny, please.'

All I had from her in reply was a low, frightened whimper.

It was agreed that we'd care for her at home. We could see in her eyes that she'd prefer it. Her stroke had in fact been a mild one, and within days her speech began to unfurl into something we could recognize. The left side of her body slowly began to tingle back into life.

'I'm not done yet,' she said defiantly, one corner of her mouth lurching up unasked. 'I'll be out in the breakers.' But just then she couldn't even get out to the bathroom.

My mother rose to the occasion and nursed her with a kind of objective professionalism. She was brisk and detached and left me to provide the other components of nursing: company and affection. As soon as I came home from school I spent every moment I could sitting in the easy chair next to Granny's bed.

'You've got to get better – please, please,' I kept saying to her. 'Please try, Granny.'

With huge effort she'd manage the words, 'You're not nagging me – are you?'

Granny's illness pushed everything else to the back of my mind. Olivia was away at school and normally I missed her every single day. We wrote long letters full of details of our days and jokes and anecdotes about school. I wrote to her still, but the letters were shorter and full of my worries about Granny. I had almost forgotten that unseen, at home, Elizabeth Kemp was dragging herself very slowly, painfully back to health. But that was something shut away from my understanding then. Olivia never even hinted to me what had happened. She tried to preserve her parents, present them to me perfect as seahorses on a bed of wax. I had no idea just how much she needed me.

Angus often came to see Granny after she fell ill. They had an affinity with each other. She liked him to read to her and I'd often go into her room and find Angus's dark head bent over Wilkie Collins or Edgar Allan Poe. ('Anything with a really good story,' Granny would say.)

One wet winter afternoon I sat listening as Angus finished off a chapter from *The Woman in White*. After a few minutes Granny coughed gently and interrupted him. 'It's all right. You stop now Katie's here. You're a good reader, Angus Harvey, I'll say that.'

'I suppose you'd like tea?' I asked.

'Of course. What other pleasures do I have left in life

now apart from my food? Well, and your company of course.'

Simmons had a kettle on the hob downstairs. I carried a tray up and we settled down by the fire. She left the light off so the room was lit only by the flames. Rain flung itself at the window. Granny sipped her tea carefully from one side of her mouth, some of it spilling into the saucer which she held underneath. She tutted with frustration until she saw Angus and me watching her anxiously. She smiled lopsidedly at us. Tiny flames danced in the lenses of her specs.

'Don't you worry about me.' I heard a mischievous twinkle in her voice. 'I must say it's lovely seeing the two of you together. You make a lovely pair. Or am I embarrassing you?'

It was too dark for me to see if Angus blushed as I did. He was still smiling affectionately at Granny.

I jumped up, anxious to find some activity to hide behind. 'Yes you are. Now – shall I do your hair for you?'

She shuffled over a little so I could sit on the edge of the bed and I pulled the pins gently from her long grey hair. It reached half way down her back, thick and soft. I felt Angus's eyes on me, watching the two of us together.

'Tell me,' Granny said to him. Patiently he waited for her to manage the words. 'What is it you want to do with your life, Angus?'

After a moment's thought he said, 'What I'd really like is to invent something. A machine or tool that would be very important to people. Make their lives better or make it easier to build something else. Or create something really beautiful that people could

81

enjoy looking at.' He hesitated. 'I don't think I'm brainy enough to go for anything really academic like William.'

Granny waved her good arm dismissively. 'Never mind William. I wasn't talking about him. William will do whatever William does. I'm interested in you. Are you saying you plan to be an engineer?'

He looked into the fire, his thin face serious. 'I think what I'd like most is to learn the basics of something really well. Get an apprenticeship somewhere.'

'What about the university?'

'Perhaps later. I want to work in the real world a bit first.' He seemed embarrassed to be talking about himself like this.

'You're good at Meccano,' I said eagerly.

Angus laughed. 'That's a start, I suppose.'

I realized with surprise that for all the years Angus and I had grown up and played together we had barely ever had a conversation without the others around, when of course there was a lot of ragging and we were always intent on cricket or some other game. We didn't have serious conversations. Self-conscious suddenly, I concentrated on the soft feel of Granny's hair sliding between my fingers. I hoped Angus would think the pink of my cheeks was only from the fire.

'What will you do after school, Katie?' he asked.

'I think I'd like to be a nurse.'

'You've made up your mind then?' Granny said.

'Only just this minute.' I laughed. 'But I've really known that's what I want to do for ages. I want to look after people. It seems the obvious thing.'

I felt Angus watching me again. I knew there were new feelings between us.

'You've always been good at looking after people,' he said. 'Your grandmother, Olivia . . .'

'Olivia?' I was startled. 'What d'you mean? Why does Livy need looking after?'

'It's always looked to me a bit as if that's how it is, that's all. Sorry. Perhaps I've had it all wrong.'

'Livy's all right!'

'Well anyway, I think you'd make a very fine nurse.'

'What's this,' Granny interrupted, 'the mutual appreciation society?' She was smiling, her face cock-eyed and rather comical-looking. 'You two want to look out.'

Seeing she'd embarrassed us again, she added, 'I think I need a doze now. And you must need a rest from me. Thank you for your company, Angus. I'm most grateful.'

She was already sinking into sleep as we left the room's cosy light and went downstairs. William was studying in his bedroom.

'I suppose I should be going,' Angus whispered. 'William's putting me to shame.'

But he stood with me in our big family room at the back of the house where there were old easy chairs, a Welsh dresser and a piano. He seemed reluctant to leave, and I found I didn't want him to. I perched on the arm of a chair, woollen skirt pulled tight across my knees, a compromise between remaining standing and committing myself to sitting down in the chair.

'She's a fine person, your granny,' Angus said.

'Everything changed when she came,' I told him. 'I love having her here.'

Cautiously Angus said, 'I suppose your parents aren't always the easiest people to talk to?'

'No.' I felt grateful that he'd noticed. His own family were freer, more scatty. 'They're certainly not. But with Granny – it's hard to explain. I know she did some peculiar things when she first came. She was so used to being in charge of her house and everything, going down to the beach for a swim, even in winter if she wanted. And suddenly she was expected to come and settle down here with everyone telling her what to do. But she's just so different from everyone else . . .'

The tears came suddenly, streaming down my face with so little warning that I couldn't control them.

'I just can't bear the thought of her dying.' I felt silly blubbing like that in front of Angus, I who had always been so much one of the boys, their games from which you didn't run off in tears. I took my specs off and put my hands over my face.

'Katie, don't – ' His voice was gentle. He took one of my hands gently away from my cheek and drew me to my feet. 'She's doing well, isn't she?' He looked anxiously into my face. 'She'll be all right.'

'But you can't just say that,' I retorted. 'She's old and sick. People *do* die. Daddy's patients are always dying.'

'I'm sorry,' he said, shrugging awkwardly. 'It was a stupid thing to say. I just wanted to make you feel better, that's all.'

I looked up at him. His face was rather blurred even at this distance. 'I must look such a fright.'

'No. You look lovely.' He spoke so kindly that I nearly started crying again, but he was embarrassed and covered it with a joke. 'My, my, grandmother, what big eyes you've got!'

We laughed together. 'I'm sorry, I don't have a hanky to offer,' he apologized. I pulled out my own and he wiped my face softly with it, then leaned forward, coming suddenly into focus, and kissed my damp cheek. It didn't startle me as much as it did him, and he leapt away from me almost as if he'd been electrocuted.

Then he went all brisk and said, 'I'd better be off now. Prep for tomorrow. Do cheer up, won't you?'

Confused, but warmed, I watched him go.

Chapter 7

'What's going on with you and Angus?' Olivia demanded. Her voice was tight and angry. 'You're all sort of stiff with each other. And he keeps eyeing you up all the time.'

I tried to look surprised. 'Nothing – really.' Even now the new emotions between Angus and me were too fresh and untried to talk about, to Olivia or anyone. And I didn't like her phrase 'eyeing you up'. It sounded dirty.

'Katie,' Olivia wheedled, putting on her very best appealing face. 'We never keep secrets from each other, do we?'

I shook my head, though I knew this was far from the truth nowadays: I couldn't talk about Angus; even less could Olivia bring any words to the surface about her mother, and I no longer dared ask. When Elizabeth had returned home she had been frighteningly thin, her face drained white with bruise-coloured dents under her eyes. Even her hair had a deadened look, its sheen quite gone. Very slowly over the months her colour had begun to return. Smiles appeared dutifully at her lips. She was forever resting. I visited. I tried to be concerned and helpful. But not once did we talk of what had happened. And I knew instinctively that I must never mention Elizabeth's visit to our house last summer. I was afraid. I could feel changes nudging at us. Although mostly we tried to put aside any difficulties and were as affectionate with each other as ever, there were times when these things which I knew, or half knew, became a burden, and an obstacle between us.

As soon as she noticed the changes between Angus and me it got much worse. It's hard for me to express my feelings for Angus, how they gradually grew and intensified. I'd known him for so long and our lives had been very much a part of each other's. Our more adult feelings grew directly out of that. But of course it meant letting go a part of our childhood which had always included Livy and William. And I assumed Olivia was jealous, simply that.

'I wondered if Katie'd like to come for a walk with me?' Angus asked shyly.

He had appeared at the front door instead of coming round the back, in the hope of avoiding William. Mummy was startled. The realization that she had a daughter who was now sixteen and who might not want to wear hand-me-downs and be counted for ever as one of the boys had scarcely dawned on her.

I was up with Granny, who beamed triumphantly on hearing Angus's invitation. I was immediately flustered. 'Me – on my own?'

'Go on with you,' Granny commanded. 'I told you he'd get round to it one day. He'll not bite you. Just relax and enjoy yourself. After all, you've known the boy since you were knee high.'

He watched me walk downstairs, smiling. He was dressed in cream flannel trousers and a pale blue shirt and I laughed nervously and said, 'Look – we match today!' My skirt was pleated cream with a print of cornflowers. I had slimmed down a bit now I'd grown taller and liked to think of myself as 'curvaceous'. I took more trouble with my hair too, curling the ends and pinning it back so that it waved round my shoulders instead of pulling it into any old Alice band. I did feel self-conscious about the size of my bust, though. It pushed rebelliously at the buttons of every blouse I wore.

'It's so heavy and embarrassing,' I complained to Granny.

'Never you mind,' she told me serenely. 'You may not appreciate it, but believe me, there'll be others who will. Now stop finicking. You're lovely.'

'I was wondering if you'd fancy a walk to Cannon Hill Park?' Angus said. 'It's such a good day.'

'I'd love to come.' Then just in case I'd got him wrong, I added, 'Shall I fetch William as well?'

'I'd much rather you didn't,' he said quickly.

It was beautifully warm outside, with lilac and laburnum coming into flower and bluebells still in some of the gardens. We walked through the shade of the mature trees at the end of Chantry Road and down the hill towards the park.

I felt very conscious that we were alone. Since Angus had kissed me that day we had scarcely had any time without someone else's company. We had all met, of course, with Olivia home for the Christmas holidays, had talked and joked together and been to the park and the pictures. And Angus had often called round at the house, but everyone assumed he had come to see William and we'd ended up as a threesome or more. But even then, I knew that every time Angus and I were close there was more between us than was spoken. We were inhibited of course. Angus was shyer even than I was, but an undercurrent of glances and thoughts developed between us, which of course Olivia had not failed to notice.

At first we walked in silence. I was acutely aware of his every movement, as I'm sure he was of mine. Eventually I said, 'So next term's your last? Things won't be the same when you get a job, will they? No more long hols.'

'I'll still be a student really. Though I don't know what we get in the way of time off yet.'

Angus had gained a place at the Vittoria Street school to learn jewellery-making and silversmithing.

'I thought when you said you wanted to make things, it would be cars or furniture or something?'

'There's a lot of design involved in those, of course. And it'd certainly be a challenge. But when I saw the sort of work you can do in the Jewellery Quarter I knew I should like that much better. I'd like to make things that are beautiful as well as useful.'

'You're lucky.' I sighed. 'I wish I was good with my hands. Olivia's clever at the piano and there's you ... Granny says William and I are doomed to be ham-fisted for life, and I'm afraid she's right.'

Angus laughed. 'Yes, I wouldn't set William loose on a lathe or any other kind of tool. But he's got more than his fair share of talents I'd say.'

I knew William often went out of his way to appear superior to Angus.

'But William's so ridiculous!' I protested. 'I know he's awfully brainy and all that, but you can't have a decent conversation with him. It's like trying to talk to a shire horse – big and strong and quite intelligent but awfully dopy. I can talk to you so much more easily.'

Angus laughed. 'Well, that's something anyway.'

We turned through the wrought-iron gates. It was

Birmingham's biggest and proudest park, the expanse of grass sloping softly down from the bandstand under the chestnut trees to the fish ponds where there were boats for hire in summer.

We strolled round the murky oval of water. Ducks slid alongside us in hope of food.

'I don't know,' I said gloomily, after a while.

'What? What's the rest of that sentence?'

I smiled. If I'd said that to William he'd just have ignored me. One of the things I'd always liked about Angus was the way he listened to you.

'I'm not sure I like growing up really. The way you realize certain things suddenly.'

'Such as?'

'Mummy and Daddy were talking about those poor people in Spain this morning.' The bombing of Guernica had reached our households in bold newspaper headlines. 'How can people do things like that? I thought the League of Nations was going to stop there being any more wars?'

'Not if countries defy the League. The Germans already have, remember.'

We found a spot to sit on the grass in the shade of a tree, near the park's large war memorial. I was frowning. I felt heavy and preoccupied when what I really wanted to do was laugh and be good company. But I was already wondering whether our walk would cause trouble.

'I can tell there's a thought in there trying to get out,' Angus said, leaning round to look into my eyes.

I laughed reluctantly. 'It's just, Angus, would you say your family was happy? I mean they seem happy to me.' I'd thought a lot about the Harveys recently.

Angus's father, James, owned a business crafting pianos and harpsichords. He was kind, jovial. There was Mrs Harvey with her friendly, welcoming face, who spent her time reading and reading, and John and Mary, Angus's younger brother and sister. I'd begun searching for undercurrents, wondering if there was something I'd missed in every family, even my own.

'Yes, I s'pose I would,' Angus said. 'You know, just normal. We rub along.'

I told him some of my feelings of unease about Olivia, though I didn't mention Elizabeth's mysterious visit. 'I don't know what it is I'm trying to tell you really,' I said. 'It's just that they can behave rather oddly. I've been noticing it more recently, but even that holiday I went on with them – you know, a couple of years ago – they were certainly different from how they seem normally.'

'Wouldn't any family be if you were living closely with them for a week or two?'

'No. Not like that. There's something not right, but Olivia won't talk to me. I can't seem to get near her any more. And I don't like that.' I looked into Angus's face. 'I know you all find her a bit of a trial at times, but she's so nice really, and so different when we're on our own. I'm really very fond of her.'

'I know. I can see. But if there's something she doesn't want to talk about then you can't make her, can you? You know Olivia, she likes attention. If there was anything she wanted you to know she'd soon tell you.'

'We used to be able to tell each other everything,' I said sadly. 'And now she's gone all chilly because she thinks you and I . . .' Face burning, I stared down at the grass, feeling I'd said too much.

I sensed Angus waiting tensely beside me. We sat in silence for a moment. Then he reached over and gently took my hand. I felt him trembling slightly.

Neither of us could think of anything to say. The silence grew longer, our shyness and lack of certainty about what to do next inhibiting us completely. We sat for a time, the palms of our hands growing sticky from being pressed together.

In the end I slowly withdrew mine. 'Shall we go back now?'

'Where were you this morning?' Olivia demanded, marching across our lawn towards me. 'I came round looking for you and your mother said you'd gone out with Angus.'

'I did. He came and asked me to go for a walk with him in the park. I'm sorry.' Immediately I resented feeling obliged to apologize.

'Did William go too?'

I shook my head. Olivia looked at me through narrowed eyes. 'You could have waited for me. I spent the morning on my own.'

'I'm sorry – I wasn't expecting it. He just came over and asked me. Look, sit down and I'll go and fetch something to drink.'

But she couldn't leave the subject alone. 'Well,' she demanded harshly when I returned to the garden with a jug of lemonade and biscuits. 'Did he kiss you?'

I flushed, annoyed now instead of apologetic. It really was none of Olivia's business, but I tried to keep calm.

'No, I told you, we just went for a walk, that's all.'

'But he's obviously sweet on you.' She looked shrewishly at me. 'Do tell me what he said.'

I remembered the awkwardness of that part of the

morning when Angus had held my hand. 'Really, nothing very much,' I said, selecting a biscuit as casually as I could. 'We talked about the League of Nations if you must know.'

Olivia brought out a mirthless laugh. 'Really? How dull of you!'

'Well if my walk with Angus was so dull, why are we discussing it?' I retorted. We teetered on the edge of a serious quarrel. But I couldn't bear to fight with Livy.

Eventually I persuaded her to go inside with me and play the Chopin waltz she'd been practising. The piano was a fine one, from James Harvey's works. Absorbed in the music, Olivia's mood softened. I watched her, my anger dying. I loved it when Livy played. I was always moved by the sight of her, taken up by it, her body no longer deliberately poised as it usually was, coy yet somehow closed. She was more fully herself than at any other time when she played for me. I'd seen her play for her father's guests and I knew she found it a torture. Then she was formal, mean with the music, giving nothing of herself. But now she was playing without a score in front of her, and at times she leaned her head back and closed her eyes, her long hair reaching down her back against her sea-green frock. She finished the Chopin and, not heeding my applause – 'That was wonderful, Livy' – moved straight into a Beethoven *adagio* which was one of my favourites. This she knew very well so she had no need to look at all. I watched and listened to the notes flowing from the piano. Olivia's eyes fluttered closed and her body swayed, taut and sensual.

She was oblivious to the fact that as she was reaching the concluding bars of the piece the boys slipped into the room, William, Angus and John, all lured by the sound of the music as they came in from cricket. They sat quietly, wiping their hands on their thighs, foreheads beaded with sweat, and waited for the end.

Olivia played the final chords and lifted her hands, wrists leading, from the keys. When she opened her eyes she leapt to her feet as if boiling water had landed in her lap.

'Oh!' she cried. 'How could you? How *could* you?' She rushed from the room, out into the garden.

'What on earth have we done?' William asked, laughing in total bafflement. 'Honestly, she gets more peculiar by the day, she really does.'

'Don't laugh at her,' I snapped. 'You probably just made her jump. I'll go and see.'

I found Olivia sitting curled on the slabs by the edge of the pond, her head resting on her bent up knees.

'How could you?' she said again as I knelt down beside her. She reached for her hanky, her face already pink from crying. 'How could you let them see me like that?'

'Like what, Livy?' I was rather frightened.

'So abandoned-looking. When I play like that I'm . . . naked. I can't bear the thought of them seeing me . . .' She began to sob, her voice rising. 'It doesn't matter in front of you because you really know me.'

'Do I?' I asked sadly.

She cried in my arms, shuddering with the strength of it like a small child. Then she raised her head and stared up at the sky, a desperate expression on her face.

'Livy – darling. What's the matter?'

Olivia didn't answer. She sat shaking her head.

'Look.' I spoke briskly, trying to overcome the disturbed feelings welling inside me. 'That lot are all as thick as two short planks anyway. All they saw was you playing the piano and making music, nothing more.

Now do come in with us, or they really will start wondering what's going on.'

'Just wait one moment, will you?'

I sat down beside her and waited as she tried to compose herself. I put a warm hand on Olivia's arm, and she leaned over and rested her head on my shoulder. I stroked her wild hair.

'I'm sorry.' She sounded exhausted. 'I didn't mean to be such a witch earlier.'

'It's all right.' The skin of her upper arm was cool and smooth where I touched it. It reminded me of when we were younger, comforting Olivia in some quiet place at children's parties when the clamour of it all had proved too much for her. 'You know I'd do anything for you, don't you?'

Olivia twisted her neck and looked solemnly round at me. 'I do believe you would.'

We walked slowly up the garden together. Olivia seemed tired, almost dragging her feet along. When we went inside the boys had started on a game of bagatelle. Olivia and I stood behind them quietly. I watched as Angus concentrated, pushing the wooden stick, flicking one of the small metal balls so that it flew round the board. I felt very tender towards him too.

When his go was finished he straightened up and turned to Olivia, deliberately including her. 'You know your piano playing is just beautiful. Have you ever thought of applying to a music school?'

Olivia let out a harsh laugh. 'Oh, I've *thought* about it,' she said. 'But Daddy would never let me. I thought you knew – when I leave school I'm to take my place as a breeder of sons.'

* * *

I wasn't supposed to go up to Izzy's attic, but she never minded and that day Mummy was out. I called Izzy by her Christian name. She liked children, was still almost a child herself, with hair the colour of rust curling round her face and deep blue eyes.

It was two days before my seventh birthday, back in those days before I had started to watch and listen at doors. I was lovely then, clean. Life was sweet, mutual adoration. Daddy. My beautiful, talented, worshipping Daddy. I was his princess in white gossamer dresses, his fairy, his angel. Comfort and trust: his embrace, his tobacco smell, the scratchy worsted of his flamboyant suits, bright checks dazzling my eyes and the strong warmth of his long, long body.

A thin carpet curved up the attic stairs, the colour of green baize. But at the top the floor was bare for the maids, a peg rug or two in their rooms. I had new shoes: black patent leather, rounded toes, with a strap and a button to fasten them. I watched my feet as I ran up the stairs, my thin brown legs beneath a cherry-coloured skirt, white ankle socks, the shoes ... They tap-tapped loudly on those wooden boards. I ran to Izzy's door, rapped with my fingers, didn't wait –

'Izzy, look – I've got new shoes!'

It was his face. For seconds as I burst in on them, Daddy was in crisis, deep in his body's pleasure. He curved back over Izzy's little body, pushing down on his arms, her knees very white drawn up each side of him as she held him. His face was thrust back, red and sweating, mouthing the air, eyes squeezed shut.

Before he could recover himself enough even to speak my name I was downstairs in my room with my birds, bent up rigid on my bed with the eiderdown over my head. I was too sick even to cry. What they were doing I knew, and I didn't know. He had showed me all his weakness.

'Olivia?'

He'd pulled clothes over himself quickly and come down to sit on my bed. He was scared and I hated him for it. He lifted the eiderdown and laid his big hand on my back, but I curled myself tighter, squirming.

'Princess? Come on – there's no need to be upset. Izzy and I were just playing a little game and it's all over now. It's nothing to worry about. You can just forget it.'

His voice was light and wheedling. He tried to lift me on to his lap but he had a new sweaty smell and I pushed him away. But then I started to cry on my bed and I crawled back into his arms. He stroked my hair. His hand smelled of her.

'We'll let that be our little secret. Mummy needn't know our secret, need she? Just you and me, my pretty angel. You're good at keeping secrets, aren't you?'

I nodded, sobbing into his chest. The birds shifted on their perches.

The next day he came to me holding a box tied with extravagant pink ribbons. 'Angel – this is for you.'

The dress was also pink – taffeta, with silky bows sewn round the full skirt and lace petticoats.

By the end of the week, Izzy was gone.

* * *

Chapter 8

Birmingham, 1938

That terrible July evening.

The four of us were at the Kemps. We had lain in the sun most of the afternoon, drugged by the heat. The boys, shirts unbuttoned, sprawled side by side on a rug. William's solid, sporty frame was tanned and muscular from a summer term of tennis, cricket and swimming, his broad chest covered by a down of fair hair. His face was freckled and rather bullish. He lay with his arm under his head, his wavy hair bleached on top by the sun, blue eyes moving over a book on the Renaissance. The pages were dwarfed by his large hands.

Angus, much slighter with only a few dark hairs visible on his chest, was reading poetry, propped sideways on one elbow, but often stopping and looking up at the mellow brickwork of the house, with Virginia creeper trailing between the windows. Sometimes he looked across at me and we exchanged a secret smile.

Olivia lay on her back beside me on another rug, her vivid blue dress pulled up so the hem barely covered her knees, and a wide-brimmed straw hat shading her eyes. She seemed to be asleep. I sat up, sated with sunshine, pulling my skirt down to my ankles. The colours of grass and sky looked dark and intense after I'd lain so long with bright light beating on my eyelids.

The garden was immaculate, laid out on two levels, the upper area where we were lying edged by tall privet hedges. Around us were the scents of guelder roses, buddleia, mock orange, and in the middle of the lawn a fountain played out from the mouth of a stone dolphin on to a bed of water lilies and fish with feathery tails. The cool, sprinkling sound of water was constant. On the lower level of the garden, screened off by conifers from the vegetable patch, stood the round summer-house which the Kemps called the 'gazebo'. It was made of varnished wood with high windows and had inside a couch and chairs. I'd spent hours playing in there with Livy, in its shadowy light, its musty, exciting smell.

Elizabeth Kemp was sitting in a wicker chair in the shade of the house, a finely woven straw hat on her head, lifelessly turning over the pages of the *Queen*. She saw me turn to look at her.

'Would you like a drink?' she asked in her thin voice. 'There's a jug on the table. Or I could have Dawson bring something out?'

'It's all right,' I said, standing up slowly and stretching. 'I think I've had enough sun for now, thank you. I'd like to go and sit inside, if you don't mind.' I saw Angus raise his eyes from his book, and knew that if I moved inside he would soon join me.

'William?' I called, making sure. 'Are you all right here?'

'Mmmm. Want to get through some more of this.'

Olivia didn't stir.

I walked into the cool of the house, poured a drink of blackcurrant juice, and took it through into the informal sitting room which looked over the garden. It was the more attractive of the two rooms, I thought, the plump settee and chairs covered with trailing flower patterns in pinks and greens, and plants on the window-sills. After a moment, holding the glass against my warm cheek, I saw Angus get up and move towards the house. I smiled, waiting for him to find me inside. As the months passed we were overcoming our inhibited shy-ness, but our time alone together still felt furtive and stolen.

Angus came in and stood behind me.

'I can feel you,' I said. 'You're giving off heat like a boiler.'

'Not very flattering!' He moved my hair aside and I felt his lips warm on the nape of my neck. 'Couldn't you think of a more attractive comparison?'

I reached round and took his hand behind my back. 'You're the poet round here.'

'I only read it.' He came and stood beside me, his arms lean and tanned. 'Olivia seems to be out for the count.'

'Good.' I turned to him. 'D'you want some blackcurrant?'

We went and fetched him a glassful and sat side by side on the settee. After a few moments his slim fingers closed round mine. He sipped the rich-coloured drink.

'That's good stuff.' He indicated the glasses on the low table in front of us. 'Homemade?'

'Oh, I should think so. Can't imagine Elizabeth Kemp having shop-bought cordial, can you?' We laughed together.

'Everything just so,' Angus said. He nodded towards the garden. 'Even out there.'

'Makes our gardens look a bit ramshackle, doesn't it?'

He looked down at me. 'I want to see your eyes.' Sliding my specs off carefully with one hand he put

100

them on the arm of the sofa. 'There, that's better.' He ran his hand over my hair, gently lifted my chin with his fingers. Both of us were nervous, and within seconds there were footsteps in the hall. We sat up and I quickly put my specs back on. Elizabeth put her head round the door and found us sitting sedately side by side, looking through a book on Wedgwood china.

'I'm just going to slip up for a wash and change,' she said. 'I'm glad you've made yourselves at home.' A few moments later we heard water running upstairs. I took my glasses off again. We laughed, our eyes meeting.

He was very correct when we kissed, as if he was slightly afraid of me. He kept his arms stiffly round my shoulders or waist, or caressed my back. Both of us sat skewed round to face the other so our legs got in the way.

'Angus?' I looked into his eyes and saw in them such strong feelings that I wanted to say something, tell him I loved him, but it felt too soon, the words too important.

We leaned back in each other's arms. Moments later, very softly, he laid his hand on one of my breasts, hesitantly at first, then more firmly, and I so big, filling his hand. He unfastened a button of my dress and for a few seconds his fingers reached in to touch my bare skin. It sent such extraordinary sensation through me that I arched my back. Angus withdrew his fingers as if he had been burnt.

'Did I hurt you?'

'No. It felt lovely.'

He got up abruptly and stood with his back to me, looking out at the garden. 'I'm sorry.'

'Whatever for?'

'For – perhaps going a bit far. I don't want to do

anything to offend you, Katie. I wouldn't dream of it. It's just that I'm new at all this – knowing how to behave and what you expect of me. I feel I ought to know exactly what to do.'

I went over to him and put my arms round him. He felt rather stiff and reluctant at first. 'Angus – I don't mind – really. Perhaps I'm supposed to, but I don't!'

Laughing now, he pulled me into his arms. We stood holding each other more easily, kissing, the house quiet around us.

'It must look very dark in here from out there,' Angus said after a while, looking over my shoulder towards the garden. 'There's no one out there now. They must have come in.'

A few moments later, hearing the sound of the front door, we sprang apart again. There were brisk footsteps along the hall and Alec Kemp appeared at the door.

'Hello, you two,' he said, with that smile he could bring out, mischievous and complicit as if he guessed exactly what we were doing there. 'Got all you want?' He stood loosening his tie and removing the studs from his collar. His suit was a loud tweed. 'Elizabeth upstairs?'

We heard her voice from behind him. 'Darling, hel*lo*. Did you have a good day?' Her tone was caressing, solicitous, as if addressing a convalescent. 'Poor thing, having to work when it's so hot.'

'Oh, it wasn't so bad. Where's Olivia? Upstairs?'

'I thought she was with you,' Elizabeth said to Angus and me. Her right hand moved nervously to her throat, fingers nipping a fold of skin. 'She'll be around somewhere.'

Ten minutes later, when Angus and I were ready to

leave, Alec came down from changing into more casual clothes.

'I gather that brother of yours is here too,' he said to me tersely. Every trace of mischief was gone from his voice.

'He was,' I told him, bewildered. 'But he must have gone on home.'

'Well,' Alec replied grimly. 'We'll see.'

Outside, the only signs of life were two magpies, stalking across the grass.

Alec strode down the lawn, tensed and threatening, his hands clenched. The sight of him filled me with a terrible sense of dread though I could make no sense of it at the time. Angus and I followed.

Our feet were silent on the grass as we approached the gazebo, neat as a doll's house in the corner of the lawn. We were right behind Alec as he pushed the handle then stood across the doorway. The scene came to me in painful, jumbled images, like a cubist painting. Olivia's face, hair loosened in thick waves, her expression frozen; long, brown arms, the blue dress startling at her waist, her white, white breasts. And William's hand, arrested in the act of touching her, looking huge and dark as it was snatched away. I found my eyes moving anxiously downwards to check the extent of my brother's embarrassment, but he was fully clothed, everything fastened. His face was enough, flushed red like raw meat, eyes childishly wide. He could not speak. The two of them sat like trapped rats.

There were no smiles from Alec this time, no knowing looks. This was his daughter, matured and ripe as a siren, legs spread on the striped couch, pulling the blue cloth up fast now to cover her nakedness.

'I knew I'd find this.' His voice came low, more broken than angry. He stood over her, trembling. 'Oh God – Olivia. You were supposed to keep yourself clean. Clean.' In an anguished whisper he hissed at her, 'Have you any idea what you've done?'

She stared ahead of her sullenly, wouldn't face him. He leaned down, provoked into anger now, and took her chin roughly in his hand. 'Look at me – ' He jerked her face up violently, but her eyes still didn't meet his. 'You filthy, disgusting . . .'

'No, Mr Kemp, no!' William cried, jumping up, his face gleaming with perspiration. 'It wasn't – that's not fair!'

'Fair?' Alec shouted at him. 'What the devil has fair got to do with it? Are you telling me it wasn't her leading you on, getting you so wound up you couldn't resist her?' William couldn't seem to deny this. 'I know what they're like.' Suddenly he slapped Olivia hard across the face. I saw the pain flare in her eyes but she made no sound. She carried on staring sullenly across the room.

I slid past him. 'Livy – are you all right?' My friend's face was hard and full of hatred.

'Course I'm all right,' she spat out. Then more softly to me, 'Thanks.'

Alec marched her to the house and the rest of us followed. He had Olivia by her upper arm and she acted as if she was oblivious to the stream of abuse that he directed at her as they crossed the lawn. She was a bitch, filthy, too clever for her own good. She looked round, up at the trees, anywhere. By the time we reached the house I was choked with helpless rage.

'Get in the house,' Alec ordered. 'You won't be going anywhere for a while, my girl.'

He tried to bundle Olivia into the house while the three of us watched aghast from the bottom of the steps. I caught a glimpse of Elizabeth Kemp, her face a terrible white in the shadowy hall.

Olivia grabbed hold of the heavy iron door-handle and held on tight, her hair tumbling all over her face. 'You know why he's like this, don't you?' she shouted shrilly. 'Because my mother won't do it with him – never – '

Elizabeth Kemp stood absolutely still behind her, her mouth open, one hand at her throat. In panic, Alec clamped a hand over Olivia's mouth and pulled her with all his strength to loose her hands from the handle.

'Just get out of here,' he shrieked at the boys. 'And take your hideous sister with you. Out – now!'

Alec finally succeeded in wrenching Olivia's hands away from the door. For a second she shook her mouth free. '. . . so he does it with tarts and whores.' She spat out the words, '*Councillor* Kemp!' and then the door slammed shut. Through the coloured glass we saw their movements receding from the door, heard Olivia's cries.

My legs nearly buckled under me. William was silent, standing quite still.

'My God,' Angus said. 'D'you think there's any truth in that?'

I burst into tears then, and felt Angus's arm round my shoulders. He put out a hand to touch William's shoulder, but William shook him off.

The three of us walked home in silence. As we passed under the sweet-smelling trees in the dusk I felt hatred sinking deep in me and settling there.

'How could you be so *stupid*?'

I felt like killing William. We'd sat through tea,

through the passing of plates of bread and butter and jam and stewed fruit and junket, saying nothing to our parents, while misery and rage nearly choked me. What was happening to Livy? I wanted to rush back to the Kemps' house and break glass to get in.

Afterwards I cornered William in his bedroom. He was sitting on the edge of his bed, elbows on his solid thighs and a book between his hands. He didn't look up at me.

'Didn't you think?' I hissed at him furiously. We didn't want anyone else hearing this conversation. 'And put your flaming book down, can't you? Don't you care what you've done? What that bastard might be doing to Livy?'

William looked up, shocked. 'Katie – language.'

'You weren't such a prig with her.'

He laid his book face down on the eiderdown and looked up miserably at me. His face with its freckles and boyish looks appeared very young suddenly, but it did nothing to melt my heart. 'It wasn't my fault.'

'Oh no – of course not. Nothing to do with you at all.' I stood haranguing him, hands on hips. 'Anyway – I never knew you liked Olivia – like that, I mean.'

'I don't.'

'So what the hell did you think you were doing?'

'Look,' he said, standing up suddenly. His face had turned red to the roots of his hair. 'You've got a nerve coming in here lecturing me when you know perfectly well that you and Angus – '

'Angus and I what?'

'Were up to exactly the same thing, weren't you?'

I stared at him, my fresh-faced, good all-rounder, oh-so-wonderful brother, and I could see him, ten, twenty years on, pompous and self-justifying. I'd never disliked William before as I did at that moment.

'The difference with Angus and me, if you must know, is that we love each other and we know when to stop. Whereas you apparently have no idea what might be appropriate and you don't care a fig about Livy.'

'It wasn't like that.' William's voice turned small and pitiful. He sank down on the bed again. 'It's true I've never felt that way for her. I can see she's pretty as well as anyone else. But recently she's been behaving so oddly. She's too moody for my liking.'

'Well, something obviously changed your mind.'

William shot me a look of appeal, then stared down at the worn green carpet. 'One minute she was asleep, or I thought she was. Then when you'd gone in, she suddenly got up and came and sat down, right next to me.' He shuddered slightly at the memory. 'She was like a snake. She started touching me, just my hands, very softly, but you know – seductively, and staring me in the eyes. Then she just said, "Come on – come with me." So I went with her to the summer-house.'

'But why did you go?'

'That's the thing.' He seemed relieved now to be talking. 'She has this way with her. You can't refuse her. If her father hadn't come in like that I don't know where it would have ended. She just took me over.' William looked away towards the window. 'She kept touching me, and I couldn't ... You always feel with Olivia as if, if you disagree with her or refuse her, she'll crack. She always seems fragile.'

I found my mind following this remark like a dog after a stick. It was true. Olivia had this quality that made you want to care for her, to succumb to her. I remembered Angus's comment 'You look after Livy.' I felt sick inside now with my longing to care for her, to rescue her from her father. My brother meant nothing to me. I could think only of her.

William suddenly burst out, 'No one ever talks about it, do they?' I dragged my thoughts back to him. 'Dad, Mum. I'm eighteen and I've never kissed a girl before and I couldn't even think straight. And girls aren't supposed to do that, are they? My mind was telling me one thing and my body wanted to do another. And Olivia wanted me to, that was the thing. It was she who took her dress off, not me. You must believe me, Katie. But now she's in such trouble and I feel it's all my fault. I should have stopped her, been stronger.'

'Yes, you damn well should,' I said heartlessly.

'What if they tell Dad?'

'Oh, they won't do that. Think about it.' I tried to be more sympathetic. 'Look, don't worry. I'm sure nothing will happen to you. In fact I don't suppose they're thinking about you at all.'

He kept Olivia locked in her room for nearly four days. Nothing was supposed to pass her lips except water. Elizabeth Kemp was under strict instructions not to let her out, and she was too afraid to defy her husband.

I was frantic. Granny was the only one who knew. I paced restlessly up and down by her chair in the garden. Nowadays she did very little but sit. Her speech was reasonably distinct, but slow. We were patient waiting for her words, like listening for the voice of an oracle.

'There's not much you can do, I'm afraid.'

'But they're starving her.'

'Oh, I expect you'll find someone's feeding her something on the quiet. After all, Mr Kemp can hardly do nothing but sit at home like a guard dog. He has a business to run. All you can do is to be as staunch a friend as you can when she comes out. Whatever's wrong in that family, you can be sure it didn't begin yesterday.'

I tried to see Olivia. Elizabeth Kemp's spidery fingers twitched along the collar of her blouse as she stood at the door. 'Alec says I musn't let anyone in.'

I felt complete contempt for Elizabeth Kemp at that time. Even in my fury with Alec I wondered whether he was owed sympathy. Was he married to a woman so cold, so selfish that she wouldn't even let him touch her? Had her illness, secret and undefined, been simply a ploy to gain his attention and keep him physically at a distance? Warmed by my own new relationship with Angus I found it hard to imagine feeling so negative. It was clear to me, though, that this woman in front of me was frightened.

'Will you tell Livy I'm here?' I asked. 'Please? Perhaps she could just come to the window?'

Elizabeth glanced wide-eyed down towards the road as if fearful that Alec might appear at any moment. Then she nodded. 'Be quick though, please.'

As I started walking round the back of the house towards Olivia's window, Elizabeth called out in a high, childlike voice, 'It's not his fault, you know.'

I didn't bother to reply. I didn't care about them any more. I cared only about Olivia.

She appeared at the window still wearing her nightie, sleeveless, in white organdie. We stared at each other in silence for a moment.

'Are you all right?'

Her face looked different: naked, like a statue from which rain has washed the dust. I could tell she had spent hours crying, though her eyes were not red. They were wide and sad, yet I could see in them something else, hints of other submerged emotions. I thought I detected a kind of exultation about her which disturbed me because it was so incongruous.

She nodded at me.

'Are you on your own all the time?'

'No.' She spoke so quietly I could barely hear her, as if she was afraid of being overheard. 'Mummy slips up and keeps me company. And she sends Dawson up with food although she's not supposed to. I'm supposed to fast like Joan of Arc. The servants think it's mad of course, and who can blame them?'

'But for goodness' sake,' I exploded, 'when's he going to stop all this nonsense? He's got you imprisoned up there – and William's feeling awful.'

She pressed a finger urgently to her lips. 'Shh – please. Sometimes he comes home to check . . .' She smiled suddenly, an odd, amused smile. I felt she was removed from me, untouchable. 'Please tell William I'm sorry. He won't get into any trouble, I promise.'

'Why on earth did you do it, Livy?'

'Oh,' she said dismissively. 'I had to know I could, that's all.' She wavered for a moment. 'I don't know really . . .'

'Was it because of me and Angus?'

'Oh no. No – I'm very happy for you,' she said smoothly.

I heard light sounds to my left, and saw Elizabeth Kemp tiptoeing round the house towards me.

'What are you supposed to do to get out?' I asked quickly. 'What are the terms?'

'Oh, I have to apologize, and give up any notion of a life of my own, and promise I'll never go near another boy again and be Daddy's little girl for ever and ever until they find the right man for me to marry. Not much really.'

'You must go,' Elizabeth said to me. 'Please. Don't keep coming. It'll make things worse.'

I looked into her pale face, lined now round the mouth and eyes and taut with fright. I wanted to take hold of her and shake her and tell her she was weak and pathetic. Instead, all I could say, contemptuously, was, 'This is ridiculous.'

'Katie!' Olivia appealed to me as I was about to move away. 'We didn't want you to know any of this. You know Daddy's a good man really. You won't tell anyone, will you?'

I stared up at her. 'No,' I said in the end. 'I won't tell anyone. But for your sake, not his.'

When Olivia finally came out of her room she looked even thinner. Her manner was taut and she was sardonic and hard to reach.

'Did you apologize?' I asked.

'Not exactly,' she quipped. 'I just told him I'd spend my days up there writing up his story for the *News of the World*. He soon let me out then.'

* * *

OLIVIA

Katie was so lonely when we first became friends. She needed me. And oh, yes, I needed her. She was the only one I ever came near telling about home. But I didn't want to spoil it. I wanted her to love me. I wanted her admiration, her worship of us, of Daddy. It meant that I could pretend, and believe in it all sometimes too, like

I did when I was a little girl, and for Mummy's sake no one should know. Katie was so innocent. Sometimes she saw things but I glossed over them. I became closed by habit and could not open myself again.

Katie gave me herself. No one took much notice of her at home, and I made her flower, I know I did. But then people kept taking her away. That grandmother of hers. She was barmy but Katie had to love her of course. That was the difference between us: she could love people properly. Before, she talked only to me. And then Angus. I could see it coming long before either of them. The way he looked at her secretly. I couldn't endure it.

What she never understood (how could she?) was that I, Olivia Kemp, had to be the one, not her. The one that men wanted. I was the pretty one. I knew what my body had to do. If my existence taught me anything it was that the way to get anywhere is to give them what they want and plenty of it and they can't resist you. You've got them caught like flies in honey. Mummy couldn't do it. It wasn't her fault, I know that. I know she spent every waking moment trying to compensate Daddy for her inability to service him. But I was going to please them, to have them. I had to be the one.

Poor stupid William. Quite handsome in an obvious sort of way, but so middling and happy with himself. As soon as I touched him I knew my power.

'Come on,' I whispered in the garden. 'Come with me. I'll show you how to enjoy yourself.' When I saw the look in his eyes my body was turning inside. I fancied I had a thick scent coming out from me like an orchid. I wanted scarlet silk wound about me.

He was so easy. I made him shudder trying to hold himself in.

'Oh Olivia,' he kept muttering in the stupid way they all do. 'Oh God, Olivia.'

I had no intention of letting him enter me, oh no. I let him kiss me, and when I undid the top of my dress – his face! His eyes were almost bulging in his head. I spread my legs to let him imagine things, let him put his hand up my skirt.

I moved my hand over his pleaser, all hard and tight. If they hadn't all come crashing in like that I would have unfastened him. Taken him in my hand – mouth even – made him lose control of himself.

Poor Daddy. His princess dethroned, if not deflowered. But he was a hypocrite locking me up like that. I couldn't forgive him. And I told them about him. I let some of it out. I didn't want to – to spoil things like I did. It was seeing them all there at the bottom of the steps – Kate and Angus all close and united of course – looking so shocked and righteous. I wanted to tear through that, to smash it all up. I'm a bad, bad woman.

But the days when he had me locked away up there, he came to me on his knees, weeping, begging me, 'I love you. I worship you. Say you'll never never ever . . .' One day he knelt with his arms around my back, face pressed against my belly like a child, his tears wetting the light cloth of my nightdress. I stood stiff as a tree, not touching him, just looking at the dark curls on top of his head. In that moment I knew I could do anything.

* * *

Part Two

Chapter 9

'Katie – darling!' Olivia gave a discreet wave, arm half extended as I panted across the polished floor of the Ranelagh Room in Lewis's department store.

'It's all right. Don't rush. I haven't been here long.' She raised herself from the chair smiling broadly and leaned across to press her face against mine. Her lips brushed my cheek. 'Oh, sorry – I've left lipstick on you. Where's my hanky?'

'Not to worry. I've got one.' I wiped my cheek, handing my coat to the waiter, stowed my gas mask under my chair, then sat beaming at Olivia. 'It's so lovely to see you.'

For a moment we were silent, looking at each other as if unsure where to begin, and finally both burst into laughter at our awkwardness.

'You're all aglow,' Livy said, once we'd settled into being with each other. 'Still in love with nursing then?'

'Absolutely.' I pulled the comfortable chair in closer to the table. 'Yes, it's marvellous, especially now they've let us loose on the patients. The classroom part's a real slog, but it's worth it once you get out there on the wards.' I had been nursing now for over a year and I knew I had made the right choice. I was being sucked into the rigours and rituals of the General Hospital

117

which took us young and unformed and bent us to its demands, its disciplines.

'I'm sure you're terrific at it,' Olivia said. It was typical of her to have such implicit faith in me.

'I just can't imagine wanting to do anything else.' I smiled back at her, taking in her appearance. 'I say, Livy – you look marvellous. So glamorous.'

She was wearing a perfectly tailored suit in royal blue and her hair was pinned stylishly, swept back from her forehead. Beside her on the table lay a wide-brimmed blue hat and leather gloves. She was made up, lips a rich scarlet, and she looked stunning.

Of the four of us she seemed suddenly the most grown up. William had taken to Oxford with apparent ease, his conversation when he came home full of rugger and student pranks. Angus was enjoying his training at Vittoria Street. But both of them seemed comparatively unchanged, except that they had moved on to something new. Whereas Olivia dressed now with sophistication, made her face up routinely in a way I never did and seemed suddenly adult.

'You'll have to take me in hand,' I teased as we sipped our white wine. 'There's you looking like something out of *Harper's* and me in my frumpy old uniform . . .'

Olivia grimaced and rolled her eyes to the ceiling. 'There've got to be some compensations, I suppose.' She picked up the menu and laid it in front of her but didn't read it. The band was playing 'Blue Moon'. A shaft of autumn sunlight fell into a warm rectangle across our table.

'The job's not getting any better then?'

'I hate, hate, hate it!' Suddenly she was storming at me. Olivia had not been given a choice. The Kemps decreed that she should do a year's secretarial training, something useful, not these airy-fairy notions about study and music. She was to become versed in Pitman and commerce. As well as the proverbial 'something to fall back on' (which I'm sure in their hearts they never thought she'd need) it was to be her entrée to a suitable marriage. She would rise through a prominent company and marry well, preferably the boss. She had worked now for six weeks at Leggett and Martin, an insurance company which occupied prestigious offices in Colmore Row.

The smile had dropped from her lips. 'It's so tedious and arid. I can't bear it.' She looked into my eyes. 'I know I may not be brilliant at music or anything else – '

'You're exceptionally good, though,' I interrupted fiercely. I felt frustrated on her behalf. It wasn't as if the Kemps were short of money. They could have allowed her more freedom to choose.

'It's what I really wanted. Was that so wrong of me?'

I reached over and squeezed her hand. 'Of course not. Look, they're far too protective. They're trying to run your whole life for you.'

I had spent much less time at the Kemps' house over the months since Alec found William and Olivia together. That summer of 1938 had felt like the end of our childhood, changing all of us. Alec and Elizabeth were civil enough to me still – more than civil in Alec's case. He was clearly very embarrassed and went out of his way to win me over. But I was on my guard now and couldn't trust him as I had before. I avoided the Kemps as much as possible.

Although I'd tried to talk to Livy about what happened after it was over I couldn't get her to open up on the subject. I knew she was aware of my stinging censure of her parents. When we met now it was nearly always somewhere away from either of our houses. It was sad. Both of us knew we had lost something.

The waiter approached our table and hovered discreetly. Olivia forced her attention to the menu. When he had taken our order and departed with dignity Olivia leaned closer and whispered across the sugar bowl, 'I've got to get away. It's suffocating me. I've got to do something.' She seemed frantic.

'Gracious, Livy – '

'I've thought about it over and over. I was going to try and find a job in London. But now with the war everything's changed. It seems so trivial and selfish to think about it. After all, we could all soon be dead . . .' She pressed one hand over her eyes, trying to hold back tears. Her nails were the same colour as the lipstick.

I reached out again and took her other cold hand across the table. 'Livy, darling – don't. I do wish there was something I could do for you. Can't you ask your mother? No, I suppose she wouldn't put her oar in for you.'

Wiping her face, Olivia said, 'Don't be too hard on Mummy. It's not her fault. Not really.'

'She said it wasn't *his* fault,' I said, more harshly than I'd intended.

Olivia looked me in the eyes. 'I wish I could hate them. I wish it so much.'

'Livy – can't you tell me what's so wrong at home? Is it – what you said that day – about your father?'

She rearranged her cutlery with nervous movements, half looking up at me, a fierce blush rising in her cheeks. 'No. I can't talk about it. I'm sorry, Katie.' She tried to sound brisk. 'I really shouldn't have said anything that day. I must have given you quite the wrong impression. Please forget I said it. Mummy and Daddy are just a bit over-protective. That's all.'

Our food was served: roast chicken and vegetables. Livy was treating me.

'This is so nice,' I said to her as the waiter spooned potatoes on to our plates. 'Thank you for it – very much.'

'Oh, I'm glad to.' Her smile was warm again now. It was such a reflex with her, being able to rally herself and change the subject. 'What are best friends for?'

We sat talking and laughing over our meal, and I enjoyed watching her pretty face across the table, thinking how the war was beginning to bring things like this into focus, things we had taken for granted.

'How's dear Angus?' she asked.

She often called him 'dear Angus', with a shading of irony in her voice.

'He's thriving. Loving the training. Of course I don't see very much of him – we're both so busy. And now, who knows what's going to happen?' In those early days of the war we were all galvanized by the expectation of being bombed or invaded any moment. 'Do you think it's all going to be over soon? Daddy's taking a very pessimistic line: Fascism is the dark force of evil in our time and won't be easily overthrown, and so on.' I imitated my father's sober Scots voice and Olivia grinned. 'Feels so normal sitting here like this though, doesn't it?'

'All these gas masks and shelters and everything certainly bring it home though, don't they?' She grew solemn again, reverting to her own frustrations. 'Honestly Katie. The only way I can see to get out of this is to get married. And that's not much of a motive for giving your life to someone, is it?'

In November Granny Munro lay dying. Another stroke felled her so that she couldn't speak and could barely move. She lay in her room, inert as lard, one side of her pallid face the only real register of her feelings.

Angus and I were able to spend time with her together one evening. We sat leaning forward so she could see us, the room lit only by the low sidelight on her bedside table. I held hands with her, with Angus on my other side. My emotions were very mixed. Here I was with two of the people I loved best in the world, together in this strange, silent intimacy. Granny's eyes moved over our faces. Her hair was white now and thinner. She was less considerable in size. I hadn't seen Angus for some time and was acutely aware of the novelty of his presence beside me: the soft curve of skin I loved at the back of his neck where the hairline ended, his hand warm on mine, eyes serious and affectionate.

Coal burned with a hiss in the grate. We talked softly from time to time, both of us telling her about our different jobs: my patients, Angus's hours cutting sheets of metal into fine shapes with a tiny fretsaw. We knew she liked to hear. Eventually her eyes closed.

'We'll be back soon,' I said softly. I laid her hand on the bedcovers. 'I'll bring you up some soup later.'

Outside the door we stopped and put our arms round each other.

'You smell of work.'

Angus laughed. 'Not surprising. I came straight here.' He looked at me sadly. 'She's very bad, isn't she?'

'She's dying. There isn't much can be done. We just have to keep her as comfy as we can.'

122

'What if there's an air raid? You can't very easily lift her down to the cellar.'

'I don't know.' The long looking-glass at the top of the stairs showed my face white with exhaustion. My legs felt weak and shaky. I'd just come from a long spell of duty on a women's surgical ward. 'We'll have to think of something.'

We went to join the rest of the family for dinner. It was unusual to have everyone at home. William had asked for permission to leave Oxford to see Granny. The house felt sombre with swathes of blackout material at all the windows. The panes were criss-crossed with tape to shield against blast. There was talk of food being rationed within the next couple of months: bacon, sugar, butter. Even the light in the dining room felt thinner, as if they were diluting the electricity.

As we ate our boiled ham with carrots, potatoes and dried peas, I stopped feeling so low and tired. We sat under the high, coved ceiling with its ornate rose at the centre, all painted white, and the walls a paper pattern of buff and brown. My father was at one end of the table and William at the other, Angus and I sat opposite each other, Mummy next to Angus.

I glanced at each of my parents as we ate. Both of them looked very tired too. Daddy was mostly silent and preoccupied. The war was constantly in our minds, yet of course at that stage no one knew exactly what it would entail. Poland was overrun, the seas had become menacing, trawled by U-boats and malevolent ships, magnetic minds floating unseen just below the surface. It was as if the world had a pall over it. And of course Daddy felt involved in every detail, as well as that of the health care of the city of Birmingham. His eyes were focused far from those around him. If he had taken the trouble to adjust them so that he could see my mother, he should have noticed the pale, pinched look on her face, her tense angry movements, evident even in the way she was eating, stabbing at the ham with her fork like a hen after corn. I watched her uneasily.

'How's Oxford?' Angus asked William, since no one was speaking, though I felt sure he must have asked him earlier. 'Still doing well?'

'I'm enjoying it enormously,' William said. He was looking very well, thinner and alight with the stimulation of it. 'I've got an absolutely first-rate tutor this term, and the chap I'm rooming with is very decent – we fit in a lot of sport together. All in all it's exceeded expectation. Pity about the war, though. Even if it is only "Bore" War at the moment . . .'

Daddy cleared his throat. 'I doubt if the Merchant Navy would see it that way.'

William gave a nervous laugh, embarrassed at expressing any uncertain emotion in front of his father. 'Yes, well I suppose we all really know our days are numbered now. Waiting to be called up and all that. It's all rather disturbing.'

'Well, it'd be terrible if anything happened to disturb your little life, wouldn't it?' I said. I saw Angus look at me in surprise.

'Kate, how can you say that?' Mummy snapped. 'Heaven only knows what your poor brother might have to go through. And Angus too, for that matter.'

'D'you think it hasn't crossed my mind?'

The terrible thought of Angus going away: it was like a hand closing tight around my heart, making my breathing go shallow. Our generation was brought up on images of the Great War. The trenches were woven in to every family history.

'If it comes to it, Angus,' William said, 'who are you going to join up with?'

My father's voice sliced unexpectedly across the table. 'You take it for granted I suppose that you have to follow the herd, like thousands in the last war who thought it was a heroic and glamorous thing to do. Have you not considered that there might be other alternatives?'

'But you weren't a conshie in the last war,' William protested, his face as usual turning red easily. 'And if you had been they'd have given you a pretty thin time of it.'

'No, I wasn't a conscientious objector then.' His voice had dropped but it was clipped and precise, his accent coming out more strongly than usual. 'I was a medical student. I chose to direct my energy to the preservation of life instead of its annihilation.'

The four of us sat watching him awkwardly. He discussed his thoughts so rarely that we felt at a loss as to how to communicate with him. His fervour usually expressed itself quietly, in his writing.

'But Father, this Adolf Hitler fellow is a raving lunatic. You can't just let him march across Europe taking away people's liberty and get away with it. Where's the justice in that?' William had assumed his debating chamber tone. 'We have to fight. Doesn't it bother you, the thought of other people doing all your fighting for you?'

'*Bother* me?' Daddy's pale blue eyes swept round the table coldly. 'Does it bother me? William, it appals me. But I can't believe there's any such thing as justice in a war. There's nothing just about it. And I have to stand against it with every fibre of my being. Can you understand that?'

William stared at him, then said stiffly, 'I'm sorry, I can't agree. When the time comes I shall offer myself to the army. I can't do anything mechanical of course, but they might find me something clerical or educational. I'm sorry I can't share your ideals, Father, but that's just the way it is. What about you, Angus?' He spoke with a note of appeal, needing Angus to support his point of view, but there was a challenge in his voice as well, the old competitiveness. I watched Angus anxiously.

'I shall volunteer for the RAF. I'm going to offer to train as a pilot.' As he spoke, his eyes met mine, but I could hear a certain kind of assertion in his voice and knew it was directed at William.

'Mummy, what's the matter?'

I'd taken the presumptuous step of following her upstairs after the meal and knocking on her bedroom door. There was no reply but I opened it and stood in the doorway. 'May I come in?'

'You already are in.' She had her back to me.

Timidly I walked towards her. 'You seem very upset about everything. Is it William – having to leave Oxford when they call him up?'

She went to her dressing table with an agitated pretence of sorting through one of the drawers, though I could see she was achieving nothing. She couldn't seem to bring herself to speak. Her thin, deft hands folded handkerchiefs, tinkered with the contents of a sandal-wood box, jewellery she almost never wore.

'Mummy?' I forced myself to move closer. My experience in nursing had at least made me more at ease in approaching people.

'You know I'm no good at talking about things,' she

said. 'Never have been. You just have to get on with life, not keep blathering about it all the time.'

I felt encouraged. Even this much expression of her inner feelings represented progress.

'You must feel very hard-pressed now you've taken on so much more in the garden – and Granny. You're doing such a good job with her. It must be jolly tough. You two never exactly got on well, did you?'

Mummy ceased her activity suddenly and stood still. Her shoulders began to shake and I could see from her twisting lips that she was trying to ram her feelings back down inside herself.

'Look, you were a nurse,' I said gently. 'You know you're doing the best job you possibly can.'

Her voice came out in a kind of screech. 'But it's not a job, is it? It's an imposition. He just takes it for granted that I'm here to do it all. He always has done. And I can't make a fuss – not with the war . . .'

'But you always wanted to carry on nursing – '

'Nursing's not the same as this though, is it?' she cried, whirling round to face me. What I had intended as a sympathetic conversation seemed to be fast turning into a row. 'It's one thing to be a professional and be paid and be able to walk away from it,' she said, slamming the drawer shut. 'It's quite another when it's family and you have feelings all tied up with it and you can't just go off duty. Oh, I can't bear it.'

Her whole body seemed to crumple and she sank down on the green sateen eiderdown. Cautiously I sat down as well, not daring to touch her. A tear ran down each of her pale cheeks and then there were no more.

'I can't tell you how much I loathe it, having to clean up day after day when she soils herself. The indignity of it – for her. And I can feel her eyes watching me as if

127

she's trying to say something and I feel it's a reproach. We're alone together so much, you see. Just her, quite silent, watching – and me. I try to be detached. I stand there wiping her up and think, "You're a nurse. This is a patient." But my patients were babies. I always loathed nursing old people. I was no good at it.' She looked round at me suddenly with frightened grey eyes. 'When I look at her I see myself. She reminds me this might happen to me. When you nurse people when you're younger it's not the same. And the worst of it is, the more time I spend with her the more I can't help admiring her. Her stubbornness, her independence. Bull-headed as anything . . . Qualities I've never . . .'

She sniffed and got up from the bed with renewed briskness. 'I never thought I'd be saying any of this. It's ridiculous and self-indulgent. Come along now, we must go down. The others will think we've deserted them. Those poor boys could be going off soon to get themselves killed.'

Chapter 10

Granny died shortly before Angus went away to begin his initial RAF training. He came to her funeral, of course, walking with Olivia behind William and me, when I would much rather have had him by my side. My father was silent, slightly stooped, displaying no emotion. Mummy looked haggard, exhausted from the nights of waiting while Granny had been lulled finally to death. To my surprise she wept at the sight of the coffin being lowered into the dark grave.

'In the midst of life we are in death: of whom may we seek for succour, but of thee, O Lord . . .'

I watched numbly then, wondering whether Granny would have been offended that she was being committed to the earth by this rite of the Church of England, but I decided she would have been amused by the irony of it. I found my sadness in our ring of black shoes round the grave, the wind flapping trouser legs and Mr Hughes' alb and rich purple stole, and Mummy having to hold on to her hat, and thinking how small and defenceless we booked standing there beneath the heavy sky.

My tears came later as I walked back between the silent stones and trees of Lodge Hill Cemetery, this time with Angus beside me. Mummy and Daddy walked slightly ahead of us, slowly, as if they had lead ingots strapped to their feet. I felt I ought to go to them, though I knew no comfort would be possible between us.

'I shall miss her so much.'

Angus put his arm strongly round my shoulders. He was wearing a black suit which made him look thin and older. 'Your house will certainly never be the same again. Even though she didn't get out of her room much by the end, it's going to feel very empty.'

'Not as empty as it'll be in a couple of days,' I said forlornly, tears running down my face. 'Oh Angus, I can't bear the thought of you going.'

I was really crying now and he stopped me and took me in his arms and I could feel his heart beating against me. He held me close, his cheek against mine, arms tight around me.

'I'm sorry.' He drew back and looked into my eyes with a troubled expression. 'I wish it didn't have to be now, so soon after this. But you'll be busy too, won't you, and I'll be back on leave like a shot as soon as I get the chance. Katie, you know I love you so much?'

'I know.' Thankfully I laid my head against his shoulder. The suit smelled strange, seldom used, with a whiff of camphor. 'I love you too. And I'm glad you were so fond of Granny as well.' I looked up at him. 'I suppose we all have to do our bit now.'

Angus grinned, suddenly, eyes crinkling at the corners. 'I couldn't help having a little smile to myself when he read that psalm – "I will keep my mouth as with a bridle", or however it goes. I think she would have enjoyed that, don't you?'

I laughed, tears still on my face, and hugged him again. 'Yes, she would, and she wouldn't like to see us being miserable either.'

Olivia approached us, dressed to the hilt as usual. She had on a very stylish black coat and hat and vivid red lipstick. Her cheeks were pink from the cold wind.

'Now now, you two,' she said archly. 'You've only just dispatched your grandmother, Katie. Surely you should save the billing and cooing for later?'

I turned to her, stung by the insensitivity of her remark, but seeing her smile I relented. It was so hard to get cross with Livy. She took my arm and we all walked on together.

'You're off on Thursday then, Angus?' She spoke to him in a caressing way, turning on the charm.

'Yes – basic training. It'll be a good stretch yet before I'm qualified to fly.'

'Have you any idea how much I envy you?'

'Really? Well, I suppose if you're that keen you could join up yourself.'

'Me?' Olivia looked astonished. 'What on earth would they want me for?'

'They need everyone they can get, especially if you've got something to offer. You could go for a clerical job, couldn't you – in one of the women's forces? I should think you're pretty well qualified by now.'

'Angus,' I protested. 'Don't give her ideas, please!'

But Olivia had stopped, excitement lighting her face. 'My goodness, of course! Why didn't I think of it? It's so obvious.'

'Oh, Olivia,' I wailed. 'You can't go away as well. Anyway, I've heard the women's forces are full of rough types who you wouldn't feel comfortable with at all. You know how you like your home comforts, the piano . . .'

'Kate,' Olivia said determinedly. 'I wouldn't care if it were full of the most uncouth Amazons to walk the earth if it means I can get away.' She ran round in front of me and kissed Angus so extravagantly that he blushed.

131

'Thank you, Angus. It's been staring me in the face!'

'Oh well,' I said gloomily. 'With any luck they won't take you.'

We linked arms again. The rest of our small party was standing by the iron gates of the cemetery. I felt a great rush of affection go through me – a sense of the preciousness of people I knew so well when everything around was changing.

'My best friends.' I reached up and kissed each of them and we walked to the gate with our arms round each other's backs. 'At least love is something they can't ration, even if they are taking you away from me.'

I spent the evening before Angus left round at the Harveys'. It was a comforting household with its littered, nestlike clutter of newspapers and periodicals, books and music scores and dogs' baskets. Two black Labradors sprawled snoozily in the hall beside a deflated football, a stack of the family's gas masks in their boxes, a carton full of Meccano and an assortment of old shoes and galoshes. John's clarinet lay askew across a chair. Mary was sitting at the table in the living room in a cone of light surrounded by algebra and *Paradise Lost*. On the mantelpiece a round-faced clock was just visible between John's swimming cups, sheaves of paper and invitations, candlesticks, receipts, ration books and good wishes cards. Mrs Harvey, who resembled Angus facially but was much rounder and had hair several shades lighter, sailed cheerfully through the mayhem apparently oblivious to it.

We all ate together. They were comfortable people. Being with them was like wearing a very old coat, so much so that I realized regretfully that evening how much I had taken them for granted. I had been beguiled by the Kemps for so long. My hatred for Alec Kemp seethed in me now, a revulsion born of former adoration. But it allowed me to appreciate the Harveys at last, and their home which was so familiar, into which I had run freely for so many years and always been made welcome.

Peter Harvey was black-haired, balding, thin. He smoked and smoked cigarettes and his chest sounded as if it was full of dried peas when he coughed. He had gnarled, prematurely arthritic hands which meant that although his firm produced beautiful instruments, he could no longer play them. But he was not downcast. He had a jovial, slightly sardonic way with him. Ruth Harvey was kind and comforting, though often with a rather distracted air, as if any question you asked her cut through a train of thought which brought her back from somewhere quite different and she was uncertain for a second quite where she was.

We didn't talk that evening of Angus going away. We sipped sherry and listened to the seven o'clock wireless broadcast, the nation's ritual. The Red Army had invaded Finland. The Western Front still ended short of France. Every bulletin was listened to with rapt attention and a strong sense of dread.

'Oh dear,' Ruth said as Peter got up to switch off the wireless. 'It's so awful not knowing what's going to happen.'

'Well, let's face it, you never know that at the best of times,' Peter said, clicking the round dial to cut off the radio announcer and picking up his glass again.

'It doesn't seem to matter as much normally, though,' Ruth said. Then she jumped up from her chair. 'Anyway, let's not be miserable on Angus's last night at home. Come on through and eat, everybody.'

We tried to keep the war out of the conversation as Ruth dished up beef casserole and potatoes and home-grown carrots and greens. We talked of the past, of childhood, until we were all laughing and joking. John and Mary both stayed quiet, though they joined in the laughter, Mary watching us all with her heart-shaped face and serious eyes.

After we had talked over coffee and it grew late, they left us alone.

'I know you'll be thinking of Angus and praying for him as much as we shall,' Ruth said to me before she retired.

'Of course.' I smiled at her.

She laid her hands on my shoulders, looking into my eyes, and I saw Angus's eyes in hers. 'It's a great support to us to know that, Katie.'

Peter Harvey gave me a peck on the cheek. 'If we don't see you again before you go back to work, come round when you can, won't you?'

They were as tactful and generous as it was possible to be. If I had stayed there all night with Angus I felt they would have passed no comment. They were open-minded people, and in any case, the war changed so many things.

'Are you scared?'

'Not scared, I don't think. Just nervous. A bit excited in a way.'

We lay side by side on the plump green eiderdown on Angus's bed. His arm was round my shoulders and I rested my head on his chest.

'I hate the idea of you doing something so danger-ous. Couldn't you have chosen something a bit less heroic?'

'Well, that'd make a change for me, wouldn't it?' His tone was ironic, almost bitter.

'What d'you mean?' I half sat up and looked at him. 'I don't understand why you seem to feel – well, whatever it is you do feel – not very able physically, or a coward or something. It's just not true. Is it because of William, because he's always trying to put you down?'

Angus shrugged. 'There are things everyone feels they have to prove, I suppose. I need to be able to know I can do this. It's a challenge. And I've always wanted to learn to fly.'

'Yes, I'd almost forgotten.' I looked round the softly lit room. Like the rest of the house it was cluttered. There were old models, childhood preoccupations: a de Havilland DH–4 bomber, Bristol fighter, planes from the last war settled like moths on Angus's bookshelf, fuselages resting on school exercise books, volumes of poetry, encyclopaedias.

'D'you think Livy will really join up?' I asked him.

'She sounded serious enough.'

'I can't really imagine it. Though God knows, she needs to get away from those two.'

'Is Kemp's going over to the war effort?'

'I imagine so. I'm sure the war will increase dear Alec's sales figures enormously. Couldn't be better for him and his reputation, could it?' I added almost automatically, 'Poor old Livy.'

Angus pulled me closer to him. 'Livy, Livy, Livy. You can't take on her life for her, you know. If anyone's going to rescue her from her stifling parents it's going to have to be herself. After all, she can do a job now and earn her own money. It won't be long before she's twenty-one.'

'I know, but the hold they have on her. They're so over-protective.'

He leaned over and kissed me to stop me talking. His lips tasted faintly of coffee.

'Let's leave Livy out of it for tonight,' he said, looking into my eyes.

Slowly he undid the buttons down the front of my dress, removed my specs and unfastened the front of his shirt, and we lay holding each other, in the shadows from the little bedside lamp, warm skin touching. The house was silent. From the garden we heard an owl.

Angus ran one finger along the strap of my bra. I sat up. 'I'll take it off.' He helped me pull it away, releasing my breasts, full and heavy. I felt the heat of him against my back as he sat up behind me, his hands reaching round to touch and stroke me.

'There's so much of you.'

'You mean you don't get many of those to the pound!'

'No – you're wonderful. Like touching life.'

We seldom allowed ourselves to go this far. Opportunities were few in any case, and it was hard to draw back, not to take it further. He kissed my neck, lowered his hands so they were round my waist.

Holding me, he said, 'Katie, what I'd really like to do now is to ask you to marry me. But it doesn't feel right with the war on and everything feeling so uncertain. So I'm not actually going to ask you, but I wanted you to know that I'd like to.'

I turned my head and pulled him close so our cheeks touched. 'Well, if you had asked me, I'll just tell you that I'd have said yes, but since you haven't, I haven't!'

We laughed, lying down in each other's arms. 'Kate,

I do love you. But I don't want to make you a war widow.'

I felt chilled. 'Don't say that, please.'

Angus pulled me on top of him, his hands stroking my body. 'I love the feel of you. You're so beautiful.'

We kissed each other hungrily and I felt him move under me, his hands pressing into my back.

After a time he said, 'Katie, I'm sorry, you'll have to get off.' He looked at me shyly. 'It's just – if we carry on like this I'll go too far.'

I moved beside him again and he sat up, sighing, running his hands through his dark hair. 'I've been longing to have you – completely – for such a long time.' He looked away from me, embarrassed.

'Darling – ' I sat beside him and kissed his face. 'I want it too.'

'Do you? Don't you think it's wrong – outside marriage and all that?'

'Probably. But that doesn't stop me wanting it.'

Angus laughed delightedly. 'I love the way you're so honest. D'you mean you'd really . . .?'

'Yes. Especially now you're going away. If it wasn't for the war it would be different. Only I'm not sure about in your parents' house.'

'I can't think of anywhere better. Trouble is – I don't have anything in the way of protection. I certainly don't want to go and leave you pregnant.'

Hesitantly, I said, 'It's all right – as long as you don't actually come into me, isn't it?'

I moved my hand down and touched him, hearing him take a sharp intake of breath.

'You don't mind – if I touch you?'

I guided his hand to my body. We unfastened our

137

clothes, timid, then bolder, learning each other, lost in it. We lay together for a long time.

Much later I let myself out into the starry darkness of the January night.

It was a month of partings. William left shortly afterwards for the army. After a restrained farewell to Mummy and Daddy, he kissed me goodbye stiffly, suddenly garbed in adulthood and self-importance in a way that I found mildly ridiculous. He'd grown a little moustache which had gingery lights in it.

'Take care of yourself, Kate.' The whiskers prickled against my face. 'Keep an eye on the parents, won't you?'

'I will,' I promised, absolving him, as required, of any guilt on that front. 'Good luck, William.'

A week or two later Olivia came to see me at the hospital. I'd just knocked off from my shift and had invited another of the nurses to my room for a cup of tea. Brenda Forbes had a room close to mine in the nurses' home and we spent quite a bit of time together. She was a sturdy down-to-earth girl from a family of nine children. Her father owned a hardware shop in Alum Rock on the east side of the city. I found there was no side to Brenda and I enjoyed her sense of humour.

'Been up and down like a fiddler's elbow all afternoon,' she groaned as we walked along the corridor to our rooms. 'My feet are killing me. Don't half stink after work, don't they?'

'Yes – since you put it so delicately, I must say washing my feet is the first thing I want to do after a shift.'

Brenda pulled the starched cap off her long dark hair. 'One of these days I'm going to get myself a glamorous job.'

Laughing together, we burst into my room. And there was Olivia. She sat on my one hard wooden chair, her hat still on, face all made up, her smart suit looking incongruous in my austere little room. I felt strangely deflated at the sight of her.

'Oh,' Brenda said rather curtly. 'You've already got company. I'll see you later then, shall I?'

'No – Brenda, do come in. I'll make us all a cuppa.' I was embarrassed that Brenda should feel she had to leave.

'You're all right,' Brenda said. 'You talk to your friend. I'll get back and sort out my washing. See you later, Katie.'

I was relieved. Trying to juggle Olivia and Brenda together would have been pretty taxing. Olivia's eyes followed Brenda from the room, bemused.

'Gracious,' she said, eyeing me up and down.

I pointed out the landmarks on my apron. 'That's sputum, that one's vomit, and this wet patch, you'll be relieved to know, is only water.'

She took in my sudden tired irritation. 'Sorry, you must be exhausted. And missing dear Angus.' I chose to ignore the arch tone in her voice.

Tears filled my eyes. 'I am. I feel so worried, and I don't even know what there is to worry about yet.' A sense of foreboding that I could barely put into words had weighed me down ever since Angus left. I missed him with an intensity I hadn't expected. Now he was gone I knew just how much I loved him, and that feeling was private and couldn't be shared with anyone else.

Not even Olivia. I had had a note from him, though, saying he was settling in and learning a great deal. Apparently he was in Cornwall.

'Poor Katie,' Olivia said. Carefully she lifted off her bright cherry-coloured hat and laid it on my table. 'Come here – ' She held out her arms to me, then withdrew them again. 'How about taking that apron off?'

I unbuckled my belt and lifted the apron off and then we hugged each other and I felt her soft hair against my cheek. She felt like someone from a different world, beautiful and sweet-smelling: Givenchy perfume, her favourite.

I held her at arm's length, smiling. 'It's lovely to see you.' Then I narrowed my eyes suspiciously. 'What are you doing here?'

'I've got news to tell you. I've got to tell someone or I'll burst.'

I stared at her. 'You haven't?'

Her face broke into a delighted grin. 'I have. I had a letter today.' She held it out for me to read. 'On behalf of the Naval Ministry I should like to invite you . . .'

'I've been accepted by the Wrens!'

'Oh no, Livy – not you as well!' I said without thinking. 'I'm sorry, I suppose I ought to be congratulating you. I'm happy for you if that's what you want. But what on earth have your parents said?'

'They don't know. I'm not going to tell them until the last minute.'

'D'you think that's wise?'

Olivia nodded emphatically. 'Oh yes. They'll be hopping mad when they hear.'

I handed her a cup of tea. 'It's been difficult at home, hasn't it?'

140

'Difficult?' Olivia shrugged as if she couldn't find the words. 'I'll say.'

'I don't understand your parents, I can't pretend I do. I know there must be things you're not telling me and I don't want to pry.'

She didn't meet my eyes. 'It's not your problem. You've made that very clear.'

I was stung both by the injustice of this and the bitterness in her voice, but before I had time to respond she had done one of her quick changes and was on to something else.

'You're nearly done aren't you – qualified, I mean?'

'Yes, in the summer. I can't wait.'

'What will you do?'

'Depends a bit on the war. I want to get out of the hospital. I'll go for the Health Visitor's training if I qualify. There'll be a stint of midwifery first of course. But I'm set on that. "Prevention is better than cure" as they say. And I could do with getting away from all the petty rules in here. Matron saw me with a bit of my hair hanging loose from my cap the other day and I thought she was going to send me to the gallows!'

We sat talking for a long time. I felt like hanging on to her, delaying her leaving because I knew I was unlikely to see her again for a good while.

'It's going to be awful not having you around,' I said. 'You will write to me, won't you?'

'Of course I shall. After all, whether we've got men in our lives or not, we're still best friends, aren't we?'

I reassured her. I knew she felt pushed out because of Angus. 'Of course we are.'

But as she left, I knew, sadly, that there were more and more things in our lives that we were unable to talk about. I couldn't automatically confide everything to her now that Angus was gone. Our lives were increasingly separate and we couldn't hold on to the absolute closeness of childhood.

Chapter 11

'For goodness' sake Katie, find something useful to do,' Mummy said, though in a less acerbic voice than she was capable of. She was almost smiling.

I couldn't settle to anything. I was home after my exams and Angus was about to arrive on leave to 'await further instructions'. Now all I could do was to wait. Restlessly I kept going to the window and pulling back the nets to look out along Chantry Road, willing him to be there against the bright flowers of the gardens.

'There are endless things need doing in the garden,' Mummy went on. 'The lettuces are going to seed already – oh, and my blue dress needs rinsing through. You could peg that out for me.'

Dreamily I stood and washed out the faded blue dress in the scullery's deep white basin, silver bubbles of water tickling up round my hands, my thoughts far away. It seemed so long since I'd seen Angus.

'I've passed!' I had written to him ten days before. 'It seems like a miracle. After all, this has hardly been the ideal time for performing in exams.'

Everything was heaped against us that summer of 1940. The Dutch had fallen, the Belgians capitulated, then Dunkirk and the advance into France. And the Italians took against us as well. The Channel saved us, and all those young men in their tiny planes. But at the time I wrote to Angus in July, the Battle of Britain was still beyond the horizon.

'How small our personal concerns seem in the face of all this. But I miss you so much, my darling. Life here has been very busy, and I'm glad of it. It's in the quiet moments that I long to see you and feel very low at the thought of how little we can be together. Brenda came in and found me actually hopping up and down with excitement when I got your letter about your leave next week! I'm certain she thought I was quite cuckoo. But I can't wait to see you, my love.'

Angus had been moved from Cornwall to Cambridge.

'I never thought I'd end up attending lectures at Clare College,' he'd joked in his first letter from there. 'That's much more William's sort of territory. But at least it's taken some of the mystique out of it for me.'

After wringing out the dress, twisting it round and round into a tight snake, I went into the hot garden and hung it, the thin straight shape of my mother, on to the washing line. Then I tried to turn my attention to the vegetable patch. Mummy, in her gristly way, had dug out, single-handed, another long strip of bedding for vegetables in the place where we all used to play cricket, and radishes were growing roughly where we positioned our homemade crease. Angus, William, Livy ... I had to hold on to each day for what it was. The future was too uncertain and frightening to think about. And what was precious about today was another of Livy's frequent letters, to which I would reply as promptly myself, keeping the threads of our friendship alive. And today – today I was going to see Angus.

For about half an hour I stooped and squatted round

the bed, tugging at groundsel and grass, my summer dress tucked round my legs. I pulled lettuce and carrots for lunch, then sat staring in a dazed way at the rows of spinach and beetroot. I heard the latch on the gate behind me and, turning, was on my feet in an instant and running to him.

'Oh darling, my darling!'

'Katie!'

Laughing, almost crying, I ran to him and we were in each other's arms, pressed close, quiet at first, suddenly shy.

'I've missed you so much,' Angus said after we'd kissed. I touched his face with my fingers, seeing his eyes full of love.

'You've still got your uniform on.'

'I've just walked in. Went up to change and I saw you through the window tinkering with the weeding.'

I laughed. 'My mind wasn't exactly on the job!' I looked at him in silence for a minute, then said seriously, 'It is so wonderful to see you. I love you.'

'And I you. More than ever.'

The week passed with terrible speed. We saw each other so rarely that Angus's leaving again seemed to over-shadow even his arrival home. In many ways it was a blissful week, but for the sense of what was brewing in Europe. And I noticed a strange restlessness in Angus.

I sat beside him one evening in the Harveys' house on their battered, comfortable sofa. Angus had his arm around me and we had been talking softly, but I noticed that he seemed tense. I leaned round, holding his slight body, trying to take in the fact that he was here with me. All that was in focus was the front of his white shirt, the row of translucent pearl buttons. I stroked my hand over his ribs. He felt even thinner than when he'd left.

'What's the matter?'

'It's odd being home.' He sighed. 'All the time I've been away I've been dying to be back here with you. That's the most important thing, seeing you.' I pushed myself up so that I could look into his face. 'It's nothing to do with you,' he assured me. 'It's just so comfortable here. I feel as if I'm being cosseted like a child again when I'm supposed to be out there doing a job.'

'But they're only trying to make you welcome. Give you some home comforts.'

'I know. It's quite unreasonable of me. I feel ... everything's changed. This wretched war has turned us all upside down. But you must know, Katie, nothing could change the way I feel about you.' He leaned towards me for a kiss.

One baking hot afternoon we caught a train to a country station outside Coventry, with our sandwiches and lemonade, fruitcake and apples that Mrs Harvey had packed for us.

'You have a lovely afternoon now,' she'd told us. 'You both deserve it.' Her voice was wistful on our behalf, knowing how rare and brief were our times together.

We walked out into the Warwickshire countryside, finding fields into which it was possible to believe the war had not yet slunk its tentacles. The corn was turning yellow. Bees moved in and out of the poppies and morning glory and a breeze moved the wheat stems.

'It's so beautiful,' I said, stopping, breathing in the smell of the fields, the air free of smoke. 'It's so long since I've been out of Birmingham. You almost forget there is anything else.'

We stood quietly for a few moments looking out over the gold field edged with the trees' black shade and sprinkled with red.

'I do think it's right to fight for it,' Angus said suddenly. 'I've thought a lot about what your father said, before William and I joined up, and I can see he's probably the most, I don't know – saintly of us. But I do feel with every fibre of me that you have to stand up to the likes of Hitler, and I want to be part of defending all that this country stands for against what they're doing.' He spoke with a forced casualness, avoiding sounding pompous as William would have done. I reached out and squeezed his arm.

After a time we came to an oak tree providing a patchy ring of shade between two fields and sat on the soft grass edging the barley. I opened the packet of beef sandwiches. Angus's mood was changeable that afternoon, sometimes joking, the next moment quiet and serious as if preoccupied, and then I could tell his thoughts were elsewhere.

'It was odd travelling up to Cambridge,' he said, pouring lemonade into our two enamel cups. 'Now they've made all the signs so small we couldn't always tell where we were. It's quite a haul from Cornwall too. We thought we must be going to Scotland, but then it all looked too flat!'

'I wonder what they'll do with you next?'

'More training somewhere. Has to be. I'm a way from getting my wings yet.'

'D'you really like flying?'

'Oh yes.' He sat eating with his knees drawn up in

front of him, shirtsleeves rolled up to the elbows. His forearms were tanned under the dark hairs. 'I enjoy it even more than I imagined. I wasn't sure when we started off, of course. All those talks. It was all airframes and aerodynamics and navigation, and the hangars were horribly cold.' He gave me his wide smile. 'But as soon as they started teaching us to fly – oh, it was marvellous. Hard to describe it – it's like another dimension to life. I'll have to take you up for a spin one day, then you'll see what I mean.'

He talked with enthusiasm about all he was learning and the other cadets training with him.

'They're a real mixed bag of course, but we've got used to each other now. We had to pull together against a couple of officers who are right – '

I could tell he was biting back a swear word, another symbol of forces camaraderie.

' – well, tough sorts, let's say.'

I laughed. 'I do have more than the odd patient who curses, you know!'

Angus grinned sheepishly. 'Of course. I'm sorry. I keep talking as if I'm the only one who's doing anything.'

'It's all right.' He'd already asked me about my plans. 'The war hasn't touched us all that much yet, except for there being so many people missing. I sometimes feel so stuck here with you all gone.'

To my annoyance, tears filled my eyes. The past months had been so lonely. I had poured all my energy into work. I didn't want to be blubbing in the few days I had with Angus.

He shifted over to me, pushing aside the packet and cups and apple cores from our picnic. The grass was soft beneath us. Crows called in the branches.

'Here, let me hold you.'

We lay in each other's arms, looking up at the thick, strong branches of the tree, sunlight skewering through into our eyes now and then as the breeze shuffled the leaves.

'I wonder what you make of it all,' I said. The solid girth of the trunk was behind our heads. 'You'll still be here long after it's all over.'

I rested my head on Angus's chest, listening to the sound of his heart, one arm across his body. A daytime moon hung in the sky, remote and white like a slice of pumice.

'How many children shall we have?' I asked playfully, making believe we lived in a wholesome world to which there was no threat.

'Oh, six at least.'

I leaned up on one elbow. 'You are joking?' But he was looking very solemn.

'Katie – ' He hesitated. 'If I wasn't to make it through all of this . . .' I wanted to stop him, not to hear, but I knew I must let him speak. 'We've none of us any idea how it's all going to go, but I want you to know – I love you. Whatever happens, I'll always love you.'

'Oh God,' I said, beginning to cry. 'This is awful. Why did this have to happen? Those damn Germans messing up everyone's lives. Angus, I love you, that's what matters. Wherever you are you know you can always carry that with you.'

He pulled me strongly towards him.

'I love you,' we said again and again between our kisses. 'I love you, I love you.'

Angus pushed himself into a sitting position, his jacket for a cushion, between the roots of the tree. I sat on his lap facing him.

He ran his hands over my shoulders, dark eyes watching my face. 'You're thinner,' he said. 'Heavens, I can feel your bones. Don't disappear, will you?'

I stroked his hair, cropped RAF-style now, smiling at the bristly feel of it. Gently he tugged my thin red blouse out from the band of my skirt and reached round to free my breasts.

'Oh God, I've missed you.' His hands were warm on my skin, holding me close.

'Katie – ' He hesitated. 'I've got some, well – protection this time. We could make love properly. That's if you don't think it's wrong?'

'You've been planning this!' I teased him.

'Not planning. Hoping.'

Without answering him I sat back, and to his surprise, unfastened first my clothes, then his.

'I take it that's a yes.' Again he slid his hands under the red cotton of my blouse. As we touched each other I was aware of the muscular strength of him, the force of another body so close to my own. We were nothing but gentle with each other, but in our excitement I understood how lovemaking could so easily fall over into a fight.

After, we lay close, quiet in the dappled shadow of the tree, our heads on Angus's brown jacket. That day is one of my most precious memories of Angus. The intent, tender expression in his eyes when he moved into me for the first time, the haze of leaves and blue sky behind his head and my hands pressing into the flesh of his back under his shirt. His cry, 'It's lovely – God it's so lovely,' at the height of it. And our 'thank you, thank you' afterwards as our cheeks touched, mine wet with tears.

Lying together, we heard the planes, the sound half

obscured at first by the breeze, then swelling towards us, engines straining across the sky. Angus sat up.

'They are ours?' I asked, only half joking. Without my specs I couldn't even see the planes, let alone their insignia.

'Yes, definitely ours. Off on a practice run, I expect.'

The sight of the planes had pulled his mind back to his training, his job.

'Can't escape it for long, can we?' I said, sitting up. 'Oh, I do wish we could see what's going to happen.'

Seldom has a wish been more ill-guided. In our ignorance of the future that afternoon we sat, peaceful and loving in our barley field between Birmingham and Coventry, cities whose solid, familiar faces would be shattered almost beyond recognition by the approaching storm.

Chapter 12

As we waited through the intense days of the Battle of Britain, Angus was sent to Canada to complete his training in Moose Jaw, Saskatchewan. The inhabitants of Apple Valley en route to Moose Jaw stopped their train and deluged the lads with the red fruit which gave the place its name. Before he left again, Angus gave me a book of poems.

'Some of them are my favourites,' he said. 'I want you to keep this for me.'

The collection was by Gerard Manley Hopkins. I found them hard to understand but for glimpses of beauty in them and my favourite was the simplest: 'Heaven–Haven – A nun takes the veil':

> I have desired to go
>   Where springs not fail,
> To fields where flies no sharp and sided hail
>   And a few lilies blow.
>
> And I have asked to be
>   Where no storms come,
> Where the green swell is in the havens dumb,
>   And out of the swing of the sea.

I kept the poem in my head as a charm, a conjuror of peace, even if there was none in the world.

'Every day I thank God selfishly,' I wrote to him, 'that you have, as yet, no wings on your uniform.'

God was on people's lips more than usual in any case. With autumn came the bombing. At the height of the blitz on Birmingham I went to church with my mother. I had moved to live back at home now my training was complete.

'Lead us, heavenly Father, lead us, o'er the world's tempestuous sea,' we sang. The church was packed and people stood in the aisles. We all needed something to hold on to.

Mummy was tense as a trip-wire. I stood with her one day while she was wrenching the pale flesh from a boiled pig's head for brawn.

'Wouldn't this be a good time for you to go back to nursing?' I ventured. 'They're short-handed everywhere.'

Daddy was working incessantly it seemed. Days, nights, any demand that came he tried to meet, as if he had something to prove.

'How can I?' Mummy said briskly. 'There's the house to run, all the garden – there's so much to do. And no Simmons.' Simmons had volunteered for the ATS.

'But I'm here to help,' I urged her. 'I thought you wanted to do more nursing?'

'What's wanting ever had to do with anything?' she snapped. She handed the bowl of pig's flesh to Mrs Drysdale. 'Here, you could finish this off for me, please.' We went through to the living room. 'She's so wasteful getting the meat off,' she murmured.

Mummy was up to her eyes in make do and mend. There were old cut up shirts and curtains strewn all over the living-room sofa. She held up a length of curtain material in a yellow and white regency stripe.

'I thought this would run to a skirt. Or do you think you'd look too much like a stick of rock in it?'

'No, that would suit me very well.' I smiled cautiously. 'It's just – I've decided to delay my midder training for a few months and work in casualty for a bit. Extra help's needed everywhere.'

Mummy stopped again and looked up at me awkwardly. 'I suppose I could fit in a few hours at a first aid post. It's not as if you and William are holding me back any more.'

'I'm sure they're crying out for you,' I said.

The first bombs had fallen on Birmingham in August 1940. The bombardment crescendoed through that foggy, blacked-out winter, right through until April 1941. So much that we had thought solid and sure, familiar landmarks made of weighty stone, caved in like plywood boxes. The bombs destroyed the Market Hall, smashed to rubble sections of Fort Dunlop, Marshal and Snelgrove's, the Bull Ring, the BSA. People pushed the remains of their belongings from bombed houses to the emergency centres in wheelbarrows and babies' prams. In November, the fires from Coventry's sacrifice bled into the sky.

I worked nights in the casualty centre at the Queen's Hospital in Bath Row. Mummy was doing two-night stints in the first aid post at Moseley Baths.

On one of the heaviest nights of the blitz I set off late for work. Pushing down feverishly on the pedals of my bike I turned into the Moseley Road. There was a light mist which made the going slower with my muffled headlamps. I breathed in mouthfuls of the damp air. Abruptly, the air-raid sirens let out their terrible wail into the night.

'Damn and blast it!' I stopped, my stomach churning with nerves. Gas mask. I couldn't go without it tonight.

I tore back home to fetch it and set off again, balancing the box in my wicker bicycle basket.

I had only gone about a mile when I heard the sound of the first planes. In panic I dismounted, and finding myself against the wall of a churchyard, left the bicycle and ducked down in the graveyard, somewhere I would never normally have gone at night on my own. Squatting, head down, hands against the lichen-covered brick of the wall, I became aware of my quick breathing, the beat of my heart, close and hard, and in the distance the drone of the planes.

They crossed the city, coming in from the east. There was a swell of sound: ack-ack guns, the impact of the bombs, muffled explosions in the distance, then the noise dying. And here was I shouting 'Damn you, damn you!' at the top of my voice, furious at having to squat terrified in my own city while they knocked the stuffing out of it. It was clear they were aiming for the centre, hoping to destroy aeroplane and weapons factories, though in fact the extra 'shadow' factories to fuel the war were built on the edges, so shops and houses took it instead.

I had not long set off again when I heard the next lot. I had suddenly grown wings. I flew down the sweeping slope of Belgrave Road as if I was parachuting and pedalled madly across the Bristol Road towards Five Ways.

What little traffic was on the roads had come to a standstill. I slowed, looking upwards. The searchlights jittered and crossed over us, lighting up the bellies of barrage balloons like bloated silver fish, and now there was extra light from fires. The planes were very close. I was only yards from Bath Row, already off my bike and pushing it, when the first wave of bombs fell. I flung myself against the nearest building, shielding myself behind my bicycle and with my free arm wrapped round my head. The gas mask tipped on to the ground. Our ack-ack guns were going again, hammering into the sky. There was a terrible pause, then the impact. In seconds there were more explosions, close, but not in my street. Panting, I waited for the one that was going to fall on me. There came what seemed hours of sound, the whistle of the bombs, the echoing, shaking impact as they fell, glass shattering and debris falling and the smell of cordite and the air thickened with dust and smoke. But the sound of the impacts grew more muffled. They were moving over. The guns held fire, no doubt predicting the positions of the next wave of planes that I could already hear. I knew this was the moment to move.

I pushed my bike upright. Flames lit the sky from the next street and I could hear fire-engine bells in the distance and shouts from firewatchers high on one of the buildings near by. As the planes roared overhead I dashed towards the entrance to the hospital, thanking heaven I could at last get under cover.

There was an ambulance parked outside. At the Casualty entrance I held the door open for two ambulance volunteers coming out with an empty stretcher.

'Won't be Bournvita and slippers tonight,' one of them said to me cheerfully. 'Not for a good few hours yet, anyway.'

I smiled at him, reassured. My legs were like jelly, but at least I would be inside now. These people had to go out and face it all over again. 'I wish I could get you some.'

'Oh, you'll have enough to do, love.'

But we at least had an illusion of safety here, the generous layers of the hospital stacked above us.

Hurriedly I hung up my coat and pinned on my white cap, feeling at home now, able to be competent. Doctors, already looking exhausted, were scurrying between the new arrivals in the reception area. 'Fractured tibia – needs casting', 'This one – theatre – quickly', 'That one can hang on for a bit'.

Nurses were collecting valuables from the wounded, writing rapid notes on casualty record cards and trying to exude calmness and reassurance. There were already more casualties coming in.

'Where the hell have you been?' one of the other nurses demanded as she rushed past me.

'I got caught out in it.'

She didn't comment further on my lateness. 'At least you can hear ours going out there.'

It was always a great boost to people to be able to hear the ack-ack guns, though we had no idea how accurate they were. Our defence was comforting. We were fighting back. But it was hard, even while rushing to and fro paying attention to the job you were doing, not to strain your ears, constantly wondering what was going on outside, wondering how close they were. Often we felt the vibrations of the bombs' impact.

I was sent to theatre to help prepare trolleys. I recited the items in my mind trying to keep my thoughts away from the bombing, from my parents, both out there working. Saline, hydrogen peroxide, sterilized dressing drum, Cheatle's forceps, tray of instruments, bandages, iodine . . . the reassurance of routine.

I'd no sooner got going on that, though, when Sister hurried over to me. 'Nurse Munro, we need you to come and help with some of the new arrivals . . .' and once I'd got started on that one of the doctors sent me scurrying back and forth for dressings. As I completed this task we heard a loud groan of pain from one of the two men lying to the side of the reception area waiting for further attention.

'Nurse!'

'Go and see,' the doctor ordered me.

A middle-aged man, face a ghastly white, was lying stoically pressing a pad to his wounded head. When I approached him, he said, 'I'm all right love. You see to 'im.'

The sounds of distress were coming from the younger man beside him. He had a padded dressing which had been hastily applied to his left cheek and was already bloodstained. The clothing had been cut from his upper torso, presumably because it was soaked in blood. There was no other apparent injury to his body.

I bent down beside him. 'What's the matter?'

Few of our patients made much of a to-do when they came in. Some, of course, were very frightened or in pain, but many of them were in shock and lay there numbly like sacrificial lambs.

'God,' he groaned. 'I'm in such bloody agony.' He twitched his body angrily from side to side. 'I can't stand it. It was numb to begin with, but now it's getting worse every minute.' He spoke painfully out of the side of his mouth, trying not to move the left side of his face.

'It won't be long,' I assured him. 'A doctor will see to you properly soon. It's busy tonight, I'm afraid.' I felt a bit irritated at the fuss he was making, but at the same time there was something about him which intrigued me. I think it was partly the strength of feeling that came from him, even though it was expressed through frustration, and partly the glimpse I caught of the side of his face not covered by the dressing. I saw the contours of a prominent cheekbone, a strong chin and eyes of the brightest blue I'd ever seen. I found myself staring in fascination.

I thought I'd try and take his mind off the pain. 'My name's Kate,' I said. 'Yours?'

'Douglas Craven,' he grunted, then added ironically, 'Pleased to make your acquaintance.' He spoke very carefully, wincing as he did so.

'It's bad out there tonight, isn't it?'

'Of course it's bad,' he snapped. 'What the hell d'you think?'

'What happened to your face?'

'Don't know exactly. I was on firewatch. There was stuff flying all over the place. Something stabbed right through my cheek – metal. I can feel it's gone into the bone ... Aagh – God!'

He started giving dry, tearless sobs, his lips contorting miserably. He had a little moustache which was clotted with blood so I couldn't see its colour. His hair was blond though, so I assumed the moustache might be. For a moment I took his hand.

'They'll soon look at you. It must be quite awful for you.'

'Damn it!' He writhed beside me. 'This is terrible.'

He communicated the powerful outrage of a fit man who has been struck down and slowed.

A commotion suddenly started up at the entrance, raised voices and more stretchers arriving.

'I'll be back.'

Everyone was talking at once, the ambulance workers, a doctor trying to be heard above everyone else. Then everyone saying 'Ssssh.'

'It's the Carlton Cinema up Sparkhill,' one of the

ambulance workers told us. His eyelashes were white with dust.

'The control centre warned us you were coming,' said a voice. Everyone had fallen silent. 'What's the damage?'

'Direct hit. Straight down in front of the screen.' The man speaking looked really shaken. 'There's God knows how many gone. The blast got their lungs. They were all sat there in the front rows as if they were still watching the film. Never seen anything like it. Eerie as hell. They're taking the rest straight to the General, and Selly Oak, I think.'

I hurried back to Douglas Craven. 'It's going to be very busy.' I told him what had happened.

'Oh damn, damn,' he groaned.

'Whatever's wrong? Was someone you knew at the Carlton?'

'I should have been over there.'

I stared at him in disbelief. 'What are you talking about?'

'I'm a reporter. If I hadn't been on bloody fire-watch I could have been over there – got the first look at it ... And now I'm stuck here with my face in shreds ...'

I knelt down close to him so that no one else could hear, and between clenched teeth I said, 'You stupid, self-pitying sod. You ought to be ashamed of yourself.'

I turned away and busied myself with what I considered to be more deserving patients.

The next day I was ashamed. It was very bad form to talk to any patient like that however much they provoked you. It had been a very hard night and I was exhausted, but I went to enquire with the casualty register.

'Douglas Craven? Looks as if he was admitted for the night.'

The morning, after the all clear, had brought news that the total dead in the Carlton Cinema was nineteen. It was the first thing my mother told me the next morning. I resolved to take this news to Douglas Craven, to show him the consequences of what he had seen as a 'story'. I suppose I felt rather self-righteous, and it didn't occur to me that the reason the city was reeling with the news this morning was that someone like Douglas had done the job of reporting it.

We didn't recognize each other to begin with. They'd cleaned Douglas up so that his hair and moustache were the same colour, and the dressing was neat and not seeping.

Now it was more reposed, his face was even more striking, with its chiselled bone structure and those vivid blue eyes. He was sitting in bed in the pale light of the ward eyeing the morning paper.

'Hello,' I said gruffly.

He looked up, baffled. I didn't have my uniform on.

Speaking rapidly, I said, 'I owe you an apology – for last night. I shouldn't have said what I did. You were in pain and in a state. I'm sorry.'

His blue eyes suddenly showed recognition. 'Kate, isn't it? My Florence Nightingale.' He appeared still to speak with some difficulty.

'Not all nurses are Florence Nightingale,' I pointed out stiffly. 'We're all different. We have personalities of our own actually.'

'Yes, quite. I'm sorry. And thank you for your apology. You're quite right, I was in a state, but nothing to some of them who came in. I'm afraid I was having a bit of a tantrum. Do sit down by the way.'

Reluctantly I perched on the chair by his bed. I wasn't at home as a visitor in a hospital, nor was I sure how I felt about being in his company.

'Surely you should be asleep in bed after last night, not visiting me?'

'I've slept. I'm used to night work. How're you feeling?'

'Oh marvellous. Actually – ' he tried a rueful smile, putting the palm of his hand cautiously against the dressing – 'my face is dreadfully sore and stiff. They managed to yank out a great shard of something.' He spoke in a sardonic tone, but I saw a blush seep across his face. 'I'm afraid I was an awful baby.'

Disarmed, I said, 'That's all right. It's the pain.' I added untruthfully, 'Anyone'd be the same.'

'You're very kind,' he said. 'Do you enjoy being a nurse? Seems a frightful job to me.'

'Oh yes – on the whole.' I told him of my longer-term plans. I found that he asked a great many questions, and that by the time I left I had told him a surprising amount about myself, my work and my family. I supposed he was at ease asking questions. It was his job, after all. His eyes watched me with intent interest. To my surprise I realized I was enjoying the conversation. I found myself telling him I was engaged, which seemed the easiest way of explaining my relationship with Angus.

'Ah,' Douglas said. 'That explains it. Your face has a kind of glow about it.'

I smiled wryly. In fact I was feeling pretty washed out and tired sitting there after a few restless hours of sleep.

'Must be the light of love I can see – lucky fellow.' For a split second as he said these words Douglas appeared vulnerable.

'You don't have anyone?'

He gave an odd laugh, somehow apologetic. 'Me? Good heavens no.'

Unsure what to say next I felt I ought to leave. I stood up, suddenly reluctant to go. As we shook hands I smiled, and Douglas made a rueful attempt to do the same. 'Well, good luck. Don't risk too much for your reporting will you?'

He said goodbye with a strange solemnity. I turned at the door as I left, half pretending I was just glancing round the ward, and saw he was still watching me. I raised my hand in a wave. As I walked downstairs from the ward I mused over the fact that I had told him far more about myself than I had imagined possible, and that about him I knew almost nothing.

Chapter 13

Olivia stopped writing to me in any meaningful way in November 1940. After sending a letter faithfully once or twice a week, she scarcely wrote now from one month to the next, and when she did, it was a note on a single sheet, brief and frothy, as if suddenly for a few seconds she had remembered me. At first I was baffled. She'd been home on leave for a week back in the summer and we'd had a very jolly time together, laughing almost as much as when we were children. It was an escape from the war, looking at the light side of things and finding the jokes.

Livy had looked healthy and full of life, showing off her uniform – 'It's definitely the smartest in the women's services. Not like that awful drab ATS garb!' – playing the piano, and we'd gone out dancing . . . And suddenly this oddness.

'Dearest Katie,' she wrote in December that year,

Guess what – I've been reposted! More responsibility, or so they tell me, though it doesn't feel too arduous as yet. All in all though a new, big adventure.

How are things in grim old Birmingham? Life here is such a lark – as I'm sure I've said. I can't think why I didn't join up at the earliest opportunity! My life before the war seems deathly when I think back on it now. Of course we're working fearfully hard as well, but I

scarcely have a night in, except when we have to –
dreary domestic nights which are a rule of the service.
But at least it's a chance to reset my hair!

I do hope you're not overworking and burning
yourself out with all your duties. Do remember to let
up sometimes won't you?!

Just dashing this off – must finish now. There'll be a
lot of disappointed faces at the dance tonight if I don't
turn up!

All love for now. Olivia.

After several letters like this I felt pretty browned off
with her, and not just because her writing to me was so
rare when I'd been making an effort to write regularly,
but because the tone of them was always similar to this
one. It didn't strike me then that anything was wrong: I
was just irritated by their shallowness. She felt so distant
and it was as if we could no longer communicate about
anything important.

Angus spent the Christmas of 1940 at home.

'Oh, look at you!' I greeted him, fingering the
embroidered wings on his blue uniform. 'A real airman!'

While he was home we announced to our families
that we planned to marry.

'We don't feel we can plan a date,' Angus explained
to his mum and dad. 'Not with things as they are. But
as soon as I know I'm going to be back home . . .'

'I can't pretend I'm surprised,' Ruth Harvey said,
embracing me enthusiastically. 'And I couldn't be more
delighted.'

Christmas slipped by far too quickly. Angus and I
treated ourselves to one night away together, deciding
not to worry what anyone thought. My parents couldn't
bring themselves to comment and Peter Harvey lent us

his car. When we signed ourselves into a small country inn it was as Mr and Mrs Harvey. No doubt couples were doing something similar all over the country.

In the small restaurant we had a magnificent meal considering the time of year and strictures of rationing.

'That's the great thing about being in the country.' I stared in wonder at the pheasant and generous helpings of vegetables on my plate. 'And she said there'd be eggs for breakfast!'

'Didn't you see the chickens out at the back when we arrived?' Angus said, smiling at my enthusiasm. 'That's what you really came for, wasn't it – the food!'

'Don't be silly.' I took his hand across the table. 'But it's all lovely.'

'We don't do badly for food. I think they give the services all the best.'

'Well I'm glad they're looking after you.'

We ordered a half bottle of wine and sat for a long time near the comforting fire in the inglenook, enjoying being with each other. Because my thoughts were often sad and questioning I didn't want to voice them, and I sensed there were a lot of things that Angus was not saying, was keeping at bay. We sat quietly holding hands across the table, and when we did talk it was often about the past because it was safer.

'D'you remember that day when your granny stripped off just as your mum was expecting all those parish bods round?'

I smiled back. That afternoon: Granny's graphic display of her frustrations, Olivia's strange mood – the start of so many more.

'I thought your mother would burst she was so angry.'

'Oh no. That'd be far too self-indulgent. She's prepared to permit herself some emotions, provided they're all brisk, positive ones.'

'You're very hard on her.'

'I've had to live with her. Your mother's so relaxed and warm compared with mine.'

Angus nodded, unable to contradict me. He watched me, head on one side. 'How's Livy getting on?'

'Oh, like a house on fire apparently.' I couldn't help the bitter edge to my voice. 'Taking the Wrens by storm, one long party, all marvellous ...' I spoke mocking the tone of those breezy notes which made me feel so cut off from her in their twittering, persuasive brightness.

'So what's wrong?'

'I don't know who she is any more. As if we can't ever tell each other anything. It used not to be like this.'

'Don't let it upset you.' He squeezed my hands, his own cupped warm and comforting around them. 'Everyone has different ways of getting through all this. Maybe that's hers.'

I was staring down at the cloth. 'It just feels as if I'm losing everyone – the people who really matter, anyway. Still – ' I loosed one hand to take a sip from my glass, looking at the flames through the deep red liquid. 'Mustn't start feeling sorry for myself.'

'Oh, go on – I was rather enjoying it,' Angus teased.

'At least you're here – that's the main thing.'

He shook his head slowly. His hair was so short now, clipped very precisely round his ears. 'I'm not certain for how much longer.' He spoke reluctantly.

'What does that mean?'

He leaned forward and whispered, very close to my ear: 'Strong possibility of an overseas posting coming up.'

'Oh, Angus, no!' I put my glass down, catching the

base on the ashtray. Red wine bled slowly across the white cloth. I sprinkled salt on the stain and it turned a sickly pink. I felt tears rising in me. Angus going away, no home leaves, never seeing him. I cursed myself for being so self-centred.

'Look – we haven't actually heard anything yet.'

I looked across at him in silence. He took my hand and squeezed it. 'Come on, Katie. Let's go up.'

He teased me out of my despondency on the way up the dark staircase, trying to lift me up, sweeping me off my feet.

'I wouldn't have even attempted this a few years ago,' he said, pretending to stagger across the landing. 'You're not quite such a lump nowadays.'

I kicked and protested, and high on the wine we found ourselves tangled, giggling on the bed in our little room. The fire was still alight, and we left the light off and settled in front of it. The playful mood lasted. Together we laid the eiderdown and a scratchy rug on the floor by the grate, then knelt opposite each other.

'The first person to laugh has to forfeit one article of clothing,' I said, immediately erupting into giggles.

'Right,' Angus said. 'That's you for a start. And the second rule is that the other person has to take it off for them.'

We didn't hold back on our laughter, struggling slightly hysterically with buttons and fastenings until Angus said, 'The only thing you've got left now is your specs.'

He lifted them slowly from my face, serious now, his grey eyes close to mine. His excitement was evident and I felt suddenly awed by it, by the responsibility each of us had for the other's happiness.

'I've missed you. I've wanted you so much.'

Our lovemaking that night was the least reserved I ever remember it. A fierce combination of need, fear and passion, not mindful of what was proper or permissible, only what was strong and right. He stayed out of me for a long time, not wanting to give himself up to it too soon, and we knelt together in the firelight, fingers on each other's skin. The tautness of his mood excited me, his eyes closed, breathing me in, touching every part of me.

We lay together, then, on the blanket as the fire faded. I could see only the closest things: Angus's face, his dark hair, chest pink in the light and the shape of my breasts falling heavily to one side as I lay beside him. He ran his hand very softly along my side, again and again, thigh, hips, waist, ribs, following the deep curves. He closed his eyes. Eventually we moved to make ourselves comfortable on the bed, lying tucked tightly together.

I woke later in the night to find him moving beside me, slight shifting movements of his head and limbs too controlled and conscious for sleep.

'Angus?'

Silence at first, then his voice: 'I think I'm going to die.'

Swiftly I turned over. 'Don't. Please don't.' I could see only the faint outline of his face. I held him close to me.

'We don't talk about it – none of us. Best not to. It's not the done thing. You can't function if you think about it, so we joke about collecting scores, flying aces and all that. None of my squadron have seen much in the way of real action of course, but we've heard enough.'

Silently I listened, my arm crooked across his flat

stomach. He spoke quietly into the darkness, in an even voice.

'You can't say the obvious, can't share it. I'm shit scared. I don't want to die. I don't want to leave you, Katie.'

Our arms tightened round each other.

'My darling, I love you,' I told him helplessly. 'I love you so much.' We slept, clinging as if afraid that the other might slip away.

That room has stayed with me always. Waking the next morning: the white bowl and pitcher on the chest of drawers, powder-blue wallpaper with trailing pink roses, the pink eiderdown with satin finish, sun through that window overlooking fields. And the shadows of the place round us the evening before, the firelight: Angus's face.

They embarked from Liverpool in early January 1941, on the *Empress of Australia* for Freetown, Mombasa, the Arabian Sea. At Bombay, the squadrons joined the *Aquitania* with its draft of a thousand service personnel bound for the nutmeg smell of Rangoon. In March the squadrons formed at Kallang Airport to aid the defence of Singapore, with their cumbersome Buffalo fighter planes.

Two days before he left, Angus sent me a postcard.

Thank you for a wonderful leave, my love. Something to carry with me in the darker days ahead.

Guess who I ran into last night – Olivia! At one of the local Naafis. We had quite a jolly time together. Good to see a familiar face in all this. Keep your spirits up, my darling. Thinking of you constantly. Love, Angus.

*

I ran into Elizabeth Kemp, forced the meeting, though I'm sure she would have preferred a pretence of not seeing me. Even her appearance grated on me. It was the spring of 1941, and the air raids were at last beginning to let up, but it had been a hard, heartbreaking winter for so many people. The city was peppered with bomb sites and we were all pale-faced, haggard from nerves and lack of sleep. But there was Elizabeth, sauntering along New Street dressed in what must have been a very expensive navy coat, stylish high-heeled shoes and an extravagant, wide-brimmed hat. So few people looked glamorous in the city. I couldn't help thinking how typical it was of her, this inability to confront even the reality of the war.

'Good morning, Mrs Kemp.' I wouldn't call her Elizabeth. I stood square in front of her in my flat nursing shoes and blue serge coat.

'Oh! Katie!' She recoiled slightly. 'I didn't see you.'

'How odd. I could have sworn you were looking straight at me.' I gave her a broad smile so that she was left unsure whether I was being sarcastic or not. I could feel her thinking what a frump I looked.

'How's Olivia? I don't hear all that much from her.'

Elizabeth's hands fiddled with the clasp of her glossy blue handbag. 'To tell you the truth, neither do we.' She looked down, watching the drab feet passing us. She had aged even since I last saw her. Her face was thinner, more lined. 'I gather she's getting along fine. Well settled in. Doing her bit – you know. To tell you the truth we thought she might soon find she'd had enough, but not a bit of it.' She forced a laugh, still unable to meet my eye.

When she looked up again it was over my shoulder at the grand frontage of the bank behind me. 'And how are you, Kate?'

We exchanged a few more pleasantries. As we said our goodbyes she looked at me directly for the first time, eyes slightly narrowed.

'Was it you that put her up to joining up?'

'Good heavens, no.' I began to turn away. 'Actually, I had the impression that it was your influence. Both of you.'

I didn't see Olivia all that year and only heard from her occasionally. My letter telling her of Angus's departure and our plans to marry provoked a brief note of congratulation. The year sped past. We were all so taken up by the war and all I could do was to hope she was safe. It wasn't until November 1941 that I knew she was home. A freezing, windy day, the breath clouding back from her face as she stood on the step in Chantry Road.

'Olivia?' My face must have shown blankness or astonishment.

'That's not much of a greeting.' She gave me a self-conscious smile. 'Didn't your mother tell you I'd called yesterday?'

She must have forgotten. Typical of her, to have let something so important to me slip her mind. Both my parents were, as usual, busy.

'No. I'm sorry, Livy.' I laughed, suddenly full of delight, and tried to hug her. 'It's so amazingly good to see you – it's been such a long time. Are you on leave?'

'Not exactly,' she said abruptly.

I was full of questions, but Olivia stood stiffly in my embrace, and as she walked in past me I took in her extreme thinness and the exhausted sag of her face. Her black coat made her skin look very white and she coughed as her lungs met the warmer air of the house.

We sat in the living-room drinking tea. Livy toyed with the spoon on her saucer.

'You look terrible. Have you been ill?'

She crossed one bony leg over the other, a tight gesture. 'Yes – a touch of pneumonia.' She spoke lightly. 'The dear old navy took pity on me and sent me home to recuperate for a couple of weeks. I think I was really on the mend by the time I got here, though. Mummy and Daddy have been clucking over me of course, poor darlings.'

'Why poor?' I said tersely. 'It's not them who've been ill.'

'Oh, they seem to be missing me rather a lot. The centre of their lives taken away by the war and all that ... Actually – ' She looked warily at me, then shifted her gaze down to her lap. 'They were asking after you. They wondered if you'd come round some time, just for tea or something. It's been a long time, Katie. It'd be so nice to have you in the house again.'

'You could have let me know you were ill.' My voice softened. 'I'd have come to see you before.'

'Oh – ' she brushed this aside. 'They were told to keep me very quiet and rested. Of course they always follow doctors' orders to the letter. Anyway, darling – tell me what you've been doing, won't you?'

'I'm doing my Health Visitor's training. I've written that to you, if you remember.' Clearly she didn't. I poured more tea, putting plenty of sugar in Olivia's. 'That's since September. Before that I did my midwifery experience.'

Olivia sat watching me, her pinched face arranged in attentive lines. Somehow I felt I was being interviewed.

'I adored doing that. I was very tempted to stay on, but I've been set on doing Health Visiting for so long.'

I had been totally absorbed by my experience of the beginning of life: the extraordinary miracle of it, the price of it. I laughed. 'I think I cried at every birth I attended. The other midwives thought I was completely cuckoo. They kept saying, "You'll soon get hardened to it. Seen one, seen 'em all."'

'How very interesting,' Olivia said brightly. 'I always knew you were a soppy old thing really.'

'The first time I was allowed to deliver one myself, I was so afraid I wouldn't be able to manage it. I laid my hand on the top of its head and guided it as it came out. I thought his mother would crack apart, you know, giving him life – ' I found myself making gestures with my hands, remembering it all. 'And he looked so cross, as if it was all a shock with the light suddenly all round him. I couldn't see a thing, my eyes were so full of tears! Livy – oh, don't!'

I leapt up and went to put my arms round her. 'I'm so sorry. I didn't mean to upset you.'

Her shoulders were shaking, the sobs breaking into coughs. I could tell even through her layers of clothes how little flesh she had now on her bones.

'I'm sorry,' she said in a broken voice. 'I just feel so very low at the moment. The slightest thing makes me go all weepy.'

'Of course. It's always like that after you've had a bad illness. I got carried away, talking like that. I'm so sorry. Poor Livy, you must have been very ill. You feel so thin.'

I sat on the arm of the chair, my arm round her and her head resting just above my waist. Here we were, back to normal, all the awkwardness and brittleness gone in these moments. I could forgive Livy anything. All my feelings of love and protectiveness washed through me. It was a relief to feel warm towards her again.

'I know I've been silly.' She turned to look up at me, brown eyes still full of tears.

'Have you? Why? You didn't write much. I haven't much idea what you've been up to.' I couldn't help the resentment showing a little in my voice.

'It was the freedom – being away . . .' She started crying again in a helpless, broken way which disturbed me.

'Livy, don't. Please don't be so unhappy. You really must rest and get yourself better.'

She didn't speak, but just cried herself out until she sat jerking and gulping like a child, wiping her eyes.

'Have you heard from Angus?' she asked eventually.

'Yes. He's well so far as I know.' I felt close to tears myself. It was so long since I'd seen him and I ached to hold him, to be held, just to feel him near me. 'I gather you met him?'

'I was in London, briefly,' she said flatly. 'He was passing through. It was good to see someone from home.'

'That's what he said. Oh, I so wish it was all over. I just want him back here with me.'

'Will you come – to the house?'

'I've only got tomorrow. Then I'm back at work.'

'Tomorrow then.'

'Katie – how marvellous to see you.' Alec actually kissed my hand when I arrived. He raised his head and looked into my eyes and I felt his charm turned on me fully. Anything that had gone before was apparently to be forgotten. My ungracious meeting with Elizabeth might never have happened. She was once again the smiling hostess, perfect in every detail, each syllable of speech and every gesture exuding the correct measure of friendliness and pleasure in my company.

How I longed to be beguiled again after my long absence. I had seen pictures of Alec, of course, but the grainy quality of newspaper print concealed just how much he had aged. It only added to his looks. The lines round his eyes and mouth gave him a kind of vulnerability. I wanted to admire, to be wooed. But I knew, as he took my hand, that I was keeping myself closed, not letting him in the way I had as a child when I blushed at anything he said.

'It's been so long since we've seen you,' he said smoothly. It was a moment before he let go my hand. 'We mustn't let that happen again.'

They had lit a fire in the drawing room, and the wind moaned outside and buffeted the window. Over the fireplace hung the De Loutherbourg painting of the furnaces of Ironbridge in a thick gold frame. We drank China tea and ate sponge and delicate *langue de chat* biscuits.

'Is business going well?' I asked Alec. I heard an abruptness in my voice. I was determined not to play along with this new situation. He must want something from me.

'Oh, not bad,' he said. 'Not bad at all.' He sat back casually in the cream chair, one leg crossed over the other. His hair was slicked back and his suit perfectly cut. The dainty tea plate and knife rested foolishly on the palm of one hand. 'It wouldn't be right to say the war's done you a favour, would it?' He chuckled uneasily.

'But it has?' I questioned him, not joining with his laughter.

'Well, let's say it hasn't been the end of the world where business is concerned.' He gave me that smile of his, its suddenness designed to dazzle.

Elizabeth leaned forward. 'Alec is thinking of standing as an MP,' she said in her soft, whispery voice. 'Isn't it marvellous? He'll have the backing of so many people. Of course there might be quite a wait, until the end of the war, but I think he'd be absolutely marvellous, don't you?'

I stared incredulously at the two of them. Was there no limit to their self-promotion, their obliviousness to whatever else was going on? Olivia was gazing at the fire, cut off from the conversation, her face so sad that I wanted to go to her and put my arms round her.

'Oh, marvellous,' I said abstractedly to Elizabeth. She saw me watching Olivia and stood up quickly.

'More tea, Katie? Let me give you another drop. It's very good, isn't it? Lapsang souchong.' As she poured from the slim spout, she said, 'Do tell us about your exciting work.' I felt her eyes boring into me as she sat down again.

Briefly I filled them in.

'How very brave of you to work during the raids!' she exclaimed. 'It must have been simply dreadful. We're so proud of both of you – Olivia working so hard in the Wrens as well. It makes me feel quite useless.'

'Oh, I'm sure you could find something to do if you were to look around,' I said unctuously.

'Well – of course Alec wouldn't hear of me working,' she said. 'Would you, darling? Not unless there was some really catastrophic reason.'

I was wondering how much more catastrophic a reason she needed than this war, when she said, 'And of course, Olivia has been so ill, I've been needed here at home. Poor darling. We were really frightened for her at one stage.'

This confused me. Olivia had said she had only been home convalescing for ten days or so. I saw her turn to fix her eyes on her father's.

'It was a bad do she's had, no doubt about that,' Alec said. 'Double pneumonia, the doctor told us. Should have been in hospital really, but we all felt the best place for her was at home. Nowhere like home when you're ill.' He chuckled. 'I bet your patients are keen to see the back of the hospital, aren't they?'

'That rather depends on the state of the homes they have to go back to,' I said. 'Of course you'd understand, with all the interest you've taken in housing, why some of them seem to find the hospital rather restful.'

Alec laughed extra loudly. 'Well, yes – I'd never thought of it like that. We're the lucky ones, of course.'

'And it's been so lovely having Olivia home again, hasn't it darling?' Elizabeth leaned over and stroked Olivia's hair. Livy accepted the caress passively.

'Proper family again.' Alec sliced more cake. 'Come on, Katie, have another go at this. You're looking a bit peaky. Not the girl you used to be.'

Not the fat, ugly one, you mean, I thought bitterly.

'Lovely to be home, isn't it, Olivia?' he went on.

Olivia nodded meekly, fingers crumbling the uneaten cake on her plate.

'Eat up, my lovely. You need some flesh back on those bones. Don't want the Wrens to think we've been starving you, do we?'

'You're going back then?' I asked, surprised. She didn't seem herself at all yet.

'Next week,' she said quietly.

'Are you sure you're well enough? You do seem pretty run-down still.'

'Absolutely,' Olivia said in a tight voice. 'I don't do physical work, you know. I'm a typist. And they need all hands on deck, as they say.'

'You're a secretary, not just a typist,' Elizabeth corrected her. 'And a very good one, I'm sure.' She glanced anxiously at me. 'Do you think she should be going back? You're a nurse – what's your opinion? Of course we'd be much happier if she'd throw in the towel and stay at home.'

Olivia stared at me with unmistakable appeal. There was a desperate look in her eyes.

'I'm sure Olivia knows whether she feels well enough,' I said carefully.

I stayed talking with them for a time, and it was polite if not relaxed. I had hoped for a few words with Olivia alone, but when I stood up ready to leave, Alec followed us out into the hall.

'D'you like these?' he asked, guiding me by the elbow to the wall opposite the stairs, almost as if anxious to delay me. 'Bought them a few weeks ago.'

He was looking up at a set of five prints. I moved closer and stared at them carefully. They were all black and white engravings of the sort you might have come across in an old half-crown gift book. One showed a couple walking through woodland, she with the hem of her high-necked dress brushing the grass, the strings of her bonnet between her fingers; a young man, casually dressed, was leaning protectively towards her, one arm round her shoulders. Underneath, the caption read *Shall we fix the wedding day?*.

Some were scenes of Victorian families with rosy-cheeked children at the fireside: *A romp with the children* and *Love is a mighty power.* There was one slightly bigger than the other four which he had arranged in the middle. It showed a bearded man with an austere expression standing in a dark street lit only by a dim gas lamp. In the background a church spire was just visible. Kneeling at his feet was a young girl, her long hair over her shoulders and her hands outstretched to him, begging for assistance or for money, it was not clear. Much more apparent was the expression of desperation on her face. Underneath the title read, *The Supplicant.*

'Marvellous, aren't they?' Alec said softly. He pointed at *The Supplicant.* 'Especially that one. Don't you agree?'

He was clearly moved by the pictures. There was even a slight break in his voice as he spoke. I turned to look at him carefully. We were standing close together and I couldn't fail to notice the magnetism of the man. I realized suddenly how exhausted he looked, the dark patches under his eyes. He adored Olivia. Her illness had evidently taken a lot from him.

I could find nothing honestly polite to say about the pictures, but he didn't seem to expect a reply. I actually saw tears in his eyes as he stood staring at the engravings. For a second I found myself moved, an instinct to comfort welling in me. Then I wondered if this was not a theatrical ploy, the kind of thing he used to approach other women, luring them to pity.

'I must be off,' I said.

'Of course. Of course. It was good of you to come.' He was flustered, eager to please.

As I left, he and Elizabeth were full of wide smiles and good wishes. Olivia and I finally got away from them, and we held each other out on the cold of the steps. Her arms were almost convulsively tight round me.

'Look – are you really sure you're all right?' I asked. 'You don't look it at all.'

'Perfectly. I'll be better when I'm back to work.' There was an unflinching braveness in her voice.

I could see she wasn't prepared to say any more. I kissed her. 'Keep well, Livy. See you soon. Try and write more often, eh?' I spoke half jokingly and didn't receive any promise in reply.

She stood waving by the door, a tiny wisp of a thing, her belt pulling in all the loose tucks of material at her waist. The sight of her frightened me. I could see she wasn't well, but it was more than that. It was as if something in her had frozen, and she couldn't help it or explain. I wanted to stay, to try and help her.

But she vanished from me again as if swallowed up by the navy and her letters were as sparse and infrequent as ever. It was a long time before I saw her again.

Chapter 14

Birmingham, 1942

I remember that morning in small details: frosted windows between the criss-crossed tape, the slightly knobbly cotton of my old nightie, my blurred impression of the sepia and white wallpaper. It was February, freezing, and I was still in bed, reluctant to face the chill room. I was making the most of the fact that it was Saturday and that I didn't have to go in for lectures: Acts of parliament affecting health and social welfare, hygiene, breastfeeding. I lay half awake, wishing Simmons was still around to come and build a fire in the bedroom, though I was ashamed of this wish. The war gave us a new awareness of the old order of things. Why should Simmons be my lackey?

Then feet hammering urgently up the stairs.

'Kate – come down quickly!' My mother's face was pale and taut.

'What's happened?'

She couldn't face saying any more. My numbness began even then. I put on my dressing gown, fastening the buttons with extreme care, delaying going down. Icy air gusted up the stairs. I could see out to the garden. Dry leaves scratched in over the step and the laurels shuddered in the wind. Only as she saw me did my mother regain the presence of mind to close the front door.

Ruth Harvey stared up at me, her face very still and white. She was holding a creamy sheet of paper.

'No!' I shrieked, as if at a torturer. 'Oh no no no. Please no!' I sank down in the middle of the staircase.

'Kate,' Mummy said sternly. 'Control yourself, for heaven's sake.'

Ruth climbed up and sat on the step beside me, taking me in her arms. When I looked at her face she seemed to have aged and shrunk.

'It says he's missing.' She held out the telegram to me. 'There may be hope. It could just be . . .'

'What?' I couldn't think at all, or make sense of anything.

'Perhaps he landed somewhere – or parachuted, and they haven't found him yet. We can make inquiries. There's a special section of the Red Cross . . .'

I only half heard what she said, but I knew then already like a doom drum beating in my mind and I could only think, Angus is dead, Angus is dead. Ruth Harvey had shiny black buttons on her cardigan and leaves stuck to her shoes. My mother stood very still, hand on the banisters, looking up at us.

'Katie?' Ruth gripped my shoulders powerfully with her arm. 'We've got to be strong – for him. We can't give up hope. He could be making contact with them even now.'

I thought Ruth was not a woman to spin me false optimism. I turned and looked up into her eyes. 'D'you really think so?'

'I have to. I can't do anything else for now.' Only then did she begin to sob, her body jerking, though no tears fell from her eyes. Her mouth pulled to one side. 'Oh my God,' she whispered. 'I can't bear it.'

I put my arms round her, noticing how much grey

183

there was among her brown hairs. My mother disappeared along the hall to the kitchen and I heard her rattling cups and saucers.

We drank our cups of tea almost in silence before Ruth left, folding her arms tightly across her chest. I saw her rally herself.

'I'll go and take this off,' she said, touching the black cardigan. 'It seems to indicate a lack of faith, doesn't it?'

If it had not been for Ruth and Peter Harvey I would have despaired during those months. There was no one else I could turn to. We all tried to get on with the business of our lives as the war reached its gloomiest. The fall of Singapore to the Japanese, the Battle of the Atlantic, people demonstrating on the streets for a second front to be opened in Europe. The Harveys spent months in correspondence with the Red Cross Wounded and Missing Relatives Department.

'I just feel sure there must be hope,' Ruth said to me one day after another ICRC missive had arrived saying that they had so far drawn a blank but would try to pursue inquiries further. 'He could be in hospital. Or lost in the countryside. If your plane lands in the middle of nowhere, how are you supposed to find your way out? It could be months, couldn't it?' Her voice rose high, full of tears. Peter came and put his arm round her, his gnarled hand stroking her shoulder. He had lost weight since the news about Angus, and his cheeks were gaunt, showing deeper shadows. He had not been a fleshy man before.

'All we can do is hope and pray,' he said. 'If Angus is alive, we know we'll hear eventually. Of course we will.'

'Suppose he's lost his memory or something like

that?' Ruth said wildly. 'I keep picturing the most dreadful things.' She put her hands over her face. Peter guided her to a seat.

I was prepared for the worst. Though I couldn't help a rush of hope at the infrequent communications from the Red Cross, I forced the feelings away each time their searches yielded nothing. Angus was dead. I could sense it. A terrible knowledge like a light going out somewhere across the world that I couldn't see, yet sensed it growing darker. I didn't voice this to the Harveys, but I could at least share other feelings about Angus with them. We remembered him together.

Confiding feelings was something I had given up trying to do with my parents. Even when I made the mildest attempts to open up to my mother, everything, down to the sharp, defensive angles of her elbows conveyed to me that she did not want to listen. Could not endure it.

One weekend during that summer, just before I started my first post as Health Visitor, I was working out in the garden. It was a humid morning. My hands were clammy. And it was sunny, poignant in the illusion of tranquillity. The hearts of the lettuces were washed in dew, and we had good crops of spinach, carrots, beetroot and onions. At one end my mother had set up bean-sticks and the plants snaked up them, mingled at one end with the bright tendrils of flowering sweet peas, her favourites. I stood looking at them, at the pinks, mauves and whites, which had always represented summer and friendship and a kind of innocence. I had not cried much over Angus. The feelings crouched inside, hurting me. I bent over and began to weed for victory between the carrots and onions.

My mother came out with a basket of handwashing

for the line. We were silent together among the buzzing insects. Then I realized she was standing at the edge of the vegetable patch next to me. She must have sensed I was close to tears.

She cleared her throat, awkwardly. 'It's been a great help having you back at home.'

I straightened up and looked at her. In the bright sunlight her sharp-featured face looked weary and lined. Her hair was still long and pinned up carelessly behind so that bits of it were always coming loose. Seeing the pain in my eyes, her face crumpled suddenly and she burst into tears.

'Mummy – what's the matter?' I stepped across the onions to stand on the grass beside her. I didn't know what to do with my hands and wished it could have felt natural to embrace her.

'I'm sorry,' she said. 'I just don't know how to be of comfort to you.' She couldn't meet my eyes. She looked down at the ground. 'I know how unhappy you are – and Ruth. I just ...' She paused with a helpless shrug. 'In some ways it would be better if you and Angus had never got so ... closely involved. Then you could just get on with your life.' She shook her head. 'I'm sorry. I shouldn't be talking like this. Not now.' Pulling a hanky from her sleeve she blew her nose on it resolutely. 'Oh, this dreadful war!' She picked up the wicker basket and quickly crossed the lawn to the house.

Watching her go, I felt a heaving sensation from inside me and thought for a moment I was going to be sick. But then instead, the tears came. I sat down on the grass, head on my knees, and cried and cried. Then I dried my tears alone.

*

'Here – you gas or 'lectric?'

'Come to read the meter, 'ave yer?'

Two scruffy boys dashed sniggering away from me down the entry into number eight court Stanley Street, their bare legs splashed with muddy water from the recent rain. Wearily I pushed my bicycle along the wet blue bricks of the entry and propped it against the wall near the yard tap, opposite the back houses. There were children playing round the gas lamp in the middle of the yard, and a woman stood mangling her washing.

She eyed me up, throwing the garment she had been about to mangle back into the maiding tub. 'They won't 'alf be glad to see you!' she called out to me, disappearing into one of the houses.

It was September, and early days in my job as a Health Visitor. It had not been a good morning. I'd already found one baby with chronic diarrhoea. Her mother was feeding her condensed milk from an old Daddy's Sauce bottle with a couple of inches of decayed rubber tubing. Another woman had called me an 'interfering cow' when I suggested she might spoil her baby when feeding it whenever it demanded and carrying it round all over the place. A feed every four hours, we were taught, and not too much cuddling and stimulation. 'I didn't ask you to come forcing your ideas on me, did I?' the woman said aggressively. The Welfare. Snoopers. That's how we were seen, though not many came out with it as bluntly as that. The majority listened politely and probably ignored a large percentage of what I said. Sometimes I looked back with longing for the hospital and its controlled environment.

Still, Mrs Callaghan, the young mother I had come to visit, was gentle enough and had a thriving week-old baby. I was just gathering up my bag with the leaflets on breastfeeding and brushing down my blue serge skirt when a voice behind me shrieked, 'Thank God you're 'ere – come on, quick, or we'll be too late!'

A young woman in a worn grey dress, with sandy-coloured hair, was hopping agitatedly from foot to foot, her pasty face taut with anxiety. 'Hurry up – Margaret's up there on 'er own with 'er.'

'You mean . . .? But I'm not the midwife.'

'I know you're not the flaming midwife. We can't find 'er anywhere. The babby's come on fast and the doctor's not 'ere yet neither.'

She made as if to take hold of my arm, but I said, 'All right, I'm coming,' and we hurried across the wet yard. As we passed through the front door, though it was much like any of the other houses, I had a strong sense of having been here before. In the gloomy downstairs room an elderly man was sitting smoking, stretched out in an armchair in a stained singlet and trousers with the fly unbuttoned. At the tinny fender sat a young boy intent on a comic, and two other tiny children cruised round what remained of the floor space. In those few seconds passing through the room, I took in that the dark shape taking up most of the centre of the room was a coffin.

God Almighty, I thought. But I was on the stairs with my heart thumping. Let this one be normal, please, I prayed as we clattered up the bare treads. And let the doctor get here soon.

'About time,' said a voice from the top of the stairs. 'Thought I'd 'ave to deliver it meself.'

A hefty middle-aged woman with a black plait coiled above each ear and a round fleshy face ushered us into the room. Our feet crackled on the floor which was strewn with newspaper. There was a pungent smell of sweat in the room.

'I'm Margaret and this is Sandy,' the older woman said. 'We're neighbours of 'ers.' She seemed very capable and had evidently helped organize the room. 'I've 'ad a good few meself,' she went on. 'But I draw the line at delivering 'em. Still – got the place sorted out too. Not too bright about keeping house this one.'

I took off my hat, glancing round. There were two narrow beds in the room. Clothes were hanging from oddly distributed hooks round the walls.

'I'll need to wash my hands.' I glanced at the silent woman on the bed. She hadn't even bothered to look round when I came in. She was lying curled on her left side, covered only by a stained sheet. Apart from one hard chair the beds were the only furniture in the room. 'Is she all right?'

'She's grand,' Margaret said. ''Ere you are – ' She presented me with piping hot water in a bucket. As I hurriedly covered my hands with the carbolic soap and rinsed them off, the woman on the bed gave a low moan.

'Awright,' Margaret said, going to her. 'Not long now.' I realized the sweaty smell came from under the arms of the tight, crimson dress she was wearing. 'Don't fret, bab.'

Tied to the end of the bed was an old strip of towelling. The woman's hands tightened on it, her whole body tensing as she panted through the pains, the veins standing out on her neck. She was a strong-looking woman, about my own age I realized, with straight brown hair.

'You're going to be absolutely fine,' I said in my

189

firmest nurse's voice, hoping to God it was true. The woman didn't reply except with a long sigh as the pain subsided, her eyes closed.

'You're getting close, aren't you?' I said.

She opened her eyes and nodded. Then her face contorted. 'Oh, not again.'

She showed the immense control that I'd seen in so many women giving birth at home, their children waiting downstairs, even though she was obviously in agony. She pulled herself up on to her knees. At the height of the pain she pushed her head into the pillow and groaned into it before lying still again.

'Least it's quiet out now,' Margaret remarked, jerking a thumb towards the window. 'We 'ad one or two come on in the bombing and oh my, what a to-do. Cissy Taylor's babby arrived in the shelter.'

'I've got scissors,' I interrupted as the contractions began again. They were very close together. Sandy was kneeling by the bed saying, 'It's all right, Lisa – you're nearly there.'

'Have you any string?'

Margaret calmly held up a twist of white twine. 'We're all prepared. All we need now's the babby.'

The woman suddenly hauled herself up from the bed on to her knees, her teeth clenched.

'Oh, lor' – 'ere we go,' Margaret said. I found her stolid calmness reassuring. 'Here, Sandy – cop 'old of 'er other arm. We can 'old her up between the pair of us.'

Once the baby started to come down it was very quick.

'It's 'er fourth,' Sandy said. 'So she ain't no beginner.'

As the two women held her in a half-sitting position, her knees up, I guided the baby's head out. I saw the strength of her body, the self-control, even in that crisis,

190

of not crying out. The little sticky body slithered into my hands. I looked up at her mother who shimmered in front of me through my tears. She craned her head up to see.

'You've got a little girl,' I told her as the child roared in healthy protest between my hands.

'Oh, a little girl – at last!' Weakly she sank back on to the pillow.

'Eh – ' Sandy was at the window. 'Looks as if the doctor's got 'isself 'ere at last.'

I had wrapped the baby in a strip of sheet, and was tying off the umbilical cord as the footsteps grew louder up the stairs. Seconds later I found myself face to face with my father.

'Katie!' he exclaimed. 'What are you doing here?'

Margaret and Sandy stared from one to the other of us, bewildered.

'Delivering a baby,' I said briskly.

He watched as I deftly knotted the string tight round the quivering cord and cut the child's lifeline from her mother.

'Placenta?'

'Not yet.'

As she began to moan a little, I went and massaged her stomach. Minutes later the birth was complete, and Margaret and Sandy washed her down and covered her up again. As they tended to her I noticed that the soles of her feet were black with grime.

She saw the direction of my gaze. 'I went down to the shops just before,' she said apologetically. 'That's what must've set it off.'

'Tea,' Margaret said. 'That's what we all need. You got time for one, doctor? Even if it was your daughter done all the work.'

'Nothing I'd like better,' Daddy said courteously.

Stately, Margaret clumped off downstairs.

I looked round shyly at Daddy, who was watching the new mother suckle her baby.

'A miracle every time, isn't it?' he said quietly to me. And to the baby's mother: 'She's a fine child. Another, I should say.'

She smiled, her face softer now. I knew there was something familiar about her, as I had about the house when we first arrived.

'I'm sorry,' I said. 'In the heat of the moment I didn't think to ask your name.'

'You don't remember each other, do you?' Daddy said. 'Katie, this is Lisa Turnbull, now she's married. She was Lisa Blakeley before. D'you not recall taking her little brother Sid home with us for a few days once?'

Sid Blakeley, the grimy baby I had ridden home with in the car that day. And Lisa, his skinny sister whose father had 'buggered off'.

'I knew there was something I recognized as soon as I walked into the house,' I said. 'Now I look at you I can see ...' She was much more robust-looking now, and her hair had grown thicker, but I could remember her in the pale grey eyes and high cheekbones.

'You've changed a bit, too,' she said, her eyes leaving the baby's face for a second. She smiled again. 'Your dad's been ever so good to us over the years.'

There was a sudden bustling around us as Margaret arrived, panting from the stairs and making a great to-do with cups of tea for us all, milky and loaded with what must have been most of their sugar ration for the week.

'You're out of stera so I got Agnes to borrow us

192

some,' she remarked. 'And Lisa, you ought to apologize for the coffin downstairs. It ain't nice with people coming in.'

'Oh, sorry.' Lisa looked at my father. 'Auntie Glad. Dr Williamson came out to 'er, more's the pity. Funeral's tomorrow.'

'No need to apologize at all,' Daddy said. 'Now, may I give the child a quick look over before you bath her? And then I must be on my way.'

I watched him handle the tiny baby, her limbs still clenched tight, feeling her soft fontanelle, checking her hips and eyes.

'I've got a scale with me today,' I remembered, pulling the spring balance out of my bag.

The baby squalled resentfully as we popped her into the weighing sack and she hung dangling as if from a stork's bill.

'Six pounds four,' I said to Lisa. 'She's a good weight. And you're going to carry on breastfeeding?'

She nodded. 'Oh yes – can't be doing with bottles and all that.'

'Much the best thing.' I closed up my bag. 'Much less chance of her picking up germs.'

'The Health Visitor approves,' Daddy joked.

'What're you going to call 'er then?' Sandy had evidently been bursting to ask.

'Daisy,' Lisa said. 'After my mom.'

My father and I said our goodbyes. 'I'll see you in a few days after the midwife's been in,' I told her.

Downstairs, Sid was sitting looking blankly out of the window, absently tapping one foot on the coffin lid.

'Stop that.' The older man cuffed him. ''Ave a bit of respect.' Neither of them seemed to have taken in the arrival of Daisy upstairs.

Daddy stood with me in the shadowy light outside. The sun had sunk behind the houses. Lines of washing were draped across the court, blocking the light even further and giving off a faint whiff of Hudson's soap. More pungently I could smell the drains.

'What happened to Lisa's mother?' I asked.

'She died. Never came out of hospital after that time we had Sid. Puerperal infection. One of the worst I've seen. Sadly we lost the baby too. Lisa's relied on neighbours all her life really, and they've been marvellous to her. And that uncle of hers – the old fellow. He's a man of few words but he's kept up the rent for her until she could manage it herself.'

'Was that his wife – in the coffin?'

'No, his sister. She's been living with them for the past year or so. She had a bad chest. Lisa looked after her – she's got a kind heart. She'd look after anyone, I think.'

We stood in silence for a few seconds.

'Well, I'd better pop into Mrs Callaghan,' I said.

Daddy started feeling in his jacket pockets as he did sometimes when he had something on his mind. 'You did very well today, Katie,' he told me awkwardly. 'I was proud of you. You'll be a very good addition to the team in this area.' He paused. 'You're looking very peaky. You won't overdo it will you?'

It was only later, when I was alone in my bedroom and found tears running down my cheeks, that I realized fully how much his words had meant to me.

Chapter 15

Daisy Turnbull was asleep, tucked in a deep drawer, taking quick, snuffly breaths.

'She's beautiful,' I told Lisa. She was sitting, dressed, but still wearing a pair of ancient slippers, a cigarette in one hand. The coffin was gone and the table now occupied the centre of the room. 'Feeding all right, is she?'

'Oh yes – loves 'er food. Can't get enough of me. Bit of a nuisance at times, of course, but it keeps 'em quiet, don't it?'

'You are sticking to the four-hourly feeds though? You know that's considered best for the child?'

Lisa cocked her head to one side so that her hair tumbled over one shoulder of her milk-stained blouse. 'You aren't married, are you? No kids?'

'No, of course not.'

'That's the trouble with you people, if you don't mind my saying so. You're full of instructions about what to do when you ain't had a go at it yourself. All this about doing it by the clock – for a start I ain't got a clock. It's broke. And even if I 'ad, if my babby starts screaming, it's not a clock I need to tell me to see to 'er, is it?'

'But we're trying to introduce the baby to regular habits – see her in good stead for the future...'

Lisa made a dismissive sound. 'She'll grow out of this. Then she'll be eating what there is, regular with the rest of us. Won't be any choice about that. The way I look at it, Miss Munro, this is 'er one chance in life to get as much grub into 'er as 'er wants. Won't be like that for long, will it?'

I could see I was on a losing wicket with Lisa. I may have been fresh out of training with all the ideals and regimens of Truby King fresh in my mind, but in the end I couldn't force anyone. I had more luck with my middle-class ladies who'd read the childcare books and took it all very seriously, but then some of them got rather over-concerned and nervy about it all.

'Cuppa tea?' Lisa asked, jumping up. 'While I've still got my 'ands free?' I was warmed by her hospitable ways, the enthusiasm with which she had greeted me when I arrived. My delivering her baby had formed a bond between us.

'That would be lovely. I've got a few minutes to spare,' I said. 'And I missed my morning break today.'

Several mornings of the week we Health Visitors made our way into the middle of town to attend to our patient records which were housed in the majestic Town Hall. As often as not we'd stay on for coffee and cakes afterwards, but I hadn't been this morning.

Lisa shuffled round in her slippers on the grimy brick floor, then planted her round behind on the chair across the table from me, much as we had sat when we first met as children. She stirred her tea and looked anxiously round the room. There were unwashed plates and cutlery on the table, a pile of dirty washing in one corner and a bucket of nappies with a stick poking out from it. On the range stood two badly stained pans.

'Sorry the place is in such a mess,' she said. 'Usually is, I'm afraid.'

As she took a sip of tea a high mewling sound came

from the drawer. Lisa rolled her eyes towards the ceiling. 'Wouldn't you know it?'

'What a plaintive noise.'

'Just like a little cat, int she?' She picked up the baby, whose face wore an expression of outrage, and lifted the edge of her blouse just enough to attach the baby to her swollen breast. The child's body was so small she could cradle it on one arm. She drank, making tiny squeaking noises. Lisa was one of those mothers who made me feel redundant. Despite the chaotic look to her house she exuded an air of competence. Nothing I might say would make much difference to her. I watched her with admiration, sipping her tea with one hand, cigarette burning on a saucer, the baby balanced on the other arm and a patch of damp darkening the material of her blouse over her other breast. There was something comforting about her.

'Where are your other three?' I asked.

'Two. Asleep.'

'But that woman – Sandy – said Daisy was your fourth.'

'We lost the first one.' Her voice was clipped 'Still-born. 'E were a lad and all. Terrible it was. Don took it even worse than me. 'E cried. Never seen 'im cry other than that.'

'I'm sorry, Lisa.' I hesitated. 'Where is Don – the army?'

'Yes, with the Warwicks. God alone knows where. I've 'eard from 'im of course but I 'aven't seen 'im for months. She – ' she jerked her head towards Daisy – 'she was the last time. 'E'll be like a kid when I've writ 'im about 'er. Always wanted a little girl.' She smiled directly at me, and I was startled by the transformation of her face. She had widely spaced front teeth, and her

197

large mouth dominated her face. The pale eyes were full of life. I warmed to her further, to that smile. It lifted me and I smiled back.

'You got a fella?' She lifted Daisy and transferred her to her other breast, stroking her little head.

'I don't ... know,' I said hesitantly. I never usually discussed my private life when I was working and few people would have been bold enough to ask. But Lisa was different. 'I think he's dead.'

The smile dropped from her lips. 'Oh, Kate – you poor thing.'

Her calling me by my name like that, like a friend, brought tears to my eyes. I cried so easily at that time.

'We had a letter saying he was missing. He's – he was – in the RAF. His parents have been in touch with the Red Cross for months, of course. We heard nothing for ages. But I've been sure, well, almost sure, that he's dead. I could feel it. Last week they had some more information. He was almost certainly shot down over the sea. They won't be able to recover his body.'

'But was it 'im? Are they sure?'

'No one's entirely sure. It seems it's the only thing that could have happened. But his parents can't accept it – especially his mother. They don't know whether to hold a service for him or to carry on hoping he might be alive. They've aged twenty years, both of them.' Tears ran down my face which I wiped away hastily. 'If we had his body we could mourn him properly.'

Lisa watched me in silence, her eyes sad.

'I'm sorry,' I said, blowing my nose. 'I shouldn't be doing this. Very unprofessional. I'm supposed to be here to help you, not carry on like this.'

'It doesn't matter,' Lisa replied straightforwardly. 'I don't think I need any 'elp really.'

I smiled, still sniffing. Daisy looked the picture of contentment. 'No, you don't, do you?' Pushing my unneeded leaflets back into my capacious blue bag, I went to the door. 'I'll come back and see you, though. Find out how you're both doing.'

'Come whenever you like,' Lisa said, standing up to open the door. I gestured at her to sit down again. 'Any time you want a natter, Kate. I'll be glad to see you. I like a bit of company. And we go back a long way don't we – sort of?'

In the spring of 1943 Mummy ran into the mother of one of my old school friends, Marjorie Mantel, which of course set them exchanging news about their daughters. Marjorie was soon expected home on leave from the WAAF. A fortnight later I got back from work one evening to find a note waiting for me.

> Home for a spot of leave and Roly too, so we're planning to hold a hop next weekend and would be chuffed if you could make it. It'll be a kind of reunion! A song and dance to cheer the Home Front troops! It'd be marvellous to see you. Do bring a friend if you can. Hope you can make it. RSVP, Marjorie Mantel.

I hadn't seen her in years and only dimly remembered that she had a brother called Roland. Marjorie was always rather 'jolly hockey sticks' when we were at school, and I was intrigued by the thought of seeing her. I found myself smiling, missing Livy. The old Livy. We would have laughed together about this invitation.

It was such a long time since Livy and I had met, let alone laughed together. Once again she had been reposted, and I wasn't sure where. I wrote several times asking if she was recovered, was anything wrong? She assured me in a tight sort of way that she was better. But there was another change in the letters: they were no longer bright and over-excited; they were determinedly factual, flat – actually dull – something which would have been unheard of before. But I kept writing. When the war's over, I thought, we'll sort this out. We'll talk properly and everything will be all right.

I took Brenda Forbes along to Marjorie's with me.

'Hello,' Marjorie brayed, swinging her front door wide open to the dark evening. 'Kate Munro – how absolutely marvellous to see you! It must be how long? And who's this?'

I introduced Brenda '. . . we did our nursing together.' Brenda said a curt 'Evening', in her rather graceless way.

Marjorie had grown from a buxom girl into a sizeable woman. She had a wide face with a large, beak-like nose and very thick dark eyebrows, and her black hair was curled and piled round her head. She wore a bright pink dress and a leafy brooch which put me in mind of a Christmas decoration. Brenda, who was short and stocky, was dwarfed by her.

'Nursing!' Marjorie boomed at me. 'How heroic. I simply couldn't do it.' An elderly black Labrador stood panting at us. 'Don't mind Wally,' she went on distractedly. 'He wouldn't dream of hurting you, would you darling?' As she patted his gaunt head the doorbell rang again. 'Oh – someone else! No rest for the wicked. Do dispose of coats . . .' She shimmered towards the front door again.

Brenda shot me a look of amazement.

'She's very good-hearted,' I reassured her.

The Mantels had a very large drawing-room at the front of the house with a smooth olive-green carpet and green curtains to match covering the blackout blinds.

The chairs had been pulled back round the edges of the long room and a row of tall red candles were burning in front of a huge gilt-edged mirror above the fireplace. The effect was a blaze of warm light adding to the more discreet table lights arranged round the room on the piano, a sofa table, a chest of drawers.

'I expect she hoped you'd bring a bloke,' Brenda said in a low voice, 'since they're probably in short supply. I expect you'll find half your school here.'

'God forbid,' I murmured. 'I must say I did get the impression we were asked to make up numbers...'

We must have been almost the last to arrive. The room was well filled by a throng of people all talking loudly, and it felt very warm. A shout of laughter met us from one corner as we walked in. There were plenty of men there, too – a few in uniform, most not.

'Yanks, a lot of them,' Brenda observed. 'Seem to look bigger than our lot, don't they?' Brenda, who wasn't much interested in men, often talked about them as if they were some queer breed of squirrel.

The two of us stood looking round the room, at a loss.

One man – small, English – peeled away from the crowd. 'Hello, you look lost,' he said amiably. He had a thatch of dark hair like Marjorie's and a chubby pink face. 'I'm Roly, Marjorie's brother. Come and have some punch? It's fearfully good. Made by her own fair hands. In fact there's homemade wine, too. We're disreputable soaks in the Mantel family, I'm afraid. Make it out of anything that's going. This is a brew from back in '38. Those fair, halcyon days...'

For a moment I thought he was going to break into poetry. More usefully he poured us some of the fruit cup.

'The fruit's a bit limited, of course. Nearly all apples and pears from the garden.'

'It's very nice,' I said politely. 'Marjorie said you're both home on leave?'

'Yes, bang on. I'm army and she's a WAAF. Marvellous spot of luck being able to take leave at the same time. Not often we coincide. I'm due to be posted soon, so I'm making the most of home.'

Looking at Roly's face, I realized he was much younger than he seemed. His manner was already so middle-aged.

'I say – it's Katie, isn't it? Kate Munro?'

A face swam towards me which I recognized instantly. The sight of her brought back the classrooms, the very smell of school.

'Celia Oakley!'

As I stood reminiscing with Celia, Marjorie appeared and pounced on Brenda, saying there was someone she 'must meet'.

'And what's happened to Olivia Kemp?' Celia wanted to know. She had a very pale face and almost white blond hair and lashes. 'You were always such friends. I found her a bit, well, odd myself. Rather stand-offish. I always presumed it was because she got fed up with people carrying on about her father. It surprised us all when you two teamed up.'

'Livy's in the Wrens,' I said. Celia made impressed sounds. 'I haven't seen much of her, of course, though she was home for a stint of sick leave – ages ago now – end of '41 it must have been. Went down with pneumonia. I think she's quite taken to service life apart from that.'

'She always did look delicate,' Celia said. 'Though as I say, I didn't have a great deal to do with her. Kept out of her way really.'

'Now everyone!' Marjorie hooted suddenly in her huge voice. 'Shall we have some music? Does anyone fancy a dance?'

'Let's have a singsong,' someone called out. 'Cheer us all up. And then we can carry on drinking!'

There was a flutter of agreement round the room. 'Come on, Marj – play us a song!'

'She's very staunch, isn't she?' Celia said, mouth near my ear. 'You know the other brother's missing?'

'I had no idea.'

'Oh yes – air force. They're all worried stiff, poor things. But Marjorie's got such guts – look at her. You'd never guess.'

Marjorie advanced on the piano, looking serene.

As people began to move towards the edge of the room to claim chairs, I suddenly saw someone sitting in the corner next to the mantelpiece, who had been hidden before by all the chattering bodies. I squinted, pushing my specs further up my nose to see more clearly.

'Excuse me,' I said distractedly to Celia.

As I walked across he looked up at me. That face with the prominent cheekbones, vivid eyes, a scar worming down his left cheek.

'Douglas Craven?'

He frowned, taking his cigarette from his mouth. 'Yes, officer?' Looking at me more closely, his face broke into a smile which seemed to take it by surprise, pulling the pink scar tissue tight across his cheek.

'Florence?' he called out loudly. Marjorie had started playing 'Hands, knees and Boomps-a-Daisy' with heavy-handed enthusiasm, and a group were bottom-bumping in the middle of the room.

'Kate,' I corrected him. 'Florence Nightingale is dead. As is Queen Victoria.' Already, before we'd exchanged more than a few words, I felt the same combination of prickliness and attraction towards him that I had when we first met.

He smiled cautiously. 'Are you always so tart with everyone?'

'Not everyone.'

'So it's my fault. Listen – take a seat. Forgive me for not getting up.' He spoke with the odd, ironic tone which I remembered.

I looked round at him, using an examination of the healed wound as an excuse to take in his appearance now his face was free of dressings. He had wiry-looking blond hair, long compared with the clipped styles of the servicemen which we were growing used to. His eyes were less blue than I remembered in the soft light from the candles above his head. The scar curved round from one high cheekbone towards his fair moustache. He obviously found the candour of my gaze disconcerting and looked down. I thought he was blushing.

'It's healed well. You're jolly lucky it missed your eye.'

'Yes,' he said sardonically. 'Jolly.' He turned and grinned at me suddenly, looking into my eyes so that it was I who felt compelled to look away.

'Not in a dancing mood?' I was glad to see Brenda across the room jigging about and laughing with a woman I didn't know. This was more her cup of tea than polite chit-chat over glasses of punch.

'Dancing?' Douglas said. 'No, most definitely not.'

Marjorie started on 'A Nightingale Sang in Berkeley Square', her hands kneading at the keys, and most people were joining in singing the lines they knew.

'Have you known Marjorie long?' I asked.

'I don't know her at all. I came with Pete over there to swell the numbers, of course.'

'We had the definite impression that we were padding as well.'

'What you're too polite to ask, of course,' Douglas said, his tone oddly aggressive, 'is why I'm not fighting with the boys in blue, khaki or any other colour? What a young male is doing here unable to make the claim that he is "on leave" from defending the nation.'

'I was wondering.'

'Of course you were.'

Awkwardly he pulled himself to his feet. I realized that I had never seen him other than lying or sitting before. His right leg was skewed at the hip, the knee bending inwards so that he had to bear its weight on the ball of his foot.

He sat down again abruptly and looked at me very directly, as if challenging me for a reaction.

'Cripple, you see. Born like it. I can get around on it like the clappers as a matter of fact, but I'm not seen as being up to the old one-two, one-two, which apparently is what matters in the services. Not that I didn't try. The army recruiting wallahs looked at me as if I was mad. Of course I only imagined they might sit me at a desk somewhere, but apparently that wasn't on either. So it was decided that since newspapers are nourishment for the nation I should be allowed to lurch around the *Mail* offices doing my job – or what we're allowed to print nowadays – as usual.'

'I'm sorry,' I said. At a time when young men felt they were proving themselves all over the country, Douglas apparently felt himself stuck like a frustrated Rumpelstiltskin, one foot trapped in the floorboards.

'Oh, don't be.' He sank back in the chair. 'After all,

I have a war wound to show for my intrepid report-age.'

'D'you always talk like that? So sarcastically?'

'You're very direct. Yes, often. It's a defence I've established. If there's something amiss with your body you have to learn to keep your end up somehow, don't you? After all, it's not everyone I allow to see me howling because I've got a lump of Christ knows what sticking out of the side of my face.'

'You don't even need to think of that. It's my job.'

He looked into my face with his disturbing gaze. 'You were wonderful, I have to say. Especially coming back to see me like that.'

I felt myself blushing. I was alarmed by the unexpected impulse I felt to put my arms round him. His eyes were extraordinary: appealing, penetrating. For a second it would have felt natural to rest my head on his shoulder. I looked away, ashamed.

But Douglas seemed to relax suddenly, as if he trusted my acceptance of him, and I found myself talking to him, animated in a way I had not been for months. He asked about my work and how I knew Marjorie and we laughed together. Then I felt caught out, laughing like that. Confused, I turned my attention to the music, thoughts churning in my head. How would I ever know if Angus was alive somewhere? Our last night together seemed such an age away. I ached to see him, for us to hold one another, yet at the same time, if that was never going to be possible, I needed to know that too. Would we have to wait until the war was over, and even then would we know for certain? And here was I, enjoying myself at a party and wishing that this man beside me, who I barely knew, would take me in his arms.

A group was standing round Marjorie, who had her back to us at the piano, all well into the swing of singing.

'I'll never smile again, until I smile at you,' they belted out with incongruous jollity. The song cut through me. Should I never smile again? Had I to wait for a homecoming that might or might not happen? And how could I feel so damn sorry for myself just having to wait when for all I knew Angus might be going through the most appalling suffering? A lump grew in my throat. It all felt so hopeless, all these months of waiting and praying when I knew in my heart that Angus was dead.

'Grim little number, isn't it?' Douglas leaned forward and spoke gently. 'I say – you're not crying, are you?'

'No, I'm not,' I said in a determined voice.

'You are – nearly, aren't you?' he persisted with ungentlemanly intrusiveness. 'Is it that – fiancé of yours?'

Dry-eyed now, I told Douglas about our correspondence with the Red Cross.

'The open grave,' he said. 'You poor girl.'

'Don't be nice, I really shall start, else.'

'I shouldn't mind.' His tone was kind.

'But I should. This is supposed to be a party.'

Fortunately Marjorie decided to move on to the ENSA tune, 'Let the People Sing', at this point, which got some of them dancing again.

'Good job it wasn't "We'll meet again",' Douglas said. 'Or the floodgates would have opened.'

I laughed. 'You're terrible.'

'Am I?' He directed an uncertain smile at me.

'Actually, no. In a funny way you've cheered me up.'

'The feeling is mutual. Most girls, once they've found out about my gammy leg, start treating me like some sort of damned invalid with only half a brain.'

He sounded so bitter that without thinking I laid my hand on his arm as I would have done with a patient, then quickly withdrew it.

We spent most of the evening talking and I found myself forgetting about everything else in a way that I only normally did when we were exceptionally busy at work. Again I found that Douglas was more ready to ask questions and learn about me than he was to disclose anything about himself. The shreds I managed to glean from him were that he had a fierce satisfaction in his job and that he was an only child whose parents lived near Gloucester.

Towards the end of the evening, Marjorie came breezing over and said to me, 'Ah, Katie, darling – I see you've been looking after poor Douglas.'

'Oh yes,' Douglas said in a mock pitiful voice. 'She's a proper little Florence Nightingale.'

Marjorie couldn't work out what we were both laughing about.

As we were leaving I moved towards the door with Douglas. I could tell he was painfully conscious that I was seeing his rocking, distorted walk for the first time. With an effort, and taking refuge in his tone of self-mockery, he said, 'I don't suppose you'd consider seeing me again?'

I knew I couldn't hold back from saying yes and giving my address for his sake. But I knew I was doing it as much for my own. As we parted, shaking hands, our eyes met and Douglas smiled, his face transformed from the sad, rather uncertain expression to one that was warm and hopeful.

After I'd thanked Marjorie I said, 'I'm so sorry to hear about your brother.'

She reddened, her only hint of emotion. 'These things are sent to try us, I suppose.'

Brenda joined me outside, glowing from the warmth of the room and her dancing. 'That Susan's a good laugh – we're going to Ivy Benson's tea dance next week if my duty hours fit in with it.' She did a little twirl on the pavement. 'That was the best evening I've had in ages,' she said as we made our way carefully along the blacked-out street.

'Yes,' I said, surprising myself. 'Me too.'

Chapter 16

Birmingham, 1944

'Dr Williamson?'

I can't say I'd have been pleased to see him at the best of times, and his presence on our doorstep in the early evening foretold trouble. He walked in brusquely with barely a glance at me, saying, 'Is your mother in?'

I showed him into the front room. Mummy was at the back with Gladys Peck and the children. Gladys, a young mother with skin the colour of curdled milk, had come to us from South London to escape the flying bombs.

'Winifred,' Dr Williamson said, stroking his little moustache uneasily, 'you'd better sit down.'

Mummy wasn't keen on Dr Williamson either. 'I don't wish to sit down,' she said. 'What's the trouble?'

'Very bad news, I'm afraid. It's Bill. He collapsed at the surgery – his heart.' He paused, looking down at the floor. 'I'm afraid he died in the ambulance. I got here as soon as I could.' My first thought was how much better Daddy would have handled this, his gift with his patients.

My mother stood rigid. She said nothing. Her knees buckled and I helped her to a chair.

Dr Williamson looked monstrously uncomfortable. 'Is there anything I can do?'

Mummy stared ahead of her as if hypnotized. Then she came to herself and without turning her head said, 'No. Thank you.'

Dr Williamson cleared his throat. 'He would have been proud to die in harness,' he offered.

I showed him the door.

Gladys Peck was a pleasant, anxious woman who was perpetually grateful. Although she had to care for her five-year-old, Eric, and Lizzie who was not yet two, she seemed to think that because she had been sent to live with us in a house which resembled the one in which she had first gone into service, she ought in return to act as our maid. We took a lot of trouble to stop her.

But now Gladys came into her own.

'What you need at a time like this,' she declared, 'is help.' She plonked fair, curly-haired Lizzie down on the floor as if trying to root her to the ground. 'Good job I'm here now, isn't it?'

And for several days, with impressive capability, she completely took over the running of our house. While Lizzie slept in our wooden cot upstairs, she scrubbed floors. She settled Eric at the table with crayons, copies of the *Eagle* and *Beano* which he was too young to be able to read properly but enjoyed the pictures, and an old toffee tin full of William's cars and soldiers. He was a quiet, pallid child with cropped, mousy hair. Gladys donned an apron, tied back her thin hair in a pink scarf and set to, humming and singing like someone who had finally found a purpose in life. Then she'd stop, tactfully, remembering that we didn't have much to sing about. I didn't mind. I liked to hear her. Mostly she sang hymns: 'The Old Rugged Cross' and 'Great is Thy Faithfulness', adding her own warbles and fragments of melody.

What was most striking was that Mummy let her do it all. She surrendered control of the house while we made arrangements, sitting in miserable silence in the sombre offices of funeral directors or in the sitting-room at home. She was like a person winded, unable to gather herself up to protest or move into action.

'Gladys is wonderful, isn't she?' I ventured one day. Mummy was sitting with Lizzie on her lap, occupying the child with a string of coloured wooden beads. Her hair was scraped back and she looked exhausted.

'She's a great comfort,' Mummy said, to my surprise. 'Hearing her singing sometimes I feel . . .' She trailed off, stroking the little girl's curls and her soft, spongy limbs.

'What?' I asked softly. So far we had said almost nothing to each other about Daddy's death. We had been to see him, hands across his chest, his face relaxed and strange to us. But the house felt as usual. He had been there so little when he was alive.

'It's as if she's a kind of messenger,' Mummy said.

'From Daddy, you mean?'

'No. I don't believe that sort of thing. You know I don't. I meant from God.'

'I hope so,' I said grimly. I got little else out of Mummy. We moved round one another, each guarding our own pain.

I wrote and told Livy about Daddy's death and she wrote me a sweet note in reply, but her letters were still rare. If she was having leave from the navy, she was no longer taking it at home.

The war was turning: Paris had been liberated in August. But it all felt so sad and futile. Life was empty of the people I cared about. The one thing which warmed me at this time was that Lisa told me she was going to have Daisy baptized.

'I wanted to ask you,' she said shyly, 'if you'd be her godmother?'

In the middle of all this came a telephone call from Douglas. Although I'd given him my address at Marjorie's party he had never got in touch, and he had slipped again from the forefront of my mind though I had quite often noticed his name in the *Mail*. In a way I was relieved. I didn't want my feelings complicated further.

My mother took the message. Would I meet him after work later that week, at Snow Hill Station?

Work was a distraction at that time, being able to go out and immerse myself in it. I didn't feel like going out socially and making an effort with someone I barely knew, but I felt that telephoning him to refuse might prove even more awkward and would hurt his feelings.

I waited for him under the clock in Snow Hill Station as arranged, nervously tapping my umbrella against my legs. Above the cluster of people standing there, the huge hands of the clock jerked the minutes round. I was wishing like mad that I hadn't agreed to meet him, that I could be at home, able to think quietly on my own. But as the big hand clicked over the twelve – seven o'clock – I saw Douglas come limping across the station forecourt, his camera over one shoulder, held close to his body. When he caught sight of me his smile lit his face with a warmth that lifted me.

'Katie, my dear – I'm so sorry.' He took my hand and his voice was the gentlest I'd ever heard it. I had left him a note at his office in Corporation Street, agreeing to meet him for a short time and telling him about Daddy. 'You poor girl. You've had enough knocks already. I mean look at you – you're a shadow of that bustling nurse who came along and swore at me.'

I smiled wryly. It was true. My clothes were hanging on me. I'd had to put a tuck in the waist of my blue uniform skirt and my face was pale, shadowed under the eyes, and too gaunt for my bone structure.

'Oh, well' – I made a Douglas-like quip – 'I always did want to be a beanpole.' Pointing at the camera, I said, 'D'you take that everywhere with you?'

'Yes, pretty much. Just in case.' He looked at me, concerned. 'I'll bet you haven't eaten yet. Come on, let's find somewhere to go.'

The thought of intimate conversation across a table suddenly filled me with panic. 'D'you know what I really feel like?' I said quickly. 'Fish and chips.'

Douglas laughed. 'There was I thinking of something really sophisticated. Oh well – fish and chips, then. At least we don't need our ration books for that.'

We crossed the busy station forecourt, both starting to talk at once and trailing off into embarrassed laughter.

'You first,' I said.

'Look – ' His handsome face grew serious and rather rueful. 'I'm sorry for not looking you up before. I've thought a lot about you since I saw you. It was a bit of a failure of courage on my part, I'm afraid.'

I was disarmed by this admission. 'I'm so glad you did get in touch. It's very good to see you again.' And I meant it, had forgotten how attractive he was, his combination of wit and vulnerability.

'Your father – ' Douglas turned to look at me. 'It must have been a terrible blow to you. What happened?'

'His heart gave out. Overwork, I suppose. He's always had quite good health actually but he worked so hard, and since the war started he's not let up at all.'

'I'm so sorry,' Douglas said again. As we stepped

214

outside he laid a hand gently on my shoulder to guide me through the crowds at the door.

We carried our warm newspaper parcels, strolling down through what remained of the Bull Ring. It was a melancholy sight in the half light, quieter than it would ever have been in peacetime, the bombed shells of buildings round us filled with queer shadows. Droves of starlings circled the wreckage of St Martin's, shrieking sadly.

A couple of boys appeared out of the gloom, tearing past us.

'Peg-a-leg!' they shouted at Douglas. 'Cripple!' They disappeared behind us.

'D'you want to catch the bus?' Douglas asked ruefully.

I felt embarrassed for him. 'I was rather enjoying walking – that's if it's not difficult for you. Does it hurt to walk?'

'Oh, no – no pain,' he said, his sardonic voice back again. 'I just look like an inebriated clown as soon as I set foot, that's all. In present company I'd enjoy a walk too. That's if you don't mind being seen out with me?'

'Of course I don't mind. You mustn't think that.'

'I get a fair bit of what we've just heard.' He jerked his thumb in the direction the boys had gone.

'It must be ghastly.'

'Oh, don't you start!' he protested cheerfully. 'I can stand the abuse, but for heaven's sake don't pity me.'

'OK. Subject closed.'

We cut up along Cheapside, climbing the steep slope up to Camp Hill. Douglas chatted about work, performing such comical impersonations of his colleagues that they came alive in front of me, and soon I was laughing as I'd begun to think I'd never laugh again. I felt warmed by the thick chips and crisp battered fish, and temporarily uplifted. It was a still evening, with the last waning light of summer. The factories throbbed on either side of us, their high grimy sides towering over us, half muffled by sandbags. A truck reversed out from a gate in front of us and roared off up the road.

'"One has no great hope of Birmingham,"' Douglas quoted lugubriously. '"I always say there is something direful in the sound."'

'Who said that?' I was still recovering from his last bout of clowning. 'D'you always mimic people? You must get yourself into frightful trouble.'

'Yes, I'm afraid I do. And in answer to your question it was Jane Austen.'

'Well, it may have been, but it's still nonsense,' I argued. 'Just listen to this place – all these people round us working away day and night. Up there and down under the ground. Listen – it's as if the city's alive. There must be more coming out of Birmingham for the war effort than anywhere else in the country.'

'All right, all right. I didn't say I agreed with her, did I? Can't say I'd want to settle here for life, though.'

'I wonder how much longer it'll all be needed.'

'I did a piece today on the Fire Guard, now they're standing them all down. The Home Guard'll be the next to go, I suppose.'

It was getting really dark as we walked down the Moseley Road. I shivered. Now we had both thrown away our greasy newspapers holding the food, it had created an awkwardness. We had nothing to do with our hands. Douglas walked with his clasped behind his back. I folded my arms, pulling my cardigan closer round me.

'I should have brought a coat,' I said. 'I keep thinking it's still summer.'

Pain washed through me suddenly. Angus. If Angus had been here we would be walking arm in arm, easy with each other, our knowledge of each other so long, deep and familiar. For a moment I felt insanely angry with Douglas for being who he was, for lurching along beside me and for not being Angus. I was bewildered. My moods seemed to switch so quickly.

I was silent for so long that Douglas said, 'Is there anything wrong?'

'It's been a very difficult week,' I said in a tight voice. 'As you can imagine.'

'Oh Lord, I'm so sorry. How clumsy of me.' He sounded quite distressed. 'You seemed in such good form back there that I'd almost forgotten. Were you very close to your father?'

I sighed. 'No. Not really. Only – it's been different recently. Since I started working on the district. We worked in the same area you see and I sometimes met him. It was the first time we've found anything in common. He was the sort of person who was happiest and most himself when he was working. We all used to feel terribly neglected at home really. Poor Mummy ... But he told me, a while ago – I delivered someone's baby you see ...' I felt myself growing incoherent, trying to hold back my tears. It felt too intimate to cry in front of Douglas. 'He told me he was proud of me.'

Douglas stopped me gently and turned me round to face him. Then, realizing his hands were on my shoulders, he hastily removed them.

'When's the funeral?'

'On Friday.'

'Would you like me to come?'

Startled, I looked up at him. 'I don't know. It's just – my mother's rather difficult, and my brother's coming home, I think. It could be a bit – it won't be much fun for you.'

'Fun?' Douglas exploded. 'What d'you think I am, made of wood or something? It doesn't matter about your family. Of course it'll be difficult. It's a bloody awful business. I'd come because I care about you, you silly thing.'

The scarred left cheek was twitching slightly and his eyes were full of an emotion which I couldn't read. It only dawned on me then that his feelings for me were much stronger than I had imagined.

'All right. That would be very good of you, thank you.'

I was very weary and wrung out. I knew if I stayed with him much longer it would end with me stepping into his arms and crying myself out. My feelings were confused and painful and could only be eased, I felt, by my getting away from him.

'Look, I'm very sorry. This hasn't been much of an outing, I know. But I'm very tired. I'd like to go home.'

Douglas was all courtesy. We waited in silence at the bus stop. All I could feel was my acute need to be out of his company. Saying nothing, we sat together on the slow-moving bus. I got off first at Moseley.

'Thank you,' I said, standing up quickly. 'See you soon . . .' I tried to smile at him.

As the bus passed me I saw him looking out, searching for me with his eyes.

*

218

At Daddy's funeral he kept well in the background. I was glad he was there, though my mind was mostly on other things. I wished Olivia could be there and that I could turn to her, but I had to be content with her brief letter.

A bewildering number of people did attend the service, though. I looked round the church seeing faces I had never set eyes on before: many must have been patients, but there were also a rather oddly dressed crew in mismatched clothes and squashed felt hats, some of whom I guessed were his Christian Socialist friends. The organ let out a bleak sound and it was raining outside so the lights had to be on in the church. The tribute all these people were making to Daddy by being there made me feel wretched and powerless, as if circumstances had cheated me. Why had I known him so little? All these people for and with whom he had worked so hard, had in fact given his life for, and I had barely known of their existence.

Mummy was dignified and calm. She was well used to buttoning up her emotions. She wore her usual brown coat since she didn't possess a black one, and a black hat with a wide brim against which her pale features looked sharp and severe. She sat beside me on the front pew, her back very straight.

William had two days' leave from his Intelligence – hush hush – work for the army. He looked older, thinner, with his cropped hair, and as ever, self-important. We were civil to each other, if not warm. I could see by the strained look of his face that he was cut up by Daddy's death.

'How's Mother?' he asked afterwards. He no longer said 'Mummy' of course.

'Oh – you know. Hard to tell. Gladys has been a gem. She's taken everything on.'

I was holding one of the plates of fish-paste sandwiches which Gladys Peck and I were handing round to the throng who were all trying to squeeze into the drawing-room. We had to spread them into the back room as well and the hall was lined with damp raincoats and umbrellas.

Gladys smiled and blushed, making her way past us. 'I'm just glad to have been here at the right time,' she said. 'Eric, don't take any more! There won't be enough to go round.' She darted off after him.

'Extraordinary,' William said, his eyes following her compact figure. 'And Mummy doesn't mind?'

'No. She's really hit it off with Gladys, odd as it may seem. I heard her crying the other day, and it was Gladys she allowed to see her. I found her with her arm round Mummy's shoulders. She's a godsend. We'd never have coped otherwise.'

I moved off to distribute sandwiches. People kept stopping to talk to me, all assuming that I knew who they were. A tiny, childlike woman in a murky green shawl seized my elbow and fixed me with watery eyes. 'Your father was a saint my dear, a saint.'

'Thank you,' I said, at a loss. 'I don't think we've met.'

'I'm Edie Webster.' She held out her hand and I could feel the raised blue veins of her wrist against my finger tips. '*Christian Health Quarterly*. Your father wrote some inspirational papers.'

A familiar face came towards me through the crowd and I excused myself from Edie's skeletal grasp. 'Lisa!' I was delighted to see her. 'How are you – and Daisy?'

'Oh, we're all right – going along.' She was wearing a patched black dress. 'Daisy's running around now. You'll pay us a call soon, won't you? I 'ad to come today – ' She took my arm in her direct way. 'Terrible, your Dad going like that. 'E were a good man. We'll all miss him.'

'Yes,' I said, still feeling overcome. 'So it seems. I've never seen most of these people before.'

'Ah well,' Lisa said. She touched my shoulder. 'You can't know everything, can you?'

This was the most comforting thing anyone had said all day. 'It means a lot that you're here,' I said. 'I'll come and see you very soon, I promise.'

'Please,' she said. 'We miss you.'

Douglas stayed until the last guests were leaving. Gladys had finally sat down with Lizzie on her lap and was gulping down a cup of tea. There was nothing on any of the plates but crumbs. Eric was dabbing at them with a wet finger which travelled urgently back and forth to his mouth.

I walked to the gate with Douglas. The rain had eased off and the ground was scattered with bright yellow leaves.

'Thank you for coming,' I said. 'I'm sorry I've barely even had the chance to say hello to you.' I had, in fact, almost forgotten he was there. The strain was telling in my voice though I was trying to sound light and cheerful.

'You've got tears in your eyes,' he observed. He had a strange, detached manner sometimes. He moved his gaze to the laurel bushes behind me, avoiding my eyes.

'Well, it's been that kind of day.'

I could think of nothing to say and felt dog-tired. I

backed away from him over the wet leaves. 'Look, I'll see you soon,' I said formally. 'It was good of you to come.'

'Kate – ' Clumsily he moved towards me and pulled me into his arms. I felt his lips, startling against mine, the pale moustache prickling against my skin. It was a hard, desperate kiss, one which I didn't have the time to return, nor the inclination.

He stepped back. 'Sorry – oh, God.' He half turned away from me. 'I just – wanted to touch you. I'm sorry . . .'

Before I could say anything he was moving off at surprising speed down the road.

Chapter 17

Evening had set in as I cycled to my last call that day, and it was all the later as I had been delayed by a punctured tyre. It was January. Fog thickened between the walls of the narrow alleys, mingling with smoke from the chimneys of houses and factories to form a smelly, sludge-coloured haze. The muffled light from my bicycle made little impression on it as I pedalled cautiously along, its frame shuddering as the wheels moved over the slippery cobbles. After a time I dismounted, tired and impatient, and walked instead.

'Damn fog,' I cursed to myself. 'Damn bicycle. Damn flaming war.'

Coughing. I wheeled my bike irritably into number eight court, Stanley Street. I wiped my damp face with my hanky. It would be good to see Lisa. She always gave me strength. Despite the cold, the alleys and yards were full of the sounds of children playing out until bedtime. A gaggle of them were shouting shrilly and from somewhere came the sound of dustbin lids being clanged together. At least now the blackout had been lifted to 'dim out', more light filtered into the yard through the thin curtains in the houses.

When Lisa opened the door she looked fraught and exhausted. She had on a washed-out fawn-coloured dress, tight across her breasts, with what looked like fat stains down the front. Her hair was unbrushed and she looked set to jump right down my throat.

'Oh – it's you,' she said unceremoniously. 'Come in.'

'Have I caught you at a bad time?' I asked, stepping into the chaotic room. I'd seldom seen her so brusque before.

'No – you're all right. It's just them little buggers out there've been banging on my door on and off all evening and it's driving me mad.' She seemed close to tears. Her two older children were fighting over the fire-tongs by the grate.

'Pack it in the pair of yer!' she yelled. 'I've 'ad enough of it!'

'What's wrong?' I asked gently. Then I caught sight of Daisy, propped in one of the old armchairs. She had grown into a rather quaint-looking two-year-old with straight brown hair and a round face. She suffered badly from eczema and was always on the move, trying to scratch at some part of her arms or legs. She was at ease with people, and normally came to me, chattering. But now she lay against the greyish pillow with her eyes closed, taking quick, fluttery breaths. Clearly she had a high fever.

'How long's she been like this?' I knelt beside her.

'A couple of days. She's not been so bad in the daytime. It comes on worse of an evening.'

'She's coughing?'

As I spoke Daisy began to give out harsh, dry-sounding coughs.

'It looks like bronchitis, Lisa.' I looked round at her. She was frowning and biting the end of one finger. 'Why haven't you called the doctor?'

With a pang I realized that for a moment I had been thinking of Daddy.

224

'I hoped she'd get better without it,' Lisa gabbled tearfully. 'I've been sponging her down. I give 'er a bath earlier with the oatmeal in for 'er skin. Thought it'd cool 'er down. The thing is, Kate – I can't abide that Dr Williamson. It's not been the same since your dad passed on. She will be all right, won't she?'

Daisy stirred again and started trying to scratch, pulling at the cotton eczema cuffs on her arms. Her movements started off the coughing again and her face puckered with pain.

'Look, if it's the money you're worried about I'll help you out. She is my goddaughter, after all.' I patted Lisa's arm. 'I'll go and see if Dr Williamson's still there – he often stops late, especially now he's on his own. It won't take long.'

I had never seen Lisa so upset before. It was usually her who had a calming effect on me. I felt anxious for her, and for Daisy, and angry with Dr Williamson. There was enough to feel helpless about nowadays without having to be terrified of your own doctor. Twenty minutes later Dr Williamson and I were on our way to Lisa's house. He had not been pleased to see me or to be asked out on another call. As I explained the situation he nodded impatiently.

'It's very foolish to bath a child in this condition,' were almost his first words as he set foot through Lisa's door. He threw his hat on the table. I saw that while I was away she had been trying to tidy up.

Dr Williamson bent over Daisy, breathing his tobacco breath loudly at her. His balding crown was shiny with sweat. He looked into the little girl's mouth, felt the glands in her neck with his pink, stubby fingers, listened to her chest with his stethoscope. Daisy coughed as he did so, barely able to open her eyes.

'Say ahhh,' he instructed her. There was silence. I could see Lisa biting her nails.

'Say ahhh, child,' he repeated, loudly.

'She's only two years old,' I pointed out. 'And she's almost asleep.' My usual irritation with him was turning to anger.

'She'll be much too hot in these,' he said briskly, unfastening the eczema cuffs from her elbows. 'I should have thought that was obvious.'

The two of us stood in silence. I could tell Lisa was close to tears and my breathing was growing shallower with fury.

'I think Mrs Turnbull would like some assurance that Daisy is going to be all right,' I translated for her.

He stood up. 'Oh, I dare say she will if she's looked after properly. Here – ' He wrote out a prescription and handed it to her abruptly. 'Go to the dispensary in the morning. In the meantime she needs warmth, fresh air and plenty of fluids. Think you can manage that?'

He walked straight out without another word and I was after him. I had seen doctors be monumentally rude to patients in hospital on occasion, but it seemed so much worse in people's homes.

'D'you always speak to your patients like that?' I demanded.

Dr Williamson jerked to a standstill, bristling. 'I beg your pardon?' I expect he still regarded me as a child.

'I thought our job was to try and make people feel better – to alleviate suffering. Not to go out of our way to make them feel small and inadequate and imply that they can't even look after their own children.'

He breathed in sharply. 'I'll thank you to keep your views to yourself,' he said in a low, furious voice. 'And when I need advice on how to do my job after thirty

226

years' experience I'll find someone qualified to dispense it.'

He strode away, quickly disappearing from view. Inside Lisa was in tears.

'I only did what I thought was right,' she sobbed miserably. ''E's an 'orrible man, he is. I'd like to see 'im try and get fresh air and warmth at the same time in here, 'cause it's bloody harder than it sounds.'

I persuaded her to finish getting the other children to bed.

'Daisy's asleep now, look,' I told her. 'Why don't you get yourself something to eat and try and get some rest yourself. I'll call by tomorrow, all right?'

She smiled faintly. 'Thanks, Kate. You know – you're very like 'im.'

'Who?'

'Your dad, of course.' She added miserably, 'I wish Don was here.'

When I visited the next evening I found Lisa standing outside her door with her apron on. In her hand was a bowl and I could see steam rising from it in the light through the front door.

'Chicken soup,' she told me. 'For Daisy.' Her face looked more relaxed, though she was sagging with exhaustion.

Daisy's eyes were open and Lisa was altogether more buoyant.

'I'm absolutely wiped out,' she told me. 'We 'ad an 'ell of a night. She was burning up – got me in a right state. Thought I was going to lose 'er. But come this morning she perked up again. Look at 'er. Don't you think she's better?'

Relieved, I smiled at Daisy. 'Hello, darling – are you

on the mend?' I went to sit by her and felt her forehead. 'She's a bit warm, but as you say, her temperature's settling, isn't it? That must've been the worst of it yesterday.'

'Let's see if she'll have some soup.' Lisa settled the other two children at the table and then went to the door.

'Sid!' she yelled into the dark yard. 'Get 'ere!'

We heard running feet outside and Sid Blakeley tore into the room, his cheeks raw from the cold. He was ten now, his brown hair cropped very short, face pinched, with not a trace left of his baby chubbiness. He had on grey shorts and a jumper and *Birmingham Mail* charity boots which looked weighty on the end of his bony legs.

'Say summat to Miss Munro,' Lisa ordered.

''Ullo,' Sid said, eyes on his bowl. He sat perched on the side of the armchair which was pulled up to the table. He was dunking bread into the soup and cramming it into his mouth.

'Oh,' Lisa groaned, 'I give up.'

'Leave him.' I smiled. 'He's hungry. Looks a healthy lad.'

Automatically Lisa handed me a cup of her tea which was as unpleasant as ever, but I drank it, standing by the range, waving away Lisa's apology at the shortage of chairs.

'This should do 'er good, shouldn't it?' Lisa spooned soup into Daisy's mouth. 'Albert,' she snapped suddenly at one of the small boys. 'Get your spoon off Danny's 'ead.'

'Albert? Is that after your father?'

Lisa gave a mirthless chuckle. 'No fear. No cowing use to anyone 'e wasn't – 'scuse my language. No –

Prince Albert. I always liked the pictures of 'im. Thought 'e were ever so 'andsome.'

For a few moments there was silence as she concentrated on the little girl. The boys were intent on their soup. She got up to give them more bread and a minute scraping of jam. I looked round the room. Clothes were hanging drying in every conceivable place – chairbacks, picture frames – and the atmosphere was steamy.

Lisa's house was hardly a model home, but I could detect a certain personal order among the chaos. She had after all had to run her family home from a young age and brought up her brother and her own children.

She smiled as Daisy finally pursed her lips and turned her head away from the spoon. 'She's 'ad a good go at it.'

'Marvellous,' I said, smiling slightly as I caught myself sounding like Marjorie Mantel. 'That's a good sign. She'll soon be up and under your feet again.'

Lisa yawned, then laughed. 'Sorry – it's not the company.'

'You must be exhausted.'

'Thanks for looking in,' Lisa said. She gestured to the boys to get down from the table and they disappeared outside. Then she looked carefully at me. 'You all right? You look a darn sight better than the last time I saw you.'

'I'm well, apart from this cold.' I sat down opposite her, amid the remains of the boys' tea.

Lisa put her head on one side. 'Who was that bloke I saw at your dad's funeral? The one with the gammy leg. I was watching 'im – 'andsome, isn't 'e? 'Ardly took his eyes off you all afternoon.'

'Oh, that's just Douglas,' I said.

'That's just Douglas,' Lisa mimicked me, her spirits returned. 'Come on Kate – 'e'd put bonfire night in the shade the flame 'e's got lit for you.' She leaned towards me. ''Asn't 'e?' I knew Lisa took pride in her directness, her knowing that she could make me open up.

I nodded. 'I suppose he has.'

'And what about you?'

'I've been trying not to have.'

Throughout the previous months Douglas and I had grown closer, though the progression was awkward. He apologized repeatedly for his behaviour after Daddy's funeral, and since then had been only charming and good-natured. We had very little physical contact, and though Douglas was very tender towards me, he behaved with nothing but restraint and tact. I was the problem, confused and guilty as I was about Angus. But Douglas was very patient and he had a gift for making you confide in him. I poured out my feelings about Angus.

One day when I was telling him about our childhood he said, 'You'd known him since you were quite small then?'

'Oh, yes. The Harveys moved in when I was seven. I thought I'd told you?'

'I see,' Douglas said, as if he had suddenly got to grips with something. 'So he was really a childhood friend?'

'Well – yes,' I said, puzzled. 'We'd obviously known each other a long time.'

Since the afternoon of the funeral he had not tried to kiss me. Sometimes the way he looked at me I thought he was about to, but he held back. The only exceptions to this were times when I cried. He held me then, with a gentleness which touched me. I didn't know whether I wanted more. I didn't encourage it. It would have made me feel disloyal to Angus. I felt safe with Douglas, restored by his sheer physical presence near me, and knowing that he was not going to be sent away. And increasingly I knew how attractive I found him. But I resisted showing too much affection. It would have been unfair to him.

Gradually, Douglas began to tell me about his own family. Evidently he did not find them an easy subject to discuss.

'I wanted to get a long way away from them,' he said. We were sitting by the lake in Cannon Hill Park, wrapped in coats and scarves. 'That's why I came to look for a job up here. Birmingham's not a place they'd be all that keen to visit.'

'Not even to see you?'

'No. My father's in the Home Guard now. He's a schoolmaster in civvy street. It should suit him. Used to giving orders.'

'And your mother?'

'A waxwork.' He stared at the grey sky. Straight-necked mallards whirred above us. 'Actually, more of a plaster saint. Never talks back to the Colonel. He never was a colonel, by the way, but that's the way he behaves at home. I had to get away – it was stifling. I couldn't breathe in that house. My mother wanted to wrap me in lint and keep me there, muzzled, because of my leg. She tried to do that pretty much all through my childhood. I had to prove to myself that I had a brain even if my leg was a joke. I loved writing and I wanted to do something active, not be some dried-up academic. They didn't even send me to school, you see – because of the way I looked. I suppose they were worried about me being teased – I'd be no good at games and so on. So my father taught me when he had time, and I had a man

231

who came to the house. Mr Lovely his name was – '
Douglas chuckled. 'Not a bad sort. Actually it was his
idea that I look for a job on a paper.'

'How very grim,' I said. 'It must have been so lonely.'

'I lived through it,' he said lightly.

Sometimes I sensed Douglas wanted to touch me, or
kiss me. I found him watching me with a kind of hunger
in his face. He would look away quickly when our eyes
met. I often wished he could just hold me and that I
could respond without fear or guilt, that it could all be
more simple.

'Go on,' Lisa urged me. 'You can tell me. You've
fallen for him, haven't you, Kate?'

'Maybe – a bit,' I admitted.

'So what's wrong with that?'

'I'm afraid I'll allow myself this – that I'll let my
feelings for him grow and then suddenly one day Angus
will come home and I'll have hurt everyone. It would be
terrible. What I really wish is that he'd come back and
things could be as they were before.'

'They'll never be that,' Lisa said drily. 'Never are, are
they? You said 'e was dead.'

'He almost certainly is. The latest from the Red Cross
is that he was shot down over the sea. I know there's no
real hope.'

'And you reckon this other feller's worth it?'

I hesitated so that Lisa put her head on one side
quizzically. 'Yes – I think so.'

'There you are, then.'

When I left Lisa's that evening the fog had intensified,
and hung dark and choking along the streets. Even
though the road was no longer completely blacked out,
it was very hard to see anything. I clicked on my

ineffective cycle lamp and decided I would be safer walking until I reached the main road where the kerbs were painted in black and white stripes to make them easier to see. I set off up Stanley Street. Muffled figures passed me in the fog, a few saying 'Evening' as they faded out of view again. After a while I decided I'd be better off without the lamp as it seemed only to reflect off the fog.

The man approached me almost silently and I ran my bike straight into him.

'Christ,' the voice said furiously. He bent down, rubbing his leg. I think the wheel nut must have caught his shin. 'For heaven's sake, if you can't ride the thing, at least walk it along the kerb so you don't do anyone else an injury.'

He had his collar turned up against the damp air and his face was in shadow, but I knew that voice immediately. Not wanting him to recognize me, I murmured 'Sorry' and quickly wheeled past him, my heart pounding.

'I should damn well think so!' he shouted after me.

I wanted to get away from him as fast as I could. As I pressed on up the street I had a strong, horrible instinct as to what he was doing there. Kemp's stood among a collection of factories several streets away. Alec Kemp always travelled there by car, and Stanley Street was not, by any stretch of the imagination, on his way home.

Part Three

Chapter 18

KATE

At dawn it was quiet, except for the dripping trees. And then the bells: church bells so long silent, the sound of them ringing across the city all the more jubilant when unheard for so long. 8 May 1945. In the night there had been a storm, thunder and lightning like the nudge of something supernatural, ending the war just as they had begun it.

The day before we had spent waiting, confused. In the morning there was a news blackout and it wasn't until three in the afternoon that they announced Germany's surrender. War in Europe was over.

I went to church that morning with Mummy and Gladys and the children. The building was packed and they were promising to put on extra services. Between us we kept the children amused and reasonably still.

'Now thank we all our God.' Gladys's clear voice rose and fell beside me as it had when she was scrubbing our floors. I knew, sadly, that she wouldn't be with us much longer. During the prayers Mummy knelt with her eyes closed. I assumed she was thinking of Daddy and giving thanks that William would be coming home safely. But thoughts of what we had lost came more forcefully to me. I tried to bring Angus's face before me, feeling panic and shame when I could barely picture him.

'Whatever's happened to you, I love you,' I told him silently. 'If you are alive, come back to me, please, my darling. And if you're not, rest peacefully knowing I'll love you always. Always.'

Many of us were in tears, especially when we stood to sing the last hymn, 'Jerusalem', the combination of joy and loss too much for us.

Afterwards, everyone was on the street, hugging, shaking hands. There was a dazed look to people, euphoria and disbelief combined with a residual irritation at the confused way in which the news of the final surrender had been relayed to us. 'They could at least have let us know what was happening . . .' But now it didn't matter. It was over.

I went through the motions of greeting the neighbours, of laughing and exclaiming, but all the time I wanted desperately to be alone. My thoughts during the service had been so close to Angus, and this had left a knot of tension tightening in me like a physical ache.

It was a showery day, the sky busy with cloud. I just wanted to walk and walk and have time to think by myself.

'Where are you going?' Mummy called after me as I took off along the road with my umbrella.

'I'm just going to have a look round for a bit,' I called back over my shoulder.

'But that nice Mr Craven said he'd come round to the house . . .' Gladys's voice wafted to me along the pavement.

I knew this perfectly well, and it was another reason I had to take off. I turned and waved vaguely as if I hadn't heard properly, calling, 'Back soon!' I knew Mummy and Gladys would be all right together listening to all that was going on on the wireless.

Without really deciding where to go I turned automatically towards the centre of Birmingham, walking fast, needing to let off steam and exhaust myself. As I did so I looked down the side streets and could see all the hurried preparations going on for street parties, the trestle tables draped with sheets and people bustling around, some already wearing coloured paper hats. Miles of bunting was going up, rippling above the tables in the side streets, and Union Jacks brightened the grimy fronts of the houses, and everywhere movement of people, shouting, laughing.

Down one street in Balsall Heath a pair of trousers adorned the middle of one of the lines of bunting. I found myself smiling as I heard Douglas's voice in my head: 'Still hanging out the washing on the Siegfried Line!' and I was startled by the way I was becoming used to his jokes, to him.

It started raining and I put up my umbrella, but the rain didn't chase anyone from the streets for long. I walked down into our battered city, hearing bursts of cheering and bands playing as I moved into the crowded streets in the heart of Birmingham. I felt a rush of loneliness at being there alone on this day, but at the same time it was fitting. It was a day of turmoil for everyone, in its way, and I could not have stood company just then, such was the tension of mixed feelings inside me. But I wanted to be out here amid the frenzied activity of the city, to be part of it on a day when we all stood poised on the rim of the future. I suppose here in all this communal uncertainty I was longing to find the way to orientate myself in my own life. To work out what direction I should take next.

Around me pasty, tired faces smiled along the streets, chattered and shrieked with excitement under the ripple of flags. People were breaking into singing and dancing. A group of women cavorted across New Street with their arms linked singing 'Knees up Mother Brown' and pushing their legs up high, and I heard 'Roll Out the Barrel' clashing with it from further down the road, and whistles and cheers and shouts of laughter.

I made my way slowly towards Victoria Square, smelling the wet pavement mingled with cigarette smoke. People were shouting at each other, someone's voice behind me, 'Edna – Edna – over 'ere!' and a woman with curlers round her head, not caring. Daredevils in uniform and out of it scrambled up lamp-posts and on to high window-sills and stood laughing and waving: another group, some of whom were still dressed for the Land Army, sang 'Auld Lang Syne' with their arms round each other. Worries were put aside, everyone throwing themselves into this uplifting, long, long-awaited morning. This was enough: today. I saw a few people crying and Churchill's words, relayed to us through loudspeakers in the streets, moved more people to tears: 'God bless you all. This is your victory. It is the victory of the cause of freedom in every land . . .'

I didn't cry, not then. But perversely, after such a strong impulse to be alone, what I did feel was an overpowering need to turn to someone close to me to share these moments. Angus. And he wasn't there. He never would be. Standing amid the jostling crowd and seeing this glimpse of what might have been gave me my most extreme moments of distilled pain in all the time since Angus was reported missing. I felt a physical sensation like an incision, too sharp and deep for tears. Yet once I had passed through it it left me lightened and relieved as if I had wept for a long time.

I bought a cup of tea from a mobile canteen on the street and stood quietly sipping it next to a lamp-post, hands tight round the enamel cup, soothed and easier in myself.

'Awright, love?' a gravelly voice asked next to me. A dapper man with a thin black moustache like Peter Lorre. 'What a day, eh?'

I smiled. 'Yes, isn't it?'

There was something in the man's stance and chirpy way of talking that Douglas would have loved to mimic, and I would have liked to see him do it. I stored the encounter in my mind as something to tell him. After handing the cup back I eased my way out of the crowds, away from the centre of the city, and began to walk home.

I experienced a sense of anticlimax, yet also of understanding. It was over – for us. I'd never imagined it like this, with war still raging on the other side of the world. It thought this day, when it came, would be a key to something. Angus would come home, somehow decisions would be made for me. But if the Red Cross were right, Angus lay in a sea grave. He was not missing. Not a Prisoner of War. Angus was dead. I had to accept the truth of that. I had to turn and carry on with the living.

Douglas didn't arrive at our house until late afternoon, so I hadn't been much missed.

'They gave me the rest of the afternoon off,' he told us. 'So I came round straight away.'

Gladys, charmed by him, actually simpered. She thought Douglas wonderful. 'It's a pity about his, well, you know, his leg,' she'd say. 'But he's ever so handsome, isn't he?'

Douglas was looking very spruce. Smart clothes were

important to him, and I often teased him, saying he didn't look seedy enough to be a reporter. His camera was, as ever, slung over one shoulder.

'I'm so glad you were in,' he said. 'I thought you might have taken off somewhere for the day.' Taking me by the shoulders he kissed me quickly on the cheek, and I felt myself blush. We so seldom touched each other or kissed. Covering his own uncertainty, he said, 'Well – this is quite a day, isn't it?'

We spent the evening pleasantly with Mummy and Gladys, Douglas and I telling them what we'd seen while we were out. Douglas went out to fetch an evening edition of the paper and we laughed together at the *Mail*'s assessment of Birmingham's VE Day celebrations: 'We are not much given to mass gaiety. We are gardeners, family men, artificers and very individualistic at that.'

'Rather austere,' I said. 'Is that what you'd have written? I thought they were having a pretty jolly time out there myself.'

'Yes, and I expect it'll hot up tonight,' Douglas said. 'Perhaps I'll go back in for a while ... Would you think of coming too? We could take a tram in – they've got some of them dolled up.'

'I think I've had enough for today,' I said. 'But thanks for the offer.'

I sensed from Douglas's increasing silence as the evening wore on that he had something on his mind and that he would rather have been alone with me. The chance didn't arise until he was leaving. We stood outside on the doorstep and he seemed reluctant to go.

'Were you woken by the thunder last night?' he asked.

'Yes, of course. But it was nice to lie awake and think and take in the news.'

'What were you thinking about?' Sometimes he asked questions in a disconcertingly clinical way.

'Oh, just the rest of my life.' I tried to speak lightly.

'Freedom!' Douglas said exultantly. 'A chance to move on at last. Get on to one of the nationals.' He was silent for a moment, hands in his pockets, looking down at the ground. 'That's if I stand a chance, competing with all our heroes returning from the front.' I felt sorry for him, for his bitter sense of separateness, of not measuring up.

'Look.' He turned to me, speaking fast and awkwardly. 'I can't carry on like this – not telling you how I feel about you.'

I pulled the front door closed behind me and stood against it.

'I need to know whether you could ever feel anything for me. Sometimes it seems you do, and then ...' He hesitated. 'You've got to face it, Katie. He's not going to come back.'

A lump rose in my throat and for a moment I couldn't speak. Douglas read his own meaning into this. With a frustrated sound he turned away from me. I reached out and put my hand on his shoulder. He jerked loose from me fiercely. 'Don't, for God's sake.'

'What?'

'Feel bloody sorry for me.'

'I don't feel sorry for you,' I said. 'Actually I was feeling quite sorry for myself. Why do you have to take it that anyone who shows you any sort of affection must be feeling sorry for you?'

'Well, why else do you keep on seeing me?' he burst out. 'You're clearly still in love with – him. There's nothing I can do about that.' He looked into my eyes and I was rocked by the strength of emotion in his. 'I feel helpless. That's what drives me mad. I've spent months watching you mourn for someone else, feeling I should keep my distance from you, when it's all I can do to hold myself back from touching you. Because I don't want you to think I'm...' He made another frustrated gesture.

'What?'

'I don't want you to think I'm a crass idiot coming crashing in when you see me as nothing more than a second-best companion.'

'That's not how I see you.' I looked away, down at the brick floor of the porch. In a flat voice I said, 'I can't tell you I didn't – don't – love Angus. And in some ways that hasn't been finished properly. But that doesn't mean I don't have feelings for you. I'm just so afraid – '

He waited for me to finish. I couldn't look at him as I spoke.

'I'm afraid of him coming back. And I'm afraid of him not coming back. It's utterly unfair on you, I know. And you've been so good to me. I'm very grateful.'

'He's not going to come back, Katie,' he repeated gently.

'I know that really. In fact today, when I was in town, I really saw properly that I have to try and put it all behind me.' I moved closer and laid my hands on Douglas's shoulders.

'Katie – ' He sounded wretched. 'Please don't do this if you don't really mean it.'

'I do.' I wanted to mean it, wanted things to be resolved and clear. I reached up and stroked his face. 'Thank you for being so patient.'

He pulled me hard into his arms. 'Katie. Katie ...' His lips pressed hard on mine. I felt firstly the comfort of being held. As I kissed him back, the desire for him I had fought against for so long lit at his touch.

On a beautiful, tranquil Sunday in July we sat together on the grass at the far end of our garden, beyond the vegetable patch and bean-sticks. Douglas often spent part of the weekend at our house now, rather than in his spartan digs, the garden of which had space for nothing but vegetables. My mother was civil to him, if not exactly warm, but he apparently saw no lack in her then, and even seemed to be quite fond of her.

Douglas was sitting up with a newspaper spread over his legs. He usually read a whole range of papers at the weekend: *Times*, *Express*, *Daily Worker*, some of them several days old. Work: always work. I lay back contentedly with my head on my bent arm. All I could see was the branches of our apple tree and the pale blue sky.

'It's so quiet without Eric and Lizzie,' I said. Gladys had departed tearfully soon after the war ended, begging us to keep in touch. 'Mummy really misses Gladys, I think. She's invited them to come back for holidays if they want to.'

Douglas looked up. 'That's good. She's a staunch character, isn't she?'

I watched a tiny curl of cloud unfold itself slowly across the sky. Only now it was over, the images of the war seemed to bombard me, a delayed realization of what we had all been through. 'Even now I keep expecting something to appear – I'm always looking out for planes.'

Douglas folded his newspaper untidily and flung it on the grass, then lay back beside me. 'You don't throw off habits like that in five minutes. I dreamt the other night that there was an air raid on, and I was all set to get out of bed and down to the shelter.'

I laughed, and we lay together looking up into the blue. Though I was happy, I had an odd feeling of disconnectedness now we had peace. It was as if we could not pick up the threads of our life before the war, that we were cut off at the roots. And now the war was not our main preoccupation I found myself missing Olivia far more acutely. She belonged to the peace. She should be here. I also missed my father.

I rolled over and looked down at Douglas. 'What about your family? Don't you think you should contact them?'

Douglas had mentioned to me only recently that his mother wrote to him without fail every week and had done all through the war. 'She knows I'm all right,' he said in the dismissive tone he always used when talking of his parents. 'I've dropped her a line here and there.'

'But shouldn't you go and see them?'

'What you should do is not always the question, is it?' he said, surprising me with his harshness. 'And besides, I don't think we've got a lot to say to each other.' He sat up and held the camera to his face, altering the focus. 'Lie still.' I waited patiently as he took yet another photograph.

'I don't understand you,' I said. 'What is it about your parents that's so terrible?'

'Don't let's talk about them.' He moved closer and we sat leaning against the high garden wall, Douglas putting his arm round me. I saw his pale, flecked lashes. As we began to kiss, sitting side by side, I ran one hand over his strong hair, then down his back, stroking the raised muscles each side of his spine. He kissed me strongly, hungrily, arms tight around me. I was beginning to respond to him, when suddenly his hand was on my breast, grasping me clumsily and hard. I gasped, drawing back. Douglas snatched his hand away again.

'Darling,' I said gently. 'You've never touched a woman much before, have you?'

His face turned red. He was twenty-five, a year older than me, and innocent. 'No,' he said very quietly, as if ashamed. 'Never had the courage – or the chance much. Not many girls go for cripples, you see.'

'And men don't make passes at girls who wear glasses,' I said, trying to joke him out of his embarrassment. But he was solemn and unsure of himself.

'I'm sorry.' He couldn't look me in the eyes. 'You're different, Katie. You're so very special. I love you.'

I leaned to him and kissed him again. I longed to show him the joy of it, to let him touch me. It would be all right here, where it was so secluded. He began to unfasten my blouse, fumbling with the top button. He looked me in the eyes as if waiting for permission.

'You don't mind? I've never – I'd like to see you . . .'

When he had undone the buttons and slowly parted the two sides of white cotton, he slid his fingers inside the lacy edge of my bra. As he touched me I let out a slight sound, wanting him to continue. I could hear his breath coming fast and his hands were not steady.

When my clothes were undone he stared, childlike suddenly. 'Oh, Kate – they're so beautiful.'

I waited for him to touch me, eyes closed and crying out with the pleasure of it as his hands reached my flesh. His breathing was fast and excited. A sudden sound startled me, a whisper of foliage, and I sat back from Douglas in time to pull the front of my blouse together as my mother advanced on us down the garden, her hands gigantic in gardening gloves. We sat feeling utterly foolish, but to her credit she gave us as wide a berth as possible and kept her eyes fixed on the vegetable patch beyond us. Passing back in front of us moments later with a garden fork she'd come to retrieve she said casually, 'By the way, there's tea . . .'

Douglas's cheeks were burning red. Silently I buttoned my blouse.

'Look,' Douglas said eventually, 'if we really care for one another, we ought to be able to wait for all that, don't you think? As a mark of respect. It should really be for after marriage, shouldn't it?'

I kept my gaze turned away from his, blushing now myself as I realized Douglas assumed I was innocent.

He misinterpreted my heightened colour. 'And I should be very happy if we didn't have to wait very long.'

Olivia didn't come home until shortly before the Japanese surrender in August 1945.

'My darling, darling!' I cried, when she first arrived to see us, all my niggles about her letters forgotten. I held her tight, tears on my face. 'It feels like a lifetime since I've seen you.'

'To me too,' she said, returning my embrace.

She smiled and kissed me, but even in my happiness I could hardly conceal my shock. She was skin and bone, her hair limp and straggly and her eyes dull.

'Livy – you look so ill,' I said gently to her, feeling I had to cajole her. She seemed so knotted up in herself.

'Well, you don't exactly look like Doris Day your-self,' she replied, evasive and teasing.

It was true. Like so many other women we were shrunken and worn down by the war. I assumed that the exacting hours the Wrens had demanded from her had taken their toll, compounded by her bout of pneumonia. But I couldn't imagine what they had done to her emotions.

One evening I went round to Park Hill to spend some time with her. I felt slightly nervous as I walked down under the trees. She was so unpredictable nowadays.

Alec and Elizabeth were evidently frantic about the state of her. They trod around her as if she might detonate at any second, while being on the other hand ferociously jolly towards me in an attempt to pretend that all was well, that 'poor Olivia' was just a little worn down after all her war work.

'What she needs is a good holiday,' Alec said. He was leaning against the polished surface of a grand piano which I dimly remembered seeing in the house on my last visit. He was leaner, his forehead lined and grey hair showing at his temples. Hearing his voice, I remembered my encounter in the fog with my bicycle, and I knew for sure that it had been him.

When Livy and I were left alone, I said, 'That's a really beautiful piano,' I hesitated. 'Look, I've barely played through the war and I'm fearfully rusty, but would you like to have a go at some duets?'

'Oh no,' she replied languidly. She seemed to find it almost too much effort to speak. She sat smoking, drawing hard on the cigarette so that her cheeks were sucked in. There was an ashtray on the little table beside her with several stubs in. 'I haven't played for months either. I don't suppose I shall. Can't think what he bought the wretched thing for.'

'But you were so good at it,' I protested. 'You mustn't just let it all go.'

She ground her cigarette stub into the ashtray. Her next words sent a chill through me, they were spoken with such flat indifference. 'What does it matter?'

'Livy – ' I went to her and knelt down carefully beside her chair and took her bony hand in mine. It felt like a starved bird. 'My dearest Livy – what's wrong? You look so thin and unwell.'

She looked into my eyes then, really stared, as if she was searching for something. But in hers I saw a kind of hard blankness so unlike the vivaciousness of the young Livy that it made me want to cry.

'What is it?' I asked softly.

She stared at me in silence and I thought she was making up her mind to say something. Then she put her head back, resting it against the chair, and closed her eyes.

'Livy?'

'I'm all right, Katie. Don't fuss. I'm just tired. I'm always so tired. It's been an exhausting war. Not just the work, you know – so much else going on.' She rallied suddenly, switching into another gear. She sat up straight, eyes open. And she was off on her old track of how marvellous the Wrens had been, the parties, all the men, the team spirit, the romance ... She talked very fast in a high, slightly childlike voice.

'I was just the belle of so many navy do's,' she giggled. She began to rock the upper part of her body back and forth. I found myself shrinking back from her. 'And when they discovered how well I could play' – she held her hand out, indicating the piano – 'well, of course I was in constant demand.'

'But I thought you said you hadn't played?'

She waved a hand at me as if I was a half-wit. 'This was earlier. And I was always top of the men's lists for dances. There were fights over me you know. One poor fellow was knocked out cold outside the Naafi one night over me. I thought it was simply terrific. So romantic!' Her laughter came out exaggerated, as if she'd been drinking.

'Livy.' I found myself speaking in a measured voice of the sort we used for patients who were confused or agitated. 'I'm glad you enjoyed it all. But it's over now, isn't it? You need to rest and settle down again. Get well properly. And you'll have to think what you're going to do. You never wanted to come back and live at home, did you?'

She sank back in the chair, suddenly limp. 'Daddy didn't get elected, did he?' She gave a malicious laugh. 'Missed the boat. He jumps on the bandwagon thinking he'll get a seat because of all dear Mr Churchill's done, and then they go and elect the Labour wallahs instead. Isn't that a joke? Don't you think it's a scream?'

'Livy – don't. Look, think about yourself. What are you going to do?'

'Oh, I don't know. What a nag you're being, Katie!' She threw herself up out of the chair and went to the piano. She lit another cigarette and offered me one. I shook my head. She sat perched on the piano stool, pulling in the smoke hard.

'I suppose I'll get some tedious little job in a tedious little company somewhere. I'll have to find a way of livening it up somehow, won't I?' Suddenly an odd, gleeful smile spread across her face. 'Come here, Katie.'

She beckoned me urgently. 'I'll tell you a secret, shall I? You must promise not to tell.'

Encouraged, I walked over to her. Putting her lips close to my ear she said, 'They think they've got me here now, all locked away. But I still do it. I do. Every week at least I do it with a man. Anywhere I can. Even once in the gazebo – like when you found me and William. I told that one he had to be a very good boy. Nice and quiet, no shouting out. A lot of them shout you see, the things I do to them. Poor fellows can't control themselves.'

I drew my head back as if from a hornet. Of course I wasn't a total innocent, but it had dawned on me only gradually as she spoke that she meant sexual intercourse. Her face wore a terrible, smug smile.

'You'll keep this all under wraps of course, won't you, Katie?'

I felt sick. I took her in my arms. 'Olivia. Oh my sweet one – whatever has happened to you?'

Chapter 19

Soon after VJ Day Douglas and I announced to our families that we were planning to marry. My mother digested this piece of information almost entirely without comment, other than to suggest that, to start with, we live with her.

'There are hardly any houses to be had and there's plenty of room here. You'd have no need to fear for your privacy.' She spoke stiffly, perhaps afraid we'd reject her.

'Are you sure you wouldn't mind?' I said doubtfully.

'I don't entirely relish the thought of living on my own. I should have to think about selling the house. And in any case,' she announced, 'I shan't be around bothering you. From the new year I shall be very busy – I've accepted a post on a children's ward at Selly Oak Hospital.'

'Mummy, that's terrific!' I said. 'Whyever didn't you tell me?'

'I just have told you,' she said, stalking off with an armful of dried washing.

Though my inclination was not to accept her offer I knew it made sense, and Douglas was delighted. 'It's such a beautiful home,' he said. 'Otherwise we'd be in some poky little place. It's very good of her to ask us.'

Douglas received a formal, tetchy note from his father, to the effect that he was glad to be informed that 'my boy' was planning to settle down, but that it was very bad form that they hadn't even been allowed the privilege of meeting his intended. It also rebuked him sharply for not visiting home. His mother had been distraught with worry. Douglas was to travel to Gloucester immediately.

'We really must go,' I insisted to an enraged Douglas. I was shaken by the impersonal tone of the letter, but also by its description of Mrs Craven's distress. 'You can hardly blame them, can you? You've barely contacted them at all and your mother's written so faithfully to you.'

'Oh yes – she's very good at giving completely the wrong impression,' Douglas snapped.

I was taken aback by his tone. 'What d'you mean?'

'Nothing.' He got up from his chair in our back room and went to the window. 'I'm not going to be summoned to Gloucester like that. I'm sorry, Katie, but I've got away from them and away is where I'm going to stay. Once you've cut ties it's better to keep it that way. That's my view of things.'

'You can be very cold.' I was upset, not wanting to begin married life with us so much on the wrong side of my in-laws. 'Look, why don't I go and see them on my own if that's how you feel?'

'No!' Douglas shouted, his face flushing a deep red. 'Don't you dare. I'm not having you going down there behind my back.'

'Don't shout at me like that.' I was furious with him for reacting like this. 'It wouldn't be behind your back, would it? I've just asked you.'

Without turning round again he said, 'Well, the answer's no.'

After a few moments he hobbled over and put his arms round me. 'I'm sorry, darling. Don't be angry – please.'

He wrote an immediate reply to them saying that we wouldn't be coming. I felt angry, guilty about treating them in such a way. Eventually I dropped them a brief note myself, trying to sound as pleasant as I could, saying I was sorry for our lack of contact, but that I hoped to meet in the near future. By return of post I received a strange note from Mrs Craven.

> Dear Katherine,
>
> I was most relieved to receive your letter. I suppose Douglas has stopped you coming to visit us, being the stubborn boy he is. He doesn't find it easy to forgive, the poor darling. He won't change, you know, they never do. If you can persuade him to let us meet you I should be very grateful of course. I'm sure you'll look after him. I shall do all in my power to be at the wedding.
>
> Best if you don't mention to my husband that I've written.
>
> Sincerely, Julia Craven.

Soon after she heard of my engagement, Ruth Harvey came to our house. She stood on the doorstep, her bag on her arm and an odd look on her face which reminded me of the day she had come to tell me Angus was missing. I showed her into the front room. She refused to sit down.

'You're marrying someone else.'

I hadn't anticipated such directness. I nodded, not speaking.

'Oh ye of little faith.' Her voice was low, almost menacing. Her belief that Angus was not dead had reached the point of obsession. She was a thinner, stranger woman, hair now pepper-and-salt grey.

'He's dead. He's not coming back,' I said, pitying her. 'It's not that I don't love him still. I shall always love him, Ruth. But we have to face up to it. We shan't see him again, however much we still feel for him.'

'We'll see,' she said, though I thought I heard the beginnings of resignation in her voice. Opening her handbag she drew out a white envelope and handed it to me. 'You'd better have this.'

I stared at it for a few seconds, unable to give any meaning to it. I saw my name written carefully in blue ink and knew immediately that the writing was Angus's. Frowning, I looked across at her.

'He left it with me. That Christmas, when he was on embarkation leave. For me to give you if he – ' she struggled for a second to steady her voice. 'He said I was to give it to you at the right moment.'

Just managing to control myself, I said, 'And if I was not now about to marry someone else, when exactly do you think the right moment might have been?'

She turned her face away from me and looked beyond, out to the garden. 'I hoped I should never have to give it to you.'

It was all I could do to prevent myself running at her, tearing my nails across her face.

'How dare you keep it from me?' I shrieked at her. 'How could you? How dare you decide when I could read it?' I flailed my arms helplessly. 'Give it to me!'

I went to take it but she held the letter clutched to her chest. 'You gave up on him.'

'And if you carry on like this you'll be giving up on John and Mary. Now give it to me.'

'Whatever's going on?' My mother's shocked face appeared in the doorway.

I held my hand out, my eyes fixed on Ruth's. Finally

she laid the envelope in my palm. I pushed past Mummy, beyond thinking of anything, and ran to my room, shaking, bewildered at the violence I had felt towards Ruth. We who had been such a comfort to one another in the early days of Angus's disappearance had grown sharply apart when I had moved forward, able to grieve, to find the beginnings of acceptance.

Before I opened the letter I let the tears come, months' worth of grief still raw in me, compounded by my rage with Ruth. I even half suspected she had chosen this moment to give me the letter in order to blight my marriage to Douglas. What a comfort it could have been having this letter when I first knew I might not see Angus again. To have his voice through these words at a time when he still felt close and recent. I sat holding the envelope, weeping and shaking.

Only when I was spent did I open it. Seeing his writing on the paper brought a new ache. He had headed the letter Christmas 1940.

Dear Katie,

I'm sitting on my bunk writing this, only just able to see as the sky is so heavy with rain outside, and I must admit to feeling as weighed down myself by what I have to say to you.

I suppose like anyone writing a letter such as this I am praying above all that you will never come to read it. The thought of you having to do so is unbearable but I know I must write. I can't assume that I shall come through all this unscathed. Unlike some of the other chaps I don't have a supreme confidence that I am indestructible.

All I know is that with every fibre of my being I want to stay alive. I love life, and above all my darling, I love you. I am only thankful that I shall not be leaving you widowed, perhaps with our young children to bring up alone and unsupported. That would be an enormous sadness and shame to me. Sometimes I dream of our having a family together, but not now – not in the middle of all this. When I am low I think of your smile and the feel of you close to me. I want to live and live, and to be back sharing this life with you.

All I can say is that you are everything to me, and I shall love you and remember your touch through life or death. But if it comes to it that you are left alone, Katie, please don't feel you mustn't love anyone else or allow them to feel for you. You are so lovable, and above all I want to think that you will be happy. You must take whatever life can give you with my blessing.

I'll end this by saying 'until we meet again' in whatever way that is possible. Pray God that it is in life.

Goodbye, my dearest love. Yours always, Angus.

I lay on my bed for a very long time with his letter pressed to my body, while calmer, quieter tears moved down my cheeks like a benediction.

Two days later, my mother told me that Ruth Harvey had agreed to hold a memorial service for Angus.

Douglas and I were married by Mr Hughes in January 1946. I would not have felt right dolling myself up in a long white dress, and in any case I've never been the frilly type, so instead I chose a cream suit which was smart and flattering, if not ethereal and virginal. My mother approved. I'm not sure Douglas did. I think he would have loved a white angel on his arm.

The evening before the wedding there was a stream of people through the house. Olivia, who was of course to be my bridesmaid, came to try on her dress for the last time. It was made of a vivid blue shantung, in a straight, elegant style which suited her. But I couldn't help noticing the painful boniness of her back as she undressed, facing the mirror. Her face looked washed out and strained and there were dark shadows under her eyes.

She was excited, nervous, and barely stopped talking. 'I so terribly want to get everything just right for you.' She chattered on, looking at herself in the long mirror. She had on a pair of high, slim-heeled court shoes in cream, and twisted herself this way and that on the balls of her feet as I sat watching from the bed. 'This is so exciting, Katie, and Douglas is an absolute love. It's got to be a perfect day. Nothing else will do for you.'

I smiled at her extravagance, happy to see her so animated. 'Livy – it's wonderful to have you around again.' I stood up and went to kiss her. 'Thanks for being such a brick.'

Peter Harvey came to see me. I found it very difficult to communicate with Ruth, despite the service for Angus which had been held just before Christmas. But Peter had been kinder and more resigned from the beginning.

He held both my hands and kissed me. 'We shall be at the service, but I wanted to see you properly while you've got the chance to talk. The actual day is such a bustle. Now, now,' he said, seeing my eyes filling. 'You deserve a bit of happiness. Ruth wishes you well really, you know. It's just taken her a long time to come to terms with it all.'

I kissed his worn face. 'It's all right. I understand. You do know if I still thought there was a chance of Angus coming home, that I'd never – '

'Oh, now – that's no way to go into your marriage.' He gave his chesty laugh. 'You're marrying Douglas. You be happy, girl. That's an order!'

Mummy helped me with my simple preparations for

259

the wedding dutifully, but without obvious enthusiasm. She had shown more vivacity when, shortly after coming home, William announced he was going to abandon Oxford and embark on a career in banking. She felt it would stand him in far better stead. Clearly he had no desire to return home, and had taken off to London acclaimed by Mummy as being very clever and sensible. I had thought Mummy and I had grown marginally closer during the war years, but as soon as William arrived home I had sensed the distance growing between us again.

'You always did prefer him to me, didn't you?' I said to her sadly, the night before the wedding.

She had taken to wearing little pince-nez for reading and close work, and she peered up at me over them, fingers still busy stitching the hem of her dress.

'It's not a matter of preference,' she said, apparently scandalized by the idea.

'What then?' I was feeling emotional, and in need of support and reassurance.

She stopped sewing for a moment, the needle poised. 'Boys are so much easier somehow. Their lives are more direct. And William's always been so clever. Not that you're not,' she said unexpectedly, shooting a glance at me. 'It's just that normally, with boys, their lives go in a straighter line. The war's made a difference to that, of course. But I knew I shouldn't have to watch William grow up, get an education and then throw himself away on a man.'

I gasped. I knew she had found aspects of her marriage frustrating, however good a man Daddy had been. I'd had no idea her thoughts were so bleak.

'Health Visitors can still work when they're married,' I ventured. 'They started allowing it during the war.'

Mummy looked severely at me. 'You think you've got all the answers, don't you? Well, you just wait. It's never how you think. You'll find you're expecting and you'll have all that on your plate. And who d'you think'll be doing all the work and worrying about the children and the house? It won't be Douglas, take that from me, whether you're in a job or out of it. Once you're married it's curtains to any ideas you might have for yourself.'

Accompanied by these cheering words I faced my wedding day.

Olivia looked stunning the next day in her dress of rich blue. She was well made up so her face wore a healthier colour. I had chosen roses for our bouquets as I loved their scent of summer and childhood – mine yellow, Olivia's white. They were hard to come by and expensive because of the time of year.

'Good luck, darling,' Livy whispered, smoothing the shoulders of my dress before I stepped into the church on William's arm. How I missed Daddy then! And I found my legs shaking unexpectedly. But I was collected enough to be able to take in whose faces were turned to watch me arrive. My mother in sky blue with white flowers on her hat, peering anxiously along the aisle at me; Lisa holding Daisy up to get a better view, the little girl's hair scraped up into tiny bunches, and Don's freckled face beside them. Just as I was taking in how smart Douglas looked waiting at the front of the church, I noticed the couple standing opposite Mummy, and realized with a shock that they must be Douglas's parents.

I had felt very uneasy in the weeks before the wedding about the fact that we hadn't been down to visit them, partly because it seemed so odd but also because I was afraid of offending them and of their having a bad opinion of me. Now, though, I felt a new sense of foreboding. If the sight of Douglas's parents was so strange and puzzling, what did this say about how much I knew of Douglas and where he came from?

His description of his mother as a plaster saint could not have been more inaccurate. I assumed this had been his ironic sense of humour. Julia Craven was a small, very curvaceous woman, dressed today in a suit of shimmering candyfloss-coloured silk. Her hair was a more vivid blond than Douglas's, and I could see from where he had inherited his eyes, his full lips and high cheekbones. She was extraordinary rather than beautiful. As I passed her, her gaze fixed frankly on me. I noticed a pungently perfumed smell.

The incongruity of her husband beside her almost made me turn my head to stare back at them. He towered over her, hugely tall and bony with wide, stooped shoulders giving him the look of a bird of prey. He fitted the part of a crusty schoolmaster: the chalky-skinned, lined face, heavy spectacles, the dull tweed suit. His mouth had a bitter slant to it and I felt immediately that I should find him hard to like.

We were married standing as it was difficult for Douglas to kneel. For the first hymn we had chosen 'My Song is Love Unknown'. Singing the beautiful melody I tried to calm my mind. The sight of Douglas's people had really thrown me. I panicked, suddenly breathless, and had to stop singing. I was glad to be facing the front so that no one except Mr Hughes could see my face as my mind raced through a whole assortment of questions.

Who was this man beside me, and what did I really

feel for him? Were those feelings strong enough to bind myself to him for the rest of my life?

'Love to the loveless shown that they might lovely be,' they sang behind me. The words pierced me. Was it pity after all that I felt for Douglas? A powerful combination of pity and desire? What about the kind of love I had felt for Angus, a steadiness between friendship and passion. That knowledge that I could not conceive of the future spent without him. Yet this was precisely what I had been forced to face up to. And now I was giving that future to Douglas.

It's too late now, I said in my thoughts. Please forgive me, Angus.

'Are you all right?' Mr Hughes whispered. I saw Douglas glance anxiously at me.

'Yes,' I replied. 'Thank you.'

I began singing again: 'Here might I stay and sing, no story so divine . . .'

Yet suddenly I had an ominous feeling that ours was not a marriage made in heaven.

Chapter 20

After our reception at a modest hotel, we travelled by train to Malvern, having decided that mid-January was no time to head for the coast. I had changed into a new wool dress in a soft mulberry colour and packed warm clothes, imagining wind sweeping the pointed hills and log fires in the hotel. The railway carriage still had its wartime feel of dinginess and lack of attention, and stank of stale smoke. My seat cover was torn and the floor was dirty. By late afternoon a fine rain had begun to fall, obscuring the first, uplifting sight of the Malvern Hills and leaving outside little to see but a grey murk.

Instead of the new relaxation into certainty I had expected once the nerves of the ceremony were over and the marriage an irrevocable thing, I found my mind jittering around, alive with troubling images.

My mother's ambivalent expression as I finally said goodbye to her: was that simply a mother's mixed feelings at her daughter's wedding? Or was she thinking of her own marriage, or of my father's death, his absence at this occasion? I knew she would never explain such a commotion of feelings to me, but I felt a perplexed need to understand.

When I managed to banish these thoughts from my mind, Olivia slid into it instead. Trotting out after William in the vivid blue shantung dress from a side corridor of the hotel, he walking with urgent speed, slipping between other guests as if trying to throw her off. She wore a tense, fixed smile. There was the exaggerated way she embraced Douglas, throwing her body close against his until he protested, 'Steady on, old girl – I'm not as firm on my feet as I might be, you know.' Even when standing still, performing in ordinary conversation, I noticed the way she held her body in the close-fitting dress. She looked posed, self-conscious, like someone fearful of being startled by a camera at any time.

From her, my mind flitted to Douglas's parents. Having no alternative, he had introduced them to Mummy and me as we arrived at the reception on the Hagley Road. Mummy, I have to say, rose to the occasion and was charming, conveying just the right balance of warmth, welcome and regret at their not having made each other's acquaintance before. In a quiet moment afterwards she murmured to me, with a subtle nod in the Cravens' direction, 'What a very odd couple. I hope you know what you're letting yourself in for.'

When I met her properly, Douglas's cameo of his mother as a 'plaster saint' did not seem quite so wild after all. Close up, the age difference between the two of them was hugely evident. Bernard Craven must have been at least twenty years his wife's senior. His hair, once presumably black like his eyebrows, was storm-cloud grey, his face lined, eyes deep-set behind the thick glasses and his manner unapproachable.

I shook his hand, saying, 'I'm so glad to meet you at last,' and received in reply a nod and a slightly absent-minded 'How do you do,' like an acquaintance in a baker's shop, while his wife watched him with wide eyes as if willing him to expand on it.

Seeing her face close up, I realized it was at odds

with the over-bright, predatory-looking clothes she was wearing. She had, like Douglas, a sensuous face, but there was more sweetness to it, and she looked as young for her years as her husband appeared old for his.

'Katie, my dear – ' She reached up to kiss me. Her skin was flawless. I had expected a heavy, brassy voice, but instead it was small and hesitant. She kept glancing anxiously at her husband as if inviting his permission to open her mouth.

'We're so delighted. We've worried so about Douglas – we have, darling.' She took his arm playfully and kissed him, standing on tiptoe. Douglas, who up until now had been smiling and affable with all the other guests, was now blushing and obviously uncomfortable, but didn't resist her kiss. 'He's such a naughty boy about keeping in touch, but we're terribly proud of him. And we're so happy to be here and meet you – aren't we, Bernard?'

Bernard Craven coughed and gave an almost imperceptible nod. Douglas stared at the ground. I saw Julia Craven watching her husband as if gauging whether he was about to speak, in which case she would desist from doing so, his words counting for more than hers. As he didn't, she continued, trying to draw both husband and son into the conversation. I sensed this was an old pattern. She addressed first one, then the other and drew so little response from them that she was left to turn to me in desperation. In her childlike way she appealed, 'I do hope we shall be able to see something of you both?'

'I hope so too,' I said. I found that I meant it.

That evening we ate beef and drank wine in the pale coffee-coloured dining room of our hotel, one of many elegant buildings in the spa town which straggled its way across the smoke-grey hills.

'Douglas,' I said. 'Tell me about your parents – properly, I mean.' Their strangeness made me feel unsure of him.

'Why? What do they matter?' he asked flippantly.

'Don't be ridiculous – of course they matter. They're who you come from – and you haven't managed to prevent me meeting them. But I'd at least like to know why you tried so hard to keep them away.'

At last he told me more, words spilling fast from his lips as if he had them all prepared.

'My father was a postmaster's son in a small town outside Gloucester. He was bright and he became a schoolmaster, even though I'm not at all sure he liked children very much. They met when she was sixteen and he was already thirty-eight. All rather a cliché really: the shy, graceless schoolmaster sinking into bachelorhood – no one interested in him. He wasn't handsome. He's the kind of man no one normally notices very much. But she noticed him – she's like that . . .' His voice softened. 'She sees things in people that others miss and brings them out. She's very compassionate, would do anything for people.' He paused and looked across the room as if stopped by a painful thought. 'She was lovely to look at then, perfect really. Pretty, innocent, very vivacious. You can see it all in the photographs. He was forever having portraits done of her. He was completely taken over by her. I suppose his life began again when he met her. She saved him, and he knows it. But she adored him as well. She was an only child, and I think her parents were reasonable enough people, but she had a great store of affection to give away. They married two years later. When she was nineteen, the next year, reality crashed in on them. I arrived, wonky leg and all. Imperfect. A disappointment. She was very good to me, of course – defensive of me. But she was so protective, she wouldn't let me breathe – give me a chance to get out and cope.

'She's always been dominated totally by my father. It was his age, his manner, and I think she felt guilty for not giving him a proper son. It was he who ruled they must have no more children because the first pot was cracked, so to speak.' Douglas gave a self-mocking laugh. 'If this one's like this, think what the next one might be like, was his attitude. He's an arrogant man, and cold. I suppose their courtship was the one aberration in his life. And she still loves him. Heaven knows why. She was so young when she married him and in some ways she still is. Didn't she strike you as girlish?'

'In a way.' I thought of her letter to me. 'She must be strong, though.'

The cheeseboard arrived at our table and we cut slices of Leicester and Wensleydale to eat with water biscuits, luxurious in this austere time.

'Your father looks so bitter,' I said, thinking back to the man's sour features. 'Why would that be? Not because of you, surely? He ought to be proud of all you've achieved.'

'Things built up over the years,' Douglas said evasively. He reached out and took one of my hands in his. 'Can we change the subject now? I'd really prefer to leave them out of tonight.'

My curiosity was still unsatisfied, but I agreed.

'You must miss your father,' Douglas said kindly. 'Especially today. It seems tragic to die so near the end of the war.'

I nodded slowly. 'He was a pacifist – I expect I've told you. When the war ended and those pictures of Bergen-Belsen and the other camps were all coming out, it was the only time my mother allowed me to see her cry for him. She was crying partly about the terrible things in the pictures, of course, but she said to me, "Thank God your father didn't live to see this." And I understood exactly what she meant. Although he had worked with so many people in all walks of life, and seen some awful things, he still had such strong beliefs in the sanctity of people. There was a kind of innocence about him.'

Douglas squeezed my hand. 'I'm sorry I didn't meet him.'

We sat talking over our coffee, well fed, warmed by the cosy room and suddenly intimate. I relaxed, unburdened of the painful thoughts that had marred the train journey. We ordered more coffee, delaying the moment of going upstairs, luxuriating in the sense of anticipation.

As soon as we were in our room our hands were pulling at each other's clothes. Our lips opened up to each other's, and I pulled his body in close to mine. He seemed startled at my passionate response to him, drew back and looked at me, and I could see the urgency in his eyes.

'Stand still,' he ordered. 'I want to undress you.'

I realized only afterwards how prominent in his mind was the thought that he was the first person to do this. I waited, my legs unsteady with longing for him. Both of us were breathing fast, shallow breaths. Douglas's physical presence had always had a strong effect on me and now I could allow those feelings to be satisfied. He slipped off my wool dress, slip, stockings, camisole and the rest of my underwear, his hands trembling as he loosed my breasts. Without giving me the chance to do the same for him, he began to tear off his own clothes, struggling impatiently with his tie and collar studs. He turned his back to me as he removed the last of his clothes. I had never seen him naked before. Shivering, I looked at the broad top half of his body, the strong straight back. His legs were very white, the bad one slightly thinner than the other. He turned, very bashful suddenly, braving both the exposure of his leg and his obvious arousal. At first he couldn't look at me, as if he was afraid that having seen, I would reject him.

But I wanted him for everything he was. 'Come here,' I said. 'Please.'

His hands flickered over my body, lightly, then with more firmness and confidence. He stood back from me a little, not allowing the lower part of his body to touch me. His hands moved over my breasts, waist, back, and then, as if he could no longer resist, his fingers stroked quickly between my legs. I responded, moving my hips forward, eyes closed.

'My God,' he cried. His voice was harsh and loud.

I opened my eyes. 'Sssh. People will hear you. Whatever's the matter?'

His face wore an incensed, cheated expression, lips tightening. 'You know exactly what you're doing! You're not a virgin are you?'

Half stunned, I looked into his livid face. 'No.'

He turned abruptly and limped towards the window. 'You've made a proper fool of me. I should have seen it that day in the garden. You'd have had all your clothes off if I'd let you. I might have known – just like her.' There was a bitter conviction in his voice.

'Who?' I was bewildered. I folded my arms across my goosepimpled breasts, shivering now from the cold.

270

'My dear sweet mother.' He was silent for a moment, then spoke very fast, his back to me.

'Go with anything she would. Almost, anyway. D'you really think she was faithful to my exhumed mummy of a father? There were a number of them on and off as I grew up. After all, she was lovely, wasn't she? Sympathy and intimacy were what she wanted. And the young men with their tight skin and vigorous bodies wanted her for her hips and breasts, those eyes, for the sparkling life she gave off. And they made her laugh and stay young. I had to lie for her sometimes and I found out how easily it comes. He always knew, of course. But they didn't stop needing each other. That's the power they've always had over one another – the dependence – each afraid of losing the other's love. The more he withdrew, the harder she tried for him. It was poison – the house was full of unspoken rage all the time. And I moved between them like a symbol of their warped marriage.' His voice began to break up. 'She doesn't know who she is. She's a child, a butterfly, a whore . . .' He controlled himself. I stood waiting, frozen.

'You went with . . .?'

'Angus. Yes.'

'I thought your relationship with him was innocent.' He seemed to force out the words.

'Douglas – ' I went closer to him, finding it unbearable talking in this distant way. 'You didn't ask. It's not something I could just come out with easily. I loved Angus. And of course, the war . . . We lived from day to day. Every time he came home on leave we knew we might never see each other again. And the last time we happened to be right. If it hadn't been for the war it would have been different.'

271

'You'd be married to him, wouldn't you?' Douglas asked miserably.

'Most likely.' I kept my voice gentle. 'But there's no point in thinking like that. Angus is dead, Douglas. It's you I'm married to. You can't go through our marriage being jealous of a ghost. It's absurd.'

'A woman should be a virgin on her wedding night,' he said peevishly. 'It's what a man expects.'

'I'm sorry.' I put out my hand and touched the top of his arm. He didn't shake me off. 'There's nothing can be done now. All I can say is, it's you I want.'

He turned and looked at me hard then, his blue eyes searching mine with frightening intensity. 'How do I know I can trust you?'

The question grated on me. 'You can't know. That's what trust is about. I shan't be unfaithful to you.'

We were both very cold and I took his hand and led him to the bed where we got in under the covers. The shock of the sheets made us shudder. I put my arms round him. This was someone I wasn't used to, this weak, exposed Douglas, deeply insecure. After a moment he laid his head on my chest and I moved my body closer to him.

'That's right,' he said, his sarcasm less wholehearted now. 'Throw yourself at me.'

Silently I stroked him with my hand until we were both warmer. He began to move his face against my skin.

'Katie – I want us to be together so much.'

And he began touching me very fast, almost per-functorily; breasts, stomach, thighs and momentarily between my legs, removing his hand with a jerk as if I'd bitten him. His face was tense.

'It's all right,' I reassured him. I raised my head and

pulled him to me, kissing him, trying to inject some warmth into our lovemaking when all I could find was a hurried kind of desperation as if he wanted it over.

His movements became urgent suddenly. He tried to climb on top of me but got caught up in the sheet and had to kneel up to free himself.

'Lie back,' he ordered abruptly.

He flung himself on me. 'Quickly – for God's sake.' He was too high, against my stomach and I arched my body under him. But he lay very still suddenly. His face creased, agonized, hands gripping the pillow behind my head.

'No.' Now he was almost sobbing. 'No, no.' He sank his head down beside me and gave a sigh which I felt right through his body. Gradually I felt the wetness between us. He began to shake and I knew he was crying.

Eventually, raising his head a little he said, 'I couldn't have deflowered you anyway, could I?'

We lay there for a long time and I stroked him like a child. He was too deep in his own feelings to notice the tears on my face.

'Don't worry, darling,' I whispered. 'We've got the rest of our lives for this, haven't we? It'll get better.'

Chapter 21

It might have got better had things been different. Had it not been for Olivia.

In May, the Kemps sent her away.

'So where is she?' I demanded of Elizabeth.

'She's having a spell in hospital.' She had invited me in, but we remained standing in that bleached, fussy drawing-room. She fiddled with a silver cigarette case, turning it round and round in her hands.

I had re-established more contact with the Kemps over the past months, especially seeing the state Livy was in. I felt for them, disturbed as they were by her depressed listlessness interspersed with loud, over-excited behaviour But now I could feel my civility slipping fast.

'Where?' I asked. 'I'll go and see her.'

'It's not that kind of hospital.'

'What d'you mean?' I was afraid of her answer.

She couldn't meet my eyes. 'She's in All Saints.'

All Saints, the mental hospital on the north side of the city. Part of an old, forbidding complex of institutions: asylum, prison, workhouse, shoulder to shoulder, only separated from each other by high brick walls.

'My God!' I was horrified. 'Why? I mean I know she's seemed very overwrought at times, but surely things weren't that bad?'

Speaking in a whisper, Elizabeth said, 'We didn't

know what else to do. You've only seen a little of what she's been like. Her behaviour has been horrible. I can hardly bear to think of it. She's been going with men like a . . .' She wrung her hands. 'Alec felt he'd lost control of her. Just a little spell in there, he said, to bring her back to her senses.' She began to sob quietly, her shoulders heaving.

'Alec says, Alec says,' I stormed at her. 'Don't you ever think or say anything for yourself, you pathetic woman? Or at least for your own daughter? He's not God, he's just a man, and a pretty unprincipled one at that.'

'It's not his fault,' she cried, gulping and sobbing. 'It's all my fault. I am a pathetic woman. I am!'

'What is the *matter* with you?' I was inflamed, unable to see anything but my fury. 'Don't you realize how difficult it is to get someone released from a mental institution once you've had them certified? And you have, I take it?'

Elizabeth crumpled. I found myself looking down on the pins in her blond pleat of hair as she knelt in front of me. 'I don't know,' she said. 'I don't even know that. Help me, Katie. You're so strong. As strong as he is. Help me. I don't know what to do.'

'Help you?' I blazed at her. 'Why should I help *you*? But I'll do whatever it takes to help Olivia. And damn the pair of you – damn you!'

I turned and left her kneeling with her beautifully coiffured head pressed to the floor, weeping with harsh, broken sounds. My feeling at the time was that it served her right.

But I also shared with her a terrible sense of guilt. I'd seen for myself that things were not right with Livy and had done nothing. I was preoccupied with my own concerns, and also I simply didn't know what to do. She had needed help – perhaps for a lot longer than I realized – and I hadn't responded. What sort of friend could I call myself?

* * *

OLIVIA

Other people can love. Katie loves, but I have not learned how. She cries when babies are born. I think that's a kind of love. She cares for other people's children. But I have never been able to make things turn out right. Everything I touch curdles. I am like brown spots on apples or the monster skulking under the stairs.

My initial training in the WRNS is at Mill Hill. The Wren officer who interviews me looks as if she is in the wrong place, as if she has just stepped out of her kitchen fresh from bottling fruit.

She asks, 'What were you up to before the war?'

'I was a pianist.' The words stride out of my mouth. I want it to be true. It ought to be true.

She frowns at my forms. 'It says here you have secretarial qualifications.'

We all hear this regulation: we are to 'be amenable to naval discipline and put service before family ties'. To me this is beautiful, a kind of psalm. I want it in embossed silver letters across my wall. It makes my life feel narrow and simplified like a nun's. I am free.

I hope freedom will make me clean. I can be a child and begin again. Like any child I need love.

My first job is at Southampton. I am Personal Assistant and shorthand typist for —. I don't want to give his rank or write his full name. People can make things out of anything. His wife lives inland in Hampshire. He is Peter. Just Peter. He is strong and lean with a face lined beyond his years, possibly by sea and weather. His nose is large, with character and authority. He has strong, square nails and I watch his hands move over paper, reach for pens, lift the telephone receiver. After days, only, alone in that small square office I know his eyes are on my hands, on my curved body, his eyes piercing me when he believes my attention is away from him. We match each other in our dark blue uniforms. I know we must touch, skin on skin.

I wait a long time because this is different. It hurts me, is fish hooks under my skin. With others it is I who decide, who take charge, because it is nothing. With Peter I am paralysed, cannot flaunt, at times can barely speak. I watch him work so hard. He is very tired and I want to comfort him. The air takes on life between us.

We are forever working late. When it happens he pushes his chair back in a rush and stands behind mine. My hands move like machines on the typewriter until I am trembling too much. My breaths are thin as wafers. My body feels scraped raw, waiting for his touch. I have never felt this before, so tilted and falling.

He says, 'I can't get through another day without touching you.'

It is not skin on skin because there's no time. It's buttons and layers of clothes and a hard floor. I no longer know what I am doing. I have not known I could want a man, that my body could cry out and hurt until it's losing me, leaving me behind. I hear myself moaning and my teeth are biting into stiff cloth and flesh and hair and the room is rocking and my head crashes back and forth and more words spill out of my mouth as he does it to me and I am there and not there.

When everything slows and the room is still he's climbing away from my body, fast. He says 'Christ', and his voice is small and frightened. When our clothes are straightened out he is giving me looks across the room from the sides of his eyes. My face is bleeding.

He has me moved to another office. I know it's his way of showing remorse because of that cold wife. He never talks about her but I know she's cold like cod on a slab. I don't take it personally. Liaisons of that kind are naturally frowned on in the forces. I leave some time before seeking him out. Then I think he needs encouraging, that he might be afraid he's hurt my feelings.

I telephone then, every day. Of course the new secretary answers. She says, 'Peter' (she doesn't actually say Peter of course) 'is not able to speak to you at present.'

And I say, in my best Wren voice, 'Perhaps you could tell him it's a matter of the utmost urgency?'

I try to see him, but he is never alone, and is colder than the winter sea. The nose takes on a look of cruelty. I write. I wait outside his quarters. His face looms in my sleep. Eventually I go to his office, in tears, though I haven't meant to cry. The secretary is still there, blond, trim and impassable as a shield for him. Following that they move me away from Southampton.

Since that I have been with men a lot. Anyone's. Everyone's. Other Wrens won't speak to me. Officers' groundsheet, and not just officers. It's something I can do well, when I don't care for them at all. There's a comfort in a man's body, but I am playing it, I never lose myself. I am supreme for those moments. I'm queen, jewelled with ice and thorns.

They never come back to me. They're coated in a thick rime of disgust. I don't allow myself disgust.

*　*　*

As days, then weeks passed, I became almost savage with anxiety about Olivia. At that time I was taken over by it and it felt as if nothing and nobody else mattered. Just as when Alec had imprisoned her in her bedroom all those years ago, my energy was all directed into thinking how I could help her and release her.

It was not a good start to our marriage. We stayed at the house in Chantry Road, which was an arrangement Douglas was happy with, but made me feel I had not yet graduated fully from being a child, and I was restless and perverse. Douglas was working very hard as ever, pushing himself on, conscientious to the point of obsession, and I suppose lonely. He found it difficult to talk to men his own age, all returning now with their stories of war. Now and then he talked about moving on, finding a job in London. Each of us seemed shut away in our own thoughts and concerns.

We lived chiefly on the top floor of the house, which in itself was equivalent to a spacious flat. We had an arrangement whereby we only ate with Mummy at weekends, if she was not working. In fact she had few weekends off and we did not see a lot of her. Mostly I prepared meals for Douglas and myself after work, chatting often with Mrs Drysdale who still came in daily, carrying them up to our living room which looked out over the garden. Douglas often worked odd hours too, covering evening meetings, and then I ate alone. Sometimes recently it had been a relief to do so.

'You're not here with me at all, are you?' he said one

evening as we ate mutton chops and vegetables. 'In your head, I mean.'

I looked across at him guiltily. He was eating fast, his tie off, shirt unbuttoned at the neck, keeping his eyes on his plate as he spoke. Our clock on the mantelpiece seemed to tick too loudly.

'I'm sorry. I'm just so worried about Livy.'

Douglas helped himself to more carrots. 'It's a shame, of course,' he said with his horrible journalistic detachment which sometimes made my blood boil. 'Terrible, those places, from what I gather. But I can't understand why it is you're so attached to her. Nice girl of course, but she is off-centre you know. She was even flirting with me at our wedding. I don't see what she's done to merit such blind devotion.' The tone of his last words was edged with sarcasm. I chose to ignore it.

'It's very hard to put it into words.' I was trying to explain it to him and to myself. 'You never saw her as she used to be. We've been friends for so long – I just can't help loving her.' My voice became high and tearful. 'And I can't bear to think of her locked away in that place.'

Seeing me cry, Douglas was immediately full of concern. He pushed his chair back and came and leaned over me, an arm round my shoulders. 'Don't cry, my darling. I hate to see it.' He stood stroking me with the immense gentleness he could sometimes summon, as I wept, feeling angry and helpless.

When I'd had a cry, I said, 'You finish your meal. I'm all right.' I polished my specs on my napkin. Sniffing, I tried to smile at him.

Douglas beamed at me across the table. 'My darling, I do love you.'

I was gradually learning that when I came to Douglas

tearful and needy was when he could best cope with me. He always did love me most in my weakness.

I went to the hospital. The walls were very high and the iron gates locked. All that could be seen of the inside was the tops of the trees. It took me some time to find the entrance, walking round the wide perimeter of the hospital grounds.

On Lodge Road I heard voices calling desperately to the unseen world. They were men's voices. One was shouting, 'Hello? Hello? Is anyone there? Can you hear me? Hello?' On and on. Another voice, high and strangely sexless, was insisting, 'Tell her. Tell Doris I'm coming, Friday. Tell Doris I'm coming.'

It was a beautiful spring day. I couldn't associate my sweet friend with this place. Nor, of course, could I get in.

I wouldn't leave the Kemps alone. I went round to the house almost daily.

At first Alec was jovial and defensive. 'She's all right,' he assured me on a day after they'd been to visit. 'A little better, we thought, didn't we, Elizabeth?' His wife nodded dumbly. 'I don't think there's any need for you to feel so crusading about all this, Kate. She's where she needs to be at the moment. None of us like it.' He gave me a challenging look. 'Her being in there isn't a fact we want broadcast, of course.'

'I bet it isn't.'

Alec stepped over to me, leaning down to put his face close to mine. I remembered for a second how I used to dream of him leaning over to kiss me. 'Look here,' he hissed. 'If you let anyone know about this . . .'

I met his gaze, steadily.

'Don't come here again,' he finished in a low voice. He left the room.

Elizabeth began to cry. 'She told us they'd put her in one of those – those things where you can't move your arms.'

'You mean a straitjacket,' I said brutally. I felt like screaming. 'What did you expect? It's a mental hospital. That's what they do.'

'But I thought – being who she is – that they'd be kinder. You know, treat her a bit differently. She's in there with all nature of people.'

'Since when has madness distinguished between classes?' Elizabeth put her hand to her head in a gesture of despair.

'Who can get her out? Just him?'

She nodded slowly. Her hands were never still as she talked. 'It's not that he wants her in there – you have to understand that. He loves her very dearly. He wouldn't let you see it, of course, but he's so afraid and ashamed of what's happening to her. Of how she is. Things in our family haven't always been – ' She stopped, silenced herself. 'We've been at our wits' end.'

Speaking more gently, I said, 'I'll go and see her. When are visitors allowed?'

Elizabeth looked up at me. 'I don't think they'll let you. They said close family only.' I saw an unusual look of determination enter her face. 'Perhaps if I were to write you a note. You might have to pretend to be her sister. If it had Alec's signature . . .'

'Being who he is,' I quipped. 'But he's hardly going to sign anything for me now, is he?'

Elizabeth looked at me with surprising calm. 'Don't you think I'm familiar with my husband's handwriting by now?'

I stared at her, only grasping slowly what she was saying.

'I daren't write it while he's here. I'll bring it round to your house later.'

As I was leaving, Alec appeared out of his study and I realized he had been waiting for me. His expression was very stern. 'You'd better keep your mouth shut, Katie.'

I was exhilarated suddenly. This man's true colours were showing under the strain and I could be free of him.

'I'll keep it shut,' I said. 'For as long as it helps Olivia.'

That evening an envelope was delivered at our house. The note inside explained that I was Olivia's friend, that we were very close and that it would be beneficial for me to visit. The likeness of the handwriting to Alec Kemp's was so extraordinary that I thought at first Elizabeth had persuaded him to put pen to paper himself. But there was a separate sheet on which Elizabeth had written, 'I'm sure this will do it. Please believe better of me. E. K.'

The following Sunday I took the note to All Saints and was let in through the gate. The hospital was a huge, stately building like a country house, with stained-glass windows above the entrance and sunlight pouring on to its soft-coloured stone.

They wouldn't let me see her. Not because I wasn't a close relative, but because she wasn't, they considered, in a fit state.

In June they had her moved to Arden.

'Alec wanted to get her out of the city,' Elizabeth told me. I always tried to visit the house when she was there alone. 'He's very much afraid it will get out somehow that his daughter's in an institution. He's still hoping to stand at the next election.'

I knew I had a kind of ally in Elizabeth, but I was wary of her. She had clearly decided that for the moment her feelings for Olivia must override her loyalty to her husband. But I saw I had never really known her at all, and she was so conditioned to giving nothing away. I was growing more suspicious about the whole situation. Clearly there was something more seriously wrong with Olivia than the odd outburst of emotion and anxiety she had shown before the war. And all these things were now beginning to build into a sequence of events that I hadn't identified before. I wanted to get to the bottom of it: her unhappiness before the war, her withdrawal from me over those years, and what it was that had tilted her so far over that she had to be speedily put away out of sight.

I knew, though, that I'd never get the answers direct from Elizabeth. Sometimes when she looked at me with those childlike blue eyes and gave her automatic smiles, I wondered what it would take truly to break her into honesty.

Olivia had been in Arden for two weeks when, with Elizabeth, I managed to get into the place for the first time. I had gone alone the week before, carrying with me Elizabeth's forged letter, but they turned me away.

We went together on the sort of day which normally makes you feel glad to be alive. The sky was almost unmarked by cloud and there was a feeling of expectancy in the strong sunlight that I always associate with early summer. But sitting in the cab in which we travelled from Leamington Spa I was churned up inside with apprehension. As we passed under the stone archway at the entrance to the drive I felt as if my heart was going to explode. Even being a nurse, like most people I regarded places like Arden with a kind of flesh-creeping horror. The surface of the curving drive was so rough I was thrown from side to side on the back seat. I watched the place move nearer, a vast brick building, the edge of its roof sculpted into points, looking dark and impersonal.

The grounds at Arden were in a shocking state. The hospital had been used for wounded servicemen during the war and it was only just in the process of adapting back to its normal use. This decrepitude only increased its grimness. It looked terrible. The grass was long and full of dandelions and thistles. The drive itself had clumps of grass growing between the wheel tracks and the flowerbeds were only just identifiable, so choked were they with weeds and branches from the overgrown bushes behind them. The wide view across the front looked more like a cattle field than the grounds of a hospital.

The brickwork of the building itself was stained in places, and the roof, half covered with moss, showed dark gaps where slates had slid off and smashed on the ground where they still lay. The windows were grimy, some of the panes broken, and I wondered if these were in windows of dormitories. The building must have been cold enough in the winter as it was. I could hardly bear to think of Olivia inside there. Already, I felt I had stepped out of the world into a terrible, removed place.

When we told the porter, a leathery-cheeked man, who we had come to visit, he said, 'Crikey – we don't get many visitors coming to see this lot.'

He led us into a large hall and told us to wait. The hall must have been very grand before the war. Its ceiling was high and decorated with ornately carved wood. There were long windows along one side with iron radiators beneath them, which I found a reassuring sight. There was a platform at one end of the room. But once again everything looked dirty and worn. The grain of the wooden floor was obscured by grime and hundreds of round black indentations showed where rows of metal bedsteads had stood.

We waited in silence, not looking at each other, as if we were both ashamed to be there.

I was prepared for Olivia looking different, but when they brought her in, her arm grasped by a muscular nurse, I actually gasped. Her removal from the world outside seemed to have become a physical reality. Everything that had made her beautiful had in a few weeks altered or faded. They had dressed her in someone's green gingham dress of a ludicrously large size which sat limp on her like a sack. Her hair, normally so glossy and curling, hung in flat, lank sheets each side of her face; her cheeks were pale and blemished. She barely raised her gaze from the floor, and when she did, her eyes were empty of expression.

'Livy?' I bent my head to intercept her gaze. I saw myself, guiltily, as I must have seemed to her: larger somehow than this place would allow, face blooming from the air outside, healthy and free in a blue dirndl dress and light coat. She continued to stare at the floor.

The nurse, with cheeks the colour of boiled ham, led her to a chair. When she made no effort to sit on it the nurse pushed her down. The woman's masculine-looking arms bulged out from the sleeves of her tight blue uniform dress and she smelled pungently of sweat. I pulled a chair round to face Livy. The nurse stood over her. 'Could you leave us, please?' I said sharply.

'I've got to stay in the room.' Her voice reinforced

the impression she gave of a man dressed as a woman. She ambled over to another chair by the door. 'You've got fifteen minutes,' she shouted across to us.

Olivia sat quite still, hands clasped in her lap, head down. The top button of the dress was missing and it was so loose that it gaped open, showing her dark, naked nipples. I leaned over and softly pulled it together and pressed it against her body.

After a moment she looked up at her mother and the tears came straight away. 'Mummy, oh Mummy.' She flung herself sideways and buried her face in her mother's shoulder, grasping on to her, knuckles white.

With surprise I watched Elizabeth's steely calm. She held Livy for a few moments, then made her sit up again, almost pushing her away. 'Listen, darling. *Listen* to me. You're not going to be here for long, we hope, but you've got to try and get better.'

'But people don't come out of here.' Livy's eyes were bulging. 'Some of them have been here years and years.'

'You won't be,' Elizabeth said firmly. 'You won't.' I felt they had forgotten I was there.

'Isn't this enough?' Olivia whispered. I watched her white, strained face. 'Haven't I done enough for him? Isn't he satisfied?'

I saw a look of panic flash across Elizabeth's face. She actually shook Olivia slightly. 'What are you talking about? This isn't a punishment. Don't be so stupid. You're here because you're ill and you need help.'

'She died,' Livy said suddenly, her eyes still stretched wide. She perched on the edge of the chair, kneading the fingers of one hand with the other ceaselessly as she talked.

'Who died?' Elizabeth asked sharply.

'Eileen.' She spoke very fast, her voice like that of a

little girl. 'They put her in the side room next to the ward when she went off. They call it going up the stick, the nurses. Eileen went up the stick. Right up – up to the top and she fell off. She shouted and shouted. All day for hours and hours. They went in and tried to stop her – men as well. Crowds of them. But they couldn't and she carried on. Then she went quiet suddenly. They tried to stop us seeing, but we saw anyway when they carried her out. They're always dying. The man comes round every day and asks if they've got any for him. His thinks we don't know what he means, but we do. And Mary says she'll be next because it's waiting for her, always there waiting for her because of what she did years and years ago. Like me . . .'

Elizabeth made a convulsive gesture towards Livy as if to silence her, but she stopped abruptly of her own accord.

'Livy?' I took her hands. Trying to speak calmly, I said, 'You do know who I am, don't you?'

She nodded, and in a tiny voice said, 'Katie.'

'Are all the nurses like her?' I asked, inclining my head a fraction towards the woman who had planted herself over by the door.

Olivia followed my glance, fearfully. 'She's not a nurse,' she whispered. 'She's a miner's wife. Her husband works in the men's side. He couldn't get a job. They're from Cannock.' She added as if incidentally, 'Everybody shouts here.'

Then the little girl voice came back. 'I think I've had some sort of breakdown. That's what Daddy says, and the doctor says so. I can't seem to – manage any more. And they give me things. I don't know what they give me.'

'Give you things?'

'Medicine. White stuff. They don't tell you.'

'It's probably to help you keep calm,' I told her.

'My tummy hurts. I think there's something wrong with my insides.'

'Did you tell the doctor?'

'He said I was imagining it.' She began rocking the upper half of her body quickly back and forth. I saw the nurse's eyes swivel towards her.

'Livy,' I whispered. 'Try and keep still or she'll make you go back now.'

To my shame I found myself half wishing the nurse would take her away from us, out of my sight. I felt utterly helpless. What could I say? It was impossible to talk about anything: the past, the future were meaningless here. Everything was foreshortened into these minutes, here between these walls.

'What day is it?' Olivia asked.

'Sunday,' Elizabeth told her gently. 'It'll always be Sunday when we come, darling.'

'The thing is,' she said, suddenly speaking calmly and firmly. 'They say I'm not well.' She directed a look of piercing malevolence at her mother. 'Nurse Tucker says she thinks I have good reason.'

Suddenly there were tears pouring down her face again. She had a terrible grip on my hands, and appealed to me, not her mother. 'I don't want people to see me like this. Help me, Katie. Help me – please.'

I was filled with panic, choking with it. 'What can I do? I don't know what to do.' I pulled my hands away and took her tightly in my arms as she cried, making loud, jarring sounds which reached higher into shrieks. The nurse was upon us immediately.

'Come on, now,' she said 'That's enough. You come with me.' With rough skill she seized Olivia and pinned her arms to her sides. She was more than a match for her in size and strength.

'I can't go back up there!' Livy screamed. 'Not through all those doors. Don't take me back!'

'We'll come again,' we told her, but she wasn't hearing us.

The last sounds I heard were her screams echoing along the dark corridor, and the sound of a large key being turned. My legs were shaking so I could barely stand.

As our taxi moved down Arden's curving drive, taking us back to the station, I said to Elizabeth, 'What d'you think she meant – about having good reason? What is all this about?'

There was a long silence. I could tell the woman next to me was struggling hard with herself, her eyes glassy with tears. But with an enormous effort she regained control. Wiping her eyes, she looked down and straightened the front of her blouse.

Finally, turning her gaze to the half-open window she said, 'I really don't have any idea.'

'Oh, so you're back at last are you?' Douglas burst out when I walked into the house. The train to Birmingham had been delayed and then I'd refused Alec's offer of a lift and had a long wait for the bus. Douglas was seething with resentment, so much so that he had come downstairs to confront me. Seeing the advent of trouble between us, my mother, with the expression of a prophet whose words have come true, disappeared towards the other end of the house.

In a peevish tone which I had been hearing from him more and more lately, he said, 'I suppose it's too much to expect that you might spend Sunday with your husband?'

I was too tired and upset to point out that often when I did spend Sunday with Douglas, a good part of it consisted of hearing the sound of his typewriter coming from the small study next to our bedroom.

'You know where I've been.' I wanted him to hold me, for something to feel normal and right.

'Do I?' he hurled the words at me. His blue eyes were hard with fury. 'Why should I believe you?'

'Oh for goodness' sake, stop being so melodramatic,' I said. 'D'you really think I'd be making up some story about carting all the way to a mental hospital half way across Warwickshire for my own entertainment?'

'That depends.' He limped badly towards me, accentuating his disability. He did this to goad me, had been doing so increasingly lately. At first it had made me feel guilty, as if I was failing him in some way. Now I was beginning to resent it. I'd certainly had enough of everything for one day.

'It all depends who you were really going to see, doesn't it?'

I stared at him coldly. 'What are you talking about?'

He stood silently for a moment, looking hard into my eyes and I met his stare, angry now.

'Oh, forget I spoke,' he said in a disgusted voice. I wasn't certain whether the emotion was directed towards me or himself.

'I went with Elizabeth Kemp. You know that.'

Ignoring this he moved towards the stairs. 'I suppose there'll be something to eat this evening.'

'Yes,' I agreed flatly. 'I suppose there will.'

When he'd gone upstairs, my mother came back in.

She'd obviously been listening. She walked across the room with a vase of flowers, not looking at me.

'It's no good.' Her tone was brisk and neutral. 'You'll have to put him first. He's not going to be the sort to play second fiddle to anyone.'

'But he's not having to,' I cried, tearful now. 'I'm doing my best. I can't help it if Olivia's ill, can I?'

Mopping a ring of water from the table, she said, 'Perhaps you should think of giving up work.'

'I'd have thought you'd be the last person to suggest that.' But I wondered wearily whether if she wasn't right. Douglas had been so demanding recently, expecting so much from me and never seeming satisfied with what I did. I kept wondering what had happened to the kind, charming man I had married. I felt tired and pulled in too many directions at once.

I told my mother that Douglas and I would eat upstairs that night, given the bad atmosphere between us. We ate our meal in silence, but by bedtime he was repentant.

'I don't know what I said all that for, darling.' He was lying with his head on my breast. 'Don't take any notice of me when I'm like that, will you? I've been alone so long I don't know how to behave with someone. You know I'm only like this because I love you and I need you so much.'

I need you. I need you. Douglas's constant refrain nowadays. He looked round at me, his expression contrite, and I was filled with sudden tenderness for him.

'Can we try it again. Please, darling?'

I'd had to be very careful, very patient with him as a lover. One hint of my own, usually unsatisfied desires, and he built mountains of resentment and insecurity. Almost as soon as he was aroused he had to be in me. Sometimes he left it just too late, and came with agonized embarrassment almost at the first contact of our flesh. When he did manage to hold back until he was inside me it was over in seconds, but he was jubilant with himself.

We did have times of great affection and tenderness, but the frustrations of the bedroom seeped out to affect everything else. It was a huge obstacle to him, something he felt he had to work at, be good at. It was equally frustrating to me, except that I learned this was something he must never be made aware of. I found I was learning to tread very carefully with his moods, tiptoeing round him fearfully.

I turned to him, and we held one another. Half my mind was still occupied with Olivia and I tried to keep it that way. I still found Douglas attractive but I tried to avoid becoming aroused by him because he seemed so incapable of giving me anything sexually. I had begun to think of our love life very much as my wifely duty, more painful in its frustrated expectations than a complete absence of lovemaking would have been.

Douglas began to take his pleasure, running his hands over my body as if testing himself. I was ready for him as he plunged into me, panting with anxiety. He thrust into me once and it was over. He laid his head next to mine as if with relief, then raised it to smile at me, searching my face with his eyes.

'That was good, wasn't it, Katie? I think it's getting better.'

* * *

OLIVIA

Things I remember about Arden

Arden is deep in the countryside, ringed by stagnant fields and petrified trees. I thought when they took me there that I was going to my death. They would have absolute control over me. They proposed to bury me alive behind all those doors. Every ten yards along the corridors, doors and more doors, unlocking, slamming, relocking. When they visit me, Mummy and Kate, I come up to them as if from a well, hauled up, up, door after door. From where they sit they can never see the bottom of it nor understand that this is where I have come from. I don't want them to see me like this. And I don't know whether it's yesterday that I saw them or last month because the days run into each other and never change.

I can't tell them. Since I've been here I learn that what we say here is twisted into nonsense to those outside and whatever words I use make them frown, further convinced of my instability. I don't try to speak about the way the staff slam and shout, treating even the doors with hatred, how they edge round the room, their backs to the walls of the ward which are the colour of dead skin, their eyes never leaving us. They are afraid of us. In my opinion they are very odd.

We have reason after all, for being here: that's what I know. Bridget has reason; she's perhaps sixty, gave birth to a dead baby all those years ago. Agnes won't eat the food. She feeds only from the pig bin outside the kitchen. She is heavy and slow like a cow. She lived among cows because she is a farmer's wife. I don't know why she thinks real food is too good for her, but she does have a reason, I know. So many of the others sit and stare, or if they talk I can't make it out; it comes in odd waves and jerks like a jumper unravelling. But I hold this tightly in my head: no one's here without a reason. I know that. The staff, however, choose to be here. What sort of reason is that?

Other things I never tell them
How it feels to wear a shroud of canvas, layers thick, stitched across and re-stitched, and to sleep in sheets of layered and cross-sewn calico, made so strong to stop us hurting ourselves with them. It chafes my skin red. Our ward is twenty strong. Like animals we rise with the light and are in bed at four-thirty, laid out under the high, blistered ceiling, our beds crammed in only a few inches apart. We breathe each other's sour air, smell all of each other's most intimate smells. I sleep between Gladys, a skeleton who wears the sweat perfume of death, and Mary who soils her bed and flies somewhere every night with massive wings and a chatter in her throat. I have never known this class of women before. They don't worry about such distinctions, each wrapped in her own cocoon. It's only the nurses who can't hear my voice and learn about my family without goading me. 'Posh cow.' 'Your Highness.' 'Lady Muck.'

It's a farm here, inside and out. On Sunday mornings they make us bath, all three hundred women, eight at a time, our shrouds in a stinking heap on the floor. The bath nudges sharply against my bones. Women scream and whip the water with their hands. The outlet pipes are four inches thick and I wonder if I could fit down them and be sucked away into the black womb of the sewer. The nurses parade among us shouting and eyeing our bodies.

At mealtimes they are forever counting. No knives

295

are allowed in the place. The prongs of the forks are an eighth of an inch long. They count them out, count them in. When they shout 'Tables!' we fight for a place at the benches round the pine tables even though we are always, in the end, sitting in the same place. At first I am numb and don't know how to survive. As the days pass I am too hungry and wrangle and cram my mouth with the rest, for one hesitation and the food is down another's throat. Food is all our pleasure here: warmth, comfort, a loving touch.

Am I a Certified Lunatic? I don't even know. No one tells me what Daddy has said to them to make them seal me in. Every morning the man comes to take away the bodies on his covered trolley. The old ladies stay in bed and die, dropping like bugs from the walls. With half-obvious relish he says, 'Any for me today?' He gets 7/6d for each corpse and he gathers them like a bunch of flowers. Will I leave here like that? Perhaps this is the beginning of it, knowing this: that within these dark walls there is another behind which I stand. It is so close it fits my skin, and behind it I am too chilled to feel even despair. The doctor said I might be schizophrenic because I'm thin. I watch others and wonder if I am already as bad. I feel lost.

Some things I don't do
I don't stand for hours in impenetrable silence. The crust of my silence can still be broken.

I don't touch myself intimately when other people can see.

I don't relieve myself in my bed, except during treatment.

When we are outside for our morning shuffle round and round the scabby paths of the airing court, I do not look for leaves, shreds of groundsel, human waste, sycamore seeds to eat, nor do I chew my shoes, the hardest of leather (no laces) which can eventually be devoured after hours of sucking.

But nor do I – their mark of a degree of trustworthiness – get led out to work in the kitchen, garden or laundry.

What I do

When I am allowed near my bed, I find myself standing there for many minutes at a time, not knowing why I am there.

I sit in the dayroom and time must be passing but I can't tell how long, nor can I solve the problem of how to lift and move an arm or leg even when there are alarms and fights on all sides. I look at the shiny wood of the floor and find patterns.

I can't sleep at night. I listen to hours of coughing and muttering and Mary's airborne chatter and women relieving themselves in the privy in the corner. I stretch my eyes open wide to see if there is any hint of light in the sky between the bars of the windows even though there is no reason to hope for tomorrow. I talk to myself as there is no one else. I summon Mozart and Brahms in my head but they refuse to be roused. I call on my Daddy dream.

On first arriving here I am energetic with fright. I charge to the walls and hammer myself against them while high sounds come out of my mouth. 'Up the stick,' they say. 'Side room for her – that'll teach her.'

I am in a room with thick Rexine walls and a curved floor so my mess slides to the gutters at the edges. I am covered by a hard canvas jacket, my arms strapped round me so that I can only buffet my sides and shoulders and head against the yielding wall until I fall. I find myself in here several times, hardly knowing how I got here. When they come to retrieve me I hear spring-loaded bolts snap back. The first time, they bring nurses from the men's wing to help. They charge in clumsily together like fat beetles and there are blue sleeves with white chevroned cuffs round me and a stench of male sweat.

'You could've managed this one, surely?' they bellow. 'She's only a little tiddler!'

After several afternoons in there and the stunning doses of peraldehyde, I sit quiet.

Nurse Tucker knows why I'm here. I haven't told her, but she knows.

* * *

Chapter 22

'Darling, whatever's the matter?'

Douglas followed me, hovering anxiously at the bathroom door as I rushed from our bedroom, still holding the empty cup from my morning tea.

'Are you ill?' He stood at a loss, toes on the edge of the lino in his pale blue pyjamas, as I retched. The tea had brought on instant rebellion from my stomach. I felt better immediately and drank a glass of water, doing fast calculations in my head once more to make sure. I'd missed my last period, I must have conceived during the first half of August, which made me about five weeks pregnant now.

'D'you think you've caught a chill?' Douglas asked, still standing back from me as if I might explode. He rubbed his hand through his unbrushed hair. 'What? What're you laughing at?'

I felt a strong sense of relief. Something I could do for him, and do right. I went and put my arms round him. 'Definitely not a chill,' I said happily, looking up into his perturbed face. 'Darling – we're going to have a baby.'

'A what?' He was so flabbergasted that I laughed even more.

'You do know the facts of life don't you? This has happened the past couple of mornings except you didn't notice. And my period's very late.'

A flush spread across Douglas's face, and I watched his expression break into a bashful kind of wonder. I realized he had scarcely thought himself capable of producing a child.

'Oh, my love.' He sounded awed. His scarred cheek twitched slightly as it did when he felt strong emotion. He held me close. Then he turned brisk, deciding to take charge. 'We must take very, very good care of you. You must give up your job straight away, of course.'

'Nonsense.' I went to the basin and splashed water over my face. 'I've got heaps to do and I can't just give it up now. Exercise in pregnancy is supposed to be good for you. Don't fuss, Douglas.'

But he did fuss. Fuss would be a gentle word for it. That Sunday I was due to visit Olivia. The hospital had agreed to me visiting on my own, and I was anxious to go as often as possible without Elizabeth. We were settling into a pattern of seeing her once a fortnight, on alternate weeks. Elizabeth was occasionally accompanied by Alec. Douglas already resented this. Now it became a symbol, an issue on which to focus his lack of trust and his need to control me in order to feel safe.

'You're not to go,' he ordered on the Saturday afternoon. I was sitting with my feet up looking through a box of books. I realized, as I looked at the old, forgotten titles, that Angus had given me several of them.

'Douglas,' I said quietly. 'Please don't start giving me orders. I'm going to Arden tomorrow. I'm sorry it means not being with you all day, but you did say you had work to do, and I simply have to go.'

'But you need to rest, not keep gallivanting about all over the place. Don't you care about our child?'

'Oh don't be so ridiculous,' I flared at him. I was

300

really needled by him lecturing me on a subject about which I knew far more than he did. 'I've been out shopping all morning carrying heavy baskets of food for your dinner, which is far more exhausting than sitting on a train to Leamington. But it doesn't even cross your mind to stop me doing that, does it?' I stood up, still holding one of the books, intending to leave the room, but Douglas seized my arm, gripping me tightly.

'Don't raise your voice at me,' he said in an aggressive voice. 'I've provided you with a child. What more do you want?'

I looked up at him coldly. 'Let go of me.'

Douglas loosed my arm and I stood before him, turning the book over in my hands. The soft, leather cover of Angus's gift to me made me feel choked with bitterness. What did I want? To be with someone who I didn't have to tread round so carefully, who didn't want to keep me in a box with a few holes punched in the lid. Someone who could love me properly and let me be.

'I'll tell you what I don't want,' I said, keeping my voice low. I was always conscious of my mother over-hearing if she was in. 'I don't want to be treated like a Victorian wife, nor like a member of the regiment. If you want me to respect you then you're going to have to stop being so mistrustful and childish about it. I'm not your mother, so there's no need to behave like your father. I'm going to visit Olivia tomorrow. If you're not happy about that, then I'm sorry, but she's my friend and she needs me.'

Douglas's face had gone tight with fury. 'Everybody needs you, don't they?' he sneered. 'You'll run round after anyone except me.'

He slammed out of the room. Feeling immediately sorry, I ran down after him to the front door, but he was already off down the street, lighting a cigarette. I saw him bend his pale head to the lighted match, watched his painful gait, his jerking angry manner, and thought how much he felt like a stranger to me.

In the railway station, among the unpredictable, jolting movements of the crowds, I felt already that I wanted to protect my unborn child. To warn off anyone who moved too quickly or advanced too close, shielding my stomach fiercely with one hand. It was a feeling I knew Lisa would understand and I longed suddenly to tell her about the baby.

On the journey, rattling through the freshly ploughed Warwickshire fields, I sat sucking peppermints, wondering in what state I should find Olivia. I had observed no change in her during the summer. She remained withdrawn, frozen, and I seldom got her to speak about anything other than the immediate facts of her state or occasionally an event on the ward. I realized suddenly that Olivia and I had never discussed having children or how we might feel about them, and thinking back on that, it seemed a strange lack. I wondered what sort of parents Douglas and I would make. Surely he would see this child as a sign of my commitment to him, make him more able to trust? But I was already beginning to see how quickly communication could break down between us. I had to admit to myself that I was becoming miserable in my marriage.

Olivia was brought in to see me not by the bacon-cheeked nurse this time, but a younger, less buxom woman with a gentle air and a very straight brown fringe between her eyes and her starched white cap. She seemed apologetic and didn't impose a time limit on us, sitting herself quietly by the door as if trying to pretend she wasn't there.

There was something different about Olivia, a slowness, as if to move at all was unbearable for her. Most striking of all was the fact that her hair was now short, lopped in a rough pageboy level with her earlobes.

I loathed asking her how she was. It seemed such an obviously foolish question, almost an insult. Instead I said, 'I like your hair.' In fact, had it been more expertly cut and more often washed, it would have suited her delicate features very well. 'Did you ask them to do it?'

She lifted one hand slowly to the back of her head and stroked her hair vaguely, as if wondering what I meant, and then shook her head. I looked round the room, already feeling desperate for something to say. I had a familiar feeling of wanting to shake her, to force her to talk to me but we had been so long out of the habit of talking, even if she were capable of it now.

'Was there a show or something on yesterday evening?' I asked eventually.

Her eyes rolled up towards the ceiling, before she looked dully down at the floor again, frowning. 'I can't remember.'

I was frightened at the way she spoke. I had tried to hold on to her, believing she would somehow revert to the person she was supposed to be. That with rest and encouragement she would surface again, break through this blankness which was all she seemed able to present to us now. But she was becoming unrecognizable as the person I had known before. I didn't know what to believe about her any more. I began to wonder whether she was really losing her mind, and whether she was, after all, in the right place.

We sat in silence for a moment. Feeling nauseous, I fished a peppermint out of my bag and offered Livy one. She refused the sweet, but suddenly grabbed my wrist, gripping me tightly. Moving closer to her, I smelled a stale, sweaty odour coming from her. Her eyes were stretched wide, terrified.

'You've got to help me.' She spoke in an urgent whisper. 'They're doing things to my head. They took me to a room downstairs and put pads on me, here – ' She let go of me then and pressed her fingers to her temples. 'And electricity went through my head. It hurt worse than anything I've ever known and I couldn't control my body. They held me down ...' She started to cry, not sobbing, but making high, mewling noises. 'They're going to do it again. They said every day. I can't – I can't – they'll kill me.' She was panting now, seeming beyond tears. 'They can do anything they want.'

I had heard of the new treatment, though never seen it. Electroconvulsive Therapy. The textbook definition: an attempt to stimulate the brain by passing an electric current through it.

'Daddy must have told them to do it.' She seized my arm again as if she thought I wasn't hearing her, or that I might get up and run away. I held her hands, despair sinking deep into me. What could I do when she was in this state? There was silence.

Then Olivia whispered, 'They're going to kill me. I shall never come out of here.'

'I don't understand.' I took her other arm with my free hand, so that we sat locked together. I wanted to keep her from moving about and attracting the nurse's attention. 'Livy, my dearest, dearest friend.' Tears ran down my face. 'Just hang on, please – please, darling. It won't be much longer now . . .'

For a few seconds she sat motionless, her cheeks very white. Her eyes moved across my face, as if searching me for solidity. But her gaze was so strange.

The nurse walked across to us with apparent reluctance. She spoke calmly, with sympathy. 'I'd better take her back.'

Olivia sagged, exhausted. I wanted to make promises to her, but could think of none I could offer honestly. Instead I kissed her as she stood passively in my arms.

As she left me, I said, 'I'll do something Livy . . .' She didn't look back as she was led away.

Outside I took deep breaths of the cooling air, leaning against the wall trying to control my rising nausea. I failed, and vomited wretchedly into a tangle of shrubbery at one end of the building.

I knew Douglas would be timing my journey back from Arden that day and, in spite of himself, adding each moment of what he considered my lateness to his catalogue of my wrongs. But I felt defiantly that his needs in this case were less important. I had to talk to someone. I also needed one of Lisa's cups of sweet tea. I got off the bus early and walked through to Stanley Street.

The light was going and in the narrow entry it seemed darker. I found the court unusually quiet. The children must have been inside eating. I could hear the sound of a wireless through an open window and cutlery clattering and voices.

'Surprise surprise,' Lisa said, opening the door to me. She was more relaxed now Don was home. She turned to him. 'Look who's come to pay us a call.'

Don nodded at me as I peeled my coat off, raising his round, freckled face for a second from the job he was absorbed in at the table. He was dismantling the clock which had long sat silently on the mantelshelf. He was a quiet man with an easy manner and I never felt awkward in his presence.

'We've just finished tea,' Lisa said. She was in her apron still and the old slippers which by a miracle were still surviving. 'Here – ' she pulled a chair out from the table, 'sit yourself down.' She chased the boys outside but allowed Daisy to stay. I gave her a peppermint. 'You look terrible,' Lisa remarked, pouring tea.

'I'm pregnant.'

Lisa stopped half way to the table with Don's teacup. 'You're not! 'Ere – d'you 'ear that, Don?'

'Course I 'eard – not deaf am I? Congratulations,' he said, giving me a shy smile.

''Appy about it, are you?' Lisa asked, sitting down wearily. She saw my face. 'Course you are. Lovely.' She looked across at her husband. 'Shall we tell 'er, Don?'

He gave her a mischievous grin across the table. 'Tell 'er what?'

Lisa tutted. 'Tek no notice of 'im, Kate. I'm expecting as well.'

We both laughed and exclaimed and compared dates. Lisa's baby was due a couple of weeks earlier than mine.

'A baby brother or sister for you, Daisy,' I said to the little girl, who was standing beside me.

'If it's a girl I'm going to call 'er Alice,' she said, cheek bulging with the sweet.

Lisa shrugged. 'Don't ask me. She's just taken a fancy to it.'

Don got up and lit the gas before carrying on with his job. It hissed quietly behind Lisa's head. She sat with her teacup in one hand and a cigarette in the other. After a time I started to tell her about Olivia.

Lisa listened, frowning. 'Olivia Kemp?' she interrupted. 'You mean ...?'

'Councillor Kemp's daughter, yes.'

'You never said you was friendly with 'er!'

'She was away most of the war. I didn't see her.'

Lisa let out her loud laugh. 'Bit different from the likes of us, I'll bet!'

I was trying to protest at this when I saw Don looking up at us, frowning.

'Kemp.' He turned to Lisa. 'Isn't that – ?' He gave a jerk with his head, eyebrows raised meaningfully.

'You mean Kemp's,' I said. 'His factory's on Birch Street.'

Don shook his head impatiently. 'Anyone knows that. No, I mean that Joyce, up in nine court – you know.'

Understanding spread across Lisa's face in the form of a blush. 'The one with the babby?'

Don's face reddened as well and he looked down again, realizing the full implications of what he'd said.

Lisa's eyes widened. 'Come to think of it, I've even seen 'im round 'ere once or twice. Course, I didn't put two and two together at the time.'

My heart began beating faster. That foggy night towards the end of the war came back to me clearly.

Lisa and Don both looked very awkward. 'Sorry,' Lisa said. 'We shouldn't be saying all this.'

I put my cup down and sat forwards. 'Are you saying that this woman – Joyce – has carried a child by Councillor Kemp?'

Lisa grew flustered, her cheeks red. 'Look, we don't want to make any trouble It was just 'earing the name

307

... I believe 'e gives 'er money – takes care of 'er a bit. 'E puts 'isself about a bit round 'ere like ... Only in 'er case there was summat to show for it. I s'pose 'er 'usband thinks it's 'is.'

'I see,' I said grimly. I sat back and automatically stroked Daisy's hair, my mind lurching from question to question. 'Look, this is very important. Can you be sure that Alec Kemp is the father of this child?'

'Well, no one can tell you that for sure, except Joyce, of course. But she ain't normally one for – you know, you wouldn't call 'er fast. And she used to work at Kemp's before the babby.'

Thinking aloud, I said, 'I wonder how I can find out.'

Lisa looked at me doubtfully. 'If it was me I wouldn't thank you for asking, but I s'pose you could go and see 'er.'

I lifted Daisy on to my lap. 'Oh, I will,' I said with such determination that Lisa looked puzzled. 'I shall be round there like a dose of salts.'

By the time I got home it was after seven o'clock. I was two hours later than usual. My mother was waiting for me.

'He's out,' she said drily. 'I gave him a meal, and he's gone to have a drink with someone from the paper.'

I felt myself breathe easier.

'Thank you, Mummy. I'm very grateful.'

She looked sternly at me. 'Why are you so late?'

'I called in to see Lisa Turnbull on the way back.' I tried to enlist Mummy's support. 'I needed to talk to her. Was Douglas getting very impatient?'

'I think for your sake it's a good job he went out. He was very short with me.' She relented for a moment.

'You look tired. It's a lot, all this back and forth to see Olivia. I've got some soup over – would you like some?'

I could have wept with gratitude. She sat with me in the kitchen as I ate.

'How is Olivia?'

'They're giving her electric shock treatment.'

Mummy winced. 'What a terrible thing.'

I nodded, my eyes filling. I looked down into my soup bowl, not finding it easy to show emotion in front of Mummy.

Suddenly, not looking at me, she said resolutely, 'It's no good. If you don't put Douglas and your marriage first you're soon going to be in trouble. You can't neglect him. He needs your attention . . .'

'Look – I do want to put it first,' I protested. 'I do. But I love Olivia too. And Douglas – ' I broke off, the frustrations of the past months welling up in me. Cheeks hot and red, I tried to talk. 'He's so possessive you see, and insecure. And it's partly because – ' I stumbled over the words. 'We have – there are some difficulties . . .'

My mother held up her hand abruptly. 'Problems in the bedroom are between you and him. It's your marriage. None of that's anyone else's concern. And anyway,' she added, 'he's managed to get you pregnant at least.'

I remembered Joyce Salter quite well. I had called to see her after the baby was born about a month before VJ Day. She lived with her mother in court nine, Stanley Street, and had told me that her husband had been called up for National Service. Thinking back to her delicate, pretty features, I could see what Alec Kemp would have found attractive about her.

Nervously I waited at her door, trying to prepare what I might say. I understood how she'd feel about me barging in to ask the identity of her baby's father. She would most likely find my questions odd and insulting.

Fortunately she was alone with the child, so I didn't have to contend with her mother, a mean woman whose features must once have resembled Joyce's, but had since spread and roughened.

For a few seconds Joyce looked very perturbed at seeing me. Then her face cleared. 'Miss Munro, isn't it?' I didn't bother to correct her. 'Couldn't think who you were for a minute then. Come in. Take no notice of the mess. It's our Maureen.' She indicated the crawling baby. 'Shocker for mess she is.'

I smiled. The small amount of confusion in the room was not such as could have been caused by the baby, who was in any case settled to play in an orange crate. Sitting down, I asked after Joyce's health and had a good look over Maureen. She was a well-covered, healthy-looking baby, bar the catarrh which dogged just about everyone in the area. She gazed at me with interested dark eyes. I had a sudden instinct that she looked very much as Olivia must have done as a baby.

'Joyce – I'll tell you why I'm here,' I said. 'I need to ask you something which I'm sure you'll think very strange and probably even rude, and I wouldn't dream of coming here like this if it wasn't very important. I'd like to assure you that I'll keep anything you tell me in confidence.'

Joyce looked very anxious at my serious tone, and took refuge in wiping Maureen's face with a cloth. 'Whatever did you want to know?'

'I need to know the name of Maureen's father.'

Blood rushed across Joyce's face. She pulled a hanky

from her sleeve and stood worrying it between her hands. 'My 'usband's away in the army. I told you...' She was a timid woman, not the sort to throw me out like some would have. She had a persecuted look, conscious of having done wrong. Trying to stand up for herself, she dared to say, 'What's it to you, anyway?'

'Look,' I assured her. 'Strange as this may sound, the reason I'm asking you this actually has nothing to do with you and I shan't want to trouble you again. I'll explain to you in a moment. What I need to know is – is Maureen's father Alec Kemp?'

Joyce grew very flustered, wringing the hanky, starting to cry. 'My 'usband mustn't find out.' She looked into my eyes, her face stricken. 'Who told you? No one was to know. I've never breathed a word. 'E said if I told a soul, 'e'd stop the money.'

I stood up and walked round the table to her. 'Joyce – I'm afraid people have a way of working things out. Look, please, I don't want to upset you.' Shyly I touched her shoulder and she gazed up at me, eyes wide, pleading for reassurance. 'I can guarantee your husband will never hear anything from me. I'll tell you what this is all about. Let's sit down, shall we?'

While Joyce listened, wiping her eyes, I explained briefly about Olivia. 'I'm sure you can understand why I'm desperate to get her out of there. The only way I can think of is to force him into it. My knowing will make no difference to your position. He won't stop the payments to you. You see, he's well aware that my husband's a journalist. We could make things rather awkward for him.'

Joyce was watching me in bewilderment. 'His poor daughter,' she said. 'What a thing.'

'Do you know of any others?' I asked her.

311

She paused. 'I know of others 'e's bin with.' She rolled her eyes to the ceiling with a hard laugh. 'Thought I was the one and only, didn' I? Jackie Flint – up at eight court. Lost a baby a month ago.'

'And she said it was his?'

Joyce looked at the floor, blushing. 'She's a pal of mine. We was both on the line at Kemp's.' She raised her eyes to me and they were red and filling with tears again. 'I never meant for it to 'appen. 'E's not like the others, you see. I can't say 'e forced 'isself on me or anything like that. 'E just has a way of making you feel sort of special – like the only person in the world. I can't explain it to you. I s'pose I were in love with 'im. I'd 'ave done anything 'e wanted.'

'I know,' I told her gently. 'Don't worry – I believe you. I haven't come here to judge you, Joyce. But I would like you to tell me one more thing. D'you know when I'm likely to find him around here?'

Chapter 23

Silence began to take root between Douglas and me. Silence which I began to imagine might never be broken. There were days when almost the only times we spoke were in response to my mother. That was when Douglas was there at all. He worked every possible hour, late into the evenings. Isolation and work were familiar havens for him.

I began to panic. I was being punished and I felt I deserved no punishment. I imagined bringing up a child in this silence.

In October it was Douglas's birthday.

'Will you be free tomorrow night?' I asked the morning before. We were both dressing, Douglas careful and immaculate as ever. 'I thought I'd book a table at the Midland. It'd be nice to celebrate properly.'

I'd caught Douglas's morning mood, brisk, already with the aura of the newsroom about him, not welcoming intimacy. 'I can be. I'll check.' He fastened his tie. 'Good idea of yours.'

I moved forward to embrace him but he kept me at a distance, allowing only a light kiss on the cheek. 'Breakfast. I need to be off.'

The next evening I put on the soft wool dress I had worn after our wedding. I wanted Douglas to remember it; the dress, the day. He was late arriving, but not enough for me to have become edgy. I waited in the bar, self-consciously a woman alone. When he finally came limping across the smooth carpet I met his eyes and smiled. We had spent too many days avoiding each other's glance. Douglas could see I was making a special effort, and with an intensity of relief which surprised me, I realized he was going to respond.

'Sorry I'm late.' He returned my smile and kissed my cheek. There was a glow about him, some pent-up excitement. 'Just fetch a drink. Another for you?'

We sat in the bar for a time, Douglas smoking and talking over the day with what felt like exaggerated courtesy. Once we had settled in the softly lit dining room and ordered some food, Douglas sat back, looking into my face 'I've got some news.' I had not imagined the excitement. 'I was talking to a chap on the *Express* today –'

'The *Daily*?'

He nodded, lighting another cigarette. 'He said there's nothing doing so far as jobs are concerned at the moment. Too many demobbed and would-be journalists. But he said he knew I'd been on the job all through the war and he's read some of my pieces – he liked the bits I did on the blitz. So he said I can send stuff in on a freelance basis, and as soon as there's a job going, he'll be in touch.'

'Douglas, how marvellous for you!' I cried. 'Well done – you thoroughly deserve it.'

Douglas leaned back and took a satisfied drag on the cigarette. 'So, we'll be heading for the big city. Not before time, I'd say. I mean Birmingham's all right, but it just doesn't have London's – ' he waved his arms expansively, 'atmosphere, excitement. Does it? Even the Hun couldn't knock the stuffing out of London.'

I watched him, trying to keep my own feelings at

bay. I couldn't leave here now. Birmingham was home. I didn't want to go to a strange place to have my baby, and above all, there was Olivia.

'How long d'you think you'll have to wait?' I asked, forcing myself to sound bright and enthusiastic.

'Anyone's guess. Weeks, months, who knows, darling. But the main thing is' – he gave a gleeful smile – 'I feel sure I'll be in there before long.'

This was not the moment to argue. Douglas, of course, took it for granted that I would do whatever suited him. After our food had been laid in front of us, I raised my glass. 'Happy birthday, darling. And I hope it turns out to be a very successful year for you.'

We ate in silence for a few minutes. Douglas's cigarette sent up a thin thread of smoke from the ashtray.

'I wanted to try and clear the air a bit,' I said eventually. 'Things have been so awkward between us recently, and – Douglas, we shouldn't be like this with each other. It's no good, especially with the baby coming. It's wretched, it really is.'

'Oh, look, I'm sorry.' Douglas reached for my hand across the table. 'I know I've seemed rather preoccupied the last few days. It's just my way of . . . Sometimes I find it difficult. Things don't feel quite right. Not how I think they should be.'

'What d'you mean?' For a moment I was encouraged. I shared this feeling. I wanted to take apart the whole puzzle of our marriage, to examine and restore it. But there were areas of it we could never reach with words. What happened between us in bed was something we could never even begin to discuss, even if this had been the place to do it. It was too fraught, too embarrassing. And the fact that I was now pregnant had apparently convinced Douglas that all was well in that department.

But there were all the other uneasinesses between us. I hoped that Douglas, too, wanted to face and alter them.

'Well, for one thing,' he began, 'I think we should move out of your mother's house.'

I was taken aback. 'But you were the one who wanted to live there!' Having chafed at our living there when we were first married, I was now resigned to it. I was looking forward to our baby being there too, to her growing up in the ample space, the garden . . .

But he was already slamming something else at me. 'And really, Kate, it's time you stopped working.'

'I am going to stop. I've only a few months to go!'

'So why not give up now? I don't like the idea of my wife working. And all those slummy houses around St Joseph's. A married woman shouldn't be out doing things like that. You should be at home, not out hob-nobbing with all those rough women. I'm sure it can't be good for the baby. Heaven knows what you might pick up there.'

I could feel a harsh outburst of temper rising. I did have feelings of guilt about being out at work, because most married women I knew were at home. My mother had already taken me to task several times on the subject. I resented this pressure to give up a job I enjoyed so much. But I knew I must keep my temper under control. If I lashed out at him now for his pompous preoccupation with his own needs the conversation would be scuppered.

'I can't see that a few more months will make any difference.' I spoke softly, squeezing his hand. 'And then the baby'll be here, and I'll be at home just how you want.'

'Then why can't you give up now?'

'I've agreed to work until February.'

'They'll find someone else. Please, my darling.' He looked imploringly at me. I saw his cheek twitch slightly. 'All I've ever wanted was a proper family. Mother at home, children. Coming home to you at the end of the day. Doing what families are supposed to do, not like mine. More like yours.'

'Mine? A father who we hardly ever saw, a mother who was mostly bored stiff, resenting every moment her talents were being wasted, and a brother and sister who despise each other? It's true that we held together and my parents respected, probably loved, each other. But that was the truth of it. The only person I could ever really communicate with in my family was my grandmother.'

I took a mouthful of wine, felt it fingering warm down into my stomach. Douglas examined my face closely in silence as if trying to find something there.

'You know, sometimes I wonder who on earth you really are, Kate.'

A wave of exhaustion swept through me. Sometimes I felt Douglas was trying to wring me dry. It was as if he could bear me to have no private thoughts: he needed total possession of me to feel safe.

There was a silence. Then he said, 'It is my child?'

I could have hit him. 'What else do I have to say to you?' I said wearily. 'Yes. It's your child.'

As we finished our meal in silence, I reflected over fruit tart and coffee that I would never have believed it possible to be married and to feel so utterly lonely.

The next Sunday when I went to visit Olivia it already felt like winter. The sun barely seemed to rise and mist hung thick over the fields, merging with the grey clouds. The train moved like a needle of light through this shadowy landscape, windows running with damp, the lights still on in the compartments even at midday.

My thoughts that morning were no less sombre than the view outside. When Douglas and I had returned home after our meal he made love to me with cold self-absorption. He was no longer apologetic about his inadequacies in bed. He just took what he wanted. I had to get used to preparing myself the way he wanted me; ready for him, on my back. He liked to test himself, leave it until the last moment. He knelt between my legs playing with my breasts like someone tuning a wireless, touching me until he was fully aroused (I wasn't to touch him), then came into me hurriedly.

I watched him that night. His heavy body lay along mine, the lion-coloured hair in childlike disarray. For a long time he didn't look into my face. I felt I might just as well not have been there. But suddenly he glanced up and saw me watching him. I don't know whether he expected my eyes to be closed. I was just lying there, looking. He brought his hand up and slapped me across the face, hard, so that I cried out, the tears stinging my eyes. Then he took his pleasure. Though his orgasm was soon over it affected him like an acute pain, his body convulsing, face puckered. He lay still, recovering. Afterwards he needed comfort. Afterwards, so did I.

During that week he had also announced from behind his newspaper, 'I'm looking for a house to rent. Somewhere we can have more privacy.'

'I don't understand you,' I said. 'One minute you say we're going to London, and the next you want a new house here.'

He lowered the paper and looked coldly at me. 'Why do you have to question everything I decide? I think it's time we moved away from your mother and got a place of our own. She can take in lodgers if she needs to and listen in on their conversations instead.'

'She doesn't.' I felt unusually defensive of her. In her way she had been good to us. Though I wasn't quite sure that she didn't sometimes stand on the stairs trying to hear what we were saying. 'Anyway, she's hardly here now she's working again.'

But Douglas wasn't going to put up with me disagreeing. 'There are a couple of houses I've seen up for rent in Kings Heath and it's no good waiting around. I'm going to see them today.'

He came back that evening saying he'd taken out the lease on one of them. I felt disappointed for myself and my mother. She was looking forward to a baby in the house. And, though I could barely admit it to myself, I was afraid of being completely alone with Douglas. With my mother there at least we had to speak.

I took a small flask of coffee from my bag, and poured it carefully against the motion of the train. It tasted nastily of the Thermos, but after it I felt a little restored. My thoughts returned to Olivia. I dreaded what I was going to find. I wanted to give her some reassurance that I could help her.

Joyce Salter had told me that though Alec Kemp did not come to see her very regularly, when he did it was always on a Tuesday evening. Lisa confirmed for me that this had also been the case with Jackie Flint.

'I'm going to have to come here on Tuesdays,' I said to Lisa. I had no clear idea in my mind of how I was going to find Alec Kemp even, let alone confront him. But it had to be there. I wanted as strong a hold on him as possible: first Olivia, and now this.

'It's like something out of the pictures, isn't it?' Lisa giggled, suddenly girlish, even with Daisy in her arms. Then she frowned. 'You can come when you like, you know that. But you know where 'e lives. Why don't you just go up to the 'ouse if you've got summat to say to 'im?'

'Because he could say anything then, couldn't he? He'd laugh and tell me the girls are making it all up. I need to be here – to see him here.'

'Catch 'im with 'is trousers down, you mean?'

'Perhaps not literally.' I laughed, holding out my arms to take Daisy. 'Come on, my lovely.' The little girl came to my arms, gripping me with her strong fingers.

'Jackie Flint was ever so bad after losing that babby. Couldn't go out to work or nothing for weeks. She's 'opping mad with 'im. Come to think of it, she's got bits of family all over the place round 'ere who could keep an eye out. I'll 'ave a word if you like, Kate.'

'Would you? That would be terrific!'

Lisa stood my me, buckling one of Daisy's little boots. 'What you need is one of them private detectives.'

I smiled. 'I seem to be fast turning into one myself!'

Three Tuesdays had passed and I'd had no luck, and none of this was helping Olivia. Although I tried to sound certain about what I was doing in front of Lisa, I was in an agony of doubt all through those weeks. Would this work, and even if it did, was I actually doing the right thing for Olivia? When I did see her, I felt I would do anything to get her out of there, away from the horror of those electric shocks. And how could I face her month after month if I was achieving nothing?

As my taxi drove away from Leamington, once more between sodden fields and bushes hanging with glassy drops of water, my nervousness grew and the sense of dread on approaching the hospital was even stronger than usual. We wound our way along the drive and Arden's angular outline cleared through the mist. The barred upper windows were dark, though I could see some lights on downstairs. Outside it was very quiet once the car engine was switched off. I could hear not a voice or a bird. I pulled my coat round me in the freezing air, trying to imagine how cold it must be inside there, and walked up the steps and through the ornate doorway.

I waited for her for longer than usual, in the weak light from the hall's high windows and the faint smell of polish. Those long radiators could not have been working, as I could see my breath on the air. I heard occasional footsteps echoing on the stone floors outside and, once or twice, the rattle of keys in the inner door. Eventually there came the sound of the door being unlocked again, the key being turned and hurried footsteps.

They came quickly into the hall, Olivia on the arm of the young nurse with the fringe who had brought her in the last time. She seemed agitated, bundling Olivia through the door at a pace with which Livy could hardly keep up. Part of my mind registered that as the nurse came in she turned to take a last anxious glance down the corridor. But my attention turned immediately to Olivia, to the ghastly whiteness of her face, her eyes enormous against the sunken cheeks, to her short hair straggly and unbrushed, and to her right arm which was bent at a protective angle across her body and encased in a fresh white plaster cast.

I was beside her in an instant. 'What's happened? What have they done?'

Automatically I found myself addressing the nurse. Olivia looked so absent. The nurse was apparently suffering such anxiety that she was unable to keep still and kept up a shuffling movement with her feet. 'There may not be very much time,' she whispered. 'I think we'd better sit down.'

I was already feeling so overwrought that for a second I thought she was telling me Livy was dying. 'What d'you mean?' My breathing had gone jagged. 'Why's her arm in plaster?'

The nurse positioned Olivia in a chair, manipulating her like a doll, then turned to face me. Her features had a certain sweetness that I remembered. 'It happened during the treatment. It does sometimes. When they give them the electric shock it makes the body seize up. All the muscles go into a kind of spasm – like a fit. They have to be restrained to stop them hurting themselves.'

I sat down. I felt as if my lungs were constricting. 'You hold them down?'

She nodded silently. I took in several deep breaths. 'Can't it be stopped? The treatment, I mean?'

The nurse made a helpless gesture. 'The doctors . . .'

'Livy?' I stood up and approached her, feeling an irrational wariness as if she were charged and I might be electrocuted if I touched her.

'She's at the end of the treatment now,' the nurse was saying. 'She's had two courses. There won't be any more – not for a while.' Her eyes flickered back and forth to the door.

I drew up a chair and placed it next to Olivia's. She sat staring ahead of her with no expression, looking completely exhausted. I reached out and took her undamaged hand. 'Darling? It's Katie.'

I felt I could not reach her. She looked so strange, so impassive and resigned. They could do to her what they wished.

'You do know who I am, don't you?' I asked, frightened.

She gave a very slight nod.

'She's ever so tired,' the nurse said. 'She'll get better.

322

It can affect their memory for a little while.' I knew the nurse had a special bond with Olivia and felt protective towards her. She gave me a sudden smile, sympathetic and wistful.

'Livy,' I implored, almost sobbing. 'What is all this about? It's been so long now – can't you tell me why you're so sad?'

I thought there was going to be no response. She was shivering in the huge, echoing room, wearing the gingham dress again, and so far as I could see she had no other garments. I embraced her bony shoulders. 'Oh Livy, I love you.' Helplessly I sat and cried, and she remained like stone in my arms.

But she turned to me then, gave me that strange, searching look of hers and said, 'The baby.' And went limp as if the words had been a rod in her spine. She folded her arms across her and began to rock, her voice tiny and plaintive.

'My baby, my baby. My little baby.' She was cradling the plaster cast as if it was a child, and this looked such a classic pose of madness that for a moment I wanted to seize hold of her and make her sit still. I glanced anxiously at the nurse. She met my eyes for a second, then moved her gaze deliberately to the high windows, light falling on her face.

'He was mine for one night,' Olivia was saying. 'Mine. He drank my milk and I held his little hands. In the morning they took him away from me.'

I struggled to make sense of what she was saying, wondering if all this was some kind of delusion. 'When?' I asked softly.

'He was born on October 15th, 1941. On October 16th they took him away from me.' She recited this woodenly, staring away from me across the room.

Things started to make terrible sense. 'But they said you had pneumonia!'

'Of course. They wouldn't tell you the truth, would they? My bastard baby. And now he's punishing me.' The high, babyish voice came back. 'It was my fault. It always was my fault. I'm filthy. I asked for it.'

Her tears came then. As she cried she made retching sounds, her whole body jerking. All I could do was hold her, feeling the grief cutting her inside. My own tears fell on her chopped hair.

I was barely aware of the footsteps in the corridor. The nurse fled across the room in a second. The heavy wooden door swept open and I heard a deep, angry woman's voice. 'Get her out of there . . .' It fizzled out to a furious whisper. There was a fierce exchange by the door, then the young woman came back to us, watched from the door by the other nurse, with oily looking skin and thick black eyebrows, who I had never seen before.

'She'll have to go back now,' our nurse said. Her cheeks were burning red, but she had an air of defiance.

'Nurse Tucker deliberately flouted my instructions,' the other woman's voice boomed from the door.

I was so shocked I didn't even have the wits to kiss Olivia goodbye before Nurse Tucker pulled her to her feet by her good arm and led her away. Olivia went without protest. But as they left, the young nurse turned to me a last time, her eyes expressing both sorrow and a kind of appeal.

'Thank you,' I mouthed at her before they disappeared.

I sat down again, listening to them, the older nurse haranguing the other in the corridor, the noises of keys, lock, door. A slam, then all but the faintest of sounds was gone. I would have liked to sit there. Just sit and try to pull my thoughts together, but I felt compelled to go out to the taxi.

Outside the clouds had not thinned and a fine rain was falling. As I stepped out of the front entrance of Arden I saw the handcarts. They were moving closer, very slowly, from across the field to my right. Three heavy wooden carts joined together by ropes. As they came closer I could see the carts were piled high with weeds and grass. At the front, two long thick ropes extended forward pulled by lines of men. There were about fifty of them, I calculated, all dressed in dark overcoats, some far too long, others obviously too tight, sleeves ending somewhere between elbow and wrist, and most of them had their collars turned up against the wet. They shambled along over the hummocky grass, stumbling in their boots and pulling on the ropes, the lines ragged and uncoordinated. They were of a wide variety of height and build but somehow all the same, the cropped hair taking a segment of identity. Some moved with an unnatural slow stiffness, others quicker, more jerky. They trudged along in silence except for someone near the back giving out panting sounds, almost sobs, as they moved across in front of me. Their breath left unearthly-looking sworls of mist behind them.

* * *

OLIVIA

The nurses who have been giving insulin therapy can be seen afterwards on the ward with a white silt of glucose down the front of their blue uniforms. Their charges are pushed down into the flabby-walled darkness of coma and then, at the given time, hauled back up through its narrow neck.

When Nurse Tucker has been helping administer ECT her eyes are wide and her hands tremble. This is her very first job and she is in shock herself. She has not been in the army or the mines. She has too much will and imagination left for this.

I believe my treatment is twice a week, but the days are so thin-edged I may be mistaken. The fear of it seeps into every moment of the week.

The treatment is performed in the basement where there are tiny cells along the dark corridor. At one end are the isolation cells, but the doors are iron-clad and so thick that any sounds from inside are tiny and muffled.

We are herded, unfed, down the steps, about thirty of us, where we meet with an icy draft of air when we are already frozen with dread. The walls have a lick of ancient whitewash and above our heads snake the metallic intestines of the hospital, pipes stretching off into the gloom of the passage. There are no windows down here. We are alive, but already entombed under the soundproof earth, in the smell of rubber and urine and the sour stench of fear.

We stand in a line hearing the animal distress of those who go before us. I am already mute with fear. What we feel does not matter to them and I have learned it is not worth protesting. Once I appealed to the doctor, put on my best voice: 'I'm afraid of what it'll do to my mind.'

He gave a half smile, actually sincere. 'Don't worry. I don't suppose you'll be needing it.'

In the cell I lie on a trolley. Their faces are a ring round me, quiet, as if they're waiting for a seance to begin. Then one jokes into the silence. 'We'll break our record this morning,' he says, rushing the machine to my head. I wish I had something to hold on to: a bead, a stone, a strand of hair, anything to call mine.

In seconds I taste rubber, still saliva-coated from the last mouth. The gag is thick and hard and punctured with holes for our sharp breaths to hiss through. There is cold jelly on my temples and immediately they are across my body, three of them lying on me as the current is applied and everything of me is seized by it, burns and blackens and I am no longer conscious to know of the wet coursing from my body adding to the vapour of urine in the room.

Return to the seeping grey light is a process of despair, in a recovery room filling with thirty bodies writhing in the incalculable dread of consciousness.

Will this be my life now, waiting for this to be done to me?

It is during the second course of treatment, while my body is in spasm, that they break my arm forcing me down.

* * *

By the time I climbed into a compartment of the train at Leamington Spa after my visit to Arden, I felt completely wrung out. My legs were weak and I was unsteady with shock at what Olivia had told me. It was as if a window had opened on a whirlwind. I understood. A baby. Olivia had had a baby. Finally I knew what it was the Kemps had kept strapped down tight all this time. A tiny, new person, the explanation for all this.

I took off my damp hat, sat down and closed my eyes. Even in my state of shock I realized that part of my shakiness was hunger and I was longing for a drink.

If I had taken the time to buy one I would have missed the train, and to keep the peace I had told Douglas very specifically what time I would be home.

As the whistle blew outside, there was a flurry of movement beside me. The compartment door slid across and there was a sound of a bag being rather frantically pulled inside. For a moment I resented anyone else's presence and then, contrarily, was grateful for the diversion. I opened my eyes to see a short man reaching up to stow his case on the luggage rack. He made a to-do of shaking water from his hat and gloves and took off his overcoat.

'So sorry,' he said, turning to me. 'I hope I didn't give you a shower?'

I shook my head. We looked closely at each other.

'I do know you, don't I – from somewhere?' he said. I shared the feeling of recognition.

He snapped his fingers. 'That's it. You're a friend of Marjorie's, aren't you?'

I managed a smile. Of course. 'Roland Mantel. Yes, I'm Kate – Munro before I was married.'

Roland darted across and shook my hand with enthusiasm, still clutching his gloves in his other hand. 'I remember you well now. How are you?'

We exchanged pleasantries and I felt myself relaxing through the sheer obligation to behave normally and make conversation. Marjorie had married a wartime sweetheart and was happily settled in Portsmouth. Roland seemed genuinely pleased to see me, and to have found a companion for the journey. I couldn't help warming to him, once I'd grown used to the quaint elderliness of his manner.

'Have a sandwich?' he offered suddenly. 'You look all in.'

'I'd absolutely love one.' I felt an absurd impulse to burst into tears and realized it was caused by hunger.

Roland stood up again. He was wearing a pair of crumpled tweed plus-fours and a jacket. I smiled to myself, watching him.

'Been anywhere nice?' he asked.

'Just visiting a friend.'

'I've just been to stay with my Auntie Sylvia out at Turnham's Farm,' Roland said, reaching up to fumble in his bag. 'She always feeds me up like a turkey cock, the old dear.' He gave a grunt of exertion. 'Where are they? Ah, here we are.' He brought down a package, firmly wrapped in layers of greaseproof and a final covering of what looked like a page from an artist's sketchpad. He sat down beside me. 'Now, these are ham, and I believe she said there's some pheasant in these. I've a flask of tea, too, and some plum cake.' He looked up and saw tears in my eyes. 'Gracious, are you all right? You're not against killing fowls and all that, are you?'

I laughed then, at the sight of his good-natured, anxious face, laughed and laughed so that he looked rather alarmed. 'It's all right,' I gasped, trying to control myself. 'I'm just very hungry. It takes me that way sometimes. I'm expecting a baby, you see.'

'Oh,' he cried, pink cheeks bunching into a smile. 'How simply marvellous! So you're – Is it...? Who's...?' He stopped, all confused. 'I'm sorry. I remember. When we saw you at the party, your – intended was missing, wasn't he? Did he...?'

I looked down at my lap. The pain of Angus's death sliced through me so suddenly, so overwhelmingly sometimes. For a moment I could barely speak. Then I managed to say, 'No. I'm married to someone else. Douglas Craven. He was at your party too.'

Roland frowned.

'Journalist. The one with the gammy leg.'

'Ah yes. I think I recall. I didn't know him at all actually, but one couldn't help noticing. But he can work all right?'

'On the *Mail*.'

'Marvellous. Well, congratulations all round then. Here, tuck in – do.'

He poured tea into the Thermos cup, and I found something reassuring, comforting even, about the way he lifted the flask, the cups – one big, one smaller – so carefully with his immaculate, white-nailed fingers. 'You go first.'

After a few sips I handed it back. 'Roland, your brother was missing too, wasn't he?'

The chubby face folded immediately into lines of misery. It was like watching a clown, except the emotion was real.

'We lost Edward as well, I'm afraid. He was RAF, of course. We're still not sure precisely what happened. It was all during the fiasco in Singapore. Don't suppose we ever shall know exactly now.'

'It was the same with Angus,' I said. 'They think he was shot down over the sea near Sumatra. That's the most information we ever had. His mother pursued it for months.' I watched Roland. He seemed so bereft that I touched his hand for a second. 'I'm so sorry. It's absolutely awful, isn't it?'

Roland nodded silently.

'When Angus was missing I felt as if everything ought to stop. That I couldn't go on until I knew for sure. But you just had to go on, didn't you? No choice in the matter. It was very brave of you both to have that party then. I admired you for that.'

'Did you?' He turned to look directly at me. 'It was the last blasted thing I felt like doing, I can tell you. Excuse me, Kate.' I waved aside the apology. 'My family is very that way you know, stiff upper lip, keep the home fires burning and all that. Edward was as well. Not me I'm afraid. Never been very good at it.' He gave a half smile. 'I adored Edward. He was five years older than me and I knew from when I was a tiny child that I could never possibly be like him. He was all the things I'd have liked to be. But he was very good to me – sort of looked out for me.' He stopped. 'I'm boring you, or worse, embarrassing you?'

'Not at all. Please go on.'

'No one talks any more, I find. Not about things like that. I suppose it's their way of putting it behind them.'

'I feel the same. And I can hardly bring it up now, not while I'm married to someone else.'

'Quite, I see that. You poor girl.'

Roland didn't question my need or see it as disloyal to Douglas. We shared his refreshments and talked all the way to Birmingham about Edward, Angus and our lives now.

'I'm with PEL,' Roland told me. 'Practical Equipment Ltd. Furniture design, though I'm more on the admin side. It's all quite exciting. Fashions are changing fast, of course, and we need new designs, a change of direction. There's a great deal to do.' He spoke of his work with infectious enthusiasm. As the train slowed, clanking into the great arching space of New Street, he took my hand suddenly. 'It's been marvellous meeting you again, Kate. You've so cheered me up.'

'Probably not as much as you have me.' I laughed. 'And thank you for the much needed food.'

'Ah – thank Auntie Sylvia for that,' Roland said, gathering up his things.

As we walked out from the platform together I explained that we were still living with my mother.

'You won't be going my way then,' Roland said. 'I've a little place in Edgbaston now.' He produced an address card. 'Keep in touch, won't you?'

'I will.' I looked into his sympathetic face and reached out to touch his shoulder. He leaned forward and quickly kissed me on the cheek. 'Goodbye then, Katie.'

Smiling, I watched him walk away out of the station. The smile locked on my face when I saw that standing a few yards away, watching me with a terrible expression in his eyes, was Douglas.

I walked slowly over, trying to turn the smile on him. 'It was very good of you to come and meet me.'

'Was it?' His voice was hard with fury, the emotion barely controlled. After only a few seconds he burst out, 'I knew it. Was that him then?'

'Who?'

'The father of that – ' He pointed towards my stomach. 'That baby.'

I lost my cool completely then, not caring who could hear us. 'For God's sake, Douglas,' I shouted. 'Don't be so bloody ridiculous.'

Chapter 24

I went to Elizabeth Kemp. I wasn't going to let on that I knew about Olivia's baby. I was saving that for the right moment. But I wanted to confirm the information I had about Alec. I also wanted to goad her. My anger with Elizabeth now was like something chiselled thin and hard. We stood, a few feet apart. She watched me warily, her face cold, aloof.

'What evenings does Alec go out regularly?'

'And what business is that of yours?'

'Tuesdays. Does he go out on Tuesdays?'

'Quite often.'

'Any other night?'

'This is extraordinary – coming here and interrogating me.'

'When did you last see Olivia?'

She couldn't meet my eye. 'Three weeks ago.'

'Not since?'

'I thought it might be better if I kept away. She looked so ill. She barely responded to me at all.'

'If she stays in there much longer I'm not sure she'll be able to tolerate it.'

Elizabeth raised her eyes with a closed, defensive expression. 'Surely you're exaggerating?'

'Do you know about the treatment they're giving her?' I experienced my habitual feeling with Elizabeth of wanting to go and shake her with enormous force. I

333

didn't know whether electric shock treatment was effective or not, but something in my very being revolted at the idea of it. 'What are you doing to get her out of there?'

Her voice was strained thin as broth. 'I've asked him – I've begged him. I don't know what else to do. He says we have to wait for them to make her better.'

'Is Tuesday the only night he always goes out?'

She made as if to think about it, smoothing her hand round the pleat of her hair. 'He does have a regular social arrangement on a Tuesday. They meet for a drink – business, you know.'

'Oh yes?' I kept my voice neutral.

Elizabeth looked at me very directly. 'Yes. It's been a long-standing arrangement.'

'Hasn't it just?'

Without changing her expression, she said, 'Please leave my house.'

'I thought you wanted my help.'

Abruptly she turned her back to me and leaned on the mantelpiece in a cringing pose. 'I don't want it at the expense of . . . of everything else.'

I was silent for a moment. 'You know just where he goes most Tuesdays, don't you?'

She lowered her head as if I was whipping her. When she spoke I heard the break in her voice. 'He is whatever I have made him.'

When I got home that evening I felt weighed down and filled with a kind of disgust at myself. Everything felt so strange, at odds. Even this house of mine would not be so for much longer. In each room there were packing cases, some already full for our move in a few days' time.

Douglas was out, working as usual. I sat for a long time in front of my dressing table, staring at my face.

I had felt like a torturer with Elizabeth Kemp. I remembered how I used to stare so often at my reflection, wishing I looked different; like Olivia. My face was thin now, severe, with my hair pinned up at the back, my oval, steel-rimmed specs. As a girl I had looked so much sweeter. Then I had dreamed of Alec Kemp, kissed my reflection in the glass, fancying it was him. I had wanted to look beautiful and alluring. I gave myself an ironic smile. Twenty years on, nearly, and I was still being goaded by the thought of Alec Kemp. Except that now my pursuit was driven by revenge; for Olivia but also – though I could barely admit it – for myself, for the bitter person I felt that night.

Now I knew about Olivia's baby I was certain in a way I had not been up until now that she was being wronged by her confinement in Arden. Through the summer I had been beset by doubts, waiting for some improvement in her that might give me hope: a grain of light through the black screen of her depression. An explanation. Instead it had grown worse until she was almost unreachable and I no longer knew who or what to believe.

But now I had reasons for the changes in her: grief, loss, anger. And now, by waiting, I had more to hold against Alec Kemp. Soon, very soon, I was going to catch him at his most vulnerable.

* * *

I have only one thing left and I keep it in my head, calling upon it like a rosary or a lucky stone. It's real and not real. That is, it never happened exactly like this. It's a summing up, a kind of poem. I call it up at night when I am once more lying awake and often in the day. It makes me ache with happiness and sometimes I cry. It's my only doorway to feeling, even if it is an illusion.

I am five years old. I live in our beautiful house in Moseley. It is a smooth, pure house, for I do not yet know its drawers and cupboards are full of squirming secrets. As the years pass the drawers are topped up until the pressure becomes unbearable.

But I am five. I am playing in the garden on velvet grass, the sun like warm hands on my face, and I am wearing a pretty white frock. Mummy likes me to wear white. I have a hoop which I am using for skipping. I twirl the smooth wood round over my head and down for my feet to jump over as it passes at the right moment in perfect rhythm. Step, twirl, step, twirl.

Suddenly I stop. I am happy, full of a deep, thrumming joy, but there is one thing missing. What I need to fill me right up to the top is indoors. I like to see my feet moving neatly one in front of the other. My white sandals clack on the path as I trot into the blue shadow of the house. Through the glass door, along the hall, clack clack still on the grey, white, orange tiles.

I know that all I need is here. Searching, I go to the back room, our refuge with its bulging sofa, for the family only. He is sitting with white shirtsleeves rolled in the heat, his strong, dark hands gripping the newspaper, legs stretched out and comfortable.

'Daddy!' Running to his arms. 'Daddy!'

The newspaper is laid down immediately. The arms are always open, as hungry for me as I for him.

'Angel! Hello there, princess!' His lips are on my cheek and I am in his smell, the best in life: crisp shirt, whiff of sweat, tobacco, man.

I lie against his body, warm, overflowing, tearful with contentment.

* * *

My chance with Alec came in November, the week after Douglas and I moved house. The night I found Alec Kemp was also the first time I saw Jackie Flint and one of his other women.

'Lisa!' We heard Jackie hammering at the door. It was about eight o'clock on a Tuesday evening. Don was at the pub, Douglas, as usual, at a meeting. When Jackie came in from the darkness, panting, I started to wonder whether Kemp's employees were selected purely on looks. She was lovely; a soft, rounded figure, long fair hair, big blue eyes and square, widely spaced teeth. In one hand she had a cigarette. Catching sight of me, she said, startled, 'Oh, it's you! I remember you from when Doris 'ad 'er babby.'

I had no recollection of her, but held out my hand to introduce myself. She ignored it, taking a puff on the cigarette. ''E's 'ere again. Me sister just saw him – up Catherine Street. 'E's after some kid at number twenty-eight. You'll 'ave to get a move on. They won't be stopping up there long.'

I was all of a dither, heart going like mad and suddenly no idea what I was doing.

'Where do I go?' I asked, breathlessly.

'After 'im of course,' Lisa said, poised as if to throw me bodily out of the door.

'Round the back of Kemp's,' Jackie told me. I could tell she was enjoying this, being in the know, and the prospect of revenge. 'That's where 'e takes 'em. We'll come with you.'

'No!' I was trying to pull on my coat, arm catching in the sleeve. 'It'll mean waiting around. I'll need to be absolutely quiet.'

'She's right, you know,' Lisa said. 'Be like a cowing 'en 'ouse with us tagging along.'

'Right,' I said, trying to sound as if I had any idea what I was going to do. 'I'll be back later – I hope.'

'Bring us 'is 'ead back!' Lisa called.

'Or summat else!' Jackie shouted brazenly, and their ragged trail of laughter followed me out through the door into the smoky air.

I turned into Catherine Street and began to walk up the sloping brick pavement. I was so wound up that every sound – a dog barking, the slam of a front door – made me jump. There weren't many people about and I certainly couldn't see Alec Kemp. Nearing number 28, a house fronting on to the street near the top of the road, I stopped. I could hardly hang about here: I might run straight into them.

A short distance away was an entry to one of the back courts, so I slipped just inside and waited, moving from one foot to the other, unable to keep still for nerves.

It was a freezing night and very still, a half moon shining clear-edged in the sky. Children were playing out despite the cold. The entry was dark, smelled of urine, and the high walls muffled sounds so that I was constantly straining my ears to hear voices or footsteps.

They went past so quickly that I only glimpsed them and for a few seconds I was paralysed and couldn't think what to do. Then I rushed after them, seeming to fly down the dimly lit slope of Catherine Street. A gaggle of children were shivering round the steps of the Catherine Arms, and as I passed there came a waft of warm, beer-fed air and a wave of noise from inside the cosily lit windows, voices singing above the talk. Otherwise the street was quiet.

They went right down to the bottom, towards Kemp's, and I slowed down, frightened that they might turn and see me. At the corner they turned down into Vaughan Street and I hurried to keep them in view.

The two figures in front of me were walking side by side but not touching. I knew the man was Alec Kemp by the height, his walk. The woman beside him looked small and slight. Now and then they appeared to exchange a word, but they were brisk and purposeful. He seemed to be urging her on. Once I saw her stop and turn to look up at him, saying something. Alec appeared to speak softly, touching her shoulder for a second. I froze, seeing him glance back up the street. I should have kept walking, looked more normal. But he can't have seen me. I saw he had his hat pulled down well over his face. They walked on.

As we neared Kemp's, I realized the factory was still running. I had not given any thought to whether Kemp's worked a night shift and had imagined him going to a place closed and deserted. Instead there were lights on, the front gates open, the hum of machines inside.

Surely to God he can't be taking her in, I thought. Round the back, Jackie had said, but so far as I could see there was only the main gate. They were going past it. There must be another entrance behind.

Walking on the opposite side of the road from the

factory, they skirted it and turned swiftly into the next street. I saw Alec putting his arm round behind her, urging her on.

Looks as if this is it, I thought. My heart was going like the clappers.

But when I turned the corner, they'd vanished. Damn and blast it! I stopped.

The street was a short one, linking Vaughan Street to the main road at the bottom. At a glance it appeared to present a uniform frontage of two-storey houses, but a short way down there was a break, a narrow alley barely wider than the entries to the back courts. The alley was pitch black and I didn't much like the look of it but I didn't see there was anywhere else they could have gone. I couldn't miss this opportunity now. I stepped into the black slit between the houses.

The first part was very dark, hemmed in by the walls of the houses on each side. I couldn't see the moon in the ribbon of sky, though I sensed the blackness thinning out ahead of me and becoming less intense. I felt my way along, moving my hands over the rough bricks, trying to tread absolutely silently. I heard a slight crunch as my foot pressed on broken glass. I stopped immediately and waited, taking in a deep breath and straining my ears to interpret the small sounds around me: the murmur of conversation from inside the houses, a distant rumble from Kemp's and, surely, a faint voice from along the alley in front of me.

I reached the end of the houses and the walls of their yards on each side and I could see fractionally better, as if hands had been lifted from over my eyes. The moon gave my surroundings a dim outline. The ground underfoot was rough and unpaved and I felt my way carefully into each step. On the right I could make out that there was now an iron fence, but not low enough to see over; behind it a silent warehouse. I realized I was soon going to be level with the back of Kemp's to my left. The high wall tapered down roughly level with my head, and over it came a faint glow of light. The yard of Kemp's was quiet, but I wondered just what sort of thrill it gave Alec Kemp to be in this particular place with a woman, so close to his daily role as grand panjandrum overseeing his laboratory and the works below it.

I heard his voice before I could see them and stood absolutely still. His tone was soft, persuasive, and they were closer than I'd realized. They were standing against the back wall of Kemp's. I made out their shapes, sensed them by the sound of their voices.

In a tiny voice, the girl said, 'Oh, Mr Kemp – it's so dark.'

'It's all right, Dolly.' That voice came back so soothingly. 'I'm sorry it has to be like this, but it's only for now. I'll find somewhere better for us to go. If I hadn't wanted you so badly ... You can see I'm in a very difficult position, can't you?'

I heard nothing. The woman must have nodded.

'That's my girl. You've no idea how I feel about you, have you? How long I've wanted to – to touch you like this. It's just – ' There was a pause. 'Sometimes I get very lonely, you see. My wife's not – well, she's not like you. She won't let me touch her, and . . .' Another pause, as if he was taking in a long breath. 'I can't live without this. Without having someone to hold.'

My eyes widened in the darkness. As he began speaking I had readied myself to hear the line being spun, the Kemp magnetism knowingly at work. What I was not prepared for was the sincerity of his distress. I felt shame wash through me at being here, hearing this.

'When you first came to work for me I saw something special in you immediately. I saw you were someone I could trust, who might give me a bit of . . . loving.'

The girl made a small 'oohh' sound, of tenderness and arousal. He'd got her well and truly. Had he spoken those words to me, my arms would have been round him as well. Clenching my teeth, I dragged an image of Olivia into my mind. I could see the faintest outline of Alec and the girl fastened together by a kiss.

I let out a cough, loud and deliberate. The sound broke into that black, tense space with all the force of an explosion.

'Who the – ? What the bloody hell d'you think you're doing?' The panic was plain in his voice. 'Come back here!'

I started to run. He was soon right behind me, grabbing at my back. I had no intention of trying to escape him completely but I wanted to get to the street so that he could see me and I could face him properly, see the look in his eyes.

'Stop right now or I'll call the police!' he shouted irrationally.

In a few seconds we were out on Vaughan Street. His hand came down hard on my shoulder.

'Don't touch me, Mr Kemp.'

He released me more in surprise than anything, standing back to look at me. 'Kate? Little Katie? What on earth?'

I suppose he was relieved for a moment when he saw me. His voice was soft again, full of that persuasiveness. I gritted my teeth against it, the way that tone could even at this moment make me want to run into his arms.

'A few things have happened since you called me Little Katie.' I injected venom into my voice.

He gave me his charming smile, gesturing with his hand back towards the alley. There was no sign of the woman Dolly. 'For goodness' sake, Katie. That didn't mean anything.'

'So what does mean something to you? Does anything mean more than getting a seat at the next election?' I took a step closer to him. 'Do I really have to spell this out? Your daughter is in a lunatic asylum. You creep around the streets at night to have – relations – with your employees and you have at least one illegitimate child to show for it.'

He was silent. I saw shock freeze into his face.

'I'm well acquainted with both Joyce Salter and Jackie Flint who – God alone knows why – have been remarkably loyal to you up until now.' I paused for a moment, watching his expression. 'I'll go to anyone I have to, you know. My husband knows all the right people to tell.'

Alec gave a kind of laugh, containing no mirth, merely an enormous tiredness. 'Oh, I see. I see.' He leaned his head back, looking to the sky for a moment, then his eyes met mine, direct again, and prepared. 'What do you want? D'you want money like all of them? How much do I have to pay you to keep you quiet?'

'Money?' I was enraged, the sensation coming as a relief. 'Is that always the first thing that enters your head?'

'What then?'

'What the hell d'you think? I want Olivia. You're the only person who can get her out. You can say the word, and – ' I snapped my fingers.

'She's not well. You've seen it – the way she talks . . . I can't tell them to let her loose. I won't take responsibility for her. She's not my Olivia any more.'

'She's not well because you snatched her baby away from her against her wishes.' I was having to hold on tight to myself so as not to become incoherent. 'It's enough to make anyone ill. Can't you see she's sick with grief? But no. All you care about is what people will think – your career at the expense of everything else.'

He put his hands over his face, slightly bent forward as if I'd kicked him in the stomach. He was distraught. 'She told you. She wasn't supposed to tell anyone. She was my girl. Mine.'

Words spilled out of my mouth like thick green slime, cleansing me. 'I don't know what you've done to her between you. You had a beautiful, talented daughter and together you've crushed and warped her and you're too much of a cowardly bastard even to go to her and see with your eyes what you've done. You sicken me, Alec. You're despicable.' I stopped, finding I was shaking.

Lowering his hands, Alec stared at me. 'I never thought I'd hear you talk like that, Katie. You used to be so innocent. So charming.'

Tears blurred my eyes. I felt the sadness of his words.

'Look,' he said quietly. 'I know what you think – how this looks to you. I can't – ' He took in a long, shuddering breath. 'I can't bear it that she's in there. It's killing me. I can't stand to see it. But she is ill, Kate. You didn't live with her. For weeks after she came home it was unbearable, the way she was. It was like a bad dream. We didn't feel we could leave her ... her moods. And then I found out she was ... was ...' He shook his head, unable to go on.

'Going with all those men?'

He expelled his breath with a sound that was half

344

sigh, half sob. I stood with my arms straight down by my sides, clenching my fists. He put his hand into his coat and pulled out a handkerchief. 'We've been at our wits' end.'

After recovering himself for a moment, he said, 'You'd do all this for her?'

I nodded, somehow unable to look into his eyes. 'I want her out. I'll take her. I'll look after her.'

'I'll have to think about it,' he said.

'You do that. You've got two days.'

He turned from me and began to walk off down the street.

'I'll be round!' I called after him.

Walking back to Lisa's house I felt not in the least jubilant. I was heavy-hearted and disgusted with myself at what I had felt forced to do.

When I went in I was startled to find four women waiting for me, their eyes darting in my direction as soon as I appeared. Lisa and Jackie, but also Joyce Salter and another woman I'd never seen before with red hair.

'This is Sarah,' Jackie said. 'She works at Kemp's.' A thick blush spread across the woman's pale skin.

They were waiting.

'Well,' I said flatly, 'I've done it.'

They must have seen the shamed lines of my face, and I didn't see in them any of the triumph I had expected: raucous, perhaps a little sadistic. Instead there was sadness, and shame in them, too. They had egged each other on, brazenly, to the idea of revenge, women drawing together against the vile seducer, all bravado. But now, seeing their faces, I knew it was not just for money that they had kept faith with Alec Kemp. He had aroused feelings in each of them which, whatever

the cost to themselves, had bound them to their silence
with a kind of tenderness.

* * *

OLIVIA

Once the WRNS have released me, six months pregnant,
with my little suitcase, and once Daddy has stopped
shouting and abusing me, he tells me, all sorrowful, 'The
only thing that matters is that no one finds out.' He
says, 'My girl, my little girl. How could you? You're
spoilt now. There's no going back.'

They keep me inside for nearly three months. Sometimes in the evenings I walk in the garden at dusk,
feeling the new weight of my body.

They polish up my story about pneumonia and,
fortunately, at the right time, when they are ready to let
me out, my chest is bad. Mummy, of course, manages to
believe the story at least half.

I am so afraid. I say to her, 'What will it be like?
What will happen to me?' And, 'I'm frightened Mummy,
the baby's getting so big. It'll never come out, I'm so
small.'

She fusses about me. 'Darling, you must rest. Have a
cushion. Eat this liver, drink that milk.' She pours
concern over me like cream, but cannot be with me in
the place where I am. The word baby barely escapes
through her lips. They keep me there, almost motionless,
in the dark like a white puffball, feeding me, waiting for
me to spill my terrible seed. Threads of feeling string
themselves between the three of us, always tangling and
knotted, never direct and spoken. Had they pulled

straight they would have snapped, spraying blood metallic red.

They buy me a new piano. I refuse to play it. I sit staring at the world outside, forbidden me. More than anything I want Katie to comfort me.

They call Dr Penn when my pains begin and Mummy leaves the house as he enters it. I am terrified and there are no women at my delivery to lead or hold me. Dr Penn strolls in and out, often leaving me on my damp sheets, the pain crushing me.

'I'm too small,' I cry to him. 'I'll bleed to death.'

'Your pelvis is perfectly adequate,' he tells me over his spectacles. He is not unkind, but he's a man and he doesn't know.

After twelve hours he is born, my son. Daddy weeps when he sees him. He has always wanted a son for the business. My body is drenched and stretched and when I look down I don't recognize it.

Dr Penn washes him and instructs me how to feed him. They leave my baby in a drawer by my bed with a thin pillow lining the base and soft squares of blanket. There is no cradle, of course, because this is not to be his home.

Before he hurries away I hear Dr Penn's murmur beyond my door, 'I'll be round tomorrow – early.'

Mummy does not come home all night.

He lies in the drawer that evening, like the poor babies do. Daddy brings me food and is soft-spoken and kind which makes me cry. He holds me and strokes me. I sit in sheets which were once those of childhood.

When he has gone I don't sleep as he tells me to. I keep the light on, just a small sidelight, like I've always done. I see the little bedclothes twitching up and down. Then he works one arm loose, although I've wrapped him well. There is his hand, so small, jerking back and forth. I watch. I can't stop looking at him. He's getting ready to cry. Then his voice, a high, sad sound, all alone in there after the warmth of me. I pick him up and put him to one breast then the other, he pulling sharply on me, full of astonishing, separate life. I keep him beside me all night though they told me I wasn't to. The house is so quiet around us. Sometimes he opens his eyes for a few seconds and looks at me. I know he sees me.

I unwrap him and take in every part of his body, every shadow of his bone and muscle, the delicate, puckered skin. He has a long strong back and a birth mark like a wild strawberry at the bottom of his spine. I feel each bit of him, arms, legs, each rib, ears, cheeks, his soft skull. I hold his head against my cheek. By the morning I know him. I want my life to be his. And they take him away, then, at first light.

* * *

Chapter 25

I was watching out for her. The ambulance arrived on a December day threatening snow, and against the grey clouds it looked very white and clean. Turning into Springfield Road it seemed to be moving in slow motion, stopping outside our door with a final shudder of the engine.

'She's here!' I cried. Aflutter with nerves, I forgot I was alone in the house, calling out only to myself.

A man wearing a blue cap jumped down from the driver's seat and scuttled round to the back of the vehicle. He opened the door at the back and I saw him reach out a hand.

Olivia was dressed in a black sable coat and black boots. Elizabeth must have seen to that. She was carrying a small overnight bag. I saw immediately that they had already removed the plaster cast from her arm. As she stepped out of the ambulance she hesitated, her face screwing up as if in pain after the darkness inside, even though it was not a bright day. She looked down for a moment, chopped hair falling forward round her cheeks, in a gesture of surrender. It was only once they had stepped inside the gate that she looked up again in bewilderment, taking in our new house, part of a long red-brick terrace, with Russian vine spiralling up the drainpipe, the green front door and wide bay window in which I stood with my hand raised to greet her. She stared at me without responding, as if she could make no sense of who I was. Her face looked so white, so haggard.

'Here you are,' the young man said as I opened the door. He handed Olivia over to me as if she were a bolt of cloth, and he was gone, striding back along the short path.

I closed the door and stood leaning against it long enough to let out a long, long sigh. I felt I hadn't been able to breathe like that for months. She was here, safe, with me.

She was still standing where I had taken her in the front room, not having moved except to stand the little case beside her on the floor. I burst into tears and went and took her in my arms. 'Livy, Livy . . .' I could say nothing but her name, over and over, holding on to her so tightly.

She stood quite still, impassively letting me hold her and cry over her. But I did hear her whisper, very quietly, 'Thank you.'

When Douglas had finally decided to move us out of my mother's house, she treated the situation with indifference, whether real or not was impossible to say. What with the hospital, the church and the British Housewives League she was scarcely in anyway. Douglas seemed to think it would be the answer to everything. He was still pursuing some abstract ideal of 'family life' which, among other things, involved having your own home. I think he hoped he would have more control over me.

In fact this short, sweetish time was the best in our marriage. A lull, when I saw glimpses of the Douglas who had charmed me into believing I loved him.

That day Douglas had seen me with Roland we had

rowed terribly. Once we'd travelled home, mute with fury, we attacked each other across our bedroom with words whose viciousness frightened both of us. I was already overwrought about Olivia, and Douglas held me guilty of wild, bizarre things, the unreasonableness of which shocked me more than the accusations themselves. He'd got it into his head that I was having an affair with the new doctor at the clinic, when I'd barely even got a grasp on the man's name. He called me filthy things, turning on me all his icy verbal power.

'You're not a real woman at all are you? You can't just stay at home where you should be. You have to be working like a man or gadding about with your friends and heaven only knows who else.' His eyes bored into me. 'You don't even respond to me properly in bed. It's like making love to a bloody corpse.'

At this I finally burst into tears, overcome by the injustice of it. 'I can't respond to you in bed,' I wailed, 'because you're so hopeless at it. You don't make me feel anything at all. It's humiliating. Can't you see that?'

The first time we'd ever broached the subject and it had to come out so harshly. Douglas was silenced. I saw the pain in his face.

'Can't you see,' I went on, 'that you're making my life miserable, spying on me and not trusting me? I don't want another man. Coping with you is too much already. I can't stand much more of it, Douglas. I'd almost rather be alone.'

'Don't say that.' He crumpled then, sinking on to the bed, his shoulders shaking. I sat beside him. He put his hands over his face. 'I can't help it. All I need is for you to want just me.'

'I do want you,' I said. I tried to believe it.

He began to kiss me, laid me back on the bed, his

eyes watching my face anxiously as he jerked my clothes off.

'I do want you,' I repeated softly.

He came to me then and made love quickly, desperately, in much the way he had always done. I felt nothing except resignation. At the time I was exhausted enough not to mind.

Strangely, the new extremes to which this row had taken us cleared something from the air between us for a time. We had been trying harder with each other since then. I had given in to Douglas and told him I'd give up my job at the end of November. And the house was a symbol of our new carefulness.

It was a three-storey terrace, reaching back from the road with rooms off a corridor from front to back and quite dark inside, but with a strip of garden ending in a row of poplars. The bedrooms let in a little more light than downstairs. I decorated one as a nursery, painting it pale yellow. I hung curtains sprigged with flowers. Douglas wanted a boy. I hoped my child was a girl.

We enjoyed the novelty of the house and discovered new skills in each other. One day I watched Douglas building a small cupboard for the kitchen, impressed with the deftness of his hands.

'I didn't know you were good at that sort of thing.'

He looked round, squatting on the floor of the back room, and grinned. 'My hands have never been the problem.' His face grew serious. 'You look lovely – with the baby I mean.'

I smiled, stroking my stomach. My pregnancy was showing by then and I was proud, excited. Except that now, knowing about Olivia's baby, I could not enjoy these feelings without a sense of ambiguity.

'You do look different, though.' Douglas lurched to

his feet and came over to me, lifting and stroking my hair which was hanging loose. 'Your face is – softer somehow. More womanly.' He took me in his arms. 'I love you, Kate. Things'll be better now we're here, won't they? New and different.'

I looked over his shoulder across our new room. I thought of Olivia. I could smell the curled woodshavings on the floor. 'I hope so.'

I wouldn't want to deny that there was fault on my side where Douglas was concerned. I was so caught up in my feelings for Olivia, and bringing her to our house seemed the natural, the only thing to do.

'Don't make me go to Mummy and Daddy,' she'd pleaded with me on my final visit to Arden. 'Please don't.'

'I'm not going to make you do anything,' I told her. 'Livy – when you get out of here people aren't going to be able to make you do things any more.' When I told her she could come to live with us it seemed to settle her mind, and especially as it was no longer to Chantry Road, which was so near the Kemps and all the associations with childhood.

I made the promise before I told Douglas. But he was all right about it. He felt safer with me then, knowing I was going to give up work, to the regret of my colleagues, and would be constantly at home.

'It'll be nice for you to have some female company, won't it?' he said. 'And both of you will need to rest. You should be good for each other.' It let him off the hook for working so hard, of course – I would not be relying only on his company. And I was relieved – I would no longer have to be alone with Douglas in the loneliness of our marriage. I would have Olivia.

Before she left the hospital, I knew I had to tell her about the baby. It was becoming so obvious and she was going to have to know.

'I'm worried for you,' I said. 'That it'll be upsetting for you living with me when I'm pregnant. I would have told you about it before, only then you'd just told me about . . .' I trailed off.

'About my baby?' Determinedly she said, 'My baby. I had a baby. He was mine.' She spoke with more energy than I had seen in her for a long time, turning to me with a kind of fierceness. 'I can't hold it in my head. It's like a dream that keeps floating away. When I try and touch him, he's gone. But I don't think it matters about your baby. That's different. Your baby is yours. It might make mine seem real when I see it.'

I was encouraged by this. It was her longest speech for a long time, and she hadn't sounded like someone trying to be brave. There was sense in it and I'm sure she believed it then. That all she needed was to be able to feel properly, to remember, and to have a period of grieving for her child.

So far as I was concerned at that time, Livy's state of health and her odd behaviour immediately before being sent to hospital were all connected with the loss of her baby. My mind carefully threaded everything into that weave, discounting things that had happened before, much earlier. Of course she'd been highly strung and moody, but nothing more. And I had a clear, substantial explanation for the state she was in now.

Douglas greeted her with surprising warmth. The sight of her in the limp new clothes Elizabeth had sent to the hospital and which did nothing to hide her emaciation was pitiful in itself. Both of us were moved in those early days, wanting to protect and indulge her.

In a strange way, for a short time, Olivia helped to bring Douglas and me closer, united in our care for her.

'It's appalling,' Douglas exploded at me soon after her arrival. 'What the hell have they done to her? When I think how she used to look! Those places must be a law unto themselves.'

I hadn't told him about Alec Kemp, though. I didn't want to do it to Olivia, nor even to Elizabeth Kemp. Alec had been worried enough about his public image – and presumably about Olivia – to keep his side of the bargain. That was all that mattered. They could go to hell apart from that.

The silence that had come over Olivia in Arden was still wrapped around her in her waking hours. It was a silence, though, that held no calm. Her mouth was full of ulcers which made it difficult for her to speak or to eat. She was slow in her movements, as if she found it hard to do anything voluntarily, was unused to making choices for herself. She ate very little, wincing at the pain in her mouth. Mostly she sat still and barely spoke.

In the beginning, she slept for hours of each day. I had prepared a room for her with a comfortable chair close to the bed. It was not a very bright room, but she could sit looking out at the garden and the changing light on the poplars. She sat swathed in blankets and extra layers of clothing, often seeming to want to be alone up there. Everything was in shortage that winter. There was barely any fuel to be had and I couldn't light a fire in her room. Often I came in to find her sleeping in the grey daylight, her head propped on a pillow tucked against the arm of the old maroon chair. Sometimes one of her almost weightless hands might be outside the blankets, and I'd cover her again, watching her face, the translucent blue like bruising under her eyes, her hair lying against her cheek.

Her dreams came to her at night. Often I heard her before she had woken herself with her screaming and sobbing. At first came the tiny mewling sounds: small signals of a distress beyond words. I came to recognize it and left my bed to be beside her when it all broke over her, the terrible cries, her eyes opening finally, bulging in her head. Every part of her would shake with extraordinary force.

I held her, night after night, saying, 'Livy, my Livy. It's all right, my love. It's all right now, Katie's here,' over and over until she could hear me. I felt so full of tenderness towards her in those days that it was like a physical ache in me. I devoted myself to this feeling.

When the snow came that winter, falling for days and lying thick, permanent-looking, we stayed in almost all the time, the muffling whiteness like a seal around the house. The city was silenced by it. Factories were being laid off for lack of fuel. I felt my energy concentrate in that house, for my friend and my child.

Livy's silence concerned me, but I felt there was activity in it, not absence. I waited for it to end.

Then one Sunday, after the snow had fallen, the Kemps arrived. Fortunately Douglas was in and answered the door.

'We've come to see Olivia,' I heard Alec say, his voice brisk and businesslike.

Olivia and I were in our sitting-room, chairs pulled close to the meagre fire. The sound of her father's voice seemed to pass through her like a physical force.

'No!' She was on her feet immediately, shaking with agitation. She ran out of the room before they had even got through the front door and took refuge in the kitchen, stumbling down the step. I followed.

'I don't want to see them. I can't. Never. I don't want to see them . . .' Her eyes were stretched open, flecked with distress.

'Livy, Livy – stop.' I took her firmly by the shoulders. 'Listen to me. What matters now is what you want. They don't matter. If you don't want to see them I'll send them away.'

She watched me mutely, disbelieving.

'I promise. You don't have to do anything you don't want to do.'

She said she'd go upstairs and I led her out, repeating what I'd said, trying to soothe her.

'Olivia!' Alec's voice cut harshly across the tiled hall. Douglas had had little choice but to let them in.

Olivia made a convulsive movement, as if the word had struck her like a bullet, and dashed to the stairs. 'No. No!' She ran up, her voice higher than a child's.

'Olivia?' her father cried after her, this time his voice containing a hurt, wheedling tone. 'Darling, come down. We've only come to see you.'

I found myself noticing small details: the smart line of his black coat collar, the white hairs beginning to outnumber his dark ones, the tiny lines like cracks round his mouth. Behind him Elizabeth, wearing a fur hat, was weeping quietly.

'She doesn't want to see you,' I told him. 'You can see that. It's not me trying to stop her, so you needn't accuse me of that.'

I knew Douglas was watching me, taken aback by the bitter tone of my voice.

'But I've come to see her. She's got to see me. We've

had quite a job getting here in this.' He waved an arm towards the door and the white light outside. 'I'm not having this nonsense.' He moved as if to go to the stairs. Elizabeth suddenly reached out, clutching the back of his coat. 'Darling, no. Don't – '

'Let go of me, Elizabeth,' he said quietly. 'I've come to see my daughter and I'm damned if these people are going to stop me.'

'No.' Douglas moved to stand across the foot of the stairs. 'You heard her. She doesn't want to see you.'

I watched Douglas's face, his powerful eyes boring coldly into Alec Kemp. Elizabeth was sobbing, no longer trying to hide the fact.

'Get out of my way.' The ugliness of Alec's tone took even me by surprise. 'Just get out of my way. I'm not putting up with this. I've come to visit my daughter. I'm not being ordered around by some jumped up cripple.'

Blood rushed to Douglas's face. He looked so broad and strong standing there. For a second I thought he was going to punch Alec Kemp but, keeping control, he blazed at him: 'Your daughter doesn't want to see you, and having seen the way you behave I'm not at all surprised. Now take yourself out of my house and don't come back until you're invited here.'

Perhaps that was the first time Alec noticed Douglas's size and strength instead of only seeing his leg. After staring at him for a few seconds, he turned silently and walked back to the front door.

Before Elizabeth could disappear I caught her arm. 'It's not been long,' I said. 'She's not ready yet.' Elizabeth nodded, face half covered by a lace handkerchief. I moved closer and whispered, 'Come on your own another day.' She gave a tiny nod before following her husband out into the flurry of flakes.

Douglas slammed the door behind them. 'What a complete bastard,' he said. He turned to me, embarrassed, needing my approval. 'Sorry.'

I went and put my arms round him. 'Nothing to be sorry for. That just about sums him up. Thank you for what you did.' We kissed, briefly. Then I pulled away from him. 'I'd better go and see what state she's in.'

The tears which followed this went on for days, and I could give her no comfort. It had punctured the great reservoir of feeling in her and she cried and cried, clinging to me in a storm of grief, *'Katie, oh Katie . . .'* her body racked with it. She wept when alone, and when I saw her afterwards her face was puffy and distorted. Sometimes when I looked in on her when she was sleeping there were tears slipping out from beneath her closed lids, rolling down the angle of her cheek towards her hair and the pillow. She couldn't eat. She cried herself sick.

At first I was relieved by this outbreak of emotion. Then I began to panic. I didn't know who to turn to. I wondered if her weakened body could stand such an onslaught of pain. Alone with her, the silence of the snow around us, I feared she might die and I would be responsible for having kept her here without looking for help. I held her tightly, sometimes for an hour or more, making soothing sounds, caressing her and pouring my own emotion into her.

'I can't bear it,' she cried to me. 'My baby. My tiny, tiny boy. I feel as if they've torn my heart out of me.'

Sometimes she took a pillow in her arms and rocked it with her body, trying to find some comfort. I couldn't

359

bear to see it. I could feel the movements of my own child so clearly now. Sometimes I cried with her.

After the thaw came her tears slowed, then stopped. She began to talk. I realize now just how little she really talked about. She had schooled into herself an inability to confide about her home life and her parents. She talked instead, on and on, about her lost baby.

We ventured out at last, walking slowly round the sodden ground of the parks. I revelled in the sensation of the cold air on my face, of using my limbs, feeling I was convalescing after a winter illness. As the days passed, bulbs pushed up through the ground, bursting colour into our grey, sad world. It felt a long time that I had been confined with Olivia. My feelings had been so exhaustingly twisted up with hers. And because of the weather I had seen scarcely anyone else, neither my mother nor Lisa. I longed suddenly to see Lisa, or someone like Brenda Forbes, someone with whom I could have a good, careless laugh. I reflected that the months of my pregnancy had been sad ones, and hoped my child would not be downcast as a result.

One day we were standing by the pond in the middle of Highbury Park, the water flooding over the lip of its normal bed after the thaw. A woman walked past us with three children, two of whom ran boisterously on ahead. The last and youngest, a little girl with straight, brown hair, sidled past us slowly, her eyes never leaving our faces until her mother called her, a sharp note of impatience in her voice.

Watching her, Olivia said, 'You know, by now he must be running around like her – talking – everything. He would be calling me Mummy, wouldn't he?'

I nodded, helplessly. Olivia turned and stared at the ducks, skirmishing on the unusually wide expanse of water. The collar of her black fur coat covered the lower part of her face. I wondered how this wound would ever heal. She had talked endlessly of his birth, every detail of what she remembered of her first and only night with him.

Standing now on the mush of leaves by the bright water, she said, 'I wonder what they've called him?'

'What was your name for him?'

'James. James Robert.'

'Good names,' I said. 'You know Angus's second name was James?'

For a second a smile touched her lips as she stared ahead. 'I remember.'

Those early months of 1947 come to my memory so poignantly. As the spring came, my body blossomed with the season. Douglas was admiring and careful. He understood it was his role to make fewer demands on me in bed and this was a relief.

Olivia's mood shifted gradually. After her time of intense preoccupation with the baby she stopped talking about him. I tried to encourage her to discuss other things: her family, the Wrens, but she was reticent about both. She grew quieter again, calmer, I thought. She did like to talk about our childhood. My mother allowed us to have the piano from her house and Olivia began to work on her music again. Her hair and skin began to show signs of life. She even encouraged Douglas and me to go out together.

'You've had a hard winter, what with the weather and looking after poor old me.' She tried to make it into a joke. 'You should go out together, before the baby comes.'

When she suggested it, it seemed very appealing.

Douglas and I decided to go and see a show, eating out beforehand.

'I do feel rather guilty about leaving her on her own,' I said to him as we were getting ready. 'After all, she's had the hardest time of us all this year.'

'It was her idea, though,' Douglas said. 'And we have had next to no time together.'

Brushing out my hair, I said, 'You've been so patient, darling. Thank you for that.' My voice sounded very polite. I often seemed to find myself being studiously polite to Douglas.

He cleared his throat. 'Well, it won't be for too much longer now, will it?'

I stopped brushing and spoke to his image in the long glass. 'Have you heard more from London?'

'Nothing definite yet.' He was knotting his tie. 'But it won't be long I don't think. And then we'll be on our own again, won't we?'

I tried to sound lighthearted. 'There will be the small matter of a baby!' But I felt desolate at the thought of being alone with Douglas, in a place where I knew no one, and with no Olivia.

Life without her here was becoming unimaginable. Sometimes, when Douglas came in from work, he would find us sitting together having already prepared a meal. Livy might be playing the piano while I rested or sat stitching frocks and coatees for the baby in soft white cotton. Now and then I'd look up at her back, loving the sight of her, absorbed in the music, her hair now gradually inching its way back to its original length and curling a little at the ends.

'Your hair's growing fast,' I'd tell her sometimes, and she'd just shake her head, sending it frisking across her shoulders. She didn't seem to care whether it was or not. I felt a warm, filling happiness at our being together there like that. Other times we sat on the couch talking or reading, Olivia resting her head on my shoulder, her hair soft against my cheek, our feet stretched across the rug towards the fire. And Douglas, walking into this scene, carrying the evening paper, hanging his coat while I fetched him a drink, would say, 'Hello, girls. What sort of day've you had?'

And while he drank down a glass of Scotch, he'd tell us how his had been, bringing some of the outside world in to us. And I knew that in this routine, his finding me always here like this, he felt safe. He had me in the place where he wanted me: an ordered household, female and domestic.

That evening, as we left to go out together, Olivia was cooking poached eggs for herself.

'I'll eat by the fire,' she said lightly. 'It'll be cosy.' She turned, as if inspecting us, and came to straighten the neckline of my frock as if I were a schoolgirl. I kissed her.

Douglas and I stood arm in arm. My coat was tight at the front, but did cover me. 'I shan't be able to do it up soon.' I laughed. Douglas put his arm round me in a show of protectiveness. And I felt very aware of us as a couple, how we must look an exclusive unit, shutting Olivia out. Her face became closed suddenly. She looked at us with a strange, frozen expression.

'Livy?' I stepped aside from Douglas, concerned. 'Are you sure you'll be all right?' I almost felt compelled to call it off, say I'd stay. But she forced a wan smile to her face. 'Yes, of course. Go along now, do. Have a lovely evening, won't you?'

I didn't have a lovely evening. Though I tried to pretend otherwise to Douglas, I felt very uneasy. There was the strangeness of being alone with him, of feeling we had so little to say. And I was worried. That look of Olivia's, something in it hard and realized, which lingered in my mind. By the time we arrived home I was taut with anxiety. I rushed through the house as fast as I could manage in my condition. There was no sign of her downstairs. I climbed the stairs and stood panting at her bedroom door, feeling so foolish when I found her settled in bed. She was sleeping with the little lamp still on, her face severe. I knew that tonight was a warning, though small, that all was not yet well, despite the warm moments with her when I might be lulled into thinking her recovered.

Chapter 26

'What d'you think?'

Olivia burst into our sitting-room which was full of April sunshine and curving tulips. She stood in front of me twirling this way and that.

'What on earth?' I gaped in astonishment at the silky, sea-green material, the close-fitting bodice and abundant, flowing skirt. The dress was everything we had longed for during the scrimping years of the war. Most of us were still longing.

'Isn't it a dream?' Olivia said, still turning in front of me so I could see its effect from all angles. 'A real Dior dress – it's the New Look. I just couldn't resist something with a bit of go in it.' On her feet were a pair of matching green shoes with high, slim heels.

'It's beautiful,' I said, lolling back wearily in my chair. The sight of her looking so thin and elegant made me feel ungainly. The baby was due in three weeks and I was huge and sluggish. 'Are you going anywhere in particular?'

She was jittery with excitement. 'Not yet. But I was thinking, it's about time I started putting myself about a bit more.' She twitched at the skirt, taking a fold between finger and thumb to pull it wide, and dancing round on our worn square of carpet, singing 'I'm gonna meet, a certain party at the station . . .' She danced too long and hard and stumbled, nearly falling, so that she had to save herself by grasping on to the other armchair.

I watched uneasily, trying to smile at her delight. There was that brittleness, the over-excitement I had seen in her in the weeks before Arden. I was not comfortable examining each of her moves for signs of unbalance, like her warder, but I was worried. Things had begun to niggle at me. I had been concentrating so hard on the thought that if she could grieve for her baby she could find a degree of healing and calm. But now the other memories, which had been pushed out during our time of intense closeness when Livy was childlike, dependent solely on me, needled my mind. Some of the difficult aspects of her behaviour even before the war forced themselves on me.

I could feel things sliding. We had been so close, so tranquil for a few weeks. Unknown to us, we had been inching along a balance, and now the ground was beginning to tilt under us.

Livy had started seeing more of her mother.

'*Darling!*' Elizabeth would say when she flurried into our house, putting on her sparkling social face and a relentless cheerfulness with Livy. 'Look what I've brought you,' she'd cry. She came with new clothes, money, flowers, even sweets, as if pacifying an infant. Elizabeth showed more vivacity than I had seen in her for years. Sometimes the two of them went out shopping together.

On the previous visit, though, it had been damp outside, and they sat in with me. The house felt cosy, smudged light coming from outside through steamed-up windows. I made tea and sat listening to them, taking refuge in knitting to avoid being drawn into the conversation.

'So how are you, darling?' Elizabeth gushed over Livy. She sat close to her, fondling her hand. 'You look so much better,' she went on without giving Olivia time to reply. 'Quite my girl again. Dear Katie must be looking after you so well.' She darted a smile in my direction, her face immaculately masked by powder and lipstick. 'We owe you such a debt, Katie.'

I managed a smile. I didn't want Olivia to know what had passed between me and her parents while she was in Arden, or quite what it had taken to get her out.

'Katie's so marvellous,' Olivia said. Her voice had gone small again: that of a six-year-old. 'I'm really feeling much much better.' I thought of her dreams, the tremor of her body, most nights still.

Elizabeth reached down for a parcel which she had been carrying when she arrived. 'Look, darling – I've brought you something to give you a bit of a lift. Nothing like something new to raise your spirits, is there?'

Olivia took the gift and unwrapped it, sliding out from the layers of paper a handbag in soft brown calfskin. She gave her mother a brilliant smile and leaned over to kiss her cheek, giggling a little breathlessly as she did so.

'It's gorgeous, Mummy, thank you. A lovely thing to have.'

Elizabeth took it from her and unfastened the catch. 'I thought these would come in handy too.' Inside she had put three Arden lipsticks, missing the irony of this completely. She could at least have chosen Helena Rubenstein.

The two of them tittered away together, trying the rich, waxy shades on the backs of their hands.

'That one's more your colour, Mummy,' Olivia said, handing her one of them. 'It's a bit pale for me. Why don't you have it?'

'Oh no, darling!' Elizabeth pronounced the 'darling' each time in an exaggerated, caressing way. 'I bought it for you. It'll look lovely. And listen, I thought after the time you've had' – this her only reference during the visit to the state Livy was in – 'you could do with a nice smart outfit for the spring. We'll go out again and I'll treat you, shall I?'

'That would be lovely,' Olivia said, though perhaps in a flatter voice than Elizabeth had hoped.

Elizabeth kissed her again. 'I'm so glad.' She glanced at me. 'I don't know if Katie would like to come? I suppose now is not the time for you to be laying out money on new clothes for yourself, is it? It'll be all matinée coats and napkins for a time ... all such a bother at that stage.' She gave a tinkly laugh, smoothing down her crisp fawn skirt. 'Believe me, you'll be glad to have your body back to yourself.'

She took her leave finally, giving me, as she did so, a look of strange coyness as if it were I, not Olivia, who was off-centre and needed humouring. Then she brought out the smile with which she had learned to embellish so many occasions of her married life.

'She does look so much better, doesn't she?' she hissed at me. 'Marvellous, really. And Katie – ' The face was carefully arranged now in lines of solemn gratitude. 'It's you we have to thank.'

I watched her walk down the path to the wet pavement, so elegant and fragile. That woman, I thought, skates round the edges of her life and never dares to reach into the middle of it.

*

When Olivia stayed out all night for the first time, I sat up in bed through the small hours, taut with worry. It was a week before my baby was due to be born.

'This is absurd!' Douglas raged beside me, after both of us had tried and failed to sleep. It was two o'clock in the morning. 'She shouldn't be depriving you of your rest like this, thoughtless little minx.'

'She's not thoughtless,' I said. 'She's off balance. She doesn't know whether she's coming or going – like grass in the wind. I really don't think she can help it.'

'Why d'you always defend her?' Douglas flung back the bedclothes and went for the umpteenth time to the window. He peered each way up and down the street, then gave a loud, impatient sigh. 'No sign. Look, shouldn't we get the police or something?'

'No!' I cried out so vigorously that I felt a kick of protest from the baby inside me. 'I don't want anyone getting hold of her like that. They'd have her back in there . . .'

Douglas limped back over to the bed. 'You think there are grounds, then?'

'Do you?'

'She's not – well – normal, is she?'

'She just needs time.' It was my turn to pull myself out of bed and hold back the curtain. 'Oh, Livy, where are you?' I stood there for a long time, willing her to appear along the road. 'At least it's not as cold as it was.'

'Come back to bed,' Douglas ordered. 'You're not responsible for her. She's an adult.'

'But I am. I feel I am, at the moment. That's the trouble.'

Douglas lay beside me, eyes narrowed. 'Where d'you think she is?'

I hesitated, hardly even wanting to admit it to myself. 'With a man, most probably.'

'But who?'

I sighed. 'I've absolutely no idea.'

'I don't think we can put up with much more of her.'

'Don't start,' I said, trying to find a comfortable position for myself. 'Not now.'

The night crawled past. I made watery cocoa at three. Douglas brewed tea at four-thirty. We lay dozing un- easily. I was sleeping badly at that time anyway because of the pregnancy. I dreamt repeatedly of Olivia, and once I was so certain that she was banging on the front door that I went down to open it and saw only moonlight whitening the houses opposite. By the time morning came, we were exhausted and full of nervous irritability.

At ten o'clock, long after Douglas had left, she came sailing in, wearing an expression of smug satisfaction, of victory almost. There was mud on her coat and her stockings were laddered. She also seemed more than slightly drunk. I felt like strangling her.

'Where've you been?' I snarled. 'We've been awake all night waiting for you.'

'Oh, how quaint – thank you,' she said, walking unsteadily to the kitchen table and sitting down. She gave an enormous yawn. 'I must say, I'm all in.'

'Where have you been?' I found myself shouting, tearful, my voice sliding up to a wail. 'Have you any idea how much worry you've caused? I'm supposed to be looking after you.'

She put on a startled look. 'Katie darling, you musn't worry about me any more. You've got quite enough on your plate with the baby coming and everything.' She stood up again and put her arms round me as I sobbed, the tension of the night releasing itself. 'I want to give you all the help in the world.'

'You smell of booze,' I told her brutally. 'And sex.'

She put on her baby voice, then, that she usually reserved for Elizabeth, and which made me feel wild with rage. 'I was just having one tiny night out,' she wheedled. 'Just for a little change. Don't be cross with me, Katie.'

I pushed her off me impatiently. 'Olivia, come to your senses. You're behaving like a blithering idiot. What d'you think you're doing? You're like a dog on heat.'

'I just wanted a little bit of fun,' she carried on, in the same silly voice.

I lost my temper completely then. 'If you go on like this you'll end up getting pregnant again. Or you'll get VD. Or both.'

She looked at me smugly. 'I'm not that stupid, Katie.'

In a hard, clear voice, I said, 'One more night like last night and you're out of my house. Understand? Out. I'm not going to put up with it.'

The tears came then, hers and mine again. She stood bereft in my arms. 'No, Katie, please. I can't manage without you. I promise I won't do it again. I love you – I've got no one else. Please don't send me away.'

And I stroked her and soothed her, my anger bleached to tenderness, and told her, as I knew I should eventually, that she could stay with me as long as she liked.

Anna. You were born in Selly Oak Hospital into a beautiful April dawn. Your birth was short and harsh, and even in my release of you I felt your energy. You wanted to be born, thrusting towards it urgently. The midwife in the hospital said, 'That's one of the best first births I've ever seen.' And you screamed with all your force, all eight pounds of you, your hair wet and smooth on your head.

I might have had you at home, but I decided not to for Olivia's sake. She was with me when the first pains began and she was the first to see you, even before Douglas, who came after work.

They had brought you for me to feed when she came in that afternoon. I was still in that exhausted, dreamlike state after giving birth, suddenly both empty and joyful, watching your face, letting your existence flow through me.

And there she was, standing in the doorway, dressed smartly in a coat and wide-brimmed hat, both of which would need shedding in the warmth of the hospital. In her hand was a generous spray of freesias. There was a look on her face which was the most genuine and naked she had allowed herself in a long time. It was both hungry and profoundly anxious. I saw that her eyes were fixed not on me, but on the tiny child at my breast.

She smiled suddenly and half ran forward. 'Katie, oh Katie, you're marvellous!' She kissed me, laying the flowers beside my bed. 'They told me it's a girl. How was it, darling? Was it terrible?'

'Not for long.' I smiled. The experience was so close to me still, yet suddenly utterly irrelevant.

Olivia's moment of exposure had passed. From then on she was the model visitor, listening, concerned. When the feed was finished there was a nurse hovering to take you away again.

'Would you like to hold her for a moment, before she has to go?' I asked.

She held you with awe, partly afraid, I could tell, gazing into your tiny, squashed face, her dark eyes wide and tender. She looked across at me and smiled. 'She's wonderful, Kate. She's a miracle. Does she have a name yet?'

'Anna.'

'Just Anna?'

'One name's enough, I think.'

'Of course it is. Little Anna.' She raised you so gently and kissed your forehead before handing you to the nurse. You let out a roar and Olivia looked taken aback and then laughed. 'Be happy,' she said. 'Little Anna.'

Later the nurse said to me, 'She's a lovely-looking girl, that friend of yours. I thought I recognized her – or was it just my imagination?'

If only Douglas could have seemed so lovely. He disliked seeing signs of human frailty and was very ill at ease in the hospital. I had hoped for him to be loving and awestruck, reaching out to his child. Instead, he was deeply uncomfortable in this public place of the ward, unable to expose any softer feelings he may have had.

His progress along the wooden floor to my bed was rather like walking across a stage. I was so used to the sight of him that I barely thought of it, but I knew he sensed the eyes of the other women on his contorted leg, the terrible graceless walk.

He said, 'Hello,' leaning over to give me a busines-like peck on the cheek, for which for a second I hated him.

'Did they tell you we have a little girl?'

'Yes.' He sat down on the chair by the bed. 'They told me. Are you all right, Katie?'

The question came awkwardly. I suppose the act of giving birth was so foreign to him, so personal.

'I feel better than I expected.' There was a silence. 'I thought we'd call her Anna.'

Douglas nodded. 'Whatever you like. Is she ... she's healthy and all that?'

He was afraid, of course, that you'd be like him: not whole. That he would have marred you in some way.

'She's beautiful.' I reached out to take his hand, which rested stiffly in mine. 'Don't worry. She's a lovely baby. I'll ask them to bring her, shall I? She'll need feeding soon.'

He was so awkward with you, Anna, right from the beginning. He watched your little form approaching in the nurse's arms with a solemn face.

'I'll give her a little bit of a feed,' I said. 'Then she'll be happy when you hold her.'

The moment I started to feed you he was on his feet. 'Look – I'll go and have a cigarette outside. I'll come back when you've finished.' And he was off again along the ward as if he couldn't get out fast enough.

When he did come back and hold you, there was no engagement in it. He held you in the stiff way I have seen some other fathers put on with infants, not wanting to expose their tenderness, not knowing how. He rocked you too hard and made you cry. He never looked into your face deeply the way a mother would. To him you were my realm, something abstract, 'a child' for which he was in some way responsible.

When I got home I was so grateful for Olivia being there. Douglas seemed to have nothing to give us. My mother called a few times, admired you in a professional sort of way, and made comments like, 'I hope you're not overfeeding her,' but seemed unable to cope with being at a remove from you, so that she could not just take over. Her visits soon dwindled. But Olivia, for the first month, was as loving and helpful as I could ever have wished.

At that time her devotion to us was so warming. I needed someone to rely on and she was always there offering to hold you, there for me to talk to. She was comfort, while Douglas was more absent than ever.

'She's an absolute darling,' she'd say, rocking you on her lap, her eyes fixed on your face. I can see her now, her hair curling on her shoulders, her look of adoration which made me ache for her. Once I said to her, 'Doesn't it make you feel sad, seeing her and holding her?'

Without taking her eyes from your face, she said, 'No, it's marvellous. I could sit and hold her all day.' She smiled, running her finger down your cheek. 'That'd be heaven, wouldn't it, little Anna?' Then she looked up at me. 'She's ours, isn't she?'

I should have taken note of the strange intensity of this, but I was happy then, feeling we shared you. She showed far more interest and feeling than Douglas, and I confided in her completely.

'It's so silly. Douglas is so jealous of the baby. He just can't seem to adjust to it all. I feel so much for her and he just . . .' My voice trailed off.

'He does seem rather stiff with her,' Livy said smoothly. She was busy now, knitting for me as we sat looking down the long garden, pansies flattening open in the sun. Now that I was a bit unsteady in myself and relying on her, she looked better, calm and secure.

She reached out one hand to jiggle the pram slightly. 'Never mind, little angel Anna. You've got two people here who love you. There's nothing to worry about. Oh Kate – can I just give her another cuddle?'

'Leave her!' I protested impatiently. 'I've only just this minute got her to sleep.'

Olivia pouted. 'All right. Better let her get her rest.' She went back to her knitting, curling soft white wool round her fingers. After a moment she gave me a quizzical look, tilting her head. 'Is everything all right with Douglas . . . otherwise, I mean?'

I knew what she was asking. 'The doctor advised us that there should be no intercourse for at least six weeks. You'll know that, of course. I think Douglas feels pushed out. He doesn't like to see me feeding her. I know that's not an especially unusual reaction, but it's still hurtful.' I found myself unexpectedly in tears.

'Poor Katie,' Olivia said, coming over to put her arm round me. 'And poor old Douglas. But still, you must do as they tell you,' she went on in a silky voice. 'You need time for your body to recover. Don't let him push you into it, will you, before you're ready?'

'Don't worry.' I was laughing now. I was supposed to be the Health Visitor. I leaned against Olivia. 'I'm sorry to be so soggy – and I'm so glad you're here. This would all have been very lonely without you.' We smiled, our eyes meeting, and I thought Livy looked happy.

'D'you feel better?' I asked.

'I think so.' She shrugged. 'I don't want to keep examining it. I just want to be here, with Anna – and you.'

I remember that month, its fractured nights, its intensity and blossoming of new feelings, only as a blur now, like a kind of illusion. There was sunshine, bright green leaves on the trees, walks pushing you in the huge, heavy pram in which I myself had lain as a child and which my mother produced in magnificent condition from where it had been stored, swathed in canvas, in the cellar. There were quiet times sitting in the park, light shimmering on the water; there was watching Olivia's face at the sight of you and feeling that you were healing her; and my own contentment: your eyes wide over the top of a white sheet, reflecting sky.

But there was also Douglas's discomfort with our new state, his absence and immersion in work, always his resort. There was my mother's stiff detachment from us. And then there was the day when I heard you screaming downstairs while I was resting, leaving you in Olivia's care. On coming down I found you beside yourself with frustration, and Olivia's face all red, her hands grabbing at the front of her blouse which was open to reveal her breasts. I stood staring with an icy fury of which I barely knew I was capable.

'I just thought I might be able to do it,' she said, in that stupid, childlike voice again. 'To save you the trouble while I'm looking after her.'

Trembling, I snatched you from her without a word, and ran upstairs, holding you close, so tight and close to me.

Chapter 27

'We thought you'd gone off us,' Lisa said, when I arrived that Sunday afternoon, baby in arms. Don and the boys were out.

'I'm sorry. I've been dying to see you.' As I spoke I realized just how true that was, how Olivia's company weighed on me. I had had to get out, to have a rest from her. I'd managed to be away from home most of the day by going to church in the morning.

Lisa and I sat side by side with cups of tea on the table and babies on our laps. Lisa had her little girl, Alice, who looked small at the side of my Anna, but whose face was full of character, her nose cheeky and snub. Daisy, a quaint, fussing little thing now in a dress at least a size too big, hovered around us.

'She's mad about babbies,' Lisa said, after we had been admiring the little girls together. Daisy slid from one to the other, kissing them and stroking their heads until Lisa had to say, 'Go easy now, Daze, eh?' The babies followed her with their eyes, giving gummy smiles.

Lisa looked robust and content. 'She was the easiest of the lot,' she told me. 'She got 'ere in a couple of hours.'

'I'll have to get more practice, obviously.' I laughed.

'You're looking all right on it, though.'

I played with Daisy for a while, giving her a Ladybird

book I'd brought with some pictures and simple words in. Daisy pointed and said, 'Dog. Flower. S'easy, this is.'

''Ow's your friend coming on?' Lisa asked.

'Bit by bit, I think. It's a slow business, though. Have you seen anything of Joyce, or Jackie?'

Lisa shook her head. 'Not really, now you mention it. Funny thing is, they said 'ardly a word about it after. I thought they'd be full of it, you making a fool of him like that. But they all just went.'

'They were ashamed.'

Lisa's brow crinkled into lines of surprise. 'Ashamed?'

'When it came to facing him like that. I was ashamed too. Wouldn't you have been?'

'Me?' Lisa hoiked Alice further up in her arms. 'Nah. There's a lot of men around'll use you for anything – wipe the floor with you if it suits 'em. Don't see why we should spend our lives kowtowing to 'em.' With her free hand she topped up my cup of tea. Then, as if a connection had been made in her mind, she said, 'How's your 'usband?'

I longed to be honest, to say, he's a detached stranger who I don't know how to be with any longer and I'm not sure I even like. But who is ever so honest?

'He's well,' I said. 'Thank you.' But I found myself adding, 'Lisa – has Don ever minded, when you're feeding Alice?'

'You mean is he jealous?' She thought about it. 'Can't say as I've ever asked 'im. 'E just 'as to put up with it. Why, is your old man?'

'It is rather difficult at the moment,' I told her stiffly. I found it so hard to confide about my marriage. Lisa was much more matter-of-fact about the subject of hers. But I had been brought up to regard this subject as the proverbial closed book. It was only Granny Munro who had let me into her feelings, shown me that her marriage had survived despite so many things.

'Course, I know some do carry on a bit. Come to think of it, Agnes over there' – she jerked her head in the direction of a house along the court – ''as some right ding-dongs with 'er old man. On and on 'e goes, and it's always worse when 'e thinks the babbies're getting 'is share of 'er titties.'

I laughed. 'That reminds me of Marj Redmond, an old Health Visitor I used to work with. She said they only ought to allow people to get married if the wife spoke only French and the husband only German.'

Lisa gave an explosive chuckle. 'That's about it though, in't it? That's marriage all over for you.'

But I could tell from her tone and from the look of her that Don and she were far happier together than Douglas and I.

'Lisa,' I told her, 'it's unbelievably good to see you.'

I would have liked a longer journey home. As the bus ground its slow way along the Alcester Road towards Kings Heath I sat with you, warm and sleepy on my lap. I wished I could just stay there and follow the route right out of the city to anywhere, in order to sit there and have some peace.

The week before there had been a scene with Douglas. After I came home from hospital I had, as promised, sent a line to Roland Mantel. He had been kind and interested that time on the train, and I hoped he'd pass on the news to Marjorie.

Roland arrived one afternoon when Olivia was out shopping. I was taken aback by the rush of pleasure I felt at seeing him.

'Got the opportunity of a little bit of time off,' he said in apologetic tones from the doormat. He rotated the brim of an old panama hat nervously between his fingers, his round face looking red and moist. 'I expect you're busy. Am I an awful bother?'

'Not at all, Roland.' I found I was smiling broadly. 'I've just put the baby out in the garden. Do come through and have a drink, won't you?'

'Well, if that's really all right.' He followed me down the hall, every gesture of his body self-effacing. He made admiring noises about the house. 'You've got it looking so nice, haven't you? I'm afraid I've been rather lazy with mine – the people before left it in reasonable repair and I've done next to nothing on it. Not one of my skills in any case.' He laughed.

In the garden he said, 'I thought I must come and see the baby before she's off to school – you know how the time goes!' He gave another little chuckle and I waited for him to relax. His nervous nature could make him sound so silly. Once relaxed out of that, the kind, sympathetic person could emerge.

He beamed with pleasure bending over to look into the pram. You were asleep, your face round and relaxed, arms flung out beside your head, hands clenched into plump fists. 'Oh, isn't she a poppet!' he exclaimed. 'Oh, Katie, I do envy you, you know. There's nothing I'd like more than a family of my own.'

I smiled gratefully at him. 'I'm sure you will have one one day. And you'll make a lovely, devoted father.'

He sat with me for a while. He declined beer, so I fetched tea and an ashtray and he sat, his short legs encased in grey flannel, smoking and chatting to me, gradually losing his twitchy demeanour. Marjorie was expecting her first child and sent her love. We spent an unruffled half hour, refreshing to me for its lack of angles or tension.

'I'd love to come again,' Roland said. He lingered by the pram before leaving. 'And perhaps she'll be awake next time?' I assured him of a welcome.

Douglas found the ashtray, forgotten between the chairs in the garden, when he came home from work. He went outside for a smoke in the summer evening air and came crashing back in again, holding the ashtray away from him like a half-decayed bird.

'Who's been here?' he demanded, in the self-righteous voice that I was coming to loathe.

Olivia sat very still watching us, the baby on her lap.

'Oh, just Roland,' I said casually. I was shelling peas in the kitchen, refusing to be ruffled by this ridiculousness.

'Roland? That's him, isn't it – the one I saw you with at the station?'

He advanced into the kitchen, his face ugly, and slung the glass ashtray down on the draining board, pettishly and too hard.

'D'you mind?' I protested. I dried my hands on my apron, preparing to walk away before I really let rip with my temper and announced that Roland had been the most pleasant and normal company I had had for weeks.

'Why didn't you tell me he was coming?'

I clenched my teeth. 'Because I didn't know. He was just on his way from somewhere I think. I didn't ask.'

'How many times has he been here before?' He leaned up against the sink, menacingly close to me. It was so silly and alienating. I felt impatience choking me.

Just controlling my voice, I said, 'That was the first time. And I don't really see it's any business of yours.

He was passing and he wanted to see Anna. Some men actually like babies,' I finished bitterly.

'It is my business.' He pushed his face too close to mine and the expression in his eyes was very cold. 'This is my house and you are my wife. I won't have you entertaining other men under my roof.'

I always felt at my most strong and perverse when he was like this. I knew I didn't have the attitude of subservience apparently expected of a 'good' wife. Even trying to have it would have suffocated me. I could hear Granny Munro saying, 'Don't let anyone take your life away from you. It's not worth it in the end. It's only convention.'

I stared Douglas in the face and said something that I am still ashamed of now for its cruelty. 'You're useless to me, Douglas. Completely useless.'

He picked up the pan into which I had been shelling peas and smashed it as hard as he could through the kitchen window, peas and all. Glass tinkled down on to the flower pots outside. I heard you, Anna, begin howling in the adjoining room, startled by the noise. At the time I felt most annoyed about the peas going out after I'd spent all that time shelling them.

Douglas stood for a second looking stunned and foolish. Then, as if it was his masterstroke, he brought out the announcement, 'What I came home to tell you is that I've got the job. We're leaving for London.'

He went out of the house then, leaving this ultimatum dumped like a tin trunk in the middle of the front room. Olivia came to me and we managed somehow to put our arms round each other, you pink and distraught between us.

Sitting on the bus that afternoon, I thought about Douglas and about how he always seemed to get it wrong. How he could never see that my feelings for my child and for Olivia were far more of a threat to him than Roland Mantel or anyone else was. I knew already that my going to London with him was inconceivable. I dared myself to imagine, for a second, what it would be like without him at home: just me and Anna and Olivia. I knew that part of this breakdown between us was my fault. But I also knew that I was inextricably tied both to this place and to Olivia.

I walked slowly along the road back to our house. Though still small, you felt heavy in my arms and were beginning to clamour for a feed. I took in the smell of flowers on the warm air, the sensation of milk aching in my breasts. I walked faster. Inside, I expected to find the house quiet, Douglas sheltering behind his news-papers, Olivia busy with her knitting or napping.

But he was upon me before I'd even shut the door. 'She's got to go!' At first I thought he was angry, but it was something a few degrees away from that. He was distraught.

'Whatever's happened? Look, I'll have to feed Anna or I can't hear you.' I unfastened my dress and Douglas waited impatiently until the room grew quiet. 'Where's Olivia?'

'Out. I sent her out. Kate, she's got to leave here as soon as possible. Tell her to go – tonight.'

I stared at him, feeling mutinous already. Douglas turned round, looking into the fireplace as he spoke to me. 'She started on me this afternoon.'

I couldn't take this in. 'What are you talking about?'

With injured dignity he said, 'She tried to seduce me.'

I fought back a wild desire to laugh. The first words which rushed into my mind were, 'Well, that must have been a disappointment for her.' Fortunately, instead I managed to say, 'Heavens, how dreadful!' Then I added, 'Are you all right?' before realizing what an absurd question that was. The awfulness of the situation began to sink in.

'Of course I'm all right,' he snapped, pacing up and down. 'But we can't very well carry on having her here. She's outstayed her welcome by a long time as it is. And she's not right, is she?' He turned to face me. 'Don't you mind that she's tried it on with me?'

'I can't quite take it in.'

Douglas came and sat down beside me, suddenly vulnerable. 'The thing was – it wasn't so much that she tried it on that worried me. I mean I know she's always been a bit, well – fast like that. I could have laughed about it, or told her to leave off. But it was her look. She was like a snake, and the things she was saying, it was frightening. I felt what she really wanted to do was to torture me. That was how she looked, absolutely intent and venomous, as if she ought to have had a red-hot poker in one hand.'

I listened, chilled. That thread of something corrupt in Olivia which kept lashing out like a poisoned tongue.

In the end I said, 'I'm truly sorry, Douglas. That's unforgivable, of course. It's just – where's she going to go? If you could just put up with her a while longer . . .'

There was a silence before he said, 'She'll have to leave anyway when we go to London.'

I couldn't tackle that one. Not now.

'It won't happen again,' I said. 'Not now she's tried it once.'

I didn't confront Olivia. I found myself unexpectedly embarrassed by the thought of it. I had been lulled, since giving birth, by her apparent steadiness, her adoration of my baby, my need of her when I would otherwise have felt so low and alone. Now, though, I was bristling and alert, on guard once more. The evening Douglas had sent her out of the house she stayed out all night again and came back with the same air of repletion and triumph. I didn't even speak to her when she came in next morning.

'Aren't you dying to know where I've been?' she goaded me. 'I do hope you haven't been waiting up?'

'I was up anyway,' I said curtly. 'Anna's been restless with this cold.' I was still pacing up and down with you fretting in my arms. By that time I was tired enough to be almost beyond feeling.

'Here, give her to me,' Olivia said, reaching out to take you. 'I'll get her settled down.'

'We're getting on all right, thank you,' I said shortly. 'She's been like this for hours, on and off.'

Olivia held out her arms again, commandingly. 'Then you need a rest. Come on, hand her over to Auntie Livy.'

'No. She's my child, not yours – especially not the state you're in. She wants her mother.'

Olivia's arms dropped to her sides. She said nothing and turned to go out of the room. As she did so she twirled round and whipped her skirt up high, showing her suspenders. On one leg the stocking was held up by only one fastening. The others were broken and the stocking was laddered down the back of her leg. With a terrible smile on her face she said, 'They can't resist me.'

We couldn't be normal with each other now. I found myself thinking of ways to get her out. I couldn't send her back to the Kemps. At that point I wouldn't have been so cruel. I still wanted to do it kindly, to ease her out, with our move to London as the excuse. My thoughts of staying here with her now seemed grotesque. But I couldn't think of anywhere she could go. I even considered asking my mother if Olivia could lodge with her, but I knew instinctively that this would be a disaster. Besides, my mother had held herself at such a distance from us over the months that I couldn't even have asked. Olivia was just going to have to find digs for herself.

I didn't want her looking after you any more, Anna. Before, I had pushed away any feelings of resentment at her swamping possessiveness of you. I had thought her feelings for you would help her heal, her holding you like that, staring into your face so long that sometimes I had almost to fight her to make her hand you over to me. At times I had wanted to shout, 'Give her to me – she's my baby, not yours!' like a child with a toy. I had been ashamed then. But now I allowed myself those feelings: a new instinct of protectiveness in me, a premonition that I did not yet understand.

Neither she nor Douglas ever told me directly how far her attempts to seduce him had gone, but that final week Olivia started making remarks, taunting me deliberately, eyes wide and brazen, and I realized it had gone further than Douglas had felt able to admit. Far enough for her to learn of his inadequacy.

'Are you sure Anna is Douglas's?' she giggled to me one evening when we were alone. She was on the gin. 'I'm surprised he could keep going long enough to hit the target!'

I no longer knew what to do with her. I could feel far more sympathy now for the Kemps and what they'd been through. All the warmth had gone. Mostly I ignored her, moving round her as if she wasn't there, preparing myself to eject her. As a last resort I knew I should have to call a doctor, and the thought played on my conscience.

Then, that one morning, I gave in to her. I felt so harassed. Your cold was no better and you were almost constantly in my arms, since I could find no other way of pacifying you. I had a huge pile of washing to do and a host of other jobs. And Livy seemed calmer that day.

'I just can't get on with anything,' I cried, tearful with frustration. 'If only she'd settle. I'm doing all the things I used to advise my mothers not to do!'

'Let me take her,' Olivia said. She spoke so smoothly, her face soft and smiling. 'We've hardly seen each other this week, have we, darling?' This last word was said in just the tones Elizabeth used with her.

Livy was wearing a cornflower-blue frock that morning. She was looking very beautiful and I relented, almost wanting to kiss her. When I handed you to her, a soft cotton sheet wrapped round you, she stood for a moment with you clasped in her arms like a madonna, her face radiant and smiling.

She turned the smile on me. I've never been able to forget the look of worship for you in her face. 'Come on, little Anna,' she said. 'We'll just go and have a play upstairs and let Katie get on with all her chores.' She left the room, humming lightly as she climbed the stairs.

I was seized with the urgency I always felt when you were sleeping or taken off my hands. I already had all the clothes heaped on the kitchen floor, napkins soaking in a pail. I spent some time sorting them, dividing whites from coloureds while the wide sink filled slowly. When I'd finished with the clothes, it still wasn't ready and I sprinkled Hudson's into the water, impatiently turning

on the tap as far as it would go. The water had slowed
to a trickle and I tutted in exasperation, staring at the
dull metal of the tap, willing it to force out more water.
Before the sink was even full I pushed in a bundle of
clothes and began pummelling at it, trying to wet
everything in the inadequate depth of water. Suddenly
the water came on again with a rush. I frowned, turning
the tap down again. Bubbles rose softly round my
wrists.

A few moments later I remembered our nightclothes
and ran upstairs for my nightdress and Douglas's
pyjamas. On my way down, I paused at the top of the
stairs. It was very quiet up there, except for a sound, a
tiny sound I couldn't place but which alerted me.
Puzzled, I looked into Olivia's room. I thought perhaps
she might be lying on the bed, trying to settle you down
beside her.

She was standing with her back to me, the blue frock
vivid in front of our dark furniture. My mind struggled
– for such a long, slow time it seemed – to make sense
of this. The chest of drawers in front of her had been
cleared, the toilet mirror now standing at a queer angle
on the bed, along with her perfume, powder, lotions. I
could see each end of the enamel baby bath, its bright,
bluish white; Olivia's elbows looking creamy against it.
Her arms were held straight, taut. And there was silence.
Then a movement of water. A tiny splash in the quiet.
It was this sound, its restrained smallness which I had
registered as odd and which now sliced across my mind.

You were never silent in the bath: you gurgled or
screamed.

I was there in a second, my body tight and violent.
Half turning, Olivia glared at me with a hard, determined expression. One of her hands was spread over

389

your face, pushing you under the water, the other holding your body down. She had filled the bath deep. Your arms and legs were moving madly, but barely managing to agitate the water's surface.

I grabbed Olivia by the neck and flung her across the room with all my strength. She fell and hit her head on the bedside cabinet, and I was pulling my baby up into my arms, completely possessed by panic, water saturating the front of my dress. I held you upside down, banging on your back, and a small gush of water came from your nose and mouth, then your choking, anguished cries reaching higher and higher. As I held you you thrust your head back, so beside yourself that there were seconds of silence between each cry, your spine bowing, rigid. I snatched up the little sheet and wrapped you in it and held you close to me, hearing distressed, animal sounds of comfort coming from me as I rocked you.

After a moment, hands shaking, I unfastened my dress and tried to let you suck to calm you, gulping and trembling as I did so, and your little body twitched convulsively as you began to latch on to me, too agitated to do so at first. I was oblivious to Olivia. I didn't care if I'd killed her.

It was only as I was beginning to come to my senses that I realized she was laughing. Sitting on the floor rubbing her head and giving off high peals of laughter. Too stunned to think, I sat staring at her, still crying, stroking my little Anna again and again.

Olivia got to her feet. 'Sorry, old girl. I've not had much practice bathing babies. Never even got to bath my own.'

She walked over to the window, standing with her

back to me, a scrawny silhouette against the light. She lit a cigarette and stood smoking it in silence.

Then she said, 'You want me to leave.' There was amusement in her voice, as if she found me ridiculous.

I didn't answer, couldn't.

She blew out a trail of smoke. 'By the way, there's one more thing I haven't told you.' The voice floated over to me, to wherever I was.

'I'd have spared you this, but truth does have a way of finding us, doesn't it?'

I waited. There was nothing worse she could do.

'That child of mine. My baby. I did know who the father was, you know.'

Indifferent to this information, I sat in silence.

'I was in London – that January – for the Wrens. Pretty beastly it was too. Then who should I run into, fresh back from embarkation leave, but an old friend from home . . .'

I was on my feet. 'No. No!'

'Dents your image rather, doesn't it? Pure, loyal old Angus. Actually, he was in a bit of a state, I thought. Terrified about the posting. And of course by the end of the night he was worse. Full of remorse, disloyal to you and all that. Katie his love, how could he have . . .' She mocked me. 'Of course I said he must think of it as something that meant nothing. I expect he wrote to you, didn't he? "Ran into Olivia. We had such a nice cosy chat."'

'I don't believe you.'

'I knew it was his, Katie. I was unusually busy that month. Very little time to spare for any hanky-panky . . .'

'You're lying to me!' I screamed at her, so that you released me and started yelling as well, Anna. 'Angus

391

would never have done something like that.' The words
fell awkwardly from my mouth. 'As a matter of fact he
didn't even like you all that much.'

Olivia laughed again, head flung back. 'Oh, darling –
they don't have to *like* you!'

'You're lying.' I could hardly breathe, was growing
incoherent. 'Why are you doing this? I've done everything for you . . . Tell me it's a lie, just a story.'

But she was silent, turned to watch me, the cigarette
held at a jaunty angle in her hand, her face exultant.

We stood like that in silence for a few seconds before
I found my voice again. 'Get out of my house. I want
you out by midday. Otherwise you'll be back in Arden
tonight.'

I left her, holding you close to my body. I couldn't
let go of you. I wrapped you up and walked to the park,
carrying you round and round in the strong sunshine,
hardly knowing what I was doing. When finally I
returned home, the house was empty.

Chapter 28

It was Lisa I turned to, then. I was in a terrible state. I couldn't bear to be parted from my baby for a second out of fear something would happen. Night after night I woke sweating, my hands grasping for you, sometimes screaming. I moved out of my bed with Douglas so that I could sleep with you, guard you. It was as if the odour of Olivia had not passed from the house and she could still harm you. And in my fear of losing you I couldn't bear to try and imagine how Olivia must have felt in parting with her child. It was too much – such thoughts sent my emotions into too great a conflict. I pushed them out of my mind.

Douglas was very impatient and thought me hysterical. 'She's all right – none the worse for it.' At least it had meant me getting shot of Olivia. That's what he was bothered about. But I couldn't have cared less about him. You were the only person who mattered to me, Anna. I saw everyone else close to me as a source of betrayal and I curled in on myself. I had a wall round me. I suppose now they would say I was traumatized and depressed

Lisa was different, of course. She was full of common sense and free of illusions.

'Look,' she suggested, when to the fascination of her neighbours I had turned up again, weeping and distraught at her door. 'When you're ready, leave the

393

littl'un with me. She can be with Alice for a bit and Daisy'll help look after 'em. You know what she's like with babbies. Even five minutes. It's a start. You can't go on like this. You're making yourself bad with it.'

I needed help and I took her advice. I had an instinctive trust in her that I felt for no one else. Sick with anxiety the first time, I left you lying there on the blanket next to Alice. Daisy was shaking an old tin with a few dried peas in for you. For ten minutes I paced with weak legs, up and down Stanley Street and Catherine Street. When I had decided to return to you I had to hold myself back from running down the road. I dashed the final few yards across the court and went in to find you laughing.

'See?' Lisa said. Then added, 'That Kemp girl needs locking up. You should've called the police. You've spared that family too much.'

'Perhaps it was partly my fault,' I said, holding you close to me, my legs still trembling. 'And I don't want them on my conscience. I want them right out of my life – all of them.'

'But she might try it with someone else's?'

I sat down, frowning. 'I don't think so.'

'Where's she gone?'

I shrugged. 'I've no idea. Away from me, that's the main thing.'

Lisa gradually weaned me off my terror. When I could leave you with her for an hour, I knew I was overcoming it. But often during that time I would arrive at her house and dissolve into tears. And she was always welcoming, sitting me down amidst all the chaos of her life and letting me be there, whatever was going on at the time.

'You're so good to me,' I told her. 'There's just no one else.'

'We're friends, aren't we?' was all she said.

My mother would be no good, I knew that. I was in a thoroughly distraught state, but couldn't have admitted it to her. And anyway, other people's nerves usually got thoroughly on hers. I knew also that she was not the person to consult about the other decision which faced me more pressingly as each day passed. If I didn't go to London with Douglas, I knew it would be the end of my marriage.

'What would you do?' I asked Lisa one day.

Lisa eased Alice up over her shoulder, the child's head resting against her cheek. Her skin looked grey and tired.

'In your shoes?' She frowned. 'I dunno. I s'pose 'e is your 'usband when all's said and done. But 'e's making you uproot yourself . . . 'Ow d'you feel about 'im?'

After a silence broken only by small sounds from the babies, I finally admitted, 'I can't stand him.'

'Well then,' Lisa said. 'You can earn a good wage on your own, can't you?'

When Douglas left we moved into our small terraced house in Florence Road in which you grew up until we moved to Drayton Road when you were eleven.

I didn't find the courage to tell him until he insisted on us beginning to pack. We were speaking so little anyway. He said, 'You've betrayed me. I always knew you would.'

I sat on our bed and replied, 'Then why marry me?'

The communication between us remained thin and stretched through those days of practicalities. I found

myself looking at him in such a detached way sometimes, wondering what, in those disturbed days of the
war, I had thought I felt for him and what had kept me
believing it. I was weary and indifferent. You were
asleep when he left and he, your father, didn't even go
to your room to look at you. We didn't speak. I watched
him walk down the road from the house with his cases
and his camera round his neck and thought that I still
hadn't been to see his parents. He didn't write. I never
pursued him for money. I could, as Lisa had remarked,
earn my own. Occasionally I saw signs of his career
developing in newspaper bylines and felt some shame at
how little I missed him.

I was happy with you, Anna, and happy to devote
my life only to us.

It was Lisa who had prepared me for my separation
from you. When I went back to work I found dear old
Mrs Busby. I suppose she wasn't so old, when you were
still a baby, but she was grandmotherly even in her late
forties. The first time she opened the door to me and
saw me standing there with you in my arms, she said, in
real tones of appreciation, 'Oh, what a beautiful baby.' I
trusted her immediately. Whenever I came to collect
you you were always clean, fed and occupied, and you
had Reni James, company which you wouldn't have had
at home. I owed such a debt to Edith Busby. I loved my
work. Life settled and didn't feel lacking. I had you, my
job, Roland. Dear Roland – he has always been such a
good friend to us.

I saw Olivia one more time, in the summer of 1962. She
was back up here for a time then. Alec Kemp more or
less paid to keep her out of the way, like a wayward son

being packed off to be shameful somewhere distant like Africa. Except she chose London.

My morning's list of calls included a visit to a Mrs Kemp, with a new baby. The name registered, of course, but it never occurred to me it would be her, not here in Birmingham, nor with 'Mrs' as the handle on the name. She was living in Moseley in one of those enormous Victorian houses that had already been sliced up inside for flats. I had to climb a flight of stairs – grand ones once, though dirty and communal now – to find the chipped door marked '3'.

She was holding him as she answered the door, her small frame wrapped in a turquoise silk robe, hair loose and falling all over the place. The child was very tiny and startlingly dark. I realized immediately that the father must have been from India or similar. His eyes were huge, brown and alert.

We never spoke. As soon as I'd realized who it was I was on my way back down those grimy stairs and out to the car. When I sat down in the seat I was shaking. I managed to drive back to the clinic, and handed Olivia's notes over to another Health Visitor. I wasn't having anything of that. Not after all this time.

For Anna

May 1981

My dear one,

I suppose I should have written this a long time ago and got it out of my system. It's our story: Olivia's and mine. You used to ask me about Olivia so often when you were a little girl, and what I used to feed your curiosity was a lie, or at least such a selective version of the truth as to amount to one.

You will see from her letter enclosed with this that Olivia didn't die during the war. In a way it was simpler for me to let you think she was dead all this time, and the fact was that for me she might just as well have died. I wanted her out of my life as cleanly as death would have taken her. She'd done such damage and I couldn't stand any more.

But I couldn't resist telling you my happy memories. When you were young and fierce with affection for your friends it made me think of her so often and how we were together. We did have those good, happy times, Anna. I shouldn't want you to think I had invented those. I always wanted you to know about Olivia as I knew her then, because I have loved very few people as I loved Livy.

I've tried to be frank with you about all aspects of my life. I've always admired your straightness and I know this is what you would want. Some of it you'll already know, but there's much that you don't. I seem to have ended up telling you my life story – but then there's not much from that period of my life which is not somehow bound up with Olivia.

I hoped to tell you all this at some point. I didn't, though, expect you to hear any of it from Olivia herself. But in 1976 Alec Kemp died, and not long after that she began writing to me. They had gone very quiet, the Kemps. He stayed on the Council for a time, but he certainly never made it as an MP. I don't recall him ever standing for Parliament again – a fact which has some-how made it easier for me to forgive him. What relations were like between Olivia and her parents all those years, I've no idea. But the letters started coming. She begged me to see her. She sent me bits and pieces which she must have written in London after she left Arden Mental Hospital. Some of these were rather disconnected, but the ones I have included for you speak clearly. They tell of things I barely guessed at the time: the hidden side of her life at home of which I felt the vibrations, but for many years knew nothing of the causes. Her father's death must have prompted her to reach back into the past and try to explain it. These fragments are, though, I have to add, stamped with Olivia's hallmark: a complete lack of remorse for her actions.

I didn't respond. Even now I couldn't bear to see her.

I hope, Anna, that I have also given you enough of a sense of who your father was. Even had things been different, I don't think we would have lasted in the end. He wanted to keep me like a cupboard full of starched white napkins and bring one out now and then to wipe his face on. Your generation would put up with that even less well than I did.

I'm sorry I couldn't just tell you this face to face, but it goes too deep, and I find I am more like my own mother in some ways than I've always hoped. I'm even glad you won't be able to question me about it. I know how ill I am, whatever they say to humour me, and that my life now measures in weeks.

But if you were to decide you needed to see Olivia, I should understand. Of course I haven't seen her properly for over thirty years and I no longer know her. I'm sure she would wish you only good – really she always did – but I still can't help feeling I want to pull you close in my arms and protect you from her as if you were still my tiny baby. This is quite irrational I realize. Even so, I would give you one warning: caution.

Now I have finished with all this I feel only sadness about the Kemps. About all of it. I'm sorry if you feel I cut Olivia's truth in half and chose to give you only the more palatable slice. It was all I could do. And now all I want is peace for the remains of my life. I want to remember the loving parts. What is forgivable by me, I forgive. Anything else is probably God's department.

I'm so very proud of you, my Anna. I hope you know that in all you have done you've been the greatest joy of my life. Go well, my darling.

Part Four

Chapter 29

ANNA

Warwickshire, 7 August 1981

'You're not going *in* there, surely?'

The ivy leaves snaking round the stone gateway were such a dark green that in the stormy light they looked almost black. Between them she could make out some of the carved letters: *Arden Mental Hospital*, and in Roman numerals, 1848.

The black cab growled rhythmically, wipers swishing away rain which was hammering on to the windscreen. The driver had spoken with his nose buried in his hanky.

'Yes – I need you to wait please,' Anna said, more sharply than she had intended. 'I shan't be long. 'Specially not in this.' She pulled a navy beret over her straw-coloured hair.

So this was the place. They had driven for some time, winding between cornfields, seeing its gaunt shape growing nearer on the rise, until they reached the entrance further round the flank of the hill among the trees.

Arden.

Trying to control her nervousness, she asked, 'When was the fire?'

'Can't remember exactly.' The driver gave a sneeze which ended in a groan. 'Late seventies sometime.'

'Anyone hurt?'

'Oh, crikey, yes. Killed twenty or more of 'em – terrible thing it was. They moved the rest out, didn't think it was worth the cost of rebuilding. What the hell d'you want to go there for? Place gives me the creeps.' He blew his nose again.

Her fingers were round the cold lever, poised to get out. 'Just give me a few minutes.'

As she turned to slam the door he called nasally, 'They're all set to knock it down soon anyway.'

Anna strode away from the taxi, glad of a rest from him and his hayfever and lamenting nature. She cursed not having an umbrella. The days before had been so intensely hot it had been hard to imagine the possibility of rain like this. She was lightly dressed – black cotton jeans and a denim jacket – and the rain was falling steadily and hard. The sound of it was all around her and in minutes she was soaked. But she was relieved to be walking.

The main building was no longer visible from here, and the drive curved up and round to the right, disappearing into what looked like a soft wall of green until she moved close up to it and saw the path straighten out again in front of her. Its surface was fractured and heaved up by quitch-grass and dandelions, puddles collecting in the cracks. Foxgloves and brambles held sway in what had evidently once been tended beds at its edges and the branches of the trees on each side were overgrown and meshed together, creating a tunnel of interlocking stems filled with the smell of wet leaves, wet earth.

She followed it round the rightward curve, then to

the left. The trees thinned, then stopped, the path opening out into an area which had been concreted over for a car park, now covered in tussocks like boils. She stopped. The building was there suddenly in front of her, shockingly black even against a grey sky.

It was lower than she had imagined, but very wide, with an impressive entrance at the centre, carved scrolls of stone above the lintel. The square brick water tower in the middle of the complex had escaped the fire, although it was blackened. The decay of the place was evident in its every line. The points of tapering brick which Kate had described adorning the parapet of the roof were now all knocked off leaving jagged edges. The windows on the ground floor were boarded up behind the rusted bars and though the upper windows were uncovered there was no glass left in the frames. Through those to the right, at the eastern portion of the building, she could see only sky. At the west end, the windows were dark, looking into the one whole remaining wing of the building. As she walked nearer, a pigeon, startled from behind clumps of thistles, lifted itself to the roof with slapping wings.

On her way along the west wing she saw a large sign nailed to the front of the building warning, 'Danger, Falling Masonry'. For what seemed a long time she made her way down the side of the building, through rampant grass and thistles which sent cool shocks of water down her thighs with every step she took. There was nothing to see. No chink of the windows was left uncovered. About half way along were two wooden doors with large rusty keyholes, and she pushed against them, relieved when they refused to budge and she didn't have to go inside.

Very little remained of the hospital's east end and the

fire had worked its way round and eaten into most of the middle wing which separated the two open quadrangles, but had stopped short of the water tower. These areas were cordoned off with flagging white plastic tape. Most of the rubble must have been taken away, leaving only some charred bricks which looked as if they had come loose since the clearance. Uneven sections of walls remained as partitions between the rooms.

Anna lifted the tape and stepped over one of the sections of wall, hearing the throaty sound of other pigeons unseen in their shelter among the ruins. She was standing in what must have been a long room. Whatever it had once been used for, its character now was quite lost. Had there been beds in this part, or were the wards only upstairs? Was this a dayroom? Squatting down at one end, she could see patches where the texture of the wooden floor showed through the silt of ash and plaster. She stroked the wet grain of it with her fingers, a tiny contact with Arden's past. With Olivia.

Ignoring the tape, she scrambled over the remains of the inner wall into the quadrangle. The hospital had been arranged in two separate halves, the men's and women's sections, each with their own airing court for daily exercise. There was the remains of a circular path, now colonized by weeds and made from uneven segments of stone, a tree stump in the middle. Following the path round, she stumbled over tufts of grass and groundsel. She stood looking at the ruined walls and the slit-eyed water tower.

The airing court. Their light on the world, this enclosed rectangle of sky. Images from Olivia's strange, disconnected account of herself filled her mind. How had she felt that June morning, moving along the drive towards this hospital? Was the sun shining, sky an exuberant spring blue and the leaves new and bright? She had not mentioned these things of course. Perhaps she had seen nothing. They arrived from Birmingham by ambulance, closed in, probably dark inside, Olivia sitting or lying in the juddering, gloomy space, watched over by iron-faced orderlies. Had she been tied in: strapped? How had they restrained her frail body? Perhaps they had already tamped her down with phenobarbitone so that she knew little of the journey. Or had her brown eyes had to face, wide awake, this place of lost souls, of strange cries and wild movements?

'I thought, when they took me there' – Anna heard the words in her mind – 'that I was going to my death. They would have absolute control over me. They proposed to bury me alive . . .'

Anna began to cry, the sadness of the past days swelling in her at the sight of these remains: hundreds of square yards of stone and brick which had been the crucible of so many lives. Raindrops on her cheeks felt cold compared with her tears. She turned her face to the sky.

She had never seen Olivia, yet she had learned, through her childhood, to love her: her mother's friend, beautiful and tragic, their affection for each other passionate and sparkling as a fairy story. The mention of her brought a special light in to her mother's eyes. Kate and Olivia – best friends. Ordinary but magical. Olivia enshrined as something Anna longed for. She was more than a girl who had been a friend: she was friendship itself.

And now she was left with the legacy of their story, this telling of the other side of Olivia so long left hidden in blue shadow. This woman with whom she was so oddly linked. She had held Anna's life in her hands and almost taken it away.

But even despite the worst Olivia had done, now Anna had seen Arden she could only feel an aching empathy with her. And coming here had not finished this as she had somehow hoped it might. Her mind was alive with questions that now only Olivia could answer. She felt the past clutching at her, filling her with a need she could barely even explain.

Her tears still coming, she folded her arms across the front of her wet denim jacket and turned away. The place had made her feel jumpy, nerves stretched taut, ready to run on hearing the slightest sound. But there was only rain falling from the low, grey sky.

Wiping her face with her hands, she headed for the drive. For a moment she turned and walked backwards watching the hospital recede, then hurried to the taxi and sat shivering on the rear seat.

'Must be out of your flaming mind,' the driver commented without turning round. His bald patch was round and pale like a peppermint. The radio was on, an over-bright voice beating from it.

They drove back through the Warwickshire country-side without speaking. Anna stared out through the streaks of water on the window, badly wanting to smoke, but a large sign in the back of the cab forbade it. She watched trees and hedges passing. Some of the corn had been flattened by the rain. Arden faded behind them like a mirage.

Chapter 30

The night after the funeral, Anna hadn't been to bed until well gone four. Apart from Richard's phone call she didn't speak to anyone. She cut slices of bread and cheese to eat with Patak's pickles and sat on Kate's velour sofa, feet up, reading and reaching for cigarettes. Every hour or two she pulled herself up and stretched, shivering a little, made coffee and ate Dairy Milk until it was all gone. Once she went to the back window and saw a bright sheet of moonlight across the golf course behind the house.

When finally she put Kate's pages of writing down and went upstairs to bed, her eyes felt dry and sore, her head tight inside. But it took her a very long time to sleep, her nerves jangling from the caffeine, images from what she had just read swirling in her mind.

Late the next afternoon, as promised, she drove their dusty blue car to Coventry and let herself into their terraced house off the Kenilworth Road.

'Richard?'

How silly. Of course he wouldn't be there. It was very quiet, the air in the house stuffy, plants drooping on windowsills. A fly droned round the kitchen like a distant bomber and the tap with the dodgy washer was dripping into the quiet, down the side of the washing-up bowl. The bin smelled in the heat.

Richard had evidently worked his way through their supply of crockery for each meal without washing up any of it. Mugs waited on the draining board rimed with coffee. There were cereal bowls encrusted with muesli and two plates with grains of basmati rice congealed in grease. Saucepans with various dribbles down their sides were stacked drunkenly against the tiled wall. Richard's ideals of intellectuals taking their turn at menial work never had quite translated into cleaning up after himself.

Anna automatically started to do what she had always done: restore order. She pulled the overflowing black bag out of the bin and tied the top. The yellow washing-up bowl was almost full of water ringed with orange grease. She tipped it away, cutlery crashing across the bottom of the bowl, and turned on the tap to run hot, staring at the bright thread of water. Then she thought, sod it, turned it off and went out to the tiny garden, to sit on the rickety bench with a bottle of beer from the fridge and a cigarette.

The house was squeezed into the long curve of the terrace, its window frames a muddy green, the built-on bathroom jutting out into the garden. The sight of it made her feel sad. She had spent too much time in there feeling low. It had been only days away from Christmas when she lost the baby. She was alone of course. Term was over for her, but Richard still had to work. The miscarriage had seemed such a violent thing: pain, blood, panic. Eighteen weeks pregnant and she had thought it was safe, established. Since then she had hardly let herself think about the child as it might have been. But now, suddenly, there was a pram in front of her on the baked paving stones, old fashioned and not the sort she would actually have had. She saw it moving, jerked by vigorous kicks from inside, tiny feet bare in the heat.

And herself leaning over, lifting, holding warm flesh, a small head with hair moist in the heat. Tears stung her eyes. The house should not have been silent this summer. She thought of Olivia, what she must have felt.

After six, when she was already angry, the phone rang.

'Anns? It's me. Look, sorry, but I'm going to be late. We've got a problem here.' He had on his harassed work voice. 'Look, I know I said I'd cook and everything, but could you maybe get something going? Otherwise it'll be midnight when we eat.'

'No, it won't, actually. I shan't be here at midnight. The last train goes before then.'

'Tonight? But I thought you were back now. Staying, I mean? Come on, at least stay the night?' Anna pictured him hunched over his desk, hand running through the wild brown hair, intense frown on his face.

'No.'

'Oh – ' He sounded very put out. 'Well, look, I'll be home within a couple of hours – definitely.'

'Sure.' She put the phone down, trembling with fury.

Kate had never openly criticized Richard. They had got on civilly enough, even had things in common. But Anna remembered her once saying, 'It's no good. He'll burn out carrying on the way he does. His work's very worthwhile, of course, but you have to keep it in perspective.'

Thinking back, Anna saw that Kate had known their relationship was at odds long before she had herself. It wasn't that she'd said anything. It was more what she hadn't said: none of those encouraging signals of hope for it to last. When the two of them had moved in together four years ago, Kate had been helpful but not exactly over the moon about it.

'We're not thinking of getting married – at the moment anyway,' Anna had confided, wondering what the reaction would be. 'To tell you the truth, Richard's not too sure about marriage – as an institution I mean.'

'I think you're very wise,' Kate said unexpectedly. 'Being tangled up in buying property together is enough of a complication without rushing into marriage as well.'

She had, back then, fallen for something Richard represented as much as for himself. After she met him, her life before seemed to have been spent in slumber, wasted in some way. She had drifted from college to teaching, unsure what else to do, had barely examined what she believed about anything. And there was Richard, fresh from his degree, embarked as a mature student in sociology and politics. Old as she was, she had been impressed by someone who could bandy terms around as if they owned them: the jargon of sociology. And Richard's ideals, which he could lay out for her like a pack of cards. But of late she had begun to notice other things: all the friends she had somehow not seen for a long time because Richard had condemned them as bourgeois or just plain boring. Friends she had once valued, who'd seen her through other times, college and teaching. And she had mistaken Richard's openness about his own feelings for sensitivity to hers.

She decided to face the rest of the house. In their room the duvet lay in a strangled twist across the pine-framed bed. There were underpants and socks and shirts left lying all over the coconut matting (Richard didn't like carpet).

She sat on the side of the bed holding a photograph in a wooden frame from the dressing table. A close up of her and Richard, both grinning foolishly at the camera. It was taken a few months after they got together. She had her hair even longer then and Richard said she looked like Mary Hopkin. She had been clowning, singing, 'Those were the days my friend – la la la la la la . . .' Richard had a cigarette hanging from the side of his mouth, a lazy half smile, arm crooked round Anna's neck and smoke threading up through her hair. His shirt was a loud check, hair curling down into his neck and chunky sideburns.

Anna put the photo back and looked round at the bed. All the nights there with Richard, his intensity even in sleep. But the more recent memory was of being alone there after the miscarriage, empty and distressed. Richard had no idea of her need for him to be there. She had wanted to keep the news from Kate, until one day, unable to bear the loneliness any longer, she phoned her, and Kate came immediately, full of comfort and understanding.

Their lives had always been dictated by Richard's timing. 'I'm-so-busy-so-much-work-this-will-really-make-a-difference.' Never there when she needed him, in her own crises at work, or when the bleeding began and she had to call an ambulance, or through her mother's death.

She thought of Douglas, of Kate's strength in ending her marriage. Turning to the photo again, she stroked dust from the film of plastic covering Richard's face, as if in order to speak to him. 'No,' she said, her voice sounding loud after the hours of silence. 'No more.'

At eight-thirty the phone rang again. She ambled across to answer it. 'Look, Anns – sorry. Meeting's running on a bit. Bit of an emergency. It'll be another hour, then that's it – definite. OK?'

413

'As you like.'

Upstairs she packed an old suitcase which had been Kate's. Richard always used a rucksack to go away, suitcases, like carpet, apparently representing something too staid. Folding clothes into the deep expandable case, Anna felt calm, peaceful almost. These few days away from Richard had allowed parts of her, long submerged, to bob to the surface like corks.

She took only what she needed most immediately, nothing like books or cassettes. This could not be finished now. There was the joint ownership of the house to deal with for a start.

She called a taxi to take her to the station. While she was waiting, she went to the kitchen and rummaged round in the store cupboard for a tin of baked beans and left it standing out on the side, the tin-opener resting on top.

Without looking round any further she went outside with her case and sat down beside it in the coppery evening light.

The next morning she went on impulse to a hairdresser's in Kings Heath and had her hair cut very short. Her head felt strangely light and she could feel the air on her neck. In the mirror her eyes seemed bigger, the cheek-bones more prominent. She looked different.

When Richard phoned she didn't tell him she'd left home for good. After her decisiveness in Coventry she found she couldn't face talking to him about it, especially not over the telephone. She found herself in a period of limbo, strung between an old life which she had to finish and a new one she barely knew how to begin.

'The thing is, I've got so much to do here,' she told

him. 'All the house to clear. And there's lots of the holiday left. I shan't be around for a while . . .'

Roland Mantel lived a street away from Kate's house, in a similar style of twenties semi. Its rectangle of front lawn was boxed in by trim privet hedges, the front door sky blue, slightly chipped and the windows huge clean panes of double-glazing with their chunky white frames.

It was a few moments before he came to the door. He was dressed in fawn cotton trousers with mud stains at the knee and gardening gloves clasped in one hand.

'Anna, my dear – how lovely!' His face lifted into a cherubic smile. 'Called in on you yesterday, but no joy.'

'Yes, I was – out,' she replied vaguely, unsure how to explain her day visiting Arden.

'I say, I do like the hair.'

'Thank you. I wanted a change.'

Reaching up, she kissed his cheek, soft and broken-veined and familiar. 'I'm very sorry it's taken me so long to get round here.' She gave a shrug, ashamed of letting the week go past since the funeral. 'Uncle Roland, I need to talk to you.'

'To me? I'd be honoured. I've missed our chats since you've been in Coventry. Come on through – I've got the kettle on. You're in luck because I've got some digestives in. Can't beat a McVitie's, can you?'

'I know I'll always get fed well when I come to see you.' Anna smiled, following Roland's plump figure into the kitchen at the back of the house, across the hall's worn brown carpet. The house had always been bare and functional, and kept in the methodical way of someone once in the armed forces. The only splashes of exuberance had been handed down from his parents' house; the standard lamp in the living-room with its huge tasselled shade, a vase shaped in deep blue glass. And the tablecloth embroidered with a riot of wild flowers which was always spread on the table when they used to come for teas of crumpets and Eccles cakes – an iced bun for Anna – all produced out of white bakery bags.

In the kitchen there were still the old wooden cupboards with blue handles which Anna knew she had run to pull open and explore when he had first moved in, some time within the memory of her childhood. He had a red and white sixties cooker with metal racks beside the grill for warming plates, an ancient Russell Hobbs kettle and a cupboard full of mismatched crockery. Coming back here after this long gap, Anna saw now only the simplicity of the house. He could have had so much more, but chose not to.

The sun was slanting through the french windows, etching a rectangle on the grey lino. Roland's cat, black and white and very hairy, was spread across its bright heat.

'Hello Maisie, old lady.' Anna squatted down and ran her hand across the inert body which just raised the energy to give a half-hearted purr.

Roland was fishing teaspoons out of a drawer, frowning with concentration. 'Yes, I suppose she'll be leaving me soon too.'

Anna looked up startled, suddenly ashamed. Roland's reserve and gentlemanly tact had kept her from appreciating how deeply he felt about her mother's death.

'I'm really sorry, Roland. You'll miss Mummy a lot, won't you?'

He paused, not meeting her eyes, a jar of Nescafé

poised in one hand. 'I don't think I can quite imagine how much yet.'

Anna wanted to go to him, give him a hug, but she held back, wondering whether she wouldn't just be piling her own emotions on him. And there was an odd feeling now, the two of them alone without Kate who had always been there.

'You were such a good friend to her – to us both.'

Roland gave her a watery smile, determinedly cheerful. He handed her a mug patterned with ears of wheat. Biscuit packet in his other hand, he said, 'Come on, let's go out. Much too good a day to be in.'

There was a covered verandah at the back of the house, where they sat on old canvas chairs, looking out over the vivid summer green of the lawn. Roland was cultivating a vine up the two supports of the verandah, its tendrils just beginning to reach across the wooden slatted roof. It was very peaceful, quiet enough to hear birds, insects even. Anna thought of the little yard at the back of the house in Coventry with its dusty slabs and tubs of bolting geraniums.

Roland sat back with a wistful sigh. 'Biscuit? Go on. Look as if you need it.'

Anna smiled, taking one. Roland always made the smallest things seem a treat, should have had a host of grandchildren to spoil. She could tell he was waiting for her to speak, clearing his throat now and then as if to do so himself but unable.

'It's so lovely just to sit still,' Anna said. 'I feel as if there are whole aspects of life I've forgotten – as if I've been underwater for a long time.'

'That's what Kate said. Work, work, work all these

417

years. She said when she retired she was going to make time to stand and stare.'

Anna chuckled. 'That's not how it sounded to me. She was so full of plans and projects.'

'Ah well – I expect she didn't want you to worry or think she was going to vegetate.'

'It never occurred to me she would.' Always some campaign with Kate, even in Anna's earliest memories. Getting people to see that the National Health Service was for them. 'All these women, so prolapsed that their insides were sleeping beside them on the bed. "Go and get yourself fixed up," I'd tell them. That's what it's for.' And sex education: working in schools, determined there should be openness, trying to combat the ignorance of young women. Recalling Kate's energetic, no-nonsense style, how much she loved people, Anna felt tears rise in her eyes.

'Roland,' she began. 'There were a lot of things Mummy didn't talk to me about, weren't there?'

Roland made a slight grimace and attended to brushing biscuit crumbs from the front of his shirt. 'I'm not sure about that, my dear. You mean your father?'

'No – not really.' Anna sat forward in her chair, reaching for the end of her hair, her habit of playing with a strand between her fingers, but it was gone – shorn and strange. 'She talked about him a bit. Enough so that I've never needed to be too curious about him. I always knew who he was. And she told me enough when I was younger – not in great detail of course – to make me understand why they were divorced.'

'Oh no,' Roland corrected her quickly. 'They were never divorced. Not formally.'

'They must have been!' She sat up straight again. 'I

418

mean it's so long ago.' Roland was shaking his head. 'I'm sure she told me...'

His gaze fixed on the far side of the garden, Roland said stiffly, 'Her name was still Craven, remember. If they had applied for a divorce I can only assume they would have been granted one after a certain time. But of course you don't have to be legally divorced if you are living apart unless you want to remarry. Presumably Douglas Craven never wanted to do so.'

Anna had the words 'And Mummy?' on her tongue, but bit them back, seeing how Roland suddenly turned very brisk, sipping his coffee, twisting the top of the biscuit wrapper to seal it up.

'D'you mind me asking you things?' she wondered anxiously. 'If you'd rather I didn't...'

'Of course you have questions, Anna,' he said, his tone gentler again. 'But I don't know that I'm going to be much help. I never met your father properly, you see. Really I saw very little of your mother while she was married. It was only afterwards we spent more time together.'

'Did you meet Angus Harvey?'

Roland startled her by suddenly closing his eyes and putting his head back for a second, giving out a long, tired-sounding sigh. 'No. I never met Angus. The first time I remember seeing your mother was after he had been reported missing.' He looked at Anna with sad eyes. 'The war. If it had not been for the damn war ... Messed up so many of our lives. Only one who did reasonably well out of the war was my sister Marjorie, strangely enough. Never looked back. Five children, running all sorts of naval wives' do's down there.' He sounded amused.

Anna had a slight recollection of having met Marjorie, a woman on a large scale with a booming voice, rather intimidating in a child's eyes.

Hesitantly she said, 'I wondered whether Mummy ever really loved my father?'

'Well that I can't tell you. Couldn't be sure.' Roland's tone had turned stiff again. 'Rather a private person really, your mother.'

After a silence, she asked, 'What about Olivia?'

'Olivia?' His brow puckered.

'Olivia Kemp. You must have met her. She was living with Mummy after I was born.'

'Ah – Kemp. Yes, school friend of hers – the councillor's daughter. I do remember someone was staying for a bit but I never met her. Course, when I saw a lot more of you both, you were already living in Florence Road.'

'It's so strange,' Anna said slowly. 'She seems to have kept bits of her life in such separate compartments. Didn't she ever talk to you about Olivia?'

'Not that I remember. She didn't hark back to school much. No real reason to I don't think. Why?'

'I just . . .' She felt weary suddenly, ready to go and lie under a tree and sleep, rest her brain from all these thoughts. 'You think you know people, don't you? And instead you only see little glimpses of them.' She could feel herself growing tearful.

'Anna, my dear . . .'

She knelt down and was in his arms, his smell of sweat and shaving cream. Sobbing as she had done as a child after scares or bumps. 'You're such a good man,' she said into his warm, fleshy chest. 'There aren't many about like you.'

He didn't speak and she could tell that he was unable. His body gave little jerks. She didn't look up at him, knowing his shyness and that he wouldn't want her to see his tears. As he wiped his pink face with the back of his hand, she said, 'My father didn't want to know me. You've been a father to me.'

He spoke softly, in a controlled voice, holding her with great tenderness. 'Nothing would have made me happier than to have been your father.'

Chapter 31

The two of them wouldn't leave her alone: Kate and Olivia. Those days immediately after the funeral and her visit to Coventry it was as if she was paralysed. She moved round the house, tired and stunned, not achieving anything. When the phone rang she ignored it now. Often she found herself standing or sitting, just staring across the silent rooms. She might wander up and down stairs opening cupboards and drawers, looking, not certain for what, but somehow unable to begin disturbing anything.

On the window-sill of Kate's bedroom, overlooking the garden, were photographs, all of Anna at different ages. A tiny monochrome print with white edges and her serious little face looking out, all eyes. This was stuck into the lower edge of the frame of her graduation portrait, the brick Italianate tower of Birmingham University in the background. 1969. She smiled at the shortness of her dress, her hair bobbed round her ears and backcombed specially for the occasion. There were the familiar snaps Kate had had on show for years: Anna in the backyard of the Florence Road house, aged about eleven, a black and white kitten cuddled close to her face. Another at nine, on a beach, bending over a metal-tipped spade and looking up to grin delightedly into the lens, hair swept to one side by the wind. Wales, and their first-ever holiday.

Revisiting herself at these young stages she tried to relearn her mother, playing through their lives together year by year like tracks on a record.

After seeing Roland she felt spurred to make a start on the house.

Clearing Kate's wardrobe and dressing table was the worst part. All those intimately shaped garments. The one bottle of cologne, sparing amounts of powder and scantly filled jewellery box. She found a pair of clip-on earrings, fifties style, round and white, dotted with tiny pink spots. She had seen them in the shallow wooden box all her life, yet now they looked so foreign, belonging to a stranger.

She worked in as detached a way as she could, a caul of practical concentration wrapped tight round her. But sometimes it slipped, or something penetrated it, and she sat and cried among this residue of Kate's life.

There were no diaries. Apart from Kate's last effort to explain herself to Anna she had not been a writer by habit. She was not an introspective woman. Too busy out there getting on with it. Nor were there a great number of books. She did find several volumes of poetry though, arranged incongruously in with Kate's few crime novels and old copies of *Reader's Digest*. They were old books, their pages almost orange at the edges and smelling musty.

'With all my love, now and always', was written on the first page of one in small, looped handwriting. 'Angus'. It was dated 1940.

The past seemed to swoop, swallow-like, through the house those two weeks. Though she was confronted at every turn by the things which had made up Kate's life, it was Olivia's voice which kept coming to her. She imagined it soft, sweet, always edged with tears: 'By the morning I know him. I want my life to be his. And they take him away . . .'

Anna thought of that loss. Unbearable. She knew she could not let this rest. Soon, when she was ready, she would have to try and see Olivia. And after all, why would Kate have left the letters, made her explanation as she did, if she had not been deputing Anna to face Olivia for her?

The only person she could stand to be with was Roland.

The first time he called round with the opening greeting, 'I thought you might like a bit of help.' Then added quickly, 'Or company?'

She opened the door in an old pair of mauve dungarees, hair standing on end from bed, and was about to say no, she could manage, but then saw Roland had come out of his own need. She saw his emotion, coming back into Kate's house again, eyeing the bin liners stacked for Oxfam in the front room in the grey light of net curtains and looking round as if memorizing the place. He took out a handkerchief and wiped perspiration from his pink forehead, talking a little too fast, trying to cover his wretchedness. She remembered how his face registered every crease and tuck of emotion. His lips twitched as they walked into the kitchen. It was the room she was leaving until last and it still felt as if her mother might walk in any moment, put on the plastic Colman's Mustard apron and start bustling around in her brown brogue shoes.

She found jobs for Roland: he spent one afternoon clearing the garage.

'You'll put the house on the market, I suppose?' he asked when she brought out a mug of tea.

Anna shrugged. 'I really don't know what I'm going to do. You see, I've left Richard.'

'Oh, Anna – ' Roland's eyes were two pools of concern. 'I am sorry. I'd no idea. How long?'

'The day after the funeral.' She held up a hand to stem the rush of Roland's sympathy. 'It's right, I know that.' She paused. 'I've also decided to resign my job.'

Roland gaped at her. 'Anna. Why? Everything at once, so hastily like this? What are you going to do?'

She shrugged, pulling dead heads from a pink rose by the garage. 'I just want things to be different. I don't want to have to decide anything else yet. I want to take stock for a while.' She looked round at Roland. 'Mummy never thought much of Richard, did she?'

Roland's brow creased. 'I wouldn't say that. She admired his drive, I think. It's just that I think she felt you weren't – what was her phrase? – building each other into more than you would be on your own. That was her idea of what a good relationship should be. She thought Richard was dragging you down.'

'I wish she'd said.'

'You wouldn't have liked it if she had.'

'True.' After a silence, she said, 'That's how it was with my father, wasn't it? She felt he was chewing away at her, diminishing her.'

Roland looked uncomfortable again. 'I suppose that was about it.'

She had found some old photographs of Daisy Turnbull and Lisa and asked Roland about them.

'Lisa Turnbull?' He chuckled. 'Now I did meet her. Kate said she owed Lisa a lot. Not sure why, but she liked her because she was rather to the point as I remember.'

'I remember her – from when I was little. She *is* dead, isn't she?' It seemed terrible, all these years passing and not knowing now whether people were alive or dead.

'Died three or four years ago,' Roland said. 'Cancer as well. Lung I suppose. She used to smoke like a power station.' He eyed the cigarette in Anna's hand.

'I know, I know,' she said.

'Lisa went to live out at Sheldon when they did away with the slums round the Birch. Kate saw more of her towards the end again.'

She later found a few other photographs. Roland appeared in some of them, the three of them grouped together like a family. In one he was holding her, aged about three, a rather slimmer but still comical Roland, smiling at her in his arms. He must have been tickling her because she was giggling, face crinkled. Anna looked at it, frowning. Exactly what her mother had felt for Roland was something she knew she would never now find out.

*

August 27th, 1981

Dear Olivia,

  I am Anna Craven, Kate Craven's daughter. I have your address from my mother and wonder if I might call in and see you some time in the next few days?

It took Anna what seemed a ridiculously long time to phrase this simple note. It was so odd to think of Olivia as a real person now, to use ordinary words. That evening she started up Kate's Metro and drove to Moseley to deliver the letter, leaving it until it was almost dark because she didn't want to be seen, to start anything then.

The house was set back from the road, one in the

426

row of looming Victorian mansions of that area, a jumble of gables and turrets which blocked out the light with its sheer size and its screen of mature trees. Creeping up the short drive under the arch of branches, she felt foolish and very nervous.

A tinny sound of music came from inside. Heart pounding, she pushed the paper through the metal letter-box, jumping as it snapped, and fled back to the car.

Her reply pattered on the mat with Tuesday morning's circulars and a seed catalogue. Anna took it into the kitchen, still dressed in her baggy T-shirt from bed. She looked at the ornate handwriting.

My dear Anna,
    I should so love you to come. Any time is convenient for me. I'm always here.
    Warmest regards,
    Olivia Kemp.

She went that afternoon. It was a fine day, with a waning feel to the light, and piles of cloud kept blotting out the sun. She drove through the slow-moving traffic in Moseley Village, its pavements crowded with shoppers.

After parking the Metro round the corner from Olivia's, outside a boarded up house, she sat for a few moments with the engine off, the windows open. From somewhere further along the road came a heavy beat of music, turned up loud. She thought of Olivia as Kate had last seen her, in the doorway of a flat only a street away from here, dressed in bright blue, alone with her child. The child – Anna had barely given him a thought – would now be nineteen. Not much older than she was when her mother came home tight-faced from work one day, going to her room in the pretence of getting changed, then crying and crying. 1962.

427

She was very nervous at the thought of meeting Olivia. Her uncertainty was made worse by not knowing how to approach her and by the baggage of conflicting emotions she was bringing to this encounter. There were those she felt obliged to carry with her on Kate's behalf: anger and bitter woundedness, a spirit of confrontation. Yet the warmth of Olivia's reply had taken her by surprise. Her own feelings were of apprehension, but also curiosity and sympathy. She wanted at least to try and get on with Olivia, to attempt to understand.

She stepped out of the car into the sleepy warmth of the street. In the gutter lay a crumpled Union Jack, a remnant of the Royal Wedding.

The house was on the corner of the two roads, and horse chestnut trees grew inside the front wall on both sides, casting the place into shadow and seclusion. It was a brick building with gables and a square fairy-tale turret at one corner. In the bright afternoon the windows looked dark and dusty.

In the shady porch she found an old-fashioned metal bell-pull at the side of the door, which gave off a tinkling sound inside.

She heard no footsteps and jumped when the door suddenly opened. A young man stood there, dressed in very tight jeans with faded knees, a T-shirt and trainers. He had collar-length mousy hair and a white acne'd complexion. There was something in his manner Anna didn't take to.

'Yes. Hello?' There was no curiosity in his manner but he seemed tense, his brow furrowed, apparently unable to keep still.

'I'm Anna Craven.' Nervously she pushed her hand back through her hair wondering if this was Olivia's son, forgetting he didn't match Kate's description at all.

'You want Olivia, I suppose,' he said, apparently resentful.

'She said I could call. Is she here?'

'Yeah. She's teaching at the moment. Come through.'

As she was turning to close the door she heard footsteps slapping madly down the wide staircase and another voice called, 'It's OK – leave it – thanks.' Another young man with tight curls, round gold glasses and a file under his arm disappeared outside in flip-flops. The door slammed.

Anna scuttled after the other one and found him standing on the threshold of a huge room. Her first impressions were the glowing red and yellow light from the windows, the honey-coloured parquet floor and a huge grand piano which dominated the middle of the room.

At one end, in the bay window, was a round table. Two women sat behind it, one plump with permed grey hair and a sleeveless, square-necked frock. The other, much smaller and dark, was dressed in something vivid and orange.

'Someone for you, Olivia.'

Anna stood in front of them, bewildered.

It was only when the smaller of the two women looked over at her that she knew it was Olivia. Across the room her face looked surprisingly young and thin, the eyes dark, seemingly bottomless.

'Thank you, Sean.' Her voice was deeper than Anna expected, with a smooth beauty like a nun's. 'Would you be a love and put the kettle on?' He gave a nod and disappeared through a door at the other side of the room.

429

As Olivia walked towards her, Anna saw that the orange clothing was a sari. She came gliding across, wrapped in the graceful folds of silk, feet bare and silent on the coloured rugs which dotted the floor. Anna's mind struggled to make sense of what she was seeing. She felt a second of panic. How should she react?

Olivia stopped a couple of feet away and searched Anna's face with her eyes. Then she smiled, a transformation, showing small, creamy teeth and an immense vivacity which shone from her eyes. She put her hands to her own face, resting her fingers lightly against her cheeks, taking in the sight of her visitor with a childlike kind of wonder.

'Anna, you're the image of your father. What beautiful hair.'

Anna smiled shyly. In seconds any anger and hostility dissolved. She was enchanted. 'Hello,' she said foolishly. She found it hard to meet Olivia's eyes, her gaze was so intense.

'I'm so very glad you've come.' Olivia reached out to shake hands with instinctive formality, and for a second Anna held her small, smooth hand. 'Come and sit with us and take tea,' she said, gesturing towards the table. As she spoke, Anna noticed an odd sing-song quality in her voice, like many Asians sounded speaking English. 'Edith and I had almost finished. You won't mind us cutting it a bit short today, will you?'

Edith, an awkward woman in her sixties, gave a nervous giggle. 'No, we've done well today, haven't we, Olivia? I think we deserve a rest.'

'I'll just go and see if Sean's fallen asleep in the kitchen,' Olivia said. 'Sit, Anna – please.'

She took a chair, noticing a strong perfumed smell in the room. Edith was stowing books into her mock-leather bag. She had tired-looking skin even in this muted light, but large, interested grey eyes.

'Are you another of Olivia's young friends?' she asked.

Just then there came an odd sound from the kitchen, a kind of muffled outburst. Edith pretended not to notice. Distracted, Anna said, 'Er, sort of.' She began to feel she was in a dream. 'What is it Olivia teaches you?'

'Bengali,' Edith said, as if surprised that Anna didn't know. 'She's very good, you know. Very gifted woman, what with all her music and everything. I've learned to speak the language quite a bit over the years what with one thing and another. Now I've retired I thought I'd do it properly and learn to read and write better.' She gave a little giggle. 'You know – Tagore in the original . . .'

There was another slam of the front door as she spoke and in seconds a black face topped by very short hair appeared panting round the door. 'Awright?' He nodded at them both. 'Sean here?'

'In the kitchen,' Edith said. 'Shall I . . .?' She made to get up but the young man, in shorts and a sports shirt, was already across the room.

'He's going to get roasted, I tell you . . . Sean – the tournament? You were supposed to be down there an hour ago. Where's your brain, man?'

There was a gasp. 'Oh shit! – Sorry, Olivia. I forgot. Have they started?'

'Course they've started. I paired up with Rob for the first set, but we need you there.'

'Look, Theo – ' Sean ran through, shouting back over his shoulder. 'You go on. I'll be down, OK?'

He was followed by a sweating Theo, shouting, 'Don't forget your racquet,' and 'See yer,' in Anna and

Edith's direction. For an odd second Anna found herself missing Richard. She felt old, vulnerable and out of place with all these new people.

'Who are these blokes around the place?' she asked Edith.

'They're Olivia's lodgers,' Edith said, bravely accepting, but obviously not quite sure about it all. 'They have the top floor, you see. There's so much space. Sean studies engineering – I think – and Theo's doing some sort of science, chemistry ... And there's Ben who you probably haven't met. He's a postgraduate. Something to do with languages.'

Anna frowned. 'Surely it's still the holidays?'

Edith looked perturbed. 'Yes, I suppose it is. They don't seem to go home though ...'

Olivia came back in with a beautifully laid tray of tea, including a plate of Indian sweets, bright with the red and green of cherries and pistachio.

'A good job I took over from Sean,' she said, 'or you'd have had a teabag in a cup and a stale Rich Tea biscuit.' She offered the plate of sweets to them, telling Anna, 'These are a treat on Bengali afternoons. Edith comes to me once a week.'

Anna nibbled a square of pistachio *barfi*, feeling its thick, milky sweetness slide over her tongue.

'Mostly, you see, I make my living from teaching music – and the lodgers, of course,' Olivia said, as she poured tea with an almost exaggerated grace.

'Does your son live with you?' Anna asked.

'Krishna?' Olivia's face took on a glow. 'Yes, he's home at last. He's just done his first year at college in London and is having a simply marvellous time.' Anna noticed that the sing-song quality had gone from Olivia's voice. Instead it had become gushing. 'He's out at the moment. He has an old friend in Kings Heath who owns a very nice furniture shop. Krish has done bits of work for him sometimes and poor Jake's marriage seems to have broken up so I think Krish is company for him. Krishna would cheer anyone up, wouldn't he, Edith?'

Edith managed, ingeniously, through a mouthful of *barfi*, to adapt concerned cluckings over Jake's marriage to noises of agreement and mirth concerning Krishna.

'He's doing his degree in anthropology,' Olivia went on proudly. 'And learning Bengali. He's adoring it. Finding out about a culture that's half his, after all. His father was from Calcutta, you see. I met him when I was studying in London myself after the war. He had a visiting lectureship.' She related this in the tones of someone telling a fairy story. 'I don't make any secret of the fact that I've been a single parent – after all, it's almost the mode nowadays. At first, though, I called myself Mrs, of course. It wasn't the same at all in the early 1960s ... It's not at all easy bringing up a child by yourself – especially as my family couldn't cope with what I'd done. But Krishna's been the most wonderful child – I can hardly begin to tell you.'

Edith nodded enthusiastically. 'He's a lovely boy. And I'm sure you've been a tower of strength, Olivia.'

Olivia accepted this compliment graciously. 'He's the one who's given me all the strength in the world. We keep in touch all the time when he's away. We're so close – sometimes it's quite uncanny.'

Anna watched her, fascinated. Sitting nearer Olivia now, she could see the slackness of her skin, a truer indication of her age. But she found herself mesmerized by her vivacity, coupled with an apparent openness and vulnerability which took her quite by surprise.

When Edith had drunk her tea she departed, full of thanks, saying, 'I'll look forward to next Tuesday!'

Olivia showed her out, then glided back into the room. Still in the charming voice, she said, 'Edith used to be a missionary in Bangladesh. With the Baptists. Now she's retired I think she's a bit lost, poor soul. This gives her a purpose.'

She moved to the piano, stood against it, her back very straight. Her face altered, as if something had dropped from it. In a tight voice, she said. 'Did she want you to come?'

Half prepared, Anna said truthfully, 'I'm not sure.'

'Then why did you?'

'Because I wanted to.'

'She told you about me?'

'All the time when I was little. About your childhood together, your friendship. It made me long to have a friend like that myself. You had something very special.'

Olivia's eyes were fixed away from Anna across the room. In their expression Anna thought she glimpsed something hard and malevolent. Then, as if roused from her thoughts, she said, 'Look, I'm terribly sorry, but I've another pupil due in a few minutes – piano this time. Would you be free to come again, say tomorrow evening? I don't have any teaching late tomorrow and you could meet Krishna.' She gave Anna one of her sudden, overwhelming smiles. 'I'd so like to have a talk with you and hear about Kate after all this time. She was, as you say, my very best friend.'

Anna found herself agreeing eagerly. At the front door, Olivia took her gently by her upper arms and reached up to kiss her. Anna felt Olivia's breath on her cheek, smelled again the pungent perfume she had noticed in the room, some sort of scented hair oil.

'You will come, won't you?' Olivia stood looking tiny under the high doorway, vulnerable again now.

'Of course. Seven o'clock.' Anna waved, backing down the drive.

In the car she sat for a time once more, breathing heavily, aware of the fast beating of her heart.

What on earth's come over me? she thought. She knew that her emotion stemmed partly from the strangeness of touching the past, of beginning to close a circle. But it was more than that. It was something in Olivia herself that had stirred her in this way, and not to anger or resentment, the emotions she had felt obliged to carry with her, but to something quite unexpected. Reaching down to try and put the key in the ignition she realized her hands were shaking. She was fluttery and energized as if newly in love.

Chapter 32

Ben opened the door the next evening, still in the flip-flops.

'Hi.' He squinted out through the round spectacles like a mole, round face pressed into an anxious look, then smiled. 'You're Anna.' He stood back to let her in. The house felt cool. She had put on an old sleeveless dress made of Indian cotton in pale blue and white stripes, long unworn because Richard said it made her look like Little Bo-Peep. She carried a bunch of white roses.

'We've heard a lot about you.'

Anna turned, startled. 'From Olivia?'

'No need to look so worried. All we've gathered is that you were the most beautiful baby the world's ever seen – after Krish of course!' Ben laughed. He spoke very fast, with a nervous fussiness about him. 'That's just Olivia. She's very extravagant – things she says.'

'I see,' Anna said, rather uncertainly. She was distracted by noises from the rest of the house: voices, laughter, the pulsing of music. The hall was filled with a delicious, spicy smell.

'Krish's upstairs with Jake,' Ben told her. 'I'll take you through. Olivia's getting one of her feasts together.'

'Are we all eating together then?' Anna frowned. From what Olivia said the day before she had expected to be alone with her.

'She does this every so often,' Ben said as he showed her into the long room again. 'Family meal she calls it. It's just hard luck if we've got things on. We have to cancel or she'll be under a cloud for days.' Anna noticed the tone of indulgence in his voice. 'As it's out of term now there's not much going on anyway, luckily.'

Anna was peeved for a few seconds, feeling childishly that she wanted Olivia all to herself. But as soon as she walked into the long room she felt uplifted and found herself smiling. She had been alone so much this week: it would be good to have company.

The round table was laid with a scarlet cloth, and Theo was putting cutlery on it, jigging around to a tune that must have been going on in his head, twirling forks in the air and catching them with a flourish before setting them down. At the other end of the room where there were a sofa and easy chairs, Sean was watching TV, perched forward on the edge of his seat. He didn't look round, sat with shoulders hunched, Rizlas and lighter on the table, a skinny cigarette held close to his face. His hair looked lank and unkempt.

'This is Anna,' Ben told Theo.

Theo stepped forward and to Anna's surprise, shook hands with solemn formality. 'Good to meet you properly – saw you yesterday, didn't I?'

Anna liked Theo immediately. 'D'you need a hand with anything?'

'No – I'm getting on fine thanks.'

Theo went back to finish his juggling and table laying. Ben was just relieving Anna of the flowers when there was a soft rustling sound in the doorway.

'Don't try that with the glasses, Theo.' Olivia made her entrance carrying a small tray of pickles. This time the sari was vivid blue, catching the light in a host of parrot shades.

'Anna, my dear... Oh, and roses – how lovely, my favourite!' She handed the tray regally to Theo and came to embrace her as if they were the closest of friends. Anna caught herself feeling gratified, her cheeks glowing, and was struck again by the contrariness of her feelings. Shouldn't she feel more hostility and reservation, at least for Kate's sake? Who was she here for after all – Kate or herself?

'Now – you must sit down and bear with us for a few moments,' Olivia was saying. 'Ben will take care of you until it's ready.' Again Anna noticed the sing-song tone of her voice.

'Oh, I don't need looking after.' She laughed.

'Will you have a glass of wine? Or *lassi*? I've made it nice and salty.'

'Wine, please.' Anna glanced across at Sean. 'All right if I smoke too?'

'No problem,' Ben said. 'There's an ashtray on the piano somewhere.'

Anna sat on the piano stool sipping red wine, a cigarette in her other hand, looking round the room. There was a beautiful lightness about it – the pale wood of the floor and the long shelves across the room – with splashes of colour: rugs on the boards, rich silk saris at the windows and also bunched and draped across the high corners of the room. On either side of the piano were leaded fireplaces, and on the walls above them, in simple wood frames, hung batik pictures, one a brightly decorated elephant, the other a scene from an Indian village in sky blue and straw colours.

Olivia bustled in and out carrying dishes, calling orders to Ben and Theo. 'And Sean,' she called. 'You're doing littlest of all. Please come and help me with the plates.' She spoke in an imperious tone.

Sean stood up slowly, pushing down the legs of his jeans, and paused to grind out his cigarette in a saucer.

'Ben – go and fetch Krishna and Jake. It's all ready.'

Anna watched, fascinated by all this activity and by Olivia's unquestioned authority over the household.

'You're working so hard,' she commented.

'I adore cooking,' Olivia said, 'especially this food. Useless doing it for one, though. Theo – water please. We'll need a jug on the side there.'

There came a burst of sound from upstairs, rock music which Anna knew she recognized but could not place before it was switched off abruptly. Then feet on the stairs.

She was having to remind herself of Krishna's existence, that Olivia had a grown-up son. She faced the door, preparing a smile. When he appeared her smile broadened. She stood up.

'Anna?' Like Theo, he shook her hand.

'Krishna? I'm so pleased to meet you.' She was looking into a face of enormous charm. He had round, boyish cheeks, the skin flawless, huge teeth creamy as almonds and deep brown eyes. He was wearing tight black jeans and a black T-shirt, and there was a ripeness about him just short of being plump, a hint of puppy fat not yet lost. There was something immensely appealing about him and it crossed Anna's mind to wonder whether this was the Kemp charm working through the generations.

'This is my mate, Jake,' Krishna said. He indicated a tall, lean man behind him with shoulder-length brown hair, a long, serious face and eyes that were beginning to hold a smile. He said 'Hello' quietly.

'What were you listening to up there?' Anna asked. 'I know I recognized it . . .'

'Van Morrison,' Krishna said. He gave Jake a playful punch on the arm. 'He reckons he's educating my musical tastes.'

'I've nearly persuaded him to part with the Donny Osmond singles,' Jake said drily.

'Surely it's not that bad?' Anna said.

'You'd be surprised.'

'Ah, Krishna – ' Olivia emerged from the kitchen, followed by Sean. 'Come and fetch the rice for me, will you, darling? The others have been doing all the work. It's time you did something.'

Krishna made a comical face at Anna. 'I see you've already met the three stooges?'

She laughed, feeling a rush of contentment and liking for these people.

They sat round the table, blood-red napkins to match the cloth folded on white side plates. Anna was between Theo and Jake, facing Olivia across the dishes piled with food, between which Olivia had lit deep blue candles.

At the centre of the table was a casserole full of scented rice, sprigged with dark splinters of cinnamon, fat green cardamom pods, and dotted with coriander seeds like game shot. Displayed round it, in blue ceramic dishes, was spiced chicken in a rich tomato sauce, a bright, mustard-coloured dal sprinkled with fresh green coriander leaves, and other vegetable dishes, potatoes and cauliflower, aubergines, okra. On a wooden board she had piled chapatis.

The boys let out whoops and whistles of appreciation at the sight of the food.

'Hey yeah,' Theo said enthusiastically. 'Come on – let's get this wine flowing.'

'I thought you were a good, church-going boy,' Krish teased him. 'No drinking, no cinema – ' He made a poor attempt at a Jamaican accent: 'No idolatry av tings av de flesh . . . eh Titty?'

Theo gave a pained though good-natured grimace, then jabbed a finger at Krish, mock threatening. 'I'll see you afterwards.'

'Don't call him that,' Olivia said. 'It's not nice.'

'I think you ought to explain to Anna,' Ben said, seeing her puzzled face.

Theo grinned, spooning rice on to his plate. 'My name's Theophilus, right? My mom's into the Acts of the Apostles in a big way – and I mean a big way. All the family's called names from the early church. Trouble is, I've got five older brothers, so by the time she got to me the decent names like Peter and John and Stephen were all used up, so I got to be Theophilus Timothy.'

'TT,' Krish finished. 'Titty.'

'Enough!' Olivia commanded.

Like everyone else, Anna filled her plate, listening to the talk around her. Her initial feeling of rawness had passed, the strangeness of being alone again in social situations. She had been everywhere with Richard for so long. Too long. She began to feel at ease, having neither too much nor too little attention paid to her. She found she was grateful that Olivia had organized this, instead of plunging them into a private, probably nerve-racking conversation, when they barely knew each other.

She sat trying to get the measure of this new bunch of people.

Sean, sitting on Olivia's left, said almost nothing throughout the meal. He ate with his pale face bent over his plate, shovelling the food in with no grace. Once or twice, though, she noticed Olivia turn to him and their eyes met. Anna watched, puzzled, unable to read the signal being passed between them. Otherwise Sean came across as preoccupied and distant, and she didn't feel prepared to try and draw him into the conversation. There was enough talk for him not to be pressurized to speak.

Krishna began the meal by creating a deep ring of rice on his plate, heaping it hugely with the chicken and vegetables and finally laying a chapati across the top like a hat. He sat back, childishly inviting everyone to look, patting his stomach with his hands in anticipation.

'I'm sure I'm getting fat being back at home,' he said. 'Next week I'm going to join the hunger strike.' He let out a laugh. 'What do I have to do to get into the Maze?'

Ben reddened across the table. 'That's not bloody funny, Krish. Everything's a joke to you, isn't it? Ha ha bloody ha.'

Krishna held his hands up, shielding himself. 'Sorry. Sorry – very poor taste I fully admit. It's all right, Ben, you can step off your soap box now.' He gave one of his appealing grins and said to Anna, 'Ben here is our elder statesman.'

Anna felt sympathy for Ben. Krishna's crassness was already grating on her. To smooth over the difficult moment she said, 'I gather you're doing research?'

'Yep. Modern French poets.'

'How's it going?' Theo asked.

'Badly,' Ben said irritably. 'Don't know why I'm doing the wretched thesis.'

'Come, now,' Olivia said. 'You're going through a bad patch. That's how it goes sometimes with research. But you don't just give up because you reach a dead end for a bit. You have to wait to get to the next notch. I promise you it'll be worth it.' Her voice held smooth, maternal concern.

'I hope you're right.' Ben's cheeks were flaming. 'Sometimes I think I'd be a lot better out there earning some money.'

'Believe in yourself.' Olivia put her hand on his. 'Look, if it's getting you down, come and talk about it.' Her tone was caressing now, soothing him. 'You know I'm always here, don't you?'

'Yeah – thanks,' Ben said, with the reluctant gratitude of a child who feels foolish crying in front of his friends.

'Anna, you've got no pickles,' Krish said. 'You should try them. She makes them herself, you know.' He gave Anna such a sweet smile that her growing irritation with him was eased a little. She accepted some of the tangy lime pickle.

'What do you do, Anna?' he asked. 'Are you at the university too?'

'No. I'm a teacher – in Coventry. History.' Simpler not to mention that she'd just resigned.

'Oh?' Krish frowned, looking at Olivia. 'But you said you knew her when she was young?'

Olivia's voice broke in across the table, somehow claiming her. 'Anna's mother and I were very dear friends, a long time ago. We've only just got back in touch.' She beamed indulgently round the table. 'We're going to have a lot of catching up to do.'

Anna felt a strange feeling of elation, of having been singled out. A flush spread across her cheeks. She kept glancing at Olivia throughout the meal, resplendent in the glossy blue of the sari, regal, presiding over the table and her admirers. She could see now what it was that had made Kate adore her so much, something in her, a combination of charm and vulnerability which made you feel prepared to do anything for her. Anna found herself waiting for responding glances from Olivia and she was not disappointed. Often she did look over, giving her a smile both affectionate and complicit. After a time Anna began to forget the incongruity of her response. It was as if the past had nothing to do with this Olivia. Whatever her problems had been she had clearly overcome them. She was as charming and lovable as the childhood Olivia Kate had known. Anna relaxed, enjoying her.

Krish spent much of the meal clowning, Theo his foil, both of them laughing, but Krish by far the loudest. Ben talked seriously to Olivia, who occasionally turned to Sean. Once, she laid a hand on Sean's and said, 'There is more bread in the oven. Would you be a darling? They're in tin foil ...' And Sean got up to fetch them, with the silent compliance of a dog.

'How're you finding teaching then?' a voice said. Anna, concentrating on watching Sean, turned, startled, to Jake.

'I'm sorry? Teaching? Well ...' She had various stock answers to this question. For Richard something upbeat and idealistic; for Kate, a more straightforward assessment of the job, but not going so far as to include the truth of how draining she found it, how hardly a day passed when she didn't feel despair; for others there were the brief social replies: 'Fine,' or 'Well, it's a challenge.'

Since she didn't know Jake at all and had no time to think of anything else, the only option was to be honest. 'I think since I've been a teacher I've lost any illusions I ever had that I'm a nice, reasonable person.'

She thought he might be tediously disconcerted, as

people so often were when she said something honest. Instead, he gave a laugh of recognition, the serious face suddenly transformed. 'Very like being a parent, then.'

'I don't know. I can imagine, though.' She tried to remember what she'd been told about Jake. 'You've got kids?'

'One. A little girl, Elly. She's just four. Only she lives with my wife – ex-wife.'

Anna groped for a response. 'You must miss her.'

Jake swallowed a mouthful of wine. 'Like hell.' He jerked his head to one side to flick back the hair from his face and forced a smile. She liked the smile and knew she was going to like him. There was something open about him, and genuine.

'You live in Coventry, then?'

'I did until recently. With my boyfriend.' She managed a comical face. 'Ex-boyfriend.'

Again, the generous laugh. 'Oh dear. You'd better have some more wine!'

Olivia, seeing Jake's hand poised over Anna's glass, called across, 'You'd be welcome to stay the night. Why not? I even have toothbrushes!'

Automatically, Anna said, 'Thank you, but I think I'd better get back. I'll get a cab.' She was so used to being tied to home, to Richard, who admired spontaneity but only on his terms. But now there was only Kate's empty house and she realized too late that she needn't have refused.

Olivia accepted the refusal graciously. 'Do whatever suits you best, my dear. Actually I teach early tomorrow, so unfortunately I shouldn't have much time to see you.' She leaned forward. 'And I so want us to have a talk.' The smile she produced actually made Anna's heart beat faster.

Jake had refilled her glass. Turning to thank him, she caught him watching her and saw an expression in his eyes that she couldn't quite read – puzzled, or worried – but before she could think about it further there was a loud outburst from Krish. She watched him, his laugh high and giggling, cheeks pink. He had drunk too much, she could see. She wondered what it was he and Jake could possibly have in common.

'Does Krish work for you or something?' she asked Jake. 'Is that how you know each other?'

He nodded. 'He has done. I've got my own business in School Road. He's worked there during a couple of holidays.' He grinned at Olivia. 'She came in to buy a dresser and by the time she'd left she'd talked me into giving her son a job. Persuaded me he'd be the best thing that ever happened to me . . .'

'Which of course I was,' Krish interrupted, his voice loud and slurred.

'No more wine for you,' Olivia said sternly. She beamed at Jake. 'And wasn't I right?'

'He's pretty good at making tea,' Jake teased.

Olivia let out a loud laugh, wine loud, Anna thought, just beyond what was called for.

'He learned a lot actually,' Jake added hastily.

'So what d'you sell?'

'Furniture, mainly. Stripped-pine stuff – do a lot of it myself. It's getting very popular. I have a few other bits and bobs in to decorate the shop, but I go for the big stuff really – cupboards and dressers, that sort of thing.'

'I like shops like that.'

Jake shrugged. 'Come and see it then. It's not far.'

She found herself talking with Jake for most of the rest of the evening, through the *kulfi* – ice cream sprinkled with shavings of pistachio nuts – the slices of mango and cups of strong black coffee.

'You all need sobering up,' Olivia said. Sean volunteered for the coffee making. Anna saw Jake's eyes follow him as he disappeared unsteadily into the kitchen.

They all moved to the other end of the room, lounging in easy chairs, congratulating Olivia on the food, and she sat on the sofa covered in its bright fabrics, between Theo and Krish, arranging the end of the sari over her shoulder with an air of cream-fed satisfaction.

Sean handed round squat cups of coffee and sat on a chair to one side, scowling. He made Anna feel very uneasy, as if he was a servant, someone without equal status to the rest of them.

Theo was telling jokes about his family, making the three on the sofa laugh loudly. Ben joined in politely. And Anna and Jake talked. They talked about films and books, comparing tastes, keeping mostly off the subject of their own lives, except that Jake mentioned having moved to Birmingham at the age of ten from Staffordshire. Through the shouts of laughter from across the room she told him briefly about Kate's death and he was sympathetic and not over-effusive. There still seemed to be a lot of things to say when Olivia stood up suddenly.

'I think it's time we broke this up, pity though it is,' she declared. The boys, except Jake, all stood up immediately. Anna wondered whether this was deliberate on his part, a refusal to jump to her orders.

'Did you bring your van, Jake?' she asked.

'Yeah, but I'm not in a fit state to drive it. I'll be back for it in the morning. The walk'll sober me up.'

Ben and Theo drifted off upstairs. Sean stood hesitat-

447

ing, as if waiting for a signal from Olivia. Eventually, indicating the kitchen, he said, 'D'you want me to . . . ?'

Olivia stared at him, silent for a moment. The look in her eyes turned suddenly icy. But she said in an even tone, 'Leave the washing up for tomorrow.'

Anna, watching Sean, was startled by Jake saying suddenly, 'Have you seen Olivia's batiks? Look – come and see this one.'

She found he had taken her hand and was leading her down towards the batik of the village at the other end of the room. His hand felt very big and warm, the skin rough.

'I have looked . . .' she began to protest.

As they turned to face the picture he said suddenly in an urgent whisper, 'Come to the shop – tomorrow?'

Finding this very strange, she said cautiously, 'Well – I'll come some time. I'm not sure about tomorrow.'

He leaned slightly closer to her. 'Don't take this the wrong way. Look – this is going to sound amazingly presumptuous of me but I'm going to say it anyway. You've been going through a difficult time recently – don't get drawn in by Olivia.'

Astonished and angry, she looked up into his eyes but they were steady, concerned. 'We should talk,' he said.

She was jolted by his seriousness, and trusted his sincerity. 'Yes, of course then. If you think . . .'

His face broke into a grin suddenly. 'Plus I'd like an excuse to show you my shop.'

'That'd be great,' she said, more reassured.

Olivia and Krish were clearing things off the table. Jake thanked them and, with a final glance at Anna, left.

'Call a taxi for Anna, will you darling?' Olivia said to

Krishna. As he went out to the telephone in the hall, Anna began to join in the work of clearing the table.

'I see those other bad boys have slunk off,' Olivia said. The two of them stacked plates and dishes next to the sink. In the big, old-fashioned kitchen Olivia chatted about practical things. 'The chicken can all go together in this dish – yes, *lassi* in the fridge, please. I'll just put a plate over this rice . . .'

She turned suddenly from the table, the rice giving off a whiff of cardamom, and gave Anna a cold, appraising look.

'You're different from her, aren't you?'

Completely taken aback, Anna said, 'Am I?'

But there was no follow-up remark. Olivia turned back to cover her rice as if the exchange hadn't happened.

'It's here!' Krish's voice came from the hall.

'Ah, go now!' Olivia said, apparently all charm again. 'Don't keep it waiting – they charge *so* much nowadays.' There was a sudden sense of hurry now the taxi had arrived.

'Do come again soon. Please.'

'I've got to pick up my car tomorrow,' Anna pointed out.

'Of course. Good.' In the hall they kissed each other, briefly, and Anna watched her glide away, the plait a slice of black down her back as the harsh blue of the sari disappeared into the long room.

Krishna was out at the front. As Anna came out he stepped over to her, took her by the shoulders and kissed her clumsily on the mouth, his lips taut and painful on hers.

He gave a foolish grin. 'Sorry. I don't know who you

are or what you're doing here. But it's lovely to see you.' And he was gone.

As the taxi took her through the dark streets she felt more and more uneasy. The odd, cold look Olivia had given her, Jake's warning, Krishna's drunken kiss – these were the things which now stood out from the evening. Caution, Kate had warned. Yet she had been so quickly beguiled. She must in future be more on her guard, even if she had no real idea against what.

On Kate's inner doormat she found a roughly folded sheet of pink paper: a note scrawled on the back of a flyer advertising cheap carpets.

'Came over to see you as you won't answer the bloody phone. What the hell are you playing at? *Call* me. Richard.'

Chapter 33

Olivia's house was quiet next morning. Sean let her in and she waited with him in the kitchen where he carried on working his way through last night's washing up, his back to her and thin elbows stuck out at angry angles.

'Have you been left to do it all?' Anna exclaimed. 'Here, let me give you a hand.'

He was turning to speak when the voice cut across from the doorway. 'No. Leave him. Sean's quite happy to do some work for me this morning, aren't you, darling?' Sean plunged a pile of bowls into the water with the force of someone trying to drown a puppy.

Turning to greet Olivia, Anna actually let out a gasp. Her hard, calculating tone accompanied another transformation so startling that she took a few seconds to manage the words 'Good morning.'

Gone were the sari, the bare feet and soft, understated make-up. Her suit was emerald green, cut in straight, sophisticated lines, the shoulders padded, the effect angular as a box, and she wore high, pointed court shoes in a matching shade. Instead of the loose plait, her hair was caught up into a perfect pleat, face immaculately made up, her lips a glistening plum red.

'Anna.' She offered a smile, but it seemed brittle and forced. Anna felt her breathing turn more shallow. Thank God she'd already decided to be more wary of this woman. 'We must spend some more time together, alone.' Olivia's heels clicked across the kitchen tiles. She leaned to touch Anna's cheek with her own and again there came a waft of perfume, this time something costly. 'I so wanted you to meet everyone last night – Krishna especially, of course. What did you think of him?'

Honesty lurked in Anna's mind: I thought he was pretty obnoxious. 'He's lovely,' she said. 'A credit to you.'

'He's my life,' Olivia breathed. Sean rattled cutlery loudly behind them and Anna stood feeling very uneasy. They were stepping too near the well of emotion. Everything was at odds this morning and she just wanted to get away from this place, back to Kate's house, and sink into a warm bath.

'I'm teaching today,' Olivia said. Her voice was clipped and precise, no trace of the rise-and-fall accent she had put on the night before. 'I like to dress up for the piano. It makes me feel professional. I really wanted to be a musician, you see. My father wouldn't hear of it until it was really too late.'

'Yes – my mother told me.'

'Did she?' There was a coldness in Olivia's eyes which brought Anna's flesh up in goosepimples. 'Come for tea,' she said abruptly. 'I've no pupils after four o'clock. We must talk. I presume you came to talk?'

The words were flung out like a challenge. Anna felt angry, suddenly, as if she was being played with, and at Olivia's assumption that she had nothing else to do but be called upon at her command.

'Yes, I came to talk,' she said stiffly. 'I presume that's what you wanted. You did write to her after all.'

The bell sounded in the hall. Sean left the sink

immediately to answer, and to Anna's relief they heard Jake's voice down the hall.

'Morning.' He smiled across at her from the doorway, so tall his head nearly reached the frame, hands in his pockets. 'Come to pick up the van. Thanks for last night, Olivia. It was a great meal.'

'Krishna's still in bed,' Olivia snapped. Anna watched her anxiously. There were stings in everything Olivia said this morning.

But Jake appeared not to notice. 'As I say, I've only come for the van. Got to get back to open up. I was wondering – ' He looked at Anna. 'Since I'm going back, d'you want a lift over, to see the place?'

'It'd suit me better to come later – elevenish? I could do with coffee and a bath first.'

Jake was flustered suddenly. 'Look – don't come if it's a bother.'

'I want to.'

'Great.' He smiled at her. 'I'll see you later, then. And Olivia – if Krish wants to drop in this afternoon, that's fine by me.'

Olivia nodded, grudgingly. 'I'll tell him.'

Anna left as soon as she could after Jake.

'Don't forget,' Olivia said. 'I'll be waiting for you this afternoon. And you can stay. I like a full house.'

It was more than a request, it was a command. Anna didn't take too easily to being ordered around.

'That should be all right,' she said coolly. 'I'll be round at four.'

Then came the smile, Olivia's disarming warmth. 'I'll so look forward to it.'

At Kate's house she lay in a deep bath and watched a silvery moth flap against the white ceiling, unable to get

Olivia out of her mind. She pictured Olivia's face, its baffling flashes of light and darkness like cloud shadows racing across a valley. She thought of the glinting malevolence she had seen in her eyes, and felt her innards turn. She imagined Olivia as she had seen her dressed that morning, malign mannequin, waiting by the bath, her hand coming down over Anna's face, the nails red and sharp, pushing her down and down.

'No,' she whispered. 'Stop. Please.' She lay in the warm water, trembling and sobbing, irrationally afraid for a time even to lie back and soak her hair.

I should go away and not get involved with her, she thought, as she dried herself. I don't need this, on top of everything else.

'What d'you want me to do, Mom?' She felt foolish talking to herself in the bathroom like that. The emptying bath inflated her words with an echo but provided no answer.

She put on clean, washed-out jeans and a white shirt and walked quickly round to Roland's house.

'Come in!' he greeted her joyfully, secateurs in hand. 'I could do with a break.'

'Roland, sorry – I can't today. I've promised to meet someone at eleven.'

'Ah. Anyone nice?' he asked, with childlike hopefulness.

'Nice?' Anna teased him. 'Yes, I think you could say nice. I just wanted to check you hadn't been round and wondered where I was.'

'No, I haven't as a matter of fact. Been to see friends then? Good for you. You don't want to be in that house alone too much, I'm sure.'

'I might be staying over in Moseley tonight. I didn't

want you to worry.' She gave him the address. 'It's off Anderton Park Road.'

'Right-o,' Roland said with his implacable cheerfulness.

'Can I pop in for a coffee tomorrow?' she asked, guilty.

'Nothing I'd like more.'

'Great. I'll see you then.'

'Anna?'

She turned back.

'Spare a kiss?'

'More than.' Hugging him tight, she gave him a big kiss on each cheek and Roland chuckled delightedly.

He stood watching her as she walked off quickly down the street amid the song of birds.

The banner across Jake's shopfront was a deep green with gold letters which read, *Jake's Pine*.

'I was looking out for you.' He appeared in the doorway, an old cloth in one hand, and came to join her in the sunshine, looking up appraisingly at the building. 'So, d'you like it? I've just cleaned the windows.'

She saw the pavement was wet and felt touched. Had he wanted her to see it at its best? The windows were still drying and behind them she could see the furniture: on one side a round table and chairs, a vase of dried teasels on the table, on the other a sturdy chest of drawers topped by a swing mirror, a rocking chair beside it.

'It looks really impressive. And I like the name. I expected something more twee.'

'Yes. Easy trap to fall into with this sort of stuff. Not

really me, though.' He talked fast and she saw he was nervous, more than she was. After all, he had asked her to come here.

'Trouble is, people keep coming in and asking me if it's getting better.'

She frowned. 'What?'

He thickened his Brummy accent. 'The pine.'

Anna exploded into laughter. Jake's dry humour confirmed why she had come. Talking to him had made her happy and uplifted after the past gloomy weeks. Such a relief after Richard.

'Come in. I'll show you round.' He stood back to let her through, his huge hands holding the door. It felt strange being suddenly alone with him, but there was a gentleness about him, about those hands, which made her trust him.

The shop was surprisingly big inside and extended up to the second floor. She followed him round, their shoes sounding on the bare boards. The downstairs was arranged carefully, without preciousness, so that items could be seen at their best. Painted wooden cats sprawled over some of the surfaces, and there were vases and stacks of wooden picture frames. Anna walked slowly among the dressers and cupboards, bedframes and chairs, touching smooth wood and admiring.

'D'you do it all up yourself?' she asked.

'A lot of it needs attention of some sort,' he said. 'Most of them are painted when I get them. Look at this – this one was in a right state when I got it.'

He showed her an elegant wardrobe with carved patterns on the doors. 'Look at the texture in that.' He stroked the smooth surface. 'It's like bringing something to life again. This was covered in brown paint, would

456

you believe – I mean imagine painting wood like that brown...'

She followed him up to the second floor. 'The top's my flat, well, hardly more than a bedsit really, but it does me fine. There's space for Elly when she comes. This floor's more for storage.'

The rooms up there were crammed full of chests of drawers, bedframes packed tightly together in rows, stacked chairs, their legs in the air. A large table was roped upside down to hooks on the ceiling.

'It looks as if you're torturing it,' she said.

Jake laughed. 'I get a bit carried away with the buying. But people often choose stuff from up here. I think they enjoy it being a bit chaotic. I don't follow them around or anything.'

Downstairs, he showed her his little office which opened into a small yard at the back and had once been the kitchen. On the desk in the middle of the room were an old Adler typewriter, piles of duplicate books, a calculator and all sorts of bits and pieces, tins and nails, rubber bands and wooden drawer knobs.

'How did you get into doing this?' she asked him.

'Took a degree in philosophy.'

She wasn't certain for a second if he was serious. 'I've got a degree in history so I'm a history teacher. Bit predictable in comparison, I suppose.'

'Thing is – what do you do with a degree in philosophy? I started off selling a few oddments out of a van. Did it from home. I got hooked on it really and it grew from there. Before that,' he added lightly, 'I had a successful career selling insurance.'

'Oh, yeah? I can really imagine you doing that!'

'I see you don't believe me.'

457

Anna perched herself on the corner of his desk. 'Does that kettle work?'

'Has been known to. Why, d'you think you're going to get a drink as well?' His grey eyes were full of amusement. He filled the kettle. 'It'd be nicer up in the flat, but I'm afraid I can't take you up just in case anyone comes in. You haven't got to rush then?'

'No. I've no plans. I'm still cleaning Mom's house but I'm taking my time over it. Actually I've just resigned from my job.'

Jake looked at her steadily. 'Wow. Big decisions.' Again she found herself grateful to him for not overreacting.

She looked back into the shop. 'I only wish I could buy something off you, but I'm already saddled with two houses and I really need to get rid of things.'

'Two?'

'Mom's, and our house in Coventry.'

'With your boyfriend?' He leaned towards the old brown kettle to hear if it was heating.

'Ex-boyfriend.' She paused. 'How long have you been on your own?'

'Year and a half nearly. What about you?'

'I left him a month ago. But to be honest I feel as if I've been on my own a lot longer. He keeps trying to get in touch but I can't face it. I'm trying to avoid him. Cowardly, really.'

He watched her, seriously. 'That's rough.'

'Yes. But I know it's the right thing, in the end.'

His eyes searched her face for a moment and she wondered with a certain amount of panic whether disclosures were about to follow, his marriage, what had gone wrong. But he looked down, pouring milk from a carton. After he'd handed her her coffee he leaned up against the old worktop.

'What did you think of Olivia's little display last night?'

'Display?'

He watched her face for a moment as if unsure what to say next. 'How long have you known her?'

'Barely any time at all in fact. But in another way I've known about her all my life. She was a friend of my mother's until they – ' she searched for a way to describe what had happened ' – fell out. Years ago. She didn't see Olivia after that.'

'What did they fall out about?' He put his hand to his forehead. 'Sorry. I don't want to put you on the spot. Only tell me what you want to, of course. It's just, there are probably things . . . Do you know much about Olivia?'

Anna sighed. 'If you've got all day, I'll tell you.'

'I actually know almost nothing about her, except a little bit through Krish. She and your mom – were they close?'

'Very. Mom loved her.'

'And she wanted you to see her?'

'I think – yes, I'm sure she did. She said she understood that I'd want to make contact. But she told me to be careful.'

'But why didn't you see her while your mother was still alive.'

'Because she told me Olivia was dead. All my life I believed she was killed in the war.'

Jake made a sound, an outward breath, half whistle. Anna hesitated. She wanted to talk about this, to share it. And she trusted Jake.

'You have to understand that Olivia's life has been, well – difficult. But she was living with us for a time when I was born. She was in a very bad state at the time. When I was about three months old she tried to drown me in the bath.'

'My God.' Jake stood upright suddenly. 'Is that true?'

'Mom wouldn't have made it up.'

'Aren't you – I mean, what the hell d'you feel about that?'

'I don't know what to feel. I don't remember it of course, not directly. I only found out about it a few weeks ago.'

'And you only met her for the first time this week?'

She nodded. 'Now I've met her I can't work out what to think about her.' She paused, looking out through the open door into the little yard. There was a neat stack of old doors covered in chipped paint, leaning against the opposite wall. 'One minute I feel drawn in, sort of ... infatuated almost, by her. I don't know if this sounds crazy to you? Then she turns suddenly and she's frightening. I don't know why. It's something in her face. It just flashes across. Then she's charming again and I can't work out whether I've imagined it, that I'm reading things into it because I know about her past. You don't really think she's dangerous, surely?'

'Only to Krish.'

'Krish? But they're so close. Seeing them together's like the mutual admiration society.'

'This is why I said I needed to talk to you.' He put his head on one side. 'Why d'you think I hang out with someone like Krish? He's fifteen years younger than me, and in many ways he's a complete pillock.'

'I had wondered. I don't know – he worked for you. I just thought you were friends.'

Jake gave an ironic laugh, shaking his head so that his thick hair shifted on his shoulders. 'Friends? Not exactly. I think I'm Krish's – resort. Refuge. He's all over the place is poor old Krish. Olivia talked me into having him here to work, just like she more or less talked him into a place at college. Not that he's not bright, but he didn't get the right grades and it's certainly not the course he would have chosen. Science is actually his thing They turned him down and she appealed – twice. Wrote letters, went down there, crusading. Eventually they gave him a place at the last minute because someone else dropped out. That was all going on while he was working here. He was OK to have around, I must say.' Jake looked embarrassed for a moment. 'I wasn't in too good a state myself at the time, and someone else working here was welcome. Otherwise I was alone all day, and up in the flat at night. I hadn't done it up then either and it was grim. Krish can be a laugh when he's not saying something crass or ridiculous.

'Anyway, after a while he started talking, confiding in me. He found it very hard I think. It made him feel so disloyal to her. Since then I've been a sort of surrogate something-or-other to him. For some reason, I feel responsible for him, as if he's a child.'

'I suppose that's how my mother felt about Olivia.' Anna picked up an old Strepsil tin from the desk and fiddled with it. Something hard rattled inside.

'Krish needs to get away from her. She's got such a hold on him. It's hard to explain. He's terrified of her – the emotion she can work up. And the atmosphere there gets very weird at times with all her boys . . .'

'The lodgers?'

'Have you wondered why they're all still there

461

through the summer holidays? Olivia never has female lodgers. Always these boys. They come and go every few weeks or months, depending on how long they stay the course. Whether they react as required.'

'Meaning what?' Anna asked, not certain she wanted to hear the answer.

'Well, it varies, I think. What she wants is for them to depend on her, to take over their lives. Did you see Ben the other night? She's set herself up as mother confessor to him. The guru. From what I gather he's got the most miserable family. Doesn't want to go home. Ditto Sean. He's the one in the biggest tangle with her, poor bloke. Like someone nailed to a log. Did you see the state of him? The reason he acts like a servant in the house all the time is because he gets his rewards later – if he's been a good boy.'

Anna let out a gasp. 'No – oh no. That can't be ... That's horrible.' She felt tearful. All her hopes of Olivia were sliding away so fast. 'Not that – not still?'

'Still what?'

Anna took in a long breath. 'She was – promiscuous. To put it mildly.'

'She has to control people. Theo's an interesting one, though. She made a big mistake there, I reckon. He's a really good thing in that household at the moment. Lightens the place up no end. But my guess is she'll get nowhere with him at all. He may make jokes about his family, but in the end Theo's got a strong core in him. He's got values, roots. That's no good to Olivia. She needs floaters like poor old Sean. People she can bend like straws and take over.'

'Jake, are you absolutely sure about this?'

'Absolutely. She's malignant. There's no other word. Krish knows it's happening, except he tries to blank it out most of the time. You can't warn them. They're supposed to be adults. They come because they want to. And Olivia can be a darling. All small and defenceless and tempting in silk robes. I don't know what's going to happen with Sean, but he can't go on like this much longer. I mean the house varies a lot depending on who's there, but Krish says it's never been as bad as it is at the moment.'

Anna put the tin down and went over to the door, leaning on the frame. She felt slightly queasy. 'God, I can't believe it.' She searched Jake's face, tears rising in her eyes again. 'When I saw her – so lovely-looking in her big house, with all these people around her, I really thought she'd managed to get her life together. That's the worst of it, that I know there's something really nasty in her, but I still feel it's not her fault and I want to protect her.'

'Look,' Jake said. 'I'd really like to know more about her. Properly I mean. You know Krish knows virtually nothing about her past. Why don't you come round this evening? I'll cook something.'

She saw it had cost him a certain nerve to ask. 'I'd love to, but I can't tonight. I said I'd go there at teatime. She wants me to stay the night.' She felt suddenly panicky. 'I don't know if I want to be alone with her.'

'Would it help if I came round? I can get a mate of mine to close up for me. I'll come over and see Krishna.'

She felt hugely relieved at the thought. 'It's all silly, I'm sure. But I would feel safer with you around.'

'Don't worry. I'll be there.'

463

Chapter 34

'There are things I need to know.' Anna found herself rehearsing in the car on the way to Olivia's house. 'Things you owe it to us to be straight about.' In this odd, contorted household, she thought, the only course she could take was honesty and directness. At least, that had seemed a good idea when she was at home. Tell me what I need to know and I'll go. We owe each other nothing. She imagined sitting opposite the icy woman she had encountered that morning, coolly asking questions.

Then she thought of the reality of those questions: *Was my mother's lover the father of your child? Why did you try to murder me when I was a baby?* And the conversation became inconceivable. Hardly questions to be tossed out over tea and cakes.

She parked the car, this time closer to Olivia's house. Her watch said four-fifteen. She should have left earlier. Walking to the house, overnight bag in one hand and a white cake box balanced on the other, it occurred to her that Olivia ought to be more nervous than herself about any conversation they might have. Perhaps she had things she needed to get off her chest. With this encouraging thought that everything might not be up to her, Anna went to the house.

Sean answered the door, looking pale and miserable.

'You're late,' he remarked.

Anna felt irritation mingled with her pity for him. 'You the butler?' she asked lightly, and immediately regretted it.

She became aware of the sound of the piano behind him. She had no idea what the piece was. It was fast and passionate and hearing it brought up her flesh in goosepimples.

'Is that her?' she whispered.

Sean's white, pitted face shifted to the nearest thing she'd seen to a smile. 'She's bloody fantastic, isn't she?'

'Should I go through?'

'Yes. She's waiting for you. Just sit down and wait till she's finished. She doesn't like being interrupted.'

Anna slipped into the long room and sat on one of the easy chairs behind Olivia, the box of cakes on her lap. The room looked beautiful, her roses in a vase on the table and the breeze wafting the coloured silks at the window. Once more, Olivia had changed. The harsh look of the morning was gone and now she had a softer, more relaxed appearance: a white blouse with a wide, frill-edged collar and a full skirt in panels of red, green and gold. The back view of her, with her hair loose, was of someone much younger. She leaned her body into the music, playing with every part of her, not just her hands. Watching, Anna saw her complete absorption and concentration and knew that the beauty of it was what Kate had seen when they were girls together. By the time Olivia drew to the end of the piece and played the long, last chords, Anna was seeing in front of her the young Olivia, before the war, before Arden, even before she began listening at doors, or being locked behind them. She saw into the sadness of Olivia's life, and the death of her friendship with Kate seemed suddenly far more terrible than the loss of any bond with a man: far worse than the end of her relationship with Richard, or Kate's with Douglas.

As the music stopped there was a discordant jangle from the doorbell which made Anna jump. She heard Jake talking to Sean and felt jarred by it. His arrival was wrong. She didn't need help. Olivia was lovely, tender, sad. Anna wanted nothing more now than to talk to her alone.

Olivia twisted round on the piano stool. 'I knew you were there. I felt you.'

'That was so good,' Anna said, wiping her eyes.

'You're crying, ' Olivia said softly. 'I used to be able to make Katie cry with my music too.'

'Oh, Olivia,' Anna cried, letting the tears run down her face. 'Why did it have to happen – you and her?'

Olivia was beside her in a second, gentle, sweet-smelling, her arms round Anna, stroking her cropped hair. The cake box slid to the floor. 'My darling Anna, my dearest.' And Anna held her too, feeling the small lightness of her, and thought she would choke with sadness.

'I've wanted to hold you for so long,' Olivia said. 'When you were a little baby I cuddled you so much. I felt as if you were mine. I knew one day you'd come to be with me whether Kate wanted you to or not.'

Anna pulled away and looked up into her face. Both their cheeks were streaked with tears. 'But I wasn't yours. And you tried to drown me.' She found her voice growing shrill. 'Why did you do that to me?'

Olivia withdrew her hands, her face stony. 'She told you.'

Anna sat in silence, waiting.

'I was – not well. You know that, don't you? She

told you that? I was destructive. It wasn't me.' She looked into Anna's eyes. 'Can you forgive me?'

'I don't know.' She thought for a moment. 'For myself, I suppose, yes. But it's my mother you really needed to ask that.'

Olivia watched her face, not saying anything.

'There are other things I want to know.'

'I know.' Olivia roused herself suddenly and stood up, becoming almost cheerful again. 'Look. We'll have a long talk. Let's go and make tea first.'

Anna stood up, offering her the box of éclairs. 'Sorry – they're probably a mess by now.'

'Oh, how sweet! What a treat,' Olivia cried.

They went into the kitchen with its huge grey stove and tiled floor. A wooden drying rack hung from the ceiling holding a row of blue and white tea-towels.

Olivia filled the kettle and then turned, taking Anna in affectionately with her eyes. 'You are so like Douglas – his eyes and that beautiful hair. How is he?'

'I've no idea,' Anna said, startled. 'I've never met him.'

Olivia stood up straight, disbelieving. 'What?'

'He left her, not long after you did. Or at least, he went to work in London and she didn't go with him. He cut off completely, never a word. That was how he was, she said. Didn't you know?'

'No.' Olivia seemed quite stunned. 'I had no idea. We had no acquaintances in common even, really. And anyway, I was in London. I only ever saw her that once . . .'

'After you'd had Krishna?'

Olivia nodded. 'She wouldn't speak to me. The look in her eyes . . . And we both brought up our children alone. We should have been able to help each other.' She hesitated, gathering her resolve. 'Anna, I need ... Will she see me, d'you think?'

Realization rushed through Anna's mind, appalling. 'Olivia,' she said gently. 'Oh God, I'm so sorry. Look, this is partly why I came now.' She could barely get the words out. 'Mummy died on July 29th. She'd been ill for some time. I just assumed you knew.'

Something stopped her touching Olivia. A glove of complete stillness had slipped over her, something impregnable which made Anna afraid. She could think of nothing to say, nor could she read the look in Olivia's eyes.

They both stood there, very still. Then Olivia said, 'No,' softly at first. She made a swift movement and grabbed the kettle beside her full of almost boiling water, yanking it so that the flex came out and water splashed from under the lid soaking her hand, and she hurled it across the pale blue table. The lid came off and water pooled, steaming, across the table, splattering down on to the floor, and the kettle took the milk bottle with it so there was a smash of glass and a diluting white pool and the tinny bounce of the kettle on the tiles.

And Olivia's cries, her hand scalded. 'No, no, no!' she screamed. 'She can't be. She can't be!' The mugs crashed to the floor and she was opening the cupboard by her head and hurling sugar, tea, coffee across the kitchen. The cries tapered to a high scream which kept coming and coming out of her mouth like thin metal tape.

When Krish and Jake came pounding down to the kitchen, Anna was pressed against the stove, eyes stretched wide. A pile of sugar was dissolving gently into the water on the table, and tins from the next cupboard were slamming against the pantry door at the opposite end of the room.

'Get her arms,' Krish ordered Jake. 'Just hold her still a minute while I talk to her.' He began making soothing noises.

Though Jake was far bigger than Olivia, he seemed to need to use a good deal of his strength to grasp her from behind and pin her arms to her sides. As soon as he held her, though, she surrendered automatically as if by routine.

Krish stood in front of her, bending to look up into her face with big, appealing eyes. '*Ma?* Are you all right, *mamaji?*' He spoke in a babyish voice, kept repeating the same phrase, hypnotically, again and again. 'It's all right, Krishna's here, *mamaji*. Krish loves you.' Then he began saying things Anna couldn't understand, in the same soothing voice, and she realized after a moment that he was speaking Bengali, and once more it was the same phrase, over and over. Olivia had gone limp.

'It's OK, Jake, you can let go,' Krish said.

Jake withdrew his arms. Anna became aware of an unpleasant smell in the room, but couldn't work out what it was.

Krish took Olivia in his arms and held her against him. The two of them were completely absorbed in each other as if Anna and Jake weren't there. Olivia was crying in a terrible, broken way, and Krish kept saying 'Ssh,' and 'It's OK. It's OK.'

'She's dead,' Olivia told him in a tiny voice. 'Anna says she's dead.'

Jake gave Anna a questioning look and she shrugged helplessly.

'It's OK,' Krish soothed. 'Don't worry now.' Anna realized he hadn't any idea who Olivia was talking

469

about. 'Let's go upstairs, shall we, and have some time together? We could have one of our talks, couldn't we?'

'I think she's scalded her hand,' Anna pointed out.

Krish nodded. He led Olivia towards the door, arm round her shoulders. As they passed through the long room Anna and Jake heard Olivia say tearfully, 'Krishna loved me, didn't he?' And Krish's reply, 'Yes, he did. Of course he did.'

Anna found she couldn't move. Her legs were unsteady and her hands trembling. Jake took her arm and pulled her away from the cooker, turning one of the taps.

'You've switched the gas on.' He was fanning the air with one hand.

'I thought I could smell something.'

Dazed, she watched Jake push the back door ajar and fling open the window over the sink. 'That's better,' he said, coming over to her. 'Smells foul in here. Are you all right?'

She was in shock, her knees giving way. Jake caught her as she was about to sink to the floor. She felt his arm strongly round her waist, holding her up, helping her to a chair in the long room. He let her down gently and she sat shaking. 'Sorry,' she said.

'That's all right. I'm used to humping chests of drawers around.'

He squatted down in front of her, eyes concerned. 'Anna, you look really rough. D'you want me to take you home?'

She shook her head. 'No. I'll be fine. I can't just disappear after that anyway, can I? Could you pass me my bag – I need a fag.'

He stood up, towering over her, passed it over. 'Here.'

'Want one?'

'I don't any more.' He frowned. 'What brought that on? I've never seen her as bad as that before. You've really touched a nerve somewhere.'

'She didn't know Mom was dead.' Anna dragged hard on the cigarette, elbows resting on her knees, one hand raking her hair. 'I feel so bad about it. I mean we just kept mentioning her and I took it for granted Olivia knew. She wanted to see her. It's all so stupid . . .'

'Don't blame yourself,' Jake said. 'She's had years, hasn't she? She's picked the wrong moment.'

'But it's not just a wrong moment, is it?' Anna retorted, angrily. 'It's never, now. *Finito*. Chance over.'

'Look, I'll go and get the kettle working,' Jake said, retreating into the kitchen. 'You look as if you could do with something.'

There was a pause, then Anna said, 'Poor Krishna.'

It was well over an hour before Olivia came down again. Jake kept making sweet cups of tea and Anna was grateful and felt relieved at being cared for, even though she could have done with a gin.

After some time, Sean came sidling round the door. 'I heard,' he said. 'Is she all right?'

'She's had a shock,' Jake told him. 'She'll be fine, I think. Krish's up there with her.'

Sean hovered for a time, abstractedly replying to Jake's questions about how were things, how was college. He fidgeted round the table, leafing through the newspaper, standing, as he so often did, with his weight on one foot, twitching the other up and down. Then he shambled off towards the door.

'Sean,' Jake said gently. 'You do know Olivia's not completely well?'

Sean shrugged. 'Who is?' And disappeared.

Theo and Ben came crashing in soon after, Theo with a pile of books. 'Best get packing,' he said, taking swigs from a can of Pepsi.

'You going somewhere?' Anna asked.

'Yeah. Mom wants me home in sunny Smethwick for the rest of the holiday. Doesn't make much sense when I have to sleep in a shoebox with two of my brothers, but she likes to keep the family together – and of course I come in handy for minding my sister, 'cos the others are all at work. Anyway, you don't argue with my mom, basically.'

Anna grinned. Theo had cheered the place already. 'Have a good time,' she said.

Theo rolled his eyes comically in response.

'Won't be the same without him, will it?' she said to Jake when Theo had bounced out of the room. Ben slouched past with a steaming mug of something.

Jake's mind seemed elsewhere. 'Look, I don't think you should be staying tonight. You've had a bad month and it can get very moody round here.'

'I'll be fine,' Anna said firmly. 'I feel all right now – really. She just took me by surprise. Come on,' she joked. 'I don't think I need a minder.'

'Sorry.' Jake looked sheepish. 'Didn't mean to take over. But look, if there's any problem – ' He wrote on a piece of paper. 'This is my number. Call any time. I don't mind.'

'Thank you,' she said, touched. 'That's nice of you.'

Again he hesitated. 'Will you come round tomorrow? For that meal I was threatening to cook?'

Anna laughed, cheerful suddenly. 'Yeah – great. Thank you.'

*

472

Despite her assurances to Jake, when she found herself alone again she felt jumpy and apprehensive. What had happened in the kitchen seemed like a dream now, but when she went back in there much of the chaos Olivia had created was still in place. She thought it typical that Ben had apparently not even noticed. Jake had sorted out the kettle and replaced the packets which had not broken open, but the floor was still wet and there was a thick sludge of sugar and coffee on the table.

Convincing herself she felt calm, she found a Tesco's bag, shovelled the mess into it and wiped the table down. She was searching for a mop and bucket when she heard sounds from the long room next door. Heart thudding, she went in there.

'Oh Anna, hello!' Olivia produced a wonderful smile which, had it not been for the white binding on her hand, would have made what had happened earlier seem impossible. 'I'm so glad you're still here. We were afraid you would have given up on us and gone.'

'Er, no.' Anna felt disorientated. Krishna appeared too, charming her as if nothing had happened.

'Jake stayed for a while. He's only just gone.'

'Lovely boy, isn't he?' Olivia gushed. She went round the chairs, plumping cushions. 'And he's been such a good friend to Krish. It was such a shame he and his wife couldn't seem to get on – so many broken relationships about nowadays. There's a sadness about Jake, I always feel. Misses his little girl terribly.'

She tidied the music on the piano. 'Have the boys got back here yet?'

'Yes. Theo's off home tonight.'

Krish looked stricken. 'I'd forgotten! I'll just go up – ' He headed for the door.

'Yes, do go, and tell him not to leave without saying goodbye,' Olivia called.

When they were alone, Olivia said, 'I'm afraid you gave me a terrible shock earlier.' She looked across at Anna, an odd, closed expression in her eyes. 'What happened to her?'

'Cancer. She wasn't well for quite a while. I wasn't keeping it from you. I thought you would have known.'

'Darling – ' Olivia swept over to her and took her in her arms. 'You weren't to know what a hermit I've been. I'm so out of touch with things. And at least we've found each other now, which is a great, great joy to me.' She held Anna's shoulders. 'We'll have a lovely evening together, the three of us – you, me and Krishna. It'll be perfect.'

By some signal, presumably from Olivia, the three of them were left alone all evening, with no interruptions from the lodgers. Theo had said his goodbyes and gone earlier. Krish clearly didn't want him to leave.

They shared a simple meal of bread and cheese, salad and pickles. Olivia sat between the two of them at the table looking beautiful and was at her most charming, but Anna now found it impossible to relax in her company. She caught herself observing, questioning, tuning in to undercurrents beneath what Olivia was trying to present to her. She moved her chair away slightly from where Olivia had arranged it close by her side and watched the spectacle of what almost amounted to a courtship between mother and son.

'I'd so like you to think of me as family now,' Olivia said after they had eaten, talking mainly of practical things, Anna's teaching, Krish's course at college. 'I always so wanted a big family, growing up alone.' She

474

leaned over to touch Krish's hand, as she had already done a number of times during the evening. He smiled back at her, his expression affectionate, adoring almost. At the start of the evening Anna had felt reluctant admiration for him, that he could cope with this woman and remain so loyal to her. But she was growing more exasperated with the pair of them, frustrated by what she saw as falseness.

'Wouldn't it be lovely to have a big sister like Anna?' Olivia went on.

'Oh, it would,' Krish said, with slightly too much enthusiasm. He gave Anna a dazzling smile, and she managed to bare her teeth at him fairly convincingly in return. 'The thing is, though, you've never told me about Anna before. Or Kate. I mean, we're not actually related are we?'

Olivia laughed. 'Not by blood, no. But Kate and I were closer than most sisters ever are. We adored each other. She was lovely, Katie was, when she was young. So kind and sweet. She'd have done anything for anyone . . .'

Anna listened, longing to be beguiled. She wanted to believe everything she was being given, to rest on the surface. And Krish was so interested and attentive, his eyes fastened on his mother's face, and she wanted to believe in that too, that this extraordinary affection was the whole story between them.

But questions kept nudging into her mind as Olivia talked and talked about her mother. 'Katie and I were inseparable at school.' Her face was glowing, her voice animated. 'And of course she loved my father. She used to come on holidays with us, because your grandfather, Anna, was a very upright man, but rather a joyless sort, I'm afraid. We had a marvellous time together, and then of course I went away to boarding school. But we wrote letters all the time, and all the holidays we just lived at each other's houses. We talked about anything and everything – quite openly for those days, I can tell you!'

On and on it went, Katie and I, Katie and I . . . Krish seemed to be drinking it all in.

'So why didn't I ever meet her?' he asked after a time.

'Oh, well,' Olivia said, face still bathed in a bright smile. 'The war came and changed everything. Nothing was ever the same. I joined the Wrens and Katie was here nursing and we didn't see so much of each other after that. And then after, I went off to London and I met your father . . .'

These last words were spoken with a worshipping tone that Anna found ridiculous. He was just a man, she felt like saying. Yet another one.

Olivia directed a wistful smile at Anna. 'If ever there was a love child – ' She leaned across and stroked Krish's head. 'Unfortunately Krishna, my Krishna, was already married. He was on a visiting lectureship, you see. He felt the only thing he could do was to return home. But he left me his child.'

Anna thought of Elizabeth Kemp, how she managed to put from her so many things she didn't like. She felt a rising anger and resentment. All this pretence at being honest and vulnerable, when all the time she was selecting what she would tell, giving her son these half-truths. And what the hell was he playing at anyway, listening with that fixed, devoted smile? She felt like a fly trapped in the syrupy atmosphere between them. She knew there were layers and layers to Olivia which made it impossible to know quite where the truth lay. Had she even been honest when she wrote her notes to Kate?

She felt tired of it all suddenly, with a frustrated urge

to smash through the brittle surface of things with which she had been presented all evening. She couldn't listen to any more.

She stretched and yawned. 'I'm sorry, I really am tired. You won't mind if I go up soon?'

'Of course not, darling,' Olivia said. 'You've had such a difficult time these last weeks and of course I hadn't even realized. Do go on. Krish and I will clear up.' She stood up with Anna, searching her face, but Anna found she couldn't meet Olivia's eyes. To have done so would have symbolized too much: an honesty otherwise quite lacking from the evening.

While Krish was carrying something to the kitchen she let the question force its way to her lips. Cheeks burning red she looked up defiantly at Olivia. 'Was Angus the father?'

Olivia's expression froze. There was a second of nakedness, fear flickering in her eyes. Then she said coldly, 'I've absolutely no idea what you're talking about.'

Chapter 35

Anna sat on the solid bed, her heart pounding. The tiredness had vanished and she felt wound up and unready for sleep. She unzipped the overnight bag and pulled out her long T-shirt and wash things, noticing as she did so that Olivia had left a small vase of flowers next to the bed, picked from the garden.

Deadly nightshade most probably, she thought. Knowing it was absurd, she found herself sniffing at the white daisies and the greenery around them to find out if there was anything amiss. Those looks she had seen in Olivia's eyes. At this time of night she could start to believe anything.

Restless, she pulled back the covers of the bed, then opened the window, lit a cigarette and blew smoke out on to the twilight air. Footsteps passed in the otherwise quiet street. After a time she heard sounds of movement in the long corridor outside the bedroom: the others coming up.

Leaving the window open a crack, she took her washbag and went out to the bathroom at the back of the house. The staircase ran up the middle of the building, joining the corridor upstairs which ran from front to back with a series of doors along it. Anna didn't know who slept where.

She washed, scrubbed her teeth, found herself thinking about Jake and the way he looked into her eyes.

Walking back to her room she admitted to herself how much she was looking forward to seeing him the next evening. A door squeaked somewhere along the corridor. Yawning, she went into her room, turned to shut the door and started with a violence that set her whole body trembling.

'What the *hell* are you doing?' she cried furiously. 'You nearly gave me a heart attack!'

'Sssh – don't let her hear.' Krish closed the door quietly and stood against it. His face was solemn and looked heavy from drinking.

'What d'you want?'

'To talk – without her.' He sat down on the edge of the bed and she thought how young he looked. 'Sorry,' he offered awkwardly. 'You obviously know a lot of things about my mother that I don't. She only tells me what she wants me to hear.'

'Yes,' Anna relented. 'I can see that.' She stood across the room from him, glad that she'd put off getting changed. 'What d'you want to know?'

'I don't know what there is to know. I mean I'd never heard all that stuff about your mom before. The only thing she talks about in the past, really, is my father.'

'And was that the great passion she'd like us to believe?'

Krish looked up at her warily. 'How would I know?'

'Of course, how could you?'

'She's got no letters though. He didn't keep in touch with her. She probably just wrapped herself round him like a creeper – the way she does with everyone.' Anna was disturbed by the harsh way he spoke.

'But downstairs you were – you seemed so close.'

Krish seemed uncomfortable at her mentioning this.

'We can be, sometimes. She's very good company, as you've seen. But there's something... She's just not normal, is she?' He spoke in a sudden rush. 'It probably sounds stupid to you but it's taken me until now to realize – these past couple of years. When I went to college I heard a lot about other people's mothers. At school she wouldn't let me go to visit other people. Wanted me to herself – ' He broke off. 'Look, can't you sit down?'

He sounded so wretched that she came and sat on the bed. 'It must have been very difficult for you.'

He sat looking down at his hands for a moment in silence, twining his fingers together. The next thing she knew, he was pushing her back on the bed, hands moving clumsily and hard on her thighs as he half lay across her, his tongue pushing into her mouth.

In reflex she drew up her knees and shoved as hard as she could. 'Who the *fuck* d'you think you are?' she yelled at him as he regained his balance. 'What is it with your family? You all think you can just take what you like. You rip into other people's lives...'

'Shut up for God's sake!' He rushed at her, clamping his moist hand over her mouth. 'She mustn't hear.'

Anna yanked his hand away. 'Don't do that to me.' She marched over and opened the door. 'Just get out of here, you stupid little git.'

Krish slunk out of the room. 'I'm sorry ... I really did want to talk.'

'Don't ever try anything like that again,' she hissed at him. She watched him disappear into his room.

Turning, she jumped again, and with even more force. At the other end of the corridor, dressed in something long and pale, Olivia stood quite still, watching. Her

480

face was set in an expression of such hatred that Anna felt her knees turn weak.

'So.' Olivia's voice snaked along the corridor. 'I can't even trust you.'

Anna felt something give in her, come flooding out. 'You're all bloody mad,' she shouted. 'All of you. I'm getting out of here.'

Starting to sob, she ran into the room and in half a minute threw all her things back into the bag. When she came out again Olivia was still standing in the same place, watching stony-faced as Anna ran downstairs. She pulled open the heavy front door and ran out towards her car, only just able to see through her tears.

The light was still on in the attic above Jake's shop. Standing outside in the deserted street, Anna realized she didn't know how to get in. There were two floors of the dark shop below, and it was as if he was out of contact with the street, high up there. She went to the door and looked for a bell. There wasn't one. Instead she tried the letterbox, which was fortunately well sprung and gave a resounding clap when she released the flap.

She waited. Outwardly, now, she was more composed, had had to control herself in order to drive. But she could feel a tight bubble of emotion inside her, only just held in. She could not have gone back to be alone in Kate's house tonight.

There were sounds from inside and she saw movement behind the glass door. He left the light off, cautious perhaps, and she could just see the washed-out blue of his jeans as he came to the door. It opened, brushing the mat. She felt she'd never been so relieved to see anyone.

'Anna?' She couldn't make out the tone of his voice. Surprised, certainly, but she thought she noticed in it a degree of pleasure, relief almost.

'I need to talk to you.'

'Yeah – of course.' He hesitated, not wanting to presume anything. 'It's too late for the pubs isn't it? Will you come in?'

'Here's fine.' She hadn't meant to sound so abrupt. As well as holding back her emotion over Olivia and Krish, she suddenly wanted Jake to hold her, and that wasn't appropriate, wasn't why she'd come.

Jake led her up through the dark shop with its comforting smell of wood polish, past the dark shapes of the furniture. Following, she thought how odd it was that she was here alone with him, somehow suddenly the closest person to her now apart from Roland. Their feet sounded loud on the bare staircase up to his attic.

When they reached the flat she forgot everything for a few moments, exclaiming, 'Jake, it's lovely up here!'

'I'm glad you like it.' He smiled. 'Only thing is, you have to go down to the next floor for the bathroom. I'm working on that. Might get a shower put in. But otherwise it does me fine.'

The room was lit only by the sidelight next to the bed, where Jake had evidently been lying. It was a long room stretching across the building, with a gabled window at each end. At the back Jake had his kitchen. The bed was at the front under the window. Music was playing softly in the background, the deep, rich sound of a stringed instrument.

In the middle of one side of the room was a wooden fireplace with space for a couple of easy chairs. Either side of it were long shelves striped with the coloured spines of books, records, tapes, and at one end a stereo. The walls were all painted a pale colour, except for the other long wall opposite the fireplace, which was a deep malachite green and covered from floor to ceiling with framed pictures.

Anna's attention was drawn to these straight away, postponing her need to talk. A section of them near the middle were photographs of a little girl: a baby, a toddler with a cap of fine blond hair and a cheeky smile.

'Is this your daughter?'

'That's Elly, yes. Of course she's changed again now.'

'She's lovely.'

'Yes – she's great.' He went to the fridge. 'D'you fancy a beer?'

'No thanks. I've drunk enough this evening already. Wouldn't mind a coffee.'

She sat on one of the chairs by the fireplace. 'I s'pose you'd rather I didn't smoke up here?'

'Sorry – I'd prefer it.'

'That's OK. It'll be good for me. I ought to give up.'

'I gave up when Elly was born.'

She twisted round to look at the pictures again. 'Are these all places you've been?'

'No. Places I'd like to go. Never had the chance, or made the chance, depending how you look at it.' He was nervous, unused to having anyone in the flat and having to be sociable.

She sat in silence for a moment, aware again of the music in the room, a melancholy cello.

'What is this?'

'Bach. Beautiful, isn't it?' He handed her her coffee and sat down.

'It sounds so sad.'

'I suppose it does. It's just what I seem to want to hear recently.' This was not spoken with self-pity, but Anna felt awkward.

'I'm sorry – I've barged in. Would you rather I went?'

'No, I wouldn't. I spend far too much time on my own.'

There was a pause, then he said, 'What happened?'

Anna put her mug on the floor and sat back. She let out a long breath.

'It sounds daft, but I'm not exactly sure what happened. Olivia came down after you left. She said she'd had a shock.' She told him about the meal, the fawning affection between Olivia and Krish. 'It was pretty sickening. I got more and more frustrated because I felt they were feeding me something, some image they wanted me to see, and I still hadn't managed to talk to her properly about anything.'

She told Jake what had happened with Krish, growing more emotional as she spoke.

'It wasn't him I really minded, though. The really horrible part was her. Krish is just young and silly . . . But when I saw her standing there, absolutely still, with that look on her face . . . I couldn't have stayed the night in that house. She'd have killed me, I'm sure. I could just see her coming round the bedroom door with a knife in her hand.' She looked across at Jake. 'I've never known anyone who's had this effect on me before. There's something – evil about her. You must think I'm being very hysterical.'

'No, I don't at all.' There was sudden quiet. The tape clicked off. 'But we'd better get hold of Krish tomorrow.'

'I'm not sure I ever want to see him again – or her, for that matter.'

'I think you'll have to.' Jake spoke gently but emphatically. 'Look, Anna, I don't know all the background to this as you obviously do, but I do know a lot about Krish. I didn't explain properly last time we talked. Your coming here has lifted the lid off something for them and it's him that's going to get the full rush of it. I know he shouldn't have behaved the way he did tonight, but you have to understand the kind of hold Olivia has on him. She's never let him out of her sight hardly, apart from school when she had to. But she wouldn't let him go out or have friends – let alone a relationship with a woman – God forbid. Anything that's started she's destroyed one way or another. She interferes in every part of his life. Possessive isn't a strong enough word to describe it.'

Anna frowned. 'But he's left home, hasn't he?'

Jake gave an ironic laugh. 'He's done three terms in London. During the summer before he went he overdosed because she made him feel so guilty about going. He was in hospital for three days.'

'But you said she wanted him to go – appealed to the university?'

'She did. But that's Olivia for you, isn't it? Nothing ever goes one way with her. Even in London she completely dominates his life. He has to phone every day, come home every other weekend. And there's barely a weekend in between when she's not down there. He's not allowed to see anyone else when she goes down. He has to devote his time to her. And if he doesn't ring there are tears, threats – the whole works, turning on the guilt. If she thought he was going out with anyone ... well, it's almost unthinkable. I think he almost believes she can see into his mind. That if he was seeing anyone, she'd know, somehow.'

Anna listened, feeling forgiveness for Krish before Jake had even finished speaking. 'I can't imagine how he's coped this long,' she said. 'She's so terrible . . .' Her voice trailed off. 'But she does make you love her, doesn't she?'

'Better not to, I think.'

'She let Krish come and work for you. She must trust you.'

'I think I was partly to distract him from other things at the time. But we get on all right, me and Olivia. She knows I'm not going to be drawn into anything. She trusts me with Krish – like a sort of old uncle figure.' He shrugged, then looked at her seriously. 'And you know her because she was your mother's best friend who tried to do away with her baby?'

Anna shook her head. 'Sounds terrible, doesn't it? But it was my fairy story when I was little. "Tell me about you and Olivia when you were little girls." Bosom pals, complete devotion and all that. The stuff she left me to read telling me the truth about what happened was awful. She'd bring out all the good bits for me when I was a child. It was like – some mothers keep their jewellery box as a special thing to show their kids. All the shiny things inside. But with her it was Olivia.' She was crying suddenly, sobbing until she could barely catch her breath.

Jake got up, flustered, knelt down by her chair.

'I'm sorry,' she said, trying to gain control of herself. 'This keeps happening.'

'No, it's OK. Don't apologize.' He went to the kitchen end and came back with some squares of kitchen roll. 'Here – 'fraid I only have tissues in when I get a cold.'

Anna laughed, blowing her nose.

'I'll make more coffee – that's if you want? Or would you rather get some sleep?'

'No.' She handed him the mug. 'I'd like to tell you about it.'

He turned and touched her briefly on the shoulder. She felt the warmth of his hand through her shirt. 'No one should be alone with Olivia.'

She talked for an hour or more, telling him everything she could remember, trying, as Kate had done, to weave Olivia's account of herself into Kate's own. She told him about Angus, about her father, and Roland, trying to keep everything in the right order. When she reached the parts about Olivia's baby and Arden, she saw a look of shocked understanding on Jake's face.

'Does Krish know any of this?' she asked.

'I'm quite sure he doesn't.' Jake paused, trying to take it all in. 'I had no idea. Poor Olivia.'

'Yes, poor Olivia. But then you think what she did to my mother. I think Mom thought it was partly her own fault for bringing her to live in the house when I was on the way. At the time she didn't see what else she could do. But there was this huge splinter of sadness through her life. Looking back, I can recognize it more clearly. When you're young you don't always spot things, or know what you're seeing. I tried to ask Olivia about it tonight – about Angus. I was getting tired of all that sweet sugary crap between her and Krish. She just blanked me out. Gave me that evil eye look of hers and said she had no idea what I was talking about.

'In a way I don't know why it matters now anyway. Except that I think Mom wanted me to find out, to deal with it for her. I can't help thinking Olivia was lying, that he wouldn't have been disloyal to my mother, but they were strange times . . .'

'You may never get the truth now, anyway,' Jake said. 'Truth with Olivia is something that shifts around. What she wants is power over people. She knows she's got power over you because you want to know things, because you care about her. You see what she's done to Sean and Ben – let alone Krish. Don't let her get under your skin. It never leads to anything good.'

'Ben as well?'

'Ben's not in anything like the mess Sean is. He's very unsure of himself academically and he confides in her a lot. There's no doubt she's bright. She's supposed to be pretty well thought of for her knowledge of Bengali culture. She's very preoccupied with it because of Krish's father.'

'She even tries to sound Indian.'

Jake looked at the ceiling, exasperated. 'The whole thing, yes.'

Anna sat back in the chair, legs stretched out. Her head was beginning to ache.

'You all right?'

'Just tired. I don't think I can think about this any more tonight.'

'But you will see Krish?'

She hesitated. 'OK.'

'We could take him out somewhere. Get him away from there.'

'She won't want him going with me.'

'I'll think of something.'

Anna groaned. 'It's so late. I'm sorry. I must go.'

'Don't,' Jake said. 'There's no need and there's not that much of the night left – it's after three. Just sleep here. I've got a folding bed I use for Elly. I'll have that.'

She looked at him doubtfully, wondering for a few

seconds what this meant. The thought of driving back now was so dismal. 'Are you sure?'

Eyes full of warmth, he said, 'Of course. No problem at all.'

'My stuff's down in the car . . .'

'Give me the key. I'll get it.'

When he came back, Jake tactfully left to give her time to undress in this strange room, his pictures watching her from the wall. But she felt trusting, almost happy. By the time he came back she was already lying down.

He had changed into an old pair of shorts and a shirt. She looked at the firm lines of his legs, his arms. He pulled the folding bed open, settling it in line with her bed, tucking a sheet round its long mattress. She took in his slenderness compared with Richard's compact body.

He looked at her across the space between the two beds. 'Have a good sleep.' And reached over and clicked the light off.

'Jake,' she said drowsily. 'I wanted to ask you more about yourself. I'm sorry. I've been talking so much.'

'That's OK. There's not an awful lot to say about me.'

'I'm sure there is . . .' She felt her voice trailing off, sleep slipping over her in thick layers.

It must have been only moments later, but felt much longer. It began with a light pressure on her head, a stroking, soft as cobwebs in her hair, but then it was hard and she was in the dream and there was the terrible pressure, pushing, pushing so she couldn't move, and she felt her breath being forced out of her until she threw herself upright, whimpering like a tiny child, sweat breaking out under her arms and behind her knees.

'Sorry,' she heard Jake saying. 'God, I'm so sorry. Anna – it's OK. It's only me. I'm sorry.'

There was a click and the room sprang up round them again in the light. She squinted, bewildered, into Jake's face. He was sitting on the bed beside her, eyes wide with worry.

'I'm sorry,' he said again.

'Why?' She was dazed, couldn't think straight. 'I was dreaming. When I was little I sometimes used to dream I was being suffocated – pushed down and down. It's come back again since – since Mom died.' She remembered waking, as a child, out of the tight hold of the dream, gasping, with Kate's arms round her and her voice, 'It's all right, you're safe now. Quite safe with me.'

Jake was saying, 'It's just – I think it was my fault. I touched you. I was stroking your hair.'

'Were you?' She looked at him stupidly. 'Why?'

'Because ... I don't know. I suppose I wanted to do something for you. I thought you were asleep. Sorry. I feel ridiculous.'

'No – don't.' She was moved by his care, felt a great need for it rise in her. 'You were being kind.' She looked up into his eyes. 'If I'd been awake I'd have liked it. I feel so lonely.'

He moved closer to her, put an arm round her and pulled her to him, so her head was resting against his chest. She heard his voice quietly, 'Me too.' He stroked her hair again, gentle as a parent, and she held his other hand and listened to the beating of his heart. After a time both of them slept, comforted.

490

Chapter 36

Birds, she thought, when she woke the next morning. Even before opening her eyes she knew she was somewhere new. The light was different, coming from high on her right, bright, no curtains.

The window had been opened above the bed, and moving air touched her face.

'Birds,' she said.

'Not the dawn chorus, though.' Jake came across, offering her a mug. 'Tea all right?'

She sat up, gratefully, trying to smooth her hair down. 'Oh, I need this. What's the time then?' He was already dressed.

''Bout half-nine. I've just been down to open up. Sleep OK?'

'Fine – thanks.' She felt herself blushing. She last remembered falling asleep leaning against him, and vaguely recalled him moving her, lying her down again. She thought of his touching her hair, of this area of need and intimacy which had opened up between them. She looked up and smiled shyly at him.

He sat down at the far end of the bed. 'Considering how little sleep we had last night, I don't feel too bad.'

'Nor me,' she said, though she did feel muzzy. Silently she sipped the tea, strong, with a tang of something, Earl Grey perhaps. A bee flew in through the window, bumped its way a short distance along the wall and back, then found the white air again and disappeared.

'Thanks for letting me stay.'

'No problem.' He smiled, face transforming. 'I was enjoying the novelty of having someone else around.'

She could tell neither of them was going to mention last night, now daylight had come, both embarrassed or afraid.

'How often does Elly stay?'

'Every other weekend usually. Unless that upsets some other arrangement her mother has made.'

Anna nodded. Jake obviously found the situation difficult to talk about and she didn't want to push it.

'What were you doing before this – before the business, I mean?'

'I told you – selling insurance.'

'What? Really?'

'Did you think I was joking?' He gave a reluctant laugh. 'I was training to be the man from the Pru. Nice safe job, suit, haircut, the lot. Life mapped out nicely.'

'And you couldn't stick it?'

His eyes moved sharply to her face, expression wary suddenly. 'You sound like Sal. Why? D'you think I should have done?'

'No!' she said, alarmed. 'Of course not. And anyway – it's none of my business, is it?'

'It's absolutely terrifying having your life stretching ahead of you like that, doing something you're indifferent to for the next thirty years. And I was doing OK at it. Personable, they called me. I was good at sales, always got on well with clients. But I got to thirty and I just couldn't do it any more. I was suffocating.'

'This seems much more you,' she said cautiously.

'I gave up work with the Pru when Sal was pregnant

492

with Elly.' Jake talked in a steady voice, eyes fixed on the floor in front of him. He talked about it as if it was something he just wanted over, needing to be told but best out of the way. Anna listened, the empty mug cradled against her chest.

'It seemed to rock the foundations of something for Sal. Some insecurity or expectation she had that neither of us had known about. My fault, I suppose. Not a good time when she was pregnant and wasn't sure how it was going to go with her own job. She works in admin over at the Poly. And I suppose she thought she was settling down with one sort of person and I turned out – in her eyes at least – to be someone very different. The business wasn't too good at first either, of course. So things were already wobbly. Then Elly was born and everything changed again.' He paused. 'I don't know. Too many changes all at once. We could never seem to reach each other after that. Even now it's not easy, having to keep seeing each other because of Elly. There's a lot of resentment. But we do it for her... I could never not see her.'

'It must be so difficult,' Anna said, feeling inane. Her mind flashed to Richard, to the miscarriage. What if she had had the baby? For the first time she was half glad. It would not have been right to have a child together.

Jake looked round and gave her a wry smile. 'Let's get off all that. Breakfast? It's toast or toast, I'm afraid.'

'In that case I'd like toast.'

She pulled her jeans on and quickly manoeuvred her way into the rest of her clothes as Jake sliced bread and clicked down the toaster.

'Shouldn't you be down in the shop?'

'There's a bell – rings up here too if anyone comes in. But yes, I should really. I'll just get this down me. I

493

don't usually do a roaring trade at this time in the morning.'

They were eating thick, slightly singed slices of toast and honey when Anna suddenly exclaimed, 'Oh, no. What's the time?'

'Nearly half-ten. What's the matter?'

'Roland. I promised I'd see him this morning.' She was flustered, driven to action, flapping round the room, toast still in one hand. 'Anyway, I must go and let you get on.' She shoved her things into her bag with her spare hand. 'Listen, thanks ever so much.'

Jake stood up. 'No thanks needed. It's been a pleasure.'

'What about tonight – Krish?'

'Fancy a *balti*?'

'Love one.'

'I'll pick you up if you like. Seven-thirty?'

She gave him the address, then hesitated. Jake looked down into her eyes. There was a moment of awkwardness, of not knowing how to part.

Anna went to the stairs taking refuge in the need to hurry. 'Bye then. See you later.'

In the street she lit her first cigarette of the day, thinking that by now she would normally have had a couple already.

The growling of Jake's Transit van sounded incongruous in the suburban street. She climbed up into the cab, slim in jeans and a round-necked navy top which followed every curve of her.

Jake gave her a broad smile. 'You ready for this?'

'Doing my best to be.' As Jake reversed into Kate's strip of drive, she said, 'Does Krish know we're coming?'

'I phoned.' The van accelerated loudly. 'He sounded very low. Didn't say much.'

'But he's coming?'

Jake nodded.

'Did he say anything about last night?'

'No. He never says much on the phone. Always afraid she's listening.'

'What a life.'

Jake inclined his head in agreement. 'My guess is he won't have had the easiest of days.'

As they drove along the Alcester Road towards Moseley, the two of them talked rather abstractedly. Had she got to Roland's in time? Had he had many customers that day? Anna was feeling nervous about seeing Krish. Not because she didn't want to forgive him, to give him support, but because those feelings had somehow to be made clear.

They saw him waving to them from the corner of the road before they even reached Olivia's house. Jake braked sharply and Anna moved up into the middle seat of the cab. Seeing Krish again she was struck once more by the enormous appeal of his puppy-like looks.

'Been forced to camp out on the pavement now, have you?' Jake joked as they pulled away.

Krish seemed slightly breathless. 'I thought if she saw you two it'd make things worse. It's been bloody awful in there today.' He shifted uneasily beside Anna, avoiding her eyes. 'She's not speaking to me – not a single word. Ben's been out all day, so there's just Sean. Jesus, is he a moody bloke. Must be living with us that does it.'

He gave a nervous little laugh and turned to Anna. 'I'm really, really sorry about last night,' he said disarmingly. 'I got completely above myself and I regretted it straight away. Can you forgive me?'

Anna smiled. There was an adroitness in the apology which made her realize that he had become well practised at saying sorry, keeping things smooth. Living with her, no doubt.

'It's OK.' To her annoyance she felt herself blushing. 'I hope you didn't get into too much trouble over it?'

'I expect you've gathered my mother's rather possessive?'

'Don't worry,' Jake said. 'Anna's on your side.'

'I thought you'd fallen under her spell like everyone else seems to.' His voice was bitter.

'Not for long,' Anna said.

Jake parked in a side street off Stoney Lane, and they walked across to the little restaurant. The street was busy, most of the shops still open, with people milling in and out of the grocer's a few doors away, leaning over the rickety trestle tables outside to select from the boxes of green bananas, okra, garlic, oranges. A string holding paper bags shifted in the breeze. One of the passing cars blared Asian film music, a woman's voice reaching high. The evening air was warm and full of the smells of cooking.

Inside many of the tables were already taken and the atmosphere was busy, full of spice and smoke, a mixed-race clientele, the waiters holding dishes high, wriggling their hips to squeeze between the chairs. A huge white man sat alone at the back of the room pulling at *naan* bread with stumpy fingers. The waiter seated them with great courtesy, a metal jug of water and a small metal dish containing chopped onions in a runny white sauce rippled with tomato ketchup. Each table was covered by a sheet of glass with the menus tucked underneath and a sprinkling of paper napkins on the top.

'You familiar with this cooking?' Jake asked.

'Oh, yes. Richard was very keen on these places and got me hooked. I brought my mom here a few times.'

Jake smiled. 'And?'

'She loved it. Said it was the nearest she'd get to travelling now.'

They ordered Cokes and food.

'Kebabs,' Krish said. 'It has to be kebabs.'

Once they'd got past the activity of ordering, there was a sudden awkwardness. Anna asked Krish about his course, whether he was enjoying it.

'It's fine,' he said 'Really interesting.' She couldn't help feeling that this, too, was a stock reply.

'And the Bengali – you obviously already speak it?'

'Some. She brought me up almost bilingual – that was the idea. She speaks it very well herself.'

He changed the subject quickly then, asking Jake how the business was going, and the two of them talked through the starters. The main dishes arrived, the dark, well-used *balti* dishes like small woks, half filled with bright, sizzling food, and thick *naan* breads and rice alongside.

'Enjoy your meal,' the waiter said, retreating.

There was a long, embarrassed silence. They tore the bread, scooped up the spiced meat and vegetables.

'So things are bad again?' Jake said eventually, with a directness which suggested they settle down to the real business of the evening.

Krish nodded. Anna expected him to feel ill at ease with her there, but he seemed to trust her. She saw that as a measure of the trust he had in Jake.

'It's the longest I've spent in the house since last summer. A few days is OK. I can cope with it. Things don't build up too much.' He looked round at Anna. 'You might think I'm being very critical of her. Most

497

people think she's marvellous – charming and sensitive, life and soul of the party. She is, of course, some of the time. In fact in some ways there's no one I'd rather have a conversation with. That's the good side of the lodgers being there. She's gifted with shy people – draws them out, makes them feel interesting and part of things. And she's very clever. I admire her a lot for all she's done. She had a hard time, bringing me up on her own and all that.'

'My mother brought me up on her own,' Anna remarked.

'Did she?' Krish looked intrigued for a second. 'But I expect she's a very different sort of person. My mother's had so much to deal with – me coming along, not only the bastard baby but the wrong colour as well, and her parents throwing her out ... She's heroic, really.'

'Why did they throw her out?' Anna asked, feeling compelled to interrupt this hymn of praise. She wondered what version of events Olivia had permitted Krish.

'Oh, they wanted her to have a nice little job, marry someone rich and influential. You know, all the respectable things. She wanted to play the piano – she's very gifted, you know – and study. Branch out. She was really a sort of Bohemian at heart.'

'I see,' Anna said, carefully. She felt Jake's eyes on her.

Krish pushed his chair back. 'I need a proper drink. Coke just isn't enough for the day I've had. Back in a minute.'

'There's an off-licence just along the way,' Jake explained as Krish disappeared. He looked at Anna. 'At least we'll be able to deliver him home safely.'

'What's going on?' Anna asked. 'We're back to the Blessed Martyr Olivia Kemp bit again.'

'He does that. When he's most angry with her he has to get all this stuff in first – how marvellous she is. It's a kind of pledge of loyalty, I think.'

'Before he says what he really feels?'

'Sometimes.' Jake offered her more rice. 'He doesn't find it easy to say anything bad about her.'

Anna refused the rice. She sat back in her chair. 'I feel I know so many things about her that he doesn't.'

'Then tell him.'

'D'you think it'd really be any help to him to know?'

Jake considered this. 'He only knows what she's chosen to tell him. Perhaps it would help to have another version of events.'

'I can hardly tell him here.'

'It's not ideal I know, but I don't think we'll get too many chances.'

Krish came back with chilled wine and a four-pack of beer. He pulled off one of the cans and drank thirstily.

'That's more like it.' He grinned at the two of them. 'Go on, help yourselves. Wine's open. I got them to do it.'

Anna took a beer and pulled the ring. Cautiously she said, 'Krish – how much do you know about your mother's life?'

'Hardly a thing,' he said, jovial suddenly. 'I mean, I have a sort of outline, without much detail. Great parents, nice house. Wrens in the war. London. My father – MY FATHER, in capital letters heavily under-lined. The great Krishna Chaudhuri. Me. That's about it. Don't know what's missing – except a screw, in her case!' He laughed, loudly, but it was drowned by a sudden cheer from one of the other tables. Someone's birthday. Krish's dark hands played nervously with the red and green can. He drained it and took a second one. 'Go on,' he said to Anna. 'Let's have it, then.'

'We could talk about it later,' she said gently. 'Get out of here?'

'That bad, is it?' he said with a foolish giggle. 'What's she done then? Hasn't murdered anyone, has she? Sometimes, the look in her eyes, I think she could. I really do.'

Anna glanced uneasily at Jake as she started talking. She began with the early parts, the friendship, easing them in. Krish listened without interrupting. His cheeks had deepened in colour and his eyes were beginning to have a slightly glazed look. As she spoke, couching what she had to say in the gentlest terms possible, Krish drank steadily, ignoring the remains of his food. He sat back on the hard chair, eyes fixed on Anna's face. In the middle of her account he leaned over and picked up the bottle of wine. Jake tried to restrain his arm.

'Go easy.'

'Piss off, Jake,' Krish protested. 'What d'you think I bought it for?'

It was only when she got to the part about Arden he began to react. He leaned across the table, clutching the bottle to his chest with one hand like a teddy bear. 'So you're saying she's a loony. It's true!' He laughed almost triumphantly. 'I knew it. My mother's a loony.' He lifted the bottle and drank it back like fizzy pop. 'That's more like it.' He offered it round. 'Go on, have some.'

'Let's get out of here,' Jake whispered to Anna. He stood up. Between the two of them they put together enough money to pay the bill. It was a struggle getting Krish out between the tightly packed chairs. He refused to give up the bottle and kept letting out bursts of laughter so that people at the other tables turned and stared at them.

'My mother's a complete fruitcake,' he told one table amiably and Anna felt their eyes all momentarily swivel to her, trying to work out if she was his mother, then concluding she probably wasn't.

Outside, Jake held him round the waist and Anna took his arm. It was growing dark, the sky a very pale blue, edged with yellow, the street still full of life, cars passing.

'Come on, Krish,' Jake said. 'Let's get you to the van. It'll be OK.'

Krish stumbled along between them. As they reached the van he was still laughing, crumpling between them, tears running down his face. Alongside the road was a small park, open space behind a low railing. They stepped over, Krish catching his foot on the rail and making them sprawl on to the grass together, him between them. A rat scuttered away nearby. They sat Krish up between them. His head was in his hands, the bottle standing between his knees. More music blared from a house opposite.

'I'm going to end up like her!' His voice was high. 'I know I will. She's going to make me like her.'

'You won't,' Anna tried to soothe him. 'You're not a bit like her.'

'But you said it last night. "You're all mad." You said so.'

'I was just angry. I'm sorry.'

Krish was silent for a moment. 'I can't be what she wants all the time.'

'And what's that?' Anna asked him. Jake sat listening quietly, an arm round Krish's shoulders.

501

Krish shook his head helplessly. 'Sometimes I think she wants me to be my father.' He paused as a motorbike roared past on the road. 'Or she wants me to be a baby for her for ever or ... I don't know. She justs wants me to be everything ... that she needs.'

'But that's not reasonable, is it?' Anna said. 'No mother should ask that of a child.'

'She's not just any mother, though, is she?' Krish took more mouthfuls from the bottle. 'Thing is – I've realized gradually that she's not like other mothers. But I've always thought, well, maybe she's not that bad. No one else thinks there's anything odd about her. I've tried to kid myself she wasn't so different from anyone else – what happens with some of the lodgers ... That she was just broad-minded, a free spirit or something. She's coped, after all. She's not got a psychiatric record – she must be OK really. So that meant I'd be all right too. But she's not all right, is she? She's even been in one of those places ...'

'A long time ago,' Anna said. 'And for a good reason.'

Krish was barely listening to her. 'She'll drive me mad herself. She'll be the one. I can't do anything without her being part of it. I can't go out, can't have friends, can't see women. If I even get near a woman it all gets fouled up because I feel as if she's watching. I don't even want to do this bloody degree. I don't know what to do ...' He was really crying now, taking deep gulps. 'I can't even talk about her normally because I feel such a shit if I do ... And I'm scared. I'm so scared of being ill – in my head. Sometimes I think I'm not right. No one should think things like I do.'

Anna also put her arm round him. 'Krish, Krish ...' The three of them sat close in the darkening evening. Anna felt Jake stroke her arm with the back of his fingers, behind Krish's back. She looked round at him and their eyes met, sadly, but with warmth in them.

'Let's get back,' Jake said. Krish was sagging between them now. 'He's past any more conversation.' He lifted the bottle of wine and held it up in the fading light. 'God, he's nearly drunk the lot.'

'We can't take him back there!' Anna said.

'He can come to mine. I'll drop you off first.'

'I'll come round tomorrow – first thing.'

They had to half drag Krish into the van. He sat slumped in the middle seat, silent now and unreachable.

'I didn't even tell him all of it,' Anna said to Jake, still outside.

'He's certainly heard enough for now, though.' Jake stopped by the door of the van. In the shadows his face looked longer, and thin, his expression anxious. He glanced in at Krish and shook his head. 'D'you think I was wrong?'

'No. I'd have had to tell him. He was going to keep asking me.'

They drove back in silence, Krish pressed against Anna's shoulder. He was asleep, but uneasily so, and kept stirring and giving long, groaning sighs. The silence between herself and Jake was not neutral either. She knew there was a pressure of emotion between them, of need and attraction. That each of them was waiting to see if the other would move forward first. Anna felt very alert, her emotions heightened, as if she could go on effortlessly all night with no sleep.

'He looks so vulnerable, doesn't he?' she said eventually, and the remark seemed to jar into the charged silence, a distraction from their thoughts.

Jake nodded. 'What you said about coming round tomorrow – that'd be really good.'

Anna smiled in the blue night light, hoping, knowing he did not just want her there because of Krish. 'I'll be round about nine-thirty,' she said.

When they stopped outside Kate's house, Jake jumped quickly out of the van and came round to open her side. He waited as she climbed down. Krish slumped further, half lying across the seat.

'Thanks for this evening,' Jake said, sounding uncertain now.

She jumped to the pavement and stood looking up at him. Each of them waited, taking courage to look into each other's face. Even in the dim light she could see the emotion in Jake's eyes, his searching her for a response. But she was afraid. It was too soon and the feelings too serious to hurry.

She looked away. 'Goodnight, then. I'll see you in the morning.'

'OK,' he said quietly. He leaned forward and gave her a brief, awkward hug. She was taken by surprise and had barely registered the feeling of him against her when he had let her go and was striding round to the other door of the van. The door slammed, the engine started up.

She stood waving as he drove away, seeing the white van recede down the street, feeling excited yet regretful.

'And who the hell was that?' a voice said behind her.

Things registered all at once. The car parked a little further along the street, the old blue Saab. The self-righteous voice. She turned to see his angry eyes behind her. Richard.

Chapter 37

He slammed Kate's front door behind them with such violence that the house shuddered. The force of it jarred Anna's nerves, set off her temper.

'Don't do that,' she snapped, switching on the hall light, then the kitchen. 'It isn't your house.'

'Oh dear.' Richard followed her into the kitchen, laughing sarcastically. '"It isn't your house,"' he mimicked. 'Just listen to you.'

Richard looked incongruous in Kate's suburban kitchen in his faded, loose-fitting trousers, grey shirt with the sleeves rolled to the elbow, the rumpled, wavy hair, hand reaching up to pass through it, a restless habit of his. She used to find his anger frightening. She wasn't used to male emotion, had once regarded it as something more valid and powerful than her own. She'd always been the one to try and stay in control and appease him; hold things together. Now she no longer cared.

'Don't imitate me.' She faced him, her tone very cold. 'I didn't ask you to come here.'

He stared at her. 'What's happened to your hair?'

'I got it caught in some heavy industrial machinery.'

Richard ignored this, already on to the next thing, pacing the floor. 'You go off one night with no explanation. You never answer the phone. I come over and you're always out ... Anna, this is ridiculous. You've been here a month and you said it'd be a few days ...'

'And you said you'd be home that night I came, and you weren't. I've had enough of that.'

'Look – ' Richard paced up and down the kitchen, palm outstretched as if explaining something really-very-simple to a perverse child. 'It was one of those things. We'd had a case conference – all sorts of added complications – one of the key social workers was delayed. It was a very unusual situation.' His rubber-soled shoes gave off a squeak as he spun round on the lino. 'It's just the way it is, Anna. I can't drop everything and come home just because you've got a meal ready, can I? There are wider concerns, and sometimes they have to come first, that's all.'

'Fine.' She could feel an ecstatic anger rising in her, her body tensing with the force of it.

'So what's going on? Why aren't you answering the phone? You must have finished packing up here by now. I thought it'd take a week, max. I'll give you a hand with the last things, if there's more to do. Take a carload to Oxfam or whoever first thing in the morning, and we can get back home.'

'And then what?' she asked, controlling her voice.

'Well – we can just get on with life again.'

After a silence, she said, 'I'm not coming home. I don't want to live with you any more. I don't love you. I want to be on my own.'

Richard stopped pacing, was actually listening. 'But you've got to be back at school any day now.'

'I've given up my job.'

He walked over to her and put his hands on her shoulders. She felt herself shrinking from him. Her life with him now felt like something from which she had woken – a trance in which she had lost consciousness.

His voice was soft and persuasive, eyes fixed on hers in a practised look of concern. 'Anna? You can't be serious? Look, I know it's been a bad month. Your mum and everything. But you can't let all this take over your life. You have to keep things in perspective. God knows, I see enough of the consequences of people letting things get to them too much. And you're too intelligent to let that happen.'

She let him have the full force of her fist on his nose, punching so hard she jarred her elbow. His eyes snapped shut instantly in pain, hands jerking up to his face. He held them out again, seeing them stained red. Blood fell in long strokes down the grey shirt.

'*Jesus.*' The hurt tone turned to fury. 'What is the matter with you?' He groped at the box of multi-coloured tissues on the worktop.

'We lost our baby,' she heard herself shrieking at him. 'And it was the worst thing that's ever happened to me in my life and you didn't say anything. Not one fucking thing. And my mother's dead and you couldn't even be bothered to come with me to the funeral. All the hours I've spent listening to you about your bloody job and you've never listened to me when I needed you to. I don't want to talk to you now – ' her voice grew quieter – 'I've got things to do. I've found Olivia and she lost her baby too and I want ... I want ...'

Incoherent, she found herself sobbing, bent over next to the sink, breathless with it, a pool of pain inside her draining out.

'Oh God,' she cried after a few moments. 'It's all so sad. Why is life so *sad*?'

Richard stood watching her warily, a pad of tissues pressed to his nose, blood on his chin.

'You didn't want us to have a child, did you?' She spoke with her back to him. 'It didn't mean anything to you.'

'I don't know. It was so sudden. It's not as if we planned it.'

'Planned it.' She turned, scornful. 'You can't just plan everything.'

'It was different for you. Maybe you were ready for it and I wasn't. And you could feel it. It wasn't real to me.'

'But you said you felt it – felt it flutter under your hand.'

'Sorry.' He gave a long sigh. 'Something I'm not very good at, I suppose. It's a long time ago now.'

'Eight months!' she flared at him again. 'What's eight bloody months? Some things stay with people for the rest of their lives, Richard, they don't just disappear all finished with. You can't just organize them away. How can you work with people like you do when you know nothing, you understand nothing?'

'My job's about practical decisions,' Richard said sternly. 'Not emotions.'

Anna turned away. 'I don't want to talk about your job. Not again.'

For a moment the only sound was Kate's clock, ticking across the kitchen.

'Look – ' He approached her again, though his voice sounded ridiculous because his hand was still clamping a pink tissue over his nose. 'You need some space, that's all. A rest. Come home and take it easy, even if you're not working. You can take your time, look for another job. We'll talk . . .'

'Richard.' She looked strongly into his eyes, her own red and still full of tears. 'I'm not coming back to

Coventry. I can't live with you any more. You and I are not good for each other.'

'Who was that I saw you with outside?' Richard's voice was even, but Anna could hear the suspicion in it. 'Is this to do with him?'

'The day I left home – not that you apparently noticed – was the day after the funeral. I'd never even met him then. I left home for myself.'

'But now it's to do with him, isn't it?'

She looked down at the floor, seeing spots of Richard's blood. 'I don't know. Maybe.'

'Who is he?'

'Someone I met through Olivia.'

Richard tutted, exasperated. 'And who the hell is Olivia?'

'Someone Mom knew.'

'Has he touched you?'

'Oh, don't be so bloody predictable.'

'Has he, though?'

She thought of that night in the flat. Jake's gentle hands. Touched, but not in the way Richard meant. 'No.' She felt humiliated having to answer these questions.

Richard stared at her, trying to decide whether to believe her. 'Five years we've been together,' he said finally. 'And now you want to go, just like that.'

'Not just like that. It's finished, Richard. I want my life to change.'

She found bedding for him and he slept in the front bedroom while Anna was in Kate's at the back. They parted for the night in morose silence. Anna lay in Kate's floral room aching with sadness, but too tired for more tears.

The next morning they were civil and distant, like acquaintances made the day before. They ate breakfast, discussed the Coventry house.

'We should sell it,' Anna said.

'You might want to come back.'

'I shan't come back. Anyway, I thought being a property owner made you feel uncomfortable.'

Richard frowned at a half-eaten slice of toast, trying to take in her decision, her strength. 'I could rent again, I suppose.'

'Or buy somewhere smaller.'

'You can't buy anywhere much smaller. Except a flat.' He looked across at her, appealing. 'Anna, this is horrible.'

'I know. I'm sorry.'

All the time she was holding on tight to her determination. Being alone there with him again it would have been so easy to slide back, not fight it, to go with him and settle into the old routine, the stifling habits. She felt she was holding her breath.

'You're not going to stay here, are you?'

The tone of ridicule in his voice riled her, brought back all her resolve. 'Probably not. I'll decide when I'm ready. I might move nearer the middle of town.'

'What about your job?'

'I've resigned.'

'Will you find another school?'

'Maybe. Maybe not.'

He put his head on one side. 'You loved that job.'

'I didn't. I put up with it. Felt I couldn't give up. I liked the kids – some of them. But I want a change.'

Richard looked concerned. 'Anna, who's behind all this? What's going on?'

Calmly she looked at him. 'I'm going on.'

He didn't stay long after breakfast. They spent some of the time in silence, some talking.

'I'll come over and collect more things,' she said vaguely. 'Don't know when. I'll ring you.'

She stood out by the old blue Saab in the bright morning as he prepared to go. She felt strong now, and certain, but Richard was suddenly emotional.

'Come with me – please? Give us another go, can't you?'

'No. I'm sorry, Richard.' And she was.

'I can't believe this.' He gestured helplessly. 'If you change your mind . . .?' He held out his arms. 'Is a hug too much for you?'

She accepted, kissed him sadly. 'Thank you,' she was saying, and then there came the sound of the loud engine, revving through the Saturday morning calm and braking outside the house.

She saw Jake's long legs emerge first below the door, then he appeared, his face white and tense, hair tied back in a short ponytail. He saw the two of them together and stopped, embarrassed.

'What?' Anna cried. 'What's happened?'

'There's trouble.' Jake made an apologetic gesture with his long hands. 'Look – sorry to interrupt. I think you'd better come.'

Jake's driving was jerky.

'What's going on?' Anna's heart was pounding, her head still thick from a night of broken sleep. She sat tensed on the slippery black seat.

'Ben phoned. It's Sean – he started a fire. I think they've sorted that, but he sounded awful. And Krish's only just functioning after last night, of course. I'd have left him to get some more sleep, but he made me drop him off home on the way.' Jake glanced at her anxiously.

'I wouldn't have come if – I mean, I haven't got your number. I feel a right clumsy idiot for barging in on you like that.'

'It's all right,' Anna said. 'Richard was just leaving. Actually I was relieved to see you. What's sparked all this off?'

'From what Ben said Sean and Olivia have been arguing half the night and no one's had any sleep. I don't know what goes on between them – some terrible version of teasing on her part, I suppose. But she's obviously pushed him too far this time. Olivia's asking for you, by the way.'

'For me?' She felt her heartbeat quicken further. 'Why?'

'I didn't ask. I thought in the circumstances I'd just do what she and Krish wanted.'

When they reached the house Ben was walking up and down, hands on his hips, elbows at an outraged angle.

'About bloody time!' he exploded as they leapt from the van. 'I shouldn't be left with all this,' he added petulantly. 'He's come down again now, too. I was all for calling the police, but Krish wouldn't let me. Sean's a fucking maniac.' Ben was quivering, babbling on as they stood by the van.

'I got up an hour or more ago. Found him at it with a lighter – stark naked, blood all down his chest as well. He was going for all those sari things – God knows what would've happened. He's completely out of his tree. And then she came down and they had another go at each other. It was disgusting, foul. I couldn't believe it . . .' Anna saw he was close to tears, the shock of it making him seem small and childlike.

'Then what?' she asked gently.

'I was the one left to put it out. Neither of them seemed to notice what was going on – they were too busy mouthing off at each other . . . I was dowsing it all down. Luckily nothing else caught.' He took a deep breath. 'Sean went upstairs saying he was going to pack all his stuff and he was going, and Olivia went to pieces. She tried to persuade him . . . crying, and she was all over him – horrible – but he said it was too late, he was going. All this time and I never saw it. I thought Sean was just moody, or – I don't know.' He shuddered. 'She's some kind of pervert. I can't handle this, Jake.'

'What about Krish?' Jake said. 'Where is he?'

Ben pointed. 'In there with them.'

With Ben following, Anna and Jake ran into Olivia's house. The front door was already open and the hall floor stippled with muddy water. In the long room they were met by a sight that Anna would never forget. The acrid smell of burning and of damp ash met them straight away. The front end of the room where the table stood was wrecked. Instead of the warm glow of light through the coloured silks at the windows, daylight poured through bare panes, harsh and white. At either side hung shreds of blackened cloth, and the wall was stained dark by the flames, as were the corners of that end of the room where there had also hung saris, which must have caught fire with the speed of tissue. The table, the floor, the sills were soaking wet and a black sludge of charred material lay at the edges of the room. Overturned on the floor were a yellow plastic bucket and a red washing-up bowl.

Olivia was sitting at the table, her elbows resting on the wet wood, apparently oblivious to the damp. Her face, stilled with shock and exhaustion, was that of an old woman, limp and grey. She still had on the long, pale pink nightdress in which Anna had seen her that night on the landing and her hair was loose round her shoulders.

Sean was standing in the middle of the room, a black Puma bag with red lettering on the floor beside him, stuffed so full of things that it wouldn't close. A pair of trainers were stuck in on the top. He had evidently just been saying something to Olivia and he was leaning slightly forwards, his body grotesquely angular and aggressive. At the other end of the room, Krish was sitting in one of the easy chairs with his legs drawn up close to him, chin on his knees, his eyes wide and staring.

Anna and Jake stood for a moment in the doorway. Jake stepped forward. 'What's the problem, Sean?'

'She's the problem,' Sean snarled. Anna was reminded of something wild: a wolf. Sean pointed a rigid finger at Olivia. 'She's sick – up here.' The finger jabbed against his head. 'Someone ought to do something about her.'

Olivia protested, her voice tremulous, 'But you loved me, Sean. You did.'

'You messed me up!' Sean shouted, his thin, pitted face contorted. 'You don't know what love is. You controlled me – sent me off my brain.' He turned to Jake suddenly. 'You ask her what she does. She leads you on and then turns against you – backwards, forwards, so you don't know where you are. She makes you so you can't get her out of your mind. You used me – ' He pointed at Olivia again. 'And last night she came at me with a razor blade, tried to slash me. Look.' Wrenching up the sleeve of his T-shirt, he showed them a ridge of Elastoplast along his shoulder. 'Wasn't deep. I got out of her way. You're a fucking crazy bitch!' he yelled at Olivia. 'People ought to know.'

Bending down, he snatched up the bag with such force that the things on top fell out and he had to stuff them in again. He backed out of the room, pushing past Ben, who was standing in the doorway.

'I should've burned the whole fucking house down. I should have burned her to death in her bed.'

The front door slammed. There was silence, then Olivia's sobbing. She covered her face with her hands.

Anna went to her, afraid to touch her. Then, tenderly, she stroked the dark hair, more streaked with white than she had realized, feeling the warmth of Olivia's head beneath it, the trembling of her body. She pulled out one of the chairs and sat down beside her, not heeding the water on it.

'Livy,' she said softly. 'It's all right, I'm here. Don't worry, my love.'

Olivia's body crumpled. She leaned over until she was half lying in Anna's lap, sobs breaking out, sometimes from a place so deep that she was rigid for a few seconds, not drawing breath. Then a great cry would come, high and terrible, and gulping sounds of distress.

And Anna held her, stroking her, trying to soothe her, tears running down her own face.

'Oh, Anna,' Olivia said when she could catch her breath. 'Anna. Anna.'

'It's all right,' Anna said again. 'I'm here. I'm here, Livy.' She was overwhelmed with tenderness, and with the peculiar sadness of that tenderness.

She didn't know how long they sat there together. She noticed nothing else. After a time Olivia sat up and put her face in her hands again. From behind them she said, 'I'm so alone.'

Anna saw Jake move across to her from where he had been sitting with Krish, beckoning her out of the room.

'I'll be back in a minute,' she told Olivia softly.

In the hall, Jake said, 'I've called a doctor.' Seeing Anna's face fill with panic, he added, 'It's just her GP. Krish told me he's occasionally given her something to make her sleep. I think he knows her quite well.'

They all helped Olivia up to bed as if she were a child. Her movements were slow and trancelike. Jake came back down to wait for the doctor and Anna was left with Olivia and Krish. Anna wanted to speak to him, worried by his silence, his troubled eyes, but somehow could not in front of Olivia. And she simply did as they asked her, lay down on the bed, her hair in waves round her pale face on the two thick pillows. There was a limpness about her, but her face was anxious.

'Krishna?' she said to him in a low voice. 'You do love me?'

'Yes, *mamaji*,' he replied.

Anna watched him lean over obediently to kiss her. His manner was exhausted and wooden. She felt very sad watching the two of them together.

'Sleep now,' Krish said wearily, as he went to the door. 'You'll feel better then.'

Distantly Anna heard the doorbell. 'That'll be your doctor.'

Olivia reached up suddenly and seized Anna's hand, gripping it very tightly. She raised her head off the pillow. 'The baby,' she said in a rush. 'My baby – I wanted to hurt Kate. I don't know why. She was always an angel to me. But I do that … I've destroyed everything I've ever loved. The baby could have been anyone's. I never knew …'

They heard feet on the stairs, and a man's voice.

Olivia fell back on to the pillow. Hoarsely, she said, 'Angus was completely hers. Not that I didn't try. But he would never have touched me.'

Anna smiled down at her, stroked her hand. 'Thank you,' she said.

'She'll sleep now,' the doctor told them, downstairs. 'Got herself into a bit of a state, did she?' He eyed the burnt curtains, evidently preferring not to ask.

'She didn't do that,' Anna said quickly.

'I know she's a bit excitable. Give me a ring if there are any more problems.'

'Where's Krish?' Anna asked when the doctor had gone.

Jake looked startled. 'Isn't he up with her?'

'He came down before I did.'

They searched the house. His room was strewn with books and papers, but he had gone.

'I expect he just wanted to get away from us all,' Anna said.

Jake frowned. 'Let's look at the top.'

They found Ben in his room with the door open, watching a portable black and white telly, its picture dancing up and down the screen. He jumped as they appeared.

'You all right?' Jake asked.

Ben stood up, clicked the set off. 'I'm leaving,' he said, standing with his hands pushed into the back pockets of his jeans. 'I can't stay here. I've never seen anything like it. It was disgusting.' He looked from one to the other of them, mole-like behind his glasses. 'I was really happy here. I don't understand what's happened. I could talk to her, and she was so lovely...' His voice started to break with emotion.

Anna was caught between pity and impatience. 'Olivia's had a very difficult life,' she told him. 'Things have just been stirred up for her a lot recently.' She looked at Jake. 'It's my fault, really.'

'No. It would've happened sooner or later.'

Ben watched them, uncomprehending. 'Where is she?'

'Asleep,' Anna said. 'Krish's gone off somewhere.'

'You're not going, are you? Leaving me alone with her?' Ben stepped forward in panic.

'I'm staying,' Anna said. 'Jake – have you got to get back to the shop?'

'It'll have to stay closed today. I can't leave you with all this.'

Anna looked at him in amazement. When Richard was forced to have time off it amounted to a tragedy. 'Isn't Saturday your best day?'

Jake gave an ironic grin. 'It's only money. Don't worry, Ben. We'll be here.'

'Good.' Ben picked up his sweatshirt from the chair with sudden energy. Petulantly, he said, 'Well, I'm off to find somewhere else to live.'

Anna and Jake stood looking round the long room, amid the mess and the sour smell. The house felt very quiet. There was an occasional drip of water in a corner by the window, a fly circling somewhere at the back.

'I wonder where the hell Krish's gone,' Jake said. He went to the front window, stepping on the squelching fringe of burnt cloth, and looked out.

'D'you think we should be worrying about him?'

'I don't know.' Restlessly he came back to her. 'God, Anna, what's going to happen to them both?'

She shook her head. 'They need someone else in on this, don't they? Help of some sort. Only it seems inconceivable after what she went through last time.'

'Things have come on a bit since then,' Jake said.

'I should hope so.'

They stood close together in silence in the desolate room. Eyes troubled, Anna saw the look in his, and she turned away, frightened by the frank tenderness she found. She stood half facing him, tousling her hair nervously with one hand.

'I suppose we ought to clear up.'

He didn't answer immediately, and she had moved to the table, started shifting the chairs away so they could work on the floor. 'Anna?'

She knew what he wanted – for her to turn and look at him, to go to him – but she felt perverse and raw. Too shocked by all that had happened. In the end, rather gruffly, she just said, 'What?'

Jake's mouth lifted gently into a smile. 'Nothing. You're right. We ought to clean up.'

They spent the next few hours sweeping and scrubbing and mopping. There was a huge relief in this activity, a physical outlet which helped ease the tension of wondering where Krish was and when Olivia would wake and what would happen when she did. And of the feelings each knew were gathering between them across the room, unspoken.

As they worked together, Anna was vividly aware of him even if she was not actually looking in his direction: of his shape, the long legs, the large, rough hands, bruised left middle fingernail, the lines of his thick brown hair. His movements impinged on her, pulled her mind off track.

519

Their conversation became foolish and self-conscious.

'It's a good job she didn't have carpet in here,' Anna said after a while. 'This should clean up all right.'

'Won't do the parquet much good though,' he replied. 'Might start curling up.'

'What a shame,' she agreed. 'Such a lovely room.'

They made sandwiches for lunch, talked about Krish, Anna smoking. By late afternoon, having cleaned the room from top to bottom with almost unnecessary thoroughness, they were running out of things to do. They stood surveying their work.

'I'll put the kettle on,' Anna said. Jake came to stand in the kitchen doorway, one hand resting on the frame.

'Olivia's been out for hours now,' Anna said, turning. 'I suppose I ought to go and have a look in on her.' She looked at him, shyly. 'I'm sorry. This is so stupid.'

'Look, Anna ... I can't believe this.' He searched her face for a response. 'Can't you say something?'

'I don't think I know what to say.' She put her head on one side. 'Could I have a hug?'

Laughing with relief, he came to her and they held each other tightly. His body felt very warm and lean, its closeness a comfort. She rested her head against him, felt his arms round her back.

'I feel so clumsy, so nervous.'

'What of?'

'Making a mess of things again. And – ' He hesitated. 'I suppose of you not wanting me.'

She leaned her head back to look at him. 'But I do. So much.' And grinned suddenly. 'Pretty unusual all this, isn't it?'

She felt his big hand gentle on her head, drawing her closer until their lips met. Anna closed her eyes.

There was a slam of the front door, and Ben's anxious voice calling 'Hello?'

They released each other quickly, exchanging a half-comical grimace. 'We're here!'

Ben strode in, morosely. 'Well, nothing much doing. Looks as if I'm stuck here a bit longer. You're not leaving now, are you?'

Chapter 38

At six Anna went to Olivia's room and found her stirring, eyes closed, her head moving from side to side. Her face was haggard. Anna waited, sitting on the chair near the bed. She watched as Olivia eventually opened her eyes, for a moment unfocusing and bewildered after this long, unnatural sleep.

Her gaze fixed on Anna, stopped, and stared hard. Anna felt a chill run through her at the dark, flinty expression.

'Anna?' She gave a faint smile. 'You've been waiting for me? That's nice.'

'We've been here all day,' Anna told her.

Olivia frowned. Then, wearily, she said, 'Sean.' She closed her eyes again. There was a pause before she spoke again. 'Where's Krishna?'

'He went out. I expect he'll be back soon.'

In a small voice Olivia said, 'Will you help me up?'

Anna pulled her gently to a sitting position. As she helped her out of bed she saw the hem of the pale nightdress was stained a grubby grey from the mess on the floor downstairs. Olivia stared at it.

'Jake and I have been cleaning up,' Anna told her. 'You won't have much of a problem, really. Just need new curtains.'

Olivia didn't seem to be listening. She leaned forward slowly and nipped the leg of Anna's jeans between finger and thumb. Anna resisted the impulse to pull her leg away. Olivia stared at the washed-out denim.

'When I was your age we never dreamt of wearing such things,' she said wonderingly. 'You're all so much freer.'

'Mummy told me you always had lovely clothes.'

'I had beautiful things. The best, if possible. My father always saw to that. Proper, tailor-made things . . .'

Olivia still had about her the aura of a past age, Anna thought, as she started helping her to dress. Kate had adapted to the years, had worn large squarish glasses, kept her hair conveniently short, shopped at Marks and Spencer, wore comfy slacks, as she called them, when she was not at work.

But she couldn't imagine Olivia in slacks. There was still a formality about her approach to clothes, the way dressing was still an activity carried out at certain points in the day rather than something incidental. And there was the dark mahogany dressing table with matching silver-backed mirror, hairbrush, clothes brush, items all formally laid out, and a passive acceptance of Anna's help which spoke of maids. Her limbs seemed to be heavy and she was slow and lethargic. Together they put on the cotton skirt in which Anna had seen her play the piano, and a white blouse. Anna fastened the buttons, her actions accepted without protest. She brushed Olivia's hair, feeling its thick softness. She saw herself in the mirror behind Olivia, her eyes serious, a sad, almost reverent expression on her face.

'Will you plait it for me?' Olivia asked. 'Then I can just coil it up at the back.' And as Anna did so, she added, 'Your hair is such a lovely colour. You should grow it long.'

Once they had walked slowly downstairs together,

Anna went to help Jake prepare food – pasta and salad – from what was available in the house. Olivia ate a little with them. She remained subdued, apparently detached from what had happened, and content to sit and watch television. They sat with plates on their knees, relieved at having the telly, at not having to talk. Every so often, though, Olivia roused herself and looked round restlessly, saying, 'I wish Krishna would come back.'

By the time it got to nine o'clock, Anna and Jake were giving each other uneasy glances. They knew Krish had few friends, had not been allowed them. 'Perhaps he's gone to see Theo?' she suggested. 'They get on pretty well, don't they?'

Olivia looked doubtful. 'We could telephone,' she suggested.

'Let's give him a bit more time,' Jake said. 'After all, it's not exactly late yet.'

They sat through the news, each of them taking little of it in.

The phone rang at ten-thirty. Jake leapt up and went to the hall. Anna heard his voice, solemn, saying mostly, 'Yes ... yes ...' He asked something, said yes again, then rang off.

He appeared at the door, his expression unreadable. 'Anna, can I have a word?' Olivia watched impassively as Anna left the room.

Jake pulled her urgently along the dark hall. 'That was Selly Oak Hospital,' he whispered. 'They've got Krish.'

'I must go to him.'

Anna expected Olivia to be hysterical, to disintegrate. Instead, she and Jake watched her transform herself. She gathered herself, seemed to gain stature, dignified and unbending as a bird of prey.

'They say he's going to be sleeping it off for hours yet,' Jake told her. 'They wouldn't let you in at this time, anyway.'

'I need to be with him. He'll want me beside him.'

'Olivia,' Anna insisted gently, 'he's unconscious.'

Olivia stood in the middle of the long room, her face set in lines like stone. She was very composed, as though all her energy was concentrated in one burning point in her mind, consuming any other thought or feeling.

'What did he take?'

'They didn't say,' Jake said. 'They only gave the barest details.'

She fired out the questions relentlessly, as if forcing herself to face the worst. 'Where was he?'

Jake drew in an uneven breath. Anna could see he was feeling terrible. 'Kings Heath Park.'

'Where in Kings Heath Park?' Impatient, as if Jake was an idiot.

'They didn't tell me. Sorry,' he added helplessly.

'He was lying there all alone in the park,' Olivia said. 'Anyone could have found him.' She turned her head fiercely. 'Who found him? Who touched him?'

Jake took a step back. 'I don't . . . They only said he was in the park. We'll be able to ask tomorrow.'

'Sit down both of you,' Anna said firmly. 'I'll make us a drink, and then sooner or later we're going to have to get some sleep.'

'Sleep!' Olivia dismissed her scornfully.

'We need to sleep.'

'I've been asleep all day. I shall sit up for him.'

Anna's eyes met Jake's. With his he motioned her

into the kitchen. As she prepared coffee she heard their voices in the other room, Jake's soft, reassuring, and Olivia's monosyllabic replies.

'I've told her we'll stay,' Jake said, when Anna appeared again.

'Of course. That's no problem.'

'We could take it in turns to sleep,' Jake suggested. There was no protest from Olivia. 'D'you want to go and get some first, Anna?'

'I'll take this up with me.' She picked up her mug. 'Wake me at three or so?'

'OK. I'll see how we're doing.'

She went to kiss Olivia's cheek, but she moved away, sitting very straight on the edge of her chair. 'No, don't touch me.'

Anna shot Jake a look which said 'good luck' and left them.

She settled down in her clothes, having nothing else, and knowing she would be up again soon. Climbing on to the high, unyielding bed, she dreaded being unable to sleep and left most of the coffee undrunk on the table. She thought of Krish unconscious on a hospital bed, nurses coming to check him through the night.

The next thing she was aware of was Jake sitting on the side of the bed. She shot up, heartbeat speeding in panic.

'What time is it? What's happened?'

'It's all right. Don't worry. It's nearly four.' His eyes were red. 'I was falling asleep downstairs, so I thought I'd better come and get a bit of proper kip before tomorrow.'

'You should have woken me earlier.' Anna looked fearfully at him. 'How's it been? What's she doing?'

'Not a lot. It's been fine, really. She's just been sitting

there – we had the TV on. No dramatics. She's quiet. She seems stunned.'

'I suppose she's not tired?'

'All right for some, eh?'

There was silence, then Anna said, 'Poor Krish.'

Jake sighed. 'Yeah.'

Anna pushed back the sheet. 'Here – it's nice and warm for you!'

'Sounds wonderful. It's a great shame my getting in means you have to get out.'

He stood up and reached out his arms and they held each other. 'I didn't want to wake you,' he said. 'You looked so lovely.'

She smiled up at him. 'That's a nice thing to say.'

He leaned down to her slowly and they kissed. His hands moved across her back, drawing her to him. Then he lifted his head again and looked anxiously into her eyes, watching for her response. 'I keep thinking, we have to be careful with each other, not take things too quickly. I don't want to steamroller you. It's taken me by surprise feeling so ... strongly, already. I didn't expect it, and I don't know if you ...'

She put her hands on each side of his face and pulled him towards her without speaking. He seemed startled by the force of her kiss, its reply to him.

'Seems almost wrong,' he said after a moment, 'feeling so happy with all this going on.'

'I don't know.' She held him close. 'Maybe. I just know I'm glad. Everything's been so sad for so long.'

After they'd stood together in silence for a moment she stepped back. 'Come on – you need some sleep.'

'I know. It's OK. I just wanted to touch you.' He stroked his fingers down her back, then released her.

'I'll tuck you in.'

When he was lying down she kissed him again, before his smile took her to the door.

The rest of the night passed, strange and dreamlike. Olivia sat upright in her chair, not leaning against the back of it, as if performing a penance. Anna made hot drinks to keep herself awake, and Olivia accepted those offered to her with a nod, but usually left them untouched. Most of the time she sat in silence, staring across the room towards the window at the back where the light began faintly to appear.

Anna kept feeling herself on the point of dozing off, and then Olivia would suddenly speak and she would be jerked into full consciousness again.

'Did Katie show you my letters?' she asked, soon after Anna came down.

'Yes. Some of them.' She wondered if now, finally, they were to have a proper conversation. 'Not all, I don't think. She didn't *tell* me anything, you see, she wrote it and left it for me to find.'

'So you know all about me.' Her eyes still didn't meet Anna's, but her voice was wretched.

'I know what you chose to tell her and what she chose to tell me herself.'

She thought Olivia was about to speak again, but there came only a clearing of her throat, then silence. She was still beautiful, Anna thought, the dark eyes in that lined face.

'D'you mind if I smoke?' Anna asked timidly. She knew it would help keep her alert.

'Do what you like,' Olivia said absently.

A moment later, she said, 'May I have one?' Anna stood up and gave her a cigarette, clicking the lighter for her, the cigarette tucked between her dry lips.

'I've never seen you smoke before.'

Olivia dragged hungrily on the cigarette. 'I have – on and off. For years.' There was a pause, then she said, 'Katie must have told you about my father?' She narrowed her eyes, breathing out smoke. 'I ruined his career. I know Kate thought he'd do anything to advance himself, but it wasn't true. He was as soft as an egg inside. When he lost me he just lost his spirit. Gave it all up – the politics, public life. Packed me off to London. He was sweet to me after the baby. Sweet and tender. He cried. My mother didn't cry – not in front of me, anyway. But he couldn't bear to have me near him, not the way I was.' She shook her head slowly. 'He got such comfort from me, you see, all those years. My mother worshipped him – really, genuinely worshipped him. Couldn't stand herself you see, so she poured it all out on him. But she closed down emotionally. I was the only one who loved him properly. I've never felt quite as much for anyone as I did him.' She looked round sharply at Anna. 'I don't want to give you the wrong idea. He never laid a finger on me in any way he shouldn't have – nothing like that. He was very honourable in his way, and besides, he was far too busy touching up all the maids or anyone else who came his way. It was more that I was an idea, a fantasy. Something he saw as pure, that he could love without all the humiliation he went through with my mother. Sometimes, the way he held me – the two of us warm and safe together – it shielded us from anything else. I should have just gone on loving him like that. But I couldn't. I spoilt it, you see. I'd seen too much, heard too much of things I shouldn't have heard or seen. I lashed out. I was dirty.'

Anna wondered if she would become emotional but

she gave no sign, just stubbed out the cigarette in her saucer. Not knowing what else to do, Anna said, 'I'm sorry – for all you had to go through.'

What seemed much later, as the light was lifting the colours round the room and the birds were coming to life outside, Olivia said, 'You were such a darling, darling baby, Anna. So sweet and pure. I wanted to keep you from it all, you see, keep you as you were. You and Krishna.'

'We don't normally let visitors in in the morning,' the nurse told them. She was petite and pretty, a black fringe curling out from the front of her white cap, but her manner was chilly and suspicious. 'Are you friends of his?'

'I'm his mother,' Olivia snapped.

The nurse looked startled. She'd probably expected a timid Asian woman with limited English. 'His...? I see. I'm sorry. I suppose as you're here... Would you follow me?'

Her feet clip-clipped on the polished floor. She led them to a little room aside from the main ward.

'We put him in here out of the way.' Her tone was ambiguous. Anna and Jake exchanged glances. Over-dose: a nuisance taking up a bed. 'I'll tell him you're here.'

Olivia stood between Anna and Jake, watching the nurse give the door a shove. She looked very small in the yawning hospital corridor. Anna had wanted to take her arm, but sensed that she did not want to be touched.

The nurse went over to the bed by the far wall. Peering through the small, reinforced window, Anna could just see Krish's dark hair and the shape of his body under the bedclothes. He was turned away from them, facing the wall. Anna saw the nurse bend over and speak to him. Krish's body moved, curling almost convulsively so that his head disappeared underneath the bedclothes. The nurse tried again, then gave a light shrug and came back to the door.

'I'm sorry. He doesn't want to see anyone at the moment, I'm afraid.'

'But I have to see him.' Olivia's voice was high, the desperation barely controlled.

'He's rather distressed.' The nurse's voice was gentler now, taking on a tone of one addressing a patient instead of a visitor. 'You have to understand, he's not long come round and he won't be feeling very well for a while. Give him a bit more time.'

Olivia broke away from them and ran towards the door of the side room. 'Krishna, Krishna!' She had it half open, and they all had to restrain her, pull her away. Jake took her by the shoulders, led her off as her sobs filled the echoing space.

Anna stood with the nurse. 'Is he going to be all right?' she asked.

'He should be,' the nurse said. She looked at Anna curiously. 'Are you a relative?'

'No.'

The nurse nodded her head in the direction in which Olivia and Jake had disappeared. 'He was pretty adamant about not seeing her.'

Anna didn't feel confident in speaking to this young woman. 'Their relationship is complicated,' she said.

'I don't know, though.' The nurse's tone of disapproval returned. 'He may look all of a heap now, but soon after he surfaced this morning he opened his eyes, looked at me and said, "Titty." Can you believe it?'

'Don't worry,' Anna said, despising her petty outrage. 'He wasn't after you. Actually Titty is a person.'

When they went back that afternoon, Olivia had dressed
in her bright blue sari and plaited her hair.

'Let's hope to God he'll see her,' Anna whispered to
Jake as they left the van and walked across the car park.

By the side door of the hospital they met Theo. He
looked shocked, preoccupied, was walking staring
down at the ground and jumped when Jake called his
name.

'Hi.' He nodded at the three of them. 'Hello, Olivia.'
He looked away, then back at her. 'This is bad. Really
bad.'

'You've seen him?' Olivia said eagerly. 'Is he talking?'
Hope shone in her face.

Theo shifted awkwardly from foot to foot. He was
dressed in a blue tracksuit and trainers and looked huge
and muscular, but Anna could tell he felt terribly put on
the spot, that there were things he couldn't say in front
of Olivia.

'He's not saying much,' he told them, avoiding
Olivia's piercing gaze. 'I think he's still a bit – you know
– sleepy.'

'Well, he's bound to be!' Olivia's voice held a note of
desperate cheerfulness. 'But he's going to be all right,
isn't he? He's awake and he's seeing people. Let's go on
in.'

Theo looked at Jake. 'He asked for you.'

As they parted, Theo gestured to Anna to stay
behind. 'Thanks for phoning me, Anna. This is . . .' He
shook his head again. 'I'll come again tomorrow, right?'

'Thanks Theo. It's an awkward journey for you.'

'No problem. The bus is OK. I can get to the outer

circle.' He stared at her. 'He won't see her, you know. What the hell's going on?'

'I'll tell you' – Anna put her hand on his dark wrist – 'when there's time.'

She watched Theo lope off across the car park.

Jake and Olivia had waited for her just inside. She took Olivia's arm as they climbed the stairs to the ward. Anna felt sick with nerves, and with sorrow at the sight of this little woman dressed up in her borrowed sense of identity, looking sad and eccentric in her sari, her gait wrong for the clothes, clinging to her hope that this costume might bring her closer to her son. She wanted to say something, warn Olivia that Krish still might not be ready, but it was too late before she could find the right words.

When they reached the middle corridor, Olivia took in a deep breath, preparing herself.

'Perhaps Jake should go first,' Anna suggested, as they pushed open the swing doors to the ward. 'Tell him you're here and you want to see him?'

Olivia hesitated, then nodded. 'All right,' she said, her voice husky.

But on looking through the window of the side room they saw that the chair next to Krish's bed was already occupied by a tall, thin man, his white coat open to reveal a moss-green shirt. Krish was still lying down and they couldn't see his face.

After a short time the doctor glanced round at the door. They saw a chiselled face with dark, serious eyes. Seeing them watching, he came out, closing the door softly behind him.

'Good afternoon. I'm Dr O'Connor.' His voice was soft, Irish. He looked from one to the other of them, trying to work out who to talk to.

Olivia could not contain herself. 'I want to see my son,' she erupted, harshly.

'You're Mrs Kemp?'

'Yes, of course I am.' She seemed suddenly enraged, as if she resented his presence there.

'We're friends of Krishna's,' Anna explained. 'I'm Anna Craven and this is Jake...' In confusion she couldn't think of his name. For a second she saw the bizarre nature of the whole situation, that she was here with these people who a week ago she hadn't even met.

'Morrell,' Jake finished for her.

'Ah, Jake,' Dr O'Connor said. 'Krishna asked just now whether you were here. He'd like to see you.'

'What about me?' Olivia wailed, her fragile collect-edness disintegrating. She went to the door again. 'Krishna, my darling – *mamaji* is here!'

Anna felt Dr O'Connor observing them all. She went to Olivia and gently held her arm. 'Livy, why not let Jake go in first, if that's what Krish wants, and he can tell him you're here and perhaps afterwards...'

Jake looked at Dr O'Connor who nodded at him. He slipped into the room and sat by Krish's bed.

'I should explain,' the doctor said. 'I've been called in to see your son. I'm the duty psychiatrist.'

'No!' Olivia recoiled from him. 'No. We don't need you. Don't you go near him. Just let me talk to him. What he needs is to be home with me. We're all right when we're together. We're safe. We don't need anyone like you...' Her voice was reaching higher, barely controlled.

The doors of the main ward swung open and a woman in a green overall pushed a huge, rattling trolley past them without giving them a second glance.

'Mrs Kemp, let's go into the side room here,' Dr

O'Connor suggested. 'We can talk about this more privately.'

'I'm not going anywhere with you,' Olivia almost spat at him. 'I'm not moving. I'm waiting here to see my son. *My* son.'

'Mrs Kemp – ' Dr O'Connor seemed to experience actual physical discomfort in bringing out his next words. 'Krishna has told me very clearly that he is not ready to see you just at the moment. I know this is terribly difficult and I'm sure he's not trying to hurt you deliberately. At a time like this people sometimes react most strongly against the people they're closest to. I shouldn't like to have to forbid you to see him. For Krishna's sake it would be helpful if you could respect his wishes. He's in a very low state and we're assessing him to see whether he needs some more specialized care. We may need to transfer him to a bed over in Rubery . . .'

Rubery Hill. The psychiatric hospital on the southern fringe of Birmingham. Olivia's face froze. In no more than a whisper she protested, 'No . . . No . . .'

Watched by Anna and Dr O'Connor, she moved to the door of Krish's room, crumpling against it, her hands splayed on the wood each side of the window. 'Krishna . . . *my Krishna* . . .' His name spilled from her mouth over and over, as if she couldn't stop, her forehead pressed white against the glass.

Chapter 39

Krishna and Olivia both went to Rubery Hill Hospital: Krishna as a voluntary patient. Olivia was not given a choice in the matter.

Anna and Jake were Olivia's only visitors over the next month. Theo went to see Krish with sombre faithfulness.

Krish's first questions now were, 'How is she? What's she saying? Is she blaming me?'

It was only recently though that he had started to talk at all. At first he had remained in a paralysed state, almost completely dumb except for whispered replies to the most basic questions regarding his needs. Anna and Jake visited every other day and Krish sat in inscrutable silence. He had been assigned a psychotherapist, and stonewalled him for hours at a time. No one could detect any maliciousness in this, but simply a need to withdraw, to be out of things. He had refused absolutely, and was still refusing, to see his mother. The hospital staff deemed it right to keep them apart.

After three weeks he had gradually begun talking to Steven, the psychotherapist. Then to Theo. Then Anna and Jake. One day when they approached him, Anna carrying a box of Rose's chocolates, Krish looked up and, very softly, said, 'Hello.' He looked exhausted, his face drawn, black shadows under his eyes. He told them he wasn't sleeping. He talked in sudden jerks about his life with Olivia, sitting childlike in pastel green pyjamas, his voice so quiet they had to concentrate hard to hear.

'I've hated her so much.' He was weeping into his hands. He shook his head from side to side as if to dislodge the thought of her. 'I do love her – but she makes my life impossible.' He looked up at them through his fingers. 'God, what the hell are we going to do?'

He held his hands out in front of him, palms down in a despairing gesture, watching their slight tremor. 'Look at me. I can't do anything any more. I can't even make a cup of coffee by myself.'

Afterwards, gloomily, they drove away from the hospital in the van. Finally Anna said, 'Well – at least he's speaking.'

The last time they saw Olivia was in mid-October. Anna took flowers to her that day: a bunch of vivid blooms, blue, yellow, pink, deliberately chosen to shout at the pallid walls of the hospital. This outcry of colour was in part an expression of her own guilt, her protest against helplessness, despite the reassurance of Dr O'Connor and the other staff that they had done the right thing. The only thing.

Olivia looked old. Older than Anna had ever seen her, the skin of her face flaccid as if something in her very being had collapsed. She was brushing her hair. Brushing and brushing. It was newly washed, long and wild looking.

'It's so grey,' she said, giving Anna and Jake no other greeting as they sat down. 'So terribly faded. I'd be grateful if you'd buy a rinse for me, Anna. Something subtle of course. I don't want to look cheap.'

In her mind there seemed to be only a small circle of illumination left, kept alight to pick out practical details. Everything else was off stage, out of sight.

'Did Ben pay his rent before he left?' she asked. She raised the brush over her head and strands of her hair lifted with it, crackling with static electricity. Her thoughts jabbed at Ben's rent book. Then at the tap in the upstairs toilet. Could Jake be a darling and fix it? Because she was sure it was leaking, and it was the hot one: such a drain on the tank . . .

'And Anna, I don't seem to have my Access card here and I'm sure to need it. Could you check in my handbag when you get back to the house? It's in the little cupboard at the side of my bed.'

These enquiries were low key, the drugs keeping her just a fraction away from calm. She didn't mention Krish.

Two days after that, Olivia walked out of the hospital. Whether by luck or canniness on her part she chose a time during the morning when the ward was unlocked, the staff busy and there was a general air of bustle in the corridors. She may have followed an instinct which told her her only mistake would be to hesitate.

She must have made her way, unchallenged, right down the drive of the hospital, wearing her blue dressing gown and sheepskin slippers. From there she was walking along the bypass, a busy, fast-moving artery feeding the M5. Who would challenge a woman in a blue dressing gown and slippers on the A38 bypass?

Just over a mile and what must have been half an hour later, she walked on to the nearside platform of the railway station at Longbridge. Within five minutes an Intercity train, moving at shrieking speed past the back of the Rover car works, dashed into a body clad in a cornflower-blue dressing gown, which was lying with a neat sense of purpose across the track.

Chapter 40

December, 1981

'Off somewhere nice?'

Anna put her bag down and watched Roland's rotund figure advancing towards her along the street, obviously anxious not to miss her.

'A day out – with Jake and Elly. Sort of winter picnic. I'm sure you'll tell us we're mad.'

'Not at all. It's a marvellous day. You'll be all right well wrapped up.'

They stood outside Kate's house. It was a dazzling morning, water droplets on the grass catching the light as last night's hard frost was beginning to melt. At one corner of the drive a freshly painted white post had been driven into the ground, topped by a 'For Sale' sign.

'Any offers yet?'

'It only went up yesterday,' Anna protested. 'Give them time.'

'And have you started looking for a new place?' Roland's attempt to sound detached and cheerful failed miserably.

'I'm not looking far away – just a little further into town, but still Kings Heath. I'd like something a bit older.'

Roland chuckled, his face reddening. Since Kate's

death his emotions seemed to come upon him even more overwhelmingly.

'Look, you're the only family I've got,' she told him. 'I don't want to lose you – if you can put up with me, that is!'

Roland laughed delightedly. 'I'm very relieved you're not planning to take off and leave me again.' He frowned. 'What are you going to do, actually? Look for a new teaching job?'

Anna stared at the house opposite, giving an absent-minded wave to a woman stepping out with a shopping bag. 'I'm not sure what I'm going to do at the moment – and I'm rather enjoying not being sure.' She took in a satisfied breath of the icy air. 'I feel as if I can start again. Use some of my earnings I never had time to spend. I think Jake's infected me with his travel bug.' She turned to Roland. 'What about you?'

'Oh – I shall potter along no doubt.' Without self-pity, he added, 'Nothing will be the same now she's gone.'

'Oh, Roland,' Anna said. 'I'm so sorry.' She went to him, and was taken up into one of his bear hugs.

She felt his breath on her hair as he spoke. 'But my dear, nothing could make me happier now than knowing you're going to be just up the road.'

Jake's van grumbled along the curving roads out into the Warwickshire countryside. Bare branches spiked black against the untouched blue sky, the fields ploughed or left to pasture. Bright, low-angled sunlight gave the furrows and tree-trunks a hard edge of shadow so that the landscape looked vivid and assured.

Between Anna and Jake, strapped to the seat with her plump legs stretched out straight, sat Elly. She was wearing a little denim skirt with woolly red tights and a blue coat with a red lining, squeezed over layers of jumpers. Her round face was edged by a mesh of fine blond hair.

'Daddy, where are we going? We've been driving for such a long time.'

'Soon be there,' Jake told her. 'Just another mile or two, and then we can have our picnic.'

Elly turned to Anna and gave her a mischievous, trying-it-on smile which showed a deep dimple to the left of her mouth. 'I want some of that chocolate.'

Anna grinned back at her. She'd taken to Elly immediately and already they'd had a couple of outings together. 'Don't worry. I expect we'll leave you a little bit.'

'Not just a bit!' Elly was outraged. 'I want lots. I want *this* much.' She held out her arms wide, red mittens dangling on strings from her coatsleeves.

'Sandwiches first though,' Jake told her firmly. 'Let's hope we're not going to freeze.' He looked away from the road at Anna for a second, giving a smile which she returned. Happiness surged through her, made her feel like singing. She had woken that morning in his bed, held by him, their eyes meeting each other's, and seeing she was loved.

They rounded the bend beneath the rise, from where she knew she had glimpsed Arden out of the taxi. She saw trees snagging at the blue, but between them a sudden shock: where the crouching shape of the hospital had stood before, there was nothing now but the naked sky.

'It's gone!' she cried. 'They've already done it!'

'What's gone?' Elly peered through the windscreen.

'There was a building there – on the hill.' Anna pointed. Still hardly believing it, she went on, 'And now it's not there.'

'Why?' Elly frowned. 'Did somebody steal it? A stranger?'

'Yes,' Anna said. 'Several strangers, I should think. And some machines.' She felt desolate. It had felt important to come back here. 'Oh, well. Can't show you now then, can I?'

'Never mind,' Jake said. 'I'll have to try and imagine.'

The stone arch at the entrance to Arden was, however, still standing, a large green and white sign next to it announcing the name of the demolition company. The arch was too narrow for the bulldozers and they had cleared a way in through the boundary fence, leaving a gash of crushed bushes and white, snapped twigs. Their tracks had mashed deep ruts along the drive, the surface churned aside and now frozen hard, still white with ice behind the broken shadows of the trees.

They left the van just inside the entrance and jumped down. Anna was disorientated. 'I was here four months ago,' she calculated as they reached into the back of the van for the picnic bags. 'I suppose it was obvious they were going to do it soon, but I still can't believe it's just gone completely. I thought it would take them longer.'

'Not once they get going,' Jake said.

They picked their way along the rough path, Anna and Jake each carrying a bag and Jake with a rug draped over one shoulder. 'Mind how you go,' he called to Elly, who was skipping ahead in blue wellies. 'Hold my hand or you could twist your ankle. It's rough here.'

'I want to hold Anna's hand,' she said. Anna felt the woolly fingers grasp hers and was flattered to be chosen. Elly looked up at her, eyes huge and grey like Jake's. 'You're Daddy's girlfriend, aren't you?'

'Yes,' Anna said solemnly. 'Is that all right with you?'

'Oh yes,' Elly said. 'I think that's all right – so far.'

'Thank you,' Anna said. She and Jake laughed together, their breath misting the air.

'You look like dragons,' Elly said, puffing a breath out herself and laughing too. Jake came and put his free arm round Anna's shoulders.

As they walked round the final bend of the drive Anna found herself feeling nervous, as she had the first time she was there. She had expected something to remain: bricks, plastic tape, skips: something of the paraphernalia of demolition. But there was nothing. The site had been cleared with great thoroughness, the rubble carted away, the ground bulldozed and flattened, so that the only thing now visible was the long area of earth frozen iron hard.

Anna walked on to it. There was almost no sound. She could feel the rays of the sun on her face. Elly loosed her hand and danced off over the inviting space.

'It was very big.' Anna pointed, swinging her arms to try and explain it. 'All across here. That wing over there had been burnt, but there was a lot of the front left – here. And it was beautiful – the façade of it, anyway – like a Victorian stately home. And there was a water tower about here. Square thing, all black . . .' She picked out as best she could the places where she thought there had been airing courts, wards, filling in the shape. They walked round in silence for a few minutes, turning, staring, trying to imagine.

As she did so Anna saw something incongruous trapped in the earth at her feet. Pale blue, icy, pressed down and half hidden. She fished a knife from her picnic bag and prised it out of the ground: a round, plastic bead, its hole for stringing blocked with a brown thread of soil. She turned it round in her fingers, cleaning the outside until it felt warm and smooth.

Olivia's voice came to her: 'I wish I had something to hold on to: a bead, a stone, a strand of hair, anything to call mine.' She slipped the bead into the pocket of her jeans.

She walked slowly over to Jake and saw him watching her, taking in the sight of her as she came to him.

'After I'd seen this place I knew I couldn't condemn her,' she said.

Jake nodded, put his hand on her shoulder, and she turned, reaching up to kiss him.

But then Elly was pulling her arm, impatient. 'Come on. Let's do something.'

'You're right,' Anna said. 'Let's get the picnic going.'

They found a spot on the grass not far away and put the rug down, laying on it French bread and cheeses, crisps and *samosas*, fruit and a Thermos of coffee. Wrapped in their coats and scarves, they sat looking across the countryside, at the gentle swell of the land and brown, scoured fields, oblong farmhouses like Lego pieces, dots of bushes. Elly was quiet, eating crisps with sudden concentration.

Anna sat back, feet stretched out, the wind ruffling her hair. She had bitten into a *samosa*, delicious spiced potato, plump peas.

Even up here there was very little for them to say about Kate and Olivia that they had not said many times already. There had had to be an inquest after Olivia's death. At the funeral Anna had been startled by the intensity of her own grief for Olivia. And for Krish struggling with his guilt, his new sense of release. She thought of him now almost as a brother to whom she owed protection.

There came to her a feeling of peace, of standing outside time, as if she could walk along the ridge of

Krish's life from up here and see that he would live through this, would surface again.

'He's going to be OK,' she said to Jake. 'I think.'

'Yes.' He unscrewed the lid of the Thermos, steam billowing out. 'Eventually.'

After their meal they shared the chocolate. Elly took her squares, relishing them slowly. She delighted in the huge flat area laid out there for her to run around on, and was soon skipping up and down in delight, her mouth ringed like a clown's with chocolate.

'Don't choke!' Jake warned her. 'Here – the Frisbee!'

He spun the thin yellow disc towards her and it lifted and arced on the breeze, Elly following as it hit the ground and wheeled away down the incline.

'Daddy, Mummy,' she cried, 'I'm flying!'

Anna laughed and turned to Jake, flinging her arms round him, feeling his tight round her. She settled, leaning against the padded shoulder of his jacket. 'She's lovely, Jake. A great kid.'

'She's coming on,' he agreed. There was pleasure in his voice. 'She's really taken to you.'

'I'm so glad.' She twisted her head to look up at him. 'In a strange way I'm glad about everything.'

He looked down into her eyes, his long face serious. 'Are you?'

'Very, very, very. Come here.' She pecked his nose, teasing, then found his lips with hers, trying to show him with a kiss. After a moment he drew back and looked at her again.

'What's the matter?'

'I don't want to lose this, Anna. It's just – we haven't said anything, actually said what we feel.'

'Didn't I show you last night?'

'Yes.' He looked down. 'You did. I know.'

She took his face in her hands, pulling him close to her so that her breath was warm on his ear. 'I love you. Thank you for making me so happy.'

He laughed and they sat for a long time side by side, watching Elly flying after the Frisbee as it curved and bucked in the air. Her cheeks were winter-pink and she chatted to herself in a constant stream, calling out to them, happy so long as they were watching.

Anna's eyes followed her, smiling. Her thoughts drifted from image to image, splinters of melancholy and joy all gathered in this place. She conjured up Arden as it had been: the handcarts, the long, sealed corridors, all the people whose lives had faded into shadows glimpsed on its walls. She watched the skipping rhythm of Elly's feet, her child's absorption and happiness. And brought before her two other children skipping there, one blond with heavy, black-rimmed glasses, the other fragile, waif-like, long hair curling, both laughing as they reached for each other's sun-warm hands.

'Daddy, Daddy!' Elly's voice floated across to them. 'It's lovely here. Can we stay? I want to stay here for ever!'

She ran and gave a leap of pure joy, her body rising, arms flung high, and the bright, gauzy hair lifting to catch the light.